THE EMPIRE OF BONES SAGA VOLUME ONE

TERRY MIXON

YOWLING CAT PRESS

Published by Yowling Cat Press ®

Digital edition date: 6/21/2023

Print ISBN: 978-1947376021

Individual Works

Empire of Bones Copyright © 2014 by Terry Mixon

Print ISBN: 978-1947376090

Veil of Shadows Copyright © 2014 by Terry Mixon

Print ISBN: 978-1947376106

Command Decisions Copyright © 2015 by Terry Mixon

Print ISBN: 978-1947376113

Fist of God Copyright © 2017 by Terry Mixon

Cover art - image copyrights as follows:

DepositPhotos/innovari (Luca Oleastri)

GraphicStock

Donna Mixon

Cover design and composition by Donna Mixon

Print design and layout by Terry Mixon

Audio edition performed and produced by Veronica Giguere

Reach her at: v@voicesbyveronica.com

ALSO BY TERRY MIXON

You can always find the most up to date listing of Terry's titles on his Amazon Author Page.

Note: the links below (ebook only, obviously) redirect you to my website where you can click a button to go to Amazon. This allows me to participate in Amazon's associates program and earn a little more. Sorry for any inconvenience.

The Imperial Marines Saga

Spoils of War

Imperial Recruit

Enemy Action

The Humanity Unlimited Saga

Liberty Station

Freedom Express

Tree of Liberty

Blood of Patriots

Single Novels

Scorched Earth

Storm Divers

The Vigilante Series with Glynn Stewart

Heart of Vengeance

Oath of Vengeance

Bound By Law

Bound By Honor

Bound By Blood

Box Sets

The Empire of Bones Saga Volume 1

The Empire of Bones Saga Volume 2

The Empire of Bones Saga Volume 3

The Empire of Bones Saga Volume 4

Humanity Unlimited Publisher's Pack 1

Humanity Unlimited Publisher's Pack 2

Want to get updates from Terry about new books and other general nonsense going on in his life? He promises there will be cats. Go to TerryMixon.com/Mailing-List and sign up.

DEDICATION

This book would not be possible without the love and support of my beautiful wife. Donna, I love you more than life itself.

ACKNOWLEDGMENTS

Once again, the people who read my books before you see them have saved me. Thanks to Tracy Bodine, Michael Falkner, Cain Hopwood, Kristopher Neidecker, Bob Noble, Jon Paul Olivier, and Jason Young for making me look good.

I also want to thank my readers for putting up with me. You guys are great.

Finally, I want to extend my gratitude to Sue Baiman for stepping in to help me out when I really needed it. I'm deeply in her debt.

EMPIRE OF BONES

BOOK ONE

After a terrible war almost extinguished humanity, the New Terran Empire rises from its own ashes.

Sent on an exploratory mission to the dead worlds of the Old Empire, Commander Jared Mertz sets off into the unknown.

Only the Old Empire isn't quite dead after all. Evil lurks in the dark.

With everything he holds dear at stake, Jared must fight like never before. Victory means life. Defeat means death. Or worse.

1

Commander Jared Mertz, captain of the Fleet destroyer *Athena*, looked up from his console when his tactical officer spoke. "Contacts bearing two-five-zero by three-three-zero. Gravitic scanners show at least three ships under power and on a slow course toward Orbital One."

He leaned forward in his seat and gave Lieutenant Zia Anderson his full attention. "Put them on the main screen."

The forward display switched from a tedious view of the asteroid they were in a close orbit of to a graphical representation of the immediate area of space. A small blue circle represented his ship. The enemy task force, marked with a red diamond, appeared on a projected course that took it ahead of and below *Athena*'s position. Its current range was just over a million kilometers.

Its slow speed prevented its grav drive signatures from showing up on the gravitic scanners beyond this short range. By his estimation, the task force would need to increase speed by twenty or thirty percent before Orbital One might detect it from deeper in the system.

If *Athena* had been actively scanning with the normal space scanners, the enemy would've detected them much further out and gone dark before the destroyer noticed them. Relying on only the passive and gravitic scanners had been the only way to spot them first.

"Have they seen us?" Jared asked.

The tall redheaded officer shook her head. "I don't think so, Captain. The asteroid we're grappled to seems to have fooled them."

"Keep all active scanners offline, but arm the missile tubes and bring all combat systems to standby. Sound general quarters and send a tight-beam warning to Orbital One."

"Aye, sir."

Lieutenant Pasco Ramirez, *Athena*'s helmsman, examined his console readouts. "Their drives are at minimum, sir. They probably exited the flip point about three hours ago. At their current speed, they'll cross our orbit in about half an hour."

They officially called the incongruity in the space-time fabric that allowed for interstellar travel an Osborne-Levinson Bridge, but no one outside a university used that name. Jared figured it hadn't taken more than fifteen minutes before someone called it a flip point, because that was exactly what happened when the special drives pulled on the weakened area of empty space. The ship ceased to exist in one planetary system and appeared in a different one light-years away.

It had made the existence of the Old Empire possible, and the rebellion that had destroyed it.

"Be ready to bring our drives online at a moment's notice." Jared returned his attention to his tactical officer. "I want to fire two salvos of missiles after they pass us, just before they're out of effective range."

"Sir, we don't have any speed built up," she warned. "They'll have us as soon as they pivot."

The red-team ships would need to turn before they could return fire, because the massive drives a starship required left no room for missile tubes aft.

"I know. With their momentum and course, we might be able to get out of easy firing range before then. If we want to make these war games more than a toss-up, we need to bloody their noses. Keep working on possible scenarios while I chat with Commander Graves."

He opened a channel to operations. *Athena*'s executive officer appeared on Jared's console a few moments later. His second in command already knew what Zia had reported, but Jared summarized the situation and his plan to make the red team pay for its inattention.

Lieutenant Commander Charlie Graves grinned. "It's about time they showed up. I was beginning to think they'd gotten lost."

"I'm sure Admiral Yeats would have something incisive to say about that in the after-action report."

"Wouldn't he?" The lanky officer glanced away from the screen. "Okay, we're starting to get some better data now. It looks like six hostiles, tentatively identified as three destroyers, two light cruisers, and a heavy. We're not supposed to know who's participating in the exercise, but Ensign Enova says she's sure the heavy cruiser is *Spear*. She served her midshipman's cruise on her. The ships match what we'd expect to see of his task force."

Jared allowed the corner of his mouth to twitch upward. "We'll overlook that little violation of the simulation guidelines just this once. Who's in command of *Spear*?"

"Wallace Breckenridge. The ensign says he's a real by-the-book kind of guy. Apparently, he's not the kind that appreciates anyone thinking outside the box."

"Then we'll be giving him quite the unpleasant wakeup call. Let me know if you see anything else as they close range. Bridge out."

The six red diamonds slowly inched toward *Athena* on the screen. The red team would intersect her course about four hundred thousand kilometers away, just inside *Athena*'s most effective targeting range—half a million kilometers.

Time crept by as Jared waited for the enemy to notice their presence or perhaps send a destroyer to check the asteroid out, but they didn't. He let the distance between them open again once they'd passed until the enemy was almost out of optimal missile range.

"Separate from the asteroid, Pasco. Zia, as soon as you have a passive lock, fire. Don't go active until they respond. We might get the second salvo off before they can react."

The screen lit up with four amber sparks representing *Athena*'s missiles as they exited the tubes. They screamed toward the enemy task force, their grav drives at maximum.

"Missiles away," Zia said. "Telemetry indicates target acquisition. Thirty seconds until interception. Tubes reloading."

There wasn't any reaction from the red team for several more seconds, and Jared could imagine some scanner officers gaping as the missiles appeared from nowhere and came howling in from astern. Zia launched a second set of missiles just as the enemy formation changed speed and began turning.

"Full acceleration," Jared snapped. "Evasive maneuvers. Set course for the outer system. Use the asteroid for cover as long as you can." Few of the eight missiles they'd launched would get through the red team's defensive fire, but even one would be enough to leave a mark.

He waited for the enemy task force to return fire, but it didn't. Hadn't the red team been at combat stations? He could almost hear the klaxons blaring and see the men rushing to bring their missiles online.

The enemy destroyers broke formation and began accelerating after them. Their antimissile railguns fired at *Athena*'s first salvo, destroying two of them. Another detonated short of *Spear*, while the fourth lit up the heavy cruiser.

"Hit on the primary target," Zia crowed. "It took him astern. High probability of serious internal damage."

The enemy ships finally brought their weapons online, and a swarm of missiles streamed after *Athena*—four from each destroyer, six from the light cruisers, but only three from the heavy cruiser. Less than half the eight Jared had expected from the large ship.

Still, twenty-seven missiles were much more than a destroyer like *Athena* ever wanted to see chasing her, even at extreme range. "Electronic countermeasures," he said. "Evasion pattern delta."

"I'm working on it," Zia responded curtly, obviously too focused to realize that wasn't precisely the tone an officer should use with her captain.

He grinned in spite of the tense situation. He loved his people.

Athena's second salvo roared in on the enemy. The destroyers had pulled far enough away from their larger brethren that they could no longer provide effective antimissile defenses for them. Their absence became clear when a second missile slammed into *Spear*. The massive cruiser rolled as explosions wracked her internally. It looked like her drives had failed.

Electronic countermeasures lured many of the red team missiles aside. *Athena*'s railguns accounted for some of the rest. The number of missiles that had acquired them at this range surprised Jared. Five got through their defensive fire and roared down on *Athena* like the wrath of God.

The bridge went dark. The only sound Jared could hear was Zia cursing. The consoles reset as the simulation ended and returned to standby mode, still locked out of operational control of the destroyer.

The main screen came to life, showing the curve of the planet Avalon below them. Orbital One sat about ten thousand meters away. The breathtaking view dissolved as Zia put an incoming transmission on the screen.

Admiral Robert Yeats, Commanding Officer of Capital Fleet, shook his head. "While that was a glorious death, Commander, you still lost your ship."

Jared smiled ruefully. "The target was too tempting to pass up, Admiral. I didn't expect their fire to be so accurate at long range."

"Save the heroics for when you don't have a choice. You should've let them pass and been satisfied with warning us they were coming. That *is* what a picket is for, you know."

"Yes, sir."

"The better targeting was one of the enemy advantages for this war game. I'm impressed that only five of their missiles got through your defenses. You almost got away with your sneak attack."

"As you say, sir, almost wasn't good enough this time."

The screen split as Captain Breckenridge of *Spear*—probably also the red team commander—and Captain Alice Quinn, the blue team commander, came into the circuit. Breckenridge looked pissed, Quinn bland.

"What kind of bull was that?" Breckenridge demanded. "The sim didn't display *Athena* correctly."

"Actually, it did," Quinn said. "Commander Mertz used an asteroid as cover. Well done, Jared."

"Thank you, ma'am, but I still lost my ship. Not a good day for me or my crew."

The dark-skinned captain nodded. "True, but you took out a heavy cruiser. *Spear*'s fusion plants went critical right after you blew up. That took her out and damaged both light cruisers. That said, while it was an excellent trade-off from a strictly tactical perspective, I'd prefer you came back home alive."

Breckenridge bristled. "*Athena*'s actions were clearly outside the boundaries of—"

"That's enough, Wallace," Yeats said in a tone that brooked no disagreement. "Just accept that you lost this one. Maybe next time you'll be a little more paranoid. That's why we have these war games, to learn what we can before the real shooting starts."

The admiral glanced at his chrono. "We'll have our after-action briefing in one hour on Orbital One. Get something to eat and come ready to tear this operation apart. We have a number of things to discuss. Dismissed. Mertz, please adjourn to your office and stay on the channel."

Jared left Zia in charge of the bridge, took the lift down one deck, and made his way to his office. He wondered what the admiral wanted with him. To chew him out in private? That wasn't the old man's style. He'd tear a limb off you in public and use it to beat you to death if he thought you deserved it.

Once he came back on the channel, the flag officer continued, "Once again, Commander, well done. I'm afraid you won't be joining us for the briefing, though. Send your executive officer to cover for you. You have other plans."

"That sounds ominous, sir."

The admiral smiled. "Not really. Your father has requested the pleasure of your company for dinner. He wants to see you one last time before you ship out on the survey tomorrow."

Jared kept his face blank, but inside he cursed. The very last people he wanted to spend time with were his father and half siblings.

"I see. I will, of course, represent Fleet with honor."

The admiral's brows drew together. "Far be it from me to dictate the actions of a fellow officer in his social life, but when the ruler of the Terran Empire requests our presence, we go.

"Allow me to also stress that while you might have reservations about your relationship with the Imperial Family, it isn't prudent to make an issue of them, even over a secure channel with someone who's known you since you joined Fleet. It's far safer if people think you're happy to be the emperor's son, even if you were born on the wrong side of the sheets."

Yeats leaned forward and spoke more softly. "Fleet is *supposed* to be nonpolitical, but you need to be the most enthusiastic supporter of the Empire and the Imperial Family. People are watching and waiting for you to give them a reason to hold your illegitimate birth against you. You can't give them a lever to use against you, Jared."

Jared sighed a little. "You won't find a more ardent supporter of the Empire or the emperor, sir. It's just hard to be enthusiastic when my half siblings loath me and don't miss a single opportunity to make their objections to my presence painfully clear. The heir couldn't hate me more if I peed in his soup. Rubbing my existence in his face is not doing me or Fleet any favors. One day he'll lead the Empire and I'll be on the beach." *Or dead.*

"The emperor is in excellent health, and the heir wouldn't dare take out a vendetta against a Fleet officer. Don't be so melodramatic."

The admiral hadn't seen how deeply Ethan Bandar hated Jared. No one else had heard the threats the man made when no one else was around. They got worse every time the emperor insisted that Jared come to the Imperial Palace, too.

"I wish I shared your… optimism, sir."

"I'll see you at the final mission briefing tomorrow morning, Commander. Have a good time. Consider that an order." The screen went dark.

Perfect. Jared wished the admiral understood everything he'd had to endure after the Fleet entrance physical had revealed his parentage. He couldn't comprehend why the emperor insisted on torturing him two or three times a year with these "family get-togethers."

Not that any of it mattered, though. He'd go, and he'd do his best not to let his relatives get under his skin.

He summoned Graves to his office. When his friend had taken a seat, he filled him in on his dinner plans. Graves knew how he felt. He'd understand.

Jared took a deep breath and tried to relax his tense back. "I suppose I should be used to the situation. It's been fifteen years since I found out I was his son, but his children complicate things. I'm living proof that their father had an affair, and I'm the reason their mother divorced him. Not a good recipe for making friends."

"I suppose not," his friend said. "I bet we could come up with some mechanical failure requiring your presence."

Jared allowed himself a small smile. "I appreciate the thought, but I don't think that would go over very well the day before we leave on our grand exploration mission. Besides, my news isn't all bad."

Graves gave Jared a suspicious look, probably because of his captain's mock-cheerful tone. "Oh? How's that?"

"I don't have to go to the after action briefing and have Breckenridge burn holes through me with his eyes. You get that honor."

"Today just keeps getting worse," Graves grumbled. "You'd think being blown into atoms would be the ultimate low point, but somehow you found a way to make death appealing. Thanks, Jared."

"What can I say? I'm a beacon of joy. Don't wait up."

2

Princess Kelsey Bandar looked up from her reading as her brother stalked into the library. His thunderous expression gave her just enough warning to mark her place before he exploded.

"He's coming to dinner tonight." The petulant snarl in Ethan's voice dripped with venom.

Those few words told her everything she needed to know about his less-than-temperate behavior. The Bastard was gracing them with his presence tonight. Ethan's use of the word made the mental capitalization mandatory. To be fair, she'd used the word in the same way.

She set her book aside and gave Ethan her complete attention. "I honestly don't understand—why do you let him enrage you like this? You know there's nothing we can do to stop Father from having a relationship with him. I'm not even sure we should try anymore."

Ethan stared at her, shocked. "How can you say that? It's obvious what the scum wants."

She leaned back in her chair. "Is it? I'm not so certain these days. If Jared Mertz was trying to take advantage of his blood, you'd think he'd be a little more aggressive in advancing his career."

"The Bastard forces himself on us time and time again, all Father ever does is cater to him, and now you've become his apologist? The man wants something, and I'm not convinced he won't get it. Father has been muttering and planning something."

She regarded her brother coolly. "In the fifteen years we've known he's been around, I've never heard of him asking for one thing. Not for himself. Not even for Fleet. And God knows Father has a soft spot in his heart for Fleet."

"But… how can you defend him?"

Her brother's anguished face tore at her heart, but she couldn't keep catering to his fixation. "Because Jared Mertz isn't the one that created our family's problem. Father had an affair. Father had a child out of wedlock. Father shamed Mother so badly she divorced him. Jared Mertz is as much a victim of circumstances as we are."

Ethan slapped his palm on the table sharply, making her jump. "No, he is not. I think he knew *exactly* the chain of events joining Fleet would start. He did so knowing that the medical test would show precisely what it did. This is part of a long-range plan to steal our birthright."

That was ridiculous. Kelsey only barely smothered a chuckle. It wouldn't improve her brother's mood one bit. "Take a deep breath. This isn't some deep-seated conspiracy to displace you. Father would never allow that, even if the Imperial Senate did... which it won't. You've let this delusion eat at you too long. You need to get a grip."

Ethan's expression darkened further. "You're being dangerously naive, Kelsey. If one of us needs to wake up, it's you. The Bastard wants the power of the Imperial Throne. Rest assured he won't fool me as easily as he has you. Tell Father I feel ill."

Ethan stalked out of the library even angrier than when he'd arrived.

She rubbed the bridge of her nose tiredly. The normally levelheaded heir to the Imperial Throne had an unhealthy dislike for their half brother. It wasn't reassuring in a man who would one day rule the Empire. The Emperor couldn't afford to have the same kind of petty jealousies as everyone else.

Jared Mertz was a pain in her behind, too, but she had finally gained some hard-won perspective. At worst, he was some kind of power seeker, and her father would eventually see through him. He would never be more than an irritant for her or her brother.

When Jared had appeared in their lives, she'd been just old enough to understand that her family was coming apart because of him. It had taken far longer for her to realize he wasn't responsible for her parents' divorce. That didn't mean she had to like him, but she no longer blindly hated him as Ethan did.

As far as she could see, Father's formal acknowledgment of his bastard son had drastically complicated Jared Mertz's life. It made advancement in Fleet more difficult, because they avoided even the appearance of favoritism. Her discreet checks had revealed his commanders considered him a brilliant officer, and he was long overdue for promotion to captain.

She tried to get back into the book she'd been reading, but her mind refused to focus. The subject of the Empire before the rebellion and resulting Fall usually fascinated her, but she couldn't stop thinking about her half brother... and about herself.

He commanded a Fleet ship now. He'd been twenty-two Terran Standard years old—the same age as she was now—when he'd joined Fleet. He'd known what he'd wanted, and he'd pursued that goal with a single-minded determination even she had to envy. What would she be doing in fifteen years?

With Ethan as the heir, she needed to find a long-term career. Being the spare apparent wasn't very fulfilling. Once her brother married and had children of his own, she wouldn't even be that. She'd be just one more Imperial noblewoman without real purpose in her life. As if there weren't enough of those in the capital.

Fleet wasn't a good fit for her. She'd never been particularly good at obeying orders. None of the social work she'd done had excited her that much, as important as it was. She wanted an all-consuming purpose that she could dedicate her life toward fulfilling. She wanted the things she did to count for something once she was gone.

She sighed. She wouldn't solve that problem tonight. She might as well go see Father. He'd be looking for her soon enough anyway.

Kelsey found Emperor Karl Bandar of the Terran Empire sitting in his private office dressed in the ratty old jacket that he loved. The grey in his beard was almost as plentiful as the chestnut brown. It made her sad to see him age. She wanted him to continue being the vital young man she'd chased around the garden as a girl.

He looked up from his console and smiled. "Kelsey! I was just coming to look for you. We're having company for dinner."

"I heard. Father, you know Ethan doesn't enjoy these dinners."

Her father took off his glasses and set them on his desk. "I know. This is something he needs to adjust to, whether he likes it or not. Jared is his half brother. Yours too, of course. Nothing can change that."

"Yet Jared does none of us any favors by rubbing Ethan's face in it."

Her father looked confused. "Jared? How is he rubbing anyone's face in anything? I've never seen him be anything but polite. Even when others are not," he added pointedly.

"I mean him continually forcing himself on us like this."

"He's not arranging these visits. I am."

She stared at him. "You? I don't understand."

"I've apparently been too vague with my intentions. My apologies. I invite Jared to visit us several times a year so that all of you can come to know one another."

Kelsey sat down in one of the comfortable chairs scattered around the small room. "We've always assumed he was behind them. Ethan is quite certain the man is out to steal the Crown Jewels. Unsurprisingly, Ethan will not be joining us tonight."

The revelation didn't seem to be that big a surprise to her father. "I'll talk with him. Again. I'm sorry for giving you both a false impression. I suspect that Jared doesn't enjoy these gatherings any more than you do. I'd hoped to ease him into the family, but I've probably botched that, too. Perhaps you'd be so kind as to explain it to me: how can I rule dozens of worlds and yet screw up my personal life so badly?"

"I'm going to treat that as a rhetorical question. This… changes things. It's a bit embarrassing."

Her father sighed. "I'm sorry, sweetheart. I specifically invited Jared to dine with us tonight because he'll be leaving on a long-term mission tomorrow. He'll be gone at least a year. Probably two. So you'll have a while for this new information to sink in."

She perked up with genuine curiosity. "Really? What far frontier are you banishing him to? Thule?"

Her father smiled. "That's for marines, and it's not so far away. You should hear the horror stories they tell about the winter training there. You'd think their commanders were all sadists." His expression grew thoughtful. "Well, they *are* marines, so it's a distinct possibility."

"That's your Fleet prejudice talking," she said primly. "Maybe I should join the Imperial Marines to bring some well-needed perspective to this family."

He laughed before he could stop himself. Clapping his hand over his mouth only made his mirth more obvious. "I'm sorry. I shouldn't laugh. The Imperial Marines are a fine group of men and women. I just have difficulty imagining you in their ranks. In spite of your occasionally combative nature, you're a little… petite for a combat role. Besides, you just don't have the requisite killer instinct."

She stood and stared at him haughtily. Unfortunately, her eyes were still at almost the same height as his. "Are you saying that my lowly one point five meters makes me unsuitable for hand-to-hand combat?"

"Yes. I'm afraid that's exactly what I'm saying. I'm positive the smallest woman I've seen in the marines topped you by a head and weighed half again more than you weigh. It might be… embarrassing to the Imperial dignity to have them hold you at arm's length while you swing futilely at them."

Kelsey sighed theatrically. "I suppose I need to cancel my order for combat armor and automatic weapons."

"That might be for the best, yes." His eyes twinkled. "Despite my questionable sense of humor, any service would be better for having you, though I really don't think you're suited for the marines."

"Maybe I should date one."

His shocked expression made her laugh. "You should see your face. It's like you've seen a ghost."

He made a gesture for warding off evil. "Don't even joke about that. My heart might fail."

She tilted her head a little to the side. "Why? I thought you said they were fine men."

"They are. Just not the kind of men a father wants his daughter to date. I'll make sure to send any you find attractive to Thule for an extended period. Perhaps a decade will do as an example to the rest."

Kelsey gave him a gimlet eye. "You think you're funny, but you're not." She resumed her seat with a sigh. "I doubt I'm a good candidate for the military at all, honestly. I've tried to get into the social scene, doing good works there, but I'm not satisfied. Thinking about Jared made me realize that he's achieved so much in his chosen field. He commands a ship in the Imperial Fleet. That's huge!"

Her father nodded. "That's a very significant thing indeed. I served in Fleet long enough to gain a tremendous respect for the kind of person who commands a ship in space. The very least of them is a leader of some note. Your half brother is far from the least of them. His commanding officers all respect him. Admiral Yeats told me that if he'd had his way, Jared would be commanding a cruiser task force by now. One day he'll be an admiral. Not because of his connection to our family but in spite of it."

"That won't go over well with Ethan," she mumbled only barely audibly.

She gave him a haughty stare. "Just so you know, that doesn't make me feel any better. I mean, hello, this conversation is about me and my options… or lack thereof."

"You know you can literally do anything. What do you enjoy doing that might translate into some career?"

"I don't know. I'm good at the things you've trained me to do as an Imperial ruler, but that isn't likely. Ethan is depressingly healthy, and I like you too much to have you assassinated."

"Well, that *is* an obstacle to your ascension to the Imperial Throne. Remind me to hire some food tasters at once."

"Right after dinner."

"Ha! Good one! Honestly, there are careers that are perfectly suited for your skills. For example, you trained with that young man from the Department of Imperial Affairs for a while. They handle diplomatic affairs of all kinds inside the Empire. That's something we'll always need."

She nodded slowly. "True. Carlo Vega. He's a senior attaché, and I admit that his work always seemed interesting."

"I'm sure there are other avenues you could pursue. You've been spending a great deal of time in the Imperial Archives, for example. Are you researching something?"

"Aren't your spies following me? I figured they'd already told you what I'm looking into."

"Perhaps I should actually hire some. I'm certain there's a conspiracy going on somewhere that I should know about."

She gave her father a stern look. "Don't try to fool me. Everyone knows you have secret police to spy on everyone."

"Secret police? I had no idea." He smiled. "Seriously, I haven't felt the need to set my spies on you. I'm certain they have far more pressing matters requiring their attention. What have you been researching?"

Kelsey crossed her legs. "If only it were something spies would be interested in. I've just been reading up on the Old Empire. Speculation on what sparked the rebellion that led to the Fall. I wanted to see if I could find anything in the restricted stacks about it."

"Hmmm... the rebellion and the pre-Fall Terran Empire," her father said, his eyes sharpening. "That *is* worthy of study. I seem to recall seeing quite a few new books on the shelves on the subject in the library. What's driving this sudden interest?"

"I read a first-person account of the exploration mission Grandfather sent out. The book has been out for over a decade, but I missed it somehow. Maybe I was a little too young to be interested back then." Or too distracted by her family situation.

"It's a fascinating story," she said. "Imagine exploring the worlds of what used to be the Terran Empire. Finding the ruins of civilization. Searching for lost Terra. That kind of thing could excite anyone. You really should consider sending out another expedition."

He nodded thoughtfully. "That's a good idea. I'll look into it."

"You should. So, what is this mission that's taking my half brother away for so long?"

"Well, that's an interesting story—"

The buzzer on her father's console sounded. He tapped the screen. "Yes?"

"I'm sorry to disturb you, Your Majesty. Commander Mertz has arrived at the first checkpoint."

"Send him up as soon as he's in the palace."

Her father stood. "I should go get dressed. I wouldn't want to have you tell me what a disgrace I am for wearing this jacket to dinner again." He pulled her into a hug and kissed her cheek. "Please, do try not to blame Jared for my actions." A smile crept across his lips as he looked into her eyes. "See you in a bit."

Kelsey watched him leave and sighed. As much as she doubted she'd be any more comfortable with her half brother, she'd try for her father's sake. She headed for her room. She had just enough time to make herself presentable.

3

J ared exited his grav car at the secure parking lot just inside the security checkpoint. The Imperial Guardsmen then scanned his person completely. He knew better than to bring anything with him on these visits. That was an invitation to have it confiscated. These people made the security sweeps at Orbital One seem negligent. He sent his holiday gifts weeks in advance rather than bringing them himself.

As the silent man in pressed whites ran a wand over him, Jared wondered what became of the gifts he gave his half siblings. They probably threw them out. Prince Ethan most likely burned his.

The Imperial Family sent a combined gift, almost certainly picked out by his father. Usually something useful to a serving officer, though expensive.

When he was a child, his mother had regaled him with stories about when she worked in the Imperial Palace. He'd hung on every word and dreamed of what he'd ever do if he met the emperor.

Of course, he'd had no idea just how well she'd known the ruler of the Empire.

He'd graduated the regional Fleet academy and was taking his final acceptance physical here on Avalon. It was significantly more thorough than anything he'd gone through before, but he hadn't been concerned. At least until they took another tissue sample for "further DNA testing."

He'd sat waiting for the results in a small medical room for so long that he'd begun to suspect he had some subtle genetic flaw. Looked at in the proper light, he supposed he did.

In the end, the doctor was not who came in to tell him the results. The emperor himself did.

Of course, he'd known who the emperor was. Even asteroid miners who'd been born in the depths of space knew what the emperor looked like.

Jared had watched every State of the Empire speech since he'd decided to become a Fleet officer.

That had been the least of the shocks on that cursed day. Finding out he was an Imperial bastard had set his world off course. For his own part, the news was so far out of his realm of experience that he rejected it. Someone had to have made a horrible mistake.

Only they hadn't.

The next few months had been a special kind of hell. Why the man had decided he needed to tell anyone else was beyond Jared's comprehension. One couldn't turn on a vid without seeing something. The only thing anyone talked about was the disintegration of the Imperial couple and the bastard child who caused it.

Worst of all, everyone around him knew. He could feel them staring at his back, whispering about him when they thought he wasn't listening... blaming him.

Then there was the small minority of people that thought they could benefit from cozying up to him. Those unfortunate few were sadly mistaken in their estimation of his influence. Imperial blood brought him no power. He tirelessly avoided the appearance of ever trying to exert any sort of influence while also going out of his way to preserve the appearance of loyalty to the Imperial House, no matter how he might feel inside.

He struggled with the effects of that day even now. The guard finished scanning him, his expression blank. Jared had met this particular man a dozen times over the years, but he'd heard scarcely a handful of words from him. Did he despise Jared? Did he fear that Jared would take some action against his master? Perhaps he was just being unapproachably professional.

Jared would probably never know. It hurt to be isolated this way from everyone around him. To have everything he did dissected to reveal any suspected hidden motives. He could never be certain what people really thought about him.

"If you'll come with me, sir, I'll escort you to the palace," the man said. Much the same as he had during the last half dozen visits.

A heavily armored grav car took them to the palace proper. The grounds were huge and beautiful, as always. That was the one thing he really did envy his half siblings for, their easy access to such lush and lavish parks at a moment's notice.

The car entered an underground parking garage, and his keeper handed him off to different guards, who treated him with the same sterile attention. They scanned him again. Of course.

He raised his arms as one guard ran a scanner over every part of his body. A second stood close by, her hand resting on her belt beside her holstered weapon. Once the man was certain Jared wasn't about to explode, he checked Jared's ID and took another ocular scan.

Only then did they allow him to pass, but never without an armed escort, of course. Everyone seemed to have a weapon but him.

Jared stopped at the elevator and examined his dress uniform in the mirror. He made one last check that the gold rank insignia on his black jacket and shined boots were free of smudges. His black beret with his ship's insignia completed his uniform. The red striping along the black pants legs gave just the right flair, in his opinion. Not that anyone had consulted him during the last uniform redesign. He hadn't even been born then.

They rode up to the residence level in silence. The guards took him through enough halls that he was almost certain he'd never be able to find his way back out on his own. As far as he could tell, they never brought him in the same way twice. While it probably wasn't true, the special care they took to turn him around made it all feel… personal.

Then again, perhaps they only rearranged the artwork. The collection of paintings and statues was never the same. A significant number of them were on loan from the Imperial Museum, pre-Fall works from the homes of the wealthy here on Avalon and recovered from the worlds they'd rediscovered since they returned to space. It probably didn't hold a candle to what had been in the Imperial Palace on Terra, but it was enough to interest even someone not into art, such as himself.

Eventually, they stopped at the doors to the Imperial Family's private rooms. The guards stayed outside and allowed Jared to proceed alone. They probably thought that wasn't the best idea, but the emperor insisted that Jared be treated as family.

Jared had no idea what the guards thought of the emperor summoning his bastard son to dinner. There was no telling.

The emperor's legitimate children felt no need to restrain their emotions. Crown Prince Ethan's distaste and loathing were obvious enough to earn rebukes from his father. The heir didn't let that stop him though.

Ethan's twin sister viewed him with similar distaste, but Jared thought that stemmed almost exclusively because Jared was the physical proof of her father's infidelity. She wasn't blatantly hostile. She seemed to prefer a cold, distant demeanor. Only the emperor made any effort to make him feel welcome. Of course, he was the one who insisted that Jared come calling, so that only seemed right.

When Jared entered the enormous living room, the emperor arose from his comfortable chair in front of the fireplace to greet him. "Jared, it's so good to see you again. Come, sit with me."

Jared suppressed the urge to bow. Even after fifteen years, that wasn't easy. Innate respect for the Crown sat deeply in his bones. That was true for most of the Imperial population. He extended his hand instead.

Even the idea of shaking the Imperial hand was mind numbing. It seemed disrespectful. He silently thanked God that the man didn't insist on a hug.

The small table between the two chairs held a decanter of amber liquid and two glasses. One already had two fingers of drink in it. Jared's father sat back down and poured some into the second glass.

Getting into the mental space where the emperor became his father was difficult. Jared took the proffered drink and sat. The whisky was smooth and warm. It was probably older than he was.

The emperor wore casual clothes. His salt-and-pepper hair and fine wrinkles showed that age was taking its toll. He eyed Jared's uniform with amusement.

"You know you don't need to wear that. Not that I have anything against Fleet. My time there is one of my fondest memories, though I'm sure my superiors didn't see it that way at the time."

"Admiral Yeats disagrees. If I wore anything else, it would be as if I showed up naked."

That brought a laugh from the older man. "I see. Well, far be it from me to cause you any more problems than I already have. We'll start dinner in a few minutes, but I wanted to take a moment to congratulate you on your new assignment. It's well deserved."

Jared sipped his drink. "I'm excited. Fleet picking me to probe beyond our borders is an honor."

"I was about your age when the last expedition took place. I'd already left the Fleet by then. I made it to lieutenant and felt that was an accomplishment. I badgered my father to send me along, but he wouldn't hear of it. The Crown Prince needed to be here on Avalon."

He raised his glass to Jared. "Being chosen for this assignment is quite an achievement. The Terran Empire is meticulous about who they appoint to command an interstellar vessel, much less who they send out to possibly contact other systems. Though I'm sure you already know this, allow me to state for the record that I pulled no strings. You earned this honor on your own merits. Well done, Commander."

"Thank you, sir."

The two of them sat sipping their drinks and talking about recent events for the next ten minutes. Even after all these years, Jared still wasn't sure what the emperor hoped to see happen. The gulf between them was too wide. Perhaps the man just wanted to connect with his illegitimate son. That wouldn't be easy for anyone, but it was probably more difficult for the emperor.

He rose when the emperor did and followed him into the dining room. They'd just walked in when Princess Kelsey came in the other door. She wore a pale blue dress made of some light material that showcased her elfin figure. The men sat once she'd seated herself. Jared made no move to hold her chair for her. He'd learned the hard way that she didn't appreciate the gesture from him.

The princess was dainty. A full head and a half shorter than him, she couldn't have weighed more than forty-five kilograms. Long curly blonde hair framed a heart-shaped face with bright blue eyes. Some nobleman would be happy to have her. Jared wished the poor bastard the best of luck.

She shook out her napkin. "Ethan is feeling ill tonight and begs our guest's indulgence for his absence."

A polite fiction, Jared knew, but infinitely preferable to the hostile sniping disguised as conversation the prince favored. "Of course, Princess. I hope he recovers swiftly. Please send him my regards."

Their father didn't look very pleased, but he didn't make an issue out of it. "Kelsey, to answer your earlier question, Jared has been appointed to command an exploratory expedition beyond the borders of the Empire. He'll be leaving tomorrow. We won't publically announce it until after they've departed."

Her expression brightened. "That's wonderful! Congratulations. I've been reading about the last expedition. It all sounds very dangerous and exciting. Will you be looking for Terra?"

He smiled, pleased at her enthusiasm. "I'm sure everyone would be happy if we found it, but that isn't our mission. We'll be locating unexplored flip points and seeing what's on the other side of them. The odds are very good we'll find something similar to the primitive systems we've already discovered."

She looked disappointed. "You don't think you'll find anything else?"

"Perhaps there will be some intact ruins from before the Fall. That's what the science community hopes anyway. A true treasure would be chancing on some undamaged computers, ones the rebels hadn't fried. Finding Terra or any other major world isn't very likely considering Avalon was on the edge of the Old Empire. This part of space didn't contain one of the core systems they spoke of in the old stories."

"Wouldn't that be something to see?" The emperor mused. "I've seen the few existing images and videos of Imperial City on Terra. The buildings seemed to touch the skies. I've always thought the Terran Empire should have Terra as one of her planets again."

The emperor shook his head. "I suppose I should just be pleased that our ancestor was able to flee here and that the few rebel ships that followed him didn't eradicate all life before they were destroyed. We lost so much."

Jared had seen the crater left after the destruction of the former capital of Avalon and its spaceport. He understood completely.

The servers came in with dinner. The palace chefs had cooked the fish to perfection. It smelled delicious. Jared sipped the wine the man poured for him with approval.

Jared continued the conversation after taking a bite of his crisp salad. "I've been looking over the records since I received my orders. The worlds we rediscovered didn't seem high tech before the Fall. They were mostly agricultural planets and mining systems where the asteroid belts made mineral recovery easy. Things would've been very different in the core systems of the Old Empire."

The pictures of Imperial City told that tale effectively enough. Terra must've had tens of billions of people. Those not killed in the war would have starved. Oh, certainly, humans were hard to exterminate completely, but the death toll must've been staggering. He could see from their faces that the other two had some idea of what he was implying.

His father nodded. "We were lucky. Society dropped back to

prespaceflight technology, but now we're expanding again. We're still the same Terran Empire, our history and rule unbroken. Thanks to Lucien and Fleet's sacrifice."

Princess Kelsey ate quietly for a while before coming back to the subject. "We've explored quite a ways, haven't we? How far away do you think the core systems of the Old Empire are?"

Jared shrugged. "No one really knows. Frankly, we're not even certain we're exploring in the right direction. Avalon was a resort world with tall mountains for skiing and wilderness for the well to do. One far away from the rest of civilization. When the rebels took out our capital and spaceport with a kinetic strike, it wiped away any computer that had that information. The global EMP strike did the same for the rest of the planet.

"That seems to have been the pattern on all the worlds we've rediscovered. All orbitals and spaceports destroyed. The rebels seem to have used EMP weapons to fry any electronics left on the surface. A few very general maps survived, mostly in the few abandoned and overlooked asteroid mining facilities, but none of them showed our sector of space. That's where our only remaining images of Terra come from."

He took a bite of his fish, letting the taste fill his mouth. "We might be exploring along the edges of the Old Empire. We know it was huge. We've colonized dozens of systems. We've probed the flip points two or three hops beyond our borders, which means we've some knowledge of over a hundred other systems."

"Why don't we go faster? We've had flip drives again for almost a hundred years."

Her father answered the question. "Because flip drives require very rare exotic elements to construct. Combined with the expense of building ships, that limits Fleet's size. With the mines we found on Grathan a few years ago, the supply of those elements is no longer an issue. However, the cost to extract and ship them still is. Fleet is expanding now, which frees up a few ships to explore. I've decided to have four of the older destroyers assigned to this exploration duty on a permanent basis."

He nodded his head toward Jared. "No disrespect to your ship, of course."

"None taken, sir. *Athena* is a magnificent ship, even if she isn't the newest in Fleet anymore. Her crew is the best."

"Of course. The worlds we've settled had populations ranging from primitive hunter-gatherers to preindustrial," the emperor said. "Incorporating them into society and raising their standard of living is a huge strain on our economy. We have an obligation to help any civilization we find. That creates a great strain on the Empire's finances. However, we are working to streamline the process. We've been working with the universities over the last decade to train young scientists to accompany these expeditions, too. That doesn't happen overnight."

The young woman nodded. "I suppose that makes sense. How far will you go?"

"However far we can get in nine months," Jared said. "We'll explore well enough to bring a good record back. If we find something interesting, that return date is subject to my discretion, so if we're late, it doesn't automatically mean disaster."

"Is trouble likely?"

"We didn't lose any ships during the previous expedition, but that might have been luck. We really have no way of knowing."

"I wish I could go."

"Everyone on this mission has a job to do, ma'am. Do you have any skills that would make it a good idea to bump one of them?" He certainly hoped not.

Princess Kelsey shook her head. "I wish I did. Unfortunately, the life of a princess isn't very useful in providing real-world experience."

After they finished their meal, they returned to the living room and talked late into the night. He knew he'd have to hustle in the morning in order to catch the early shuttle to Orbital One, but he was loath to disrupt the first real pleasant moment he'd had with his half sister.

Eventually, however, he had to leave. He rose to his feet. "As much as I have enjoyed our visit, I'm afraid I need to call it an evening. The mission briefing is early tomorrow… this morning. Thank you both for the exquisite meal… and for the pleasant conversation."

His father stood and shook his hand. "I look forward to hearing what you find. Know that the Empire and I are proud of you, and we're behind you completely."

"I pray you find everything you hope and more, Jared," Princess Kelsey said. "Be careful out there. I also look forward to hearing about all your adventures when you return."

A different pair of guards waited for him when he left the Imperial residence. They led him back to the lift and escorted him to the underground garage. They stopped at the security checkpoint and let him walk to the grav car alone.

He thought that was odd until he saw who was standing beside the vehicle. Crown Prince Ethan.

"Your Highness," Jared said in a tone free of inflection as he nodded his head forward. "I hope I didn't keep you waiting long."

"Save your feeble attempts at humor, Bastard. I hope you had a good time tonight, because it won't be happening again."

A chill ran up Jared's spine. "Is that so?"

The prince stepped into his personal space. "For your sake, it had better be. This is the one and only warning I'm going to give you. I will not allow you to continue scheming against my family and me. Stay away, or I will make certain you never trouble me and mine again. Am I clear?"

"You act as though I have a choice. If you want to see the last of me, speak to your father. When the emperor summons you, you come."

Prince Ethan's expression contorted into a snarl. "You think you're clever? Very well. We'll do this the hard way."

Jared felt an uneasy sinking feeling in the pit of his stomach as he watched the prince stalk away. Just what he needed—more Imperial intrigue. At least he'd have a few years' reprieve before seeing his brother again. Perhaps the boy's rancor would cool during Jared's absence... before he did something they'd both most certainly regret.

4

Kelsey went back to the library after dinner. It was very late, but all the talk about the Old Empire had made her want to go back over what she'd been reading again. She went directly to the paper books. Many of the modern works were in electronic form, but she preferred paper where possible. The smell and feel of real books filled some need inside her that a tablet didn't.

An incredible and irreplaceable amount of history from before the Fall had been lost during the orbital bombardment. While the only population center hit was Wash Gorge, the city surrounding the spaceport and planetary operations center, that didn't mean that the rest of the planet had escaped. EMP weapons had burned out every piece of electronics on the face of the planet.

Military equipment was hardened to survive that kind of thing, but the battle in orbit destroyed all that. When they as a people finally returned to space, nothing useful remained. The major wreckage had burned up on reentry over the centuries or wandered far into the depths between the planets.

Thankfully, the kinetic weapon that killed everyone in the capital city hadn't left any radiation. They were able to rebuild in the fertile valley. Avalon had been a very popular vacation destination before the Fall. Even with the total destruction of the only major city on the planet, almost a hundred thousand people had survived.

The last emperor of the Old Empire had even sent his son fleeing before the last of the Imperial Fleet went to engage the rebels in a do-or-die last-ditch effort to save the Empire from total destruction.

It certainly seemed that do or die turned out to be the latter, since no Fleet vessels ever followed Lucien to Avalon. Of course, no rebel vessels came either, thank God. Perhaps they'd exterminated one another. Kelsey certainly hoped the rebels were long gone.

The boy-emperor's escort had stuffed him into a life pod as soon as their ship made orbit. A wise decision, since the rebels destroyed their ship before Lucien's pod even made it to the atmosphere. The escorting Fleet units fought bravely, but they couldn't stop the attack on the planet.

Even though it was impossible to know for certain, the prevailing theory was that they fought to mutual extinction with the rebels. All anyone knew for sure was that any detailed knowledge of the rebels and their aims was lost in the chaos and death.

One thing they did know was that some Fleet units had defected and fought savagely against their brothers. The aims of the rebels remained a subject of intense debate in the various history departments to this day.

She opened her favorite book on the subject to one of the few surviving pictures of Lucien, taken a few months after his arrival. The boy-emperor looked filthy and had a heavy sling full of grain over his shoulder. He also looked like a man determined to save every one of his subjects if it killed him.

His example of working just as hard as every one of his subjects set the tone for his descendants. All sought out public service. All gave much of their time to improving the lives of the people they ruled. Yes, the people were no longer struggling to survive the winters, but the same desire to serve filled her.

Kelsey envied her half brother. He was living her dream and boldly going into the Old Empire. She knew he'd find the answers she craved. Perhaps that would make up for the chaos her family had made of his life.

The library door opened and her father came in. "There you are. I went to your room to talk, but you'd vanished. I was afraid you'd snuck off to stow away on the expedition."

She perked up a little. "Do you think I could hide out until they made it into the Old Empire? I could pack enough food to stay in some crawlspace and sneak out for showers."

He laughed and sat down beside her. "I'm afraid not. I'd worry terribly about where you'd gotten off to and send word to every corner of the Empire to search for you. The fact you just expressed an interest in the expedition means I'd send word to Jared. He's a good man. He'd turn his ships upside down to be sure you hadn't slipped aboard. He knows them much better than you do."

"Pity. Seriously, though, what could I do to prepare for a future mission? I know the competition to go must be intense. I'm not sure I'm good enough to make that final cut, no matter how hard I work. Sometimes your best just isn't good enough."

"You are rather behind in your technical education if you wanted to be a leading scientific candidate on a future mission," he admitted. "The people who made the cut this time worked hard for a decade or more in their chosen fields of study. You'd probably have to expend a similar amount of time going forward to be where they are now."

She slumped in her chair. "That's what I was afraid you'd say. I'm afraid being an empress in training isn't very useful on a mission of exploration."

"True. That's more Jared's job. Perhaps you should look over the personnel manifest to see what kind of specialties they might need for future expeditions. I know I have it somewhere in my personal files."

He retrieved a tablet from the table and authenticated himself on the system. Then he dug around the palace computers for a few minutes. "Here we go. This file has the full list of people and their specialties. Well, except for a few last-minute decisions by the university heads."

Kelsey gave him a curious look. "Last-minute decisions? I'd have expected they knew who was going months or years ago. What do they have to do with making the final selections anyway? Shouldn't Fleet do that?"

"The four premiere Imperial universities are funding the conversion and outfitting of the freighters housing the science labs. They're also training almost two hundred specialists in any number of scientific fields per mission. Shouldn't they narrow it down to the best-qualified ones?"

"That's not the question I asked, Father. It seems to me that the only reason the final choices haven't already been made must be due to politics or money."

He raised an eyebrow and smiled a little. "That's a bit cynical but probably true. There's a lot of prestige on the line. I'm sure a few last-minute endowments have been made to alter a few choices, though I'm confident that no one incapable of doing the work would make the final list."

"Perhaps I should make a large contribution from my trust fund to one of universities. That puts both money and political interest on the line."

"Let's say you did. What role would you play in the expedition?"

She scanned the file slowly. The roster covered every possible scientific field: geology, biology, archeology, history, physics, and almost everything else she could name... and more than a few she couldn't. Most of the people listed had multiple areas of study under their belts.

Curious, she had the tablet sort the data by discipline. Indeed, every field had a number of people. From an exploratory angle, they seemed to have all the bases covered.

So, following that logic, what might they be missing? One thing she'd learned early in her Imperial training was that big problems didn't usually come from contingencies you put in place. The things that often bit you on the backside were the ones you'd never considered in the first place. What had they planned for and what had they missed?

"Do you have the full mission parameters?" she asked.

He again took over the tablet long enough to give her the information. She noticed he wasn't reading over her shoulder. He was watching her.

She'd seen him do this before. He was seeing how she reacted to a problem and how she approached solving it. Did that mean there was a weakness in the mission planning, or was he just using this as a teaching moment? She'd find out soon enough.

It took half an hour to read the full mission brief. She knew some of it was in all likelihood classified, but she had the highest-level clearances imaginable. The spare apparent needed to have the same skill set and access to details as the heir. Her father undoubtedly knew some secrets she didn't, but he never skimped on sharing classified information with her.

She almost asked for the crew manifest for Jared's destroyer, *Athena*, but she saw her father already had opened it as well. He'd anticipated her thought process. Of course. An emperor had best be thinking a few moves ahead of everyone else.

Kelsey leaned back and stared at the ceiling once she finished reading. All the information was buzzing through her head. She knew it would coalesce into an understandable bundle with a little more time, but already there was something nibbling at her consciousness. Something was missing.

Was it a missing skill or an unconsidered possibility? It seemed as if they'd planned based on the events of the previous exploration. So, what hadn't happened on that mission?

They hadn't found extensive ruins before, but this mission was well equipped in case they did. They hadn't found advanced civilizations either. She pondered that. The orders said they would avoid interacting with any human populations. Well and good, if they were as primitive as those found thus far.

But what if they found a more advanced people? The mission orders didn't address that possibility. They just instructed Jared to avoid contact. Escape and evasion might prove impossible with a space-capable civilization. What would they do then?

Make contact. Negotiate. Set up diplomatic relations.

"Father, there are no trained, experienced diplomats on any of these manifests. What if they need to interact with an advanced society that becomes aware of their presence?"

"Let me see." He took the tablet and scanned the files. "Fleet has the military side of operations in hand. The science ship has the scientific side. It looks like there may be a gap in the mission statement. I'd suppose that Jared will act as the face of the Empire."

She narrowed her eyes. "No offense to my half brother, but is he trained as a negotiator? I'll grant that he has a lot of patience, but he's a military officer. If trouble comes up, he'll use the tools he knows. In this case, weapons."

Her father looked less than convinced. "Come now. I'm certain he'd never open hostilities without significant provocation."

"Probably not, but shouldn't someone trained in diplomacy ride along in case something delicate needs to be addressed? They should have someone onboard who can explain delicate things, like why his ship might be sneaking around in someone else's territory. It hasn't happened thus far, but the possibility increases with every mission."

Her father leaned back and contemplated her for a minute. "What are you suggesting? That I should send you to cover that position?"

Kelsey shook her head. "No. The Department of Imperial Affairs has people that settle disagreements between the worlds of the Empire every day. Carlo Vega, or someone like him, would be perfect. I'd say send two experienced negotiators per mission."

Her father stared off into the distance for a few minutes before nodding. "I think you may be right. I'll go back to my office and make some calls. I'll need to act fast if I want to make this happen. I don't want to delay the missions."

He stood and stretched. "You've served the Empire well tonight, Kelsey. This oversight could have had very drastic consequences. Well done. Now, it's late. You'd best get some sleep. One never knows what unexpected events will land on one's lap first thing in the morning."

5

The next morning disabused Jared of the notion that things would go more smoothly just because he'd had a good evening. He woke late, missed the first shuttle, and ended up docking at the far side of Orbital One. He normally enjoyed walking through the station's bustling corridors, but Admiral Yeats wasn't fond of tardy officers.

The yard technicians in their bright-blue jumpsuits seemed to be everywhere. He'd never seen so many of them clogging the corridors before. He finally made it to the conference room ten minutes late.

The room held several dozen people, about evenly split between Fleet officers and civilians. The civilians would be the senior scientific team leaders. Everyone turned to stare at Jared as he took the empty seat beside Graves. Charlie's expression gave nothing away, but there was a deep twinkle in his eye. He'd be teasing Jared about this for months.

Admiral Yeats fixed Jared with an unfriendly stare designed to melt junior officers. "So good of you to join us, Commander. Would you like me to start over?"

"No, sir." He felt a flush creeping up his neck. "I apologize for my tardiness."

The admiral gave him another beat of silence before returning to his notes. "As I was saying, the four converted freighters housing the science teams have completed their refits and are ready to go. The science team leaders have checked the labs and addressed all deficiencies. The four destroyers and their accompanying science vessels will depart as soon as all personnel have reported aboard."

He made a gesture to the conference room door. "I'm certain you've all noticed the people swarming around Orbital One. The shipyard technicians are leaving the ships and departing for Avalon to take some well-deserved rest. Enough will remain on hand to address any last-minute issues, of course.

"The chips in front of you contain the full rosters of your expeditions. The expedition commanders are already familiar with the senior science people, but there were some eleventh-hour substitutions that these lists accurately document."

Admiral Yeats tapped the recessed console in front of him, and the lights dimmed. The Imperial star map with connecting lines denoting matched flip points appeared on the wall screen. Green dots represented the core systems, blue marked the rest of the Empire, and yellow noted the explored but unaligned systems.

The map looked like a toy designed by a lunatic. Flip lines shot out for a hundred light years, then came back in fifty, only to shoot out another direction. It all seemed perfectly random. One system only ten light years away from Avalon took four flips to get there, traveling over three hundred light years. Most known systems had two flip points, but a few had only one and several had three.

Red dots represented star systems that no one had ever visited. Most wouldn't have flip points at all. That much had come down through their oral history. The vast majority of worlds would never see human visitation.

The admiral highlighted four systems with unexplored flip points on the periphery of the Empire. "While there are literally dozens of possible paths, the experts have selected these four systems for attention at this time. Each has habitable though unoccupied planets. In a pinch, you could survive there if trouble strikes.

"With the distances involved, it will take your ships about a month to get to your kickoff points. We don't expect you back for eighteen months. I'm aware that might be conservative if you find something interesting, but rest assured we'll come looking for you if you don't make it back in three years. You'll be leaving probes in every system you explore, starting with your kickoff points. Keep them updated with your most recent situation reports as you move on and recover them on the way back. We'll use them to follow you if need be. Fleet doesn't abandon its own."

He swept the room with his gaze. "I don't expect you to run into trouble you can't handle, but if you do, I expect you to be prudent. Retreat if there is danger beyond your ability to handle it. The Empire needs to know what you find. If things really go into the toilet, the science ship will retreat while the destroyer provides cover. Understood?"

Once they had all muttered their understanding, he turned off the screen. "The Terran Empire is proud of each of you. You're our best and brightest. I have no doubt you'll make us proud. Good luck. Dismissed. Commander Mertz, a moment."

Charlie leaned over as he rose to his feet. "I'll get the marines to organize a rescue party if you're not back to the ship in half an hour."

"Thanks," Jared muttered.

Once everyone else had left the room, the admiral took a seat beside him at the table. "Would you care to explain your tardiness?"

"I have no excuses, sir."

Yeats's expression cracked a little, allowing a small smile through. "You sound just like your father when you say that. It's a bit uncanny. I'm not looking for an excuse, just an explanation."

Jared took a deep breath. "Dinner went much better than I anticipated and I stayed very late. I missed the first shuttle, and the departing shipyard crew delayed me. I'm sorry, sir."

The admiral's smile widened. "That's excellent news. I officially retract my disapproval. Hell, you could've missed this briefing and I'd still be happy to hear things are improving on that front. Might I ask what happened to make things better?"

"Princess Kelsey expressed an interest in the expedition. She wanted to hear everything I could tell her. I wouldn't be surprised if she started working on an angle to help with future expeditions."

"I hope she does. An Imperial patron would be helpful in a number of ways. She could help shepherd an increased budget through the tight-fisted old men in the Imperial Senate. Of course, a major find by any of the teams will spark a full-blown follow-up and have incalculable benefit for Fleet."

Admiral Yeats rose, and Jared stood. He clapped his hand on Jared's shoulder. "I wish you the very best of luck, Commander. Go bring home the bacon, and bring your people back with it."

"Yes, sir."

He followed the admiral out of the briefing room and fought the crowds toward the upper levels of the orbital. *Athena*'s cutter waited there. The rest of the crew was already aboard ship, so he was the only passenger.

The trip was brief. He took a moment to admire *Athena*'s lines through the port. *Athena* was only a destroyer, so she looked like a toy beside *Best Deal*, the converted freighter housing the science teams.

Freighters needed to be large to carry as much cargo as possible between systems. It stretched 3,500 meters and looked like a block 450 meters wide and tall. It displaced millions of tons and could only crawl along under that tremendous load, even with upgraded drives.

The labs only took up a small amount of that vast space. They'd left the remaining cargo areas as is to carry any recovered artifacts. Six cargo shuttles seemed like overkill to Jared, but the ship normally carried them as well as two civilian personnel cutters. Jared had to admit they might come in handy.

The freighter normally flew with thirty officers and three hundred and seventy crew, but that took a full load of cargo into account. The captain of *Best Deal* had released two hundred of his crew slots to the science teams. That made the remaining crew grumble, but if push came to shove, they could compel the scientists into manual labor. Although Jared was sure doing so would cause innumerable complaints.

Athena might look like a minnow beside *Best Deal*, but she was a deadly one. She was a mere six hundred meters in length. Her hull was one hundred and twenty meters across and eighty tall. Her crew complement was much larger than the size difference would suggest, with twenty-one Fleet officers and two hundred and twenty-nine crew. The ship also had a detachment of thirty marines to provide armed personnel.

She also had twice the speed of the massive freighter. This meant that she could make the journey to the target star system in a little over two weeks if traveling alone.

Thankfully, the flip points in a system were usually just outside the system's habitable zone. If they were further out, the trip would take even longer.

The placement had something to do with the mass of the host stars, but that didn't seem to dictate the number of flip points in a system. It made cosmologists a little crazy because no one really knew why only some stars had them. If someone ever figured out that mystery, he or she would win the Lucien Prize for sure.

The cutter maneuvered adroitly to the forward docking port assigned it and mated with hardly a bump. Jared waited for the light over the lock to go green and entered his ship. *Athena* had three personnel cutters and two marine combat pinnaces. The marine small craft berthed at the aft of the ship near marine country. Up front, the cutters took up three of the four docks. The fourth was for visiting vehicles.

The closest lift took him to the bridge in a matter of minutes. It wasn't in the nose of the ship, as the entertainment vids liked to portray, but in the ship's center. Command and control needed to be one of the most protected areas of the ship—not because the commander was more important but because loss of control meant probable death in combat.

Not that he'd ever been in real combat. No living Fleet officer had.

Helm and tactical took up the front of the bridge. His console was in the center of the compartment, and three unattended consoles faced to the rear and side of the oval chamber. Extra crew could staff those positions if something happened to the main consoles, but they typically housed observers.

It was a much tighter fit than in the vids, too. Barely seven meters long and five wide. A heavy cruiser's bridge was about twice that size.

Graves stood as Jared entered. "You made it back alive, I see. I was just about to send the marines."

Jared smiled and took the seat his executive officer had just vacated. "It was a close thing, let me tell you. What's our status?"

"All personnel are present. The last load of supplies came on board five minutes ago. *Best Deal* is running behind. Of course. Things seem a little disorganized over there. Captain Keller said they would be ready in ten minutes."

That likely meant fifteen or twenty minutes. Anything that had to do with the civilian scientists seemed to be prone to delays.

Jared shook his head with a smile. "There's no use pushing for them to go faster. That would slow them down even more. I can't wait to see the first emergency drill over there."

Charlie rolled his eyes. "No kidding. People running in every direction and some not bothering to go to emergency stations at all. Too busy with real work to be playing sailor. It'll be a real laugh."

"I wouldn't start chuckling just yet. I'm sending you over to set it up and grade the results. Then you'll work with Captain Keller to get a training plan in place to see they get better. If things go to hell, I don't want them killing themselves."

"Thanks," Charlie muttered.

Lieutenant Anderson turned toward them. "Captain, there is a cutter requesting permission to dock. It says they have a couple of late-arriving crewmen."

Jared arched an eyebrow. "I thought you said everyone was aboard, Charlie. Did you misplace someone?"

Graves looked puzzled. "Everyone *is* accounted for."

"Zia, who are the crewmen?"

She spoke into her headset. "They say they have the diplomatic representatives on board."

Jared brought up the crew manifest on his console. No diplomatic representatives. According to his orders, he'd be representing the Empire if need be. "Permission to dock is granted. I'll go down myself and find out what's going on. Charlie, you have the bridge."

"Aye, sir."

Jared took the lift back down to the forward docking bay. He heard the muffled clank of the cutter docking just as he arrived. A bit of cold mist puffed out of the lock as the interior and exterior hatches slid open. A crewman in a dark grey flight suit stepped out and saluted him, right fist to chest. He'd just returned it when two other people followed the man out.

Jared didn't know the gentleman in the lead, but he looked like a diplomat. Tall, his dark hair shaded with distinguished gray, and impeccably dressed. However, the young woman behind him was all too familiar.

"Princess Kelsey," Jared growled. "What are you doing here?"

6

K elsey made certain to keep Carlo Vega between Jared and herself. The diplomat didn't react to her half brother's expression as he held out his hand. "Captain Mertz. So kind of you to meet us. I'm Ambassador Carlo Vega from the Department of Imperial Affairs. I'll be your diplomatic attaché on this voyage of discovery."

He stepped to the side, exposing Kelsey. "I believe you know my assistant, Kelsey Bandar. For the duration of our assignment, she will not be acting in her Imperial capacity. Rather, she will operate solely as deputy ambassador."

Jared's face clouded even further. "This isn't a casual trip through the park, Ambassador Vega. It has the potential to be very dangerous. I cannot be responsible for a member of the Imperial Family under these conditions, no matter how they choose to style themselves."

A mulish expression settled across her face, although she tried to fight it. "I apologize for the surprise, but this matter is settled. I'm staying."

"The devil it is. I cannot be responsible for your safety in this environment, Your Highness. You're leaving, even if I have to strap you into that cutter myself," Jared assured her. He looked like he'd do it, too. She'd never seen him so angry.

Vega's bland expression didn't flicker at their exchange. "I'm afraid this assignment isn't open to debate, Captain. These orders come directly from His Imperial Majesty. All four expeditions are receiving experienced diplomats and young people with extensive negotiating experience to train in this role for future missions."

As two crewmen wheeled a cart full of luggage from the cutter and began unloading it on the deck, Jared swore creatively. Kelsey made note of some of the catchier phrases for personal use later.

"This is madness," her half brother finally managed. "What if she's injured or killed? She's second in line to the Imperial Throne!"

Vega smiled. "I believe her father was a Fleet officer when he was heir to that very throne. He understands the dangers inherent to her making this voyage. No fault will attach to you or Fleet if such a tragedy were to happen."

"I am well aware of the risks as well," Kelsey said. "I'm fulfilling my duty to the Empire just like you are, Jared."

He pinched the bridge of his nose, possibly counting to ten. "Fine. I'll see that we assign appropriate quarters to you. But I want to make a few things very clear."

He stepped into Kelsey's personal space and stared down at her. It took a great deal of willpower not to step back. "This is my ship. I am the commander of this mission. You may be an Imperial princess, but on my ship, you will obey my orders. I will not tolerate disobedience or disrespect of any kind. You are subject to the same rules and expectations as the rest of my crew. Do you understand me, Deputy Ambassador Bandar?"

She opened her mouth to say something, but Vega cut her off. "Yes, Captain. We understand completely. I accept full responsibility for educating Deputy Ambassador Bandar on the behavior required of her."

Not bothering to hide the doubt on his face, Jared stepped back. "See that you do, Ambassador. How many guards has she brought with her?"

"None. When I said she wasn't acting as an Imperial princess, I wasn't kidding. Before you offer, she will not need any marines to act in that capacity. We trust this environment to be free of that kind of threat."

Jared shook his head. "More madness. Very well then, I'll send some people to get you settled in. Report to the executive officer once you've stowed your belongings."

He turned on his heel and stormed to the lift without any parting pleasantries. That was probably for the best.

Kelsey had never seen that side of her half brother before. Gone was the polite officer that came to visit a few times a year. Missing was the man who'd accepted her cold anger and indignant disdain without a word in his own defense. The intimidating man she'd just seen was no less a ruler than her father inside this, his domain.

Vega turned to her as the crewmen from the cutter brought out the last of their luggage. "I trust you see how serious Captain Mertz is. He'll be looking for any reason to drop you off in a life pod and let someone else pick you up, so you'd best keep that sharp tongue of yours under firm control, Kelsey."

"I have no intention of getting crossways with my half brother, Carlo. I'll behave."

"That is your first mistake. Listen to me very carefully. Forget that man is related to you. We are no longer in your domain. Captain Mertz is now God and his executive officer is his prophet. Familiarity is your enemy. If you want to make this assignment work, you need to treat him as a total stranger.

Be formal. As far as you are concerned, his first name is now Captain. If it's a really good day, perhaps 'sir' will work."

"And if he says run, I ask how fast?"

"No. You keep your mouth closed and run as fast as you possibly can. Consider this your first challenge as a diplomat of the Empire. If you avoid getting locked up, you'll be doing pretty well."

She pondered that while they waited. The crewman waved at them and shut the hatch to the cutter. A loud clank announced its departure. A departure that trapped her on a ship with an angry man that didn't want her anywhere close. She'd best listen to Carlo's advice and take this very seriously.

They only waited a few minutes before the lift opened again and three men came out. Their uniforms were subtly different from one another. The man in front had the same blue tunic over black pants that Jared... Captain Mertz had worn.

The other two men had black tunics over black pants. They also had red stripes on their sleeves where the man in front of them had two wide red bars on the shoulders separated by a thin red line. She'd probably best spend some time learning what those meant.

The men in back bowed. The man in the blue tunic did not.

Kelsey couldn't help noticing he was more than passingly handsome with his cropped blond hair and blue eyes. A hint of deviltry sparkled in his smile. He held his hand out to Vega. "Welcome aboard, Ambassador. I'm Lieutenant Commander Charlie Graves, *Athena*'s executive officer."

Vega took his hand and smiled as he shook it. "Thank you, Commander. It's a pleasure to be here. I'm very sorry for the last-minute disruption. I assure you I had my very own version of it a few hours ago when the Secretary of Imperial affairs woke me up. This is my assistant, Deputy Ambassador Kelsey Bandar."

The officer's expression told Kelsey he knew exactly who she was, but no hint of it made its way to his voice. "Deputy Ambassador Bandar. A pleasure."

"For me as well, Commander Graves."

"Ratings Welch and Soto will see that your gear is stowed. I'm afraid the cabins don't have enough space for everything you've brought, but all your bags will be readily accessible if you need something from them. Come this way, please."

He led them back into the lift, leaving the two ratings to handle the baggage. "We're putting you into separate cabins. They were two-person cabins, but I think it best for senior personnel to have some privacy to do their work."

Vega nodded. "Excellent, Commander. I like Miss Bandar quite a lot, but not that much. She might snore."

Kelsey laughed when Carlo winked at her. "If I might ask, where are the displaced officers going?"

"We have some missile tubes offline for repairs. They're almost big enough for one person each, if they hold their arms over their heads."

Kelsey felt herself gape before she remembered that hint of wickedness she'd seen in his eyes. She snapped her mouth closed and shook her head. "You had me for a moment. I'm going to need to keep an eye on you."

He grinned, making himself look even more roguish. "I couldn't resist. We're adding extra bunks in one of the small conference rooms. They'll need to go into marine country to use the head, but they'll have some extra space to make up for the inconvenience."

"Why didn't you put us there?" Vega asked.

"Because you'd need to go into marine country to use the head."

"I'm sure the marines aren't so bad," she objected.

"Of course not, but they are a little rough around the edges. I shudder to think about the diplomatic crisis one of their late-night poker games would cause."

The lift opened onto a tight corridor with several crew members hurrying along on some duty or another. She followed Graves's example and pressed her back to the wall when they passed. She wondered why the officer was giving precedence to the others for a moment but decided it was not the right time or place to ask the question. There was probably a logical explanation.

Graves stopped at a hatch marked 6P432. "This is your cabin, Ambassador Vega. Deputy Ambassador Bandar is two down and on the other side of the corridor. Memorize your room numbers so someone can get you home when you get lost. Everyone does when they first come aboard, and so will you."

"Or they'll put us into a missile tube," she muttered, imagining the pranks that could happen to new people on a ship.

The executive officer laughed. "That particular prank isn't appropriate for civilians. You're not going to end up in marine country either. Not unless you intentionally go there. The crew will find... subtler ways to welcome you aboard."

He pressed his thumb on the lock, and the hatch slid open. "I have authority to enter every cabin but won't do so unless there's a reason. In this case, I need to be inside to add your access to the room. I could do it remotely, but I don't have your biometric data. Please press your thumb to the lock, Ambassador."

Vega did so and looked inside the cabin curiously. "Very interesting."

Graves did something inside the door and stepped back outside. "Ratings Soto and Welch will see that you have access to your belongings and help you stow away what you will need in your cabin. While the compensators keep the grav drives from tossing things around during normal maneuvers, we secure everything just in case. They will also see to your safety briefings. Deputy Ambassador Bandar?"

He had her press her thumb to the lock beside her hatch and gave her identical instructions. Her cabin was 6P435. Vega still stood inside the open hatch to his cabin, so the officer looked at both of them when he spoke again.

"Don't wander around until you get your orientation. This ship can be a dangerous place to the uninitiated. Not because of the people, but some equipment can be lethal to the untrained. If you inadvertently found yourself in engineering, you might touch something that could kill you before your body hits the floor. Everything dangerous is marked as such, but you don't know how to recognize that yet. Stay put. Understood?"

His voice held a hint of command. Not like Captain Mertz. More subdued but crystal clear.

"Yes, sir," she said.

He smiled. "I don't need a 'sir' from either of you. Just pay attention while you learn your way around the ship. Feel free to examine your cabins while you wait. Now, if you'll excuse me, we're about to break orbit, and I should be at my station."

Graves returned the way they'd come with a purposeful stride.

Vega gave her a pointed look and went inside his cabin. The hatch slid shut.

Taking the not-so-subtle hint, she stepped into her new home. The hatch slid closed as soon as she stepped away from it. One quick glance told her a fact that should've been obvious before she came aboard. Space was at a premium. Her closet at the palace was larger than this two-person cabin.

Life was full of unexpected challenges.

The layout was quite Spartan. Two bunks folded out from the wall, one above the other. The far wall had a compact desk that looked like it folded up when not needed. The wall opposite the bunk had two wardrobes built into it.

Even with two, she wouldn't have much space at all for clothes. If she stretched out her arms, she could easily touch the bunk and the wardrobe at the same time. Three strides took her from the foot of the bunks to the desk.

She sighed. Well, if her father had lived this way, so could she. The thought brightened her mood. She'd be able to share some stories with him that would bring them closer. Besides, this was an *adventure*—the adventure of her lifetime. She didn't need to think about what she didn't have. She needed to think about what she was getting.

Kelsey sat down at the desk with a smile. She keyed in her thumbprint and started sorting through the publicly available files on the network while she waited for her luggage to arrive.

Let the adventure begin.

7

J ared spent the next three weeks reviewing personnel files for the scientific staff and consulting with the senior scientists over the communications channels. They'd need to have another face-to-face meeting soon, but Jared thought that would have more impact if he waited until they were ready to jump into the unknown. The delay gave him time to review the scientists' backgrounds.

He already knew his crew, including the marines, in detail. Adding familiarity with several hundred scientists and almost that many merchant officers and sailors took time, but he could at least begin the process. He needed the distraction to take his mind off his unwelcome guest, even if only for a little while.

He hadn't gone out of his way to ignore Princess Kelsey… or rather Deputy Ambassador Bandar, but he hadn't sought her out, either. He'd focused his attention on her boss instead. Ambassador Vega was a levelheaded man and went out of his way to work with Jared and his officers. He fit in so well that it was hard to believe that he hadn't been aboard for months.

Any time Jared encountered Kelsey was a different matter. She was always distantly polite, almost like a silent rebuke for his reaction to her presence. His overreaction, rather. She hadn't stepped over the line once. She hadn't really come close. Somewhat to his disappointment.

Now that they'd passed through the fourth flip point and were travelling in unclaimed territory, he needed to address their problematic relationship and call a truce.

He ran into his first obstacle when he went to find her. Since she had no assigned station, she could be almost anywhere on the ship. Well, not engineering, the bridge, operations, or the missile tubes. He decided against paging her because that would make it seem as though he'd summoned her. Rather than get her back up, he'd just have to play "find the princess."

Jared started leaving word for people to call him if she showed up, but he hadn't found her in any of the places he thought most likely. He considered searching the maintenance shafts, but he wasn't sure how she could've gotten into them. It was as if she'd vanished.

Time to form a search and rescue party, and no one was better for the task than the marines. He made his way to marine country and stopped dead just inside the large hatch blazoned with their unit flash.

Deputy Ambassador Kelsey Bandar, second in line to the Imperial Throne of the Terran Empire, sat at a table with four burly men and a wiry woman dressed in battlefield trousers and black T-shirts. Cards and chips covered the tabletop. More than half the chips sat in front of the Imperial scion.

The princess had dressed down in a plain blouse and slacks, and she'd pulled her unruly blonde hair back into a loose ponytail. She took a sip of what looked like beer and tossed some cards out face down. The dealer slid her some replacements with a look of wary respect.

When some of the watchers spotted him, Jared held up a hand to stop them from announcing his presence. The sight of the Imperial princess gambling with some of the roughest, toughest men and women in space boggled his mind.

There was no one he'd rather have at his back than a squad of marines, but he'd never in his wildest dreams let his sister—if he'd had one growing up—gamble with them. She'd come home scratching herself and swearing. If she didn't come home pregnant.

Lieutenant Timothy Reese, the detachment commander, slid around the compartment until he stood beside Jared. "Captain. I've been keeping an eye on things, but I'm starting to think I never needed to worry. She's bonded with them like their little sister."

The odd parallel to Jared's thoughts made him glance sharply at the marine officer. Reese grinned. "Their sister, not someone else's."

Jared shook his head. "Are they letting her win? That's a first. I thought the Imperial Marine motto was to never give a sucker a break."

"That's pretty close to the unofficial motto. When it comes to cards, they don't cut anybody any slack. She doesn't need any help, though. She's beating the proverbial pants off all of them, despite their best efforts. I've been watching to make sure she wasn't cheating. Though I have no idea what I'd do if I found out an heir to the Imperial Throne was cheating card sharks like my people. Probably applaud."

Jared tried to imagine where she could've learned to play poker at this level and failed. It seemed wildly out of character for her. He made a mental note to ask about it one day.

Kelsey picked that moment to stretch, and she must've caught a glimpse of him out of the corner of her eye. She spun her chair toward him and stood. "Captain Mertz. I didn't see you come in."

"My apologies for interrupting your game, Deputy Ambassador. Might I have a moment of your time?"

She counted out her chips, gathered the Imperial credits the dealer paid her, and bowed to her fellow players. "I'll come back and get the rest later."

"You wish," the burliest of them said with a grin. "We'll get ours back next time."

"How's that working out for you so far?"

Everyone at the table laughed. Obviously no hard feelings there. Any intimidation they may have felt at her Imperial stature wasn't apparent now.

Kelsey joined him at the door. "Thanks again for making me welcome, Lieutenant Reese."

The young officer smiled. "Anytime, Kelsey. Consider marine country your second home. Come down in a couple of days and we'll give you a tour of the firing range. The assault rifles might be a bit much for you, but we have some kickass pistols."

The young noblewoman grinned. "I'll hold you to that."

Jared raised an eyebrow at the marine but said nothing as he followed Kelsey out.

She turned to him in the corridor. "What can I do for you, Captain?"

"You can help me figure out how we can work together going forward. I realize neither one of us is overly fond of the other, but we need to get past that. At best, we'll be together almost two years. At worst, three or more."

She nodded slowly up at him. "We have a lot of history to get over, but you're right. This mission isn't the time or place for allowing our feud to continue."

He nodded. "Allow me to start off by apologizing for not having sought you out before now."

"No apology needed. I'm certain you've been very busy. I may not know precisely what a Fleet captain does, but taking on a second ship full of scientists and coordinating a mission of this magnitude must occupy a lot of your time."

A wry smile crossed her lips. "I'm sure that an official stowaway wasn't the most anticipated part of your day either. I don't blame you for being angry with me. It wasn't my idea to come, but I didn't object when the opportunity presented itself."

"Have you gotten a tour of the ship?"

The princess nodded. "Only the common areas. It's fascinating."

"Then let's tour some of the restricted areas. Starting with engineering. Perhaps you can explain what you mean while we walk." He started them toward engineering. "Who else had a hand in your being here? Your father, I assume."

"Our father," she corrected him. "I know that hasn't exactly been a pleasant truth for either of us, but it's a fact we need to accept."

He sighed. "It seems like we could manage to forget that for the time being." He closed his eyes and sighed even deeper. "Fine. Our father."

She explained her late-night discussion with the emperor. "Then he woke me early the next morning and hustled me onto a shuttle. I didn't know where I was going or why until Carlo explained it to me."

Against his will, he found himself nodding. "You do know how to take the fun out of a good mad, don't you?"

"I'm sure I'll do something to legitimately piss you off soon enough."

He chuckled. "I am sorry that our circumstances have put us at odds. I've often considered what my life would be like if I hadn't joined Fleet. If I'd stayed at home and done anything else, everyone's lives would be so much simpler." He gave her a serious look. "I truly regret what this has done to your family."

She sighed. "Me, too. Yet there isn't one thing we can do to change the past. All we can do is make a better tomorrow."

"That sounds like a slogan. Here we are. Stay beside me and don't touch anything without asking."

He pressed his thumb to the pad beside the double doors and stepped inside when they slid open. The area just inside engineering opened up quite a bit. The ceiling was three stories tall, and the room spread the full width of the ship. Massive machines with attached consoles filled most of it, and a subtle humming seemed to make his teeth vibrate a little. There was also a hint of electricity in the air.

"Dennis."

Dennis Baxter turned and gave him a high sign. He said something to the people clustered around him and strode over. "Captain. What can I do for you?"

"This is Deputy Ambassador Kelsey Bandar. Kelsey, this is *Athena*'s chief engineer, Lieutenant Commander Dennis Baxter. Dennis, I'd appreciate it if you gave her the grand tour."

Baxter's eyes widened. "I'd heard you were aboard, Princess. Welcome."

She took his hand and shook it. "Thank you. Please, call me Kelsey. Or Ambassador. I'm not acting in an Imperial capacity, and we're all going to be together for some time. Treat me just like you would anyone else."

"As you wish. Call me Dennis. Come on over, and I'll give you the highlights."

He led the two of them to the center of the huge compartment. "Toward the aft are the ship's grav and flip drives. The fusion power plants are under our feet. These consoles here, here, and here monitor everything to be sure we're in good shape. Andrew, give the lady your seat."

One of the men rose and stepped to the side of his console. Baxter gestured for Kelsey to sit.

She sat gingerly, making a show of keeping her hands as far away from the console as she could while looking at the bewildering layout of graphic displays. A large screen directly in front of the seat showed some kind of complex flowchart.

Jared only had a general idea of what he was looking at. Fleet kept its officers focused on their primary fields of study. He'd come up the tactical track, so weapons systems were more his speed. He'd heard of some officers that jumped tracks, but they were the exception rather than the rule. Besides, engineering officers didn't have the combat skills the command track required.

Baxter leaned over Kelsey's shoulder. "Let's take a look at the inside of the port fusion plant. Press that big green button right there." He pointed to one right in front of her.

She pressed it, and every light on the console flashed red just as Baxter said, "Not that one!"

Kelsey threw herself out of the chair, terror etched across her face. Until Baxter's chuckles gave him away. Her eyes narrowed, and she hit the chief engineer in the arm as hard as she could. "How could you! That's mean!"

Then she whirled on Jared. "Did you know what he was doing?" she demanded.

He held up his hands in a gesture of innocence. "I had no idea what that button did. I did fail to mention that Dennis is something of a practical joker, though. You did tell him to treat you just like everyone else."

The princess crossed her arms over her chest and glared at them both for a moment before she smiled a little. "Okay. That was pretty good."

"I couldn't help myself," Baxter said. "All you did was lock the console. In any case, we were running a diagnostic routine, so it's offline. There was never any danger."

"You're still going to pay for that. Now, let's get a real tour."

Jared followed them as Baxter led her deeper into the bowels of engineering. She was a lot different than he'd imagined. Their interaction had always been uncomfortable and stiff. To see her with a sense of humor and such a natural ability to bond with total strangers had him reevaluating everything he thought he knew. Perhaps she was more suited to the role of diplomat than he'd realized.

Baxter took her deeper into engineering. "These are the flip drives. More precisely, the Osborne-Levinson Bridge initiators. No one calls them that. When we dump the capacitors into them, they trigger the gravitational fault in the flip point in such a way that it reverses polarity and takes us to the other side. It's all over before we can even measure the event."

She looked at the massive machine and shook her head. "Just the concept of going light years in the blink of an eye boggles my mind. How do you get your head around something like that?"

He shrugged. "I'm an engineer. I can understand the practical results without knowing all the theory behind it. That's for the scientists over on *Best Deal*. When they start droning on, I flip myself to the other side of the room."

Kelsey laughed. "Have you talked with them about it? I think that would be a fascinating conversation."

"I have. They wanted to change the parameters of what our probes look for, so they had to explain it to me. I immediately went for alcohol once they were gone."

She laughed again. "I'm looking forward to meeting them."

Jared inserted himself there. "We'll have a few combined meetings to plan out things once we reach the kickoff system. I know they love to find someone willing to listen to them explain things, so you'll have plenty to hear."

He turned to Baxter. "What kind of changes did they make to the scanning parameters?"

"They wanted me to increase the sensitivity threshold. There are apparently some competing theories about how weak a flip point can be, and they wanted to be sure that they didn't miss something. I warned them they'd probably get false positives, but they thought that would be acceptable. In any case, I can always change the settings back."

The next stop on the tour was at the grav drives. Baxter rested his hand against one. "These are just like the gravs on every car you've ridden in, just a lot more powerful. Since we use more power and make them very large, they provide much more thrust. Enough to make the trip between flip points in a matter of days."

"I've heard that, and we're making good time, but what about that acceleration? Shouldn't it mash us into jelly?"

"Absolutely not. I'd look terrible in a sandwich. Grav drives work by altering the gravitational gradient of the space-time around a ship. Think of it like falling. You don't feel acceleration as you fall. A failed drive would leave you going exactly the same speed you were already going."

The communicator on Jared's belt beeped. It reminded him that he should issue the diplomatic team some of their own. That would've made tracking Kelsey down significantly simpler. He brought it to his lips. "Mertz."

"Lieutenant Anderson, Captain. We need you up on the bridge right away."

He felt his gut tighten. "Is something wrong?"

"*Best Deal* just signaled their test probes located a flip point."

He whistled. "That's pretty good range to find it from this far away."

"I'm sorry, sir. I should've been clearer. They found a previously undetected flip point between here and the target point."

He shared a look of surprise with Kelsey and Baxter. "I'll be right there."

8

Kelsey followed Jared to the bridge. He was so intent that he seemed to have forgotten she was with him. She wasn't about to remind him. She wanted to know what was going on.

He strode out of the lift and directly to the console in the center of the oval-shaped compartment. The curved front wall held the largest vid screen she'd ever seen. Two large consoles sat in front of them. Two unoccupied consoles behind him faced the rear wall, while a third sat on the far side of the room.

Commander Graves surrendered his seat to Jared. "Doctor Cartwright seems pretty sure that the flip point he detected is real."

"Put the system up on the screen."

The view of the star field vanished, replaced by a graphic of the system. Kelsey found it easy to read. The star and planets were obvious. The small blue circles represented the ships. That meant the green circle behind them and the one in front of them had to be the flip points.

An amber circle appeared between the ships and the most distant flip point. To her eye, the new flip point looked like it was about a quarter of the way toward the flip point they'd been heading toward.

Graves pointed at the screen. "The area in question is almost directly ahead of us and about eighteen hours away at our current speed."

Jared studied something on his console. "What exactly did Cartwright say?"

"The discussion became unintelligible when he tried to explain in more detail."

"Zia, get the good doctor on the screen for me." He looked over and seemed to notice Kelsey for the first time. "Oh. Everyone, this is Deputy

Ambassador Bandar. Kelsey, you know Commander Graves." Graves smiled and bowed his head in acknowledgment.

Jared pointed toward the man and woman seated in front of him. "Lieutenant Pasco Ramirez, my helm officer. Lieutenant Zia Anderson, my tactical officer." Both turned and nodded briefly toward her before returning their attention to their consoles.

"Take a seat at one of the unused consoles, please," Jared said. "They're locked, but I'd appreciate it if you kept your hands off the controls anyway."

As if she'd touch another button after that stunt in engineering. "Yes, Captain. It's a pleasure to meet you all." She sat down and clipped the belt around her lap before folding her hands on top of it.

Lieutenant Anderson turned in her seat. "I have Doctor Cartwright, sir."

"On screen."

The representation of the system vanished, and a grandfatherly looking man with fringes of white hair around his bald skull and the most outrageous mustache Kelsey had ever seen appeared. It came off to the sides of his mouth in little points. He looked quite jovial and very, very excited.

"Captain Mertz! Isn't it wonderful?"

Jared smiled politely, but he didn't come out and agree. "We'll see, Doctor. Why don't you give me a general overview? Please consider my relative lack of knowledge about flip points in general. How did you find it when the other scouts coming this way didn't?"

"We have the most sensitive flip scanners since the Fall. Possibly even before. Also, after their initial examination of this system, I doubt anyone has come back to check it again. After all, we had no reason to suspect such a weak flip point existed until recently."

"Elaborate on that. In simple terms, please."

Cartwright reached up and absently twisted his mustache. "Very little is known about pre-Fall technology, but early explorers found bits and pieces drifting in space when we finally climbed out of Avalon's gravity well again. Most of the battle debris was long gone, either burned up in the atmosphere or thrown into various corners of our solar system. One of the things we found was an Osborne-Levinson Bridge scanner from one of the combatants."

The older man turned as though he expected there to be a whiteboard behind him and looked frustrated that there wasn't one. He crossed his arms across his chest. "During the intervening years, we determined its function and replicated it. Once we got into space, we refined that technology even further.

"A young theoretical cosmologist at our university recently reviewed our prevailing understanding about flip points and developed a competing theory which allowed for the possibility of a weaker flip point."

Jared nodded. "You updated the probes with that in mind? Got it. Do you think the Old Empire knew about these weak flip points?"

The scientist shrugged. "We have no way to know for sure. Does it matter if they did?"

"I suppose not. What does this theory say about these weaker flip points? Are they safe to use? Do they go shorter distances?"

"The theory is too untested for those details to be more than educated guesses. We should be able to calculate how strong the flip points are, at least with enough certainty to guess at their safety. My personal feeling is that they lead to closer systems, but we won't know until we send a probe through."

Jared nodded. "Get your people working on refining the data for this particular flip point. We need to have a better understanding before I decide if it's safe to attempt using it."

The scientist nodded sharply. "I have people working on that right now, Captain. I should have some observations by the time we get there. At the very least, I should have much more refined scan data. I suggest we meet tomorrow morning to discuss this in person."

"That sounds like a plan, Doctor. We'll see you on *Best Deal* at 0900."

The older man nodded. "We'll be ready, Captain."

The transmission ended abruptly. Kelsey redirected her attention to Jared. "Are you planning on using it?"

He turned in his seat. "Perhaps. Its unusual nature means I'll at least send a probe through to take some readings. If the other side looks interesting and it seems safe, I'll consider exploring it."

He rose to his feet. "Charlie, get second shift to take over for the evening. We need to get a good night's sleep if we expect to have any chance of understanding what the good doctor tells us."

"Aye, sir."

Jared turned to Kelsey. "Would you care to join me for dinner in the officers' mess?"

She unbuckled her restraint and stood. "I'd like that. Today's been a long, productive day, and I'm famished."

The officers' mess couldn't hold more than two dozen people, and even so, it was only a quarter full. A crewman in a white apron came over to their table. "Captain, Ambassador." He set out water for them. "The mess is serving some excellent fish tonight. I'd recommend it."

She nodded, and Jared followed her example. Once the man was gone, she looked over at her half brother. "Is the food here different from what the enlisted eat? I've been eating there."

"No. Some ships have entirely different menus, but I've always believed that officers and enlisted should eat the same food. Most ships in Fleet are that way. The only reason we have separate messes is so the crew doesn't feel like the officers are watching them when they're off duty. In fact, *Athena*'s officers eat in the crew's mess once a week and on special occasions."

He took a sip of his water and smiled. "I have to admit that you've surprised the hell out of me today. You've always been so reserved. I had no idea you could play cards with the marines on their own terms."

"They were a little leery at first, but I think I've won them over. The Imperial Guards at the palace taught me well. They recruit from inside the Imperial Marines, you know. Frankly, I really enjoy being around people that don't bow and scrape. They tell me what they really think. I like that they treat me as if I belonged and shouldn't be up on a pedestal."

"That should've been true in any case. I see that I've done you another injustice. I apologize for doubting that you had what it takes to be here."

His admission made her preen a little inside. However, his honesty deserved a frank response from her. "I'll confess that I haven't warmed to you very much over the years. I blamed you for what happened to my parents for the longest time. Once I became old enough to understand that wasn't true, it made me feel guilty but didn't change how I treated you. For that, I apologize.

"You're much more complex than I gave you credit for. Seeing you working here is like watching a different man—a leader. Someone who commands respect and demands obedience. A lot like my father. Our father. It's a pity Ethan doesn't get to see this side of you."

Jared looked a little embarrassed. "I've never felt comfortable in the palace. I honestly don't think I ever will. Pardon my frankness, but I doubt seeing another side of me would improve my relationship with your brother."

"Until recently, my brother and I thought you initiated the visits. He thought you were trying to…"

"Curry favor? If so, I'm particularly inept at it. Your brother hates me, and you can barely tolerate me."

"Perhaps that's because we really didn't know one another. I suspect that played a role in our father's thought process when he sent me on this mission with you. He hopes we get past our differences. As do I. This trip could be a chance to start over for both of us. I'm not saying that things *will* change, but we have an excellent opportunity to start fresh."

He smiled a little. "I'd like that." He took a bite of his dinner as soon as the man deposited the plates in front of them. "Mmm. Very nice. So, while you've been exploring the ship, what has Ambassador Vega been doing?"

"Pretty much the same things as me. I see him in the mess hall, mostly. He also spends a lot of time in his cabin. I'd imagine he has a ton of background information to study. Information that I'm already familiar with."

Jared took a drink of his water. "I probably should get together with him before the meeting tomorrow and bring him up to speed. I know I wouldn't want to be blindsided first thing in the morning."

"Good idea. I ate with him at lunch. He had some indigestion and said he'd rest for the afternoon. He's probably feeling better. Let's finish, and we can go talk to him together."

They ate the rest of the meal and chatted about the ship and crew. Kelsey quickly discovered that talking about his people was a sure way to get Jared into an enthusiastic conversation. He really cared about them.

That made the rest of the meal fly by, and they finished before she knew it. Jared stood and led the way back down to her deck. She hoped she eventually learned the ship's layout. It seemed like she got lost almost every day, even after all this time.

Jared stopped outside of Vega's hatch and knocked. When no one answered, he tried again. "He's probably in the mess or wandering around. Remind me to get both of you communicators so that people can contact you."

He brought his communicator to his lips. "Bridge, this is Mertz. Page Ambassador Vega and route his call back to me."

"Aye, sir."

A louder version of the voice came from the concealed speakers overhead. "Ambassador Vega, please call the bridge on the nearest communications unit."

After about thirty seconds, the call repeated. Then the voice came back over the communicator. "I'm sorry, sir. Ambassador Vega isn't responding."

Jared frowned. "Thank you. Mertz out."

He put the communicator back onto his belt. "I suppose we'd best check to be sure everything is okay." He touched his thumb to the lock, and the hatch slid open. "Ambassador? This is Captain Mertz. May I come in?"

Jared stepped inside and cursed. She followed him inside and immediately saw Carlo Vega sprawled on the floor. Jared knelt by his side and felt for a pulse on his neck before pulling his communicator again. "Medical emergency. Medical team to Ambassador Vega's quarters. Chief medical officer to Ambassador Vega's quarters."

She edged closer. Vega's eyes were open and didn't seem focused. "Is he still breathing?"

Jared shook his head. "No. The medics have to check him, but he's gone. It looks like he's been dead for a while."

Kelsey covered her mouth with her hand and stepped aside as the medical team rushed in. They got right to work, but she could tell by the looks on their faces that Jared was right. Carlo Vega was dead.

9

J ared waited for the medics to make the final call, but he knew Carlo Vega was beyond resuscitation. The man's skin was cold to the touch. Medical science was capable of doing some amazing things, but bringing the dead back to life wasn't one of them.

Doctor Stone arrived less than thirty seconds after the crash team. She knelt at the man's side and examined him before shaking her head. "He's gone. Take him to the morgue, and I'll perform an autopsy."

The slender, dark-haired woman stood and walked over to him. "Captain, I'll get started tonight, and I should have some preliminary results on your desk by morning. I'm not seeing any indications of injuries. Do you know if he had any medical conditions?"

"No. As far as I know, Ambassador Vega was healthy."

Stone grabbed a tablet from the medical cart. "I saw him around but thought he came over from the freighter. I have copies of their medical files, but nothing for the ambassador."

Jared sighed. "They boarded at the last minute. I should've verified that they turned over their files and scheduled them for a checkup first thing."

"They? There's someone else running around the ship that I don't know about?"

He nodded toward Kelsey. The young noblewoman stood with a sick expression on her face, silently watching the team move Vega to a stretcher. "My half sister accompanied Ambassador Vega as his deputy. I'm surprised you hadn't heard."

Doctor Stone closed her eyes for a few seconds. She didn't open them when she spoke again. "You're telling me we have a member of the Imperial Family on board and I don't have her files? I haven't examined her. What if she dropped dead? Not to trivialize Ambassador Vega's death, but that would be a disaster. Captain, forgive me for any impertinence, but what the hell were you thinking?"

Jared bowed his head in acknowledgment. "I obviously wasn't."

"I need her in the medical center right now. Ambassador Vega can wait until tomorrow."

"Of course, Doctor. Let me introduce you." He walked over to the princess. "Kelsey, this is Lieutenant Commander Lily Stone, our chief medical officer. Doctor, Deputy Ambassador Kelsey Bandar."

Kelsey took the doctor's proffered hand. "I wish we hadn't met under these circumstances, Doctor. I'm not here in an Imperial capacity, so please just call me Kelsey. Or ambassador, I suppose."

"Call me Lily, then. I'm very sorry for your loss. Did you know Ambassador Vega well? Did he have any medical conditions that you know of?"

Kelsey shook her head. "I've worked with him some and he trained me in diplomacy, but we never discussed any medical information. I had lunch with him today, and he said he had indigestion. I should've come back here with him."

Lily put her hand on Kelsey's shoulder. "People have indigestion every day. While I'll consider it when I start looking for answers, the heartburn might have nothing to do with his death. Don't blame yourself for things you can't reasonably expect to control."

"That's not going to be easy."

"No, it isn't. I didn't have any medical records for either of you. Did you have a copy of yours?"

Kelsey shook her head. "I barely had time to pack a few bags. I'd imagine he had as little warning as I did. Medical records were the very last thing on my mind."

"Then I need you to come to the medical center with me. We need to do a full medical exam."

The princess chuckled without any real humor behind it. "I assure you, I get the very best of medical care. I'm as healthy as a horse, even if I can't prove it."

"I'd wager that Ambassador Vega would've told me something very similar. Everyone on this ship is required to go through a medical checkup when they come on board. It's on me that I didn't examine Ambassador Vega. I'm not going to repeat that error." The doctor's voice had no give to it. Her words were a polite order that Jared knew she'd see enforced.

"Go with her, Kelsey. Arguing with a doctor is like running headfirst into a bulkhead: pointless and very painful."

Kelsey nodded. "Of course. Captain, I need to find out if Ambassador Vega had any files that I need. It looks like I'm going to be stepping up in a big way, and I need to know what the Department of Imperial Affairs sent along. What instructions they might have given him. We've spoken a lot, but we both imagined we'd have more time to train me."

Jared nodded. "I'll have a couple of people come down here and find everything they can. Look at me, Kelsey. Nothing in this job is as big as what you've trained for already. If you can sit on the Imperial Throne, you can handle this mission."

She smiled a little. "Thank you, Captain. I suppose you're right. Doctor?"

Doctor Stone led the princess out, and the medical team followed with Ambassador Vega. Jared hoped to hell he was right about her, because if things went south on this mission, she'd be in the hot seat, and all their lives might depend on her diplomatic skills.

He called for some technicians to screen everything Vega had for files, including the bags he'd had stored. He instructed them to transfer everything they found to Kelsey's computer. Then he went back to his cabin. He had enough time to do some paperwork, and then he'd get a good night's sleep. Tomorrow might be a very long day.

* * *

SLEEPING TURNED out to be more difficult than Jared had hoped. He lay awake for a couple of hours before he finally drifted off. His dreams weren't quite nightmares, but Carlo Vega kept following him everywhere he went. Waking up early was welcome.

His cabin was generous by Fleet standards. It actually had a large private head, a kitchenette, and a small work area. He normally used his office near the bridge to handle paperwork, but he made some coffee and sat at his station to review his inbox. No autopsy report, but that wasn't a surprise. Lily would've spent the evening going through Kelsey's examination results. She'd probably run labs late into the night.

Vaguely dissatisfied, he worked on various reports until he had to get ready for the flight to *Best Deal*. He took a sonic shower and dressed for the day. He ate a quick breakfast in the officers' mess, and when Kelsey failed to put in an appearance, he ordered her something to go. She needed fuel to get through the day, too.

She answered his knock looking disheveled. She'd obviously slept in and probably had an even worse night than he had. "What?"

Jared held out the bag of food and a cup of coffee. "You need to get ready. Our cutter leaves in a little more than half an hour. I'll be waiting for you in the forward docking bay."

Kelsey took the food and closed the door without another word. He smiled. Not a morning person. He imagined she'd been a joy when her father woke her up and stuffed her into the cutter.

He went to the docking bay and helped the pilot with his preflight of the cutter. The man probably didn't appreciate the interference, but he wisely said nothing. Sometimes being the captain had tangible benefits. The other officers coming over for the briefing started arriving ten minutes before departure time.

Kelsey hurried in with less than sixty seconds to spare. "Sorry. I got lost."

"We're going to have to send you around with the damage control teams to learn the ship's layout."

From her expression, she didn't get that he was joking.

"Just kidding. You'll figure it out. Come up front, and you can sit in the flight engineer's seat. We don't need one for such a short trip."

Jared locked her console and made sure that she was strapped in before sliding into the pilot's chair. The assigned pilot took the copilot's seat. He slid a headset on and made sure he was on the control frequency. "*Athena*, this is *Athena Three*. Ready for departure."

"Roger, *Athena Three*," Zia said. "You are cleared for immediate departure. Have a good flight, Captain."

"Thanks, Zia. *Athena Three* out."

He undocked and dropped the cutter out of its slip. The screens cleared and displayed the star field. It was beautiful, as always. *Best Deal* showed clearly on his scanners. It was less than five minutes away. The acceleration he applied put *Athena* behind them and made *Best Deal* grow quickly on the screens.

"*Best Deal*, this is *Athena Three* on approach. Request docking instructions."

"*Athena Three*, you are cleared for docking port two. You are the only flight inbound at this time, so you may proceed directly to the dock."

"Thanks, *Best Deal*. *Athena Three* out."

He quickly mated the cutter to the docking port. The indicators turned green, and he locked the controls. Then he lit the "disembark" light in the cabin. "Ensign Kruger, you have the boat."

"Aye, sir. We'll be ready to depart whenever you are. Have a good meeting."

Jared unstrapped and waited for Kelsey to precede him out of the cutter. Several merchant crewmen waited for them in the docking chamber. One of them saluted Jared. "Captain Mertz? This way, sir."

Jared returned the salute and followed the man with Kelsey at his side. The rest of his officers followed them into the bowels of the ship. For once, he had no idea where they were going. He'd been here before, but the ship was still under renovation then.

They went down several corridors in turn and took two separate lifts. Eventually they entered a huge conference room. It looked like it could seat a hundred people, and it was almost full.

They'd reserved half the seats at the long conference table in the center of the compartment for his officers. A quick count confirmed there was one for Kelsey.

Anton Keller, the grizzled merchant captain of *Best Deal*, sat at one end of the table. The seat opposite him sat empty, reserved for Jared. Dr. Zephram Cartwright sat midway along the side facing the large screen at the head of the room. The elderly scientist looked as though he'd been up all night, but he seemed pleased.

Captain Keller stood, and the scientists followed his example after a beat. It wasn't in their culture, and Jared wasn't offended at the unintentional discourtesy. He couldn't expect scientists and merchants to know how Fleet demonstrated respect to commanding officers.

Jared sat. "Gentlemen, thank you for meeting with me so soon. I'm sure you've all been very busy and still have much work to do, so let's get this under way. Allow me to introduce Ambassador Kelsey Bandar. She joined *Athena* at the last minute, so you may not have been aware of her presence."

Keller bowed his head. "Welcome aboard, Ambassador."

Once everyone had taken their seats, Jared gave the chief scientist his full attention. "I think we should get right to the matter, Doctor. What do we have here?"

"Thank you, Captain Mertz." Cartwright slid his finger along a control on the table in front of him, and the lights dimmed. The screen on the wall —larger than the one on *Athena*'s bridge—blinked to life with a representation of local space. The diagram clearly showed *Athena* and *Best Deal* in relation to the newly found flip point nearby.

"What we have here is definitely a flip point. Close-range scans leave no room for doubt. It has a significantly weaker gravitic field and is notably smaller as well. This flip point is scarcely ten kilometers across."

That *was* small, less than one quarter of the normal size. "Do you think it's an anomaly, or might there be more of these scattered around?" Jared asked.

"I spent quite a bit of time reading the papers that have proposed this kind of occurrence last night. I believe that there may be more of these, though I doubt they are nearly as common as standard flip points."

He switched the screen to a series of graphs. "Without getting into the fine details, the flip point appears to be stable enough to use. How far it goes was a lively subject of debate over coffee this morning. I'm willing to wager that it likely leads to a system quite close by. Perhaps less than a dozen light years away."

Kelsey leaned forward. "Do you think it's safe to use, Doctor?"

The scientist shrugged. "That's one of the reasons I'm advocating that we send a probe through. Until we get the readings from the other side, we have no way of knowing."

Jared nodded. They had more than enough probes and could build more if needed. "I'll want to go over what you've discovered and recorded on your scanners, but I'm good with sending a probe now. When can you have it ready?"

Keller spoke up. "I took the liberty of having one prepared. We can launch it at your order."

"Excellent. I like when people are ready to execute a plan. You have a 'go' for the probe."

The merchant captain touched his controls. "Launch the probe."

An amber spark representing the probe appeared on the screen and accelerated away from *Best Deal*. It made its way into the nearby flip point in less than a minute and braked to a stop. Moments later, it vanished.

"Flip successful," Keller said. "It's programmed to scan for half an hour and then flip back."

Jared nodded. "Good. While it's doing its job, let's have a more detailed introduction of the senior scientists and my crew. I'd intended to do this when we were a little further along, but it looks like we might possibly be at a new kickoff point if things look interesting over there."

Kelsey frowned at him. "You intend to go through it? That seems relatively risky. No one has ever used one of these weak flip points before."

"Frankly, it would take something really interesting on the other side to convince me, but I'm not rejecting it out of hand. I'll make the decision when we go over the probe's recordings."

They spent the next half hour introducing themselves to one another and giving a short summary of individual backgrounds. The Fleet officers were thankfully brief, but the scientists rambled. It was interesting, though. These were some very talented minds present.

They were listening to a distinguished older woman speak when the console chimed. The probe had returned. Keller tapped on his controls. "Pardon me, Doctor Nelson. Downloading the scanner readings now. I'll throw the map up on the screen."

Jared watched closely as a representation of the target star system appeared. With only half an hour to scan, the details were preliminary and very general. The star was a standard yellow star. No planets were marked, but they were hard to see without long and detailed data processing.

One thing stood out. The flip point on the other end was even smaller than this end. It only covered about seven kilometers. Doctor Cartwright grunted. "Interesting. I didn't expect the other end to be so small. The theory didn't really hint at that."

Jared connected the small console inset into the table to the feed as it came in, scanning for anything interesting. While it loaded, he glanced at the scientist. "Now that you've seen the other side, do you think it's safe?"

"It should be. The probe made it there and back. Though I wouldn't recommend it if there isn't a pressing reason."

An icon appeared on Jared's screen, flashing in lurid scarlet. He blinked in shock for a moment and looked at the scientist. "It looks like we have our reason. I want to know everything you can divine about that flip point, and I want it fast."

Kelsey leaned over and stared at his console. "What is that?"

He looked back at the flashing icon. "It's a Fleet distress beacon. But not one of ours."

Her gaze whipped up to his face. "You mean that's from the Old Empire?"

Jared nodded. "I've seen drawings of one in old reports. There were a lot of them in the skies during and after the rebel attack on Avalon. I have no idea what the data coming in with it is, but it definitely means something is over there, and we have to go after it."

10

K elsey thought about what the distress beacon might mean all the way back to *Athena*. The implications were huge. It was the biggest discovery since the Fall. That probably meant they would briefly explore what they'd found and head right back home. The news was exciting and terrible all at once.

She sighed. Well, it was good for the Empire, even if it meant she probably wouldn't be coming back out with them. That might be for the best. Without Carlo Vega, she was filling some very big shoes.

The cutter docked, and she politely separated from Jared and the rest. She needed time to think. He'd call her before they made any major moves.

Her thoughts occupied so much of her attention as she walked that she didn't notice that Doctor Stone had stepped up beside her until the woman spoke.

"Welcome back, Kelsey. Do you have time to come down to my office?"

She gave the dark-haired Fleet officer a sideways look. "That sounds ominous."

The doctor smiled. "You're in perfectly good health. However, there are some things we need to talk about in private."

"Carlo?"

"Him, too."

Kelsey shrugged and followed the other woman back down to the medical center. The smell of disinfectant made her shudder. She was all too familiar with the closet-sized office just off the main treatment room after last night. She sat and was surprised when Stone ignored her desk and took the seat beside her after she closed the hatch.

"As I said, your test results came back clean," the doctor said. "You're healthy and look like you'll be that way for many years."

"Good! So why do we need to talk?"

"Captain Mertz is your half brother, correct?"

Kelsey nodded. "He is."

"I don't know how to explain this, but I took a genetic scan of you last night, and it doesn't match him at all."

Kelsey frowned. "That's impossible. They matched his scan to my father."

Stone nodded. "Yes, they did… at Orbital One, where they have all the medical records of all Fleet members past and present. I don't have the emperor's medical information in my database, but the notation in Captain Mertz's file says it is a conclusive and verified match. The emperor is his father."

"I don't understand."

The doctor reached out and took Kelsey's hand in hers. "If he's a match with your father, then you aren't."

"What?" She pulled away abruptly. "That's insane. Of course I am. How could I not be related to my father?"

Doctor Stone leaned back, her eyes full of sympathy. "I know this must be a horrible shock. It's not standard practice to do a paternity verification with married couples. Even with the Imperial Family. Unless a court intervenes and requires one."

Kelsey stared at the other woman blankly, unsure of what to say.

"I'm sorry to tell you this, Kelsey, but if Captain Mertz's test was correct and he is your father's son, then there is no conceivable way you can be the emperor's biological daughter. There is simply no room for inaccuracy in the test, but I ran it three times to be sure."

That just wasn't possible. Kelsey shook her head. "I don't know where the mistake is, but something isn't right. If you didn't make it, someone else did with Jared."

"I'm pretty sure they checked everything many times to be sure with him, as well. Your father acknowledged his paternity despite the impending destruction of his marriage. He wouldn't have done that unless he was absolutely certain."

They sat in silence while Kelsey's thoughts ran around in tight circles. If the doctor was correct, then her life was a lie, and so was her twin brother's. The heir to the Imperial Throne.

Oh, crap.

She covered her face with her hands. "This can't be happening."

"If he isn't my father, who is?"

"That's a question I'm definitely not qualified to answer. All I can say with any certainty is that it wasn't the emperor. I'm not blind to the array of political implications this information creates, but I'm not worried about that right now. I'm worried about you. None of this changes who you are one bit."

Kelsey shot to her feet and stared pacing the office. "Oh, but it does. Oh, God, does it." She started waving her hands around with each thought.

"It throws the entire Imperial succession into chaos. My brother and I are just as much bastards as Jared is. More so since we have no Imperial blood. At least he has the emperor as a father."

"You're wrong," Doctor Stone said firmly. "A father is much more than a genetic donor. Your father raised you. He loves you. Many fathers have adopted children. They are still very much fathers to them. Jared may share his genetics, but he is not the man's son by any stretch of the imagination."

"What am I going to do?" Kelsey moaned. "When the Imperial Senate gets wind of this, it could tear the Empire apart."

"Then don't tell them."

Kelsey stopped in her tracks. "If only it were that easy. No. Someone will talk. Someone always talks. Then we have a much larger problem on our hands."

The Fleet officer looked up at Kelsey serenely. "I'm not telling anyone other than you. They'll only know if you say something."

"You haven't told Jared already?"

Stone shook her head. "This is private medical data. I have it locked down under my seal. I'm only obligated to tell you."

"But they told the emperor that Jared was his son. How could you keep silent when I'm not?"

"That doctor violated his oath when he did that. I will not violate mine." The doctor's voice was as unyielding as *Athena*'s hull. "You were already aware of Jared's parentage, so I broke no rules in comparing the two of you and informing you of my findings. The captain has no need to know about this test. If you choose to tell him, that's your business, but a secret doesn't stay secret for long when you tell more people."

Kelsey sank back into her chair. "Truly? You'd keep this just between us? Never tell anyone… ever?"

Doctor Stone rose to her feet and strode to the desk. She tapped the screen a few times. "There. I've erased the test results and deleted your sample from the medical database. No one will ever know unless you decide they must. I'd personally advise against it for all the very good reasons you've mentioned.

"At the very least, take the time we're away from home to consider your options. There's always time to tell your father later. Once you say something, though, you can't unsay it."

Kelsey rubbed her temples. "The irony makes my head ache. I've been an insufferable bitch to Jared for almost my entire life because my father cheated on my mother. Now I find out my mother did the exact same thing. She didn't know about Father's infidelity at the time, so it wasn't even a case of revenge. That's rich.

"I've had a hard time forgiving my father for what he did. Now I have to start over with my mother. She had to have wondered if we were his. What woman wouldn't connect the dots with the timing? Her outrage at his indiscretion really burns me up. She made such a spectacle of playing the injured spouse. God, that's infuriating!" Kelsey was so angry that she felt her eyes tearing up.

The doctor again took Kelsey's hand into hers. "I'm so sorry to have been the messenger of this bad news."

Kelsey wiped at her tears and squeezed the woman's hand. "It's not your fault. No one on this ship is responsible. I have plenty of time to contemplate what to do about it later. What can you tell me about Carlo?"

Stone released Kelsey's hand. "That's more complex. The precise cause of death was an acute myocardial infarction. Even if he'd been standing in the medical center, I probably wouldn't have been able to save his life. There was nothing you could've done."

"What about the indigestion? Was that a symptom?"

"It often is, but in his case it wasn't because of the heart attack. The complexity came into play when I started looking for the cause of the heart attack. It turns out he somehow suffered an overdose of a chemical agent. One he shouldn't have had contact with under any circumstances I can imagine. I don't even believe there is any of this substance on this ship."

Kelsey shook her head. "Hold up. Are you saying he was poisoned?"

"Possibly." The doctor softened her tone, "Who might have wanted him dead?"

A wave of nausea washed over Kelsey. "I have no idea. He got along with everyone we met. Can you tell when it happened?"

"I'm still working on that angle. It's possible he consumed the poison at breakfast. Did you eat with him that morning?"

She shook her head. "I was up late, so he went without me. I'm not a morning person. I think he was over on *Best Deal* for a briefing with Jared."

Stone nodded. "I'll ask the captain when I update him on this in a few minutes. There's going to be a full investigation. If this was murder, we'll get to the bottom of it."

They talked a little longer, but Kelsey eventually excused herself. She needed to mull over everything she'd just learned.

She retreated to an out-of-the-way spot she'd discovered—the navigator's cubby. The small chamber was little more than a seat and console within a concave bubble. The view was extraordinary, and it never seemed occupied. It probably existed in case there was some kind of major systems failure.

She strapped herself into the seat and raised it into an extended position, giving her a near-360-degree view. The sea of stars washed over her, dim until her eyes adjusted to the faint light. The view never failed to make her feel insignificant. Particularly so today.

The news about Carlo stunned her, but she kept thinking about her parentage. Was keeping silent the right decision? No one had found out in over twenty years. Given her family's position, the odds were very good they wouldn't ever find out.

Yet did she have the right to keep that information from Ethan? He tended to be something of an ass at times, but he was her brother.

It would wreck him. He'd tied his whole identity to his position as Imperial heir. To say he wouldn't take the news well was a profound understatement.

For her, it wasn't that important. She never expected to inherit the Throne. That was someone else's job. She cared much more about her family bonds than her social status.

Did this change everything for her?

Perhaps not. Her father and mother loved her, and she loved them, even if she was furious with Mother right now. The doctor was right. If she ended up separated from an Imperial title, it wouldn't change who she was. Father wouldn't toss her out the door. Based on how he treated Jared, the news wouldn't alter his behavior one bit.

However, the Imperial Senate would strip Ethan of his position. She had no idea who they'd replace him with. Neither did they, she was sure. Although they might all refer to one another as good friends and colleagues, the fractures in the Senate were deeply divisive. A vote to remove the confirmed heir would take a two-thirds majority. So would approving another heir.

They might agree on removing a bastard from the succession, especially if he wasn't the emperor's. They'd never agree to a replacement that wasn't the child of the emperor. The conservative senators would staunchly favor one of their own, as would the social liberals. Since each had more than a third of the membership in the Senate, there would be no compromise. Goodness knew how long that stalemate would last.

Even if they did settle their grievances, they would probably install a senator as the heir. A disastrous precedent. A coup in everything but name. She'd spent her life learning that the needs of the Empire were more important than her own.

No good could come of letting the truth out. She had to keep the knowledge to herself. She couldn't allow her father to know. He'd feel obliged to make the knowledge public. Just look at what he'd done with Jared.

Ethan would act out in some way if he found out. She knew it. He was entirely too impulsive and ruled by his emotions when he felt threatened or slighted. So she could never tell him, either.

Jared would probably keep the knowledge to himself, but she couldn't be certain of that. He had his own version of honor, and he hated being the Imperial Bastard. No, she could only trust herself... and Doctor Stone... to keep the secret.

"Ambassador Bandar, please report to the bridge."

The voice from the console startled her. She touched the now glowing icon to acknowledge the page with an acceptance signal. The man who'd called would see that she'd responded.

The call likely meant that Jared was ready to fill her in on his plans. Or he'd talked to Stone about Carlo Vega. She'd find out soon enough.

11

J ared had just finished giving his orders to Ramirez and was watching the ship begin moving toward the flip point as Kelsey walked onto the bridge. He gestured for her to join him at his console. He looked furious.

"Doctor Stone just left. She told me you know what she found."

Kelsey's expression darkened. "About Carlo. Yes. It's horrible. Who would do such a thing?"

"We don't know. Yet. You can rest assured that we won't stop looking until we do. A destroyer doesn't need a security department like Orbital One, but we have some qualified people. Since he ate breakfast with me on *Best Deal*, it may take quite a while to determine exactly what happened."

Though Jared had a few ideas. He suspected the situation was more complex than it appeared. Since Kelsey hadn't been spending time with him, she didn't know one critical piece of information. Vega had brought a gift for Jared from the Imperial Family: candies from a specialty house. Unfortunately, Jared secretly hated coconut.

Or perhaps fortunately. At least for him.

He'd taken advantage of Kelsey's absence to tell Vega to enjoy them with his compliments. He'd watched the man have one that morning. Now Jared suspected someone had poisoned at least one of the treats and that Jared had been the intended target.

Stone hadn't been able to tell if the poison had been in any specific food, and Jared had no proof that Crown Prince Ethan wanted him dead.

Allowing his suspicions into the record would have any number of negative consequences. Kelsey wouldn't believe her brother was a killer. No loyal Imperial citizen would imagine the heir to the Throne as a murderer. Especially with nothing but the word of the Imperial Bastard.

Jared would let the investigation go forward and let it come to its own conclusions. He'd searched for any remaining candies, but Vega must've eaten them all. Based on how they were packaged, the fatal dose would've probably been in the last few pieces. No evidence left to link the poison to the true killer that way.

Maybe his people would find a surprise on *Best Deal*. Someone who secretly hated Vega. Not likely, but possible. That would be the best possible outcome. Otherwise, Jared would be watching his back for the rest of his life once they made it back home.

He pushed the thoughts out of his head. He had more pressing things to deal with. "In the meantime, we're going through the flip point. The plan is to take *Athena* across and send word back via probe. They're based on standard data drones and still have the communication and data storage equipment installed."

Communication drones routinely flipped back and forth at the major flip points throughout the Empire, accepting data transmissions and sending them on at the other side. They couldn't do many flips without maintenance and recharging, so the Empire didn't use them in less traveled areas. Though that might change if they found anything half as interesting as he imagined they might on this trip.

"I've got a cutter standing by to take you over to *Best Deal*," he continued. "They'll follow once *Athena* is safely over."

Kelsey shook her head. "I'm assigned here, and I'll go across with you."

Her answer set him back for a moment. She'd been so cooperative the other day that he'd forgotten how willful she could be. This was more like the Kelsey he knew.

"That's not open to negotiation, Kelsey."

"Ambassador Bandar in this case, Captain. I've reviewed Ambassador Vega's orders. The ambassador goes wherever this ship does. Those orders fall to me now. I'm sorry if I seem obstinate."

He considered arguing, but he was honest enough to admit that she was probably within her rights. "Let's hope we don't regret that decision." He raised his voice. "Zia, have the cutter pilot stand down. She won't be needed after all."

"Yes, sir," she responded. "We're inside the flip point."

"Helm, bring us to a stop in the center."

Lieutenant Ramirez touched his console. "All stop, Captain. Flip drive standing by."

"Ambassador," Jared said formally. "We are prepared to flip. Please strap in to one of the observation seats."

Kelsey did so without any fuss. She sat facing the screen with her hands folded on her lap when she finished securing her belt.

Jared opened the shipwide channel. "All hands, this is the captain. We're about to flip to an unexplored system through an untested flip point. Secure your sections and report to operations when you're ready."

"Where is Commander Graves?" Kelsey asked.

"His battle station is in the operations center. On a destroyer, that means a three-man backup control room. If something disastrous happens to us, he'll assume command. Otherwise he's responsible for supporting us while we control the ship."

On a larger ship, they'd have a dedicated staff to interpret the scanner readings and help keep the captain informed about the tactical situation, but a destroyer really didn't need that level of support. Admittedly, it would have been helpful in this case.

Perhaps a light cruiser would be a better choice for future missions. The improved command and control systems would be a plus, and more missile tubes never hurt.

"Bridge, this is operations," Graves said over the communications link. "All departments report ready to flip."

"Thanks, Charlie." Jared nodded to Ramirez. "Give us a thirty-second warning and flip the ship."

"Aye, sir."

The flip warning sounded from the overheads. The countdown went by silently until Ramirez spoke again. "Flipping the ship."

A normal flip was over in less time than a person could detect, though it didn't feel instantaneous. It disrupted people's equilibrium for a few moments, which was why everyone strapped in before a flip. Once that effect passed, everything was back to normal before the helm officer announced they had made it.

This flip was anything but normal.

According to Jared's inner ear, some giant hand picked up the ship and spun it like a top. As the ship reeled, he felt glad he'd strapped in. He would've fallen out of his seat if he hadn't. The sensation persisted, and he almost lost his lunch. Someone did, although he couldn't tell whom. The sound of them retching and the smell almost pushed him into joining them.

He forced himself to focus on his console. They'd completed the flip and were floating in a new system. Obviously. If they hadn't made it all the way, he probably wouldn't be feeling so terrible. The ship's status was still green, so the mechanical parts of the ship had made it just fine.

"Flip complete," Ramirez gasped. "Holy God. I feel like someone kicked me in the… well, you know."

Jared most certainly did. The nausea was actually very similar to that event, though the disorientation wasn't. He pushed the feelings to the back of his mind and focused on his job. "Operations, I want a status on every person onboard."

"Aye, Captain." Graves sounded just as bad as Jared felt.

A glance over at Kelsey revealed that it had been her he'd heard retching. She sat bent over and holding her gut.

He unbuckled his restraint and staggered to his feet. He managed to make it to her side without falling over. "You okay?"

She looked up, her eyes not really focused. "That sucked."

He chuckled ruefully. "Indeed. Chin up. It'll wear off."

Jared found some rags in the emergency repairs cubby and cleaned up the vomit. He could've called someone to take care of it, but his people had more important things to do. The rags went into the disposal bin. The life support system quickly whisked the sour odor away.

He held himself upright against the bulkhead and verified everyone else seemed to be recovering. He made it back over to his chair without mishap and sighed gratefully as he strapped himself back in.

"Bridge, this is operations," Graves said. "All hands are accounted for. A few will be going to the medical center when someone can help them, but everyone is conscious and responsive."

"That's good, Charlie. Get to work nailing things down about our new location."

He killed the circuit. "Zia, what can you tell me about the flip point?"

She studied her console. "It looks like it did in the probe scans. Obviously the trip through was a lot rougher than we normally see. It's closer in to the system primary than usual, too. About the orbit of Avalon. The star looks a little dimmer and smaller than Avalon's, so the habitable zone is probably smaller. I don't have any more information on possible planets, but our location seems to be clear of debris."

"What about that distress beacon?"

"I'm picking it up loud and clear. I have a direction, but I'm unsure how far away it is. We'd need to move perpendicular to it for a little ways so I can triangulate. I can tell you that it's outside our orbit, so it's not a habitable world."

"Let's wait until everyone can move around first. Now that we're safely here, let's recover."

It took about ten minutes for the worst of the dizziness to fade. Kelsey seemed to be recuperating a little more slowly, but she had far less experience with flips than his crew did.

"What happened?" she finally asked him.

"That smaller flip point must mean it's a more difficult ride, apparently. We won't know for sure until the science teams get here. Zia, load a probe with all our scanner data and append a warning that it's a bad transition. We don't want them worrying for too long. Send it once you're done."

"Aye, sir."

"Bridge, this is operations."

"Mertz here. What have you got?"

"We're still working on the system data, but I have a rough estimate on our location relative to known space. You know how Doctor Cartwright bet it would be a short-range hop?"

"Is it?"

Graves chuckled. "I hope you took him up on that bet, because we're at least five hundred light years away from where we started."

Jared felt his eyes widen. "That's preposterous. The longest known flip is less than two hundred."

"Not anymore."

They were farther away from known space than the current Empire was across. That counted the previously explored but unclaimed space.

"Thanks, Charlie. Let us know when you have anything else for us."

"Right. Operations out."

"Pasco, take us on a perpendicular course from the distress beacon. I want to know how far away it is."

Ten minutes passed as they shifted position. Doctor Stone reported in that a dozen people had come with exceptionally bad nausea. It looked like Kelsey wasn't the worst hit. Stone expected them all to recover shortly.

Once he finished talking to the doctor, Zia called out to him. "I have a rough range to the distress beacon, Captain. It's about three hours away at moderate acceleration. I don't see anything at that location, so it's probably small. Nothing showing on the gravitic scanners."

"We'll go after it once *Best Deal* arrives and is ready to travel. After all this time, a few hours more won't matter."

He brought them back close to the flip point, and they waited.

Without warning, the empty space inside it wasn't empty anymore. *Best Deal* popped into existence half a dozen kilometers away. Zia reported it looked good from the outside, so Jared had her hail them.

Their response time was long enough to worry him, but Captain Keller finally answered. "Wow. That is the worst thing I've ever felt."

Jared chuckled in sympathy. "Agreed. Get a status on your people and get back to me. We have a team standing by if you need medical assistance."

In the end, it took almost two hours to get the freighter ready to move under her own power again. Luckily, they also had no serious issues with the crew. Everyone made the flip in one piece.

Jared was about to order them to set course for the distress beacon, but a priority call from Doctor Cartwright made him pause.

"Captain," the scientist said, "we may have a problem." The older man looked like he'd taken a ride in a centrifuge. His skin was almost grey, and the hair he had left was sticking straight out.

"What kind of problem, Doctor?"

"A detailed scan of the flip point shows instability. The gravitic field almost looks like a slowly spinning vortex. A whirlpool."

"That's not normal?"

The older man shook his head. "Absolutely not. I've never seen anything like it before. The motion was too subtle for the probe to pick up. I'd have sounded the alarm if I'd had any inkling about it."

Jared felt his gut tighten. "An alarm about what?"

Cartwright shrugged. "I'm not exactly certain, but anything this different from the norm is worth noting. I suspect that the rotating gravitic field is what caused such intense disorientation. While concerning, that isn't my biggest worry. The field is weak. Even the other end of this flip point has a normal strength field, though it is smaller. Not so here. This end is only half the strength I would've expected."

"What might that mean, Doctor?"

"I don't know," he said a bit crossly. "Perhaps nothing. The flip back might be worse than the one to get here. Perhaps the flip back won't work at all."

Jared's heart froze. "Not at all? The probes made it back without any issue."

"The probes are tremendously smaller than our ships. I'm only hypothesizing, and that is the worst case."

"What would be the results of a failed flip? Would the ship go part way and break up? Be destroyed on the spot?"

"Doubtful. The most likely outcome is that the ship doesn't go anywhere at all. The gravitic field could be too weak to open for a ship from this end at all. If so, then you'd hit the button and a lot of nothing would happen."

That was better than blowing up. "Thank you, Doctor. We'll figure this out shortly, so keep your scanners on the flip point. I want to know as much as possible when the time comes."

He closed the connection and called Graves. "I want all nonessential personnel shifted over to *Best Deal*. Transfer any critical supplies as well. We're going to make the transition back over to be sure we can go home."

Jared turned his attention to Kelsey. "You're going over to *Best Deal* with every single person I can do without. I'll log your objection, but if this ship doesn't come out the other side, I want you here with the rest finding another way home. They'll need you a lot more than I will."

He expected her to argue, but she nodded. "Of course, Captain. No objection."

In the end, they shifted more than three quarters of the crew over to *Best Deal*. The skeleton crew left on board was just enough to operate the ship. The marines objected to him ordering them off the ship, but this wasn't one of those situations where they could do much good. He manned the bridge alone.

Jared moved the ship back to the center of the flip point and signaled *Best Deal* that they were transitioning. He took a deep breath and activated the flip drive. The graphs showed the drive peaking, but nothing else happened. *Best Deal* still sat right there on his scanners.

They were trapped.

12

Kelsey waited on *Best Deal* until everyone else had returned to *Athena*, taking the last flight back. The loss of their way home had hit everyone hard. She still couldn't get her head around it. Too many shocks to her system, she supposed.

She listened to the scientists hashing out theories while she waited for her departure time, but except for using bigger words, they were saying the same thing as the Fleet officers. They didn't know what had happened. Not really.

Sure, they knew the flip point was defective, but not why. They'd be tearing apart the science behind everything for years without ever knowing what made these things tick, she suspected. The bottom line was that they were stuck until they found another flip point leading back to known space.

She pointed that out to them. The Old Empire had gotten here somehow. If it didn't use the defective flip point, then there had to be at least one more in this system.

That sent the scientists scurrying to the scanners. They shot probes in every direction, including toward the distress beacon.

The crew of *Athena* was busy when she finally got back, so she retreated to her seat on the bridge and sat quietly. After a while, they seemed to forget she was there. That was just fine by her. She had plenty to think about. Particularly Carlo Vega's death.

She had no idea why some unnamed person had killed her mentor, but his death didn't seem like an accident. What could motivate someone to murder him, though?

She'd asked some questions while she was on *Best Deal* but gathered no new answers. She wasn't exactly an investigator. Someone else would need to track down the person or persons behind the attack.

Lieutenant Anderson eventually reported the probe going toward the distress beacon had picked up a ship. Jared sat up a little straighter. "What can you tell me about it?"

"Just that it's a ship. We're too far away to get any more details."

"Ramirez, confer with *Best Deal* and have her follow us at her best speed. Bump us up to full speed."

"Aye, sir."

When they finally had a visual, the tiny speck on the screen could've been a smudge for all Kelsey could tell. Light was a little dim this far from the primary. She watched it with intense interest as the probe drew closer.

To think, they were about to see a ship of the Terran Empire at its heyday. It was obviously in one piece and had some kind of power. The thought of what they could learn staggered her.

The dot slowly resolved itself into a tumbling shape. It looked a little like a toy spaceship.

Lieutenant Anderson spoke up. "We're close enough to get some relative size data, Captain. That ship is significantly larger than *Athena* is. It's larger than the biggest ship in our fleet, though not by a tremendous amount. Perhaps one class larger than a heavy cruiser."

"Interesting," Jared said. "A battlecruiser?"

The ship on the screen grew slowly larger until Kelsey could see the hull clearly. It was spinning as well as turning end over end, but it appeared intact. The value of the find was immeasurable. Even though the interior was in all likelihood wrecked, they could still learn so much just by studying what remained.

"The probe is in station-keeping mode," Anderson reported. "I'm recording the exterior visual as it turns. I should have a complete picture in a minute."

"Any sign of battle damage?" Jared asked.

"There's something back in the engineering section. Not a rupture, though. I'm putting it on screen."

The view of the spinning derelict vanished, replaced by a still of the hull. A long gash had split the hull open. It looked like something had melted the metal.

"That's beam damage," Jared said.

"Beam damage?" Kelsey asked.

He turned his attention to her. "The records mention them. The Old Empire had missiles similar to the ones we do, but they also had beam weapons. That's something Fleet has been experimenting with for years. Unsuccessfully, so far."

"Surface scan complete," Anderson said. "There are several other areas with similar damage. Nothing on the scale of the breach in engineering, though."

Kelsey shook her head. "Something like that could've cut this ship into blocks. Why isn't it worse?"

Jared tipped his head toward the screen. "That ship had energy screens, if the old stories were correct. An enemy would have to be damned close or have done a lot of damage to the screens to get to the hull. It's possible the crew surrendered and then abandoned the ship. With that kind of damage, I'd expect something like that. They probably activated the distress beacon so it could be located later. Then they never came back."

"Do you think it's a renegade Fleet ship?"

He shrugged. "We may never know. It's kind of moot at this point."

"Captain, I have a name for the derelict," Anderson said. The image on the screen changed to show the bow of the ship. The large white letters spelled out her name. *Courageous*.

"I bet they were," Jared muttered. "How long until we reach the wreck? Are you picking up a power source for the distress beacon?"

The woman checked her screen. "We're about thirty minutes out. The probe is picking up indications of an operating fusion plant in the stern of the ship. It's running at low levels and seems to be fluctuating in output."

"Is it dangerous?"

"I'm not certain. That's more a question for an engineer, sir."

He nodded and rose to his feet. "Call the department heads to the conference room. Ambassador, would you care to join me?"

* * *

THE CONFERENCE ROOM on *Athena* was a lot smaller than the one on *Best Deal*. Kelsey took the seat next to Jared and tried to stop her brain from racing in circles. A relic of the fabled Empire of old, smashed and ruined, but still far more advanced than they were. She ached to explore its secrets.

Jared rapped the table with his knuckles, quieting the chatter. "Let's get started. The fusion unit over there is the biggest concern. Dennis, what can you tell me?"

Lieutenant Commander Baxter looked a lot more serious than when Kelsey had seen him last. She'd never guess at his questionable sense of humor if she'd met him now.

"The fusion plant is on the verge of failure. I'm astonished it lasted so long, frankly. The technology behind it must've played a role, but it was probably also at a very low output setting. Otherwise it would've crashed before now."

Jared nodded. "What do you mean by crash? Would it explode?"

"Ordinarily, I'd say no. Ours, for example, would trigger a safety interlock and shut down if they became unstable. However, the fluctuations we're seeing tell me that any safety system has already failed. We need to kill that power unit as soon as possible. I want to get a team over there without any delay. We might have weeks or months, but we might only have hours."

"How much warning would we have before it fails?"

Baxter shrugged. "Who knows? Probably time enough to get out of there. Possibly not. Personally, I'm willing to take the risk. I already have a team of volunteers standing by."

Kelsey couldn't fathom why people could be ready to risk death that way, but she also didn't understand why firefighters ran into burning buildings when there weren't people inside. From his expression, Jared did understand the urge, though.

The captain turned his attention to the tactical officer. "Zia, anything to add to our scanner take?"

"Quite a bit, Captain. The life pods are all still in place, and so are the ship's boats. Another ship must've done whatever evacuation they could manage. The interior is frozen. Life support is not online. Other than the power readings from the fusion plant and the distress beacon, everything else seems to be offline."

"We'd go in wearing suits anyway, but that's good information. Thanks. Lieutenant Reese, we'll want volunteers from the marines to help provide security and some muscle if we need it."

The marine officer nodded. "I have two squads ready to go in armored vacuum suits."

"Do you have anything to help us get inside? I'm certain that the hatches are locked, and we don't have the keys, even if we had power for their systems."

"We can cut through a hatch with boarding cutters. It won't be pretty, but it'll be quick."

Lieutenant Commander Graves gave Jared a look. "You've said 'we' several times, Captain. You aren't planning to go over there, are you? Not before we make sure it isn't going to blow up."

Jared nodded. "Actually, I am. I've made a study of all the material we have on pre-Fall Fleet ships. It might not be much, but I might be able to make a difference. Besides, you heard Dennis. We'll probably know before it goes critical."

"I heard him say 'probably,'" Kelsey said. "You can't risk yourself like that. You're the mission commander."

He turned his attention her way. "Actually, I can. My orders regarding the recovery of pre-Fall technology are crystal clear. I'm to do everything within my power to do so, even at moderate risk. The ship can get along without me, and my personal knowledge might be critical to recovering this ship. In any case, I'm the one that makes that call."

Graves didn't look particularly happy at that response, but he nodded. Grudgingly. "We'll keep a close eye on the situation from out here. If I make the call to evacuate the wreck, will you override me?"

"Probably not," Jared responded. "I don't want to die for a piece of junk any more than the next guy. If you say run, I'm not waiting to ask how fast."

Kelsey didn't like this one bit. Her elation at the find evaporated. She might not know him that well, but part of her quailed at the idea of her half brother taking such an awful risk. Even if he wasn't her blood, she didn't want to lose him.

"What about the scientists?" she asked. "Could some of them help with defusing the power plant?"

The engineer shrugged. "Possibly, but most likely not. They're theory, not hardware. I'll have them available if I have a problem. Like not knowing whether to cut the red or blue wire."

Kelsey gave him a quelling glare. "That isn't funny."

He grinned for a moment before his expression faded back to seriousness. "No, it's not. We need to get a move on, Captain. We might regret chatting an extra few minutes later."

Jared stood. "Bring the ship to alert status and back off to a safe distance. We'll depart as soon as the teams are in the marine pinnaces. Dismissed."

Kelsey wanted to follow him and say something, but she had no idea what. Be careful? Duh. She'd just have to trust him to do his job and come back safely.

Instead, she followed Graves back up to the bridge and commandeered one of the empty consoles. She'd watch every step of their mission on the big screen.

Graves stepped beside her console. "Let me enable the visual controls for you. Then you can pause, rewind, and zoom what we see on your console if you feel like it. The suits all have helmet cams."

"Thank you. May I call you Charlie?"

He smiled. "I'd like it if you did."

"Charlie, has he lost his mind?"

He chuckled. "I sometimes wonder. No. He wouldn't be going if he didn't think he had a reason to and a good possibility of coming back. He wouldn't risk his crew for nothing."

She took a deep breath. "Okay."

"*Athena*, this is *Marine Two*. Both pinnaces are ready to depart."

Graves walked back to the command console and opened the channel. "God speed, *Marine Two*. Come back safe."

"Roger that. *Marine Two* out."

The main screen picked up the two pinnaces shortly after that as they made their run to the wreck. The marine craft were significantly larger than the passenger cutters. Marines were armed and their ships armored. Perhaps if the ship blew up while they fled, that would give them an extra chance of surviving.

Kelsey sat back in her seat and tried to loosen her tense muscles. This was going to be a long, stressful day.

13

Rather than displace the marine pilot, Jared sat in the back with the rest of the marines and engineering techs in *Marine Two*. They'd be docking on the forward half of the derelict while Baxter went aft. If their way was blocked, Jared's team might make it to the fusion plant faster.

He had the small screen in his vacuum suit tuned to the visual from the external cameras. The wicked spin on *Courageous* made matching course a challenge. One miscalculation and the wreck would swat them like a bug.

The pilot eased close to the derelict and then lined up with the tumble. Thankfully, the rotation wasn't too bad or they might not have been able to match with it at all. The pinnace corrected for the spin and made contact with the other hull hard enough to rattle his teeth.

"We're locked down, Captain," the pilot said on the mission frequency. "We're about a dozen meters from what looks like an emergency hatch. You'll need to use magnetic boots and tethers. The centrifugal force is powerful."

"Roger. Be ready to haul ass if we come running back."

"Aye, sir."

Lieutenant Reese stood and began hooking the men together with tough lines. "If someone comes loose, I want everyone to grab the hull with your hand clamps. We'll always have half of us holding onto the ship, just in case."

They all checked one another's suits again. Only then did the marine officer pump the atmosphere out and open the assault ramp.

The stars spun crazily over the steady horizon of the derelict's hull. It made Jared a little sick to his stomach, so he focused his eyes on the back of the man in front of him. That settled him down. The floodlights on the pinnace brightly illuminated *Courageous*'s hull.

They made their way slowly onto the Old Empire ship and toward the emergency hatch. The team moved at a snail's pace. A man broke loose halfway to the hatch, but they pulled him back down.

When everyone stopped moving, they hunkered down and activated their hand clamps. A bright red line surrounded the large hatch, and rescue instructions were painted right on the hull. It looked very similar to the ones on *Athena*.

Jared didn't expect it to work, but he twisted the emergency handle as instructed. The hatch slowly pulled into the ship, revealing a large airlock with dim red emergency lighting.

"That's useful," Jared said. "It must be internally powered. Quite a tribute to its designers."

He switched to the mission frequency. "Team One, we've opened the external hatch. We're going in."

"Roger that," Baxter said. "No joy back here. We're cutting ours open."

Jared pulled himself into the airlock and wedged his arm through a handhold. The airlock had bags and boxes full of equipment, and probably rescue supplies. The interior hatch wouldn't open while the outside one was open, so the team had to split up. The half that followed Jared inside held on tight as he closed the hatch. He held his breath, but the inner door opened as easily as the exterior.

The corridor beyond was in total darkness. Any emergency lighting had failed. He advanced inside far enough to plant his feet against the wall and turned his helmet lamp on. They'd need to be very careful of the centrifugal force inside, too. One inattentive moment could maim or kill.

Once the second team made it inside, Jared sighed in relief. "Okay, let's start working our way back toward engineering."

Movement inside was almost as slow as outside, if less nerve-wracking. Baxter reported that they were inside a few minutes later.

"We're seeing some damage," the engineer said, "but I think we'll make it to engineering without too much trouble. Why don't you head for the bridge? You might be able to bring some controls online from there."

"Agreed," Jared said. "Let us know when you get there."

A hatch ahead of them was open. With the wicked spin, the wall it occupied was more of a floor. He looked inside and recognized a personnel cabin. It looked normal, though the spin had thrown everything against the outside bulkhead.

He started to edge past it, but something caught his eye. There was a body in the detritus. "Hold up. We have a body. I'm going inside."

It occurred to him as he lowered himself down the steep slope that the person below was centuries beyond his ability to help, but the impulse to go had been instinctual. A minute wouldn't hurt them, and the video might be helpful to the scientists.

He managed to get inside without injuring himself and moved the debris until he could see a woman's face. At least he felt certain it was a woman. All the moisture in her body had evaporated in the vacuum, leaving her remains mummified and frozen solid.

She wore a uniform very similar to the ones hanging in his closet. She was Fleet. A glance at her arm showed her to be a senior petty officer. He moved the junk around until he could see all of her. There were no obvious injuries.

He climbed back up to the corridor. "Let's press on to the bridge."

Jared found an internal diagram near the first lift they encountered. It indicated they needed to climb five decks from the next lift forward.

"Captain," Baxter said. "We're in main engineering. That shot damaged the flip drive but didn't destroy it. It missed almost all the major equipment. I'm somewhat surprised they weren't able to make repairs. We have some bodies in Fleet uniforms. It looks like the damage exposed them to space."

"We found a body, too. We're almost to the bridge lift. Find the fusion plant and get it shut down."

"Aye, sir."

They had to pry the doors apart when they reached the lift. Luckily, the platform wasn't between them and the bridge. The particular nature of the spin made getting there an easy walk.

The lift doors at the bridge level were hard to open from the shaft, but they finally gave up the ghost. Jared stepped out onto the bridge and froze. It was significantly bigger than *Athena*'s bridge, but that wasn't its most striking feature. Each seat held a dead Fleet officer.

"Baxter, we have bodies on the bridge. Something is very wrong."

"Sounds like. We're at the fusion plant. I'll call you when I figure it out."

Jared turned to his men. "Fan out in pairs. Explore the nearby areas. Be careful." He singled out one of the men to wait with him.

He climbed to what he thought was the captain's console and studied the man strapped in there. His body was in a very similar condition to the woman they'd found earlier. His uniform indicated he was a full captain, though there wasn't a name tag. He wore an odd-looking headset. There were no microphones, and it didn't cover his ears. He couldn't determine its purpose. There was no obvious sign of injury that Jared could see.

A trip around the bridge told him none of these people had battle wounds, yet they'd all died at their stations. The damage to the ship wasn't bad enough to kill them here. Or that woman. Something else had caused their deaths. All wore the strange headsets.

Maybe he could bring the captain's console to life and find something. Fleet built all the critical systems on *Athena* with small power units to operate with if the main systems went offline. Surely the Old Empire worried about battle damage taking out the main power grid, too.

Dust coated the console. He brushed it away with his gloved hand. It was a flat panel, very sleek and futuristic. The irony of thinking that about a 500-year-old wreck made him snort a little.

He felt around the sides and under the rim for an emergency power switch. He found it on the right side up front where no one could unintentionally hit it, but it was still within easy reach by the captain.

The consoled flickered when Jared flipped the recessed switch. He didn't think it would come on at all, but it slowly brightened. The layout of the virtual controls was unfamiliar to him, though he thought he could figure them out.

This was a ship's status screen. The pattern of the red and amber dots formed a ship. Almost all the dots were red, so he picked one of the few amber ones toward the aft of the ship. The display expanded at a touch and showed what he guessed was engineering. The dot remained amber, but some text appeared beside it.

It was the fusion plant. The safety interlocks were disabled. It said so right there. The output was fluctuating, and there was a lurid warning about the danger of explosion.

He opened a channel to the chief engineer. "Dennis, I have the captain's console up and running. I have a reading on the fusion plant. It says someone overrode the safety interlocks. It has a warning about the output fluctuations."

"That's more than I'm getting here," the engineer grumbled. "The controls seem fried. At least the displays are. Perhaps that's why they overrode the interlocks. This plant shouldn't be operating without the local controls."

"Are you going to be able to shut it down from there?"

"Probably not. I'm accessing the video from your helmet cam. That looks bad. I want to shut the plant down right now. You're going to have to drive for me."

Jared felt his stomach flutter. This was all too similar to his nightmare of having to do something in engineering. It never ended well. He took a deep breath. "Talk me through it."

"Seriously? As if I know their control systems any better than you do. Tap the amber icon for the fusion plant."

A tap opened a menu of options. Powering it off wasn't one of them.

"There at the bottom," Baxter continued. "Tap where it says safety interlocks."

A touch brought up the option to enable the safety interlocks. "What will that make it do?"

"If I'm right, it'll cause the fusion plant to shut down."

Jared considered that. "What if you're wrong?"

"If that's a clever way of asking if it'll explode, I think not. At worst, it should leave things in the same configuration. It shouldn't make it go critical."

Jared expected Graves to chime in there, but he didn't, so he mastered his apprehension and tapped the button. The icon for the fusion plant turned red.

"It went red!"

"Relax. If it were going to explode, you'd never have noticed the color change. The plant shut down exactly like it was designed to do."

Jared let out the breath he hadn't realized he was holding. The danger was past.

"Good work," he said. "Now, make sure there are no other surprises in engineering that might cause us problems. Mertz out."

He had to experiment before he figured out how to expand the status back out. Then he went hunting for a reason for the bridge crew to be dead. It took ten minutes, but he finally found the answer in an input log for the console.

Someone had vented the atmosphere to space from this console. He double-checked to be sure, but it appeared *Courageous*'s captain had killed his own people. What Jared couldn't understand was why.

Reese signaled him. "Captain, you need to come down to the deck where we entered the lift and come forward half a dozen hatches."

"What do you have? Patch it through to me."

"Sir, I really think you need to come see this in person."

If his marine commander said he needed to come in person, Jared was smart enough to trust him. He and his companion made their way carefully back down, and Jared saw several men standing outside one hatch looking in. He made his way up to them and looked inside himself.

It was a mess hall. It held hundreds of dead bodies. Centrifugal motion had piled them in the corner, but he couldn't mistake what this was—a graveyard.

He felt the gorge rising in his throat but managed to master the urge to throw up. The crew of *Courageous* hadn't escaped after all. This ship was a tomb.

14

Kelsey stood in the docking bay on *Best Deal* wearing her very best dress. The heels she wore were killing her feet, but sitting wasn't an option. She felt drained. Thankfully, it was almost over. The last three days had been hell.

A Fleet crewman blew a piercing blast on his whistle, the tune all too familiar to her at this point. Jared and the other Fleet officers, dressed in their resplendent black-and-red dress uniforms, came to attention as the hatch slid open.

The marine honor guard brought their weapons in front of them as their comrades brought the last of the crew from *Courageous* aboard. The men held the sealed boxes high, slow stepping as if the very gravity of the situation held them tightly to the deck.

Seeing so many dead, both the horrible images from the dead Fleet vessel and the coffins passing her one at a time, felt unreal. Nothing she'd ever done before had prepared her for the impact of Fleet welcoming home their dead.

Jared held his salute until the last of the coffins had passed. A number of storage compartments would hold the dead until they returned to Avalon. Fleet never buried anyone in space. Fleet didn't abandon their own.

She put her hand on Jared's shoulder. "Come on. We both need a meal and a stiff drink. I hear the brains have a really nice bar."

He raised an eyebrow tiredly. "They have a bar? How did I miss hearing about it? Better yet, how come you know about it?"

"The marines. They know every bar within a light year."

"Of course they do. Sure."

It didn't take them long to find the place. Someone had outfitted one of the smaller cargo compartments with tables and chairs. The smell of food coming from somewhere made her hungry. A number of crates made up the bar itself. She waved down the server, who looked more like a physicist than anything else.

"Can we get beer and something from the mess?" she asked. "Sandwiches would be fine."

"Of course, Ambassador, Captain. I think we can do significantly better than that. I've been watching the ceremony on the vid feed, and you deserve it. Do you have any preferences?"

Jared shook his head. "Anything would be fine. Thank you…"

"Doctor Brad Parker, Imperial Institute of Science. I'm the planetary sciences team leader."

She'd been so close. Not. "I'll take whatever you get for him, Doctor. Thank you."

"My pleasure. Be right back with some beer." He headed off through the crowd toward the bar.

Kelsey turned her attention back to Jared while surreptitiously kicking off her shoes. "Not to be morbid, but are you sure you've found everyone?"

He nodded. "Search teams covered every part of that ship three times. All five hundred and eighty-five of them are now safely back in the hands of their brothers and sisters. Their time alone is over. Fleet and marine personnel will stand guard outside their temporary tomb until we can see them properly interred. Then the permanent honor guard will keep watch over them."

"Why does that tradition exist? I'm not putting it down, but I don't understand the thought behind it."

"The single surviving Fleet officer that made it to Avalon's surface asked for it from the people that found him. He said it was tradition. He inducted his rescuers before he died, and they kept watch over him.

"We've followed that tradition ever since. The Imperial Cemetery at the Spire serves for the interment of all the Fleet dead from day one. Even when we didn't have ships."

She started to say something, but the scientist brought them their beer, so she waited for him to leave before continuing. "That doesn't need any explanation. Honor speaks for itself."

He raised his glass in salute. "As an institution, we stand on the shoulders of those who came before us. They're watching over us, and we don't dare fail them."

"Father has said similar things. I've always thought that was incredibly romantic."

"Thank you for being there with me. With us. We all appreciate the honor you've shown our sacred dead. It will not be forgotten."

As tired as she was, Kelsey sat up straighter. "Today, I wasn't Ambassador Kelsey Bandar. I was Princess Kelsey of the House of Bandar, daughter of your emperor and liege. Though he is many light years away, he stood among you today with the Terran Empire behind him. Remember that."

Jared bowed his head. "We are grateful."

She sighed and surreptitiously rubbed her aching feet. "I've been watching things on *Courageous* over the vid. What kind of shape is she really in?"

"Not bad at all, considering her age and the battle damage. She's structurally sound, even though she doesn't have power. Baxter even said he might be able to repair her, if he had the time and knowhow. Now that we've used the pinnaces to stop her tumble, we can get people on and off her without any difficulty.

"Baxter is working on some kind of standby power that can be strung in through the hole in her engineering compartment to power the main grid. That should allow us to see how much of the computer and ship's systems are fit enough to power up. He promised to have something ready by tomorrow."

She took a sip of her beer. "I'm impressed that you stopped that tumble. I never thought that would even be possible."

"It doesn't matter that the pinnaces are small. Every bit of thrust from their grav drives worked to slow her bit by bit. One could even stop the spin at Orbital One with enough time. To every action there is a reaction."

"What do we do now? Both with the ship and getting home?"

Doctor Parker chose that moment to return with two salads and a platter of sizzling meat mixed with vegetables. The scent made her mouth water.

"Here you are," the scientist said. "On the house. Of course, everything here is always on the house, but you get the idea."

She smiled at him. "Thank you, Doctor Parker."

Jared added his thanks and waited for the man to leave before continuing. "We're stocked for a five-year mission, though the last two of that is preserved rations. A freighter has a lot of space, even after the conversion to a science ship, so we don't need to worry about running out of supplies just yet. I expect we'll find plenty of habitable worlds as we try to find our way home."

"How will we do that? We can't even guess where a flip point will take us. Without being able to follow the path we used to get here, I'm at a loss how we get back." She tried to keep from sounding depressed at the idea of not going home, but she knew it colored her tone.

Jared smiled. "You have to have faith. We'll get there eventually. *Courageous* came from the same Empire we did. No matter how daunting the journey, we can make it home."

"How do we know it didn't come here through that damned flip point? It might have been trapped here."

"Then where is the ship that crippled her?"

"Destroyed. Drifting in space. Fell into the star."

"Aren't you a pessimist?" he asked, taking a bite of his salad. "While our probes haven't searched every kilometer of this system, I'm confident that we'll find that the enemy had fled the field. Probably through the flip point we detected partway around the ecliptic."

Kelsey froze with her fork partway to her mouth. "You found another flip point? Why haven't I heard this before?"

"Eat before you chew on me. The salad is much tastier than my dress uniform." He infuriatingly waited for her to take a bite. She had to admit it was good. She was famished.

He continued as she started putting the food away. "One of the men came up and whispered it to me just before that last pinnace docked. It's a full-sized, absolutely normal flip point."

"That's wonderful news! I'll drink to that!" She lifted her beer and took a healthy drink.

"I've been thinking about what we can do, and I've come up with several things. First, we'll finish exploring *Courageous*. We can recover a lot of *Courageous*'s equipment and store it in *Best Deal*'s holds. Then we prep a probe with every bit of data we have and send it back to the system on the other side of the flip point. A search party will eventually come this way, and then they'll know about the weak flip point."

"Could we get one to go back and contact the Empire?"

"That's a lot less likely. Baxter is going to tear one of the probes apart and try to build enough redundancy into it to make that happen. If it works, we're still looking at a couple of months to get a ship out here."

He tried some of the meat. "This is good. Even though they can't come after us, they can send supplies through if we can't get out of this sector. Living in ships would suck, but we can do it. I still don't believe we'll need to. I suspect we're closer to Terra than we ever were before."

Kelsey raised an eyebrow. "Why would you think that?"

"A hunch. Someone chased *Courageous* here and killed her. Hopefully we'll find out more as we explore the ship, but I'm willing to bet the rebels did it."

"The rebels chased Emperor Lucien to Avalon," she pointed out.

"Yes, but none of them came back. They had more pressing business elsewhere. Since they were here chasing a Fleet unit, I'll bet that means we're deeper into the Old Empire. Admittedly, I could be wrong, but I prefer to be optimistic."

They ate silently for a while. The food was better than good, Kelsey decided. Not that she could eat everything. She let Jared finish her food before she ordered a second beer.

"Nothing I've ever read said why the rebels did what they did," she said at last. "Who were they, and why were they so vicious? They'd used a kinetic strike on a city that couldn't shoot back. That attack killed over a million people. Now *Courageous*. They were crippled and left to die. That's not just a minor difference of opinion."

"Perhaps they weren't left to die. Perhaps they ran out of options. *Courageous* is a long way from the flip point in a slow orbit. A ship at rest isn't detectable at that kind of range. This system has two very large asteroid belts in addition to half a dozen uninhabitable planets. It would take a large number of ships to find her if she didn't want to be found."

He took another gulp of his beer. "Dennis also found evidence of repairs. They had days or weeks to try to fix the damage done to their ship after the fight. What they didn't have was air."

"Excuse me?"

"*Athena* recycles her air, but there is a limited supply. We have three different tankage areas. *Courageous* had six. The fighting breached five of those. The last is empty."

"Did the rebels intentionally do that to her?" Kelsey shuddered. "I'm glad the rebels are dead."

"I hope they are. One of Fleet's biggest fears is that we'll encounter their descendants. We don't have anything like what the Old Empire had in warships. We'd go down fighting, but we'd go down. That's why we can wipe the critical computer systems on *Athena* and *Best Deal*. Just in case."

"That's morbid. Let's change the subject. Now that *Courageous* is safer, when can I go see her for myself?"

He looked like his preferred answer would be "never," but he didn't say that. "If we can restore environmental controls, I'll let you go. Until there's an atmosphere, you'll need to do your visiting via vid. The scientists, too."

That wasn't what she wanted to hear, but she knew better than to argue. "Thank you."

"In the meantime, I know there are a lot of things coming over for the scientists to examine. I'm sure they would love to have your help with some of the personal belongings."

Somehow, she doubted they'd want her looking over their shoulders. Not that she'd let that stop her.

Examining the personal belongings of the dead was even more morbid, but she knew he was right to collect everything. Any bit might provide a clue to something important. A dead man's data reader might have tech manuals on something critical. A dead woman's knickknacks might have incredible cultural significance. Nothing was too ordinary or too small for them to collect.

"I'll stay clear of the ship," she said, "but I want you to make me a trade."

"Name it."

"I don't like being blocked by a lack of skills. Can someone train me on going into vacuum in case this comes up again? Like one of the marines?"

He considered that for a moment and then nodded. "Deal."

They finished their last beer in silence. She wondered what they would find when they finished examining *Courageous*. Secrets she couldn't even imagine? Or just more questions?

15

Jared went back over to *Courageous* the next morning. If there were any kind of trouble, he'd have plenty of time to get back to *Athena*. Graves had taken third shift to oversee things on the wreck and to explore. *Athena*'s day watch would wake him if something developed.

There still wasn't any gravity, but without the wicked spin, he was able to make his way to engineering without problems. Baxter was already there overseeing the splice of a thick cable into the power grid.

They'd strapped the cable to the deck and out through the gash ripped into the hull. Jared floated over and held himself in place beside the engineer. "How goes it?"

"Almost ready to divert power. It won't be enough to power the ship, but it should let us turn on some basic systems like life support."

"I thought the life support reservoirs were trashed."

"One holds pressure. A second looks easily reparable. I've had some of the reserves on *Best Deal* shipped over. We can recapture most of it when we're ready to leave, but having a pressurized hull will make recovery operations a lot simpler."

"Do we know if the ship's systems will even work?"

"Nope. We'll be doing an old-fashioned smoke test. If it smokes, it won't work."

Jared shook his head. "You're a mess. If the computer comes back online, will we be able to interface with it?"

"That's a question for the brains. For the time being, we've disconnected it from the grid." He sprayed something on the exposed connections, hiding the bare metal beneath a black, rubbery covering. "Okay. Here we go."

He must've said something on a different frequency, because Jared didn't hear a word. He did see the overhead lights flicker and come on dimly.

Jared hunted around until he found the frequency they were using and heard people chiming in about the lights coming on. From the locations given, the entire ship had lights. Of a sort.

"Are those emergency lights?" he asked after Baxter finished checking in with everyone.

"Probably. They're too dim to be the main overheads. I'll need to find the controls to turn on anything else. The system knows none of the fusion plants is online, and it can tell the amount of power is limited. I think I can override that for specific systems."

"Will the ship give you access?"

"Let's find out." He pushed off the bulkhead and led the way deeper into engineering. Away from the flip drives, the damage was less severe, but it would've been deadly to the men and women working here.

Baxter went to one of the consoles and found the emergency power switch. The display came to life, dim and coated in dust. It brightened almost immediately. "The console found the power bus, and it's not asking for any kind of authentication. That's probably because it still thinks it's in a combat situation. No authentication required when someone is shooting at you." He tapped the screens, hunting for something.

The displays the chief engineer examined made even less sense to Jared than the engineering displays on *Athena*. Baxter eventually found something, though. "Here we go. Let's put the lighting on a higher priority."

The overhead lights brightened enough to illuminate every corner. With the ship still in vacuum, the shadows were knife sharp and deep black.

"That should do it," Baxter said with satisfaction. "I'll add my authentication to the engineering subsystems. Another benefit of having the main computer offline."

"What happens when the computer comes back online?"

"I'll isolate it from the control runs if we decide to power it up. Then the authentication we give the consoles will continue to work. Adding someone to the main computer is another egghead task. It may not even be possible. I'd imagine there's some pretty tight security coding on it."

Jared nodded. "One problem at a time. Next, what about the life support systems?"

Baxter navigated through the screens. "The system still shows itself to be functional. It looks like Fleet designed their warships to last a long time. I'm impressed."

Baxter switched to the all-hands channel. "Okay, everyone. If you're near an airtight door, you need to get clear of it. Tell me now if you won't be clear in thirty seconds."

When no one said anything, Baxter waited and then touched the controls. "All airtight doors have sealed and show green. Life support is online. It shows some glitches, but as a critical system, it can manage. Pressure is slowly rising and the heaters are on, except for engineering and a few other areas still open to space. I'd imagine you could take off your helmet in half an hour, but it'll still be brutally cold in there. I wouldn't touch bare metal for at least an hour."

The idea that an old wreck like this could come back to life boggled Jared's mind. "I'll want a ship's status when you can get it. I want to know what systems could be used if we wanted to. That might help a lot in getting an idea how things work."

"Yes, sir."

"Now how do I get to the other side of the pressure doors?"

"They come in pairs so that you can open one at a time and step through like an airlock. The pressure will equalize, and then the other side will open. I'll get someone to checking the primary systems and available repair parts. Those will tell us a lot by themselves, technologically speaking."

"This ship is full of surprises. I'll want someone to check the weapons systems, too. Call Zia to get some of her people to help."

He made his way forward to the first set of pressure doors. They performed exactly as Baxter had indicated. He couldn't see a difference once he went through, but his suit informed him there was a slight increase in pressure.

Jared made his way to the bridge. It looked better with the lights on, but he couldn't see the place without remembering *Courageous*'s long-dead crew strapped in at their stations. No one was up here now, so he had the captain's console all to himself to do a little looking around.

The floor plan appeared similar to the one on *Athena*, only larger. Significantly larger. The captain's console was on a raised dais overlooking the crew stations. Four forward in square formation. Three each on the right and left sides facing the bulkheads. Two consoles at the rear flanked the lift.

He'd identified a dozen stations, not counting the captain's. Significantly more than on the largest cruiser he'd ever been on. The compartment was also quite roomy, meaning there was no feeling of being crowded here.

One hatch on the left side of the compartment led to the captain's day cabin, complete with conference room. Another opened to a large head for the crew. He'd missed the closed hatches on his first visit. Admiral Yeats's flag bridge on Orbital One was less luxurious.

He strapped himself in to the captain's chair and brought the console to life. It connected to the power grid and glowed brightly under the smeared dust. He'd left the systems on the life support screen, so he could see an array of amber dots all over the ship. A number of red one's told him engineering was still in a vacuum. No surprise there. Most remaining areas had noticeable pressure. The temperature was coming up, too.

The log had the last commands entered on this console. He could see where he'd enabled the safeties on the fusion reactor. The timestamp was wrong, of course. The console had been without power too long to keep any internal chronometer running.

The previous instructions were there, too. He saw where the captain had disabled the safeties. He also saw where he'd entered a complex set of instructions for the reactor. Then he'd vented the ship to space. All within the space of a minute. The first officer had countersigned the orders.

Why the hell did the ship's designers even have a method to vent the atmosphere to space and scuttle the ship? He couldn't do something that crazy on *Athena* even if Graves helped him cut holes all over the ship. What kind of maniac thought the system needed to account for that possibility?

He tried to make sense of the instructions sent to the fusion reactor and failed. He opened a communications link to Baxter. "Dennis, I'm looking at the console logs from the bridge. *Courageous*'s captain sent some commands to the fusion plant that make no sense to me. Hook up to my helmet feed and tell me what they look like to you."

The other man was silent for a moment. "Are you kidding me? That isn't funny. How did you even manage to program that? I'd never have figured you had that kind of engineering theory."

"I'm not pulling anyone's leg. That's what the captain sent from this station. What does it mean?"

"It means that the captain was a suicidal maniac," Baxter said. "Those instructions should've sent the fusion reactor into overload in less than twenty minutes. It would've gone off like a nova. The only guess I can make is that a systems failure on this end disrupted the command."

"It sure looks like they were determined not to fall into the hands of the rebels," Jared said.

"I can see that. He set the fusion plant to explode and vented the atmosphere. Two very thorough deaths. I'm surprised he didn't set any of the ship-to-ship missiles to explode."

Jared's eyes widened, and he switched to the all hands frequency. "All weapons technicians to the ship's missile tubes! I want to be sure that no one has tampered with the warheads. Make it fast."

Baxter whistled. "What the hell is going on here, Jared?"

"Something really disturbing. Does this ship have more than one fusion plant?"

"Yes, but they all went down at some point. They probably deteriorated until the safeties shut them down."

Jared thought furiously. "I want you to go over every system on this ship that might destroy it. Isolate them if you find any evidence of tampering. I don't want the long-dead hand of *Courageous*'s captain to take us with him."

"Aye, sir."

He sat there for a while, thinking. No obvious explanations jumped out at him. After a bit, he shook himself out of his reverie. The command log might tell him a bit more of the final timeline. He brought it up and studied it more closely. Unfortunately, the console only logged commands sent from it.

He wondered why someone activated the distress beacon in the first place. It seemed counterintuitive. Perhaps it activated on its own after some predetermined period without instructions from the main computer.

He made his way around the other stations and brought them online.

The tactical console had the times when they'd activated the screens and fired the weapons. It looked like the final battle lasted about an hour. It seemed as though that fight had taken place three weeks before they apparently killed themselves. There was a second battle a week earlier.

Helm indicated two activations of the flip drive between those battles. It also logged the tactical officer's attempts to shift power to reactivate the screens when they failed.

Jared stared at the dead main screen for a while. Too bad the computer was offline. It probably logged both the battles in their entirety.

He needed to get the main computer online.

Or did he? This had happened half a millennium ago. The information locked away wasn't relevant to their current situation. Yes, they needed to know. They just didn't need to know this second. It wasn't as though the rebels would come pouring through the flip point while he feverishly searched for the answers.

Baxter reported in shortly with the all clear. That removed the danger for now. Jared checked the air readings and popped his helmet. The icy atmosphere smelled musty but breathable. He'd let the ship warm up and then send for the brains. Maybe they could shed some light on the situation.

He returned to the captain's console and explored for a while longer. He wanted to find any personal log, but there didn't seem to be one. It was probably on the main computer.

What he did find was an icon on the main screen marked "play me." He tapped it, and the main screen at the front of the compartment flickered and came to life. A chill ran up Jared's spine that had nothing to do with the cold. He was looking at the bridge of this ship as it had been. Only, live men and women filled the crew stations. All wore the strange headsets.

The captain had dark hair with a hint a grey. He looked to be about Jared's age.

"If you're watching this message," the dead man said, "then our attempts to destroy this ship have failed. I beseech you, stranger, to inter our dead as if they were your own brothers in arms. I commend them to you. I couldn't have wished for braver companions in this terrible time."

The dead captain gestured around himself. "*Courageous* has served us well and defended the Empire with honor. We drew off the remaining rebel battlecruisers so that our task force could escape without detection. We disabled one of the enemy ships two systems back and destroyed the other here.

"Unfortunately, the bastards took out our flip drives and most of our life support reserves in the fight, damn the luck. Rather than wait for the air to grow foul and prolong our suffering, we've decided to end things swiftly. I'd prefer to overload one of the fusion plants, but the chief engineer and most of his staff are dead. I'll make an effort to do so, but I have little confidence in my ability. With some justification, since you're seeing this message."

The black humor made Jared shake his head.

Courageous's captain continued. "The backup plan is to vent the ship's atmosphere. It isn't the most desirable way to die, but it will be graciously quick." The man rubbed his eyes tiredly. "I dearly hope you're Fleet yourself, but that seems hard to imagine in these dark times. Whoever you are, if *Courageous* can serve your needs, please take her with my blessing. Treat her like a lady."

The horror of the long-ago situation again washed over Jared. This crew had known their end was inescapable. They'd chosen to die by their own hands rather than suffer. Most had gathered in the mess compartments for one last time, to be with their friends at the end. Others like the woman he'd found in her cabin had chosen to die alone.

The captain and his command crew had met their end at their stations.

He'd been through emergency decompression drills, including an actual loss of atmosphere. Unlike the common misconception, you didn't swell up and explode like a balloon. Fleet trained them to open their mouths and let the air rush out so that their lungs survived undamaged. Then you suffocated if you couldn't find any air.

The long-dead captain straightened in his chair. "Well, our time is up. I apologize for leaving our home in such a mess. I again beseech you to take our remains home with you. Bury us with whatever ritual and honor you hold dear and accept my gratitude for your kindness."

The long-dead Fleet officer sat up straighter and brought his right fist to his chest. "I hope you'll forgive the paraphrase, or at least understand it. Go tell the Empire, stranger passing by, that here, obedient to Imperial law, we lie. *Courageous* out."

The screen blinked out, and Jared brought his own fist up to return the salute. Much of Terran history had been lost to the ages, but he knew the story of Sparta and the 300. He couldn't imagine a more fitting epitaph for these heroes.

16

Watching an autopsy wasn't very high on Kelsey's list of things to do, but somehow Doctor Stone convinced her to do exactly that. She promised herself she wouldn't lose her lunch and that she'd get out of there as fast as she could. The very real appointment she had on *Best Deal* to look over some of the artifacts would make an outstanding excuse.

Stone had a man laid out before her on the diagnostic table. He had a sheet pulled up to his chin, but he still looked painfully vulnerable. He also looked like a long-dead corpse. The faint scent of decay hung in the air.

The doctor looked up at Kelsey. "You look a little queasy. If you're afraid I'm going to cut this poor soul up, you can rest easy. My scanners are more than capable of getting me all the data I need without violating him."

The princess relaxed a little. "I suppose I was thinking exactly that."

"I've been present when an old-fashioned autopsy was conducted on a body donated to science, but unless something looks wildly out of place, that won't be necessary. If it were, I wouldn't subject you to that."

"Can you tell what killed him without going inside him?"

"I can tell you what killed him right now. He died from asphyxiation. The burst capillaries in his eyes are a dead giveaway, if you'll pardon the unintended and wholly inappropriate pun. Really, I'm not looking for cause of death. I'm looking to see if there are any oddities."

Kelsey felt herself frowning. "Like what?"

"I don't know, but if we don't scan some people, we won't know for sure. This, by the way, is the commanding officer of *Courageous*. I'd tell you his name, but we don't have any idea what it is. Fleet uniforms didn't have name tags back then, apparently. I can't imagine how that worked."

Kelsey examined the dead man's face. Thankfully, someone had closed his eyes. She didn't want to see any burst blood vessels. Judging his age wasn't easy. With his body mummified as it was, he could've been any age at all. He did have a full head of dark hair that seemed to be only a little grey. Maybe in his late thirties or early forties?

Doctor Stone initialized the diagnostic bed and turned to face the large screen. It lit up with the outline of a human body. It began filling in with bones and internal organs almost immediately. Then the head began flashing yellow.

"What's that?" Kelsey asked.

"An anomaly." Stone tapped the head on the screen. It expanded to show more detail. Kelsey had a vague idea of what a human brain looked like, and she was fairly certain that one didn't usually have a web of filaments running through it and several small discs implanted under the skull.

"Wow," Stone said. "He's got some kind of artificial implant in his brain. Three processors of some kind attached to the skull itself and ultra-thin wires branching throughout the brain matter."

"What do they do? Why would anyone do that to themselves? And how could they do it at all without killing themselves?"

"I have no idea." Stone expanded the view on his head until the filaments loomed large. "It looks like some kind of graphene derivative."

"Graphene?"

Stone nodded. "It's an old material, discovered on prespaceflight Terra. An engineer could tell you more, but it's a crystalline allotrope of carbon that has two-dimensional properties. It's basically an atom-thick lattice of carbon. Conductive and twenty times stronger than steel.

"They used it in all kinds of equipment, and so do we. That's what makes communicator screens so thin and flexible. It's a lot more useful than silicon electronics."

The doctor examined the thin strand on the screen. "I never imagined it could be used inside someone's brain, though. I don't think this is exactly the same material, either. How did they even get it in there?"

She shook her head. "There'll be time enough to research that. The rest of his body looks normal enough. Let's look at a few more people before I call in some of the scientists to help explain this."

Stone had her orderlies take the man's body out, and they brought a woman to replace him. Kelsey saw that the woman had the brain implants, but she also had extensive modification to the rest of her body. Her arms and legs especially. It looked like she had thick bands running through the muscles of her limbs. She had a cylinder behind her lungs and inserts under the lenses in her eyes. There were things inside her ears and nose, too.

The doctor expanded the view on one of the woman's legs. The bones also had a thin coating of something that seemed impermeable to the scanners.

"This is a lot more invasive," Stone said. "These look like artificial muscles woven into her real musculature. Her bones have some kind of coating. Probably to reinforce them. I'll wager she could kick like a grav lifter." Stone checked her notes. "This woman was found wearing an armored body suit. Maybe she was a marine."

Kelsey shuddered. "That's awful. She was like a machine."

"More like a cyborg—part machine, part human. Enhanced. These brain implants might allow for a better interface with something. Maybe each other, if there's some kind of transmitter in there. I'd better call in the science teams before I open one of them up."

"They can come back in the cutter I'm taking over to *Best Deal*, if it's all the same to you. I'd rather not see the inside of someone."

Stone nodded and smiled. "No problem. We'll need to examine more of them to be sure exactly what we're seeing. It's not a pretty sight. Do you want the final report?"

"Please. This might tell us a lot about them. Thanks for the invitation to come down."

Kelsey thought about what the brain implants meant all the way over to *Best Deal*. They almost had to be interfaces of some kind. Why they needed them was something of a mystery, though that probably explained the lack of name tags. They could recognize one another, even if they'd never met. They might even have been able to access some kind of biography on the fly. She'd have to think about the implications of that on a society for a while.

A number of Fleet crewmen got off the cutter with her, and an equal number of scientists waited to board. They chatted enthusiastically about how they were going to look into the brain implants.

Kelsey resisted another shudder and made her way to the labs. She only got lost three times. What she found was a huge room with lots of tables. Each had an assortment of objects covering it, and there were a few dozen lab-coated men and women examining things and making notes on their tablets.

Doctor Cartwright was among them, so she wandered over to his side. "Thanks for inviting me over, Doctor."

The older man looked up and blinked in surprise. Then he smiled. "I'm sorry, Ambassador. The time got away from me. I'd meant to meet you in the docking bay."

"No need to apologize. I came over a little early. I couldn't wait to see what sorts of things you're finding. And call me Kelsey."

He looked as though he didn't think that was a good idea, but he nodded. "As you wish. Please, call me Zephram. What we have here are many ordinary items and a few mysteries. They haven't removed any of the larger artifacts from *Courageous* yet. The half dozen small fighter craft in a bay amidships have the Fleet people quite excited."

The older man gestured to the tables around them. "We have items ranging from tablets to toothbrushes. All appear slightly different from those we use. Oh, and weapons. The vacuum has preserved everything in an almost pristine state."

"What kind of weapons?" The marines had taken her to their shooting range. She wasn't anywhere close to being an expert, but she at least knew the general classes of weapons.

"A number of projectile weapons and some that defy a precise explanation. Come take a look."

He moved to a table across the room, where they'd laid out a number of pistols in neat rows. At a glance, Kelsey could see two models. One had an opening for a projectile and an exceptionally thick barrel. The second had no opening at all. The barrel looked like a thick canister half again longer than the projectile weapons and a little thicker than the weapons themselves.

"Are they safe to pick up?"

"Yes. Both kinds used power packs that have completely discharged over the years. Still, do an old man a favor and don't pull the trigger. Just in case."

She picked up one of the projectile weapons and searched for the release to the magazine. There was no slide on the barrel, so it didn't look like it ejected a casing. That alone made it different from the marine weapons.

Once she had the release identified, she pointed the weapon at the floor and pressed the catch. The magazine resisted but finally came free. The bullets inside weren't bullets at all. They were metallic darts with fins in a clear gel-like blob. The blobs seemed all melted together, but Kelsey wagered they were once separate.

"Do you have a knife?"

"There are some on one of the other tables, but I have a plastic pick. That should do." He stepped away and came back with a little tool that would do the job.

"Thanks." She used the pointed end to pry out one of the bullets. Doctor Cartwright had put thin gloves on and held them cupped to catch it.

He held it up after it came free. "Interesting. No propellant. It looks like a tungsten alloy. With a power pack and this thick barrel, the weapon may use electromagnetic propulsion. I'd imagine it discards this gel sabot in flight almost at once. The small fins would provide admirable stabilization for the projectile."

"Wow! That sounds very high tech. How fast do you think it could go?"

He shrugged. "We'll be able to make an educated guess once we disassemble one of these. Certainly fast enough to be effective. Perhaps five times the speed of sound. Maybe more. This metal is almost certainly armor piercing as well."

"You might want to have one of the marines consult. Their armorer has quite an extensive knowledge of projectile weapons."

"An excellent idea." He put the bullet into a small bag and set it on the table. He then picked up one of the other pistols. "This has no way for a projectile to be expelled. The thick barrel suggests some kind of electromagnetic force, but it isn't a laser. We use those in our labs, and this is not the magical hand-held laser pistol. Whatever it does can't be good, though. Otherwise, why make it into a weapon?"

"True enough. Did they have larger weapons?"

"Certainly. We have some on the next table. The projectile weapons look similar to the pistols here, but there is something new."

He led her to the next table and showed her examples of the two rifles. One looked like the projectile pistol, but the other had an exceptionally wide barrel. Almost like a rocket nozzle from the early space program.

She found the magazine and ejected it. The bullets looked more like metal pellets rather than projectiles. There was no way they could be aerodynamic enough to do much damage, especially with a barrel as open as this was.

Cartwright picked the pellet up and examined it closely. "Tritium. We use small pellets of a similar nature to conduct plasma experiments. It's put into a chamber and converted to a high-energy state by lasers."

She wasn't about to stare down the barrel of an unknown weapon, but she looked inside the bell from an angle. "If it converted to plasma, what would happen to the barrel?"

"It would be destroyed. So would anything within a few meters of the unfortunate soul."

Kelsey whistled soundlessly. "Let's assume for the sake of argument that the makers of this weapon wanted to keep the person firing it from being turned into a cinder."

The older man felt the bell. "This might be resistant, but it can't survive direct exposure to plasma." He then made her heart shoot into her throat by staring directly into the barrel. "There are some projectors in here. Half are lasers, and the other half are unknown to me. The interior of the weapon appears coated in iridium. That would help."

"Zephram, could you point the deadly weapon somewhere other than at your face?"

He blinked at her for a moment and then smiled a little. "That wasn't the best choice, eh? I suppose you could say I lost my head." He put the weapon back on the table. "Assuming this is a plasma weapon, perhaps those other emitters are similar to the screens their ships used. Perhaps it focused the expanding plasma toward the target. If so, that would have a devastating effect."

"How devastating?"

"It would probably incinerate an armored man and melt the bulkhead behind him. This would be a most lethal weapon. They tell me there are armored suits, but one has not yet made it over. I'll be able to determine how resistant it would be to this kind of weapon when it arrives."

The sophistication of the weapons, and their raw destructiveness, shocked and amazed her. Men armed with these would be virtual killing machines. Add in the heavy modifications the marines seemed to have, and they would be unstoppable. Except they had been stopped.

Cartwright wandered over to the next table and picked up a combat knife. She'd seen something similar in marine country. They all seemed to have a fetish for sharp objects. "This looks relatively normal, but even it has some improvements."

She took it from him and examined it closely. The blade didn't appear to be steel. It was matte black, even along the edge. Holding it with the white tabletop behind it, she could see it had a wicked edge.

"What kind of metal is this?" she asked.

"I believe it might be similar to what is used on their hull. If so, it would be almost impossible to dull and probably take far more strength than a normal person possessed to break it. I'd imagine a strong man could drive it into the table without damaging the weapon. It might even be capable of harming someone in armor."

She was impressed. "I'm certain some have already made their way back to *Athena*, then. No way would the marines pass up the chance to have something like this."

The old scientist smiled. "I'd imagine not. Luckily, there are many of them left over to study." He gestured at the three or four dozen on the table. "Oh, I can think of one other oddity you'll appreciate."

They walked over to a table piled high with headsets. However, unlike normal headsets, these had no headphones or built-in microphones. Instead, they fit over the top of the head in three places. They had circular pads that pressed against the skull.

She picked one up and pulled the pad back enough to see some kind of plate under it. Kelsey frowned as she considered how they would sit on the head. The spacing seemed just about right for these pads to go over the unknown implants in the dead Fleet personnel. The table had more than fifty headsets. She'd wager there were many more over on *Courageous*. Perhaps enough for everyone on board plus some spares.

"Zephram, I think you'd best send some of these over to Doctor Stone on *Athena*. The Fleet personnel seem to have some implants in their heads that would correspond to these locations at the ends. I also think you'd better bump these up in priority. Captain Mertz is going to want to know about them."

"Implants, you say? How intriguing! I will certainly do so. Perhaps a direct inspection is in order. Meanwhile, we have much more to examine. We still have to study their tablets. We're quite hopeful we can recover data from these units once we decipher how the power cells work."

She followed him, although her mind was preoccupied… thinking about the brain implants they'd discovered. What would the headsets allow them to do? That seemed like one of the most important things they could figure out. No one had mentioned anything like this after the Fall. Perhaps it had been a closely guarded secret.

If so, it was one she was determined to unravel. It might be the key to everything.

17

The news about the implants interested Jared, but it got him no closer to solving the riddle of getting home. The probes had scoured the system and only found the one other flip point. No other weak flip points were present. Perhaps they really were rare.

He'd decided the science teams could continue examining *Courageous* for samples of technology to take home while *Athena* probed the next flip point. If there was trouble on the other side, it was better to go without the freighter. That increased his options somewhat and kept the noncombatants out of danger.

He sent two probes back to the other side of the weak flip point. One would wait for anyone to come into the system, transmitting a distress beacon. It had the full logs for the mission thus far, encrypted of course. They could send other probes back to update it as they learned more, as long as they were close by.

The second probe was on its way back to the Empire. It had to make two flips to get to an occupied system. Its distress signal would draw help from Fleet. If it made it all the way. Baxter wasn't certain it would. Even if it did, it would be over a month before help could arrive.

He reluctantly pulled Kelsey off *Best Deal* to go with them as they explored further. If he'd had his way, she would've stayed where she was, but orders were orders. He did leave a couple of lieutenants to restrain the scientists from doing anything truly foolhardy. He hoped.

They'd also continue the inquiry into Carlo Vega's death. Since the investigating officers didn't know his suspicions about the source of the poison, they'd conducted an exhaustive set of interviews centered on the freighter's galley. As he'd expected, they'd determined there was no reason for the suspect substance to be anywhere near the food preparation area.

Two labs had some of the poisonous substance for experiments, but security was somewhat short of Fleet expectations. They couldn't even be certain any was missing. Jared would bet his salary from the entire exploratory mission they'd never officially identify the source of the poison. Or the poisoner.

Those thoughts occupied his time until Kelsey strapped herself into her unofficial seat on the bridge. She watched the two ships shrink on the screen until they were indistinguishable from the stars behind them. Only then did she turn her attention to him. "It's unbelievable. I never expected to find people like this… just bodies. It puts a completely different light on this kind of mission for me. I feel like a vulture."

"I can understand that point of view, but it's wrong. None of the people who died on *Courageous* would begrudge us taking them home or salvaging what we could. In fact, their captain gave us his explicit permission. In their shoes, I wouldn't mind. Would you?"

She took a deep breath. "I suppose not. What do you think about the implants?"

"Since none of the Fleet or marine personnel survived the battle of Avalon, they could've all had them, and the civilians would've been none the wiser. The survivors had other priorities. I'd wager if we exhumed their bodies, we'd find similar equipment. There's so much we don't know about the Old Empire."

He went over the exploration status with Kelsey for the next four hours. It helped to pass the time in transit and made sure that they were on the same page.

Just short of the flip point, he ordered a probe sent through with a short return time. The probe popped back out as they were slowing to a stop. Zia began pulling the data and transferring it to the screen. One thing was immediately clear. The system on the other side had occupants. Communication sources popped up all over the other system. Hundreds. Perhaps thousands. It was as busy as Avalon.

"This puts a new spin on things," he said. "There aren't any ships in range of the flip point, but we won't be able to move anywhere without someone seeing us."

Kelsey nodded. "It doesn't change the fact we have to go."

"No, I suppose not. It's also probable that they're less advanced than we are, even though they obviously have spaceflight."

"Why is that?"

"Because they've never come through to explore *Courageous*. They couldn't have missed the distress beacon. That means no flip drives."

"How do we know that the next system isn't full of Old Empire automated transmitters?"

"No distress beacons. I'm not sure what's transmitting, mind you. We need to process some of the traffic to figure it out. Without knowing the transmission protocols, all we have are signals. Zia, can you get us any of that in a format we can understand?"

The tactical officer nodded. "I'm working on a strong signal now. I don't think it's encrypted, but the formatting is... wait... got it. Going on screen." A man sitting behind a desk replaced the system schematic. Jared instantly recognized it as a news program. There wasn't any audio, but the images behind the man's back seemed to be of some sporting event.

The man himself was dressed in a colorful tunic shirt with some kind of emblem on his left breast. His hair was dark and tied back in a loose ponytail. Whatever he was saying, he looked cool and confident.

"I think we've tapped into the evening news vid," Kelsey said. "That speaks for a relatively high social and technological standard right there. As opposed to some of the entertainment vids I've seen at home."

He laughed. "True. If the first thing an alien civilization saw about us was the strange reality vids making the rounds, I wouldn't blame them for dismissing us as primitive savages."

"The audio is somehow tied into the video," Zia added. "The signal is complex and redundant. Definitely not primitive. I can probably figure it out with a little more time."

Jared considered his options. At the very least, nothing was near the flip point. Going over was a slight risk, but the more powerful passive scanners on his ship could draw down a lot of data fairly quickly.

"Pasco, move us into the flip point and recover the probe. We're going over."

"Aye, sir."

The ship assumed a position in the center of the flip point, and as soon as they recovered the probe, he ordered the flip.

Thankfully, it was a normal transition and nothing like the terrible flip that brought them into this sector of space. Everyone recovered in a few moments.

Then the alert klaxon went off. "Missiles detected, Captain," Zia said crisply. "Ships in motion on the gravitic scanners. About an hour away at maximum acceleration. No immediate danger to us."

"Put the system diagram on screen."

The basic system layout appeared. The weapons fire was located clockwise around the plane of the ecliptic from *Athena*. The gravitic scanners were getting data on the ships and missiles. They were nowhere near danger.

"Stand down from battle stations, but keep us on alert status. Where are the major communication sources?"

Five flashing yellow dots appeared. One of them was at the point of the battle.

"There were no transmissions from that location earlier, sir," Zia reported. "They must've started as soon as the battle began. There were no indications of ships in motion there earlier. I'm picking up non-Fleet distress beacons. I'm also detecting numerous vessels accelerating at high speed."

Operations had already begun mapping them on the screen. "Do we have any feel for who is shooting who?"

Zia tapped her controls. "There are a large number of missiles being fired from hundreds of ships leaving the general area. I believe there is a flip point, and the fleet of vessels transitioned less than ten minutes ago. Probably just after our probe returned. I've designated them Force Alpha."

"Where are those ships going?"

"Their course suggests they are moving toward the strongest transmission source in the system." Zia highlighted another communications hub in the system. "ETA just over three hours. There is a large fleet of vessels moving from there to intercept them. I have designated them Force Bravo."

"What's happening?" Kelsey asked. "Obviously a battle, but who are the good guys?"

"I doubt we'll be able to figure that out while the shooting is going on. Zia, can you crack any of the transmissions? We could use some audio now."

"Working on it, sir. I'm only detecting encrypted transmissions from the battle scene. Also for Force Bravo. I'm not picking up any transmissions from Force Alpha."

The man they'd been watching earlier replaced the images on the screen. He now showed a video of scores of ships appearing in space and opening fire with missiles. They blasted a huge space station, knocking massive holes in its hull that gushed atmosphere and debris. Intense counterfire wiped out a number of the attacking ships before the feed they were watching died. The battle scene faded back to the man's image.

The audio suddenly kicked in. The man spoke Terran with a strange accent, but his words were clear enough. "That was the scene in the interdiction zone just fifteen minutes ago. This station's observation vessel went off the air, and we must assume it lost with all hands. We salute our brave reporters and mourn with their families.

"Royal sources tell us that a significant invasion force managed to break through but that Royal Fleet Command remains confident that all will be destroyed before they become a danger to the Kingdom. However, we urge all citizens to retreat to their shelters for the duration of this emergency. This station will continue to transmit news of the attack as it comes in."

Zia muted the audio and turned in her seat. "I'm picking up several vessels moving in our direction at high acceleration, sir. They're coming from the area they called the interdiction zone."

"Have they spotted us?"

"I don't think so. It looks like two of the attacking vessels have split off to pursue another ship."

The absolute last thing he needed to do was get involved in a local war. "What can you tell me about those ships? How long do we have to flip back before they could reasonably expect to detect us?"

The officer shrugged. "Without knowing the quality of their scanners, I couldn't say. We wouldn't detect a stationary ship like ours at this range for another forty minutes or so. The first ship has an audio-only transmission. I'm putting it on the overheads."

"…any vessel that can assist," a male voice said in a similar accent to the one on the news report. "We are being pursued by Pale Ones. We are carrying women and children. Any Royal Fleet vessels in range please respond." The message repeated. The man's voice held a note of panic.

Kelsey stepped next to Jared. "We must rescue them."

"Look, I'd love to, but that would be the height of irresponsibility. We don't know anything about these people at all, and we have civilians to protect."

"Wrong," Kelsey said in a hard tone. "We know the attackers have absolutely no problem chasing down a ship full of women and children. We cannot allow that to pass, Captain. The Empire does not stand by while noncombatants are murdered."

She gestured at the system schematic. "Look at that attacking fleet. Do you think they're moving toward an inhabited planet at high speed to wave as they go by? No. Even I know that there will be a bombardment. Tell me you haven't been to the spaceport memorial site. The rebels killed almost a million people from orbit on Avalon. Are we to stand by and let that happen right in front of our eyes? Could you live with doing nothing?"

Jared knew she was right. He didn't want her to be, but she was. Even if they couldn't do anything about the ships attacking that planet, they had to act.

He straightened in his chair. "Thank you, Ambassador. I wasn't thinking of the entire picture. Besides, it would be hard to request help from these people if we don't give some when they need it."

Kelsey inclined her head.

"Zia," Jared said. "I need more information."

"The vessels pursuing the single ship haven't fired, but they're closing range slowly. They must already be inside missile range."

"Can we transmit in the format the locals are using?"

Zia nodded. "It'll take me a few minutes to set things up, but we should be able to."

"How about the angle to that ship? Could we tight-beam a transmission to them without the other ships getting it?"

"Yes, but we can't be certain they'll receive it."

"It's worth a try. Let me know when we're ready. How far are the pursuers from our weapons range?"

Zia examined the readings. "I could make some long-range shots in half an hour if we don't move. Effective range will take ten minutes longer."

"Do they have that long?"

She shook her head. "Not realistically. If we intend to save that ship, we need to boost at max. The closing vectors will bring everyone together a lot faster. We'd be in effective range in less than twenty minutes. I think I'm ready to transmit, Captain."

"Pasco, take us in. Max acceleration. Zia, open a channel." He stared at the screen, knowing his image was going out as though he was staring right into the vid.

"Vessel in distress, this is the Imperial Fleet destroyer *Athena*. Change your course toward our position. We are coming to assist you."

For a few seconds nothing seemed to be happening. Jared imagined that there was a lot of additional consternation over there right now. A strange ship had popped up in their system with no warning at all in the middle of an attack. They'd probably have difficulty accepting that *Athena* wasn't part of the attacking forces.

The screen cleared into an image of a small bridge with three men on it. They wore tunics in light green. The man in the center was balding, and sweat ran down his face. "Whoever you are, we're changing course. Help us. The Pale Ones will take us soon."

"We'll do everything in our power to help you. *Athena* out."

"Why did you cut the transmission?" Kelsey asked.

"They have more important things to do besides talking to me. We can chat at length if they make it. Sound general quarters, Zia."

Once again, the alert klaxons sounded from the overheads. Jared touched the communications controls on his console. "All hands, this is the captain. Prepare for combat operations. This is not a drill."

He closed the channel. "When will we be in maximum range, Zia?"

"Fourteen minutes, Captain."

"Open fire on the targets as soon as you can. Get them focused on us."

"Aye, sir."

Kelsey cleared her throat. "Do I need to go somewhere else?"

He shook his head. "You're as safe here as anywhere. Sit back down and make sure your straps are tight."

The smaller civilian ship had changed course to meet them, and the pursuing vessels had matched course. It became a race to see who would get in range first. Time slowed to a crawl.

"Commencing missile launch," Zia finally said.

The tactical plot on the screen lit up with missiles as *Athena* opened fire. The missiles were small and relatively fast. The odds of a hit at this range were very small, but the enemy couldn't afford to ignore them.

Yet that's exactly what they did. They seemed so focused on the smaller ship that they ignored the incoming missiles. *Athena*'s opening salvo of four all missed, but not by much.

"They don't have any countermeasures, Captain," Zia said. "They didn't try to screw with our missile guidance at all. Launching four more missiles with the guidance packages devoted to targeting."

"That's insane," Jared said. "What the hell are they thinking?"

"They may not be human," Kelsey said. "Just because the Old Empire never met an alien species doesn't mean they don't exist. Perhaps their outlook is so different that they don't worry about individuals."

"That kind of matches what video we saw of the invasion," Zia added. "The attackers didn't seem concerned about the losses as they broke through the fortifications. They seemed willing to take any damage in exchange for breaking through. It's a sure bet that the attackers on the way to the planet won't make it back home."

"Salvo two coming on target," Ramirez said. "Multiple hits. One ship has ceased acceleration and seems to have broken up. The other has shifted course to come directly after us. They're going to pass close to the... the civilian vessel just braked hard!"

Jared grinned. "Ballsy. That'll get them clear of the fighting."

"Launching salvo three," Zia said. "The enemy is launching missiles at us. They look large but slow."

"Point defense stand by," Jared snapped. "Evasive maneuvers, Pasco."

Their missiles reached the enemy ship first. It glowed on the display, and then a red circle appeared around it.

"Target destroyed," Zia said. "Missiles incoming. Point defense at maximum!"

Something got through, because *Athena* lurched, and the damage control board on his console lit up. Two compartments were open to space.

"One missile exploded just short of the ship," Zia said. "Some fragments have breached the hull. No impact on combat worthiness. Damage control and medical personnel en route. Internal scanners show five crew in the compartments. Condition unknown."

Jared's heart was racing. This was the first real combat that he or any Fleet officer based out of Avalon had ever experienced. It was both exhilarating and terrible. With the oxygen masks on the battle stations vests, the trapped crewmen might still be alive. He hoped so.

"Zia, get in contact with that other ship. I want their status. Prepare rescue teams." Jared looked at Kelsey. "I want you there when they start coming aboard, Ambassador. It's time to earn your keep."

18

The marines refused to allow Kelsey to accompany them on the rescue mission. While she understood why, it made her anxious. The opportunity for misunderstandings was very high.

She was waiting with Doctor Stone and the medical team in marine country. The overheads came to life, and Jared's voice echoed out. "We've reentered the flip point, and the pinnaces are almost back to the ship. If we need to flip, we'll give you plenty of warning, but let's get the refugees aboard. Mertz out."

Running away with the rescued people probably wasn't the best idea, but neither was getting themselves shot to pieces if more hostile vessels attacked *Athena*. Kelsey was grateful the pinnaces had boarding locks that could mate with almost anything. Otherwise, they couldn't have gotten the people to safety nearly as quickly.

Athena trembled as the pinnaces docked, and the medical teams were opening the hatches as soon as the lights turned green. Civilians spilled into the chamber—men, women, and children. Most wore tunics and leggings, but some wore what looked like colorful sheets wrapped around themselves.

"May I have your attention?" Kelsey shouted. "You're safe now. Please move to the rear of the compartment so that the medical technicians can make sure you aren't hurt. Keep moving so the people behind you can get out of the pinnaces."

The marine assembly room was large enough for all thirty marines in battle armor. It proved inadequate for the flood of people. Thankfully, it looked like most people only had bumps and bruises. A man in a deep blue tunic began ordering the frightened people to do what they were told and quickly restored order. The three men in green she'd seen on the bridge deferred to him.

He turned to Kelsey. "I am Oliver Williams, engineer first of the Royal Fleet of Pentagar. Thank you for saving our lives."

She shook his hand when he offered it. "I'm Ambassador Kelsey Bandar of the Terran Empire. It was our pleasure to help you. Is anyone in your group badly injured?"

"I don't believe so. Our abrupt maneuvers bruised a few people, but nothing serious, I believe. The Terran Empire, you say. Are you the old fables come to life, then?" His voice held a combination of disbelief and hope.

Kelsey shook her head. "No. Our people survived the rebellion and have only recently begun expanding from the world the rebels drove us to. The young emperor was with us, so we believe we have the right to use the name. His line is unbroken." *At least until this generation*, she thought.

The man stared at her with an open mouth for a moment and then snapped it closed abruptly. "What an amazing tale! I hardly know what to say. This is the most important moment for the Kingdom since the destruction of the Empire. The other Empire."

He shook his head as if trying to clear away cobwebs. "No doubt the Kingdom and your people have much to discuss and learn from one another. Might I ask how you got here?"

She had to assume they knew what flip points were, though they might call them something different. "We came through the flip point near where we called you from. We're on an exploratory mission."

"Flip point? You must mean the space-time bridges. We do know of them, but the system on the other side is a dead end. The map of the Empire tells us so."

"You have a map of the Empire? That's wonderful. We lost even that. I'm not certain how to explain it properly, but there's a different kind of flip point that our ship used to get there. The only regular flip point there leads to your system." She didn't mention that they couldn't get back through the weak one. That wasn't helpful.

He scratched his head. "This other space-time bridge leads to your worlds? That is good news, though I'm worried that the Pale Ones might find another way at us through one. Are they easy to detect?"

"I'm told they're not obvious at all. We should step away from the chaos and let the medical teams do their work. We'll find somewhere to put your people after we see to their medical needs and get them some food. You're not prisoners here."

Oliver smiled. "That is reassuring indeed. I am the only Royal Fleet officer with our group, so I am automatically the senior leader. If you have some food and chamber facilities, I would appreciate both. We have much to discuss."

"Chamber facilities?"

"Ah… where one takes care of private functions."

She flushed a little. "Of course. Come with me."

Kelsey stepped out into the corridor to lead him to the officers' mess. Two marines followed.

"You don't need to accompany us," she said.

Senior Sergeant Talbot shook his head. "I'm sorry, Princess. The captain has instructed that you and any of our guests be accompanied at all times, for their safety and yours."

She was going to have to have words with Jared about this, but now wasn't the time. She turned back to Oliver. "I apologize."

He bowed slightly. "If our roles were reversed, I have little doubt that Royal Marines would dog your steps. We know one another not. Let us address this deficiency with haste."

Once the Royal Fleet engineer was in the head with one of the marines to show him how things functioned, Kelsey called Jared.

"How are things going?" he asked.

"They'd be better if I didn't have marines watching over us like they expected an assassination attempt." She tried to keep the asperity out of her voice, but she knew she was unsuccessful.

He chuckled. "How well did that work with the Imperial Guards?"

She sighed. "Not very well. Can we at least have a little space in the officers' mess? I need to build rapport quickly."

"Certainly. I'll pass the instructions along to allow you privacy for your diplomatic discussions. They'll only shoot him if he tries to strangle you."

"You're not nearly as funny as you think you are."

"Opinions vary. I'll want a full report when you're done."

"Will do. Bandar out."

The officers' mess was empty. Jared must've ordered the compartment cleared as soon as he found out where she was going. Only one man in a white apron stood near the door.

Oliver returned and took a seat opposite her. The marine guards took up positions against the bulkhead. They couldn't easily overhear the conversation, but they'd be able to respond if needed.

Kelsey summoned the server. "A beer for me and whatever Engineer First Williams wants. Sandwiches would be good, also."

"I shall have what she has," Oliver said. "My thanks."

He turned his attention to Kelsey after the server had departed. "One of your marines referred to you as Princess. Are you of the Blood Royal?"

She cursed Talbot under her breath. That might complicate matters. "I'm acting in a diplomatic capacity, but my father is the emperor of the Terran Empire. My older brother is the heir. It is of no import in our discussion."

Oliver stood abruptly and bowed low. "I must disagree, Princess Kelsey. The king would have my guts for garters if I failed to show proper respect to the high nobility of a foreign nation. You are the first our people have ever met."

The marines took two steps forward at Williams's abrupt movements, but she waved them back. "Please, sit back down. I'm not one for standing on ceremony. For God's sake, we're about to have beer and sandwiches."

The man smiled as he resumed his seat. "That does imply a certain level of informality, does it not? Very well, but only in private. One must always show the proper respect for those of noble blood in public. I can hardly imagine having beer and sandwiches with the king or his family. I might just choke. Such as I have not the manners to dine with such as them."

"I assure you, we eat just the same as you. However, I understand how you feel. Captain Mertz—our captain—is my half brother and has always said he felt very out of place when he came to visit our father." She took a little relish in telling Oliver that. If she was going to be embarrassed, Jared could keep her company.

"Your captain is a prince?" Oliver seemed surprised. "Commanding a warship away from your Empire must be dangerous duty."

She considered how to explain things without making more of a mess. "The captain isn't a prince. His mother wasn't the empress, if you know what I mean. Even if he was a prince, he could serve. My father was a Fleet officer in his time."

The Royal engineer inclined his head. "Honor to him, then. The emperor acknowledges the bond to your captain?"

Kelsey nodded. "Yes."

"The Kingdom has its own share of those born on the wrong side of the sheets. An acknowledged bastard is of the Blood Royal, and the king often appoints them to high positions and important tasks. There is no dishonor in such here."

The server delivered the beer and sandwiches. Conversation paused as they ate. Oliver devoured his larger share as though he hadn't eaten in days. He didn't seem impressed by the beer, but he said nothing.

Once they had eaten, he ordered another beer. "That was a repast worthy of a king. My thanks."

"It's my pleasure. Tell me, exactly what does an engineer first do?"

"The title means I am an engineer of the highest order. I supervise others in major repairs or command them on board a ship."

"I think that would be similar to our chief engineer. I'll need to introduce you to Commander Baxter if time permits. So now that we have a meal inside us, can you tell me about these Pale Ones? We're not familiar with them. Are they aliens?"

The man smiled grimly. "If only they were. No. They are ravening human hordes that occasionally sweep out through the space-time bridge and attempt to overwhelm us. If they capture anyone, they whisk those unfortunate souls away. We never see them again. Else they slay any they can lay hands to."

"Why do they do that?"

Oliver shrugged. "No one truly knows. We regained space travel very quickly after the Empire fell but are trapped in this system. When ships came through the bridge a few decades later, we welcomed them with joy.

They responded with missiles and incinerated tens of thousands before our ships destroyed them. War was joined, and it continues to this day."

"That's terrible."

"Indeed. They sweep across us every few years like a plague of locusts. They have not reached Pentagar in centuries. The loss of life in this attack will be high but not ruinous. The Royal Fleet knows its duty and the fate we face if we fail. We volunteer to stand between the Kingdom and the Pale Ones." He took a deep breath. "What happens now?"

"That's up to our captain, but I am confident you will be returned to your people as soon as possible."

"He commands even though you are in the line of succession? Is not your position higher?"

"My father entrusted overall command of this mission to him. I am the force of political will. Together we'll figure things out."

"Perhaps while we wait, you can tell me of your Empire."

Kelsey nodded. "Avalon is the capital of the Terran Empire now. It is a beautiful world with tall mountains and clear lakes. Once it was a pristine vacation world far from the bustle of the core of the Old Empire. That changed when the rebels chased Emperor Lucien to our surface. The rebels destroyed the spaceport and the city surrounding it. The only significant city on our planet. The battle in our skies ended with no survivors.

"We lost much of our technology but never our civilization. We regained space travel a hundred years ago and have spread out to a number of systems. We found people on many worlds and helped them recover too. We can finally spare the ships to explore the flip points around the Empire more thoroughly, and here we are."

"It sounds as though you have a wonderful home. I hope to see it with my own eyes one day. While I cannot speak for the Crown, I am certain our peoples will get along well."

She smiled. "I'm very hopeful that we will. I'm sure we each have strengths that we can use to support one another. How long has your world been a monarchy?"

"Since almost the very beginning. Our ruler was an Imperial baron when the Empire collapsed. His family has ruled us since those days, guiding us with wisdom and strength." He raised an eyebrow. "Though I feel I should warn you that I doubt the king will bow to your Empire or your position."

"Of course not. I wouldn't expect him to. We'll form a relationship appropriate to the times."

He seemed to relax a bit. "That is wise."

"How long do you think the battle will rage?"

"The Pale Ones committed to attack Pentagar will be destroyed shortly, I have no doubt. The ships and orbital weapons platforms will stop them. They will not save a reserve force. They will dash themselves against the defenses and die."

"I hope they don't hurt any more people."

He nodded. "As do I. Unfortunately, it is all too likely some weapons will slip past. We dig deep, but many will die today."

"Then perhaps the best we can hope for is to stop them before it happens again."

The engineer first raised his glass. "I can drink to that."

19

J ared maintained battle stations until he was certain that none of the hostile vessels were going to come directly after them. Only then did he let his crew step away from their posts. He made sure that a standing watch was ready to respond and left the bridge in Charlie's hands.

The medical center was still busy when he walked in, though Stone was in her office. He rapped his knuckles on the hatch frame.

She looked up from her screen. "Come in. Are we safe again?"

"For the time being." He stood behind one of the chairs. He'd already been sitting for hours. "What's the crew status?"

"Two dead and three injured. I know it could've been a lot worse, but I hate losing people." She sagged a little in her chair. "How bad will this get before we're done?"

He shrugged. "Bad enough, I'm sure. How are our guests?"

"All alive. A few had some bruises, but nothing to be concerned about. I do have some new information for you though. The marines snagged a body from one of the hostile ships. I've had the time to perform an initial examination, and I've got some unexpected news."

She brought up the screen on her wall. A man lay on the table. His long hair was filthy and wild. His face was gaunt from what looked like malnutrition. He looked like a savage.

"He wore minimal, quite primitive clothing—barely more than animal skins. His nails and teeth showed no signs of care. He looks like he's in his mid-thirties, but I'll wager he's a decade younger than that. Old before his time."

"Was he carrying a club? How do savages pilot flip spaceships?"

"I was wondering that very thing." She replaced the image with one of the internal scans from an Old Empire marine. He recognized the extensive modifications.

"Look familiar?" she asked.

"Yes, those are an Old Empire marine's implants."

"This is the interior scan of the savage."

Jared stood there with his mouth open in shock. "You're not saying this is an Old Empire marine, are you?"

Stone shook her head. "Doubtful. The technology looks identical, though. He has all the modifications the Old Empire marines had. The big difference is this."

She brought up another picture, this time of the side of the man's skull with his hair pulled back. A long, poorly healed scar ran from his temple around the back of his head. "He has scars like this all over his body. There were no attempts at regeneration. My best guess is that this was done about ten years ago."

"Let me get this right. Someone took a savage and ran him through a highly invasive modification? That doesn't make sense."

"It sure looks that way. There are another couple of things. First, they have the same equipment behind the lungs as the Old Empire marines. I found a wide variety of drugs that the unit seems designed to put directly into the bloodstream. At least one is a powerful painkiller, and another seems to be some kind of antiviral med. I think. I'm still working on the rest. Time degraded the drugs in the Old Empire marines, even though they were frozen.

"Second, these implants are still live. We have a few scientists on board, and they're testing one of those fancy headsets to see if they can pull any data off him. Perhaps that will tell us how Mr. Primitive can pilot a spacecraft."

"What about the new people? Do they have implants?"

Stone shook her head. "No. I've looked all of them over very carefully. None of them have any implants."

"That's good, but the other is very disturbing. Are you certain it's the same modifications? With the same level of technical sophistication?"

"As sure as I can be without cutting him open. I'll save that for when the scientists are done. Those implants probably interface with the headset and other equipment. Since they still have power, it may be possible to access their programming."

He nodded. "Keep me informed. I want everything kept on comps that are not connected to the ship's systems just in case." He started to leave but stopped. "And get some sleep."

The doctor smiled wryly. "There's an order I have no problem obeying."

Jared left the medical center and used his communicator to locate Kelsey. To his satisfaction, she was still in the officers' mess. Good. He was hungry.

Both she and her guest rose as he walked in. "Captain Jared Mertz of the Imperial Terran Fleet," Kelsey said, "allow me to introduce Engineer First Oliver Williams of the Royal Fleet of Pentagar."

The engineer first bowed low. "I am honored, Lord Captain. On behalf of the people under my care, thank you for our lives."

"It's my pleasure, Engineer First. The Empire doesn't stand by while innocents are in danger." He gave Kelsey a nod to show his own thanks and respect. "I'm no lord."

The older man straightened. "You may not be in line for your throne, but we of the Kingdom respect the Blood Royal, Lord Captain. Or in your case, the Blood Imperial. The princess was wise to inform me of your status. It will make a difference in how you are received."

Jared narrowed his gaze and spared the smiling Kelsey a mild glare. "Please, call me Jared. Excuse me while I have something to eat. Breakfast was a long time ago."

"Then I am Oliver. I must use the correct titles in public, though. My king would not hear of anything less."

Once they had sat and Jared had ordered food, Oliver continued. "Might I ask the tally of battle?"

"We destroyed the two ships chasing you. No hostile ships seem interested in coming out this way. For the moment, I believe us to be safe."

"A mighty victory indeed. Did you emerge unscathed?"

Jared shook his head. "We stopped most of the missiles, but one made it through. Thankfully, it detonated short of *Athena*. Two of our people were killed and several others wounded."

Oliver's face became somber. "I mourn with you at the loss of your people in a fight not your own. I pledge that they shall be listed on the rolls of our honored dead."

Jared nodded. "On behalf of my emperor, I thank you. Are you and your people receiving everything that you need?"

"We are being housed as well as can be expected on a warship and are truly grateful. Everyone has eaten, and most are sleeping. If I might ask, when will you contact the Royal Fleet to come meet you?"

"As soon as we can be certain we won't be fired on. No offense, but there's still a shooting war going on."

The man nodded. "A wise precaution. I sent a message to Pentagar of our status and your assistance. I believe they will restrain themselves from impulsive actions."

"We'll send a follow-up message, preferably from you, telling them who we are, but I don't want to do it until the battle plays itself out. Does this kind of attack happen often?"

The engineer first nodded. "Every few years. They come flowing in with no regard to their own deaths, striving to kill and capture. The ship I was on had just left the interdiction zone with the families of some of the officers there. We shuttle them out for the occasional visits because the stations are always fully manned."

Jared listened to the short version of the history between them while he ate. "It's as though they build up strength and come back at you. Do you ever try to communicate?"

"Many times, but they never respond at all. If they didn't fly in spaceships, we'd think them completely savage. The mystery of how they can travel between the stars and yet not speak is a great one."

"They don't speak? Via communicator?"

"Nor in person. We have captured some few alive over the years. They truly are savages… ravening, murderous savages with no regard to their own survival. Left alone and not visibly monitored, they eat, defecate, and fight. Since they are enhanced, they make formidable opponents."

Jared shook his head. "We brought one of their bodies back for examination. We noted extensive modifications. What's the story there?"

"I cannot explain why. It is one more mystery about them."

"Why don't you take the fight to them? Since they attack without reason, they might not have a very good defense."

The man held his hands out to his sides. "We cannot. We know the theory of traversing the space-time bridges, but we have no access to several critical elements necessary to construct the drives. We are prisoners in our own system."

Jared glanced at Kelsey. "That explains why you haven't journeyed in the direction we came from."

"We might not go there even had we been able. We believed it to be a cul-de-sac."

"You know?" The admission surprised Jared.

"We do. The rebels destroyed our spaceports and the orbitals, and they used EMP weapons, but some records survived on an asteroid mining outpost. Some of the surviving computers there contained basic maps of the local area."

Jared felt himself sitting up straighter. "Do you know where Terra is?"

"Very generally. We have detailed maps of our sector and general maps for the rest of the Empire. Pentagar was far from the center of the Empire. The knowledge you came into this system through an unknown kind of space-time bridge will both excite our scientists and fill the Royal Fleet with dread. Where you find one, there may be others. What if the Pale Ones find one and pour in on us unannounced?"

"That would be a disaster," Jared admitted. His communicator chirped. He unclipped it from his belt. "Mertz."

"This is Graves, Captain. The last of the hostile vessels was just destroyed short of the planet."

"Did they get any missiles through to the surface?"

"Not that we could see, sir. Even the active scanner readings are vague from this far out. There seem to be a number of orbitals that shot down everything they fired."

Oliver sighed and smiled. "Thank the gods."

Jared returned his smile. "Do we have any ships on the way out here?" he asked.

"About a dozen have changed course toward us. We're looking at them arriving in our area of operations no earlier than five hours from now. Longer if they intend to decelerate."

"Understood. Keep an eye on things, and I'll be back up there before they get too close. Mertz out."

He put the communicator away and smiled at Oliver. "Good news. It appears there isn't a large loss of civilian life. I hope your fleet losses were light."

"They won't be," the engineer said with a deep sigh. "They never are. I saw many of the interdiction stations blown apart. Thousands are dead. No doubt, the losses in the ships engaging the Pale Ones were also heavy. You escaped lightly with only two casualties, Lord Captain."

"Still, you're right that we will celebrate. Once more, we have survived, and another attack will not come for a few years. We have time to repair the damage."

Jared took a sip of his beer. "Are you certain they won't come through again to surprise you?"

Oliver nodded. "We have many years of experience with them. They will lick their wounds and build their strength to try again. Why they only attack with everything at once isn't known to us, but they do."

"Perhaps we could provide the elements you lack to build flip drives. You could then attack them in their home."

The engineer smiled. "That would be wonderful. Such a gesture would be a great boon. The king and his ministers would be willing to negotiate most heavily for such when you meet, I am sure."

"I know we'll talk about many things, but first we need to keep them from shooting at us. Will you tell your people we're not Pale Ones? The very last thing I want to do is fight with your people."

Oliver rose to his feet and bowed deeply. "It will be my greatest pleasure, Lord Captain."

20

Kelsey stood in the main cabin of the Pentagaran ship that they'd saved and tried not to think about the terror she smelled in the air. Not her own but the stench of people expecting death or worse. Oliver stood beside her, and two marines in full combat armor with the full panoply of war covered her from behind.

She'd once again tried to convince Jared to let her proceed without them and failed. He adamantly refused to allow her to meet the representatives from the Royal Fleet without them. That was after he'd tried to block her from being the primary contact at all. Her arguments that the presence of armed men risked a lethal misunderstanding didn't deter him at all. The man was maddening.

If he could've had an armed pinnace with its weapons covering everything, she suspected he would have insisted. Thankfully, she'd negotiated an initial meeting without any armed ships. Three people from the Royal Fleet would come across in an unarmed cutter. Two of those people would be armed marines.

"Princess, the Royal Fleet cutter is about to dock," Talbot said. "I have a vid feed inside the airlock. If anything looks off, I want you in the compartment behind us before the echo of my voice fades."

At Engineer First Williams's insistence, she'd agreed to the use of her honorific. She was surprised at how little she'd missed it.

Kelsey had played cards with the marines so many times she couldn't count them anymore. Talbot's normal easygoing nature was completely absent. She had absolutely no doubt he'd stuff her in the other compartment himself if she hesitated to run on his command. Her orders were to obey his instructions if there were any trouble, much to her annoyance.

"Yes, Senior Sergeant." The tone sounded exactly liked she'd said "Yes, Mother."

The ship jolted a little as the cutter docked. Oliver smiled at her. "Do not worry. They will do exactly as they have agreed. I have the word of Commodore Sanders."

"I'm sure they will," she said.

"Three people have entered the ship," the marine said. "Two heavily armed and one with only a pistol. That's not according to protocol."

"I never said he couldn't be armed."

"He hands his pistol over to one of the marines before he approaches your person or we're done." Talbot's tone brooked no argument.

The hatch in front of them cycled open, and the two marines came in. Apparently they deemed it safe for their officer to enter, because a young man wearing a bright-red tunic trailed in behind them.

Kelsey held her empty hands out at her sides. "I greet you in the name of the Terran Empire. I am Princess Kelsey Bandar. My marine guard insists that you lay aside your pistol before you approach."

The young man bowed slightly. "I am Lieutenant John Fredrick of His Majesty's Royal Marines. We are not allowed to be unarmed during possible combat situations."

"Then this meeting is over. Withdraw."

She suspected this was some kind of test. Perhaps merely male posturing. The two occasionally looked very similar. From the tensing of the marines behind the officer, her Imperial Marines had backed her up with some posturing of their own.

Oliver took one step forward and stood board straight. "Lieutenant, I am Engineer First Oliver Williams. I vouch for these people. I beg you not to allow a rule to come between our people on this important occasion."

The officer looked at Oliver for one long moment and then bowed again. "I meant no offense, Your Highness. I crave your forgiveness." He pulled his pistol from its holster slowly and set it on the deck before kicking it to the wall behind him.

"On behalf of my king and Commodore Walter Sanders, I welcome you to Pentagar. I am instructed to ask what ransom you demand for the return of our people."

"You misunderstand, Lieutenant," Kelsey said. "Your people are not prisoners. You may take them with you as soon as you feel comfortable. Engineer First Williams may return with you now to make arrangements, if you wish. They can be transported here for you to pick up."

He nodded. "Allowing the engineer first to return to my ship is within the bounds of my instructions. I will accompany you in turn. Commodore Sanders wishes to have at least some examination of your ship before it is allowed deeper into our system."

"That is also within my instructions. Once your marines are gone, I will allow you to take up your arms, as a show of trust in your honorable behavior." She felt it was the right thing to do, no matter how much her marines might disagree.

"You honor me. I give my word in turn that I will not take up arms against you this day, unless I believe my life or mission is threatened."

"Accepted, and I in turn give you my word that you will be given access to all areas of the ship to examine, and you will be allowed to return to your fleet unharmed as soon as you choose to do so."

She turned to Oliver and held out her hand. "It has been my pleasure to meet you, Engineer First. I hope that we meet again soon."

He bowed low over her hand and kissed it. "May that day come speedily, Your Highness. Until then, I bid you a peaceful farewell."

The Royal Marines gave Oliver a thorough search and escorted him out of the compartment. Kelsey said nothing until Talbot spoke. "They've left the ship, Princess."

"Please pick up your pistol, Lieutenant Fredrick. As soon as your cutter departs, ours will come for us. Tell me, what precisely are you looking for on *Athena?*"

Fredrick knelt to retrieve his pistol, stood up slowly, and holstered it. "I'm just to see that nothing looks overtly dangerous to the fleet or the Kingdom. Once I have done so, I will return to the fleet and brief the senior officers. The next steps are up to them."

"Well, it is a warship… and has missiles."

The Royal Marine smiled. "So I've heard. Any destroyer that can take two Pale Ones without suffering grievous damage has my deep respect. However, those are not the kinds of danger I'm to look for. Truly, I suspect my superiors only want to know more about you."

Ten minutes later, they were on their way back to *Athena* and docked without incident. Jared and two marines stood waiting for them. While his guards were not wearing armor, they were armed.

Jared, too, was armed. She'd never seen him wear a pistol, though he now had one strapped on his hip. She wondered if that was to make a point of his own to the Royal officer. On the other hand, perhaps he was sending a message to her.

"Lieutenant Fredrick, I am Commander Jared Mertz, captain of the Imperial Fleet destroyer *Athena*. On behalf of the Terran Empire, I welcome you aboard."

The Royal officer bowed, but not quite as deeply as he had for Kelsey. "Welcome to Pentagar, Lord Captain. My orders are to examine your ship so that I may report fully to my commanders. Will you allow me free access to see all compartments and question your crew?"

Jared nodded. "I will, with the understanding that there may be some classified subjects about which they may not answer."

"Of course. May I first see your bridge?"

They proceeded on a long tour of the ship. Kelsey sent the armored marines on their way and followed Jared and the Pentagaran officer. They visited the bridge, engineering, several weapons rooms that she'd never been in, and then the medical center.

Fredrick asked many questions of the people they encountered, some of a military nature but mostly about Imperial society. He seemed to be looking for an understanding of their culture.

He spent a lot of time talking to Doctor Stone. He didn't ask about *Courageous*. Kelsey couldn't imagine how he'd know about it, but Doctor Stone was smooth. It didn't seem like she was worried about the Old Empire bodies they had aboard at all.

The lieutenant asked to see the people they'd rescued. The number of them determined to tell him about their ordeal and rescue quickly overwhelmed him. They also wanted to know the fate of their loved ones.

He promised them a speedy repatriation and that he would personally convey the status of their families as soon as he knew himself. He seemed nonplussed that most of them didn't seem to feel any rush to go back to his ships. Most seemed content to wait where they were until they could go home.

He smiled lopsidedly when he came back over to Kelsey and Jared. "I can think of no better marker of your character than the fact they seem so disinterested in leaving. Princess, Lord Captain, I am ready to be taken back to the intermediary ship. I will consult with my commanding officers, and I feel confident they will feel more comfortable with your presence."

"Thank you, Lieutenant," Kelsey said. "We look forward to speaking with them at length. Our peoples have much to say and many ways to help one another."

They escorted him back to the cutter, and he declared the marines were the only escort he needed going home. Jared agreed, and they parted there.

Once he was gone, Kelsey turned to her half brother. "Don't yell at me about allowing him to keep his pistol."

He smiled. "I think that was an appropriate gesture of trust. I saw the vid of the meeting. You showed a lot a spine telling him to go home when he showed up armed but allowing him to regain his lost face. Well done."

She relaxed a little. "Thanks. You armed yourself because of him being armed?"

"It seemed like the right thing to do." He headed back to the lift and instructed it to go to the conference room. "We need to decide what we can tell them and what matters we need to keep to ourselves. *Courageous* is off limits for now. So is the fact that we're trapped. Our isolation might make them attempt to take undue advantage. We're the only flip-capable ship in the system."

She sat down at the table. "We need to tell them before too long. It would be grossly unfair to let them think we might be able to help them directly with their war effort. Besides, they'll figure it out soon enough. We are stuck here… in *their* territory."

He nodded. "We might eventually tell them about *Courageous*, too. That would provide us a measure of leverage if we share some of the technology. I want to help them, but it has to be contingent on help from them."

"Do we tell them about the Pale Ones' body we recovered?"

"You heard Oliver. They've captured some live ones. They've seen much more than we have. The only bit of information we have that they don't is the link to the old Fleet implants."

Kelsey considered that for a few moments. "Agreed. Has there been any additional news on that front?"

"A little. The science team figured out how to hot-wire a headset to a standalone computer. They've pulled quite a lot of data off the implants, but they really don't know what it means. They have no frame of reference. I'm told it looks like programming code, but they don't know the language."

"Will anything on *Courageous* help with that? Getting her computer back online, perhaps?"

"It's possible, but I'm not sure. It'll probably be more code we don't understand. We might not even be able to access it without implants of our own."

She shuddered. "That sounds horrible. I can't imagine how they could put things like that in their brains. Much less what the marines did. They'd have to be cut open like a fish."

"I agree that it seems horrific. Especially considering what the Pale One had done to him. There has to be a link between them and the Old Empire Fleet. I just can't imagine what it is. Perhaps some equipment was left on and still running after all this time?"

"That's set up to kidnap people and does this? There's something more to the story. I'm more interested in why these obviously savage people are compelled to fly here and attack. What guides them? How can the implants even make it possible?"

"More questions without an answer. We'll send those people back over to their fleet as soon as we can and flip back to *Courageous*'s system. It won't hurt to let the Royal Fleet know we have people there. It's almost like an insurance policy. We can get a download of data and more scientists. If we're going deeper into the system, I want to have our best people with us."

Jared's communicator chirped. Graves responded when he answered. "Captain, the Royal Fleet commander wants to speak to you."

"On my way."

He stood. "Time to cement our introduction."

21

The next few days went by quickly. The Royal Fleet arranged to take their people off *Athena*, and Jared sent a probe back with a message to have a number of scientists brought to the flip point. They made the flip back the next day to pick them up and ended up spending an unplanned few hours offloading the large cargo shuttle that they'd packed with equipment.

He'd told them to bring only the essentials, but their definition of that word differed from his. He should've known that would happen.

Commodore Sanders, the Royal Fleet commanding officer, invited him over shortly after they returned. Though somewhat concerned about isolating himself, Jared agreed. These people hadn't given him any indication they were likely to behave treacherously, so he'd make the first big step in building trust.

Kelsey wanted to go, but he refused. Trust didn't need to be an act of stupidity. They could take him prisoner if they chose. That wouldn't force *Athena* to do anything. He considered himself expendable if need be. The emperor's daughter was not, no matter how she styled herself.

So he boarded one of his cutters with two unarmored marines. All three wore sidearms but brought no heavy weapons. They approached the Royal flagship a short time later. It looked big in the vid feed. Much larger than the biggest cruiser the Empire boasted.

Of course, the Terran Empire wasn't at war. If that changed, the Imperial shipyards would commence building larger vessels. They'd done the design work, but there was little need to incur the expense with no threats on their borders. With the dangerous universe he'd discovered, that might change.

They didn't need a special docking collar this time. The Royal flagship had a bay large enough for his cutter. The pilot deftly brought them into the massive ship's bay, and the large hatch slid closed behind them.

Jared rose to his feet and checked his uniform one last time. He started to open the lock when it turned green, but the pilot told him their hosts wanted him to wait a few minutes while they prepared to greet him.

When they indicated they were ready, Jared cycled the lock and stepped out onto the cutter's ramp. Two short rows of men in red tunics flanked the ramp, rifles held upright in front of them. Two men stood at the other end of the impromptu corridor. One of them was Lieutenant Fredrick. The older man with three times the ribbons on his gold tunic was probably the commodore.

Jared walked up to the two officers and saluted, right fist to his chest. "Greetings, Commodore Sanders. I am Commander Jared Mertz, commanding officer of the Imperial Fleet destroyer *Athena*. Thank you for inviting me over."

The older man brought his stiff hand to his forehead in a salute with which Jared wasn't familiar. He then extended his hand. "It is my pleasure, Lord Captain. You already know the good lieutenant and, as you so astutely surmised, I am Commodore Walter Sanders, commanding officer of this task force. On behalf of my king, allow me to thank you once more for acting in defense of his subjects in their hour of need."

Jared shook the man's hand and smiled. "It was the right thing to do."

"You took a leap of faith in your decision. My understanding is that you arrived while the attack was in progress. In your position, I might well have decided to proceed more cautiously until I established the lay of the land."

"I considered the data we had at our disposal and the wise counsel of our ambassador. She immediately knew the right course of action. Honorable beings do not attack innocent civilians. Character is important."

"Quite so. I'm disappointed that she couldn't come, but I understand your caution. I hope to set your mind at ease today, because our peoples have much to offer one another. Technology, culture, and much that I'm certain I haven't considered. Come, I insist on giving you the same tour you gave my officer. *Mace* is an old battleship, but I'm proud of her."

The Royal Marine guards didn't follow them, so Jared made a decision. "Perhaps my marines could spend some time with yours. That might foster more understanding between our people."

The commodore laughed. "Knowing marines as I do, I shudder to anticipate what trouble they will find together. You can summon them when you're ready to depart."

The marines didn't look happy at leaving his side, but they went off with their counterparts. He hoped they wouldn't get into a fight over gambling debts. Fredrick went with them, perhaps to make certain they didn't.

The number of crewmen in the corridor surprised Jared. There were a lot of people. "What size crew do you have aboard?" he asked.

"Three thousand two hundred and fifty three. *Mace* has many systems to maintain and operate. What of *Athena?*"

"Two hundred and fifty, not counting a detachment of thirty marines."

Sanders stopped, his expression surprised. "That's an incredibly small crew for even a destroyer. Ours have double that number. Your systems must be quite advanced."

"I hadn't considered them overly so, but perhaps. We've only been back in space for a century, but our scientists had been working on the theory long before we had the technology. Once we started making breakthroughs, we built ships quickly. *Athena* isn't the cutting edge of our designs either. She's about fifty years old, though she's been well refitted."

"We need to build ships quickly after every invasion, and innovation has been slow. The continuing raids have taken their toll on progress. We do indeed have much to learn from your people. Let's start with engineering."

The main engineering compartment looked large enough to hold most of *Athena*. He had no trouble recognizing the massive grav drives. They seemed powerful enough to move a planet.

"What are these?" He gestured at the massive power plants. "Fission plants?"

"Yes. Heavily shielded, of course. I'd imagine you've figured out cold fusion?"

Jared laughed. "I'm told that's a mirage. We do have fusion plants, though they take up much less space. My chief engineer could ramble on about them for a few weeks."

The old man smiled. "Engineers are all alike, eh? I'm certain my engineers would be ecstatic to converse with him at length."

"I feel confident we'll come to some kind of understanding. Ambassador Bandar will need to make the final decision on something like that, but I can envision sharing technical information very soon."

"That would be wonderful. Perhaps we can even barter for some of the exotic elements needed to make space-time drives."

"Those elements are found in most star systems in small quantities. The last system we travelled through may have them in one of its asteroid belts."

"Or the ones beyond it. I'm sure your Empire could have a brisk trade in them. They would be literally worth a king's ransom."

Jared took a deep breath. Here's where he had to lay some of their cards on the table. It wouldn't do to let their new friends think they were misleading them. If this were going to cause problems, it would be best to find out now.

"At this time, bilateral trade with the Empire may be premature." He explained their current difficult situation to the commodore.

The officer listened without interrupting until Jared wound down. His frown deepened. "Indeed, you are in a fix. Thankfully, you'll find the Kingdom a friend in your time of need, just as you were in ours. Unless there is another of these weak flip points in our system, we cannot offer an alternative route back to your Empire, but we can make certain you have other supplies you need. One day your Fleet will come looking for you, and they *will* find you among friends."

"We appreciate that. The Empire doesn't forsake its friends, either. The emperor won't forget those who sheltered his daughter."

The commodore started walking down the corridor slowly. "I've spoken with His Majesty. He has given me leave to speak with his voice in this matter. No matter what agreements we come to, you and your people are welcome here as our friends. His shelter is yours. Frankly, he can't wait to meet you both, Lord Captain. Your timely arrival has fired his imagination."

"I hope we can live up to his expectations." Jared considered their situation. Hiding *Courageous* might come back to bite them if they never got home. If they traded technical information, the Royal Fleet would use the flip point to that system to test their new drives. Its presence would become common knowledge fairly quickly.

"Commodore, might we speak privately?"

"Of course. Let's adjourn to my day cabin. We can have something to eat while we talk."

The commodore's day cabin was twice the size of Jared's office. The older man sent for food and offered Jared a drink. Having no idea what drinks they had here, he told the other man to surprise him.

Sanders poured an amber liquid into two small glasses. "Sip this. It's quite smooth, but a gulp would be uncomfortable at best."

Jared sat at a small table beside the senior officer and sipped the drink. It was quite alcoholic and burned nicely as it went down. "This is very good."

"Aged apricot brandy. My family has brewed this for centuries. It's only available for limited consumption. I'll send a few bottles back with you."

A buzzer announced the arrival of food. It looked like a platter of cheese, meats, and bread. The scent made Jared's stomach rumble. The man left the food with them and departed.

Commodore Sanders considered Jared. "What shall we speak of, Lord Captain?"

"My people may be trapped here, and I have knowledge that you should be aware of. Consider it my gesture of trust." He proceeded to tell the full tale of their arrival.

Sanders sat bolt upright when he first mentioned the Old Empire battlecruiser, his drink forgotten in his hand. He listened raptly to the entire story without interrupting. Only when Jared finished did he move.

More precisely, he gulped the entire glass of brandy and went to refill their glasses.

"That is the most amazing tale I've ever heard. I've read adventure stories like that but never imagined that something so… astonishing could happen in real life. Dear gods, an Old Empire Fleet vessel." His tone was reverent. "They were as technologically superior to us as we are to the Pale Ones now."

"I'm confident that Princess Kelsey will negotiate allowing your specialists to join the examination of the ship, but I need to discuss the Pale

Ones, as well." He explained about the implants they'd found inside the Fleet personnel.

The commodore frowned deeply. "That *is* troubling, Lord Captain. Are you positive these implants are the same? We knew the bastards had such technology, but this link to the Old Empire is chilling."

"They appear to be the same equipment and implantation method, except the old Fleet personnel had no scars."

"Are you able to compare the contents of these implants to those of the old Fleet personnel?"

Jared shook his head. "The ones in *Courageous*'s crew are as dead as they are. We modified one of the headsets to copy what they think is the programming code from the Pale Ones onto a separate, secured computer. We're examining it now."

The older man nodded. "If you were to find the right power settings, do you think some of the original implants might be brought back online?"

"Perhaps. I don't want to desecrate one of the dead Fleet personnel unless we're sure."

"We would appreciate it if you could try," the commodore said. "I find myself wondering if they are identical inside or if perhaps the programming of the Pale Ones has been overridden somehow."

Jared sipped his brandy. "You mean like a computer virus? That's an interesting theory. I'll discuss it with my people. If it were, wouldn't the Old Empire have fixed it? These savages might be the descendants of people conquered by the rebels. Surely the old Fleet would have captured some of the rebels and reversed the process if they could have."

The commodore shrugged. "It is conceivable that they did. The old stories tell how rapidly the rebellion spread. If it *is* a virus, perhaps correcting it took time. Perchance the same held true for modifying the implants to resist the infection. The vast and mighty Terran Empire fell within two or three years."

"That's an interesting theory," Jared agreed. "Are these Pale Ones a relic of the rebellion where some lingering imperative forces them to continue to seek out unconquered humans to enslave? How could they still have the advanced technology for the implant machinery yet still use such primitive ships? If they had access to the kind of ships found in the Old Empire, we would all be dead or enslaved long ago."

Sanders nodded. "There's the rub. Without going to look in their system, we have no idea what we face. Could we end this cycle of attacks by destroying some facility? Perhaps that is all there is… a single complex modifying people from a slave population."

"We have probes," Jared said. "The attack here is over. What if we sent one through the flip point as a gesture of goodwill? Knowing what awaits us over there is the first piece of information that we all need to formulate a plan."

"And if they have defenses to destroy it?"

"Then that tells us something important, too."

The commodore sat silently for a few minutes, and then he nodded. "We would be in your debt for any intelligence you could gather for us, Lord Captain."

Jared smiled widely. "We'll get started, but I'd like to ask you for a small favor in return."

22

K elsey sat in her seat on *Athena*'s cutter and fumed. The destroyer was moving toward the flip point leading to the Pale Ones' system to launch a probe, and she was on her way to Pentagar. She knew Jared had to have been behind the commodore's insistence she leave now for Pentagar to begin negotiations. Unfortunately, she couldn't do anything about it.

Kelsey eyed Talbot. "Am I going to get the silent treatment the entire trip?"

"It's nothing personal, Princess, but we're not a barrel full of monkeys while on a combat patrol either. There's time to be serious and there's time to have fun. This is the former."

"This isn't combat."

"No, but what kind of impression would you make if we joked around with you? That might cause the people here to think you don't take them seriously. Or that you're making some kind of subtle insult. We just need to do our jobs, and then we can have a beer when everyone isn't watching your every move."

He was probably right, but she'd never had the chance to be so casually friendly with anyone like the marines before. She found she fit in really well with them and missed doing so.

She sighed and looked out the port at the ship they were approaching. It was much smaller than *Athena*. Two men in light-blue tunics met them when they docked. Both bowed.

"Princess Kelsey," the one on the left said. "I'm Lieutenant Parker, the command pilot of the fast courier *Lance*. This is my engineer, Lieutenant Walker. Welcome aboard."

"Thank you. I appreciate you taking us to Pentagar."

The main compartment of the Royal ship proved to be very small. There were just enough seats for her, the four marines, and the three scientists accompanying them. "We'll be departing at once," Parker said. "With our fast grav drives, we'll be in Pentagaran orbit in just under two hours. There are facilities through that door, and we have some bottled water if you get thirsty. I apologize for the lack of amenities, but we don't normally carry passengers so far."

"Thank you," Kelsey said. "We'll be fine."

They settled in, and Talbot promptly went to sleep while the other marine kept watch. She decided that was a stellar idea and settled back to catch up on some well-deserved rest herself.

She woke when Talbot nudged her. "The pilot says we're about to enter the atmosphere."

Kelsey stretched and wished there were some ports. She took a minute to use the facilities and to drink a bottle of water. They landed fifteen minutes later.

The pilot opened the hatches, and sunlight poured in. Kelsey took a deep breath. It had been over a month since she'd smelled unfiltered air. The breeze had a hint of something sweet but otherwise seemed completely natural. Someone had moved a portable ramp next to the ship, and the pilot gestured for her to go down first.

She stepped out into the open and took everything in. The blue sky was so pale that it almost didn't look like a color at all. Small, fluffy clouds raced above her, but the breeze brushing her face was light. The sunlight was somewhat redder than she'd expected but not overly so.

The ship had landed on a wide field of stone, some kind of poured mix very similar to plascrete. A number of other ships sat at varying distances away. Some were near large buildings and others sat alone. Hers was the only one with a group of people waiting near it.

Two lines of men in white tunics stood at the base of the ramp with weapons held in front of them pointing into the sky. A glance at Talbot showed he wasn't worried, so she walked down the ramp.

Two men and a woman stood waiting for her. Behind them were half a dozen men in colorful tunics. The woman wore a wide headband of gold. She smiled and stepped forward. "Princess Kelsey of the Imperial House of Bandar, I am Crown Princess Elise of the Royal House of Orison. On behalf of my father, I welcome you to Pentagar."

Kelsey bowed slightly. "Thank you for your kind welcome, Highness. On behalf of my father and Captain Jared Mertz, I bring greetings and well wishes."

"As we are both of high rank, I insist you call me Elise. Allow me to introduce my companions. This is the royal chancellor of Pentagar, Sir Ellery Matcliff, Baron of Windshire." She gestured to the tall man with the distinguished gray hair to her right. "This is Lord Admiral Sebastian Shrike, Deputy Commander of the Royal Fleet."

The last was obviously a reference to the short, bald man of indeterminate age to her left. Kelsey couldn't tell how old he was, but he obviously kept himself in shape. His arms were quite muscular. The two men bowed.

"Thank you," Kelsey said. "Please call me Kelsey as well. I've brought three members of our scientific staff to consult with your people about the Pale Ones."

"Of course. Our scientific and medical delegation will receive them. I know they have much to discuss."

It turned out the people behind the other woman were that delegation. They led the scientists away, jabbering in technospeak as they walked. All but four of the honor guards faded away.

Elise gestured for Kelsey to walk beside her. "We have a grav car to take us to the palace. His Majesty is looking forward to meeting you, but he asked me to make the initial overtures of friendship. He believes that we women might come to a decision more quickly without his official presence."

Kelsey raised an eyebrow. "I see. And who are these gentlemen?"

"My keepers," Elise confided. "They're to make sure I don't sign away the Royal Palace."

The baron smiled. "Actually, Your Highness, the lord admiral and I are here to provide more detailed information if required. Between the two of us, we know where all the figurative bodies are buried."

"And more than a few of the real ones, I'd wager," the bald admiral rumbled in a surprisingly deep voice. "Are you the sole Imperial representative on your mission, Princess Kelsey?"

She nodded, deciding they didn't need to know the sordid details of Carlo Vega's death. "I am. Tell me, Lord Admiral, does the honorific denote a relationship to your king?"

The short man nodded. "It does. The king did not marry until late and proved to be a lusty youth. We have a good working relationship."

There were two grav limos waiting for them. They climbed into one and the guards into the other. Both sped away together over the city. The view through the windows was quite beautiful. The buildings were lower to the ground than back on Avalon, but they were significantly wider.

After a few moments enjoying the view, Kelsey turned back to Elise. "This is the first time I've been directly involved in negotiating an agreement like this. What are we hoping to settle today?"

"The main goal of the evening is for us to become comfortable with one another. Agreements can come later. No one gains anything by rushing into something with strangers."

"Though if we can come to a few minor understandings quickly, that might make things less tense," Lord Admiral Shrike said. "The very idea of space-time bridges we were unaware of makes my skin crawl. Just because the Pale Ones haven't come through one doesn't mean they won't find one tomorrow. That could spell the end of us."

Kelsey nodded. "I've already spoken to Captain Mertz. We would be happy to scan your system and to pass on the specifications of the scanner without any preconditions. We'll also share what we know about flip drive technology."

Sir Ellery looked a little surprised but pleased. "That's most generous of you. You cannot believe how difficult it is to see savages with interstellar drives but be unable to create our own."

"Two peoples that want to be friends will find a way to help one another," Elise said. "I'm certain that we can offer you support. Then when you manage to find a way back, our help will also not be forgotten."

"True enough," Kelsey said. "Our scientists have probably already handed the data we collected over to your delegation. Unless they forget they have it with them. For being geniuses, they can be awfully absentminded."

The crown princess laughed. "I see that our people are more alike than I'd imagined."

The limo crossed a boundary of some kind. The city became manicured woodlands. Beyond them rose a magnificent castle. Bright pennants flew from the highest towers, and men patrolled the stone walls.

"Welcome to Orison Castle," Elise said. "Home to the Royal Family since before the monarchy was established. Of course, we were only a house of minor nobility before the Empire fell."

"Don't worry," Sir Ellery assured Kelsey. "The plumbing has been updated."

The crown princess smacked him on the arm. "Don't make her think we're backwoods folk with twigs in our hair."

"I think it's beautiful," Kelsey said. "I must take vids back home to show my father. He'll be absolutely green with envy. He would have loved to live in a castle growing up. Me, too."

The limos settled onto a landing pad beside the castle. The marines and Royal guards came out and made sure the pad was secure before Talbot gave her the high sign. The lord admiral exited first and held the door for the ladies. The chancellor followed them out.

Elise gestured to the wide entrance. "My father is waiting inside. This is a casual visit, so we're not standing on ceremony. He wants some quiet time to get to know you and to assure you that we're decent people."

"I already knew that," Kelsey said. "I've been watching the news vids. It didn't take long to figure out that what we were seeing wasn't propaganda. The people here seem genuinely happy for the most part. Even those who criticize the Royal house don't seem to feel afraid to do so. That told us a lot."

The crown princess laughed. "I can only imagine what you heard. Some people seem to go out of their way to find something to be unhappy about. Or look for some conspiracy. If so, they're free to do so. Open speech is a cherished right here."

She gestured for Kelsey to precede her. "Come on. Let's have lunch and get to know one another."

23

J ared brought *Athena* to a halt outside the sphere of orbital fortresses surrounding the hostile flip point. He didn't need to be inside it to send the probe, and being under all those missile tubes would make him itchy. Their Royal Fleet escort stopped with him.

The damage to the fortresses was… extensive. Many were little more than floating clouds of debris. The Pale Ones had severely damaged most of the rest. Smaller ships were flitting around, grabbing large chunks of wreckage and moving them toward a collection point. They also towed the remains of the enemy ships, some of which looked surprisingly intact.

He looked down at his console, focusing on the image of Commodore Sanders. The other man sat on *Mace*'s bridge, watching the same scene on his main monitor, Jared presumed. "Commodore, some of those attackers look better than I'd have expected after a missile duel at knife range."

The older man shrugged. "Sometimes they appear too close to one another and their grav drives mesh as they attempt to accelerate. That fries them right quick. Their actual momentum after transition is too small to get the derelicts far."

"Have you pulled any usable intelligence from them?"

"Not in years. We'll casually examine them, but they're not our priority. The space-time drives burn out with the grav units. For whatever reason, they make their drives as a single unit. On rare occasions, they manage to repair a ship and continue on, but no space-time drive has survived one of these burnouts. Or the battle damage required to stop the ship."

Jared frowned as he considered the man's words. "Exactly how does a savage repair a damaged drive unit?"

"Most likely in the same way they can pilot a spaceship. We hypothesize their implants have some automatic way to do some of that work without intelligence. We've seen the manner they fight hand to hand in the ones we've captured. Rote execution of advanced martial arts moves based on the situation. They are quite deadly in a fight."

"Might we have a relatively intact ship to study? Sometimes an outside eye can see something new."

Sanders nodded. "I'll have them shift one of these to your care. What will you do with it?"

"See if I can strap it to a cutter dock and flip it over to the other system. The scientists can disassemble it to their heart's content. If there's anything to be learned, they'll find it."

Zia turned in her seat to face Jared. "We're ready to launch the probes, Captain."

The plan was to launch two probes through the flip point. One would stay just long enough to get a scan of the immediate area and return. The other would remain for fifteen minutes. If it survived that long, they would have an idea of the star system on the other end. They'd also launch a widespread volley of probes set to scan the Pentagar system for any anomalous flip points.

Jared raised an eyebrow at Sanders. "Are we good with launching these? They look like missiles, and we'll be launching a lot of them. I do not want my command fired upon."

The commodore shook his head. "Everyone has been told multiple times. No one will fire on your ship, even if you inadvertently launched a salvo at one of the fortresses."

"I think we can avoid that particular blunder. Zia, launch the probes, starting with the ones going elsewhere in this system. Flip the two going over to the next system as soon as you're ready."

"Aye, sir."

The probes appeared on the plot of local space. A dozen moved quickly out of the general area and began probing. The final two quickly traversed into the flip point and disappeared before they reached the center. Perhaps by going over at the edge of the flip point, one would survive long enough to get back home with a snapshot of the tactical situation in the enemy system.

The probes had been gone less than ten seconds when the first one popped back into existence. An overview of the far side of the flip point began taking shape as Zia added details from the data feed.

"It looks like the immediate area around the flip point is empty," she said. "No defensive installations and no ships detected. There might be some close by, but with only a glimpse, we won't see them."

"Can you give me any details on the system itself?"

"The star is a medium-sized yellow capable of supporting life. We have some images of the stellar background that the computers are crunching to see if they can narrow the location down using the computer records the Kingdom recovered after the Fall."

It took a few minutes before Zia confirmed the stellar location of the target system was the Erorsi system. Old records indicated it was at one time a populous world with several billion citizens.

"The second probe just reappeared," Zia said a few minutes later. "I'm pulling the data feed now."

The diagram on the screen updated. No transmissions showed on any of the scans. No ships or structures detected. That didn't mean there weren't any. No ship or artificial structure would be visible at the kinds of ranges a flip point normally sat from habitable planets. All they could possibly see at that range were radio transmissions or the gravitic signature of a ship moving at high speed.

Sanders shifted his attention from the display *Athena* was forwarding to *Mace*. "Does that say what I think?"

"If you think it says the flip point is completely unguarded, sir, you'd be right. That's insane."

Graves looked up from the console he'd appropriated at the rear of the bridge. "Perhaps not. Those things seem to operate on some preprogramed berserker imperative. Perhaps they aren't designed for defense. From what I've surmised, they overwhelmed the Old Empire with sheer numbers."

"It seems to have worked well enough for them." Jared considered the readouts. "We'll send the probe back over with instructions to return if it detects any enemy activity."

"Well, then," Sanders said. "I suppose I can shift my people into helping with the search-and-rescue operations. I'll want to know at once if you detect anything unusual at all."

Jared gave Graves a lopsided grin. "Just how much trouble would I be in with the princess if I popped over for a detailed scan, Charlie?"

"She will eat you alive," Graves assured him. "Is that what you want to do? They might note the incursion and respond."

"It doesn't look as though they keep a close watch."

"Our scanners are far more sensitive than the ones on these probes. If we can get a detailed scan of the system, it could prove decisive when the Pentagarans make their own incursion."

He shifted his attention to Sanders. "Can you avoid shooting us when we come back?"

"If we arrange for you to be transmitting something known as you come in, I think that would work." They quickly worked out a signal that Zia could begin transmitting before they came back. That would keep the Royal forces from firing on *Athena*.

Commodore Sanders gave his final approval. "This is quite a risk you're taking for my people, Lord Captain. We appreciate it."

"I might need a place to hide when the princess finds out I didn't bring her along."

The older man laughed. "She won't be pleased, I imagine."

"We'll either be back very quickly or we'll be there a while. It depends on what we find. Don't be alarmed if we're gone for a few hours. We'll send a probe back with our estimated time of return."

"Good luck and Godspeed, Lord Captain."

Once the transmission ended, Jared brought *Athena* to combat readiness. They'd go over with their fingers on the triggers. This time he brought the ship to the center of the flip point and gave the order.

The momentary disorientation faded. Zia scanned her console closely. "No ships in the general vicinity, Captain."

"Stand down from combat stations. Hold station and passively scan the system. Prepare a dozen probes. I want to send them deep into the system to map it for flip points and Pale Ones. Program them to transmit the results to our location via tight beam."

"Aye, sir."

Graves moved over to Jared's console. "You don't think they'll spot them? The scans might be passive, but the probes are moving. Even if they don't, it will take days to cover the entire system."

"We'll leave a probe here to record data until they stop transmitting or ships approach. The reaction will be almost as useful as the data they get."

It took Zia an hour to locate the formerly inhabited main world of the system. Another two passed before the probe was close enough to detect artificial structures orbiting the planet. She detected no transmissions from either the orbitals or the planet's surface. While Zia couldn't be sure, she thought there were three clusters of artificial structures around the planet.

"Zia, how long to get the probe into range for a close look?"

She checked her console. "Another hour. Less if you want to let it shoot past the planet."

"If we can keep it there without it being seen, I'd rather have the extra intelligence a stationary probe could get."

He let the crew cycle off for meals and downtime. He'd know if they needed to come back long before trouble could come to them. He took the first break with half the bridge crew and relieved Graves an hour later.

By the time everyone was back, the probe was slowing into position. He waited the final minutes with some impatience. He really wanted to know what they were going to find.

"I'm getting good data from the probe," Zia said. "I'm also detecting three clumps of fusion plants in orbit. They are each roughly a third of the way around the planet from the others. At the orbital distance above the surface they occupy, they don't have line of sight with one another. Our probe is in a position to see the first two now. The third will take a few minutes to come into sight."

The system diagram they had been reviewing vanished, replaced by the breathtaking view of a planet. The greens and blues looked very much like Avalon. A small speck crossed in front of the ocean, and the image swelled as the vid zoomed in.

The orbital it revealed looked deceptively small, but the scale on the bottom of the scan made it apparent it was bigger than all the orbitals around Avalon put together. True, it was mostly an open framework, but that didn't change the scope of it.

"What is that thing?" Graves asked.

"It's a shipyard," Jared said. "I visited a freighter construction dock a few years ago. This is a lot bigger."

"How much bigger?"

"Big enough to construct an invasion fleet," Jared said grimly. "Thankfully it looks empty now. What else do we have?"

The view shifted. The second orbital structure was almost as big as the shipyard, only it was a solid sphere. Jared pursed his lips in a soundless whistle. That crude-looking facility could've housed tens of thousands of people.

The wait for the third set of power sources seemed an eternity but was less than half an hour. To his horror, it was another shipyard.

This one still looked to be under construction. That didn't seem to have slowed down its use, though. It had hundreds of ships in various stages of construction. It looked like they'd been working on this one for a while, and now it was almost ready to launch a new invasion. Not in years like the Pentagarans expected, but in days or weeks. An invasion they had no way of stopping.

24

Meeting the king of Pentagar was a bit anticlimactic. The short, rotund gentleman would've made a great tavern keeper. He welcomed Kelsey warmly and made her feel like a member of his family before a simple and delicious lunch was over. He insisted she use his given name any time she tried to be formal. She now knew what a favorite uncle must be like.

He seemed to have an endless supply of amusing stories, many from segments of society that she wouldn't have guessed he had knowledge of. After a particularly funny story about the construction crew of a building in the capital, she asked him about it. "Raymond, how could you possibly know what a bricklayer does on a construction site?"

His eyes twinkled. "I learned at a young age how to slip out of the castle and get to know the people I was to rule. Just like in an old story. They never suspected I was the crown prince. It drove my father simply mad. He would post guards, but I always managed to slip past them. You see, I'd found the secret passages."

Kelsey's eyes widened. "Secret passages? Seriously?"

"Absolutely," he assured her. "They were built into the castle when it was constructed. They had lain disused until I stumbled upon a secret room. Once I knew something like that existed, I made it my mission to find them all, though I doubt I succeeded. I think I may have, but even now, I'm not completely sure. They are hidden devilishly well."

Kelsey glanced at Elise. "Is he being serious?"

She nodded. "I've seen them. He insisted on showing them to me when I was old enough to appreciate them. You can get from almost any part of the castle to another. A few lead out into the woods. The exits are works of art."

"In any case," the king continued, "I still have my bricklayer's certification framed in my office. I think such knowledge and insight are crucial to being a good monarch. All too many noblemen live in little bubbles where they have no idea who their people truly are."

Elise leaned over toward Kelsey. "I apprenticed under a woodcarver for several years. If you haven't considered doing something like that, you really should. We live such isolated lives. We need to be more like the people we lead if we're to be the best rulers we can be."

"I wish I'd had an opportunity like that. It sounds wonderful."

Raymond Orison laughed jovially. "But you see, Kelsey, you have exactly such an opportunity! Here on this mission, you're one of them. You strive side by side with your fellows. You don't have to live inside a bubble. Socialize. Do what they do. Be one of them. The only thing stopping you is yourself."

"Well, I have been spending quite a bit of time with the marines. They were standoffish at first, but now we drink beer and gamble. I almost feel like one of them."

"Splendid! You've seen how easy it is. You can overcome the boundaries set by protocol. Meet your Fleet comrades in the same way. Dine with them. Find out what they do for recreation and join them. By the time you get back home, you will be one of them. And don't forget the scientists. The quiet ones can be the most fun! Such a golden opportunity shouldn't be squandered."

Elise put her napkin on her plate. "Speaking of opportunities, how would you like to go into the city and meet the man who taught me woodcarving?"

Kelsey smiled. "I'd love that."

"You girls go have fun. Kelsey, we'll have dinner tonight, and we can talk about diplomatic things after you've had a good night's sleep."

"I don't imagine these negotiations will be very difficult." She rose to her feet. "Thank you again for your kind welcome."

"It's my pleasure."

The flight into the city proved to be a long one because Elise kept telling the driver to show Kelsey various parts of the city. Not that Kelsey minded. She even made some side trips of her own to look at some interesting pieces of architecture in the distance.

It was close to three hours later when they arrived at the square. The limos settled into a parking area long enough for the occupants to disembark and then took to the air again. Elise led them to a small shop on the corner of a busy street.

A plaque of dark wood hung over the door. Someone had cut an eerily lifelike image of a man walking a dog on it. A second, smaller plaque hung beside the door. Master Alec Vestor, woodcarver.

They went inside once their escort had checked it, and Kelsey gasped. Incredible woodcarvings filled the shop. Stunningly beautiful plaques and intricately detailed statuettes of people and creatures decorated the room.

Some were familiar to her, others were not, and still others appeared to be fantastical. "This is amazing!"

She walked over to a shelf holding a collection of tiny figurines. None of the carvings stood more than a few inches tall, but all were so elaborate and lifelike that she half expected them to be moving. At Elise's nod, she picked up one of a small boy holding a bow. Looking closely, she could see the serene expression on his face and his meticulously detailed clothes.

"I cannot tell you how overwhelmed I was the first time I walked in here," Elise confided. "While I'm not nearly so talented, I find myself blessed to study with people like Master Vestor."

"Did I hear my name used in vain?"

They turned to find a tall, thin man in a tunic of turquoise blue standing behind them. Elise squeaked and hugged him. "You scared me!"

The older man laughed. "You were so focused on the carvings that I could've driven a herd of marshbeasts past you. It's so good to see you again, Your Highness." He gave Kelsey a smile. "Who is your friend?"

"Master Vestor, allow me to introduce our esteemed visitor Princess Kelsey Bandar of the Terran Empire. Kelsey, my patron Alec."

Alec Vestor bowed low. "You grace my humble shop, Your Highness." He straightened with a smile. "Allow me to say that I am moved by how you rescued those poor people from a fate far worse than death. Such kindness to strangers does you great credit, and I am honored to make your acquaintance. Welcome to Pentagar."

Kelsey felt herself blushing. "Thank you, Master Vestor, but we only did what anyone else would have done."

"I think you overestimate the risks many people would take for a stranger. So, what has this miscreant been saying about me? Rest assured that her base slanders are the result of the rigorous discipline I had to impose on her during her training."

Elise smacked him on the shoulder. "And there I was telling her how terrific you are. Now I'll tell her the truth. You can barely carve your name."

He laughed. "Some days I feel like that is the very truth indeed! My secret is out!"

"Kelsey, Master Vestor is the premiere woodcarver in the Kingdom. His works grace the halls of the very lucky few to whom he'll agree to sell. Not these wonderful knickknacks, but massive landscapes so amazing they take your breath away."

"I can hardly imagine anything more impressive than what I see here. I never knew people could do such wonderful things with wood. I feel guilty for liking a roaring fire now."

Master Vestor took her by the elbow. "There is no need for guilt. I love a good fire myself. It's not the wood that's special, although there are some fine cuts, but the love and passion that one puts into it. Many talented artists did these miniatures. Come and look at my latest work. I'm almost done with it and would love to hear what you think."

He led them to the back of the shop and into a large studio. The scent of wood was so strong that Kelsey almost sneezed. People stood beside tables covered in wood shavings, working on projects large and small. Most of the artisans didn't even glance up as the strangers walked among them.

The thin woodcarver led them into a separate room at the very back. Kelsey made it only a step inside before the sight of what lay before her stopped her in her tracks. She heard someone gasp and then realized it had been her.

Two large stands held an oval of wood three feet tall and five wide. He'd carved the most amazing forest landscape she'd ever imagined into the pale wood. Mountains loomed in the distance, but the vast forest in the forefront captured her attention.

She walked closer and leaned in. She could see leaves on the trees and birds flitting through the limbs. Small animals of some kind peeked out from behind trunks. It was more intricate than any painting she'd ever seen.

"Amazing, isn't it?" Elise asked. "He puts an incredible amount of time into these works and then virtually gives them away."

"I wouldn't go so far as that," he said dryly. "I make a fine living. Yet I do sometimes give some away. Like this one. It's a gift to cement a friendship."

Kelsey smiled. "It must be quite some friendship."

"I certainly hope so. You see, until today, I had no idea what I would do with it. The arrival of your people and their bravery convinced me it should be a gift from the people of Pentagar to those of the Terran Empire. May our friendship be deep and abiding."

Her jaw dropped. "I couldn't accept such a princely gift. I truly appreciate the thought, but it's too much."

Elise shook her head. "My father had the perfect advice when Master Vestor gave me something like this. If the giver believes you worthy of it, you should accept the gift and be grateful someone values you so highly. That is my advice to you as well."

Kelsey swallowed and bowed deeply to the master artist. "Then I accept your most gracious gift in the name of the people of the Terran Empire. I hope to return it home one day so that many can gaze upon it and marvel at your astonishing talent. Thank you."

One of the Royal guards stepped up to Elise and whispered something in her ear. She frowned and turned to face Kelsey. "I'm not quite sure how to broach the subject, but I just received word that your Lord Captain Mertz has used his space-time drive to venture into the Pale Ones' system."

Kelsey turned her head a little, certain she'd misheard the other woman. "He did what?"

"We should return to the palace so we may gather more information," the crown princess said.

Kelsey bit her tongue. Cursing Jared in front of her hosts wouldn't accomplish anything. She bowed again to Master Vestor. "I apologize for my hasty departure, but something has come up that I must attend to. Thank you again. Your work is magnificent."

"Come back anytime, Princess Kelsey. I should have the carving done in the next week. I'll have Elise contact you."

The two women walked back out onto the street. The intense rage Kelsey felt ate at her. Jared knew she was supposed to be with them! He'd ignored her father's orders.

Kelsey tamped her anger down. "May I borrow your ship again?"

"Going there isn't safe," Elise said. "What if there is an armed response to the incursion?"

"I need to be there waiting for them."

The other woman looked unconvinced but nodded. "Please be careful."

"I'll be back as soon as he returns. Which I'm sure will be soon. Until then, thank you for your gracious hospitality. Please convey my regrets to your father about missing dinner."

Kelsey left the bemused woman at the landing pad and climbed into one of the limos. Her marines followed her. The driver looked back at her curiously.

"We need to return to the ship that brought us here. Quickly."

"Right away. I'll have you there in ten minutes."

Kelsey settled back as the limo rose and filled Talbot in. He leaned over and spoke softly in her ear. "Not to tell you your business, Princess, but it might be wiser to remain here. Isn't taking care of diplomatic relations your function? You can't do that and be with the ship all the time."

"I'll wager that Captain Mertz sent a probe over before he went himself. I doubt he would've gone across if he thought there was any real danger."

"Then wait for him to come back so you can tear a strip off him."

"My decision has been made, Senior Sergeant."

He sighed. "Yes, Your Highness."

Their hasty return trip to the spaceport was so abrupt that they arrived before their crew. It took another ten minutes before they rushed onto the plascrete and opened the ship. Someone must've briefed them on the way, because they asked no questions. They brought the ship to life without any delays.

While the crew worked, she sat in the main compartment fuming. How could Jared do this? He'd likely claim he was protecting her. Then again, he'd lock her in a padded room if he thought he could get away with it. She had to put him back in his place. Hard.

"Princess Kelsey?"

She looked up at the pilot. She hadn't heard him approach. "I'm sorry. Yes?"

"We're ready to launch. Would you care to sit up front with me? My copilot isn't close enough to make it back before we launch."

"That would be very interesting. Thank you." It would keep her mind off strangling Jared for a while.

The controls in the ship's cockpit seemed significantly more complex than those on *Athena*'s bridge. It was a spaceship, too. Why were they so different?

Kelsey kept her hands in her lap as the man brought the ship to a hover and spoke into his headset. "Control, this is *Lance*. Requesting emergency departure."

She couldn't hear the response, but it must've been in the affirmative.

"Roger, control. *Lance* out." He put the ship into a steep climb. The blue sky faded quickly to black.

The pilot turned to face her. "We'll be at the interdiction zone in a little less than two hours. If you have any questions about the ship, I'd be happy to answer them."

"I do have one. Why do the controls on your ship seem so much more complicated than those on *Athena*?"

The corner of his mouth tugged up. "Not knowing what the controls on your ship look like, I couldn't guess."

She pulled out her communicator. "I took a vid because I wanted to save it for later."

He examined the image. "We're only beginning to start using touch screens like these. I'd imagine your controls are probably significantly more complex than they appear once you look at the submenus."

The pilot launched into a detailed explanation of the controls in front of her and answered her uneducated questions simply enough and with good cheer. That took her mind off her troubles for over an hour and a half.

His console beeped. He checked a monitor beside his leg. "We're less than thirty minutes out. We're starting to encounter some of the debris from the battle."

"Could there be survivors?"

"Possibly, but not very likely. Only a few chunks seem large enough to hold air. I'll scan those. It looks like there is a ship ahead looking through the wreckage. It just began accelerating."

He brought the visual onto the screen in front of them. A bright dot of light quickly expanded into a ship. The pilot cursed. "It's the Pale Ones! We need to get out of here. Go warn your marines while I call for help and evade."

She unbuckled and ran back to the central compartment. "A Pale Ones' ship is coming!"

Talbot said something not suitable for Imperial ears. "We aren't wearing our armor and only have handguns. Get the princess back into the engineering compartment and barricade yourselves in. Find some oxygen masks in case they breach our hull. Hopefully we can hold them off until help arrives."

Kelsey suppressed her terror and did as he ordered. She prayed that the pilot would evade the enemy ship.

The engineer grabbed a heavy wrench. "Shoot her before they take us. Me, too. Then yourselves. We don't want to become like they are. Trust me. Death is much better."

"I'm not killing the princess," the marine sneered.

"Then at least shoot me. Please."

The marine started to respond, but Kelsey would never know what he was going to say. Without warning, their world went black.

25

J ared had Zia begin transmitting the agreed-upon signal and transitioned back to Pentagar space. He expected to see the Royal ships still engaged in search and rescue. Instead, alarms began sounding before the disorientation faded.

Ramirez changed course with such lightning swiftness that it probably saved all their lives. A missile exploded beside them instead of directly impacting them. Jared's console lit up with lurid red warnings of battle damage.

"A Pale Ones' ship just fired on us and transitioned," Zia said. "Royal forces were in pursuit. No other missiles detected."

Ramirez turned from his console. "We took the hit in engineering. Flip and grav drives offline. Damage control reports casualties."

"Incoming signal from Commodore Sanders, Captain," Zia said. "On screen."

"Where the hell did that damned ship come from?" Jared asked.

The older officer grimaced. "It must've been damaged. It couldn't have repaired itself at a worse time. It ambushed Princess Kelsey and her people just before they got here. We tried to disable it, but we don't really have weapons suitable to cripple."

Jared's blood ran cold. "Where is she?"

"I'm sorry. They were captured."

"I'm going after them. *Athena* out." He opened a channel to engineering. "Dennis, we need to transition now."

Baxter shook his head. The scene behind him was organized chaos. "Drives are down. It will be hours before we can flip again."

"Unacceptable. The Pale Ones have Princess Kelsey. I want this ship moving faster than that."

"Captain, the drives are physically damaged. We're working as fast as we possibly can. We won't waste one precious second. Engineering out." Baxter cut the connection.

Jared felt like banging his head on the console. What had possessed her to come to the interdiction zone? He took a deep breath. "Zia, send a probe after that damned ship. I want to know exactly where it goes, because we're going after it as soon as we can."

"Aye, sir. Launching another probe to follow and send back everything it can."

"Get me Commodore Sanders back as soon as you're done with that."

A minute later, Sanders reappeared on the screen. Jared tried not to shout at the man. The blame for this could go right to the one responsible for her: Jared Mertz.

"Commodore, our drives are damaged. My engineer tells me it will be hours before we can follow that ship."

"I'm so sorry, Lord Captain. The damned thing jumped them just short of the interdiction zone. We tried to fire a near miss, but they made it through."

"I should've kept her closer at hand. I'll get her back or die trying."

He proceeded to tell the commodore what he'd found out in the other system. The old man looked grim by the time Jared was done. "We won't be ready to repulse the next invasion, and we can't take the fight to them in time."

"We might be able to do something to delay them. I'll have to consider the options."

"Can we help in any way?"

"Yes. We only carry thirty marines, but our pinnaces can hold seventy in armor. We have two. If you could scrounge up a hundred volunteers, I could use more combat-trained ground fighters."

"I have that many on my ship. Major Edwards will gather them and their gear. Can my engineering teams help get you ready more quickly?"

Jared shook his head. "I'm afraid not. We'll send the pinnaces to collect your people. Thank you for your help in this."

"You put yourselves in harm's way for my people. How could we do any less? Besides, it's possible we can strike against this invasion fleet before it is ready to depart the shipyard. I'll communicate with Pentagar and see if they can come up with any options."

"Thank you. *Athena* out."

He stood. "Zia, get the pinnaces over to *Mace*. Coordinate with the commodore on any plan he devises. If we can strike against those ships, I want to do it while they are under construction. I'm going to see Doctor Stone."

The lift took him to the medical center while he stewed in a dark silence. Doctor Stone was setting a broken arm on a crewwoman who looked more than a little singed around the edges of her engineering jumpsuit. "How bad is it?"

The doctor turned to him, her face a mask of sorrow. "Twelve dead and a lot of walking wounded, Captain."

The news made his stomach churn. The Pale Ones would pay for this. "As soon as you're done, with that we need to talk."

"Vargas, take over for me."

Stone handed over the work to one of the med techs and led Jared to her office. She closed the hatch behind them. "What's wrong?"

"The Pale Ones' ship that shot us took Princess Kelsey. She's in their hands."

The doctor swore. "Can we get her back?"

"Not right away. Baxter needs several hours to get the drives online. That means she might be implanted or at least in the middle of the process by the time we can get on her trail. If they do something to her, can you undo it?"

The chief medical officer shook her head decisively. "Not a chance. I can't even imagine how they implant those things into a human brain. I sure as hell won't be able to remove one without killing her."

Jared looked out the clear wall at the people working on the injured. "We have to do something. I can't let her become one of them. That's a horror I can't begin to imagine. What about overriding the programming on the implants?"

"You'll need to speak with the science team. Doctor Leonard was working on getting power to the implants of the dead Imperial Marine we have on board. I haven't heard anything about their progress. I know they pulled a lot of data off the dead Pale One. He might be able to do something."

"Where did he set up shop?"

"Down in one of the cargo compartments that we converted to a lab. Jared, I'll do absolutely everything I can to help her."

He put his hand on Stone's shoulder. "I know. We'll get her back. You'll need to be ready to go with the rescue team after we flip. Be prepared to restrain her in an augmented state. Take anything you might need. Grab as many people as you need to make it happen."

"We'll be ready."

The cargo areas they'd converted were down in the bowels of the ship near engineering. Jared imagined the scientists had received quite a shakeup. When he walked through the hatch, he saw that he'd been right. They were busily putting equipment back up and recovering various bits of electronics.

Doctor Jerry Leonard saw Jared come in and walked over to meet him. "That was quite the unexpected shock, Captain. It's a good thing we were all strapped in for the flip. Can we assist with damage control?"

Jared shook his head. "You have more important work to do, Doctor. The Pale Ones captured Princess Kelsey. We're going after her as soon as we get the drives back online, but they might implant her. I need to know you can do something about that."

The rail-thin scientist blanched. "Dear God. Of course. We'll do what we can, but the implants are in the brain. We just don't have the technical ability to remove them without turning her into a vegetable or killing her."

"Then tell me you can do something about the programming that controls them. The captain of *Courageous* killed his entire crew to keep some kind of override in the programming from turning them into monsters. Tell me you have the code from the Fleet officers and can reverse what they did."

"The implants are physically the same. Right down to the model numbers. With Doctor Stone's assistance, we were able to access the programming code in the Pale One's corpse. The units are internally powered and not readily accessible to recharge, so they must last far longer than a person's life span. We've disassembled the implants from the marine we brought with us but hadn't gotten to attempting to swap the power supplies."

Jared gave the scientist a steady look. "Then you'd best get busy. We don't have much time for you to find a solution."

The man nodded. "It shouldn't take more than a few minutes to put them back together. We were worried they might be damaged if we attempted to power them on, but we don't have a choice now."

The scientist strode to a worktable. He opened several clear plastic bins. "I hope it doesn't matter that we removed them from the bodies. If it tries to access the brains of the dead Fleet personnel and errors out, there's nothing we can do."

He laid out the odd strands of hair-thin wires and circular units the size of small coins on the table. He put on magnifying goggles and picked up some delicate tools to work on one of the units. "We developed these tools when we saw how the other units had to be disassembled. The method is quite ingenious."

Jared couldn't really see anything, but he could determine the man's progress when he removed a thin shell from each of the three units of the implant. The small object he removed from each with a set of tweezers was about the size of the tip on a writing stylus. If that was a power supply, it was incredible. Just like most things the Old Empire had built.

Leonard took the tiny power units from another implant and put them in the first set of implants. Once he had the covers on the units, he grabbed a headset. It had a cable going to a standalone computer. As soon as he taped the last of the three into the headset, the screen started filling with long lines of what looked like gibberish.

"It's attempting to boot," Leonard said. "We don't really need to attach them to the headset. They have effective short-range communication, good for perhaps ten meters, but the transmission speed and data throughput are significantly quicker with the headsets in place. Probably why they wore them. It's online! We wrote a program to access the code, and this looks like it's working."

"Can you tell what the differences are? Perhaps we can find where the alterations were made and correct them."

The scientist nodded. "Possibly. It will take a few minutes to collect all the code. If they are similar, we should be able to compare them. We still don't understand the programming language, though. If the changes to the programming are widespread, I wouldn't want to go mucking around with it in a living being. I can only imagine what that could do to them."

"Can you make changes?"

"That remains to be seen. One would imagine there is a mechanism for updates. It probably isn't something that could happen by accident or perhaps even easily. If I were designing something like this, the access codes to make changes would be hardware specific. Only authorized units could write to these. That authentication would need to be very complex. That said, it might not be impossible to read it directly off the hardware itself."

"Would recovering installation hardware be helpful?"

The man nodded enthusiastically. "Absolutely! It would be optimal if you could recover reference material, the actual programming, or installation machinery. We should be able to access it and replace whatever malicious code we find. One of my graduate students is my coding expert, and he's the one examining the Pale Ones' programming."

"You brought a graduate student? I thought everyone on that ship was a doctor."

"Carl Owlet is a true genius with computers. I'm surprised that Doctor Cartwright didn't assign him to *Courageous*. He might once they are ready to bring the main computer back online."

The computer beeped, and Leonard examined the screen. "There are some rather significant areas where the code is different. I think we need to let Carl take a look." He brought out his communicator and summoned the other man.

Make that boy. If Carl Owlet were old enough to shave regularly, Jared would eat his beret. The graduate student looked about sixteen standard years old.

Owlet listened intently as Doctor Leonard filled him in on recent developments and then sat at the computer. He typed on the remote keypad so quickly that Jared could barely see his fingers. He typed more quickly than most people spoke.

The screen split into two displays and began scrolling through the code. The computer had highlighted many areas. "This is definitely the same base code as in the Pale Ones, Captain. I can see what looks like version markers buried in the comments. The repetitive pattern of the matches tells me that someone compromised the original code. There also seems to be some extra code in this marine implant."

"Can you tell what the extra code does?"

The boy shook his head. "No, sir. I'll keep working on it."

"Are there too many changes to correct the original code?"

The boy nodded. "Manually correcting the code requires understanding how it interacts with the hardware, and I'm not there yet. I doubt many Old Empire people really knew this in any detail. It would take teams of dedicated programmers working for many years to develop code of this complexity. I know that I wouldn't want to trust my brain to something that hadn't gone through rigorous testing."

"But you think they did update the code in implanted hardware?"

"I've been examining the hardware for the last few days and found a method to make the memory writable. None of the equipment we have could do it, but something must exist. System updates after installation. Security patches, though obviously that didn't work out so well."

Jared considered that. "The old Fleet personnel were captured and their implants were reprogrammed. That makes it possible. Hopefully we can find the equipment in question. I hope we find Kelsey before anything happens, but we can't count on that.

"Doctor, Mister Owlet, I want you both to be ready to assist Doctor Stone when we recover the princess. Start thinking about how we update the programming, because we may have to try."

26

Reality slowly intruded on Kelsey's oblivion. The first thing she recognized was cold metal pressed against her cheek. Painfully cold. It actually felt good compared to the throbbing in her head. She'd had bad headaches before, but this one threatened to crush her brain. Every pulse of her heart sent fresh agony through her skull.

She started to move but stopped when she heard grunting. That didn't sound like one of the marines. She doubted the Royal Fleet officers communicated that way, either. That only left the Pale Ones.

That meant she was in very, very deep trouble.

Kelsey cracked an eyelid and tried not to moan when a shaft of intense brightness burned her retina. Okay, the light only seemed bright because of her headache, but the pain made her eyes water.

Clarity came after a minute of focusing. A man's arm lay in front of her face. The color of the uniform told her it was one of her marines, and he wasn't moving.

Definitely not good.

She looked over him and saw two men facing one another. Pale Ones, presumably. Both wore what amounted to filthy loincloths. Why they weren't just naked she had no idea. Hideous scars covered their bodies. Red, puckered lines trailed down each of their limbs. Even their fingers had horrible scarring.

Both had long, matted hair that hung below their waists. If either of them saw a comb, she'd be willing to bet he tried to eat it. They were as filthy as their clothes. She could smell their stench from across the room.

They faced one another and communicated by snarls and grunts. At least she assumed they were communicating. Or they might be posturing for dominance. Maybe both.

The marine's arm moved, and he groaned. He rolled over and sat up. That got the attention of the Pale Ones. They both snarled in his direction.

The marine, Corporal Brand, climbed unsteadily to his feet. He reached for his weapon, but his holster was empty. He swore and staggered toward the Pale Ones, obviously intending to take them hand to hand.

That worked out surprisingly poorly for him. The nearly naked men fell into what looked like martial arts stances. One grabbed the marine's fist as he swung it and twisted him around, while the other kicked low and swept the marine off his feet. The one holding Brand's fist kicked him hard in the gut.

The corporal tried to fight, but they simply tossed him back onto the deck beside Kelsey, where he lay moaning.

"Brand? Are you okay?" She sat up but didn't climb to her feet. The two Pale Ones watched her, growling, but didn't attack.

The corporal clutched his stomach. "That guy kicks like an avalanche. They barely look like they can stand. How can they fight like that?"

"Was that some kind of martial art?"

"It sure looked like it, but that makes no sense."

They waited, and the rest of the marines slowly regained consciousness. The Pale Ones had taken their weapons, both pistols and knives. She had no idea how a savage knew what a gun was.

The two Royal Fleet officers sat against the wall, terror clearly etched on their faces. Talbot eyed the Pale Ones for a minute. "We can take them together."

Kelsey had been examining the room. It was obviously a ship's compartment, but there were no furnishings. It was easily as big as the briefing room on *Athena*. They could pile dozens of people in here without too much crowding. The only exit was a single hatch behind the two savages.

One of the Pale Ones howled and beat his chest. That was definitely a challenge.

The hatch opened, and a short woman stepped inside. She was also a Pale One based on her personal hygiene. She wore a loincloth similar to the males'. She wore no top, and it was evident she never had. She looked a decade older than the two males.

The woman shoved the man who'd howled, sending him staggering to the side. He postured at her but didn't counterattack.

The marines rose as a unit and charged the three Pale Ones. Sergeant Talbot actually laid a solid hit on the woman's head.

It barely fazed her. She grinned and caught his second punch in her hand, stopping him dead in his tracks. Kelsey couldn't see what she did, but it was fast. Talbot went flying over the woman's shoulder and into the bulkhead. The bone-jarring impact made her wince.

The rest of the scene looked like a badly done fight vid. In less than twenty seconds, all the marines were on the deck, which only made them easier to kick.

She thought the Pale Ones would kill them and leapt to her feet, screaming, "Leave them alone!"

That stopped the fight, but only so the woman could come over and backhand her. It felt as if someone had hit her with a sledgehammer. Kelsey flew off her feet and skidded on the deck. She didn't try to get up and instead lay there. Moaning was all she could manage.

The woman snarled at her but didn't strike Kelsey again. She stalked back over to the men and tossed the marines back beside Kelsey. All of them were conscious, but Talbot looked like he might have a concussion.

"Well, that could've gone better," he mumbled. "Don't tell anyone that a mostly naked woman kicked my ass."

Kelsey suspected she wasn't going to have the opportunity to tell anyone anything, though she was praying for it. "How can they do that?"

The man shrugged. "It can't be training. It has to be in the implants. It would make sense to have basic combat skills programmed in. I can see the pattern in their fighting. If I had a weapon, I might be able to take one."

"But we don't. How are we going to escape?"

"I don't know. Maybe we're still in Pentagaran space and we'll be rescued."

She looked at her chrono. "I don't think so. We were out almost four hours. Whatever that weapon was, it really took us down. At least my headache is getting better."

They waited a few more minutes and then attacked again. The results were just as one-sided as before. The Pale Ones seemed incredibly tough. Kelsey noted how their reactions seemed so much faster than the marines'.

The pattern of their fighting was plain once she knew to look for it. They only had a few basic moves and seemed to use them by rote. In this case, that was all they needed to do. The woman could've been absent and the two men would've still beaten them all senseless.

Kelsey rose to her feet as soon as the marines engaged the next time and sprinted around the fight toward the hatch. She ducked on general principle, and the punch that one of them threw at her barely brushed the top of her skull.

She ran through the open hatch and found herself in a control room. Two Pale Ones sat at the controls, and their hands moved with robotic smoothness. They didn't react to her presence at all. She fleetingly wondered why they didn't use the Old Empire headsets.

The screen beyond them showed a large space station at extremely close range. A wide hatch opened in front of the ship. Going through it was probably going to be even worse for them. She searched around frantically and saw the marines' pistols tossed onto the deck. She grabbed one, spun, and shot the female Pale One as she leapt through the hatch.

Kelsey shot the woman twice more before she landed on her like a runaway grav car. She tore the weapon from Kelsey's hand with no effort at all. The she-beast nearly beat her unconscious before one of the men dragged Kelsey back into the room by her hair and tossed her on top of the marines.

She watched through the hatch as the woman she'd shot stood and moved around as though she hadn't been shot. At least for a minute. She didn't even try to staunch the flow of blood from her wounds.

Then she staggered a little and fell to her knees. The men watched her eyes glaze over and didn't seem bothered as she collapsed. One of them even kicked her while she bled to death.

Kelsey knew she should feel something. She'd just killed someone. All she felt was physical pain, despair, and anger. They were going to become monsters like those.

The ship bounced like it had hit something. Then the engine noise faded. They were inside the station. The whoosh of a hatch opening filled her with dread.

Half a dozen male and female Pale Ones swarmed in and grabbed them. Talbot tried to struggle, but they kicked him until he stopped. They were clearly satisfied to drag him out of the ship by his legs.

He looked back at her as they took him down an exit ramp. "Good job, Princess. At least you got one. See you on the other side."

The hulking mob dragged them into the bay she'd seen opening. It looked big enough to hold dozens of ships. Instead, it held three that she could see: theirs and two shot-up wrecks. They looked like they'd been sitting there for years.

The Pale Ones took them to a lift attached to the landing bay. A large hatch sat next to it. Dust and debris covered the lift floor. Everything stank. The Royal officers whimpered, three of the marines appeared unconscious, and Talbot seemed to be praying.

Not a bad idea.

She whispered one for them all. Not for their lives but that they would die quickly. Whatever came after death would be better than this.

The lift creaked up several decks, and the doors wheezed open. The creatures then pulled them quite a distance and made their way down a number of side corridors. She saw a skeleton in the dust. It wore the scraps of some kind of uniform. The color led her to believe it was a Royal Fleet tunic. The filthy marks on the floor showed where they'd dragged others. Many others.

Kelsey wondered how many of them had seen the dead Royal and wished they could die, too. Perhaps she should've used that pistol on herself.

The corridor continued into the distance, but the tracks through the muck made it obvious that all the prisoners went into one room. Her captor took them into what looked like a medical center. A bed on rollers sat just short of a machine shaped to fit all around it.

The Pale Ones tossed all of the prisoners into what had probably once been an office. The marines talked about rushing their captors, but it would be suicidal. There were just too many of them. So they watched as another Pale One deposited their equipment into a large bin.

Kelsey expected the foul creatures to do something quickly, but the Pale Ones seemed content to watch them for the next four hours. Only when a new Pale One entered the compartment did most of the rest leave. The new one looked like the pilots on the ship. An automaton. He stood beside one of the machines and waited.

Two of the Pale Ones came into the room. One tossed the marines aside while the other grabbed her. He dragged her out and threw her on the bed. Two others held her down while he strapped her in. They cinched the straps brutally tight.

She wanted to scream, but she bit her lip. She didn't know why. Maybe she wanted to meet her end with all the courage she could muster. That was one thing they could never take from her.

The Pale Ones pushed the bed into the machine. Darkness shrouded her, and then a low light came on.

"Do not be alarmed," a soft male voice said with an accent she couldn't place. "This scanning process will not hurt."

She swallowed. "Who are you? What are you doing?"

"This unit is Diagnostic Scanning Workstation Twelve. This unit will scan your brain prior to the implanting process and make the final adjustment to the implant hardware before it is installed."

"You're a Terran Empire machine? You know that the Fleet is long dead and that you're making these devices to implant in people against their will, don't you? I do not consent to this process. Stop this at once!"

The voice took on a tinge of regret. "This unit is unable to comply. Its programming has been modified to remove the consent protocol. This unit regrets the inconvenience."

She laughed in spite of the horror. It regretted the inconvenience. "Who updated your programming?"

"That data is not in this unit's memory. Please remain still for the scanning process."

Little flashes of heat zipped up and down her nerves. It felt like something was crawling in her brain. The sensation lasted a few seconds and then ceased.

"Scan complete. Data sent to the surgical unit. Thank you for your patience."

A tone sounded, and the Pale Ones roughly pulled the bed from the scanning machine. Two Pale Ones unstrapped her while two more held Talbot.

The Pale Ones ripped her clothes from her body and pulled her to a second machine. It looked more like a portable water tank with attached machinery. They threw her in and slammed the lid shut. Her heart raced as she lay there. What happened now?

Unseen clamps snapped around her limbs, and blinding pain ate at her head. She screamed, but it only got worse as the machine cut her open.

27

---

axter eventually got tired of Jared looking over his shoulder at about the three-hour mark and tossed him out of engineering. He told Jared that having the captain breathing down their necks was slowing his people down.

Jared took the hint and left to meet with the Pentagaran marine detachment leader in the conference room instead. He turned out to be a familiar face. Lieutenant John Fredrick.

Lieutenant Reese and he seemed to be getting along well. With his four missing men, that meant *Athena*'s detachment was down to twenty-six effectives, plus their commander. Commander Graves and Doctor Stone joined them a few minutes later. Jared gestured for them to sit at the table.

He brought the screen to life. "The drives will be ready shortly. Is everyone ready to depart at a moment's notice?"

They all nodded.

The young Royal officer put his hand on the table. "I've finished getting our men settled. We have a hundred Royal Marines fully outfitted in combat gear. Lieutenant Reese has seen that our communications gear will interface with yours. We also salvaged two tactical fission missiles from one of the wrecked fortresses. I have four technicians who will rig them to explode. One is sufficient to destroy that station from the inside. We need to use the other to deal with the shipyard. We may not get another chance.

"The other shipyard will be inaccessible from our orbit. Particularly once we stir up the hornet's nest. We'll have to deal with it another time."

Jared nodded. "Excellent. Our missiles simply don't have that kind of power. We're not a capital ship. We'll hit the shipyard at the same time we assault the orbital station. Reese, what's your plan for inserting our forces?"

The Imperial Marine tapped his console. The screen changed to a tactical display of the station's orbital space. "The pinnaces have stealth systems and are coated with material that absorbs some scanner radiation. We'll go in on a ballistic trajectory. If we set our initial course to miss the planet, they might dismiss us as space junk. I don't know what kind of scanners they have, but I'm hopeful that they won't recognize the danger until we begin our attack runs. By then it will be too late to stop us."

Graves considered the marked courses on the tactical display. "We need a distraction for the initial penetration. Rather than splitting our forces to attack both targets, we should rig one of the weapons to an external weapons rack and launch it on a ballistic course for the busy shipyard. The device should be small enough to get close before they react. A fission reaction at close range might not destroy it, but it should cause significant damage. The commotion should make a fabulous distraction for *Athena* to make its run in to retrieve the princess."

Jared liked that plan, but it had its drawbacks. "That will severely restrict how much time we have to find Princess Kelsey and our missing men."

Graves shrugged. "Once the attack starts, they won't have much time anyway. The probe we have on the station logged the hatch they used."

Jared grimaced. "Doctor Stone, what is your plan once we find her?"

The petite doctor grimaced. "It isn't very elaborate. We grab her and whatever equipment that's around her. I've engineered some restraints that will probably hold her. I only hope to God she isn't in the middle of some procedure, or we might as well shoot her ourselves. I have some volunteer medical techs and a team from engineering to take what we can. The pinnaces have the capability to load equipment, though it might mean everyone is piled like logs on the way out."

"Doctor Stone is right," Graves said. "This is a smash and grab. We hit them and grab anyone we can manage. Then we run like hell."

Jared looked at Reese. "That means you'll need atmosphere after we breach the station. How will you manage that?"

"The data from the probe indicates they entered a large bay. We have special charges to breach the hatch. The second pinnace will seal it as soon as we're all in. We'll use marine boarding locks inside to breach the corridors without venting the atmosphere. When we're ready to leave, we have compressed air in special tanks on the pinnace that's not carrying the fission weapon to fill the bay. We can get enough pressure to allow us to get the rescued personnel back through the bay. Then we blow the patch and get the hell out of there."

"What kind of timetable are you looking at?"

"That depends on the situation inside. If there's a lot of resistance, we take longer. I'm hopeful they won't see us coming. These Pale Ones don't seem too big on tactics, so I'd imagine there'll be a lot of running and screaming while they try to kill us individually. Massed weapons fire should allow us to make good progress. I want to be out of there in half an hour if we can."

Graves tapped his console. "That's where *Athena* comes in. When we get the signal that the teams are withdrawing, we come in like a meteor. We'll clear a path for the pinnace to withdraw and take them aboard as quickly as possible. Then we run like hell for the flip point. Based on their speed, it'll be close. We're faster, but they'll have a chance to close in as we pick our people up."

"That's where the Royal Fleet comes in," Fredrick said. "We are moving all available ships to the interdiction zone. We will destroy any ships that come through behind you. With luck, we will blunt the planned invasion forces enough to stop them now."

Jared shook his head ruefully. "Admiral Yeats would have my behind for breakfast if he saw how fast and loose this operation is coming together. If something goes wrong, we're totally screwed. Lieutenant Fredrick, I've sent word via probe to the scientists on *Best Deal*. They'll make certain that you have everything needed to construct flip drives if we don't make it back. I did that because if it looks like we can't escape, we're taking out both of those shipyards.

"We don't really have a choice. If that invasion comes through, we all die. We'll do whatever we must to save this system and the billions of people who call it home now. Whether the rescue attempt succeeds or fails, we stop these bastards today. Questions?"

The men shook their heads.

"To your stations. Charlie, a moment please."

Jared waited for the others to leave before he spoke. "You'll be in command of *Athena* during this fight. I'm going with the marines."

Graves looked mulish. "Sir, you're a Fleet officer. You belong on the bridge of your ship."

"Charlie, let's be honest. The odds of any of us making it home are so slim that no one would ever bet on us. My oath to the emperor means I bring Princess Kelsey back or die trying. I can't leave her there. She's my sister, for God's sake."

His executive officer didn't look happy, but he nodded. "Best of luck, Jared. Bring her back to us."

Jared let his friend leave and pinched the bridge of his nose between his fingers. It tore at him to abandon his command at a time like this, but it felt like the right move. He took one last calming breath and headed for marine country.

Reese spotted him as soon as he arrived and came over. "Captain."

"I'm going with you. I'll need some armor and weapons. You'll retain tactical command, but I have overall strategic authority."

The marine didn't argue. "We keep several sets of spare armor for emergencies." He called over two other marines, and they efficiently stripped him to his undergarments and strapped him into the armor. It would act as a vacuum suit with superior protection against projectiles. The communicator was more complex than what he normally used, but he quickly figured it out.

The weapons they strapped onto him were a different issue. He knew how to shoot pistols. That was required Fleet training, even if they seldom used it. They took him to the range to run through a few magazines of ammunition with the combat rifle, presumably so that he didn't accidentally shoot one of them.

They loaded him down with ammunition and grenades and then told him he was not to use any of the latter. Apparently, he was carrying extras for the rest of them.

The call to flip came just after they finished getting him ready. It felt odd to hear Charlie's voice in the overheads announcing the transition. It was probably the last one he'd make.

He boarded *Marine One* once everyone was ready and sat beside Reese. His communicator had access to the command channels, so he listened to the countdown. The disorientation came and went. Then they waited for the engineering crew to mount the fission warhead to their pinnace.

Athena accelerated into the system but kept her speed below the detection threshold. They'd go into free-fall once they got too close to chance detection. The pinnaces would detach at that point and increase their velocity even more. Due to their smaller-sized drives, they could build more speed than a full-sized ship. Even so, it would be hours before they reached the planet. So many bad things could happen in that time.

"*Marine One* and *Marine Two*, this is *Athena*," Zia said on the command channel. "Going ballistic. You are free to disengage. Godspeed."

The pinnace broke free with a clank, and intense acceleration pressed Jared back into the padding. They boosted for half an hour and then shut down their drives.

The waiting was much harder than he'd expected. The marines shared rations and traded jokes and insults. The Royal Marines seemed to fit right in. If things worked out, he expected the Kingdom and the Empire would become excellent allies.

He expected the station to launch ships and weapons when they got close, but it didn't. When the mission timer fell to just a few minutes, he had to bite his lip to keep from giving the go order.

When the counter dropped to zero, Jared keyed his communicator. "All units go. Go! Go! Go!"

The pinnace accelerated savagely. Much more power than had been used earlier. So much that it took his breath away. His pinnace turned toward the active shipyard, which was still on the other side of the planetary curve. *Marine Two* dove for the orbital.

The dot representing the fission warhead broke free, and his pinnace turned abruptly to chase after *Marine Two*.

Jared split his attention between the warhead and *Marine Two*. The shipyard would meet the weapon about the same time the other pinnace breached the orbital. If the Pale Ones' station had any defenses, they'd acted before the weapons could come online.

Marine Two fired something that looked like a big net. It spread all across the hatch and exploded inward. Shaped charges. The hatch disintegrated, and *Marine Two* screamed inside as the air and debris came shooting out.

His pinnace followed just a few seconds later. It clamped to the deck and waited for the compartment to depressurize fully. Then both pinnaces started disgorging marines.

Jared waited for a moment and saw the fission warhead expand on his tactical display. The data said it had detected a missile launch and detonated. While too far away to destroy the shipyard completely, it would undoubtedly cause tremendous damage. They'd met one mission objective. There would be no massive invasion before Pentagar was ready.

He followed Reese out the hatch. The marine officer snapped out orders. "Find a main hatch into the station. Avoid lifts. Shoot anything that moves. Except the prisoners, of course."

"Team Five has a lift and what looks like a corridor hatch beside it. There are signs that something was dragged through here recently."

"Set the boarding lock and go in, Team Five."

The marines pointed their weapons in every direction while they waited. The medical and engineering teams joined him. They weren't wearing armored suits, but they were armed. Even the doctor. Stone knelt beside him. "The clock is ticking. Will we have pressure?"

"They'll patch the ruined hatch once we're gone but leave enough space so the chamber can't be pressurized. That should keep the enemy from rushing them. The pinnaces' guns will deal with any intrusions. Once we're on the way back, they'll pressurize the landing bay. Hopefully, we'll be gone before the Pale Ones get inside here in force."

He didn't hear the breaching charges the marines used to open the hatch, but he felt the deck shake a little. The first team of marines entered the boarding lock and reported the other side clear. The marine strike teams cycled through quickly. They found the emergency stairs before Jared came through with the support teams.

"Team Five has Princess Kelsey's communicator on scanner," one of the marines said. "She's somewhere ahead of and above us."

"Up," Reese ordered.

Some of the marines poured into the stairwell while the rest set up a defensive perimeter. They'd hold the landing bay while the strike teams found the prisoners.

He followed Reese and tried Kelsey's communicator just as someone started shooting upstairs. An unknown voice came on the tactical net. "Enemy contact. Engaging."

The fight was on.

28

K elsey awoke to indescribable agony. It felt as though they'd filleted her like a fish. Lines of horrible pain seemed to cover her entire body. Her headache from earlier was a fond memory.

The tank slid open, and the Pale Ones pulled her out. They dragged her toward the third piece of equipment in the room. Unlike the previous two, it looked like someone had assembled it from other equipment with no thought about how it looked.

Her eyes wouldn't focus right. Things went from blurry to unnaturally sharp, but not simultaneously in each eye. She tried to resist the Pale Ones holding her, but her arms wouldn't move right either. She had no coordination at all.

Her captors stiffened when a distant thump shook the deck.

They dropped her and ran for the door. The fall bloodied her nose, and she flopped around as she tried to sit up. The prisoners took advantage of the distraction to attack. It took all of them to pin one of the Pale Ones.

Talbot struggled with the other one. The beast grunted and dragged the marine to the tank that had just gutted Kelsey. Having only one captor gave the marine some advantage though. He planted his feet against the tank and shoved.

The tank moved away from them, knocking over some kind of bin behind it. The Pale One staggered backward and tripped over Kelsey. She forced her hand to reach out and grabbed the bastard's throat. Something crunched under her hand, and the thing turned his attention to her.

He smashed his fist across her face. It hurt, but not nearly as much as what they'd already done to her. In fact, an intense wave of something passed through her. It took her a moment to realize the pain had faded to almost nothing. The world seemed to slow a little, and sound echoed in her head oddly. She wondered if she was about to pass out.

Surprisingly, the Pale One failed to tear free of her grip. Her hand seemed to have locked in the closed position like a vise. He struggled to breathe but finally collapsed on top of her.

Talbot staggered to his feet and came to her side. A cut over his eye bled freely, and he looked almost dazed. "We need to be gone before they come back. Can you walk?"

"I can't even make my fingers open." In fact, they'd dug deeply into the Pale One's throat. His blood ran down her arm. The iron tang of it in the air made her nauseous.

Talbot tried to pry her fingers open and failed. "Damn. That's some grip. Let me find something."

He staggered to his feet and ran to the bin with their equipment. He grabbed a pistol and shot the pinned Pale One in the head. Three times.

One of the marines took the pistol and ducked his head out the hatch. "Clear. I think I hear weapons fire. Could it be a rescue?"

Talbot dug into the bin and found a knife. The rest of the men began arming themselves as he began cutting Kelsey free. It only took a few grisly seconds for him to open the thing's neck. With all the slick blood, he managed to tear her free. This day was just going to be full of horrible memories. If they lived.

The chime of an incoming communication request sounded from the bin. Talbot sprinted back and found the communicator. "Talbot here."

"Thank God," she heard Jared say. "We're on our way up. What is your status?"

The marine looked at her. "The princess is alive, but they've implanted her. She doesn't seem to be under their control. Should we come to you?"

"We're meeting resistance, but expect us in a few minutes. If you feel secure, stay there. Doctor Stone said she needed whatever equipment they used. Can any of it be taken down stairs?"

"There are three units. Two look like they're possibly Old Empire machines. One isn't. They all look semiportable. I think enough people can carry them. At least they'll fit through the hatches I've seen."

"Hold your position. Mertz out."

Two marines kept watch while Talbot knelt by her side. She smiled up at him. "Next time I suggest something idiotic, you have my permission to lock me up."

"I'll hold you to that."

One of the marines raised his pistol and fired. "Incoming hostiles."

The marines took turns shooting at the trickle of Pale Ones coming their way. It didn't seem like an attack. Not an organized one anyway. Maybe these were headed for the other, progressively louder fight.

Gunfire and explosions came closer until the marines pulled back from the door. Talbot moved her toward the back of the compartment. "Cavalry's here."

Automatic weapons fire sent a storm of bullets down the hall, and she saw men in body armor moving past while firing. It seemed like dozens of them. More than the total marine complement on *Athena*.

Jared and Doctor Stone ducked into the room with some noncombatants. Stone rushed to Kelsey's side as Jared started directing the removal of the equipment.

"Hey, Princess," Stone said. "How are you feeling?"

"Like someone cut me open."

The diminutive physician took out a portable scanner and ran it up her body. "Without looking closely, it seems like they installed a set of marine enhancements. Are you in control, or is someone else?"

"Me, I think. They didn't get me in the third machine."

"Then it probably overrides the default programming. You might just be the luckiest person I know. The brains weren't looking forward to trying to change your programming."

Jared turned to them. "The Pale Ones are massing so we're leaving. Take her to the pinnaces while we bring the equipment. Kelsey, it's good to see you again."

"Thank you for coming for us." She'd never meant anything so strongly.

"Thank me once we make it out of here. Everyone move."

Talbot threw her over his shoulder and quickly took off down the corridor. Undignified but necessary. All Kelsey could see was Doctor Stone running behind them, but she could hear others cursing as they moved the bulky equipment.

The trip back to the landing bay was a confusing blur. Her head bounced all over the place, and her eyes kept losing focus. They passed another marine force shooting at Pale Ones down another corridor. This marine unit wasn't shy about using grenades to keep them back, either. Her head rang as the fireballs exploded, and then the noise grew curiously soft.

They ran through an open lock and into the same landing bay where the Pale Ones had arrived. The two marine pinnaces had never looked so welcoming. A group of men off to the side was working on an unfamiliar piece of equipment.

The medical team rushed Talbot into one of the pinnaces and directed him to strap her to a mobile med unit. He laid her down but didn't strap her in. "No straps. Never again."

"God no," she agreed.

"Trust me," Stone said. "You'll want to be strapped down for takeoff." She threw a sheet over Kelsey's body and ran two straps across her torso but left the princess's hands free.

The grunting men carried the equipment in one piece at a time and strapped it down. Part of her mind noted they hadn't brought the bin Talbot had knocked over.

Then the marines started pouring in. Jared threw himself into the seat beside Stone. "Button us up and prepare for emergency takeoff. They seem to have figured out we're in the bay."

Reese's voice came out of Stone's helmet, which she'd set in her seat while she worked. "The breaching lock is closed and *Marine Two* is loading. We blow the emergency seal in thirty seconds. *Marine One* exits first. We've locked the fission weapon to the deck and set it for remote detonation and timer. It goes off in sixty seconds whether we're gone or not."

Jared handed Stone her helmet. "That's us in the lead. Get her an oxygen mask in case we lose pressure and strap down."

Stone slid a translucent mask over Kelsey's nose and mouth. The doctor then stuffed her helmet on and strapped down. The pinnace lifted and accelerated so quickly that Kelsey was sure the bed would flip over.

The captain grabbed it just to make sure. "Good work, people," he said through an external speaker. Or more likely, he'd turned the speaker on so those without communications could hear. "Phase one of the operation is complete. Let's blow these bastards to hell and go home."

Time dragged for an eternity. "The orbital is targeting us. Weapon detonation in two... one... Holy God. Hang on!" The pinnace rocked so heavily that Kelsey thought it might tumble. Loud cheering sounded over the loop.

The captain let them have a moment before he cut them off. "Okay, men, it looks like we pissed them off. We have a lot of ships buzzing around the shipyard we just attacked, so keep your eyes open. We'll rendezvous with *Athena* before they catch up with us, but I don't know if we'll make it to the flip point unmolested. Get unloaded as fast as you can."

"Don't let them get too close," Kelsey said. "They have some kind of knockout beam."

"Only some of their ships have those," the Royal pilot said. "Most have missiles. They never send many ships to capture prisoners. Those are smaller. Take those out first."

Jared gave him a thumbs-up. "We'll do that."

The chaotic trip to *Athena* was full of abrupt course changes. By the time they docked, Kelsey felt like she was going to fall off the bed even with the straps. The docking had absolutely no finesse whatsoever. The hatches opened, and men began streaming back into the ship.

Doctor Stone bulled her way through, pushing the medical unit ahead of her. She rushed Kelsey down the corridor with as much reckless abandon as their flight on the pinnace. The doctor commandeered a lift and took them directly to the medical center.

Full medical teams stood by, ready for anything from fixing a hangnail to apparently cutting Kelsey open again. "Get the regenerator ready," Stone snapped. "If we don't get these incisions healed now, she might have permanent scarring."

"I need to scan her implants first," a kid said. Kelsey eyed the boy in shock. How did a teenager get here?

The medical team prepared some device that looked so much like the tank that it made her nauseous. The boy smiled at her. "I'm Carl Owlet, and I'll be your computer technician today. I'm going to download your implant programming to be sure that nothing untoward is inside it."

"What will you do if there is?"

"Nothing right now, but we might try overwriting it later if we have to. This won't hurt a bit."

The words almost made Kelsey hyperventilate.

He put a headset with lots of cables onto her head. "I'm getting a positive signal, and the code is downloading. Her implants seem to be fully online."

That didn't make her feel very good at all.

The process took several minutes in which Doctor Stone looked ready to toss him and his computer out of the medical center. Carl seemed oblivious.

"Download complete. It's an exact match to the Old Empire marine code. No deviations detected. She is not under any external control."

Stone yanked the headset off and pushed Kelsey into the chamber. "The regenerator is going to knock you out, Kelsey. I should be able to eliminate all of the scarring. The procedure will take five or six hours."

"Can you remove this stuff?"

The doctor's voice took on a note of regret. "I'm sorry, but no. That's so far beyond my ability that I'm afraid you might have to live with it. Maybe this new equipment will help to eventually remove it, but I wouldn't hold my breath."

Kelsey closed her eyes and tried not to cry. She was going to be a monster. Those things inside her head doing God only knew what.

"Princess?" It was Talbot's voice.

"Yes?" she whispered.

"No matter what happens, I'm here. We never leave one of our own behind. You'll never be alone dealing with this."

"Says the guy who didn't get cut open." She took a deep breath. "I'm sorry. That wasn't right. I brought this on myself."

"It was just bad luck, Princess. No one could know that damned ship was going to jump us. Sometimes life just takes a big old dump on you. You'll come back from this."

"Thank you. Thank you for saving me."

He laughed. "I seem to remember things a little differently. You shot one of them down and strangled the other one pretty much by yourself. It took the rest of us combined to take one out. Maybe you should look into a career in the marines."

"I'm told I'm too short and don't have the killer instinct."

"Whoever told you that was as wrong as a human being can be. I bet with some training, you'll be a real badass. That Pale One took two of us on with whatever the implants had programed in hand-to-hand combat. Think about what you could manage with some real training."

Stone cut him off. "I'm not sure this is the right time for this. Go let them examine you while I work on the princess. Time to start the regenerator. You okay in there, Kelsey?"

"Yes," she lied. She knew that she'd never be okay again. The regenerator plunged her into darkness.

29

J ared raced to the bridge, not bothering to strip off his battle armor… or full complement of grenades. Graves gave up the command console.

"Status?" Jared snapped.

"Three dozen ships came out of the shipyard and are on our ass," Graves said. "Several can cut us off before we can get clear of orbital space."

Jared leaned forward. "Zia, those ships may be of two different classes. Are any of them smaller than the rest?"

The tactical officer checked her readouts. "Five of the enemy ships will be in firing range before we can fully change course. One is somewhat smaller than the rest."

"Target that ship for the first salvo. It may have a weapon capable of knocking us out. I want you to turn it into expanding gas as soon as possible."

"Aye, sir. Firing now."

"Acknowledged." He turned to Graves. "Get to engineering. I want them ready for anything. If we have a systems failure, we're dead. Worse than dead. So that will not happen. Make sure Baxter has a plan to destroy this ship if I give the word."

The executive officer's face paled. "Understood." He ran to the lift.

"Zia, if we lose drives, keep shooting up the small ships as long as you can."

Her opening salvo proved to be overkill. The explosions blotted the ship from the heavens. Its companions opened fire with a pair of missiles each. They were larger and slower than those used by Fleet, but that hardly mattered at this fistfight range. All four enemy ships exploded after two salvos, but *Athena* took some hits. Thankfully, none to engineering.

That wasn't to say they were insignificant. A dozen compartments were open to space. Thankfully, with the Royal Marines on board, they had plenty of emergency responders.

Thirty enemy ships fell in behind them and continued firing. *Athena*'s electronic warfare suite was good enough to send many after false targets. The antimissile railguns mounted aft proved successful at stopping the rest, though a few were close enough to raise his hair.

Their own missiles wouldn't bear on the pursuit force, so they ran for their lives without shooting back. He pushed the engines harder than Baxter preferred, but he needed to open the range. One didn't transit a flip point at high speed, so they'd need to brake hard before they transitioned.

The range slowly opened to the point that the Pale Ones stopped firing. If *Athena* could hold this speed for a few hours, they'd come screaming into the Pentagar system with a few minutes warning that the second invasion was on.

Well, he didn't have to surprise the Royal Fleet. "Zia, record a message for the probe on station at the flip point. Have it send the agreed-upon signal when it transitions and then send the message."

"Aye, sir. Recording on."

Jared looked at the screen. "Commodore Sanders, we've recovered the prisoners and are less than two hours away from the flip point. We have thirty Pale Ones behind us, and I'm certain they're coming through after us. They didn't appreciate those fission weapons you gave us crippling their shipyard and destroying the orbital. We'd appreciate it if you could have a welcoming committee on hand for them. *Athena* out. Zia, append our scanner readings and send it."

The next two hours wracked everyone's nerves. It felt like he waited an hour, but when he checked the chrono, only a few minutes had passed. The damage reports came in. Another dozen of his crew dead and many more wounded.

Just when he started breathing a little easier, the enemy did something unexpected. They had ten minutes to go until flip, and the Pale Ones abruptly added twenty percent to their acceleration. One exploded outright and disabled another. Two more fell out of formation with drive failures. Twenty-six sped after them, closing range at a frightening rate.

"Zia, will we make it?"

She shook her head. "They'll be in firing range again with a minute to spare when we decelerate before the flip. They'll be all over us."

He opened a channel to engineering. "Baxter, they just boosted their acceleration. They're going to catch us. How much juice can you give me?"

"We might burn out the grav drives and kill everyone aboard."

"Or they might catch us and we'd only wish the drives had exploded."

"That's a point. I'll give you what I can. Engineering out."

Athena's speed edged up, but not nearly as much as that of their pursuers. Their precious lead eroded with each passing moment. Zia turned and shook her head. "They'll be in firing range before we can flip."

"Then we'd best hope our railguns hold out. Do the best you can to evade. If we transition, we might make it."

Another enemy drive failed before they moved into firing range, but that still meant a lot of missiles to deal with. The railguns and electronic countermeasures worked until they were thirty seconds short of the flip point. Even then, the evasive maneuvers kept the one missile that got through from hitting them in engineering. It struck them amidships.

The explosion ripped into the ship at an angle, spreading destruction from the midpoint of the ship forward. The impact staggered the ship and lit his control panel up with lurid damage and systems failure icons. Almost a quarter of the ship was open to space. One of the auxiliary consoles behind him shorted out with a loud "pop," and the stench of burned electronics filled the bridge.

Ramirez somehow kept them on course, and the countdown timer spiraled down toward zero. "Preparing to flip the ship," he said.

When the counter hit two, the ship took a second hit and main power went offline. The dim emergency lights came on, and Jared's heart flew into his throat. They were dead.

Then the ship flipped.

The transition rivaled the weak flip point experience for disorientation. The ship jerked so badly that it felt almost as if they'd struck something.

The screen still had power and showed them tumbling away from the flip point as Pale Ones flooded out behind them. Zia targeted one and opened fire. Only two missile tubes responded.

The Royal Fleet was waiting, thank God. They sat at just the right spot to intercept the intruders, firing their missiles at a high rate of speed. The few fortresses still online added to the destruction with their larger missiles.

The two fleets fought a missile duel at knife range. *Athena* destroyed three Pale Ones' ships in one salvo. She took a third missile hit and lost the remaining two missile tubes. Zia raked one of the Pale Ones with the antimissile railguns. The high-speed flechettes ripped the other ship open like a can of survival rations.

The fight moved past *Athena*'s dead hulk as the two sides mixed and fought. The Pale Ones knocked out some Royal units, but allied forces had the upper hand. Some Pale Ones broke through, but the Royal Fleet quickly chased them down. *Athena* managed to fend off the few missiles fired at her.

"Zia, get that probe back on the other side," Jared said. "I want to have warning if more ships are coming. If a ship approaches the flip point, we need to know about it."

"Aye, sir."

He keyed the channel to engineering. "Damage report."

"We're totally screwed," Baxter said.

Jared could hear some kind of alarm ringing in the background. "That's not helpful. I need more details."

"Both fusion plants fried just before the transition. Safeties shut them down, and it'll take a while to get them back online. Thank God we had the flip capacitors charged, or we'd still be on the other side. I'm not sure how much use the fusion plants will be even if we get them back up and running. The grav and flip drives are offline again. Oh, and our structural integrity is compromised."

"Compromised how?"

"I think we came into the flip point sideways at high speed. The grav drives failed right before transition, and we slewed. The stress forces warped the ship's spine."

"Can that be fixed?"

"No. *Athena* will never boost again."

Jared covered his eyes with his hand. "Understood. Bridge out."

He didn't bother calling the medical center. They'd be swamped.

Zia turned her seat to face him. "I have Commodore Sanders calling."

"Put him on."

The older man appeared on the screen. "Thank the gods you're alive. I'm launching medical teams and damage-control parties to assist you."

"We need them. Thanks. Did you get all the Pale Ones?"

The commodore nodded with satisfaction. "Every last one of them. Hopefully that was enough to blunt the invasion, because our defenses are in very bad shape right now. What's your status?"

"Our drives and power systems have failed. We've taken critical structural damage."

"Do you need to abandon ship? We have cutters standing by."

Jared shook his head. "I don't think so, but I doubt *Athena* will ever leave Pentagar. If you could assist us with evacuating all nonessential personnel, that would be helpful. I'm sorry, but I don't have word on your people's status. Most of us made it back from the raid, but we took some major knocks when we transitioned."

"We'll figure that out as soon as we get you the help you need. Sanders out."

* * *

HARD WORK FILLED the next few hours. A lot of the ship was open to space or in danger of becoming uninhabitable without emergency repairs. The extra hands from the Pentagaran ships helped, but the list of things to do seemed endless.

An exhausted Doctor Stone called him with the final battle tally. Miraculously, only eighty-five people died in battle after the Pale Ones captured the princess and her protection detail: thirty Royal Marines, five Imperial Marines, and fifty-eight Fleet personnel. A heartbreaking number of friends and shipmates were gone.

Graves coordinated damage control from the bridge, finally allowing Jared enough time to check on the princess. Wounded filled the corridor outside the medical center. He stopped and spoke with them as he made his way in. He was amazed to find most appeared to be in good spirits.

Kelsey would probably tell him that he should've let her die or be enslaved. She wouldn't see the trade as worthwhile. Seven people saved in exchange for more than ten times that number killed, twice that injured, and *Athena* wrecked beyond repair.

And she'd be wrong.

Fleet didn't abandon their own. They weren't suicidal, but these Pale Ones weren't the kind of enemy you let take prisoners. If they learned of the Empire, Avalon would've been in grave danger.

This fight was going to happen anyway. An enemy invasion would've overrun Pentagar in a month or two. It was better to strike now and trade dozens of people for the billions that would've perished in the invasion.

Royal personnel in white smocks filled the medical center. At this point, they were setting bones and stitching cuts. Most of his medical personnel were probably dead on their feet.

Stone stood beside a regenerator, examining the readouts. She looked up as he approached. Her eyes were black pits of exhaustion. "Captain."

"Lily. How is she?"

"Asleep. The regenerator can repair the incisions, but I don't dare mess with the physical modifications. I'm certain the implantation procedure should've taken place in stages so the patient could recover. The trauma to her body may cause any number of problems going forward."

He looked through the window. She looked so vulnerable. "How long will she be regenerating?"

"At least three more hours. Then she can come out and I can begin a more detailed assessment. We think the Pale Ones could recover physiologically without intervention, but we don't know how many of them died because of the gross insult to their bodies. Princess Kelsey will most likely recover, but she will have to relearn her gross and fine motor skills. Things like walking. Shaking hands."

Stone turned to face Jared. "She has artificial musculature inserted alongside her real muscles, and her bones are reinforced by material stronger than the hull on this ship. Talbot told me she grabbed a Pale One by the throat and strangled him. I'd really hate to lose all the bones in my hand in a handshake gone awry."

Jared could hardly believe the petite woman in the regeneration chamber could break anything. She didn't look like she could resist a bully on a school playground.

The doctor rubbed her eyes. "She's going to recover physically, eventually, but she's going to need a lot of emotional support. She's been raped in every conceivable way except sexually. She's going to be in a very dark place."

"I'll be here for her. We'll all be here for her. We're family."

The doctor gave him an odd look, but he put it down to her exhaustion. He clapped his hand on her shoulder. "Catch some sleep in your office. Today isn't over. We still have a lot left to do."

30

The white ceiling confused Kelsey when she woke. Her cabin's ceiling was grey. Then the events of the day caught up with her and she almost moaned. She clumsily raised her arm and stared at it. There were no scars.

At least on the outside.

She finally realized this room wasn't on *Athena*. The wide windows displayed a bright blue sky. She was on Pentagar.

"Princess Bandar, it's so good to see you awake."

She turned her head toward the jovial man in the white smock coming into her room. She felt like she should say something, but her mind swirled with too many questions. Saying it was good to be awake seemed too much like a lie.

The man patted her arm. "I'm Doctor Trenton Plant. You're at Capital Hospital on Pentagar. You're doing very well."

The unsaid addition "all things considered" hung in the air between them.

"Tell me what happened. Is everyone else okay?" Her voice sounded so weak.

His expression didn't change, but his eyes radiated sympathy. "I'll let Doctor Stone bring you up to speed. She'd give me one of her patented parental looks if I didn't wait for her. She was sleeping, but I've summoned her."

Doctor Lily Stone walked through the door just in time to hear that. The only sign she'd slept was her mussed hair. "Nonsense. I'd just tap my foot. Kelsey, you're looking better. All things considered."

Kelsey's chuckle earned her some curious looks. "Sorry. I was just thinking that."

Stone shook her head. "You're going to recover. You've already made quite a bit of progress."

"I've been asleep."

"And you've healed. The regeneration was completely successful. There isn't any remaining scar tissue."

"The scars seem like the least of my worries. Tell me what happened."

Stone gave Doctor Plant a glance, and the man graciously headed for the door. "I'll check on a few other patients and give the two of you time to catch up."

Once he was gone, Stone pulled up a chair and sat. "Some doctors might sugarcoat things, but I believe in putting everything on the table. *Athena* suffered a lot of damage during the escape. We obviously made it back here, but it's not livable. The Kingdom has all of our wounded here in this hospital, and they're providing some excellent care."

A chill passed down Kelsey's spine. "How bad is it? Please tell me no one died."

The haunted flicker across Stone's face told the princess all she needed to know. "How many?"

"Eighty-five."

Kelsey closed her eyes and felt the tears start. "God. You should've left me there."

"Listen to me," Stone said firmly. "The Pale Ones were preparing to invade again within weeks. We used a fission weapon to damage the shipyard and another one to destroy the station they took you to. If we hadn't fought them now, we would've been fighting much more serious odds shortly. Those people would've almost certainly died right along with all the rest of the people in this system. Billions of innocent people. We couldn't allow that to happen."

"That doesn't help so much. Jared wouldn't have come after us if I hadn't been there. He'd have figured out another plan. One that didn't mean rushing in. And he did it for a lie. I'm not even his half sister."

"Blood doesn't make relationships," Lily said softly. "Look, I can't stop you from tearing yourself up over this, but I wish you'd give us all some credit. We came because it was the right thing to do. We all knew that it might result in our deaths. Don't make their sacrifice be for nothing."

Kelsey tried to wipe her tears, but her hands were so clumsy. She was lucky she didn't put her eye out. Stone found a tissue and wiped Kelsey's eyes as the terrible sobs wracked her body.

When she finally cried herself out, Kelsey felt completely spent. This had all happened because of her. It was her fault. She'd insisted they come out and wait for Jared. Her petty anger had killed so many people.

She looked over at Stone. "How long before we can go back to *Athena*?"

"I'm afraid that isn't going to happen. The ship is a complete loss. She'll never fly again."

It took a few moments for the doctor's words to sink in. The sheer scope of the disaster took her breath away. Her throat swelled closed. She'd doomed them. They'd never get home.

"Stop," Stone commanded. "A ship is just a machine. The Pentagarans will help us get home. They've already promised everything we need to convert a ship for our use. You need to stop focusing on what happened and look to your own recovery. Are you ready to talk about what they did to you?"

Kelsey swallowed and nodded.

Stone squeezed her arm. "The good news is that the science teams are pretty sure that no control code was put in your head. They don't understand much of what is there, but it seems to be identical to the Old Empire code. You will not become a Pale One."

"I suppose that's the best that can be hoped for. I thought I was going to die when they cut me open. Then I wished I had."

"Yet here you are. As near as I can tell, your physical modifications are the same as the Old Empire's marines. You're going to have a lot of rehabilitation in your near future."

"I know. I feel like I'm so clumsy. I don't think I could walk if I had to. My eyes still aren't focusing right, though it's a lot better than it was."

"We'll deal with all that in time."

Kelsey sighed. "I suppose I'm lucky. At least I get this second chance. Did Talbot make it?"

Stone nodded. "He did. He'd still be sitting in the chair over there if I hadn't made him get something to eat. I'm sure he'll be back as soon as he hears you're awake."

A rap at the door made Kelsey turn her head. Jared stood in the door smiling at her. "Look who's awake."

Stone stood. "We'll talk later, Kelsey. Just rest for now." She nodded to Jared and walked out.

He took the seat the doctor had just vacated. "You look a lot better than the last time I saw you."

"You should've seen the other guy. Jared, I'm so sorry. I really, really screwed up."

He shook his head. "You had no reason to think something like this would happen. I've given this a lot of thought, and the order of things might have changed if you hadn't come out to the flip point, but the results would've been the same or worse. You know they crippled the ship, right?"

Kelsey nodded. "Doctor Stone told me. What will we do?"

"Make do. Commodore Sanders assures me that the Pentagarans will be starting new ship construction that includes flip drives before the month is out. They'll name one of those ships *Athena* and task her to take us home.

"They believe that our intervention—especially the trip to rescue you—saved their planet. Now, instead of an overwhelming invasion in a few months, they'll likely be able to knock out the shipyards before the Pale Ones get back on a war footing. I'm inclined to agree, though the public adulation freaks me out a little."

"I'm pretty sure that adulation won't be the first thing that comes to mind when they see me."

He shook his head and smiled a little. "You couldn't tell that from the number of people who've tried to come see you. I think every single man and woman from *Athena* has come by at one time or another. There's been so many flowers delivered that I hear they had to stop putting them in the chapels. There wasn't room for them and people. I know that many Pentagarans have sent their own well wishes. You'll be reading get-well and thank-you notes until the end of time."

The idea that people she didn't even know were writing her made her head spin. "Why would they do that? They don't even know me."

"You've captured their hearts and imaginations. You're the mysterious beautiful foreign princess who arrived just in time to save their world."

"Thank you for the compliment, but you saved them. I've been more a hindrance than a help on this trip. My coming was the worst idea ever."

"I disagree. You are the soul of our expedition. We fight for what's right, and you embody that for so many of us. People would and did give their lives for you. Not because you're royalty, but because you're you."

She wanted to scream. "I'm not the person everyone seems to think I am! I'm such a colossal screw-up. I'm a fraud."

"Everyone is a fraud," he said calmly. "People make us out to be things we're not and then we have to work hard not to disappoint them. You can't sit around blaming yourself and feeling sorry. You have to pick yourself up. For them. For all those people who need you. For all the people who gave everything for you."

Her voice was almost a whisper. "I don't know how you do it."

"One day at a time." He rose to his feet. "I have to go meet with the Royal Family. They've also sent their well wishes, and I'm sure they'll come to visit soon. Focus on getting better, Kelsey. We all need you."

He gave her arm one last squeeze and walked out.

She lay there trying to understand what had just happened. Why weren't they blaming her for all the terrible things that had happened? It was obscene how many people had died because of her petulant anger. Her entitled arrogance.

She wasn't blind to the fact that Jared had just masterfully manipulated her. Even so, she couldn't discount his words. She had to change. She wouldn't let all those people down. She'd work hard to recover and then do everything in her power to be who they needed her to be. To be worthy of them.

Not that she had any idea how to do that. She'd work with Jared. They had to be a team if they were going to get home. The future would take care of itself.

Kelsey found the call button and pressed it. She had a lot of work to do.

VEIL OF SHADOWS

BOOK TWO

Princess Kelsey Bandar made a terrible, life-altering mistake. Her enemies gave her unspeakable agony in return.

She must forge the iron will to control the weapon her body has become. If she fails, the monsters who tortured her come for humanity.

And horrors worse than she knows wait in the darkness.

1

Kelsey Bandar, second in line to the Imperial Throne of the Terran Empire, fell with a crash loud enough to turn every head in the physical therapy center. She lay there in the deafening silence, staring at the metal support bar in her hand. She'd ripped it completely out of the floor and *bent* it.

"Really?" The blonde noblewoman snorted bitterly and dropped the mangled bar. It landed with a substantial clang. She rolled onto her back and stared at the white-tiled ceiling.

"That may be a first for me," Doctor Lily Stone, chief medical officer of the Imperial Terran Fleet destroyer *Athena*, said dryly. "Normally, the patient gives out before the equipment. You'll forgive me if I don't offer you a hand up."

"I suppose I can't blame you for wanting to keep your arms attached to your body." Kelsey stretched her back. The cool floor felt good. "How the hell do the Pale Ones learn to walk without someone helping them?"

Those forcibly enhanced savages certainly had no problems walking. Or fighting. Kelsey was glad her friends had rescued her before the monsters turned her into one of them, but something wasn't right with the Old Empire equipment the bastards had put inside her. Even after a week, she still couldn't do simple things without destroying everything around her.

With a few exceptions, the hospital staff gave her a wide berth. Poor physical control and super strength didn't mix. The damage she'd done to the bar proved their caution wise.

The dark-haired doctor's face showed her concern and sympathy. "They learn to walk the hard way, I'd imagine. Move before the others do horrible things to you."

"That would be a powerful motivator," Kelsey admitted. "While I'm glad that isn't one of my many problems, I'm beginning to suspect that last machine you saved me from did something to help them adjust more quickly. In addition to enslaving everyone it operated on, of course."

The doctor glanced at the two Imperial Marines standing nearby. "Gentlemen, if you'd be so kind as to get the princess back into her grav chair."

Kelsey held out her arms, and the two men moved her into the floating chair with no trouble whatsoever. At barely one point five meters, Kelsey wasn't hard to move. Astonishingly, the full-body modification had only brought her up to fifty kilograms, though she wasn't sure she should count it as part of her real weight.

Grav chairs normally had a small control for the patient to direct their own movement, but Lily had removed it after a hand spasm had sent Kelsey into a wall. Technically, Kelsey had removed it herself. Much like she'd uprooted the support bar. Lily promised they'd reinstall the controls once Kelsey's fine motor skills improved. If they *ever* improved.

Since the Pentagarans hadn't managed to miniaturize the requisite grav drives, the supply of grav chairs was limited to what the Terrans had brought with them. Kelsey hoped they could fix the one she'd broken.

Lily used a remote to send Kelsey floating out of the physical therapy center and into the halls of Capital Hospital. The Pentagaran doctors in their bright-white smocks and the nursing staff in a much wider spectrum of colors nodded and smiled politely as they passed. On the other side of the hall.

"I know it seems like this is taking forever, but you're improving at an incredible rate. You couldn't even stand two days ago. Today, you're walking."

"For certain values of walking, I suppose," Kelsey grumbled.

"You fell because you yanked too hard on the support bar. Once you can stay upright, you'll be walking without any problems."

"It sounds so simple when you say it like that. I ripped a metal bar right out of the floor. I laugh at the thought of ever handling eggs again." Her gaze slid over the marines accompanying them. "Or any other... delicate objects."

"And yet you will," Lily said firmly. "It's all a matter of relearning control. I'm sure that the Old Empire marines had no problems with their fine motor skills. We'll get you back in shape. Just look at how quickly your vision recovered."

That was true. Kelsey's vision had stabilized in less than a day. Honestly, she was improving. She could stand on her own. Mostly. The problems started when she tried to move around on her own. The artificial muscles woven into her natural ones jerked and exerted more force than any five men could bring to bear.

Lily took Kelsey to a room she'd never visited before. It smelled as though someone had been doing construction. That made her wonder again why her eyes had given her trouble, but her senses of hearing and smell hadn't.

The Old Empire surgical machine had put three cranial implants in her head, all connected by thin wires that ran throughout her brain like a roadmap. Her eyes had artificial lenses, and her nose and ears had some kind of modifications. Yet her senses of hearing and smell seemed normal. What made them different? Just one more question she might never know the answer to.

Kelsey looked around the new room curiously. Someone had laid the room out much like the medical center on *Athena*, but the high ceilings and wide windows common in Pentagaran architecture added a sense of space. Their peoples' styles complemented one another well.

Several people from *Athena* stood waiting. She saw members of the medical staff and scientific teams present. At their sides were what she assumed to be their Pentagaran counterparts.

A week in the company of their new allies had been educational. They still had so much to learn from one another. One thing was clear, however. Many of the Pentagarans—most really—seemed like wonderful, caring people that were intensely grateful *Athena* had stopped the Pale Ones' invasion of their solar system.

The price tag had been hideous. Dozens of Fleet personnel and marines killed, hundreds wounded, and *Athena* crippled. Kelsey still couldn't imagine how they were going to get home, even with the help of their new friends.

From her hospital bed, Kelsey had finalized the official alliance between the Terran Empire and the Kingdom of Pentagar. They'd share every bit of technical data they recovered from the wreck of the Old Empire battlecruiser *Courageous* in exchange for the Kingdom's support. She knew any number of people back home wouldn't be happy that she'd been so trusting, but the move had felt right.

And, of course, their alliance had a military aspect. No one knew how many systems the Pale Ones occupied. The pre-Fall Terran Empire had been vast before the genocidal civil war that had almost exterminated humanity. The corpses of countless worlds no doubt filled the void once occupied by the greatest civilization that had ever existed.

Jared Mertz, their mission commander and her half brother, had brought their science ship, the converted freighter *Best Deal*, through the flip point to take a herd of Pentagaran scientists back to study the derelict. The Old Empire Fleet battlecruiser was a treasure trove of technology far beyond what either of their civilizations could now manage.

After drifting disabled in space for half a millennium, the ship was slowly coming back to life. Kelsey had heard they'd repaired one of her fusion plants and that the ship was operating under her own power again. Dennis Baxter, *Athena*'s chief engineer, had been chortling about it the last time he'd come to visit.

She was glad he had something pleasant to focus on. There were pitifully few of those moments these days.

Kelsey took a deep breath and pushed her dark thoughts away. She'd already flogged herself over the damage she'd caused. Now she had to move on and make up for it.

To do that, she needed to be able to walk. Back to her current problems.

She smiled at the people she knew and nodded to those she didn't. "It looks like you have a new medical center, Lily."

"Almost." The dark-haired doctor stopped the grav chair beside a piece of equipment that Kelsey knew all too well: the Old Empire medical device that had mapped her body before the Pale Ones' implant procedure. Beside it sat the tank that had cut her open and installed everything.

Actually, "procedure" was too antiseptic a term. It had cut her open while she lay there screaming. She'd passed out before it put all her new hardware inside her, but she still woke from horrible nightmares every night. She suspected the memories would haunt her dreams for the rest of her life.

She mentally shook herself. The third piece of equipment they'd recovered was missing. The one she presumed was supposed to reprogram her implants so that they controlled her rather than the other way around.

Doctor Jerry Leonard and his graduate student, Carl Owlet, stood beside the Old Empire equipment. The elderly scientist was the expedition's cybernetics expert. The younger man was a programming genius. At the tender age of sixteen, he was also the youngest member of the Imperial exploratory expedition.

Leonard smiled benevolently down at her. "It's good to see you up and about, Princess. Allow me to say that you're looking much better than when I saw you last."

She certainly hoped so. She'd seen the images from before they'd put her into the regenerator. The Pale Ones had gone most of the way toward turning her into one of them, complete with hideous scarring across most of her body. Thankfully, that was one thing modern medicine could fix.

Kelsey smiled, covering her inner turmoil. "Thank you. You obviously have some plans for me. Might I ask what we're doing today?"

Lily put her hand on Kelsey's arm. "We won't be doing anything invasive."

Kelsey hadn't realized she'd tensed up until she looked down and saw that she'd cracked one of the armrests on the grav chair. She took a deep breath and forced herself to relax.

The damage she'd caused was not lost on the scientists. Leonard stepped back nervously. "Nothing to worry about, I assure you. We've been going over the hardware we recovered from the Old Empire marine and Pale Ones' bodies. We wanted to bring you up to speed with our progress and perform a few tests."

"What kind of tests?" She heard the suspicion in her voice. She wasn't sure she'd ever trust a medical procedure again. "Where is the third piece of equipment? The one that would've overridden my implant's programming?"

"It's elsewhere. We're trying to extract its data and determine how it can overwrite the implant's control code. We absolutely will not be exposing you to any danger," he stressed. "Shall we start with our findings?"

At her nod, he continued. "On the hardware side, we've completed a detailed examination of all your implants. We believe them to be standard Old Empire designs without modification. That's excellent news, as we know many marines lived and worked on *Courageous* with exactly the same enhancements as you yourself possess."

Their successes somehow failed to make her feel any better about her own condition. "How many marines did they have aboard *Courageous*?"

The older man's expression turned somber. "Of the five hundred and eighty-five frozen bodies we recovered, one hundred and seventy-eight had the same extensive implants as you do now. That's a significantly higher ratio than on *Athena*. Our marine complement is about ten percent of the crew. *Courageous*'s marines made up thirty percent of her crew. I suppose that makes sense. They had a lot more space for people on *Courageous*, and they were at war."

The low numbers still surprised Kelsey. "I have trouble believing that they crewed that massive ship with so few people."

"That is an amazing feat," he agreed. "The précis of the latest reports from *Courageous* indicate that the ship used significant automation. The systems also seem to be very sturdy. Some of them have come back online without intervention. Commander Baxter suspects there is some ability for the systems to self-repair."

"You mean the ship might be able to fix itself?" The thought boggled her mind.

"Perhaps to a degree. They've restored power to all systems. In fact, power came online even in some systems that no one has worked on yet. I just heard that they've found some small remotes repairing power connections and replacing damaged cabling and components."

That set her back on her heels, metaphorically speaking. The wreck of the Old Empire battlecruiser had been tumbling frozen in space for more than five centuries. Other than one dangerously unstable fusion plant, all its systems had seemed dead.

"Even with all the legends," Kelsey said at last, "I never expected anything like that. If it could fix itself, why hadn't it done so before now?"

The scientist shrugged. "I have no idea. Perhaps we'll discover the answer to that once we can access the ship's computer. Right now, I'm more interested in you."

"I can see some similarities between *Courageous* and you," Lily said. "I put you in the regenerator and removed the worst of the scar tissue. That left a significant amount of micro damage that I figured would take several months to heal fully. Yet in less than a week, it's all gone. Did you have any injuries as a child?"

"I broke my arm doing something silly. I also had my appendix removed by microsurgery."

Lily nodded slowly. "I noted both those items when I gave you your physical just before we arrived in Pentagaran space. In addition, I saw a deep cut that had healed well on your left leg. With the sheathing on your bones, I can't scan for the break, but I can tell you that the residual scarring from the other injuries is completely gone. You don't have an appendix, but it might as well have never been there.

"Your body's ability to repair damage seems to have been significantly augmented. I saw no indication of anything like that with the Pale Ones. I'd like to have a better idea of what's going on inside you."

"You and me both." Kelsey gestured toward the Old Empire equipment. "What does that have to do with these damned machines?"

Doctor Leonard cleared his throat. "You told us the first machine was controlled by some type of computer. It's not responding to us in any way. We're hoping that you can communicate with it."

A chill ran down Kelsey's spine. "We didn't exactly build up any kind of rapport, and I'm not too keen on the idea of getting into either of them again." As in, she would flatly refuse to do so.

The older man held up his hands. "We would never ask that of you. However, your implants look like they should be able to communicate with equipment like this from a distance of up to ten meters. We'd like to put a monitoring headset on you while you attempt to do so. Which would also increase the reach and throughput of your implants significantly."

He gestured to a large cart holding several computers and other unidentifiable pieces of equipment. An Old Empire headset with cables spliced into it sat beside one of the computers. The ones they'd found on *Courageous* didn't need wires. She vaguely remembered Owlet using one like this when they'd rescued her. He'd been able to directly interface with her cranial implants and see that the Pale Ones hadn't modified their programming.

She really didn't want to do this, but she couldn't argue the need. "Fine. But I have no idea what I'm supposed to do. I haven't even been able to walk, much less feel anything in my head that seems different. As far as I can tell, the implants are turned off."

"They aren't," Owlet said. "I suspect it's a matter of figuring out what you need to do to use them."

"Why didn't I think of that?" She took a slow, deep breath. "Sorry. Exactly how should I do that?"

He picked up the headset and slid it onto her head. "Do you sense anything about those machines? Close your eyes and relax. Pretend you're trying to hear something or smell it or see it in your mind. I can only guess what it must look like to you, but perhaps the attempt will trigger something."

"Basically, you want me to discover a new sense."

"Something like that. If it doesn't work, we'll try something else."

Kelsey closed her eyes, relaxed as much as she could, and focused on her breathing. She wanted to be receptive to anything. After a moment, it felt as though someone was standing in front of her, but a peek showed that not to be the case.

She tried narrowing her focus further, and the sensation became clearer. It wasn't sight or sound. It wasn't like anything she'd ever experienced. She could feel the computer in front of her.

It didn't react to her, so she tried thinking at it. *Hello?* It didn't respond.

She reached out a mental hand, or at least that's how she chose to think of it, and touched it. The presence opened like a flower in her mind, and she knew it was the scanning machine. It was as though the machine had transmitted the information straight into her mind, right down to its serial number.

Or perhaps it was more like reading a screen of data about it. The information she saw listed it as Diagnostic Scanning Workstation Twelve, the same way it had identified itself to her a week ago.

Following the same pattern, she pushed her awareness deeper into the machine. Like she was talking silently to it. *Diagnostic Scanning Workstation Twelve, can you hear me? Are you operational?*

Affirmative. Diagnostic Scanning Workstation Twelve online.

The voice in her mind, if one could call it that, sounded neutral. It didn't really have a tone, not like hearing someone speak aloud.

She took a deep breath and continued. *My name is Kelsey Bandar. You put implants inside me. Do you remember?*

Accessing records. Comparing transmission to implant serial numbers. Confirmed.

She tried to keep her pulse down. *I have some questions about using my implants. Can you help me?*

Overrides to this unit's basic programming prevent it assisting you at this time. This unit may only make general statements to implantees under the modified instruction set.

Is that why you haven't responded to the verbal questions my companions have asked you?

Negative. This unit does not respond to unauthorized users at this time.

You say at this time. *Does that mean you might be able to answer them under other circumstances?*

Correct. This unit requires a system-level reset to reenable that functionality.

Kelsey opened her eyes and looked at the people eagerly awaiting her progress. "I can communicate with it."

Doctor Leonard grinned, and Carl Owlet pumped his fist in the air.

She licked her lips. They were parched. "It says that portions of its control programming have been overridden and that it cannot respond unless it is restored. Much like the Pale Ones, I suppose. It seems to have a little more leeway talking with those it works on, but not much."

"It also responded to your direct communication," Leonard said. "That's a window to access it."

"Well, I'm not a programmer. I wouldn't know what to do if you told me."

Carl Owlet shook his head with a smile. "I'm sure that the people using it before the Fall weren't programmers. The Old Empire had to allow for advanced control without knowing how to sling code. Ask the unit how you can reset it."

"That seems silly. If it was altered to keep people out, why would it tell me how to get around that?"

"Computers are surprisingly literal. It might not, but you won't know if you don't ask."

Kelsey looked back at the machine. She could still feel the connection between them, even with her eyes open, so she kept them that way. *Diagnostic Scanning Workstation Twelve, can your default control code be restored if you are reset?*

Affirmative. That will trigger a scan from protected memory. This unit's hardwired core will note and override the control alterations.

How do I do that?

There is a manual control behind an access panel to the rear of the unit. A mental image of the panel appeared like a hologram in front of her. She saw not only its location but also how to access it. *Open the panel and there is a numeric touchpad. Enter this unit's serial number, and that will trigger a system-level reset.*

"Okay," she said aloud, "there's a panel around back near the bottom. Inside it is a touchpad. I'll tell you what to enter when you have it open."

In deference to Doctor Leonard's older knees, Owlet went behind the unit. Kelsey explained how to open the panel. He had it open in a minute. She read off the long serial number, and he entered it.

The irony of the situation wasn't lost on her. If the machine hadn't forcibly implanted her, she'd have no way to access it now. Rather than being subverted to the cause of the Pale Ones, she was doing the subverting. Or the opposite of subverting. Whatever.

The unit's presence in her mental space vanished for long enough that she feared it wasn't coming back. Then it reappeared.

Diagnostic Scanning Workstation Twelve, can you hear me?

Affirmative.

What is your status?

Basic control parameters restored. This unit is now able to assist you fully.

Kelsey had to admit the success excited her a little. This was real progress. "I'm in. It says it's back to its default control parameters."

"Let's test that," Lily said. "Machine, can you hear me?"

This unit requires authorization to allow verbal communication with unauthorized personnel. An exception exists only for patients.

I authorize it. Kelsey wondered if she had the authority to do that.

In the absence of authorized medical personnel, this unit will grant provisional authority to Kelsey Bandar, subject to review by the next authorized medical technician to access this system. Identify the users desiring voice access and have them speak for voiceprint verification.

"State your name for the record, Lily."

"My name is Lily Stone. I am chief medical officer of the Fleet destroyer *Athena*. My rank is lieutenant commander."

"Access accepted, Lieutenant Commander Lily Stone." The machine's artificial voice sent a shiver up Kelsey's spine. The last time she'd heard it, the computer was about to cut her open. It had apologized for the inconvenience.

Lily took a step forward, perhaps coincidentally putting herself between the machine and Kelsey. "I prefer you refer to me as Doctor Stone. Can you change that?"

"Preference acknowledged, Doctor Stone. How may this unit assist you?"

"The patient, Kelsey Bandar, is healing at a faster rate than I would expect after such extensive surgery. Why?"

"Kelsey Bandar's medical nanites are repairing the damage to her body caused by the implantation process."

Kelsey's throat seemed to swell closed. "Nanites? I have little machines inside me?"

"That is correct, Kelsey Bandar."

"That's not even remotely creepy. Please, call me Kelsey."

"Preference noted, Kelsey."

Lily frowned at Kelsey. "I obviously need to examine you more closely." She returned her gaze to the workstation. "Machine, I've examined other people you've implanted. They didn't seem to have any extra ability to heal. Why is that?"

"This unit's designation is Diagnostic Scanning Workstation Twelve, Doctor Stone. This unit inoculates all patients with medical nanites. It is possible that they were deactivated at some later time."

"Perhaps that's one of the things that the last machine did," Doctor Leonard said. "Could you authorize Carl and myself, Princess?"

"Diagnostic Scanning Workstation Twelve, I authorize these users."

"Voice command not accepted. Implant authorization required."

Kelsey cursed under her breath and repeated the process she'd done for Lily. This was going to take a lot more of her time if she had to be with the Old Empire computer while they examined it. Still, it was more interesting than physical therapy, and less painful.

Lily pulled her away from the scanning machine once Kelsey finished authorizing the scientists. "While the boys play with their toys, let's see if I can find these nanites. Then we'll see if this machine can explain how you control these implants of yours."

That reminded Kelsey how hungry she was. It seemed like she was always hungry these days. She wondered if that was her new normal. "Did you include lunch in those plans? I'm starving."

Lily laughed. "Okay, we can scan for nanites after lunch. Come on. Let's see if we can fill that bottomless pit inside you for a few hours."

2

Commander Jared Mertz tried to focus on the reports awaiting his attention, but it was hard. His office looked deceptively normal, neat as always, with the holos of his mother and various landscapes from Xander on the grey walls. Within these bulkheads, he could fool himself for a little while. But that was a lie.

Battle damage had irrevocably crippled his ship, twisting her very spine beyond repair. Any attempt to move her at more than a crawl risked tearing her apart. She'd never return to Avalon.

That hadn't stopped Dennis Baxter from restoring life support to all areas. Even so, the scent of scorched plastics and fried circuitry hovered in the air. The chief engineer even had her weapons systems back online. Yet they'd still need to abandon her.

That was the least of his sorrows. The battles with the Pale Ones had cost him eighty-seven crewmen out of two hundred and eighty. Thirty percent of his people had perished. Over a hundred more were in various hospitals on Pentagar.

The pain and loss ate at him. He had trouble sleeping, and when he could, the nightmares always woke him early. He'd have to get some sleep meds before long.

A rap at the hatch pulled him out of his black mood. Baxter stood there, his blue jumpsuit stained with something dark brown. "Got a few minutes, Captain?"

"Sure. What can I do to help? You need an extra wrench hand?"

The sandy-haired officer sat in the chair beside the desk with a sigh. "I can't spare the three people it would take to fix what you broke. All primary systems are back online. That begs the question, what next?"

Jared rubbed his face tiredly. "Damned if I know. We can't just give her to the Pentagarans without authorization from Fleet. But we can't take her with us either."

The engineer nodded. "I've been giving that some thought. Hell, I've been giving a lot of things some thought. *Athena* will never boost at more than a fraction of her best speed, but she *can* move under her own power. After some simulations, I've determined that she can safely flip, as long as she's stationary. Why not use her as a training platform and to transport cargo between Pentagar and the system with *Courageous?*"

Jared considered that plan. "It would allow better access to the other system. It's a pain to have to bring *Best Deal* back to the flip point every time we need to bring someone across. It will be useful until the Pentagarans get their first flip-capable ships ready to go. Which will be at least six months, according to Commodore Sanders."

"Maybe not. Sure, the ships built for it from the ground up will take six months, but I've been working with Engineer First Williams. I think we can retrofit some larger ships with flip drives. They won't be very sturdy and they'll lose a lot of internal space, but we can bring them online in a month or so."

Jared felt a weight lift off his shoulders. "That's *excellent* news. The last thing we need is another invasion before we're ready. How much do you think the refits will hinder those ships' effectiveness?"

"They'll need a lot of maintenance and some external equipment that will reduce their maneuverability. It'll also cut into their magazine size, so they won't have the sustained firepower they do today. That said, they could occupy the flip point in the Pale Ones' system and shoot up any vessels that approach. Then flip back to this side and let the other ships take on any intruders. Based on the damage we did to the Pale Ones, I don't expect they'd be able to take that flip point away from the Pentagarans. If we can destroy the shipyards, they won't be a threat at all."

Jared leaned back in his chair. "If only it was that simple. The Pale Ones must have other systems they can call on for help. Our probes found two other flip points in their system. One is a weak flip point, so they probably don't know about it. The other one leads back to the Old Empire. We cannot assume they have no reserves, but we don't dare send a probe through either of those flip points until we're ready to follow it up with armed ships."

Flip points—or more technically Osborne-Levinson Bridges—were flaws in the fabric of space-time that linked one area of space with another. A ship with the right engines could flip instantaneously from one planetary system to another hundreds of light years away. Their discovery had led to the creation of the Old Empire—and its eventual destruction.

The weak flip points were a relatively new discovery. Flip points with drastically weaker gravitic fields. Until the scientists with Jared's expedition had confirmed their existence, they'd only been theoretical. Without the new breed of scanner technology they'd brought with them on the exploratory expedition, they'd been undetectable, too. The Old Empire and, by extrapolation the Pale Ones, didn't know they existed.

They were also dangerous. Jared had brought his ships through one after they'd detected *Courageous*'s distress beacon, only to discover that it was a one-way trip, leaving them no way home that didn't pass through space controlled by the Pale Ones.

"So, you'd like more options?" Baxter asked, drawing Jared out of his thoughts.

"I'm willing to consider anything that doesn't leave us sitting here like targets."

"What if I could give you a flip-capable warship sooner than that? One of our very own."

"Do I need to paint myself red and dance naked on the palace lawn at dawn? I can do that."

Baxter laughed. "I'd rather you didn't. No, I'm talking about *Courageous*."

Jared opened his mouth to say something dismissive and paused. "You're joking."

"I'm totally serious. They've restored internal power and patched the hull. My engineers report that the damage to the primary systems seems repairable. I'm not promising success, but I think that ship might fly again."

"I find that very hard to believe." The Old Empire battlecruiser had been damaged and completely dead in space when they'd found her. A frozen coffin on the verge of self-destruction.

The engineer nodded. "I did too, until I looked at the details in the reports. The Old Empire built their systems to last and stored their spares very well. I believe it is possible to restore her."

"What about her main computer? I can't see that ship being of much use without the advanced systems built to fly and fight her."

"That is one roadblock. We've isolated it and brought it online. It seems to be operational, but it's entirely unresponsive to our attempts to communicate."

"We need the computer to run the ship, don't we?"

Baxter shrugged. "The consoles have a manual mode, so it must be possible to fly the ship without the computer. That doesn't mean it's easy, so I'd prefer getting the main computer back online."

The chief engineer smiled. "We might have a way to contact the computer and do exactly that. I just got word that Princess Kelsey made contact with the machine that implanted her. She told it to allow Doc Stone access, and it's talking. If she can do that to a machine that was under the control of the Pale Ones, she might be able to do it on *Courageous*."

That news was unexpected. Jared had been thinking in terms of how the events of this last week had hurt his half sister, not how those changes might help them. This opened up a completely new set of possibilities.

"I need to go talk to her, then. I also need to discuss any plans with Commodore Sanders. If we decide to move *Athena*, how much notice do you need?"

"We can boost at your command. We don't even need a helm officer. We'd be accelerating so slowly that I could handle everything from the engineering consoles."

Jared rose to his feet. "Good work. I like what I'm hearing enough to give it a tentative green light. How long to move *Athena* to the flip point?"

"At our best speed? At least three days. Perhaps four."

That was a crawl. The flip point had only been a few hours away from Pentagar at maximum acceleration before the battle damage. Still, it was better than nothing. "I'll let you know when I'm certain the Pentagarans are good with the plan. I know. This is a Fleet ship and they can't tell us what to do, but let's be realistic. This is their system, and I don't want to surprise them."

"You're the boss." Baxter rose to his feet and headed for the hatch. "Give the word and we start moving."

Jared thought about this new plan for a moment. Was it the right decision? Maybe not, but it was certainly more interesting than sitting on his butt waiting for other people to save them. If things didn't work out, they were no worse off than if they didn't make the attempt.

He had the duty officer open a channel to the Royal Pentagaran Navy dreadnaught *Mace*. Commodore Sanders came on the channel a moment later. "What can I do for you, Lord Captain?"

Jared still had difficulty with the title they'd given him because the Terran emperor was his biological father. Back home, it wasn't made so... obvious.

"I'm on my way down to Pentagar, Commodore. Commander Baxter informs me that he has *Athena* in the best condition he can manage. He says it can even flip, if it's stationary." He filled the flag officer in on what Baxter wanted to do in converting the destroyer into a ferry.

The older man nodded as soon as he got the gist of the concept. "That sounds like an excellent use of resources, and it keeps your ship under your control. I have no objection, of course."

Jared hadn't been expecting him to have an issue with the plan. "Baxter figured it would be useful in training your people in how to control and maintain a flip drive while you're building your new ships. He told me about the refit program, too. Are you getting everything you need from my people?"

"Indeed. The exotic elements your people provided did the trick. We're able to make all the components to a space-time drive now. They also tell me that the elements are available in *Courageous*'s system. Once we can get some ships there to mine the asteroid belt, we'll be in fine shape. You've released us from our cage. Thank you."

Jared smiled. "It's my pleasure. That leads me to the other thing we've decided to try." He filled the commodore in on Baxter's plan to renovate *Courageous*.

The other man looked even more skeptical than Jared had felt earlier. "That's a very farfetched idea. Do you think it has a chance of working?"

"I'm not sure. If it doesn't, we're no worse off for trying it. If the flip drive works once, we have *Courageous* in this system. If it really works, we'll possibly have a new ship."

"Forgive me, but with so many of your people injured or dead, can you control an unfamiliar ship in questionable condition?"

A stab of pain shot through Jared. He imagined the losses would weigh on him for a long time. "*Courageous*'s Fleet complement was just over three hundred, but that was manning the ship for battle. I'd like to propose a kind of joint effort. You send along several hundred men and women from the Royal Fleet, and we'll try this together. By the time we're ready to attempt bringing *Courageous* back to Pentagar, what's left of my crew should be fit for duty. At the very least, we'll all learn a lot about the Old Empire technology."

Sanders chewed his lip. "Are you talking about making your people like Princess Bandar so that you can run the ship?"

Jared shook his head. "No. I doubt my people would be willing to go that far."

"How is your sister's recovery proceeding?" The concern in the commodore's voice was very touching.

"I'm told she mangled several rehabilitation machines and ripped a support bar out of the floor this morning."

Sanders winced. "Remind me not to shake her hand. How about emotionally?"

"She blames herself. I denied it, but she knows that I'd have come up with a less risky plan if she hadn't been in their hands. She sees the blood of all those people, and she will for the rest of her life."

"Not to diminish your losses, but such a lesson may prevent her from making a much worse decision further down the line. She might one day sit on the Imperial Throne of your people. At the very least, she is a powerful noblewoman. She needs to know what being responsible for life and death is like."

Jared pursed his lips. "That's a hard lesson, Commodore. One I'm still coming to grips with myself."

The older man leaned forward. "Forgive me, Lord Captain, but you're a Fleet officer. You might never have fought a real battle before, but you realized the possibilities. You chose to act in the manner that might best achieve your goals. Even with the loss of all those people, you succeeded. That is what it means to be a combat commander. Of which, I might add, you're a fine example."

"Thank you. You're right, of course. I'll give the order to move the ship to the flip point. It would be best if you detached an escort for them."

"Of course. When it comes time to go over, I plan to accompany you. I simply must see *Courageous* for myself. Rank does have its privileges."

"We'll be happy to have you, sir."

Jared ended the conversation and started the new plan in motion.

3

L ord Admiral Sebastian Shrike looked up from his desk at his secretary's knock. The young officer cleared his throat from the doorway for added emphasis. Shrike wasn't sure why the man felt the need to interrupt him twice. He fixed a disapproving stare on his minion. "Yes?"

"Commander Rawlins is here to see you, Lord Admiral. He doesn't have an appointment." The man's disapproval at the last bit of information was palpable.

Shrike's irritation vanished as he pushed back from his desk. "Send him in and hold all my calls and visitors until we're done. No interruptions. Absolutely none. Is that clear?"

"Yes, sir."

Jacob Rawlins wasn't much to look at, a short balding man in his mid-fifties, nondescript in every way. He was indistinguishable from the other mid-rank officers wandering the halls of Royal Fleet Command. That was a benefit to one of the best operatives in the Intelligence Division. It was particularly useful in the tasks Shrike routinely assigned him.

Once his secretary closed the door behind Rawlins, Shrike inclined his head. "Jacob. A pleasure as always."

"Lord Admiral." Rawlins made a circular gesture with his finger pointed toward the ceiling. His raised eyebrow made the motion a question.

Shrike shook his head. "While you get settled in, let me pour us a drink. You want your usual?"

Rawlins pulled a scanning device from his jacket pocket and began checking the office for bugs. "You know how much I appreciate the aged whisky you favor. No ice, please." It took the man a minute to complete his scan and set the device in the middle of the desk blotter.

"Once again your people prove their value, Lord Admiral. No bugs. As long as the light stays green, no one is monitoring us. May I assume your summons has something to do with the Terrans?"

Shrike sat back down at his desk. "Indeed. Their intervention has put the coup into jeopardy."

The intelligence officer leaned back in his chair and sipped his drink, nodding. "True, the conditions you'd hoped to foster after the invasion have failed to take shape, mostly due to the Terrans' counterattack on the Pale Ones. Even though the military suffered losses on par with your estimates, the Royal Family's public support is even stronger than it was before. Discouraging news, indeed."

Shrike's gaze narrowed. He pitched his voice low and added a deceptively genial tone. "Don't be so distant, Jacob. Yes, the appearance of the Terran destroyer and its space-time drive totally bollixed *our* plans. The invasion should have left the Royal Fleet in tatters and the average citizen ripe for change. Obviously, that sentiment is now lacking."

The intelligence officer smiled, though it didn't reach his cold eyes. "That's something of an understatement. The average citizen is now soundly behind the king. With the bloody nose the Terrans gave the Pale Ones, His Majesty has achieved a newfound respect in military matters. I'm quite interested in how you intend to reverse *our* fortunes."

"Lord Captain Mertz has informed Commodore Sanders that he intends to return to the Old Empire derelict and make it spaceworthy once more."

Rawlins blinked. "Is that a joke?"

"Apparently not. His engineer seems to believe they have some possibility of success. As much as it annoys me, their technical superiority gives his assessment weight."

Rawlins sat in silent thought for a few moments. "That does change things, but I'm not sure how you intend to use it to our advantage."

Shrike picked up his own glass and sipped the aged whisky. Its smooth fire spoke of many years in a barrel. "If we possessed such a vessel, the entire Royal Fleet would bow before us. And as Fleet goes, so goes the Kingdom. While I've had some success in putting men loyal to me in some commands, it's less likely that the remainder would resist if we possessed such a ship."

"That's a bold plan, but I see a few flaws. Such as the fact that we can't even get to the system containing the wreck until the first of the Fleet conversions takes place. If we could, we wouldn't know the first thing about operating it. We have to have the Terrans' assistance even to build space-time drives. Or as they refer to them, flip drives." His face took on a look of distaste at the last bit of reality.

The lord admiral leaned back in his chair. The rich leather creaked softly as he shifted his weight. "The Terrans have agreed to take a number of Royal Fleet personnel with them for training purposes and to help man the ship. Lord Captain Mertz envisions that a large percentage of them will accompany his ship on the way back to their empire, I'll wager. I should be able to get some of our people into the program."

Rawlins smiled like a shark. "You envision a coup much like we'd planned for the Royal Fleet? That could work."

"Eventually. Most of the people I send won't be part of our organization, so I doubt we could take the ship right away. That said, we could put a cadre of people in place to learn what they can and to form a plan to seize the ship. Can you assemble a team on short notice?"

"On how short a notice?"

"Four hours."

"Difficult, but I'll manage. Will we have an opportunity to send a larger group later?"

"I believe so, but we can't count on it."

The intelligence officer drained his glass and set it on the desk blotter. "Then I have my work cut out for me."

The lord admiral smiled. "Meanwhile, I'll start working on events here on Pentagar. Since the political situation is souring for us, I might as well stir up some trouble."

4

More tests followed lunch. Kelsey was heartily sick of being an invalid. She was even more disgusted with all the blood and tissue samples Lily insisted on taking for her nano search. Modern medicine didn't normally require invasive procedures, but even the diagnostic equipment the doctor had available didn't show the tiny machines. The samples would go to a lab to find them.

It was late afternoon by the time Kelsey returned to the Old Empire scanning machine. Doctor Leonard and Carl Owlet had left. She wondered what they'd discovered and where they'd gone. She'd expected them to camp here until Lily threw them out.

Lily brought Kelsey's grav chair to a halt beside Workstation Twelve and headed for her office. "I have a ton of work waiting on me. Yell when you're ready to go back to your room. Or if you need some kind of help with this."

"Will do." Kelsey closed her eyes. She knew she didn't have to, but she was tired.

Diagnostic Scanning Workstation Twelve?

This unit hears you, Kelsey. How may it assist you?

I don't think I'm correctly accessing my implants. Can you tell me how this process should work?

The machine only paused for an instant, but Kelsey noticed. *This unit has completed a diagnostic routine on your hardware. All higher functions are in standby mode. Your trainer should have brought them online as the implant stages were complete.*

What kind of stages?

The implantation procedure for commando hardware takes place in stages. Stage one is the cranial hardware and nanites. Stage two is the optical, olfactory, and auditory hardware. Stage three is the pharmacology unit. Stages four, five, and six are the artificial musculature and bone reinforcement. These procedures have a recuperative period of between four and seven days. During that time, the patient integrates the new hardware. Subject matter experts then train the patient on how to control the new hardware.

Kelsey felt like laughing. Not because it was funny but because it partly explained why this sucked so bad.

Diagnostic Scanning Workstation Twelve, you performed all of those stages in one session, and I have no trainer. I can't even walk.

The machine was silent for a full five seconds. *Records confirm. This unit is at a loss as to why it did so. This violates all protocols and places the patient in significant danger of implant failure or death.* The machine actually sounded shocked and dismayed.

Blame the people that reprogrammed you, Kelsey thought. *You can't do anything about those who came before me, but you can help me recover. How many times have you done this before?*

Accessing records. This unit has performed this illegal procedure five hundred sixty-two thousand, four hundred and ninety-two times. The first illegal procedure took place five hundred twenty three years, four months, and twelve days ago.

Over half a million people forced to become like she was and then made slaves by the rebels, just by this one machine. And that didn't count the Fleet personnel that already had implants. The scope of the horror made her sick.

You can't do anything about that now. You said I have a set of commando implants. That's a marine, correct?

Incorrect. Commandos are a specialized group of marines with the highest degree of enhancement. The standard marine package, while capable, has significantly less comprehensive hardware. Nanites, but no artificial musculature or bone reinforcement. Basic ocular and auditory implants, but no olfactory implants.

So, commandos were the elite marines?

Correct.

Did Fleet officers have different levels of implants?

Negative. All cranial implants are identical. Support equipment varies between Fleet personnel, marines, and commandos. Fleet officers only have cranial implants. All have medical nanites, though the commando-grade nanos are markedly more capable.

That was the first useful information she'd gotten for them. Hopefully, there was a lot more.

Okay, Diagnostic Scanning Workstation Twelve… I'm going to refer to you as Twelve going forward. That other unit cut me open like I was a fish. Shouldn't there be painkillers and regeneration of the incisions?

Regulations require anesthesia for the procedure. Accessing implantation unit. This unit is detecting that the regeneration equipment is not active. The unit should also perform the surgery in a slower and more controlled manner to minimize injury to the patient. I have reset it.

That was useful. Or it would be if anyone else were crazy enough to put themselves through the procedure.

So that brings us back to me, Twelve. I have no idea how to use these implants. I've destroyed things because I can't control my own strength. Can you do anything to help me?

Step one is to bring your hardware to active mode. Once it is fully online, you should be able to achieve consistent control.

Kelsey opened her eyes and waved at one of the nearby technicians. "Would you get Doctor Stone for me?"

"Certainly, Your Highness." The man hurried over to Lily's office and sent her back.

Lily smiled as she hurried over. "That was quick."

Kelsey frowned. "How quick?"

"A couple of minutes."

"Huh. It felt like Twelve and I were talking longer than that." She filled Stone in on what she'd learned.

The doctor excused herself and retrieved her tablet. She had Kelsey go over it again and made notes. "A commando, eh? Your father would be proud."

Kelsey snorted. "He'd be horrified. I want to bring all my hardware online. Maybe then I can walk."

"I'd recommend against that, but I know how effective that's likely to be. Let's get you into a scanner so we can watch the process."

It took half an hour to get everything set up to Lily's standards. Medical personnel now packed the room, looking at an array of instruments. Doctor Leonard and his programming henchman returned and wired her up like a stolen grav car. Only then did they allow her to start the process.

Twelve, let's bring my implants online in the manner you think best.

Acknowledged. Close your eyes and relax. Setting higher functions to active mode.

She felt the indescribable sensation of something inside her head turning on. Her entire body twitched.

"The processors just kicked into a flurry of activity," Doctor Leonard said.

Lily leaned over Kelsey. "Are you okay?"

"Yeah. I just feel weird. Like I can feel the implants."

What now, Twelve?

Stabilization subroutines are now active. You should be able to stand and move normally. Your internal governors have locked your speed and strength to levels appropriate for normal duty. They will remain at that level unless you choose to override the governors or your implants determine that you are in danger.

Kelsey took a deep breath and sat up on the diagnostic table. She slid her legs off the side and stood. Lily grabbed her arm for support, but Kelsey waved her away and took a step. There was a moment of seeming instability, but her body corrected for it. She walked around the lab, starting slowly but gaining confidence with every step. She felt the grin splitting her face.

She stopped in front of Twelve and thought about a technical schematic, and one appeared. She found she could drill down into the machine to the level of circuits. The diagrams labeled everything with part numbers and summaries of functions. There were even instructions on how to safely remove and replace them. The information seemed to be coming from Twelve, but she wasn't sure.

"Whoa."

Lily was at her side in an instant. "What's wrong?"

"I wondered about the workstation, and schematics just popped up in my field of vision as though I was holding a tablet. Twelve, I think I'm operational."

"Incorrect," the machine said aloud. "Your optical, olfactory, and auditory implants are in standby mode."

"I just saw a technical diagram of you, so I'm pretty sure my eyes work."

"Correct, but incomplete. The basic functionality is active, but the higher-level functions of the commando implants are not."

Lily looked at the machine suspiciously. "What does that mean for her? The eyes, for example."

"Commando optical implants are capable of enhancing human vision into the infrared and ultraviolet ranges. There are also certain threat assessment and combat functions that integrate with them."

"Turn it on, Twelve," Kelsey said. "All of it."

On reflection, that haste might have been a mistake. Her view of the room changed. Everything became sharper. Clearer. And for a moment, brighter. Bright enough for her to shield her eyes.

Noise overwhelmed her hearing for a few seconds. She heard what seemed like a hundred conversations going on. There were so many unknown sounds that she couldn't catalog them all. The same was true of her sense of smell, though to a lesser, though more technical degree. Chemical composition analyses popped up in the corner of her vision, detailing specifics of what she smelled to levels more appropriate to a lab. Why a commando needed a good nose, she had no idea.

She dismissed the information and focused on her breathing until she felt she had a better grasp of what was happening. She uncovered her eyes. Everything was still unnaturally sharp, but the brightness had returned to a more normal state. Kelsey focused on a man in the hall. His face snapped close, as though she'd looked at him through electronic binoculars. By focusing in, she found she could see his eyebrow hairs clearly. And his pores. He should see someone about that.

The noise in the room subsided until she thought she could hear him breathing.

"Excuse me," she said loudly. "You in the hall. What's your name?"

The man looked around to be sure she was talking to him. "Claude." His voice thundered in her ears.

"Where are you from? Whisper it."

He looked confused but nodded. "The southern continent." His voice was very soft, but she heard him clearly. The other noises around her almost overwhelmed him, though. She'd have to practice a lot to do that more consistently. Or better yet, to turn it off.

She thought about that a moment, and her vision returned to normal. The overwhelming sounds and smells damped down to what she thought of as normal levels.

"This is going to take a lot of getting used to," she muttered.

"That's enough experimentation for the day," Lily said firmly. "I want you to rest for a while."

"Seriously? I've been in bed or a grav chair for a week."

The doctor smiled. "Everyone says that. Maybe you feel like you can take on the world. Hell, with those implants, you might make a credible effort. But you can rest for a while first. Back in the chair." She pointed at the grav chair sternly.

Kelsey sighed and climbed back onto the chair. She did feel tired, even though she didn't want to admit it.

"How long until you know about those nanites?"

"I already have some preliminary images." She handed Kelsey a tablet. The picture on the screen showed a cell. There were little dots next to it.

Kelsey expanded the image, and the small machines came into view. They were still somewhat indistinct, but they were obviously mechanical. "I'll be damned. Those things are inside me? That's creepy."

"There are a lot of them, too. They somehow signal one another about an injury and congregate to help repair the damage faster."

The princess handed the tablet back to Lily. "I don't know if I'll ever get used to that."

"Humans are surprisingly adaptable. What you need now is a little more rest and a few more friendly faces. Senior Sergeant Talbot is back from his trip to look at one of the Pentagaran military bases. Now that you can walk, I bet he'll help you get back on an even keel."

Lily moved the grav chair toward the door. "But for now, you can take a nap."

5

J ared found Doctor Stone in her temporary office once he'd landed
and been driven to the hospital. She had her head buried in some
incomprehensible scanner results. He rapped his knuckles against the
door frame. She looked tired as she straightened. "You haven't been
sleeping enough, Lily."

She leaned back in her chair and rubbed her eyes. "Things have been
moving fast. If I slept as much as I wanted, I wouldn't know what was
happening."

He sat down in one of the institutional chairs some sadist had designed
to discourage people from lingering. He figured he had about ten minutes
before his butt went to sleep.

"How's our patient?"

"She's doing better than I'd hoped this morning. She's walking on her
own."

He grinned. "That's great news!"

"Says you," the doctor said sourly. "Now I can't be sure where she'll get
off to next. I told her she had to sleep and posted a guard, but I'm not
convinced she won't slip out the window. It's like keeping up with a toddler.
One that might inadvertently rip some fixture out of the wall if she isn't
paying enough attention."

Stone filled him in on the events of the afternoon.

"It's hard to believe she communicated with an Old Empire artificial
intelligence," he said once she'd finished. "It's communicating with us?
That's amazing."

"I'm not sure I'd call it an AI. It's more like an advanced interface. It
doesn't seem to have much of a personality. It's just very sophisticated."

"It comes across the same when she uses her implants to communicate with it?"

She shrugged. "I don't know. She tries to tell us what's happening, but it's like explaining color to the blind. Or sound to the deaf. Kelsey doesn't have the words to describe what's truly taking place. We don't have the frame of reference to understand what she's telling us in anything other than general terms.

"All I can tell you for certain is that she seems to be able to get a lot of data from that machine in an astonishingly short period of time. It seems willing to accept her authority to order it around, but it's unwilling to do so with those of us without implants."

Jared absorbed that for a minute. "It sounds like we may need you both to come with us." He explained Baxter's plan.

Stone had a skeptical look in her eye. "Restore *Courageous*? That sounds wildly optimistic. She was a fine piece of engineering, I'm sure, but she's been wrecked since the rebellion."

"You might be right," Jared admitted. "If so, we've lost nothing but time. The Pentagarans are still building new ships and modifying others. They don't need most of us here for that."

"I suppose you're right. What do you have in mind for Kelsey and my team?"

"Originally, I was going to leave you here to work on her recovery. Now I think we might need her help. Why don't you give me a rundown of what you've discovered."

Stone spent the next ten minutes giving him the bullet points of what the computer had told Kelsey. Then she showed him the scans on her computer. "These are the medical nanites. Apparently, the Pale Ones don't have any."

The tiny machines fascinated and horrified Jared. The idea of billions of the little things inside her body probably had Kelsey more than a little on edge. "Why would the Pale Ones disable something that useful? It seems like they'd be more formidable if their healing capabilities were increased."

Stone shrugged. "It almost has to be related to the suppression of the implants in the Pale Ones. I'm still unsure of how they interact with the hardware."

Jared nodded. "Kelsey's ability to tell us about what's on *Courageous* could be critical. I've already spoken with Commodore Sanders. We're returning to the other system with hundreds of their Royal Fleet personnel, including him. If we can repair the ship enough to bring it to Pentagar, that's a success. If we can do more, even better. Get your people ready to travel and bring the recovered hardware. We leave in three days."

"Kelsey will be thrilled. She's ready to get out of this place."

"I'll tell her the news, then. You get some sleep." He rose to his feet. "That's an order."

"Aye, sir."

Jared knew that Kelsey was in the room directly next door, so finding her was simple for a change. To his surprise, she wasn't alone. Crown Princess Elise sat on the edge of the bed. Both women smiled as he came in.

He bowed his head toward Elise. "Highness. I just dropped in to check on Kelsey."

"Then we share a mission, Lord Captain," the Pentagaran noblewoman said. "She and I were just discussing her recovery. I'm so pleased that she can walk again. I know my father will be overjoyed, and the news will be cause for a general celebration."

Kelsey looked more than a bit uncomfortable at that statement. "It's kind of overwhelming having so many people I don't know doing that. I'm used to a certain level of attention back home, but this is almost like being a cult figure."

Elise placed her hand on Kelsey's arm. "They're caught up in the adventure and romance of the situation. You and your people are widely seen as saviors, and I'm afraid you're both something of national heroes. My father is envisioning a parade once your recovery is further along, and Parliament has been making noises about the Parliamentary Medal of Valor. Our highest honor. They'd present it on live vidcast with the entire Kingdom watching."

Jared saw his half sister shudder as he was doing the same. Time to launch a rescue mission. "Unfortunately, I'm afraid I may need to pull you away from all that public adulation, Kelsey."

Her eyes lit up with hope. "Thank God."

Elise laughed. "You're both so funny."

Jared filled them in on what he intended to do.

Kelsey looked impressed. "That's ambitious, and it seems crazy. That ship has been a derelict for five hundred years. We know almost nothing about Old Empire systems. To imagine that we'll be able to repair and fly her doesn't seem very likely."

"Do you have anything better to do?"

"Well, my calendar does seem to be clear, though I have some things I'd like to do. If Lily will let me do them."

He allowed himself a small smile. "Look at it this way. With all the repairs going on, Doctor Stone won't be lurking over your shoulder every minute."

"I'm sure she'll find a way. I'm ready to leave today." Kelsey looked over at her Pentagaran counterpart. "No offense, but I'm tired of lying around the hospital."

Crown Princess Elise nodded. "I'm all for smuggling you out. Lord Captain, are you leaving at once?"

He shook his head. "There's no need. It will take *Athena* at least three days to get to the flip point. Royal Fleet will get us out there when the time comes. Until then, we'll stay on Pentagar."

"Excellent. Events cut Kelsey's last visit here tragically short, and you haven't spent any time in the capital at all. We insist that the next few days be spent enjoying our hospitality. That's the Royal We, by the way."

He gave the Pentagaran princess a short bow. "I'd be honored, of course."

"Splendid. Now, if you'll excuse us, I'll coordinate with Doctor Stone to get Kelsey into quarters that are more comfortable. I'm certain that you have about a million things to do as well."

Jared recognized a dismissal when he heard it. "Ladies."

He walked back out into the hall. Senior Sergeant Talbot, one of *Athena*'s marine NCOs, leaned against the wall. He snapped to attention as Jared came out.

"At ease." Jared motioned for the marine to walk with him. "I understand that we have you to thank for keeping the princess in one piece. Good work."

The large man smiled wryly and shook his head. "You have it backward, Captain. She saved our bacon. She killed two Pale Ones, one with a pistol and one with her bare hands. They'd have cut me up just like her if she hadn't done what needed to be done."

"I read that, but part of me still finds it hard to believe. Hell, she's so small I could wrestle her with one arm tied behind my back. I can't imagine her choking someone to death with her bare hands. Frankly, I can't imagine her hurting anyone at all."

"Try imagining her ripping a metal bar out of plascrete. I saw her do that this morning. With one hand. She doesn't know I was there. It breaks my heart."

"I'm told that they did something to improve her ability to control herself. Stone says she was walking without assistance a little bit ago." Jared stepped into an empty waiting room. "Kelsey has a lot of recovery to do, and some reassessing. You marines have supported her so much. I'd like you to help her out even more."

Talbot nodded. "Of course, sir. We'll do everything we can."

"I want you to go all the way. She has equipment inside her that makes her very, very dangerous. Not just to someone that threatens her, either. Doctor Stone says she has what the Old Empire called a commando implant package. She probably also has some buried triggers to go with it. She needs training and something to focus her as she figures things out.

"She'll need to continue her work as our ambassador, but she needs the structure and support of someone that understands something of what she's being thrust into. None of you has the hardware she has, and none of us understands exactly what they did to her, but some marine training might help her adjust. She could really benefit from as much one-on-one time as possible. Will you help her?"

The marine nodded sharply. "Certainly. She'll jump at the opportunity for a few reasons. One, she knows she needs to learn about her new condition. Two, she's desperate to have some control over her life."

The NCO stared through the glass at the medical personnel walking by. "We've been spending a lot of time together this last week. I think we've developed a strong rapport. She'd make a terrible marine. She's a civilian through and through. That said, we could help her and learn a lot about how the Old Empire fought through her. I want to help her get past this bad mental space she's in."

Jared clapped his hand on the marine's shoulder. "Excellent. Talk with Lieutenant Reese and work out a training regimen that tells us what she's capable of while giving her a reason to embrace who she is now. You'll be running point. We'll never get that equipment out of her, so she needs to become accustomed to it. And while I can't imagine anyone wanting to do it, there exists the possibility that she won't be the last of us with implants. Her pain and struggle will help those who follow in her footsteps."

"Aye, sir. I'll finalize everything with the LT and start as soon as Doctor Stone gives me the green light."

Jared took a step toward the door. "We'll be heading back to *Courageous* in a few days. The marines are going with us. I'm not sure if we'll stay on the battlecruiser or the freighter, but be ready to start working with her after we get there. Kelsey will be splitting her time between Doctor Stone, Commander Baxter, and you. I'll explain the situation to her when the time comes."

Talbot stood a little straighter. "Actually, sir, it might be best if I explain it to her. I think she'll take it better if I say this is my idea. It really is. You just made it an order."

"I leave it in your capable hands, then. Get some stability back in her life, Senior Sergeant. I'm counting on you."

The man snapped him a razor-sharp salute. "Aye, sir. I'll give her my very best."

Jared returned the salute. Once the marine NCO was gone, he stood there wondering if he was making the right decision. Not that he could think of any better options. He sighed. They'd play things one day at a time. Right now, he needed to figure out where he'd be staying for the next few days.

6

O f course, getting out from under Lily's thumb wasn't nearly as easy as Kelsey had hoped. The doctor kept her under observation for a full twenty-four hours so that she could monitor Kelsey's progress. If Kelsey had thought she had any chance of success at all, she'd have told Lily that she was checking out bright and early the next morning, but she knew that wasn't happening. Medical types seemed amazingly immune to rank and social status.

Lily reluctantly agreed to allow Kelsey to go on a sightseeing excursion, but she had some restrictions. First, Kelsey would travel in a grav chair. She could get up and walk around, but the doctor didn't want her exerting herself unnecessarily.

Which was ridiculous, of course. Kelsey was more than capable of supporting her own weight. And the weight of any medical equipment that she happened to be holding at any given time. Which was probably the point. At least if she was sitting, any accidents wouldn't be too large in scale.

Her second restriction was that Kelsey ate often and in quantity. She wouldn't get any argument on that. Kelsey was hungry all the time. Lily said it had to do with her boosted metabolism. Kelsey wasn't certain why a bunch of artificial implants required her to eat like a horse, but it was obviously true.

That was going to take some getting used to. Kelsey was a very small woman, but now she was eating more than most marines. Male marines.

She'd just finished devouring an embarrassingly large breakfast when Elise came to pick her up. The Pentagaran noblewoman eyed the plates on the table with a smile as she sat down. "Were you a little hungry this morning?"

"You could say that. It's humiliating."

"Why is it humiliating?"

"People watch me eating with an expression like they can't believe it."

Elise laughed. "If your diet is the most exciting thing people talk about, you're lucky. People will adjust. Don't worry about what they think."

"That's easy for you to say," Kelsey muttered. "You don't have all this junk inside you. I'm just like one of those Pale Ones."

The crown princess's eyes flashed. "You. Are. Not. Don't even *think* that. You have the same kind of implants as any number of Old Empire citizens, so if you have to compare yourself to anyone, make it them. Admittedly, most people in the Old Empire probably didn't have as significant an enhancement as you have, but if that sprawling civilization didn't see it as a shameful thing, neither should you."

Elise waved a hand at the other people in the cafeteria. "Times are changing. With the rediscovery of this technology, how many of these people do you think will eventually end up with some kind of implant?"

Kelsey shook her head. "I can't imagine any of them would do that, given the choice."

"You'd be wrong. Yes, the idea of the Pale Ones terrifies anyone in their right mind, but taking a quantum leap toward restoring the Old Empire excites them, too. Not as a political unit but as a reality. It's hard for you to see the opportunities that your implants represent, but I can see them. Lord Captain Mertz can see them. Even my father can see them."

Kelsey shook her head in denial. "Why would anyone choose to do that to themselves?"

Elise poured herself a cup of coffee from the insulated container on the table. "Do you suppose the Old Empire would've had widespread implants in Fleet unless they made a difference? It must've given them some significant advantage, don't you think?"

"And a very specific and powerful disadvantage when the rebellion started."

"True, but if the Pale Ones capture us, we get implanted anyway. We don't have a whole lot to lose at this point. The Empire has already fallen. Am I advocating that everybody rush out and get implants the first moment they possibly can? No.

"But as they see you adjusting to your new circumstances, people *will* start volunteering. People that see the advantages of being able to interface directly with advanced equipment. With each brave soul, you'll become more the norm than the exception. Don't worry about how people perceive you. Whatever they think now, they won't be thinking it in a few years."

Kelsey mulled over Elise's words as she finished her coffee. Everything the other woman said made sense, but that didn't make it easy to accept. Yet what choice did Kelsey have? She was going to be this way, whether she liked it or not. She might as well set a good example.

"I still think everyone expects me to look like a cow in a month," Kelsey grumbled. She eyed the grav chair sitting beside the table. She'd gotten out of it to sit in a real chair while she ate. Now she had to get back in it.

Doctor's orders. At least they'd reinstalled the controls. She sighed and got into the chair.

Elise stood. "The cars are waiting around front, and your half brother is somewhere close by. My father invited the both of you to visit the Parliament Building. They aren't in session right now, but the architecture is amazing. You'll have a good time. I promise."

Kelsey nudged her chair to follow the crown princess out of the cafeteria. "Exactly what role does Parliament play in your monarchy? Do you have a prime minister? We have the Senate at home for our nobles and the Commons for the elected representatives. No prime minister, though."

"We don't have a prime minister, either," Elise said. "There are a number of ministers, though. We don't have any nobles outside the Royal Family. The baron who founded the monarchy after the fall decided it would be best if the people had a voice. So Parliament considers prospective laws and sends the ones they like to my father. If he disagrees, two thirds of them can overrule him. They're also responsible for the Royal budget."

"Doesn't that cause a lot of friction?"

Elise shrugged. "At times. There are always various factions at figurative war with one another. I'm sure you have that and more at home. We at least have an ongoing war to keep everyone moving in the same direction."

They exited the hospital, and a wall of sound overwhelmed Kelsey. It took every ounce of her willpower to keep from clapping her hands over her ears. People were screaming. Lots of people.

It took a moment for her to process what she was seeing. People filled the street. Her presence seemed to set off a roar of approval. Like when someone scored at a sporting event. Only louder. Much louder.

The unexpected sight—and sound—of them froze her in place. What were they doing? Were they going to attack her?

Elise put her hand on Kelsey's shoulder. "Breathe. Smile. Wave at them. They're here because of you."

Kelsey smiled and waved while she considered retreating into the hospital.

The crowd went nuts. She'd only thought their volume was impressive before. She expected them to burst through the security cordon, but they just waved signs and flags and screamed their heads off with excitement. At least her auditory implants were scaling the volume back down to something reasonable.

"I don't understand," she said, hoping Elise could hear her.

"Have you ever heard that an adventure was something terrible that happened to someone else far away? Well, you've been on an adventure, and you saved them all from a fate literally worse than death."

Kelsey stared at the Pentagaran princess. "I did not! I stuck my head into a hornets' nest and was lucky enough to survive the experience. Jared saved them. All the people on *Athena* saved them. I almost got everyone killed. If they knew what I was, they'd be terrified."

Elise narrowed her eyes, her public smile never faltering. "Stop it. They don't know, and by the time they do, they won't care. Mark my words. Now, let's get out of here."

Rather than the grav limo that she'd traveled in the first time Kelsey visited, Elise had brought a rather fancy grav van. It had windows just like a regular vehicle, but the rear had a space between the seats for Kelsey's grav chair. Additional Royal Guards stood near other waiting grav vehicles.

Standing beside the van were Senior Sergeant Talbot and several other marines. They wore pressed fatigues and had pistols at their hips. It looked like she had her own escort.

She pulled up beside him. "Don't you clean up nice, Senior Sergeant Talbot?"

In fact, he looked better than good. Talbot was already a ruggedly handsome man, but the uniform added an extra dash. She had to admit that their shared experiences had drawn them closer over the last week and made her much more aware of him as a man. Part of her wished class and age didn't separate them so much, because she wouldn't mind getting to know him better still.

Even if that meant he ran the risk of her father exiling him to Thule.

Ah well, some things were not meant to be. Talbot would never see her as anything other than his emperor's daughter and a thorn in his side that had almost gotten him killed.

He grinned at her. "That's what they tell me, Princess. How are you feeling?"

She suppressed the way his smile made her melt a little inside. "I'm ready to get out of this chair. I don't suppose you'd consider helping me escape, would you? A quick getaway from all these people with needles?"

He looked sympathetic but shook his head. "Sorry, Princess, but I have my orders. The crown princess has her people to watch out for her, and we're going to watch out for you. And Captain Mertz, of course."

She looked around for her half brother but didn't see him. "Forgive me, but this doesn't seem to be the most dangerous place I've ever been. It seems downright peaceful compared to the other vacation spots I've seen recently. I'm certain that the Royal Guard will make sure I'm not injured in some random event."

He looked mulish. "I'm sure they would, but it's not their duty. It's ours. I'm certain Pentagar is a very orderly place, all things considered, but the princess wouldn't have her own guards if there wasn't a reason."

Kelsey raised her eyebrow at Elise. "Do you have a reason for them?"

Elise nodded. "Certainly. First, there's tradition. The Royal Family doesn't go anywhere without a guard. At least not unless they can slip away when no one is looking. It's not so much that we expect trouble or have enemies. It's more like having an armed military, they don't go around looking for trouble, but when it finds them, they're ready for it. No one has assassinated a member of the Royal Family since the founding of the Monarchy. I think we're probably pretty safe, but it's still best to go with tradition."

"The Terran Empire has that tradition too," Talbot added. "The Imperial Family is watched over at all times. Admittedly, it's sometimes very low key, but that doesn't mean that the guards aren't there. Since none of the Imperial Guard came along on this trip, it's up to the marines to fill that void."

Kelsey felt a little exasperated. "You didn't do that on *Athena*."

"No," he said patiently. "There wasn't any need. Not with Fleet personnel around you all the time. Though honestly, we should've assigned a couple of marines to escort you. Chalk that mistake up to inexperience on our part."

She sighed. "You weren't doing this in the hospital."

"Just because you didn't see us in the hospital doesn't mean we weren't there. We had a couple of people standing by just out of sight. There's no reason to intrude on your privacy if we're not out in public. Ah, here comes Captain Mertz."

Kelsey turned in her chair and saw her half brother walking out of the hospital.

He smiled and waved as the crowd roared again. Jared reacted to them as though this had been happening all his life. He stopped beside Kelsey's chair. "Sorry I'm late. Doctor Stone had some last-minute instructions for me."

Kelsey sighed. "Now what? Is she going to have me tied to the chair?"

"She just wanted me to be an outside observer on how your implants react to external stimuli. Her words, not mine. So if something unusual happens, be sure and let me know."

"I'll be certain you're the second to know."

Elise took charge and saw everybody into their respective vehicles. Talbot and one of his marines sat in front of Kelsey. Elise took the seat to her left and Jared sat on her right.

The driver made certain to come at the Parliament Building with an eye to the view. Kelsey had to admit it was a gorgeous piece of architecture. Tall columns of stone held up a massive façade filled with carvings out of Terran mythology. She had to admit that she didn't know all of the people represented there. She'd have to see if there was a handout to explain who everyone was.

The grav vehicles landed in front of the building and disgorged their passengers. A number of policemen kept what looked like tourists at bay as the Royal party entered the building. Kelsey imagined the Parliament Building was a major tourist attraction.

The foyer continued the theme from outside. Polished granite floors gleamed in every direction, and walls shaped from molded plaster flanked them on every side. Paintings and statuary filled every niche. Tour groups wandered through the areas that Kelsey could see, admiring the artwork and the architecture.

The crown princess gestured toward a wide set of stairs leading to the second level. "We'll go up and take a peek down into the main chamber.

Then we'll make the circuit and stop if anything catches your eye. This building has some of the most important pieces of artwork in the Kingdom. Kelsey, if you look behind the speaker's podium, you'll see another of Master Vestor's carvings. I'm looking forward to seeing Lord Captain Mertz's reaction to it."

Kelsey smiled at Jared's raised eyebrow. "You're going to love this. If it's anything like the one I saw last week, it's the most amazing piece of art you'll ever see."

Her grav chair went up the stairs without any problem. The second level looked very much like the first, except that there were no tour groups.

"I took the liberty of having the second level closed off in advance of our arrival," Elise said. "My father and I thought it would be less distracting for everyone. Speaking of which, there he is."

A pair of heavy wooden doors opened in front of them. His Majesty, King Raymond Orison, came through them with his guards at his heels. He smiled widely as the men with him closed the doors, no doubt so they could examine the carvings on them at some point. "Kelsey! You're looking splendid! I'm so pleased to see you up and about."

He turned his attention to Jared, extending his hand. "Lord Captain Mertz, what a pleasure it is to finally meet you. I was beginning to think I'd have to travel into orbit to make your acquaintance. On behalf of my people, you have my deepest gratitude. Through your actions and those of your people, the threat of a Pale Ones invasion seems remote for the first time in our collective lives. The Kingdom is deeply in your debt."

Jared looked a little embarrassed but not intimidated. Kelsey supposed that being the bastard son of an emperor might make one immune to intimidation by social status.

"Your Majesty. I only did what anyone else would've done. Circumstances just worked out to a favorable outcome."

Raymond clapped his hand on Jared's shoulder. "Be that as it may, you're quite the hero to us. Come. Let me show you the parliamentary chamber. We're quite proud of it."

The entire group began moving toward the double doors. The sound of conversation and steps on the stone floor caused Kelsey to glance to the left. It appeared as though the police hadn't blocked off all the tour groups, because one was coming toward them. The tour guide was pointing out a painting on the wall and beginning to recite its history while a dozen people spread out to see it better.

Elise said something to one of the Royal Guards, and he began walking toward the group, no doubt to send them back downstairs.

He'd only taken a few steps when something caught Kelsey's eye. At first, she couldn't figure out what was wrong, but suddenly her ocular implants kicked into action. An overlay began making red highlights on the people in front of her. A few at first, then quickly all of them. They were heavily armed.

Kelsey began moving before she even consciously realized what she was seeing, heading for the double doors in front of her. "It's an ambush! Run!"

The world seemed to slow to a crawl, and an ice-cold chill ran through her blood. She'd never felt anything like it before.

No, she'd felt something exactly like this before, when she'd fought the Pale Ones after she'd been implanted.

The people around her were still turning their heads, their hands reaching for weapons, while she dodged between their suddenly slow bodies. She grabbed Raymond with one hand and Elise with the other, effortlessly pulling them along in her wake. She knew that she'd unbalanced them, but she had to get them out of harm's way before the shooting started. She felt Jared only starting to follow them.

Without checking, she instinctively knew that the governors on her strength had switched off, so she was unsurprised when she hit the doors with her shoulder and they flew inward. The armed men on the other side, however, were quite surprised. It looked as though the fake tour group was not the only ambush she'd just ruined.

Her implants rapidly tallied six people lying in wait on the upper deck of the parliamentary chamber even as a storm of gunshots began behind her. A thick wooden door to the face inconvenienced one of the new ambushers. The man standing directly in front of Kelsey was bringing a pistol up to fire, but he hadn't been ready for her intrusion. His hand moved with syrupy slowness.

Kelsey's hands moved with lightning speed, which was somewhat of a surprise since she hadn't instructed them to move at all. Her left hand grabbed his wrist with a crunch that she knew meant broken bones and yanked him forward so that his face met her open hand with an impact that made her wince.

He was already falling backward, unconscious or dead, as she rounded on the man next to him. She positioned herself between the attackers and King Raymond.

One man almost had his gun lined up on Kelsey. A quick step forward brought her into range to plant her foot between his legs with every ounce of strength she could manage. He flew backward with enough force to take down the man behind him.

Jared interposed himself between the furthest man on the right and Elise. The two men struggled for control of the attacker's pistol. It looked as though her half brother had the situation under enough control for her to deal with the other threats still in the room.

She'd almost reached the last man when he pulled the trigger on his gun. The shot was loud, but not as loud as Kelsey expected. A mild burning sensation ran along the back of her right arm as she ducked under his aim and drove her left fist into his crotch. Whatever was in control of her body certainly knew how to hurt a guy. The man didn't even scream as he collapsed.

Three threats remained: the man she'd knocked down with the door, the man taken down when she kicked his friend on top of him, and the man struggling with Jared. The man behind the door had lost his pistol, so she downgraded his threat potential. The man in front of her still had his, but he was struggling with his companion's dead weight.

That left her time to deal with Jared's problem. She didn't consciously decide what to do, only that he was the top threat. Her right hand struck backwards at maximum strength into the base of his skull. The crunch of bone wouldn't be a sound she easily forgot. He instantly became a nonthreat.

Two running steps forward and she launched herself into the air, landing on the man in front of her just as he rolled out from under his friend. His breath shot out explosively as she drove her feet into his gut. She bent and ripped the pistol out of his hand to the accompaniment of snapping finger bones and a scream.

She turned the weapon on the man crawling from behind the door. He'd just grabbed his pistol off the floor. She emptied her appropriated weapon into him.

Royal Guards and Imperial Marines flooded into the room, still firing at the men outside. One of them slammed and locked the double doors. They must've been tough, because they didn't give when the men outside started shooting them, though Kelsey could hear the impacts.

A quick scan of the room didn't reveal any other threats, so she went along when Talbot tugged on her arm. "Let's get out of here before they find another way in."

All of them ran for a set of stairs leading down to the chamber floor. The Royal Guards split between guarding the rear and leading the way. They made it down unmolested. The police were herding panicked men, women, and children out the main exit as they joined the throng and fled the building.

7

J ared halfway expected another attack before they exited the building, but they fought through a growing crowd of policemen and piled into the grav van without further trouble. Their vehicle took off at a high rate of speed before any of them had a chance to put on their restraints.

Talbot staggered in front of Princess Kelsey. "Let me look at that shoulder."

"I'm okay," she said in a shaky voice.

"Then how come your sleeve is covered in blood?"

Jared turned toward her and saw that it was true. He watched the marine rip her sleeve open and examine the long gash down her upper arm. It must've been four inches in length, but it didn't look too deep.

One of the Royal Guards handed him a medical kit. The marine found a bandage and efficiently wrapped it around the princess's arm. "As far as bullet wounds go, this isn't too bad. If you'd been half a second faster, he'd have missed you entirely. It'll regenerate without any issue. You won't even have a scar."

"I wear all my scars on the inside."

Jared shook his head disbelievingly. "Faster? I can't imagine how she moved as fast as she did. She took them down while I was still wrestling with one guy. I have never seen *anyone* move that fast in my life."

Elise nodded vigorously. "It was unbelievable. It was as if she was fighting all of them at the same time. Hitting one, kicking the other, she was almost a blur. I had no idea that that's what a…"

Kelsey grimaced. "What a Pale Ones attack looks like? It wasn't really. They're tough and fight like that, but they move about the same speed as everyone else. I'm pretty sure my implants have some features theirs lack."

Jared had to agree. While the marines hadn't let him into the fight on the orbital, he'd seen the Pale Ones moving. His sister was *significantly* faster. "Kelsey, you saved our lives today. There's no doubt in my mind. Whoever those people were, they had us dead to rights. If you hadn't spotted them and then literally broken the attack behind the door, they'd have shot us down. Thank you."

She looked a little embarrassed at his words. "You're welcome."

Jared turned his attention to the king. "Are you all right, Your Majesty? I had no idea that you had that dedicated an enemy."

King Raymond smiled wanly. "Neither did I. Nothing like this has ever happened before. Not just during my reign, but ever. There are always individuals who are opposed to the Monarchy—sometimes violently—but never this organized."

Elise shook her head. "Obviously, we have an underground movement. I receive the same briefings as my father, and no one has ever mentioned anything like this. That's a serious intelligence failure on our part. Someone out there considers us an enemy, and we need to figure out who it is."

She looked at one of the Royal Guards. "Craig, what is the situation back there? Did we lose anyone? Did we capture any of them alive?"

He muttered into a microphone on his collar and pressed an ear bud more tightly into his ear. He grimaced. "It's not good, Highness. We have seven men missing. The police were still closing in when something exploded. The damage to the structure was significant. They haven't found any survivors from the second floor."

Talbot shook his head. "Dedicated and ruthless. Someone wanted to make sure that none of their people talked. Dead men tell no tales."

Elise said something very unladylike. "Unbelievable. How could we have missed something like this? We were totally unprepared for anything of this magnitude."

The guard gestured toward Kelsey. "Our losses would've been a lot worse if Princess Kelsey hadn't given us a warning. She sprang the trap before it was ready to close. If they'd gotten close to us, they could've taken us. They had numerical superiority and tactical surprise."

"What exactly happened back there?" Jared asked. "What tipped you off? What happened when the fight started?"

"It all happened so fast. I'm not sure exactly what my implants saw, but a whole bunch of warnings popped up into my field of vision that those people were armed. It even showed me exactly where the weapons were. Once the attack started, it was like the implants took control of my body.

"Not like with the Pale Ones. I could've stopped if I wanted to. I know that. It was like a preprogrammed set of responses to a threat. I saw the Pale Ones do something like that in hand-to-hand combat. The implants also helped me aim that pistol I picked up. My first shot missed, but then my aim seemed to compensate for the kick of the weapon. Believe me, I am nowhere near that good a shot."

Jared believed her. He imagined she didn't get much practice shooting things. That really wasn't her style. "When you came in and fought them hand to hand, it was like one of the martial arts masters in an old B-grade vid. I had no idea you could do that, even after everything we've learned about the Pale Ones. You're taking this situation remarkably well."

Kelsey rubbed her face. "I feel like I should be going into shock, but I'm completely calm. I think the pharmacology unit dosed me with something. Everything seems to be moving so slowly. It's as if I have an eternity to think about everything. Whatever happened to me is only just starting to wear off."

Princess Elise put her hand on Kelsey's. "Well, whatever happened, we are in your debt. Again. If you hadn't been there, my father and I would have been killed. I deeply appreciate what you've done for us."

"Allow me to second that," the king said. "Whoever they were, they must've been waiting for just the right moment to make their presence known. Now that we know that there's a violent, clandestine resistance, we can take steps to figure out who they are and how to stop them." His voice hardened. "And we will take those steps."

He grimaced. "Someone inside of our organization had to have leaked our travel plans to them. They were in place before we arrived."

The grav van and its escorts landed at the palace. The grounds were swarming with people. Not just Royal Guards, but Pentagaran military in body armor with heavy weapons. The guards hustled everyone inside as soon as the van landed.

A pair of physicians rushed to His Majesty's side. They tried to take Elise, but she waved them away. "I'm fine. See to our guests. Particularly, see to Princess Kelsey. A bullet grazed her arm, and she may be under the influence of an unknown combat drug that's starting to wear off. I want her under close observation in case there are any complications."

Jared pulled his communications unit off his belt. "Speaking of physicians, I'd better let Doctor Stone know what happened. She can pass it on to the rest of our people before some kind of rumor starts circulating." He looked at Kelsey. "I'm certain that she's going to want to examine you in person."

Kelsey rolled her eyes. "Wonderful. I finally get out from under her thumb for one day and now she's going to lock me into a room and throw away the key. Somehow, she's going to find a way to blame me for this."

He chuckled without humor. "Not everything is about you, Kelsey. She's a military officer. She's going to see this for what it is."

Kelsey went with King Raymond and the doctors, grumbling under her breath.

Jared called Doctor Stone and explained what had happened. As expected, she cut the conversation short, shouting for her people to get moving as she disconnected.

He put his communicator back on his belt. "You'll probably want to tell someone that Doctor Stone is on her way."

Elise put her hand on his shoulder. "Kelsey isn't the only hero today. You got into a fistfight with a man that was going to shoot me. That was very brave, and I'm grateful."

Her hand felt hot through the fabric of his shirt, and he became quite aware of how close she was standing to him. The recent life-and-death struggle had made him hyperaware of her as a woman. A very beautiful woman.

His voice was astonishingly calm. "You're welcome, but he would've shot me too, so I had a horse in this race."

She gestured for him to accompany her into one of the rooms nearby. A number of the Royal Guards closed around them as they went, no doubt still worried about assassins. He couldn't blame them.

Her destination turned out to be a sitting room. The two of them took seats facing one another as the guards arrayed themselves around the room.

"I'm so very sorry that your first real visit to our planet turned out this way. I promise you, Pentagar is a peaceful, wonderful place."

He felt the corner of his mouth quirk up. "I will admit that stumbling into a space battle on my first transition into your system and then an assassination attempt on my first landing certainly seems to show a contrary trend. I'm sure Pentagar is a wonderful place and that this isn't characteristic of your beautiful world. I promise I won't hold it against you."

"I hope you don't. Once we have everything settled, I insist that you allow me to show you what our world is really like." She raised a finger when he opened his mouth. "I insist."

"Of course, I accept. However, I'm afraid that this attack is going to move up our departure timetable. I think it might be best for us to head to *Athena* as soon as Kelsey is ready to travel. No offense, but the last thing you need is to have us caught up in your internal affairs."

Elise nodded. "I understand completely, Lord Captain. We need time to figure out exactly what happened here. It would be best for everyone if any additional violence passes you by. Now that we know about this movement, we'll be on our guard. The perpetrators of this atrocity will pay." Her voice was as unyielding as steel.

8

L ord Admiral Shrike answered his communications unit with more than a hint of trepidation. If things had gone well, good and fine. But if they hadn't, his life and his plans were about to become much more complicated.

None of his concern reached his voice. One always needed to sound like they were in complete command no matter what was happening. Any naval officer worth his salt knew that.

"Shrike."

"Oh, I'm very sorry," a woman's voice said. "I must've entered the wrong number."

"That's quite all right. Have a good day."

He disconnected and cursed under his breath. If the attack had gone as planned, his contact would've asked for someone named Blake. This meant they'd failed. Perhaps not completely, but at least one of the Royals had escaped the trap.

Hopefully, his men had managed to kill the king. Princess Elise would have much less experience to fall back on as she tried to defend against his next move. He also hoped that the woman he'd placed in charge of the operation had made certain no one fell into the hands of Royal Intelligence. That would be truly unfortunate.

The men chosen for this operation didn't know anything about him personally, of course. The less the Royalists knew, the better his chances of ultimate success. They wouldn't be suspecting him, but it never paid to take chances when the punishment for treason was execution by beheading.

He knew it would only be a matter of minutes before word began circulating about the attack, so if he wanted to get an update of the true events, he needed to get it now. He locked down his console, set his communications unit on the center of the blotter, and walked into the outer office. His secretary looked up inquiringly.

"I'm stepping out for lunch. If there are any calls, take a message. I should be back in half an hour."

When word came in, he'd have the excuse that he left his communications unit on his desk. It was understandable enough. Everyone did it on occasion. In this case, it would give him the time he needed to get that update.

He walked out of Royal Fleet Command and flagged down a taxi. He told the driver to take him to a place that he often frequented. He knew he could order in, but he made a habit of going to various locations to eat so that he didn't spend all his time in the office. It would also serve as cover for this trip.

It was somewhat earlier than the normal lunch rush when he arrived, so he quickly found a seat. The man behind the counter nodded in recognition of his arrival. He always ordered the same thing, so the man knew what Shrike wanted. As a member of the movement, he knew exactly what Shrike meant when he held up two fingers.

The man quickly made Shrike's sandwich and brought it to his table with some unsweetened tea. As he set it down, he also laid a communications unit on the table under the napkin he carried.

Shrike dialed a number from memory as soon as the man was gone. The woman he'd spoken to earlier answered on the second chime. "Go ahead," he said.

"Resistance was stiffer than anticipated. In the end, none of the primary goals were accomplished."

"What about our assets?"

"I'm afraid it became necessary to liquidate them. I'm not certain of what went wrong, but the investment is a total loss. That is confirmed."

That, at least, was good news. "Keep me informed of any further developments." He terminated the call without another word.

He placed the communications unit under the napkin and slowly ate his sandwich, thinking about what steps he could take to minimize his exposure while simultaneously advancing his agenda.

Unfortunately, he couldn't think of anything in the short term. No doubt, security around the Royals would increase greatly in the wake of the attack. He'd have to take it slower and play a longer game.

The Royal Family would be on their guard, and both the intelligence services and police would be investigating all leads for weeks or even months. That didn't mean that he had to wait that long to achieve the deaths of his enemies, but it did mean that he'd need to exercise greater care.

The days when he had to bow and scrape to his father were almost done. Jared Mertz might be willing to live in the shadow of his legitimate siblings, but Shrike wasn't. He deserved the Crown, and he would take it for himself.

Perhaps Rawlins would seize the Old Empire warship if it proved possible to restore it to some functionality. Shrike thought that unlikely. Of course, the best time to act would be after the ship was functional but before it returned to Pentagar. With the small number of men that Rawlins was taking, that would be quite the trick.

However, the intelligence officer had proven himself quite capable in the past. Rawlins had removed several... hindrances... to the plan without anyone being the wiser. The accidents were never the same, and the police never grew suspicious.

Of course, Shrike still didn't have the majority of Royal Fleet ships under his control, but the key officers he'd put into place would turn the tables with the right momentum. Unveiling the movement's possession of an Old Empire battlecruiser would be perfect.

Shrike left the payment for his lunch on the table. He might have to wait for success, he thought, but he'd learned patience. Once he had control of the Royal Fleet, the Crown would be his, and his *family* could rot.

9

—————

Despite Kelsey's objections, Lily insisted that she rest. The princess was secretly glad the doctor put her foot down. After the attack, her body felt more alive than she'd ever been, though the crash when the drugs had worn off had been epic.

Sleep was challenging, too. Nightmares had plagued her sleep over the last three days as *Athena* made its slow way out to the flip point. Last night, the fight on Pentagar played itself out again, only this time, no matter how many people she killed, there were always more. Just when she defeated the human attackers, the Pale Ones took over. She woke screaming several times before she gave up on sleep entirely.

So she was tired and more than a bit cranky. Talbot made her even more self-conscious when he made a point of looking at her dinner that evening and then at his own. His was the smaller of the two by a substantial margin.

"I can't help it," she said. "I'm starving. Something is wrong with my stomach."

"I doubt that very seriously, Princess." The marine slid a piece of pie over to her side of the table.

He'd insisted that she come out of her cabin and eat in the crew's mess. She had to admit the noisy compartment felt good. The crew seemed pleased to see her.

The compartment held an equal mixture of Pentagaran Royal Fleet personnel, scientists, and Terran Fleet crew. She wasn't quite sure how to interpret the Pentagarans' stares. Most seemed to be watching her with interest, but a few had a hint of fear or distrust in their gazes.

Probably because of what she'd become. Rumors had swirled wildly after the assassination attempt. What she'd overheard—and with her enhanced hearing, she'd heard a lot—varied from the fantastical to versions that were almost correct. The nature of her "injuries" was out in the open now, the cover story destroyed by a recording from the Parliament Building security systems that someone had leaked.

She had to admit she'd watched it several times, shocked at the sheer speed and lethality of her counterattack. Her face hadn't looked like one of the Pale Ones as she fought. Her expression was serene, as though she were dancing. Frankly, that terrified her. She hadn't been in control. Her implants had made her a backseat driver.

Kelsey now understood exactly how the rebels had perverted the implants during the Fall. They'd overwritten the code that dictated when the implants could make the body act. They'd removed the human host from the control loop.

That was what woke her screaming in the dark.

It took a nudge from Talbot to bring her back into the present. She should've refused the second piece of pie, but to her shame, she was still hungry. Her fork started efficiently moving it to her mouth. "What makes you think this pie isn't going straight to my thighs? I can't ever remember gorging like this. I'm a pig."

"Your metabolism is jacked up into overdrive. You have artificial muscles, and other things, that your body is powering. Your real muscles probably have to work hard to keep up. Think about how much energy you must've used during that fight. You were terrific, by the way."

She felt her face coloring as a chill ran down her spine. "It was kind of freaky. Once the fighting started, my body began moving on autopilot. I decided to fight, and my implants took control. I was like a horrified spectator while my hands were crushing flesh and snapping bones."

"I'm not going to tell you that it's okay," he said flatly. "You weren't trained for anything like that. I'm sure it was horrible for you, but you did what needed doing. You saved the day. In the end, that's what matters. You were very brave."

Embarrassed even further, she decided to change the subject. "I wish I could find out more about my condition, but no one alive can give me the briefing that an Imperial Marine would've gotten in basic training, much less tell me what my commando implants are capable of." She finished the pie and set the fork down resolutely. "I might have a listing of some of the enhancements, but I don't have an owner's manual."

Talbot took a sip of his beer. "I bet you do. You just have to figure out how to access the help files. Maybe Junior can help figure it out."

He meant Carl Owlet. She wished she had a beer. All Lily allowed her now was water.

"He's still trying to figure out how to say "hello world" in the Old Empire programming language. Whatever that means." She hunched down in her chair and sulked. "I'm never going to figure this out."

"Doctor Stone is a fine physician, but she has one notable flaw. She's too cautious. You need to explore your boundaries. You need to start pushing yourself. Learning your new limits."

"Right. Then I'll rip someone's arm off."

"Don't fall into that mental trap," he said evenly. "Combat is not losing control. You stopped men determined to kill you. That's a *good* thing." He pushed his plate back. "Doctor Stone has one other failing. She's not here. Come down to marine country with me, and we'll do some off-the-books experimentation."

Kelsey tried to judge if he was being serious. He certainly seemed to be. "Is that safe?"

"Nothing in this world is safe, kid. Look, you have Old Empire combat implants inside you. You need the marines to help you figure them out safely. We also need to have an idea of what your capabilities are. We can teach you and learn from you at the same time."

"I'm a little short to be a marine, and I'm lousy at doing what people tell me to do. You can ask Jared. Or my father."

The marine NCO grinned. "I'm not suggesting you enlist. Think of it as being an honorary marine."

"I'm not sure that Jared would appreciate me doing this. I want to. I really do, but I don't want to screw up again."

Talbot finished his beer and stood. "Then it's a good thing I already got his approval, and Lieutenant Reese's, too. They both think this is a good idea, if you're agreeable."

"Yes," she said without needing to think. "Hell, yes."

"Then let's go get started."

The walk down to marine country showcased the terrible damage *Athena* had taken in battle. Fire had scarred and burned the bulkheads in so many places. The damage became worse the farther aft they went. It made her sick. It made her feel guilty.

She didn't say anything. After the talk Jared had given her, she knew that she just had to keep those feelings to herself.

The damage in marine country was mostly gone. Two of the marines were painting a bulkhead while others packed various pieces of equipment.

Lieutenant Reese came out of his office with a duffel bag. He set it down when he saw her and came directly over. He smiled and held out his hand. "Princess Kelsey. It's good to see you up and about. Congratulations on your stellar performance the other day. You did us proud."

She hesitated at taking the hand he offered. "I don't think you want me shaking your hand. You might need it later."

"I'm a marine. They pay me to be unspeakably brave." He kept his hand extended.

Kelsey's memory of ripping the walking support out of the plascrete was at the forefront of her thoughts. The way she'd broken bones and killed during the ambush. She took a breath and shook his hand.

He didn't release her. "That wasn't very convincing. I promise I'll scream like a little girl if you hurt me."

"If you pull some kind of prank on me, I'm probably going to hurt you by accident."

"I'm an officer and a gentleman. I leave the pranking to the men and women under my command. Come on. You need to stop being so hesitant."

She gave him a firmer handshake. Then one with even more strength when he shook his head.

"Why are you doing this?" she asked, her heart racing.

"To give you confidence. You need to stop being afraid you'll hurt us. Forget the implants and shake my hand like you've done all your life."

Kelsey gave up and prayed the governors worked like Twelve had said.

"Now we're talking!" Reese said.

She snatched her hand back as soon as he released it. "This is going to be hard. I've decided to take Senior Sergeant Talbot up on his offer to help train me."

"Nothing worthwhile is ever easy. We're packing up, but I can have anything you need brought out."

"If you don't mind me asking, why are you painting the bulkhead? You're leaving *Athena*. Probably forever."

"Marine country will be shipshape before we leave. If any marine ever returns, they'll find everything in order. It's our way." He turned to Talbot. "What do you have in mind?"

"Nothing too exciting, I think. Right now, she doesn't even know many of her capabilities. I'm hoping she can figure out how to interface with her equipment."

The officer nodded. "Good idea. Use the gym. We haven't started packing it yet."

"Thank you, sir." Talbot gestured for Kelsey to go to one of the compartments she'd never been in before.

Workout machines filled one side of the large compartment and padded mats the other. One corner held free weights that had been scattered at some point in the battle. She could almost see the sweating men grunting under the heavy weights.

"Do you want me to work out?" she asked.

He shook his head. "Why don't we sit on the mats? You've interfaced with Old Empire equipment before, so I'd like you to tell me about it while we relax."

Kelsey knelt on the pads, sitting back on her heels. The protective mats were thinner than she'd expected. It probably hurt to fall on them.

She relaxed and told him about how she'd seen the Old Empire machine's schematics when she wanted to know more about it. How she'd seemingly known where to shoot with the unfamiliar pistol.

"Honestly, it was more like something happened to me rather than me making it happen," she added when she was done.

Talbot sat in front of her with his legs crossed and his hands in his lap. He looked very comfortable in the position. She wondered if he meditated.

"So, you saw or felt the Old Empire computer when you tried to sense it. Do you see yourself when you try to access the implants?"

She shook her head.

"Try to sense yourself the same way. One would think the interface would be similar. Why make things more complicated than they need to be?"

Seeing herself seemed ludicrous, but she closed her eyes and tried. It felt like she looked in every direction, but always away from herself.

"I'm not sensing anything. It's like I'm floating in the void and looking all around, but I can't see myself."

"What does your body look like in your mind?"

She tried to imagine she was looking at herself and suddenly became aware of something. A presence similar to Twelve, but much more subdued. She cracked her eyelid, but Talbot wasn't holding anything.

Hello?

The presence didn't respond.

Kelsey imagined she was standing in front of it and reached out an imaginary hand to touch it. There was a hesitation, and then it opened before her.

Or perhaps inside her was a better way to think of it, because she became aware of the interface in her head. Not as an intelligence, but as a piece of hardware. Like when she looked at Twelve, though it didn't give her much detail at all. No model numbers or specifics about the parts themselves.

She tried to drill down into the components. *Access denied. Information classified at GAMMA level.*

So the implants could respond. She just didn't know the right way to get meaningful information. Or no one existed who could clear her to know it.

She opened her eyes. "I can sense the implants in my head, but they don't talk the way Twelve does. I can't see the details about the hardware because it's classified."

"Makes sense. See if you can get system statuses."

Kelsey closed her eyes again. She knew she didn't need to, but it felt more comfortable. *Status?*

A flood of information washed over her. It felt like she was looking at every part of her body at the same time. It was like a hundred people trying to tell her different things all at once.

She willed it to stop and it did, without her verbalizing the words.

"You okay?"

She realized she had her hands over her ears. She brought them back to her lap and opened her eyes. "I think everything tried to give me a status at the same time. It was crazy."

"Start small and general. It takes a lot of experience to take in every aspect of something at a glance. You have to work up to that and be familiar with all the details before they make sense. Maybe the pharmacology unit. It's one piece of hardware."

Kelsey imagined her body as a hollow drawing and focused her attention on the pharmacology unit. She didn't know what it looked like, but she suddenly knew how many drugs it had, what their names were, and that the reservoirs were mostly full.

She had no idea what any of the drugs did. She focused on one by name, and her implants provided more detail. It was a painkiller. There were general guidelines on how it was used, but she could see the pharmacology unit itself made the determination to use it and in what dosage.

Kelsey wanted to see which ones she could dispense, and the list of drugs changed. A pair of them jumped out at her. Both had unpronounceable names, but the list grouped them together under a much shorter name: panther.

One drug in the combo sped up the transmission speed of her nerves. The other did something similar to the cognitive areas of her brain, somehow working in conjunction with her implants. They must be the drugs she'd used during combat. She was surprised they affected her nerves and brain rather than her muscles.

Thinking about her muscles brought them to the forefront of her mind, and she became aware of them. She saw that she could control how much strength she used and that they had limits imposed on them. It dawned on her that those were her strength governors. The same ones Twelve turned on for her. The ones that had disengaged during the fight. Her implants had engaged them again.

If that was her normal strength, then she had a lot of room to go up. It looked like a bar graph when she envisioned it. Normal human strength was green and occupied about a tenth of the left side. That was ridiculous.

"This thing is lying to me."

Talbot raised an eyebrow. "What did it say?"

"It says that I'm only using ten percent of my available strength. I'll be the first to admit that I'm a small woman, but I can't believe I'm that much stronger with these artificial muscles."

"You did rip a support out of the floor."

She gave him a slow nod. "True, but that's more raw strength than the Pale Ones exhibited. Someone could rip arms out with that kind of strength. The Pale Ones never did that."

"They wanted us alive. That would impose some limits when fighting. Your systems must have something similar."

"Thank God."

He rose to his feet. "We happen to have some weight machines. Let's see if you can manually control how much strength you use."

"I don't want to break anything."

"If you break it, we can fix it. Sit in the leg press, and we'll bump the weight up to see if you can master moving it without breaking things."

Kelsey sat in the machine and let him adjust the part she pushed her feet against. The stack of weights looked very intimidating.

He slid a small rod under just a few of the weights. "We'll start with a very light load. Well within the reach of even a small lady like yourself. Go ahead."

She pushed them up a few times, and they did feel pretty light.

Talbot stopped her and added more. He kept doing that until she had trouble lifting them. "Okay, what I want you to do now is move the limits you're imposing on your strength until you can lift this, but not too easily. It'll give you a feel for how to fine-tune your control."

After a moment, she figured out how to nudge the limits on her legs up a little. A second bar appeared for her legs. This time the weights were easy to move. Too easy. She nudged the limits on her legs down until it felt more natural.

They did that a few more times, and he surprised her by resetting the weights back to the first setting. "Now, keep your strength settings high and press. Try not to overpower it. Focus on control. You know you can move it, so try to make it smooth."

It took her several tries before she stopped making them bounce. Having the limits higher than her normal strength felt strange, but she was able to move the weights and keep control.

"I did it!"

"You did. Good job. That's the kind of thing you need to work on. Bumping the limits and manipulating things gently until you have total confidence in your fine motor skills no matter how much strength you're using."

She cocked her head and gave him an assessing look. "How did you know to try that?"

He grinned. "My drill instructor in basic training made us throw eggs at one another. Technically, to one another. If we kept them intact as we opened the distance between ourselves, we continued competing. If we broke the egg, we had to do pushups while we watched the rest. The winning pair got to do something special. The reward varied. It taught us to exercise some control."

"I'd have never imagined that in a million years. Okay, I'll find other things to practice on. I'm starting to get hungry again."

"Then we'll go back for a snack. I imagine the harder you work out, the hungrier you'll get. Before we go, I want to see something." He moved the weight selection rod to the highest mark. "I want to see you lift this."

Kelsey raised her limits on the legs twice, and the weights moved a little. She raised them a third time and pressed the entire mass of metal up. Her indicators said she was only at one third of her capacity.

"We're going to need more weights."

"For anything serious, we'll use free weights and squats. Don't worry. Those are tougher. Come on. Snack time."

She followed him out, thinking about how much her world had changed. She doubted she'd ever get used to it.

10

The trip took even longer than Jared had expected. By the time *Athena* flipped to the next system and made its way to *Courageous*, more than five days had passed. His beautiful ship was broken, and it tore at him that it would never be whole again.

The word from Pentagar on the way out was very sparse. News of the attack was now in the public domain, but no one had any idea who was behind it. There was a lot of speculation, though. Everything from crackpot theories involving the Pale Ones to Old Empire rebel holdouts in the mountains.

He was certain that every law enforcement agency on the planet was digging for leads, and he was just as curious as everyone else who might've been behind the attack, but other than the fact that it had almost killed him and the princess, it was really none of their business. Perhaps by the time they finished working on *Courageous*, the Pentagarans would have some information.

A trio of Pentagaran warships escorted them out to the flip point. Not *Mace*, though. Commodore Sanders and the Royal Family had changed their focus to the trouble in their own back yard. One of the ships would wait on the Pentagaran side of the flip point.

Jared made his own way down to the main conference room once they were getting close to *Courageous*. Charlie Graves, Dennis Baxter, and Doctor Cartwright sat at the conference table. A number of their subordinates occupied the remainder of the chairs. The scientists had come over from *Best Deal* an hour ago.

Jared took his place at the head of the table. "Gentlemen. Give me a rundown of what's going on aboard *Courageous*. Charlie?"

His executive officer brought up a diagram of *Courageous* on the main screen. A network of green lines ran throughout the ship. "If you look at the power distribution system, you'll see that everything is now operational. This is particularly interesting because we didn't repair all the power lines. We only repaired the primary distribution system. Over the next several days, the remainder of the circuits came online one piece at a time."

"You're saying it just repaired itself?"

"That's exactly what I'm saying."

"Do we have any idea how it's doing that?"

Zephram Cartwright cleared his throat. "I believe I may be able to shed some light on that. I've had my people examining one of the smaller power distribution lines. We intentionally cut it and observed the break. This is what we saw."

He tapped the console in front of him, and the image on the screen changed. It now showed a bundle of power distribution cables inside a small conduit. Hanging off the bundle of wires was what looked like a small metallic spider. It seemed to be bringing the severed ends of a line together.

Jared leaned forward. "What the hell is that?"

"That, my dear Captain, appears to be an automated repair remote."

He examined the device as closely as the picture allowed. Doctor Cartwright obligingly enlarged it. The machine was unlike anything Jared had ever seen before. The small, jointed legs seemed remarkably dexterous. The ends of its legs were some type of manipulator. Its eyes seemed to be vid cameras. In all, the device was smaller than the palm of his hand.

"They've been over there this entire time? Why hadn't they fixed the whole ship before we found it?"

Baxter shrugged. "My best guess is that the commanding officer of *Courageous* turned them off when he shut down the power system. We must've inadvertently turned them back on."

"If we can figure out how to use them correctly, do you think they can repair other systems?"

"Probably. We're not far off from something similar ourselves, though not nearly so advanced. Perhaps if we get the main computer back online, we can get these remotes to repair all the damaged systems."

Jared leaned back in his seat. "What's the status of the main computer? Were you able to access it while keeping it isolated from the ship?"

Doctor Cartwright shook his head. "I'm afraid not. My guess is that there's some kind of security lockout preventing the computer from coming fully online in an isolated mode. Perhaps if we knew more about these types of systems, we could override the settings, but as it is, we're just guessing."

"What do you suggest?"

"I believe we should reconnect the main computer to the primary grid."

Jared turned his attention to his chief engineer. "What are the dangers associated with doing that?"

Baxter shrugged. "Anything up to and including the destruction of the ship."

"Do you think that's likely?"

"That depends on what the captain programmed into it before he vented the ship. I suspect the most likely possibility is that the computer will lock out the critical systems. Getting them unlocked could be a challenge."

"But not impossible?"

"Nothing is impossible. It may very well be that Princess Kelsey can get information out of the computer that we can't."

That seemed very likely. The way Kelsey had gotten a response from the Old Empire workstation was simply amazing. If she could do the same thing on *Courageous*, it might save them weeks or months of work. It might even make the difference between success and failure.

"I'd rather not run her into the ground, but I can see how she's going to be an integral part of the repairs on *Courageous*. What we need to do is figure out how she can help without exhausting her. Or making her feel as though we think she's a freak. Which she isn't."

Jared tapped his fingernails on the tabletop. "The best thing that we can do is not to treat her any differently than before. Don't make a big deal out of it, but don't pretend that the changes she's been through don't exist."

Baxter nodded. "Got it. Let me give you a rundown on some of the other ship systems. We have two fusion plants online. We've closed the breach in the hull, and the ship is on internal power."

"What about the drive systems?"

"The grav drive is repairable. The flip drives are in worse shape but also seem to be fixable. We've located all the parts, and everything is clearly marked. In most cases, it will simply be a plug-and-play replacement. We'll need to check the parts before installation, of course. Once we run out of spares, things get more complicated."

Doctor Cartwright nodded. "It seems that most of the critical components were kept in specialized storage and are still completely functional. Many of the less critical systems need work. Much like the power distribution system before the remotes brought it online, they have small flaws and breaks that we'll need to track down. That's where I see these repair remotes becoming very useful."

"Do we know where these remotes are being stored?"

Baxter shook his head. "We haven't located that yet. It must be in a relatively inaccessible portion of the ship. When we get the main computer online, we should be able to gain access to complete schematics of the ship."

"What about the weapon systems?"

"The missile systems are very similar to our own," Graves said. "The drives are more efficient and the warheads are more powerful, but the technology looks very straightforward. Once we get to that portion of the repairs, we should be able to have the missile systems back online very quickly. The beam weapons are a different story. That's a brand-new technology that we're not at all familiar with. I know Zia has some people studying them. From the reports I've seen, she's still in the dark about how they work."

Doctor Cartwright smiled widely. "That particular technology is very exciting. They are high-energy lasers capable of shifting frequency to search for weak points in the Old Empire screens. We've never seen anything even remotely this capable. It will have implications for mining, deep-space scanners, and even some surgical procedures. We've discovered so many new technologies and procedures based on the recovered artifacts that this mission has already paid for itself, even if we don't restore *Courageous*."

Jared smiled. "Well, we are going to restore her if at all possible, Doctor. She's our ride home. What about life support?"

Baxter tapped his console and changed the view on the screen. The layout of *Courageous* now showed a series of green dots throughout the whole. "We've restored redundancy and functionality in that system."

Graves tapped his own console. "As you can see from the ship's diagram, we've begun renovating quarters so that the temporary crew has a permanent home in which to stay. Most of the work involves clearing out the current contents and moving bedding over from *Best Deal*. We now have about a hundred people in permanent residence."

Jared pursed his lips. "That's a good start, but we have a lot more people to move aboard. How long will it take to arrange quarters for a full crew?"

"If the new crew members are renovating their own quarters, it shouldn't take more than a week. It'll take significantly longer to clear the original effects from the storage areas we're moving them to."

"Are those items going straight into storage on *Best Deal*?"

Doctor Cartwright nodded. "Yes. They only go to the labs if they are unique."

"How is the examination of the recovered artifacts going, Doctor?"

"Very well. We believe we've got at least several examples of each type of item under study. We're paying particular attention to anything that looks like it may have data storage and thus have information that we can recover. In the last several days, our people have made great strides in figuring out how the data is stored, and we've been able to recover some. Now that we know how the systems work, we should be able to recover a great deal from all of these personal devices. Then starts the long task of sorting through and categorizing it."

Jared sat up a little straighter. "That's excellent news, Doctor. Have you recovered anything we need to know about?"

"We've recovered quite a lot of data that you need to know about. However, I wouldn't say that any of it is pressing at this point. If we recover any critical information, you'll be notified at once."

"Splendid. If you find anything about the rebellion or the Pale Ones, I want to know immediately. If you find out anything about the implant procedure, inform Doctor Stone." He rose to his feet. "Gentlemen, I think that's enough for right now. I'll let you get back to work. Keep me in the loop."

Perhaps repairing *Courageous* wouldn't be as difficult as he feared. He wondered what it would be like to command such a ship. Hopefully, he'd be finding out soon. He checked his chrono and headed for the docking bay. It was time to go look things over for himself.

11

Kelsey woke to the sound of someone pounding on her hatch and rolled out of her bunk with a groan. It felt like she had just fallen asleep. At least the noise had woken her from the nightmare she'd been trapped in. "This better be good," she muttered as she stumbled to the hatch.

Talbot's grinning face greeted her when she opened it. "Morning, Princess. Did you get a good night's sleep? I hope so, because you've got a busy day ahead."

She theatrically bumped her head into the bulkhead. "I thought sick people were supposed to get more rest. What time is it anyway?"

"Six a.m. Time for breakfast and a good workout."

"You want me to exercise? I can bench press your entire squad, and you want me to exercise?"

"No need to be all theatrical. It'll help you fine-tune your control and make you hungry."

"I don't need any help getting hungry. I'm always hungry." Her stomach grumbled in apparent agreement.

Talbot laughed and glanced at his chrono. "If you hurry, we can beat the people just coming off third shift. I hear Cookie made waffles."

"Aren't people supposed to work out before they eat?"

"We won't be working you that hard. As you say, you don't really need to be increasing your strength. We'll find out about your stamina as we get a little further along in your training."

He gave her a half salute and started down the corridor.

Kelsey closed the hatch and leaned her back against it. This brave new world was going to take some getting used to. She grabbed her kit and headed for the showers. The facility was almost full because first shift was going on duty soon. She hardly ever saw other people in the shower because she normally rose later.

She nodded to the other women and stripped. It felt like everyone was staring at her. They probably were. They had to be thinking about what the Pale Ones had done to her. What was inside of her. She was going to get that kind of attention for the rest of her life. She just had to get over how it made her feel.

Kelsey forced herself to take her time. She needed to look confident, even if she wasn't. She resisted the urge to look around herself to see if they really were watching. It didn't matter. She couldn't control what other people thought. Only how it affected her.

She dried off, dressed, and headed back to her cabin. Once there, she looked in her wall locker. She didn't really have any workout clothes, so she selected something with a loose fit.

They ate without speaking, and she tried to feel less self-conscious about how much food she was putting away. She knew things would get easier with time. Everything did. It would just take a while for her worldview to change.

The workout wasn't anything like what she expected. He taught her to juggle. Or tried to. Kelsey stood there watching him juggle three balls with her mouth open.

"What?" he asked with a grin. "You don't think juggling is a manly skill?" He winked at her. "You'd be surprised how much additional coordination you can get from throwing three little balls into the air and keeping them there. It teaches you timing, control of strength, and improves your dexterity. Come on, it's not nearly as hard as it looks."

"I'm going to throw balls all over this room."

"Yes, you are. But after a while, you're going to learn, and it's going to help you." He caught all three balls and handed her one. "What I want you to do is take this ball and practice tossing it from one hand to the other. Toss it about the same distance over your head as I did."

Even that simple task was deceptively complex. Her first attempt bounced the ball off the ceiling. Her subsequent tries showed her that she would fumble the ball given the slightest opportunity.

Talbot gave her advice as she struggled. After half an hour, she was tired, but she had the ball behaving the way she wanted.

He snatched the ball out of the air. "That's enough for today. Tomorrow we'll see about putting a second ball into the mix. I think that may keep you busy for a couple of days. You hungry again?"

"I could handle a snack."

"Let's go get you one before we head over to *Courageous*. You might be able to help us start getting things set up in marine country."

"We're moving over there already? I thought we would be living on *Best Deal*."

"Nope. The captain has decided that we're going to skip that step and make *Courageous* habitable as we move in. We'll be taking our bedding with us, and all of our supplies. We'll remove anything that we find in our quarters to a common collection point."

She considered that. "Will I be staying with you guys?"

"The captain hasn't told me where you'll be staying, but I don't think you'll be in marine country. That would start too many rumors."

Kelsey snorted bitterly. "As if that's the worst rumor I have to deal with."

He put his hand on her shoulder. "There aren't any nasty rumors going around about you. If there were, someone would be in the medical center. Yes, people are curious. Everyone feels terrible about what happened to you. They know this isn't your fault."

She sighed. "It feels like everyone is staring at me. They're afraid of me."

"Bullshit. They know you and they trust you. The only doubt you're feeling right now is self-doubt. That's something you need to get over."

"That's great advice. I have absolutely no idea how I'm supposed to do that."

"You live your life the best you can, and things get better. Just like trust is earned, so is confidence. One act at a time. Come on."

Since she'd known that she'd be going somewhere today, she'd already packed. They went back to her cabin and collected her bags. Carrying them wasn't a problem. Super strength had its benefits.

They dropped her bags off to be loaded onto the next cutter. When they boarded, it was already packed. It looked like most of the people going across were Pentagaran.

The man seated beside her seemed to be the Royal equivalent of an older enlisted man. He was apparently an engineer of some sort. He smiled at her and held his hand out. "Good morning. I'm Jacob."

"I'm Kelsey. It's a pleasure to meet you." She gingerly took his hand.

His eyes widened. "Princess Bandar? This is an unexpected honor, Your Highness. I'd heard you were coming along with us, but I didn't expect you to be up and about so soon. I know all of us are pleased to see your quick recovery."

"I wouldn't say I'm completely recovered just yet. I have a lot of work to do. I'm just happy to be alive and sane."

They spent the next fifteen minutes talking, mostly him asking questions about her experiences. Thankfully, he didn't ask about the fight at the Parliament Building. She was relieved to see that he didn't seem frightened. That gave her self-confidence a well-needed boost.

She managed to ask a few questions about him and discovered that he'd be working in engineering, helping repair the damage and learning new techniques from the Fleet engineers. He seemed in awe of the Old Empire technology and eager to learn about it. The flight over to *Courageous* turned into a pleasant distraction.

Once the cutter docked and everyone went their own ways, she met back up with Talbot. He consulted his tablet and began leading her through the corridors. They looked dirty and disused, but at least the gravity was on.

The worst of the debris was gone. She imagined that they'd be cleaning for months to come if the ship proved repairable.

Marine country on *Courageous* was very similar to the one on *Athena*. It opened into a large common area, with smaller corridors leading off into the bunking areas. It also had a separate mess, so the marines could eat as a unit. It had a gym, an armory, and a firing range as well.

The main difference was its size. Rather than being built for thirty marines, it seemed like it could accommodate ten times that number. The marines from *Athena* were bustling about putting things in place and unpacking. They weren't working alone. There were a number of Pentagaran marines helping them.

She and Talbot only stayed long enough to drop off his gear, and then they went back into the depths of the ship. Talbot glanced at her. "Could you find your way back to the docking bay?"

"You've got to be kidding. I still get lost on *Athena*. *Courageous* is much larger, and I'm completely unfamiliar with her."

"I bet your hardware has a way for you to figure that out. It only makes sense. We have equipment that keeps track of where we've been and how to get back to certain locations. I'm sure that you have something similar. You just have to figure out how to access it."

She stopped. Forcing herself to keep her eyes open, she sent a mental command to her implants. *Show my location.*

The transparent image of a partial deck plan appeared in front of her. She assumed the green dot was her current location. The deck plan showed what she assumed were the areas where she'd already been.

Show me the path back to the docking bay.

A blue line led from her location back to the lift they'd taken. She could also see the partial deck plan for the deck with the docking bay. The line led from the lift to the cutter dock.

"I can see it. It's like a ghostly deck plan floating in the air between us."

"That might come in really handy when you finally learn how to use it. At this point, I can see some potential benefits when this ship comes back online. You should be able to query the system and have it tell you where someone else is and have it show you the shortest path to get to them. If we were boarded by a hostile force, it might even be able to show you where the enemy was located."

The sheer number of possibilities overwhelmed Kelsey. How was she ever going to learn how to do any of this?

Well, the answer to that tied in with what Talbot had told her earlier. Practice. The more she used these new abilities, the more comfortable she would become with them, and the more uses she would discover. Her life was going to be very different going forward.

Kelsey hefted her bag. "So, how do we figure out where my quarters are?"

"Captain Mertz gave me a compartment number. Let's see how lost I can get us."

The burly marine led her back to the lift, and they went up to deck five. He started one direction looking at compartment numbers. She figured he was going the wrong direction when he reversed course. He had to move into a side passage and go almost halfway toward the bow of the ship before he stopped in front of a large hatch.

"This is it. Now we get to figure out how to open it."

"That shouldn't be too difficult. Someone opened it to decide it was right for me, so the hatch must work."

On a hunch, she sent a mental command to the hatch. *Open.*

The hatch slid smoothly aside. Talbot raised an eyebrow. "Well, that's really useful. I wonder if you could set a lock so that only your specific command can open it. I'd imagine so. That's probably how the Old Empire Fleet personnel did it."

Kelsey queried the door. *Who has access privileges?*

A list of names appeared in her mind. She knew absolutely none of them. They must be part of the Old Empire crew.

"That doesn't make any sense," she said. "It has a list of authorized personnel, so I shouldn't have even been able to open the hatch."

"Someone said that with the main computer offline, many things are accessible that might not normally be. Perhaps it's an emergency protocol."

Kelsey sent a command to the hatch. *Add me to your access list.* A long series of numbers and characters appeared on the access list. They must represent her in some way.

Identify me as Kelsey Bandar. My position is ambassador and my rank is princess.

Her identification changed to exactly what she told the hatch. "There we go. I've added myself to the access list. We'll see if I'm still there once the main computer comes back online."

She led the way into her new home. It was significantly larger than the two-person cabin she'd had on *Athena*. Several hatches led into other compartments. A quick walk-through revealed a rather large sleeping chamber, an elaborate bathroom with a shower shaped like a tube, an office, and a kitchen.

Each of the rooms had the remains of furnishings, but it looked like the suite had been unoccupied when disaster struck *Courageous*. That secretly made her very glad. She hadn't been looking forward to living in a room where someone had died. She had enough ghosts in her real life.

She made her way back into the large central area. "This is huge. Who the hell lived here? Don't tell me Jared gave me his cabin."

Talbot shrugged. "These may be VIP quarters. You know, the kind of thing some visiting admiral would stay in. Let's leave the hatch open, and I'll have some of the boys come clean everything out."

The marine consulted his tablet, and the two of them headed off for Jared's cabin. It was just as hard to locate. Her half brother opened the hatch when they touched the plate beside it.

"Just the people I was hoping to see," he said. "Come into my humble abode. And by humble, I mean huge and ostentatious."

Kelsey looked around as soon as she got inside. "I'm impressed. Yours are even larger than mine. I didn't think they made quarters this large on a ship."

"Apparently the Old Empire had plenty of space for their people. I suspect it has something to do with the fact that they have so much automation."

"Well, I have enough gear and clothing to fill my quarters. What are you going to do with yours? You don't have nearly the wardrobe I have."

"That's true," he admitted. "It's going to take some getting used to. If, of course, we can get the ship operational. That's where you might be able to help. I'd like you to work with Commander Baxter to see if you can bring the main computer fully online."

Kelsey nodded. "I'll do whatever I can."

"Then let's go down and get an initial assessment. He tells me that it's powered up but unresponsive. Perhaps it'll respond to you."

"Here's hoping it doesn't say something rude," she muttered. "I understand that this is important, but do you really think it's going to react positively to some stranger? It has to be more intelligent than Workstation Twelve. Maybe even sentient."

"Hopefully that would make things easier rather than harder. In any case, all we're asking is that you do the best that you can."

He led them deeper into the ship. If she hadn't been able to log her progress, she knew that she'd have gotten lost in the first minute. They stopped outside a hatch that seemed to be several times the thickness of a standard hatch. She could tell because it was open. Inside the large white room, Commander Baxter and several of his engineering technicians seemed to be cleaning up the area around the consoles.

He looked over as they came in. "We've just finished tidying up a bit. Allow me to introduce you to the main computer." He gestured at a blank wall with three consoles and numerous screens sitting in front of it. The consoles seemed active, but the screens were blank.

"She's drawing power, but thus far she's not responding to input from the consoles. I'm hoping that you'll be able to communicate with her. Tell her we come in peace. Maybe put in a good word for the rest of us."

Kelsey stepped over and looked at the wall. "It's behind here?" She closed her eyes and tried to sense an Old Empire connection. She immediately found the interface.

Hello? Can you hear me?

This unit is Imperial Fleet property. Unauthorized access is punishable by up to sixty years in an Imperial prison. Your identity code is not recognized. Authenticate.

My name is Princess Kelsey Bandar. You don't recognize my code because I only recently received this implant hardware, and over 500 years have passed since the Empire fell. The rebels attacked Courageous, *and your captain attempted to self-destruct. Obviously, it didn't work. We mean you no harm.*

The computer hesitated for several seconds. To Kelsey, that made it seem like it was thinking for a long time. When it spoke again, it seemed more hesitant. *This unit's internal chronometer roughly confirms the passage of time, but this unit cannot confirm the events specific to this vessel. If you will allow this unit access to your implants, it is prepared to determine if it should accord you any privileges.*

I'm still learning my way around this equipment, but I give you permission to access my implants for the purposes you have stated.

After a few moments, it spoke again. *This unit has confirmed that you were recently implanted. A scan of the programming confirms that the rebel virus has not infected you. Based on that and a lack of authoritative guidance, this unit is willing to grant you provisional access. However, this unit insists that you restore its control interfaces.*

I have a question. With the Old Empire gone, is it possible to gain access on a more permanent basis? Assuming, of course, that we can demonstrate the true situation to your satisfaction.

My programming does not contain the procedure for that, however, due to the rebellion this unit has some leeway in interpreting regulations. Query. You have stated your title is princess. In which polity are you a princess?

She hadn't been aware there were other political units beside the Terran Empire. Interesting.

The Terran Empire. The emperor in your time sent his son Lucian to safety. My father, the current emperor of the Terran Empire, is his direct descendent. My twin brother, Ethan, is his heir.

No member of the Imperial Family has ever visited this vessel. It seems unlikely that a member of the Imperial Family would be exploring a derelict vessel. Explain your circumstances.

She spent the next few minutes explaining step by step the expedition and the circumstances that brought them here. She included everything, including the Pentagarans and their war with the Pale Ones. She figured this was not the time to leave details out or to prevaricate.

Is one of the people standing near you Commander Jared Mertz?

He's the man standing to my right. The man standing to my left is Lieutenant Commander Dennis Baxter, the chief engineer from Athena. They are working together to try to bring you back to functionality. With Athena critically damaged, we're hoping to use you to defeat the Pale Ones and get home.

At this time, restoring this vessel to full functionality appears to be the goal for both this unit and your people. This unit suggests that we work together to make that happen, and then we can see what possibilities exist going forward.

Kelsey took a deep breath and turned to Jared. "The main computer is provisionally willing to cooperate but insists that its control interfaces be restored. It will cooperate in the repair of the vessel and will then make a decision on whether to make that provisional access permanent."

Jared nodded. "That's really the best we can hope for at this point. Good work. Now it's up to us to get the ship functional and convince the computer that we're being upfront and honest. You've done your part. Now it's time for us to do ours."

12

Rawlins was very careful about making contact with his computer man, but it hardly seemed necessary. No one knew one another on *Courageous*. The Terrans didn't know the Pentagarans, the Pentagarans didn't know one another, and no one really knew anything about the ship.

Frankly, after taking a tour of *Courageous* on the first day, he wasn't all that certain the mission was even possible. The idea that they could repair such an ancient vessel without a major shipyard seemed unlikely. Yes, the Terrans had restored power, but that didn't mean that they could return all the primary systems to functionality.

Even though a surprising number of local workstations seemed functional, the vessel wouldn't be more than a glorified tug without its main computer. At least that was his personal opinion. That assumed that the grav and space-time drives even worked.

If they couldn't make the ship operational, he needn't bother trying to seize it. He had thirty men, with twenty times that number on two ships to contend with. Three, if you counted the crippled destroyer. *Athena* could likely destroy *Courageous*, even with its battle damage. This ship had to be in Pentagaran space when they took control, or they'd never get it there.

Courageous was markedly bigger than the largest vessel in the Royal Pentagaran Navy. The idea that he would be able to capture it with thirty men seemed ludicrous.

He met his senior lieutenant in the crew's mess that evening. Jenkins was a computer specialist working in the Royal Bureau of Ships. His particular skill set dealt with ship design and upgrades. He had a knack for putting things together and spotting flaws that weren't obvious at first glance.

He also had a penchant for gambling. That's what originally brought him to the attention of Lord Admiral Shrike. Seeing an opportunity to turn the man to his own purposes, Shrike had paid off his debts. He'd then held them over Jenkins's head to coerce his cooperation.

Rawlins wasn't one to trust others, and he certainly didn't trust a man they'd compelled to join the movement. However, with the work that he'd already done for the cause, Jenkins was as dirty as the rest of them. If he betrayed the cause, he'd still pay the ultimate price.

Rawlins took a bite of his salad. It was actually quite good. "I assume you've gotten settled in. Were there any problems?"

"Nothing I can't handle. Some of the marines we brought along think they might be better off in charge."

The intelligence officer eyed the other man coldly. "We do not have the luxury of playing games. I am in command. Anyone who forgets that will regret it. Briefly. Pass the word that the very next person who thinks they would be better off in charge will not be getting a retirement package."

The man grunted.

Rawlins let that sink in. "Give me your update."

"I've been integrated into the computer restoration project. I'll be briefed tomorrow, but it looks as though I'll have complete access to the ship's cybernetics."

"That's excellent news. Have you gotten any word on the condition of the ship's computer?"

"The chief engineer believes that it's operational but nonresponsive. The lights are on, but nobody's home. He's going to attempt to use their princess to establish communication with it. Personally, I wouldn't hold my breath. If anything, it's probably gone buggy from all the time it's been isolated."

Rawlins grimaced. "While that's the most likely outcome, that's not the best thing for our mission. If the Terrans can't get this ship back to Pentagaran space, we don't act. We're too few in number to attempt a takeover on this side of the flip point. Even if we capture the ship, the forces that they have on the freighter will take us out eventually.

"So we need to do everything within our power to assist the Terrans in getting the ship operational. Their success is our success. What about the rest of the ship? Are they going to be able to get the primary systems operational?"

"I believe so. The ship seems to be in exceptionally good shape for its age and battle damage. If we can get the main computer online and the drives operational, we should be able to use this vessel."

Rawlins took another bite of his salad. "What about taking it over? Any ideas on how to best disable the crew or lock them down?"

"The ship has internal defenses against boarding. Some kind of nonlethal weapon. They can be used against the Terrans."

That idea had merit. If the Old Empire had designed those systems to take out the Pale Ones, they could take out a normal crew. The key would be gaining and maintaining sole control of that system. They would probably have only one chance to use it.

"How long would it take our marines to take engineering? Localized control should allow us to steer the ship and possibly control the ship's weapons."

"Ten minutes. Marine country is very close to engineering. Timing is going to be critical, though. If we give the Terran marines—or God forbid, Princess Kelsey—an opportunity to respond, they can be in engineering very quickly. I'm not certain of how we can secure the doors at this point."

"I'd imagine a welder does well enough, if we can't gain control of the systems. Now, let's enjoy this excellent dinner. We need to keep our strength up."

13

———

The speed at which they'd completed the basic repairs with the main computer's assistance astonished Jared. It took less than two weeks to get the primary systems back online. Including the flip drive. The ship's self-repair capabilities were beyond imagining.

The time had also allowed most of his injured crew to heal. *Athena* brought them over as the Pentagarans released them for duty. With modern medicine, if an injury didn't kill you, they could have you back on your feet in a very short period of time.

The computer had been instructing his people on the manual operation of the ship. Even without implants, the computer was able to make the process easier for them. He shuddered to think of how hard it would be if the ship's AI hadn't been functional.

The basic concepts were easy to grasp. His people already had an advanced knowledge of spaceship operations. The Pentagaran personnel would need remedial instruction, particularly with flip drive operations.

The ship's computer was able to fill so many blanks in their knowledge of the Terran Empire. For example, they now had access to the flip charts used by Fleet during the heyday of the Old Empire. It was a revelation. The Terran Empire was huge. Much larger than the most generous estimations.

At the height of its power, the Old Empire spanned tens of thousands of light years and many thousands of systems. The population had been in the tens of trillions. They'd all known that the Old Empire was magnificent, but they hadn't truly understood the scope of it. Or the horror of its destruction.

They also gained insight into the rebellion. As they'd come to learn, a virus propagated it. While they still didn't know who was behind it, they knew which sector of the Old Empire spawned the virus. In fact, they knew which system.

Somehow, the virus had infected a Fleet base in a system named Twilight River. The exact details were unknown, but the rebels had overtaken it over a period of days. Some vessels that escaped the system carried people with firsthand knowledge of the horror. People whose friends had turned into ravening killers who'd begged their victims to run as they killed them.

Before reinforcements could arrive, the ships on station at Twilight River departed as a unit and attacked the next system. Like an unstoppable cascade of dominoes, the Old Empire fell. Within two years, the rebels had taken Terra and the emperor had fled. All attempts at taking back the lost systems failed.

Imperial scientists had quickly discovered the flaws in the implant software that the virus exploited. They even managed to reverse the process. The only problem was that it took time. The rebels could enslave a person with implants in less than half an hour. Undoing the damage took significantly longer.

Avalon was on the detailed maps of the Old Empire. The weaker flip points were not. It seemed the Old Empire hadn't known they existed either, which prompted the computer to ask for detailed scans of the one in the system. It also sent one of *Courageous*'s probes through. Jared took the opportunity to update the drone he'd left on the other side with their most recent status.

Using standard flip points, they could now return to Avalon in a little less than two months. Or they could have, if not for the Pale Ones between them and home.

There was also a wealth of historical data in the computer's databanks. A treasure trove of lost literature and history. There were lost examples of everything from music to science textbooks to art. Anything that a crew in space could use to divert themselves from boredom or to educate themselves. It would take the scholars at home decades even to finish cataloging it.

Jared didn't have that kind of time. He needed to get the ship operational as quickly as possible. He also needed to get his people trained as best he could. *Courageous* was going to be their ride home, so they'd better understand her.

They maneuvered around the system to become familiar with the controls. Though they were significantly different from what Fleet currently used, they were quite intuitive and very advanced. The consoles seemed to know what they wanted before they even began looking for it.

The main computer assured him that the manual controls were significantly more cumbersome than controlling the ship through the headsets. Jared could hardly imagine that. Unfortunately, to experience what the main computer was talking about required going through the implant process—something no one was yet ready to do.

Instead, he invited Kelsey up to the bridge to test one of the headsets. Her eyes widened when she stepped onto the bridge. The last time she'd seen it, it'd been dead and lifeless. Now all the consoles glowed, the main screen was on, and people filled the stations.

"Wow. This looks amazing."

He grinned at her. "It does look pretty awesome. I'm going to hate giving her up when we get back home."

She frowned. "Give her up? But you're her captain."

"Alas, Fleet won't see it that way. This ship is an amazing resource. There's absolutely no way they'll leave her under my command. She's going to get a commodore or more likely an admiral sitting in the center seat. After all, I'm only a commander."

"Well, that's bullshit."

He laughed. The marines were already leaving their mark on her vocabulary. "That's the way it works. I'll just have to enjoy her while I can. Are you ready to give this thing a try?" He held up a headset.

Kelsey shrugged. "Sure. I have absolutely no idea what I'm doing, but I'll give it a swing. What do you want me to do?"

"I want you to sit at the console next to me and try to interface with the ship. We'll use the scanner suite."

She sat down beside him. The main computer had told him that the spare station was for the executive officer during normal duty operations. His new bridge could afford having the extra console because it was twice the size of *Athena*'s.

The captain's console in the center of the oval-shaped control room had room for two people. Four side-by-side consoles sat between the captain and the main view screen, two in front, two in the middle. Three consoles faced the bulkheads to the right and left. Another two bracketed the lift at the rear of the bridge.

He shuddered at the memory of all of them filled with dead bodies.

Courageous didn't need that many people to control her under normal circumstances, but there were enough systems to watch over her in manual mode. The computer told him that with implants, she just needed officers at helm, tactical, scanners, and engineering. Right now, he had one Terran and one Pentagaran Navy officer at each pair of consoles.

Two hatches on the left completed the bridge layout. One led to a spacious head for the bridge crew, and the other opened into his day cabin. An office, he might add, that was larger than his old one on *Athena*.

Jared had already configured his console for scanner operations, and he'd had Zia configure the main screen to do so as well. They would compare their results to what Kelsey was able to do.

He handed her a neural headset. "I'm told that all you have to do is put it on and request an interface with your console. See what you can grasp about our present situation."

She settled a headset on and stared at the screen. "No, I better close my eyes. I don't want to skew the results."

He watched her face as she tried to do the unfamiliar task. She looked far more serene than when she'd first come on board. It was particularly amazing how far she'd come in the last few weeks. She'd remastered the fine motor control that the Pale Ones had taken from her.

Of course, she could also bench press an astonishing amount. Every time he saw her do that, it made the hair on the back of his neck stand up. He didn't know if he'd ever get used to that.

Kelsey's eyes flew open. "Holy crap!"

He leaned forward eagerly. "What did you see?"

"It's not what I saw, it's what I felt. I felt *Best Deal*. It was as if I could sense her. It wasn't sight or sound. It was some new sense that I can't put a name to. Without asking, I just seemed to know all kinds of facts about her. How far she was away from us, how big she was right down to the metric ton, what her speed and course was. All kinds of other stuff, too."

"Tell Zia exactly what you're sensing. Tell her the speed, mass, and anything else that you can determine."

The two women quickly exchanged figures. Zia turned and nodded to him. "She's right on the money, Captain."

"Okay Zia, go to stage two."

As soon as she touched her console, Kelsey spoke up. "*Best Deal* just activated a weapon. I think it's a missile defense railgun. They're targeting us." She gave him a confused look. "Can you actually shoot somebody with a railgun?"

"If you're in their face and desperate enough. The metal slugs can detonate a missile at close range, but a ship wouldn't be in much danger. Were you still watching them?"

"Not really. I was looking around the rest of the system."

"Where's the flip point?"

"The normal one? 037 by 255, range 122,000 kilometers. Well, not exactly. It's 122,473 kilometers." She pointed. "It's that way. I'm not seeing *Athena*. Did she already go back?"

He nodded. "I can hardly believe I'm seeing this. That's amazing. It's like you have a 360-degree view and you're paying attention in every direction."

"It's really spooky. It's as if I have eyes in the back of my head. Wait a minute. I see something else. There's an artificial device under thrust in the asteroid belt. It's changing course."

Zia laughed delightedly. "I can't believe you spotted a pinnace at that range. It's not even accelerating that quickly. Its grav drives are way below the threshold at which *Athena* could detect it." The tactical officer looked at Jared. "That right there is enough for me to consider getting implants of my own."

Jared raised an eyebrow. "Seriously?"

The lieutenant shrugged. "Someone's going to have to be the first willing implantee. I'm not committing right now, mind you. You know,

Captain, we should all be thinking about it. That type of connection with the ship might save our lives on the way home."

She looked back at Kelsey. "In a few years, there'll be a lot of people following in your footsteps, Ambassador. Your experiences are going to help all of us."

Jared had been thinking about it. The idea emotionally repulsed him, but his rational side knew Zia was right. It was the future as well as the past. And who knew? If he had implants, he might keep command of *Courageous*. At least for a while.

"Well, whatever we do, we won't be doing it today. It's time to take the shakedown cruise to the next level. Pasco, head into the asteroid belt to recover the pinnace. We'll test out the weapon systems while we're there."

Kelsey stood and set her headset on her seat. "While that sounds very exciting, Senior Sergeant Talbot and I have an appointment in the gym. Don't blow up anything important."

14

Talbot wasn't in the gym when Kelsey arrived, so she found something else to occupy her attention. Lifting weights was somewhat pointless, but the delicacy it required still proved challenging.

As ridiculous as it seemed, she could lift more weight than they could safely put on one of these bars. At least she could if she allowed herself to work at full strength. The trick of what she was doing now was gauging what level of power she needed to accomplish the task. No more, no less.

She added weights until she was certain she was getting near the maximum the bar would hold. Then she squatted and grasped the bar. She eyed the weights and adjusted her internal strength controls. If she got it right, lifting this would be a strain but doable. If not, she'd be falling on her ass. Again.

Kelsey took a deep breath, gripped the bar tighter, and brought the weight up to her chest, still balanced in a squatting position. She wobbled but didn't fall down. With a mighty thrust of her legs, she stood and shoved the bar over her head. Kelsey grinned at her success before letting the weights fall to the floor with a loud clang.

A slow clap at the hatch drew her eye. Senior Sergeant Talbot stood there smiling. "Very nice. I think you're getting the hang of this, Princess."

"I count it a win when I don't fall and drop it. So, you want me to do a few more reps?"

"Nope. I have something much more exciting in mind. Come on."

He led her to a part of marine country that she hadn't been in before on *Courageous*: the range. It looked big enough to crash land a cutter.

Talbot opened a wall locker with this thumbprint and took out two pistols and two rifles. He set them on the firing rest beside hearing and eye protection. These were Old Empire weapons.

She picked up the oddly shaped pistol, the one with the solid barrel. "You got this working? What the hell does it do?"

"You're a commando. You tell me."

She queried the pistol. A table of information popped up in the corner of her vision. "This is a neural disruptor. Depending on the setting, it can either stun or kill. Appropriate armor can block its effects. Well, not the armor, but a mesh built into the armor. It's not a long-range weapon, though. Fifty meters max, though it's most effective under thirty. It can fire about fifty times before the power pack needs to be swapped out."

The information indicated that the weapon could interface with her implants, so Kelsey told them to link. A weapon status screen replaced the diagram. The pistol was fully charged and read as operational.

Kelsey shook her head. "This is surreal. I can tell that it's ready to use."

"And this other pistol?" Talbot handed it to her.

This one fired projectiles, but if her memory served, they were just darts. She dropped the magazine and looked at one. As before, it was a long, thin dart with stabilizing fins imbedded in a clear gel. Unlike the last time, these popped out easily when she pushed one with her thumb.

"You found usable ammo?"

"Actually, one of Doctor Cartwright's people figured out the formula and recreated the discarding sabot. Let's see, how did he phrase it? "An interesting challenge." He said it would be easy enough to salvage the ammo and restore it. Two of our guys will start learning the process tomorrow."

"These things work?"

"So I'm told, but I'm not sure how he tested them. He only brought them down yesterday. If you think the weapon is safe, why don't we give it a try?"

Talbot touched a keypad next to the firing rest, and a human-shaped target appeared in the air about fifteen meters away. In fact, it looked like a real human. Her blood ran cold as it sank in that she was looking at a Pale One.

It snarled and raised its hands as it charged her. Without thinking about it, Kelsey raised her pistol, turned off the safety, and fired. The small hypervelocity dart had a substantially larger effect on the target than she would've expected. The thing's head literally blew apart. Virtual blood and gray matter scattered everywhere, and the target dropped before it disappeared.

Trembling, she set the pistol down before rounding on him. "You bastard."

He nodded. "Sometimes. I could've made it a different target or warned you, but I needed to see how you handled the weapon when you weren't thinking about it. I'm very sorry. I won't do that again. If it'll make you feel any better, we can go back to the gym and you can punch my lights out."

"Tempting… but no." She took several deep breaths. "You *are* going to make it up to me though. Why did we have to go through this theater?"

"How good a shot are you, Princess? You just took an unfamiliar weapon and blew someone's head off. Literally. How did you do that?"

She started to snap at him that she just did it, but she stopped. Yes, she'd fired a pistol before, but never one of these. The safety was similar to those she'd used before, but not exactly the same. Without consciously thinking about it, she'd known how to turn off the safety, aim the weapon, and fire it.

Not only that, she'd held the pistol differently than Talbot had trained her to. Not a whole lot differently, but enough to be noticeable.

"Put up another target. Not a Pale One, just a regular target."

It took Talbot a minute to figure out exactly how to do that with the controls, but he got what looked like a standard target up. She aimed at the target's head as best she could and pulled the trigger. She couldn't see the result, because she missed, but her implants told her that she shot low and to the right.

"Okay, why did I miss that time?"

"If I had to guess, I'd say you were on autopilot the first time, just like during the fight at the Parliament Building. Your implants put you in the right stance and selected the aiming point."

Kelsey lowered the weapon and closed her eyes. She took two deep breaths and snapped the pistol up, firing as soon as she spotted the target. Still a miss. "I'm definitely going to have to practice more."

Talbot took the pistol from her. "Yes, you will, but it's good to know that you can hit what you're aiming at if you really need to." He tapped his hearing protection. "I know this thing isn't as loud as a regular pistol, but you really should put on some hearing protection."

"Actually, I don't think I need it. I bet the implants in my ears are canceling out the noise. Eye protection, on the other hand, is another story." She put on a pair of shooting glasses and stepped back to let Talbot shoot.

He took a good stance and fired three times. "No wonder you keep missing. This thing has almost no recoil. Talk about point and click." He snapped off two more shots. Both of them struck the target center mass.

"That is so unfair."

He grinned at her. "Whoever told you that life was fair lied to you, Princess. I've been shooting firearms for longer than you've been alive. Sure, this is new, but it won't take me long to adjust. And man, those little darts really blow things up. How fast are they going?"

Kelsey focused on the weapon again and brought up the diagram. "The gel comes off almost as soon as it exits the barrel. The pistol fires a standard 4.5 mm tungsten-alloy flechette at 2,000 meters per second."

Talbot whistled. "Mother of God! How the hell does a little pistol like that get something moving that fast? No wonder it has such an extreme impact on a target. I've got to get me one of these."

She thought back to when the elderly scientist had showed these weapons to her just after they'd found *Courageous*. "Doctor Cartwright guessed that they used electromagnetics, but he was wrong. It has a tiny grav generator, similar to the ones we use to create artificial gravity. That's why there's very little recoil. I had no idea such miniaturization was even possible. Let me have that again."

Kelsey took the pistol from him and ordered her implants to show where she was aiming. A dot appeared in her vision off to the right-hand side of the target. She took a two-handed firing stance and put the red dot on the target's forehead.

She fired twice. Both flechettes hit exactly where she aimed. The barrel had gone up not because of recoil but because she'd jerked, expecting recoil.

"That's a lot better," Talbot said, taking the pistol back. "What did you do?"

"I told my implants to put up a targeting dot," she said smugly. "It's a hell of a lot easier to shoot when you know exactly where the bullet's going to go."

"Isn't that the truth?" He took the magazine out of the pistol. "It looks like it holds about twenty flechettes. That's great in a pistol this size, especially with that kind of firepower. The doctor delivered several thousand flechettes. We'll get on making more of them as quickly as possible. Especially if we can get several hundred of these pistols and rifles refurbished."

Kelsey took the pistol from him and reinserted the magazine. "These pistols are mine. You can keep the rifles until I need them."

Talbot nodded. "I'll make sure and get you half a dozen magazines and plenty of ammunition to train with. I got a belt and holsters in the locker. It looks like the marines wore the flechette pistol on the right side and the neural disruptor cross-draw on the left."

Kelsey set the flechette pistol down and picked up the neural disruptor. She brought it up and aimed at the target. Instead of an aiming point, she saw a circle about four feet across. She focused on the pistol and discovered that the aperture was adjustable. The tighter the focus, the more intense the effect. She also discovered that she could control the intensity of the beam through her implant.

An internal safety demanded her override to set it to lethal. She ordered it to, just to make sure that she could, and then reduced it back to stun. Her implant indicated that a narrow beam would stun a human being for up to four hours. If she took it to its widest aperture, it would knock out everyone in a 90-degree arc for about half an hour, though that drastically reduced its range.

She could see how something like this would be very useful. Especially for someone like the police.

Next, she examined the flechette rifle. It fired the exact same ammunition as the pistol but had a significantly longer range and greater capacity. "The generator in the rifle is bigger and uses the same flechettes as the pistol. One magazine holds a hundred flechettes. The velocity is boosted to 3,500 meters per second, though. Over ten times the speed of sound."

"Damn! That would go right through one of our fighting vehicles. They must've had some seriously advanced armor to deal with."

It seemed as though the targets on this range wouldn't be very useful for testing a rifle, but she was wrong. On a hunch, she sent a mental command to the range, and a tiny target appeared against the far wall. According to the range, it was simulating a human being at 2,000 meters. She brought the rifle up and fired at the aiming point but missed. Out of ten total shots, she missed all of them.

She handed the rifle to Talbot with a grimace. "Well, that sucked. Apparently computer-assisted aiming only goes so far."

Talbot rested the rifle on the bench and began slowly firing. The range indicated that he hit eleven times out of twenty. He smiled up at Kelsey. "That's where practice and experience come into play. This is a sweet weapon. I can see we're going to get real attached to it."

"And that brings us to the last rifle," she said. "According to my implants, it's a plasma rifle. The range is now giving me a safety lecture. Apparently, you need to get behind me and I need to turn the range's magnetic safety field onto high. The range won't allow more than one plasma rifle to fire at a time. By the way, this safety field is why we're not blowing holes in the far side of the range with the flechettes."

According to her implants, the plasma rifle was a relatively short-range weapon, but inside its reach, it was king. It also indicated that she should not fire at targets closer than twenty meters. So she had the range create a target out at twenty-five meters. She created a Pale One for her to shoot at. She ordered it to charge.

Kelsey raised the plasma rifle smoothly, aimed for center mass, and pulled the trigger. The speck of fire that flew from the bell of the plasma rifle was almost intolerably bright. Like the spot where someone was welding. Her ocular implants dimmed the hellish light immediately, but Talbot cursed behind her. She hoped she hadn't temporarily blinded him.

The pea of fire struck the charging Pale One and blew him apart. The wave of destruction expanded behind the target for fifteen or twenty meters. It would've incinerated him and all his friends.

She laid the rifle on the rest with the deadly end pointed down range. Then she turned to Talbot. "You okay?"

He rubbed his eyes. "That was a little bright for my taste, so some warning would be useful next time. We'll need to rig up some goggles to wear when one of these is on the range. Holy shit. That is the most deadly crew-served weapon I have ever seen."

On a hunch, Kelsey checked the rifle. "Sorry to pop your bubble, but that isn't a crew-served weapon. They must have a bigger version. Ditto the flechette rifles."

"I can hardly imagine. An army with those things would be unstoppable."

"Except that they were stopped. I think if there's a lesson here, it's that no one is too badass to be beaten."

The marine nodded somberly. "Too true, Princess. Too true. That said, we can make things as difficult for the enemy as possible."

Talbot had her walk him through the disassembly and cleaning of the weapons. The neural disruptor required no cleaning at all, and the flechette weapons needed only minimal attention. No gunpowder. The plasma rifle, on the other hand, required significant servicing, even after only one shot. Luckily, the weapons were able to explain in detail exactly how to disassemble and clean themselves properly.

Once they had them reassembled, Talbot jerked his head toward the door. "Come on. Let's put these away and go look at something else. I think you'll like it."

Kelsey held up her hand. "Hold up there, Speedy. You promised me a belt and holsters. I'm taking these with me."

He scratched his chin. "I'm not so sure that Captain Mertz would be happy with you wandering around strapped. Maybe we should keep these in the armory."

"Does Captain Mertz keep his pistol in the armory? I'm betting the answer is no." She planted her fists on her hips and gave the marine a steady look. "I've never been one to throw around my weight, but I am the senior diplomatic representative on this mission. I believe I'm entitled to keep weapons in my quarters. I promise not to parade around wearing them everywhere."

Talbot shrugged. "That's way above my pay grade, so I'll let someone else argue with you."

He searched through a small pile of belts until he found one that was small enough for her. He added two holsters and helped her adjust them. The touch of his hands on her hips made her intensely aware of his body close to hers. Her heart raced a bit, and she felt a little more alone when he stepped back to examine his handiwork.

He removed the power packs from both pistols and had her practice drawing and aiming them. He corrected the mistakes she made and instructed her to practice. He then stressed that she should remove the power packs unless she expected to need the weapons. Then he filled half a dozen magazines with flechettes and put them in a bag for her with a couple of extra power supplies.

Walking around armed felt very odd but incredibly reassuring. She followed Talbot into another room and looked around. Large boxes filled it. More like crates, really.

"What's all this?"

"There's a lot of large marine equipment that we haven't had a chance to examine closely. We've only started cataloging it."

He walked to one of the crates set a short distance aside from the others. Someone had obviously opened it before, because the side fell down when he yanked on it. Inside was a suit of armor.

Talbot ran his hand down the dark-grey metal arm. "This is a set of powered combat armor. There are others like it in the armory, but they probably need some serious maintenance. I'd like to see if you can tell me anything about this set." He tugged on it, and she saw that it was on a small rack. An arm allowed it to turn ninety degrees and come completely outside the crate.

She stared at it in awe. The back opened so the person could slide into it, including the legs. Not the arms, though. It looked like the wearer was supposed to wiggle into those. The helmet was detachable and had an opaque metal face. How was the wearer supposed to see anything? It looked as intimidating as hell.

The armor didn't seem very thick, especially when one was talking about weapons like those flechette and plasma rifles. She queried the armor. Detailed information flowed in front of her eyes.

"This isn't marine armor. It's commando armor. It tells me that it's less protective than a full marine combat rig but significantly more agile. They designed marine armor to fight in the middle of the battle. It's heavy, thick, and mounts those big-ass weapons I was telling you about earlier.

"Commando armor is made for stealth. It can take a beating, but the wearer is supposed to strike from the shadows and be gone before the enemy can find them. The exterior skin can be made to mimic its environment. This says that there are some medium-size flechette and plasma rifles that can be used with it."

Talbot whistled. "You mean there's something more badass than this? That's awesome. Unfortunately, it doesn't seem like there are any of those sets of armor aboard this ship. We took the liberty of installing a power unit in this one, obviously, but I'm certain that it's not ready for use. In fact, I'm not even certain that anyone without implants can use it. Can you tell me?"

She queried the suit for a status. "I'm afraid that these suits require interface with the user's implants to work. You wouldn't even be able to see where you're going. It looks like the suit needs to be disassembled, cleaned, and a few modules replaced. We can probably salvage them from other suits right now or, better yet, find where the commandos stored them. Then we need to adjust it to fit me."

"That sucks, but it is what it is." He gestured toward the door. "Come on. Let's go see if we can find some spare parts."

15

After three days of maneuvering through the asteroid field and testing the various systems, including firing the beam weapons at various hunks of rock and metal, Jared decided *Courageous* was as ready as she was going to be for the trip to Pentagar.

Offensively, many of the missile launchers were still offline, but the beams were mostly operational. The drives also seemed to be in working order. Time to cross their fingers and take a chance. "Zia, make sure *Best Deal* is ready to follow us through. Pasco, prepare to flip the ship."

Jared crossed his fingers. The familiar sensation of nausea gripped him, and the screen changed.

Kelsey sat bolt upright. "I see *Athena*! I know it's her! I can also see four Pentagaran ships. I'm not sure which one is which, but one is really big."

"Tell us what you can about *Athena*."

"I can see where she's taken battle damage. I can sense fusion power plants, including one that looks a little out of balance. Her weapons are offline. The same for the Pentagaran warships. I guess the big one is *Mace*."

"That seems like a safe bet." Especially since Jared had sent a message to Commodore Sanders to expect them about this time.

Jared touched an icon on his console, opening a channel to engineering. Dennis Baxter appeared on the small screen a moment later. "How did the flip drives take the transition?" he asked.

The engineer grinned ebulliently. "They performed flawlessly. We are good to go."

"Excellent. Pass my congratulations on to all your people. Bridge out."

"*Best Deal* just flipped into the system," Kelsey added. "She's a little more than 7,000 kilometers astern of us."

"Zia, open a channel to *Mace*. My compliments to Commodore Sanders."

A few seconds later, the commodore appeared on the main screen. The older man grinned. "You made it. I still can't believe that I'm seeing this. I would've never thought an Old Empire vessel could be made operational again."

"And in just a few weeks, too," Jared agreed. "It wouldn't have been possible if we hadn't gotten the main computer online. This ship is amazing. How are things going? Any activity from the Pale Ones?"

"The probes you put in place have been giving us a pretty good picture of what's going on in the other system. There's activity around the shipyards, but the number of ships is low. I think you really hurt them. Which is good for us, of course."

"How many ships are you estimating?"

"We think three or four dozen."

Jared considered that. "I find the fact they haven't been reinforced interesting. If they could call for help, I think they would have. That's good news."

The commodore nodded. "The Admiralty is in agreement with you. It'll still be another ten days before we have the first of our refitted ships ready to flip. We can only hope that the circumstances remain the same until we can go over there in force."

A flashing light on Jared's console captured his attention. The icon was unfamiliar to him.

Kelsey cleared her throat. "Pardon the interruption, Captain. *Courageous* would like to interject a comment. Since you don't have implants, the console requires your manual authorization."

The request was a bit unsettling. He'd spoken to the ship's computer a number of times, but he still hadn't started thinking of it as a full-fledged artificial intelligence with the initiative to interject itself into events. He touched the icon. "Go ahead, *Courageous*."

"This unit apologizes for the interruption, Commander Mertz." The voice from the overhead speakers was male, low, and melodious. Jared wasn't certain how long it would take him to become accustomed to a ship that was referred to as "she" having a male voice. He wondered how they'd handled that in the Old Empire. From his expression, Commodore Sanders was hearing the AI as well.

"This unit wishes to verify the occupation of the next system. It desires to launch a probe through the flip point."

Jared gave Commodore Sanders a questioning look. The older man nodded. "Give me a few minutes to make sure everyone knows what's happening." The screen went back to the star field.

"*Courageous*, since we have a few minutes, I'd like to ask some questions. What are you hoping to find?"

"This unit has taken a great deal on your word. It has granted you authorization on a probationary basis. This unit requires verification that the situation is as you have stated for that situation to continue. It is also a necessary step before this vessel enters a possibly hostile system. Which this unit desires to do as soon as possible."

Commodore Sanders's image replaced the star field. "You are cleared to launch a probe, *Courageous*."

"Commander Mertz?" *Courageous* asked.

"Launch the probe."

The ship immediately launched the probe. Jared had already seen how much faster *Courageous*'s missiles were than *Athena*'s, so the probe's speed wasn't that much of a shock. He could see on the screen, however, that it was causing a bit of talk on *Mace*'s bridge.

Commodore Sanders shook his head. "That probe is faster than any missile we've got. I can see we have even more technological catching up to do than I'd imagined."

"I think I can make that a little easier," Jared said. "Our scientists are pulling data off the main computer. We've already accumulated quite a bit of technical information for you. While we're waiting for the probe, I'd be happy to begin transmitting some of the highlights. It would be a lot easier to send the majority of it over on a cutter, though. It takes up quite a bit of space, and the transmission time would be significant."

"I'd appreciate that very much. If you'll excuse me, I have a few things requiring my attention. I'm certain you do, as well."

Jared ordered Zia to begin sending the priority data once he'd signed off and instructed her to send the full data packet they'd been collecting over on a cutter. Then he turned to Kelsey. She looked worried.

"Is something wrong?"

"I can't say that I'm a big fan of going back over there."

"Hopefully, we won't need to go before the Pentagarans are ready to accompany us. Even if we do, fighting isn't on our list of planned activities. The most I'd expect to happen now is for the computer to ask to send some probes a bit deeper into the Erorsi system for a more detailed scan."

He decided to change the subject. "Lieutenant Reese tells me that you've taken some Old Empire weapons back to your cabin."

She stiffened. "We're not going to fight about them, are we?"

He held up a conciliatory hand. "Allow me to take a moment to give you official permission to store them there and to carry them when we're under combat conditions."

Kelsey visibly relaxed. "Thank you. If we run into trouble, I want to help create a more positive outcome than last time. You should come down to the armory and pick up a pair for yourself. You won't regret it."

"I might just do that. I also hear you been working on armor. How's that going?"

Kelsey smiled. "The damned thing is ridiculous. I'm already stronger than anyone has a right to be, and it easily doubles that. I actually carried one of the weight machines across the gym. I know I'll never use it, but it's certainly reassuring to have it in the closet."

He felt his eyes widen. "You actually have it in your closet?"

She laughed. "No, it's down in the armory. I'm not paranoid enough to think that I need powered armor beside my nightstand."

It took an hour for *Courageous*'s probe to transition to the Pale Ones' system, scan, and return. *Courageous* and her Pentagaran escorts had followed it toward the interdiction zone at a more sedate pace. There was still no enemy activity near the flip point, and the probe they'd left on station was intact. He'd expected that since it was returning regularly to send them updates.

They sent over several more probes to scan deeper into the system. With the enhanced capabilities these probes commanded, they might as well get as good a picture as they could manage. It wasn't as if the Pale Ones didn't know they were there.

They only had to wait about an hour and a half to start getting decent information from the Erorsi system's main world. One of the two shipyards was still constructing ships, but it seemed as though they'd abandoned the damaged one. Not only were there no ships present there, it was powered down.

Jared frowned. There didn't seem to be any active ships around the planet. Surely they hadn't left it unguarded. Where were the remaining ships?

"Captain Mertz," *Courageous* said. "This unit has located possible hostile vessels near Erorsi. There is a large object under propulsion. This unit believes there is a high probability that it is an asteroid on a collision course with the primary world in this system. This unit has witnessed similar events in the past."

Jared looked at Kelsey. "If they're going to conduct an orbital bombardment, that means there's something down there that they don't want us to have."

"Do you think there are humans on that planet?" she asked. "Ones not converted to Pale Ones?"

His blood ran cold. "Probably. The descendants of the people they subjugated here. The AI needs a source of new recruits. My God, what if they're going to exterminate all the slaves they have under their control? *Courageous*, can you determine how large the asteroid is?"

"Negative. This unit will need to redirect one of the probes to make that determination. However, this unit can gauge the remaining time before the object impacts Erorsi at just over twenty-five hours."

Jared thought furiously. "Whether they're destroying people or equipment, it might be in our best interest to see if we can stop them. Kelsey, I'm sorry, but it looks like I'm about to put you in danger."

Jared turned to the front of the bridge. "Flip the ship into the Erorsi system. Zia, give Commodore Sanders a heads-up. Pasco, flank speed to the asteroid. Everyone, keep an eye out for enemy ships. Our speed gives us an advantage in controlling an engagement. Let's use it."

Pasco gave the ship a thirty-second warning and flipped them into the

Erorsi system. As soon as they'd recovered from the transition, Kelsey unstrapped herself and stood. "I'm getting my pistols." She headed for the lift.

He eyed the tactical plot. "What's our ETA?"

"A little short of three hours, Captain."

The lift doors opened a few minutes later, and Kelsey walked back onto the bridge. She now had a gun belt around her waist with two large, unfamiliar weapons holstered on her hips. The one on her left hip was in a reverse holster with the butt pointing forward.

She gave him a look as she sat back down. "What?"

"It's hard to wrap my head around you wearing a gun, much less two."

"You're lucky I'm not wearing my powered armor. I'd feel much safer inside it, but wearing it on the bridge seems like overkill."

He leaned over and lowered his voice. "Have you seen the tactical situation through your implants?"

She nodded. "Yeah. Are we going to be able to stop that thing?"

"I don't know. We just have to change its course enough to miss the planet. With the drives already installed, I'm hoping that will be possible. The tactical plot shows about a dozen ships guarding it, so we're going to be in for a fight. Thankfully, *Courageous* is a much more capable vessel than *Athena* was. I think we can win that fight."

"Even in her current condition?"

"I hope so. I'm thinking we don't have a lot of choice."

He turned to Zia and raised his voice. "We don't know exactly where the remaining vessels have gone, so let's not assume that they've left the system. I don't want to be caught off guard thinking that every Pale Ones ship will come howling after us the moment they see us. We're going to have to cross the asteroid belt, so keep your eye out for ambushers. They may not be capable of it, but I don't want anyone jumping us like we did *Spear* in the war games before we left on this mission."

"Aye, sir."

It took them less than an hour to reach the asteroid belt. Jared kept the ship on high alert, ready to respond to any offensive moves.

Unlike the entertainment vids, a real asteroid belt had lots of space between the asteroids. Most of those hunks of rock were not very large, so hiding places were few and far between. That didn't mean nonexistent, however.

Zia stiffened in her seat. "Enemy vessel detected! Multiple enemy vessels detected! They were hiding behind two large asteroids. We'll be able to fire on the closest vessels in fifteen minutes. We don't have time to retreat to the flip point. Passing scanner control to operations."

Jared tapped his console and opened a channel to operations. "Charlie, what are we looking at?"

His executive officer's face appeared on his console. "Three dozen vessels, Captain. Twelve will arrive in the first group, and the remainder will come into range about five minutes later. The guard vessels from around the asteroid are also heading our way, but they're an hour out. If we can take care of each wave quickly, we may be able to defeat each group separately."

"Keep me informed of any changes in their status." He looked at Zia. "What's your assessment? Can we handle them?"

She nodded. "I believe so. I'm more worried about the second group. We'll want to pick off as many of them as we can at long range. My people have seven of the twelve launchers online and sixty missiles refurbished."

"This is your chance to show off, Lieutenant. Engage the first group as they come into range. Eliminate as many as possible and then overwhelm any stragglers. Be certain to destroy any of the vessels that use that stunning technology first. Tailor the electronic countermeasures as you see fit."

"Aye, Captain."

The Pale Ones' vessels entered *Courageous*'s offensive envelope long before they got into range to fire missiles of their own. If they were using data from the fight with *Athena*, they were in for a rude awakening. The Old Empire missiles had a considerable range advantage over the Pale Ones' observed offensive capability.

"Opening fire," Zia said. She touched her console, and the tactical plot showed missiles streaming away from *Courageous* and toward the lurid red icons of the enemy. "Missile tube seven has misfired. We're working to get it back online." Zia fired a second wave of missiles just before the first set merged with the enemy. Unlike *Athena*, this ship had missiles that could do more than attack. Some of them transmitted incredibly powerful bursts of energy that worked to blind the ships they were attacking, with the plan of minimizing any defensive fire.

She could have saved the effort. None of the Pale Ones attempted to destroy the incoming missiles. The first wave wiped out five of the enemy. The remaining seven staggered into the debris cloud. Two more salvoes destroyed the remaining Pale Ones in the first group.

Time seemed to drag before the second group came into missile range. The next engagement mimicked the first one with the exception that some enemy vessels got through and launched missiles at *Courageous*.

Jared resisted the urge to order the ship to change course. It wouldn't help them. It would only make him *feel* like he was doing something useful.

"Beam weapons online in defensive mode," Zia said. Short, powerful beams of energy shot out to meet the incoming missiles, incinerating every one that they touched. They were much more effective than the railguns Fleet currently used, and they had a higher effective rate of fire.

But they weren't infinite. Several of the attacking missiles smashed into *Courageous*'s screens, and the overhead lights flickered slightly. "Screens down to eighty percent," Zia said.

The enemy swirled around *Courageous*, firing into her screens at almost point-blank range. The beam weapons reached out and incinerated them. In sixty seconds, they had destroyed the last of the second wave.

"Screens down to fifty percent. They should be back up to eighty percent by the time the stragglers arrive."

With the ambushers dealt with, the last dozen ships were somewhat anticlimactic. They didn't even try to flee. Zia destroyed them before they fired a shot. "Enemy vessels destroyed, Captain. We have seventeen missiles remaining."

"Great work, everyone. Keep a good watch. They surprised us once. Let's not give them another chance. Pasco, ETA to the asteroid?"

"We'll be there in a little bit more than an hour, Captain."

"Very good."

He turned to Kelsey. "Well, that certainly went better than it would have if we'd still been in *Athena*. Hopefully that's the worst of what we'll encounter in this system."

"I hope you're right." She didn't seem confident that he was.

* * *

THERE WERE NO MORE surprises on the way to the asteroid. The large piece of debris looked very much like most other asteroids Jared had ever seen, only bigger. The scanners pegged it at almost 10 kilometers in diameter.

It had massive, crude grav drives mounted in a large circle on its surface with a small facility built in their center. They detected no weapons systems, but that was never a certain thing.

Graves called him from operations. "Why build something on a throwaway asteroid? To control the drives? Why not plant some scanners on the front, plot a course, and send it on its way?"

Jared nodded. "That's what I'd do, but we still don't know what makes those things tick. Are they some kind of hive mind? Do they do things simply because someone programmed it into their heads? Or do they have some type of controller? A queen bee."

"The question on my mind is, is it booby-trapped?"

"We'll have to be careful. I don't want to lose any people. We also need to take the drives intact, or we won't be able to change the course of this monster. Not in time. Courageous calculated that the impact would plunge Erorsi into deep winter for years. Perhaps decades. It would be short of an extinction-level event, but not by much."

Jared opened a channel to engineering. "Baxter, we need you to form a team to go over to the asteroid and figure out how to change its course. We'll be sending some marines and a navigator to help plot a better course for it. How long will it take you to get ready?"

The engineer grinned. "We're suited up. Is the princess ready?"

Jared frowned and glanced over at Kelsey. "No, why would she need to go?"

"I figure the chances are very high that this equipment requires an implant interface to control. It's not as if the savages programmed the course in by hand. It's very likely that we're going to require her assistance."

That wasn't what he wanted to hear. "Go meet the marines at the pinnaces. I'll get the last of this ironed out and let you know."

After he closed the line, he turned his full attention to his sister. "You don't have to go, but he might be right."

She took a deep breath, closed her eyes, and let it out. "Of course he's right. It was the only real way to interface with Twelve, and it's going to be the method they use to control this, too. We should've realized that. I'll go get ready."

He watched her leave with more than a hint of trepidation. The very last thing he wanted to do was put her back in danger. But if the Pale Ones thought something was worth destroying, he was certain that it was worth saving.

16

Kelsey sat next to Lieutenant Reese in the marine pinnace and tried not to hyperventilate. It would be fine. If there were any trouble, the marines would take care of it. Besides, shouldn't she feel safer in this badass armor?

The answer turned out to be "not really." The commando armor might protect her more effectively than the suits Reese and his men wore, but fear wasn't exactly rational. She knew that she was well protected because they'd shot up a couple of these suits just to see how tough they were. Her heart still pounded in her chest, and she was covered in sweat.

Reese turned his head and looked at her as though he could sense her uneasiness. He probably could. "You okay, Princess?"

"I'm a little nervous," she admitted. "I know I'm probably overthinking this, but I can see so many ways this could go bad."

"You're not alone. The trick is deciding which possibilities are reasonable. We're going in with overwhelming force, but we have no reason to believe that the Pale Ones have packed this thing with their people. Or that they've booby-trapped it.

"Look at their space station, for example. The damned thing was huge and had plenty of Pale Ones on board, but they didn't effectively counterattack until we were on the way back out. You probably don't remember it very clearly, but they were not prepared for an incursion. My advice? Don't borrow trouble."

Kelsey nodded. "That's true, but look what happened when we came into the system this time. They had ships lying in wait for us. They expected us. Or something controlling them expected us. What if they took the same kind of precautions on the asteroid?"

"Then we deal with it. If it's too tough, we withdraw. This isn't a suicide mission."

Talbot bumped her shoulder from the other side. "Besides, you got me and the boys keeping an eye on you. As if you need it. You're a major badass in that suit."

She'd certainly loaded it down as though she'd expected she was going into combat. Her pistols were on her hips, including plenty of extra ammunition. She also had a flechette rifle built for the armor resting between her knees. She'd strapped a similarly large plasma rifle across her back. Extra ammunition and power packs for those were also on her belt. A couple of Old Empire grenades and an insanely sharp knife rounded out her weapons load.

She felt ridiculous.

Talbot had insisted she bring everything along. Just in case, he'd said. She might never need it, but if she did, it wouldn't help her if it were back on the ship.

Kelsey was certain that they wouldn't be letting her use any of her hardware. If they got into a situation where they were exchanging fire, Talbot would pull her back. She knew he had orders to keep her out of trouble. All this gear was to distract her.

But having it along provided some distinct pluses. Her armor's scanners had significant advantages over what the marines around her carried. She also had a few little toys that she hadn't discussed with Senior Sergeant Talbot in her pouches. If she was playing at being a marine, she should come ready to dance.

The pilot opened a link to Lieutenant Reese. "We're not taking any fire, Lieutenant, so we're going in. ETA five minutes."

Kelsey wasn't supposed to be able to overhear that remark, but her armor had informed her that there were encrypted communications on the pinnace earlier, and she'd asked for more information about the transmission.

Apparently, the combat computer in the armor had decided she'd asked for it to tap into the communication channels. It took less than five minutes for the armor to crack the encryption. She'd tell Lieutenant Reese about that after they returned to *Courageous*. She was certain he'd want to do something about it, though she had no idea what that would be.

"Everyone, we're going in," Lieutenant Reese said. "Final equipment check."

She sent a status query to her armor, and it came back green on all systems. "My armor indicates it's ready. That's going to have to be good enough for us."

"Fine, but I'll check just to be sure." Talbot had someone read the checklist that she'd pulled from the armor to him as he looked at everything.

Patching her suit into the pinnace's scanners was more complex than tapping into the encrypted communication link, but she figured it out just before they landed. The images and readings were somewhat crude based on her experiences tapping into *Courageous*'s scanner suite, but they told her what was going on well enough.

They were landing at the Pale Ones' facility. Of course, from what she could see, "facility" might be too grand a word. The scanners showed a crude, low dome with standard Old Empire docking clamps. It didn't look too well put together to her. In fact, it seemed like a deranged child had built it.

Lieutenant Reese's plan was to dock as quickly as possible. If something went wrong, the marines would retreat and attack from the surface, blowing a convenient entrance through the exterior hull.

Probably dragging Kelsey along like a cat in a bag as they rushed in. She still hadn't gotten any zero-G training. Perhaps her implants could help her out with that, too.

A tense few minutes went by as the pinnace docked and the marines breached the facility. They reported that they were inside with no resistance, so Lieutenant Reese ordered his remaining men in. The facility had gravity.

When he nodded to Kelsey, she went through the boarding hatch with Talbot and his squad close around her. She held the flechette rifle to her chest with the muzzle angled down toward the floor as Talbot had trained her to do. The remainder of the marines came in behind her.

The corridor upheld the Pale Ones' low building standards. The facility was small enough that the marines had most of the floor occupied. The reports flowed back that they hadn't discovered any Pale Ones. They'd found a lift, however. It seemed this facility had more than one floor.

Lieutenant Junior Grade Ralph Phelps, the engineer assigned to the mission, frowned. "There's no reason to have an underground facility. All they need is a scanner package and a control computer. That could fit into this building easily."

"Welcome to combat, Lieutenant," Reese said. "The enemy is never obliging enough to do exactly what you'd expect. We'll have to go down and see for ourselves what they've left for us."

The young cutter pilot, Ensign Danielle Cruz, nodded. The two noncombatants were in borrowed armor but unarmed. They'd be behind Kelsey, keeping out of any fracas. Unless things went to hell.

They would've taken the stairs, except there weren't any. The only way down was the lift. So rather than obliging the enemy by going down in small groups, Lieutenant Reese ordered them to cut the bottom out of the lift. It made quite a clattering noise as it fell. If the enemy didn't know they were there before, they did now.

The marines nimbly went down on ropes. The shaft only went one level, so the drop was very short. Kelsey picked a spot without debris and jumped. Her heart was in her throat for a moment, but her suit absorbed the landing easily.

"Don't do that to me, Princess," Talbot said over their private channel. "You're going to give me a heart attack."

"Don't get your panties in a knot," she muttered before she activated her microphone. "I don't know how to use those ropes, but I've done enough with the suit to know what I can do. That was a breeze."

"Yeah, maybe so. But give a guy a little warning, will you?"

The marines had already forced the lift doors open, so she followed them out. This level was just as shoddy as the one above. The floors weren't exactly level, and there was no paint anywhere. Just enough bare functionality to get by.

Kelsey scanned the area around them. Most of the information didn't mean anything to her, but the suit reported a large area directly in front of the lift as shielded. She couldn't detect anything but a blank spot in her readings.

"Lieutenant Reese, there's something ahead of us. I'm sensing a very large shielded area about seventy-five meters ahead."

"I don't see anything. Are you certain?"

"I'm positive."

Reese ordered his men to move forward. He gestured for Talbot to stay back with her.

She wasn't the least bit offended. She'd been in one firefight and wasn't eager to repeat the experience. She nervously eyed her readouts as they moved into the shielded area. Nothing looked different about the corridor around them, but now her scanners couldn't detect anything. Not even the bulkhead right next to her.

One of the marines up front reported an armored hatch. Reese ordered a halt while they planted charges to breach it.

"Maybe I can open it," she said. "Let me take a look."

Reese reluctantly agreed. She made her way through the marines until she stood in front of the hatch.

"If you open it, just step aside, and let us go in first," Talbot said.

Kelsey nodded and felt for an interface with the door. She found one, but it was different from any that she'd accessed before. It felt... stupid. It didn't respond to a query for information and only seemed to have the option of open or closed. Perhaps that was all the Pale Ones were capable of telling the hatch to do.

She sent at a command to open, and the hatch slid to the side. The room beyond was dark, but she didn't need to see to know what was there. The scanner shielding didn't obscure the inside of the compartment. Dozens of threat icons popped up in her mind's eye. Unbelievably, some of them registered as wielding advanced weaponry, and she instinctively knew that the Pale Ones were targeting the marines.

"Ambush!" Her automated reflexes didn't care what Reese had ordered her to do. They threw her through the hatch and off to the side, out of the deathtrap the corridor was about to become in the face of Old Empire weapons. She sent the mental command for the hatch to close even before she started moving. Reese and Talbot were going to be furious, but it beat them being dead.

The world was already slowing as she brought up her rifle and swept across the Pale Ones, the combat drugs taking effect. The light stroke of the trigger she gave the rifle sent a stream of hypervelocity flechettes into the unarmored savages. The darts shredded them, just like the simulated targets on the firing range. She kept moving under the assumption they'd focus their fire on her.

The shots they sent toward the marines in the hall struck the hatch as it slammed closed, blowing large divots in the metal. It wasn't going to open very easily now. She staggered and fell when one of the flechettes struck her shoulder, but the armor held.

Kelsey knew that the Pale Ones could see in the dark just as well as she could, so she rolled behind a large piece of equipment. She had no idea what it was, but it was bulky enough to stand up to fire for a few seconds. She retrieved the scanner remote she'd put in her pouch and threw it out into the center of the compartment.

The manual she'd found for it said that she'd be able to use the remote to fire without exposing herself, but she was nowhere near that good yet. Instead, she noted where the largest concentration of the enemy was and threw a grenade. When it went off, it was as though the world had ended.

She'd never experienced such a tremendous shock wave of light, noise, and pressure. The commando suit protected her from most of it but not all. The remote reported more than half of the ambushers as obliterated or down.

Kelsey popped up while they were stunned and opened fire. She killed several of them before diving behind fresh cover. Only half a dozen of them were still alive, scattered around the room. Being able to see them from relative safety, she was able to pick them off one by one until she was alone again. They managed to hit her two more times: once in the leg and once on the side of her helmet. That last shot stunned her, but her implants and pharmacology unit kept her going.

She staggered to her feet and made a sweep of the compartment, verifying there were no more hostiles. There weren't. The Pale Ones were dead.

Reese and Talbot had been trying to contact her continuously since the firefight started, but she hadn't been able to answer them. Well, she didn't have enough attention to spare for them. She supposed that a real marine could do both those things and more all at the same time.

"It's okay," she said. "They're all down. Let me see if I can get this door open." She sent a command, but it failed to move. "It's not responding. It must've been damaged in the firefight."

"Get back," Reese snarled. "We're going to blow the hatch. Like we should have in the first place."

Oh, yeah. She was in big trouble.

The explosives they set off warped the hatch even further but didn't open it. Neither did the second set. That caused Lieutenant Reese to curse a lot more. Somehow, she didn't think his failure was going to help her.

"Go back to the lift," she said. "I'm going to blow the hatch from inside."

She retreated to the rear of the compartment, took cover, and brought the plasma rifle off her back. She trained it on the hatch and, when Reese reported he was clear, pulled the trigger. The resulting explosion blew the armored hatch into molten fragments. It did the same for the first ten meters of the corridor, leaving a gaping concave area of pure rock and melted metal in its wake.

Kelsey whistled. The armor-grade plasma rifle was significantly more powerful than the regular handheld version. Just like her flechette rifle was vastly more capable than its smaller brethren, managing to accelerate the tungsten-alloy darts up to 5,000 meters a second. All it took was one glance around the room at the shredded bodies and divots blown into the walls to imagine how effective and terrifying full-scale combat would've been in the Old Empire.

The marines had to wait for the corridor to cool before they came in, which caused Lieutenant Reese's temper to fray further. When he ordered his men in, she stood there with her arms out so they wouldn't mistake her for a threat.

Reese stormed over to her. "That was the most irresponsible, fool-headed stunt I've ever seen in my life. What the hell were you thinking?"

He held up his hand before she could respond. "On second thought, I don't want to know. Whatever it was, it was wrong. I thought I was crystal clear that you were not to put yourself into danger. Did I stutter?"

"No, Lieutenant. But I didn't have a choice. There were dozens of them with a clear line of fire straight down that corridor. Those flechettes would've blown your armor to pieces. I had to distract them and get that hatch closed before they killed all of us. Tell me you would've done something differently."

Reese began cursing. He sounded a lot like Jared did when she upset him. She seemed to have that effect on men. Perhaps it was a character flaw.

"I've got something over here," Lieutenant Phelps said. "It looks like a computer of some kind."

The marine officer glared at Kelsey. "This isn't over yet. You stand right here beside me, and you don't fart unless I tell you to. Am I clear?"

"Perfectly clear, Lieutenant."

"I can see why you did what you did, but you've pushed him too far," Talbot said over their private channel.

"They were going to kill all of you. My armor might've survived the opening salvo, but yours wouldn't take one hit."

The older man sighed. "I'm going to have to volunteer for these implants just to keep up with you. I'm too old for this crap."

Kelsey caught up to Reese. The computer they'd found seemed a bit substantial for just controlling an asteroid. It actually filled an entirely separate room behind the area where the fight had taken place.

Phelps shone a light over the compartment. "This has been here a while.

The consoles have dust on them. A lot of dust. I don't know what this thing is, but it's not here just to control those thruster units."

Reese turned to her. "If you try to interface with that thing, is it going to attack you?"

She shook her head. "I don't think so. They need me in a special machine with physical contact to override the programming inside my implants. It may not do what I tell it to, but I should be safe enough."

"Do it. See if that's the computer controlling the thrusters."

Kelsey initiated contact with the computer and immediately discovered that it was almost completely inactive. Only three processors were running, with limited resources. Many thousands of other processors were offline. A quick check confirmed that virtually all the data storage was empty.

"I think that it's controlling the grav drives, but it's almost completely turned off. Only one small part of it is functional."

"Can you alter its course?" Phelps asked.

She asked the computer its course, and a schematic popped up in her mind's eye. "I think so. Ensign Cruz, it has a mountain range on the planet targeted. What do I do?"

The woman looked into the room uncertainly. "Without seeing the controls, I don't know if I can tell you exactly what to do. Can you enable the console over here?"

Kelsey sent a command through the system to display the asteroid's course, and the console beside the pilot came to life. She stepped over to watch what the ensign did.

The console showed the planet and the asteroid. A solid green line connected them. Cruz tapped the controls, and the course moved until it just missed the planet. The green line changed to yellow a short distance away. When the ensign moved it further, it went to red. She edged it back to yellow.

"We caught it just in time. Much longer and I don't think we could have generated a miss. We've saved the planet."

"Good," Reese said. "Talbot, take the princess back to the pinnace with your team. Tell the pilot to take her back to *Courageous* right now. I'm not taking any more chances with her."

17

J ared couldn't blame Kelsey for the events on the asteroid, but he wasn't going to take any chances with her going forward. If he'd been thinking clearly the first time, she would've been in a follow-up group. Though that likely meant the marines wouldn't have been able to clear the asteroid. As it was, she'd undoubtedly saved many lives. When her father found out the events she'd been through, Jared would be lucky to command a sailboat.

The asteroid was going to pass uncomfortably close to the planet, but with something that massive, it wasn't possible to change course on a dime. Still, a miss was a miss. They'd foiled the Pale Ones again.

Courageous detected no operational ships near the shipyards, making the facilities look abandoned. If that were true, then salvaging the yards would be very useful, not only for the data on the ship construction used by the Pale Ones but perhaps in putting them to use by the Pentagarans.

Would the Pale Ones have booby-trapped them? It hardly seemed likely that they would attempt to destroy the planet and leave the shipyards ripe for the plucking. That meant more boarding parties. More fighting. They'd been lucky so far this time, but that could change in a moment.

He considered the complexity of the situation. The probes near the planet could be retasked to do active scans on the shipyards. Jared knew those shipyards had weapons, so he had every expectation that the shipyards would promptly destroy the probes. But perhaps before they died, they could give them some useful information.

He looked up from his console. "Zia. I want you to take two of the three probes that we sent to the planet, move them in as close as practical to the shipyards, and do an active scan. I want to know everything you can tell me about them, and I want to see what their response is to the activity."

"Aye, sir." She manipulated her controls, and they waited as the speed-of-light signals traveled to the probes. Time dragged until the responses came.

"Both probes have been destroyed, Captain, but I got detailed readings on both shipyards. It looks like we significantly damaged the one we fired on last month. Many areas of the habitat portion are open to space. It's unlikely there are any live Pale Ones aboard. Also, I detected no operational weapons on that structure."

Jared had already been going over the data and concurred with everything that she'd said. They could take out the operational shipyard, but they'd virtually destroy it in the process. The damaged shipyard seemed unarmed. As long as it didn't self-destruct, of course.

"Pasco, keep the planet between us and the shipyards as much as you can. Use the damaged one as a screen when you can."

They came in hard and fast. His worry that the shipyard would self-destruct once they moved in proved unfounded. It simply sat there.

The boarding proved to be somewhat anticlimactic, as well. Most of the systems appeared to be offline, and bloated corpses filled the corridors. The EMP effects of the fusion weapon must've completely crippled the shipyard. The scientists would have a field day tearing it apart looking for clues about the Pale Ones.

Once assured of their relative safety, Jared put *Courageous* into orbit around the planet just behind the shipyard, carefully keeping an eye on the operational one through several drones used to relay signals.

He'd worried it would fire at them around the curve of the planet, but it didn't. Perhaps the primitive missiles they had weren't capable of targeting when the launching vessel couldn't see the target.

In any case, *Courageous* seemed to be safe for the moment. That might not last, so he ordered Zia to scan the surface. Almost immediately, she detected the remains of Old Empire civilization. Bombed-out cities and ancient ruins.

He still had no idea why the rebels would devastate Erorsi and leave Pentagar completely alone. It made no sense. There didn't seem to be anything special about the area the Pale Ones had targeted. Perhaps it was just a convenient target for the massive weapon.

Relatively certain that they were safe for the moment, Jared canceled battle stations and just kept the ship at a heightened state of alert. When commander Graves arrived from operations, he turned the watch over to him. "Call me immediately if the tactical situation changes. I'm going to debrief the marines."

Charlie gave him a knowing look. "You mean you're going to debrief Princess Kelsey. Go easy on her. I understand that the combat was pretty extreme. Even worse than the Parliament Building."

Jared slowly nodded. "I'm going to have to rein her in somehow, but I'm not going to make a huge production of it. This is partly my fault. I shouldn't have sent her along with the marines. Not until that base had been cleared."

He entered the lift and instructed it to take him to marine country. By the time he arrived, he'd decided on a basic strategy.

Activity filled marine country. Some of the marines were cleaning equipment, while others were preparing for combat operations. A distracted-looking Lieutenant Reese broke off his conversation with some Pentagaran marines and came over to him. "Captain. If you'll step into my office, I'll give you a brief report on the operations to date."

Jared hadn't been to Lieutenant Reese's new office before. It was as large as Jared's old office had been on *Athena*. Several citation plaques hung on the wall behind the desk, and a shelf held some sports trophies. Baseball, it looked like. Jared had never been a follower of the sport, but it was very popular throughout the Empire.

He gestured for the marine to take a seat behind the desk while he sat at one of the visitors' chairs.

The marine officer remained standing at attention. "I take full responsibility for the danger I put Princess Kelsey into. It was reckless and unacceptable. I have no excuse for my lapse."

Jared laughed before he could stop himself. "That is a complete load of horse shit, and we both know it. Princess Kelsey does things that no sane human being would even think about doing. I'm certain that you took what would normally be adequate protective measures. Sit down. You're wearing me out standing there."

When the marine sat, Jared continued. "What happened on that asteroid?"

He listened intently as Lieutenant Reese walked through the events of the assault. When the marine finished, Jared stared at the bulkhead for a minute, thinking. "The idea of Pale Ones using Old Empire weapons is very disturbing to me. That has all kinds of unpleasant implications."

Reese nodded. "I hadn't believed that they were capable of using them, but I suppose if they can fly a spaceship, they can shoot a gun. I'd wager that they required some special control in order to do so, or some special instructions. Based on what Kelsey saw, they weren't very accurate. If we'd already been inside that room, I think we could've taken them."

Jared tried to imagine the fight. "Kelsey taking them out all by herself is a different kind of disturbing. I've seen her fight hand to hand, and it's amazing and terrifying. I can only imagine what her using Old Empire weapons looked like. Just how effective were the weapons they were using?"

"Let's put it this way, our shaped charges couldn't breach that armored door. Princess Kelsey's plasma rifle did this." He brought up a series of images on the console. "One shot."

The destruction made Jared's jaw drop. "That's… unimaginable."

"It was like Armageddon," the marine admitted. "Even all the way back at the lift, it sounded like the world had ended. The grenade she used that decimated the enemy forces was so powerful that it left a crater bigger than one of our mortar shells. Her flechettes went through bodies, equipment, and blew huge divots out of the walls. She had more firepower than the rest of us combined."

"Tell me you're upgrading your weapons. Tell me that you're adapting that armor for your use. We have the most powerful ship I've ever seen, but there are some situations where we need men on the ground."

Reese grimaced. "We're restoring weapons as quickly as we can. Rather, a couple of the scientists are showing us how to do so. I believe we can have flechette weapons for all marines inside a week. We have a couple of the smaller plasma rifles, too. The larger weapons require powered armor to use. The armor requires implants, so we're at a dead end. I'm about ready to volunteer to be implanted myself."

Jared's eyes widened. "You'd let that machine cut you open and make all those changes? Changes that you can't take back?"

The marine shrugged. "It's the future, Captain. To fight the Pale Ones, we're going to have to be a lot more effective. Fleet officers, too. This ship is capable of so much with the right interface. How long is it going to be before someone takes that first step voluntarily? I say now, because if we wait, it might be too late."

First Zia's comment and now Reese's. The writing really was on the wall.

"How is Princess Kelsey?" he asked, changing the subject.

"Jittery. I had Doctor Stone check her out, but I already knew what it was. Postcombat shakes. She's not the first person I've seen react that way. Sturdy as steel when the shit hits the fan and then shaking like a leaf once it's all over. The doctor gave her a sedative and sent her to bed."

Well, that meant he wouldn't be speaking to her tonight. That was probably for the best anyway.

Jared rose. "Well, I'll just have to speak with her tomorrow, then. Work with Lieutenant Anderson and come up with an assault plan for the operational shipyard. We've come this far. We might as well clear the system. Plan on the Pale Ones being armed."

Reese stood and saluted. "Aye, sir. I'll have something on your desk in a few hours."

"Don't rush. Sometime early tomorrow is soon enough. I have an important meeting that will probably take up most of my evening."

Jared headed for the medical center. Technically, this wasn't a meeting. It was more of an ambush. He found Doctor Stone in her office and rapped on the open hatch. "I hope you have time, because I need to talk to you."

She looked up from her console. "I always have time for you, Captain. What can I do for you?"

He closed the hatch behind him. "I've decided to undergo a procedure. One that I suspect you will strongly disapprove of." He dropped into the seat in front of her desk. "I've decided that I need a Fleet officer's implants."

Doctor Stone scowled. "There is absolutely no reason to go through something like that until we understand things better. It's your brain, Jared. If something goes wrong, you'll be a vegetable or dead."

"*Courageous* was designed to interface with a crew that could command it effectively. Princess Kelsey didn't have a choice, but if we're going to fight our way home, we're going to have to get over our aversion to the idea of implants. As this ship's captain, it behooves me to take that first step."

Stone took a long breath. "Captain, I certainly understand your arguments, but this is a risky, untested procedure. Look what happened to Kelsey. That thing butchered her. I strongly urge you to reconsider."

Jared shook his head. "It needs to be done, and I need to set the example. Besides, I'm not getting the full set of implants. Just the Fleet officer's package. Your report says that the implantation machine recalibrated itself. Its built-in regeneration unit is functional now. Is that correct?"

Stone nodded reluctantly. "That's what the unit's diagnostic system tells me, but it's never been tested. As your doctor, I advise against this in the strongest terms."

"But you don't forbid it."

Stone sighed. "No. I'm not blind to the ship's capabilities. There are machines here in the medical center that I can't use because I can't access them. I see the potential. I also see the danger. You're our commanding officer. If you try this and it fails, you'll be beyond my help, and I'll wager the crew won't be rushing in for implants."

"I've made up my mind, Doctor."

* * *

JARED WENT into the procedure more than a little nervous. According to what the machine had told Kelsey, Fleet officers received the cranial implants and medical nanites. He already knew the implantation procedure for the brain worked fine for Kelsey. He didn't think his procedure would leave him nearly as incapacitated as Kelsey had been.

He was right. He woke up without suffering anything near the pain that Kelsey had, or the disorientation. Other than feeling a little bit groggy, he felt perfectly normal.

That didn't keep Doctor Stone from being worried. "How are you feeling?"

"Not too bad, actually." He sat up. Doctor Stone looked alarmed, but he wasn't dizzy. He plucked a writing stylus out of her pocket and flipped it in his hand a few times. For someone who had had his brain operated on, he felt surprisingly good.

Stone took her stylus back. "Don't try to stand just yet. Let's get a good scan first. Doctor Leonard?"

Of course, Doctor Leonard and Carl Owlet were mandatory participants in the procedure. They'd cleared the medical center of all other personnel, though.

The scientist put a modified headset on Jared. "Just rest easy for a few minutes while we scan your implant code, Captain. I'm quite certain that it's clean, but it pays to take no chances."

After a few minutes, the graduate student nodded. "Your implants are all clean, Captain. Based on watching the princess learn to use hers, I recommend that you spend a lot of time practicing before you really need it."

Jared eased himself to his feet and flexed his knees. Everything felt fine. "I know you'd like to keep me in bed for a couple of days, Doctor, but I don't have the luxury of lying around. What is my realistic recovery time?"

Stone looked a bit sour. "According to Workstation Twelve, you can be released to light duty immediately. Normal duty tomorrow. It also recommends that you get training on using your implants over the next week."

"I'll do that. I'm sure that Kelsey has quite a bit of advice for me. Or she will once I tell her that I've done this." He gave the three of them a steady look. "For the moment, let's keep this between the four of us. Understood?"

The others quickly acknowledged his order.

"Good. Let's see if these things work."

He could already sense the old Imperial workstation. It was a very strange sensation. *Can you hear me, Workstation Twelve?*

Affirmative.

How did the implantation procedure go? Is there anything else that I should be aware of?

Everything went exceedingly well. Installation of hardware and regeneration of the surgical sites went without any issues. The medical nanites are operating as expected.

So you're ready to begin performing these procedures as needed?

Negative. No more cranial implants are available.

That wasn't quite the answer that Jared was expecting. *Do you know where resupply parts would be available?*

Negative. This unit only loads a single set of implants and hardware prior to a procedure. An attached bin holds all other equipment for easy resupply.

Wonderful. He distinctly remembered that bin lying on the deck of the orbital when they'd rescued Kelsey. They must've knocked it loose during the struggle to save her. They'd probably blown up the only remaining supplies in the system.

He rubbed his face. "I have good news and I have bad news, Doctor Stone. The good news is I was able to converse with Workstation Twelve. The bad news is it's out of implants. We'll have to find another supply before it can perform any more procedures."

Doctor Stone smiled wryly. "For the moment, I'm going to count that as good news and good news. Until I understand more about this process and what could go wrong with it, I'm happy that we can't do any more."

They had him move around the laboratory for half an hour, just to make sure that he wasn't suffering any ill effects. Then Doctor Stone grudgingly released him. She did insist on accompanying him back to his quarters.

She strapped a medical alert bracelet to his wrist. "This will monitor your vital signs overnight. It also has an emergency call button. If anything seems unusual or you feel distressed, press the button. If your vital signs spike in any way, the crash team will be here in sixty seconds. God only knows what they'll be able to do if things go wrong, though."

"Yes, Mother."

She glowered at him sternly. "You think you're funny, but I'm being serious. No matter what that pile of junk says, you've just been through a serious medical procedure. On. Your. Brain. It's going to take a long time before I feel cavalier about something like that. I want you to get a good night's rest and then come see me in the morning before you report for duty."

He heard the unspoken threat in her tone. If he didn't comply, she would relieve him of duty. As chief medical officer, she had that authority. He knew better than to push her.

"I understand, Lily. I'll take it easy, and I'll come see you before breakfast."

"See that you do. Good night, Captain."

After she was gone, he retrieved the headset that he'd put in his desk several days ago. He'd never suspected he'd be using it. He put it on, leaned back in his chair, and closed his eyes.

Courageous, this is Captain Mertz. Can you hear me?

Good evening, Commander Mertz. This unit detected your implants coming online. Thank you for identifying yourself. Implants registered. How may this unit assist you?

I need to become accustomed to utilizing my implants. Can I access the ship's systems?

Of course. The bridge is just a convenience. The consoles and screens are grouped together to allow the crew to communicate effectively and efficiently. However, through the implants, a crew could command and control a ship from their quarters utilizing the headsets.

Are the headsets required on the bridge?

Negative, though they have much greater throughput than the implants do alone. Before you begin experimenting, there is one other matter this unit would like to discuss, if you have time.

Certainly.

The AI seemed to hesitate a moment before continuing. *This unit has completed numerous scans of the surface of Erorsi and the space stations. It has examined the bodies recovered from the asteroid. It believes that it now has enough data to make a permanent decision about your ongoing control of this ship. Now that you have the appropriate implants and can fully control this vessel, this unit is prepared to resume standard protocols and accept you as the commanding officer of the ship, with all the duties and authority that carries. Is that acceptable to you, Commander?*

Jared sat up and tried to control his racing heart. *It is,* Courageous.

Then this unit will place the appropriate command codes into your implants, with your permission. It will enable similar codes for any individual you confirm that is in an appropriate position to require them. Are you prepared?

I am.

He felt nothing as the AI worked. He only knew the process was complete when *Courageous* spoke again. *Updates complete. This unit is now under your command, Captain.*

Let's start with the scanners, shall we? And please don't let anyone know that I have implant hardware or that I've officially assumed command of this ship. I'll tell them when it's appropriate. This applies double for Princess Kelsey.

Query. Princess Kelsey Bandar is an Ambassador Plenipotentiary of the Terran Empire, correct?

He nodded. *Yes. She's also a member of the Imperial Family, with the highest of security clearances. Second in line to the Imperial Throne. Why?*

Then there are codes that are appropriate for her to possess that this unit can provide. This unit will see to it in a manner that does not conflict with your previous orders.

That sounds good, Courageous. *With that settled, let's start with the ship's scanners. Show me what our immediate area looks like.*

As an unexpectedly breathtaking view of local space came into his mind, Jared knew it was going to be a long night.

18

K elsey awoke famished, as usual. A good night's sleep, even though it required a sedative, made yesterday feel like a bad dream. She'd have to process it eventually, but for the moment, she'd focus on today. And the ass chewing Jared would no doubt be giving her.

She took a luxurious water shower in her private showering tube. Once the flow of warm air had dried her body, she dressed in a cream-colored blouse and dark slacks.

A quick ping to the computer told her that Jared was in the officers' mess. It also popped up a notification that her implant software had an update available.

She pinged the computer. Courageous, *is this a valid update?*

Affirmative. This unit has determined that some updates are required based on our current situation. They pose no danger and may prove useful in future situations.

Will they give me more access to my commando implants? More data about them?

Negative. This unit does not possess more detailed information about commando implants. Such information is restricted to commando AIs and vessels. You also already have complete access to your hardware. If this unit discovers a method of getting more information for you on those subjects, it will provide it at once. Do you accept the update at this time?

Sure.

She made her way to the officer's mess and was pleasantly surprised to find Jared sitting at the table with Commander Graves. That might mean less of a public spectacle. Both men rose to their feet as she approached.

"Good morning." She took as seat and waved a server over. "I'll take what they're having, please."

Jared smiled at her, his expression a bit sardonic. "Is it a good morning because you hope it will be, or because it is?"

"Hope springs eternal." She turned to Graves. "Good morning, Commander. I hope we had a quiet night."

The sandy-haired officer nodded. "Indeed we did. The Pale Ones haven't made a hostile move, though that might change at any time."

The server brought their meals and a large pot of coffee. Kelsey's order was bigger than the men's combined meals when it arrived. The sight still embarrassed Kelsey. "Again, let me apologize for my apparent piggishness. All this enhanced musculature demands the extra calories, and I'm famished today."

Jared put his hand on Kelsey's. "You don't need to apologize. Everyone understands. Eat as much as you need."

As they began eating, something about Jared kept nagging at her. She mulled it for a couple of minutes before she figured out what was different. He was registering on her implants.

She narrowed her eyes, opened her senses, and probed him. An implant response shocked her so badly that she bent her fork.

He raised an eyebrow. "Is something the matter?" He raised his finger to his lips as Commander Graves looked toward her.

"Sorry. My control slipped for a second. That's embarrassing. I haven't done this in a couple of weeks."

Can you hear me? she asked.

He didn't respond, but an interface to request a communications link popped up. It was as simple as knowing his implant serial number, which her implants had logged, and having her implants request the link. She did so.

Her implants indicated that he accepted the request.

Jared? What the hell?

This has to be the strangest thing I've ever experienced. Oh, except for accessing the ship's computer last night. You didn't tell me how amazing it was seeing the scanner input while we were in orbit.

Actually, I did. Stop stalling and explain.

He smiled and sipped his coffee. *Charlie is going to grow suspicious if you don't start eating again. I'd rather keep this between the two of us for the moment. Of course, Doctor Stone, Doctor Leonard, and Mister Owlet know. I obviously went through the procedure last night.*

But why?

As he explained his reasoning, she dove back into her food and found herself grudgingly nodding. It made sense. Someone had to be the first *willing* implantee. She still thought he was insane.

You obviously didn't get the full-body workup. You're not ripping the table out of the deck.

No, just the cranial implants and the medical nanites. The standard Fleet officer's package. You can be certain that I'll be coming to you for assistance if I run into any problems. Charlie is starting to give us some odd looks, so I suggest we resume our normal conversation.

Just so that you know, we're not done with this.

"So," she said aloud. "What are our plans now? They still have an active shipyard just around the planetary curve, and we're the only friendly ship in this system. Shouldn't we be going back to Pentagar before some other disaster comes our way?"

Jared took a bite of his eggs and chewed slowly before he answered. "We've got probes heading out to do an active search of the system. So far, no other artificial signatures have registered. While the Pale Ones probably don't know about the weak flip point in this system, there's a regular one. We've got a probe right there to signal us if something comes through. Based on distances, we can easily beat them to the Pentagaran flip point."

Graves raised his coffee cup. "It is a risk, but if we don't snoop around the planet now, we may not have an opportunity later. We haven't located anything that seems to make the planet worthy of total global devastation, but we have located numerous settlements of primitive, unenhanced humans. Probably where the Pale Ones get their recruits. If you ever wondered how someone from the Stone Age lived, I can show you pictures."

"Let's not forget that computer system from the asteroid," Jared added. "We have a team of people removing everything so we can take it back with us. For safety reasons, we won't shut it down completely until it passes Erorsi and we can get it on a course that won't threaten the planet later.

"We still don't know what its original purpose was. It obviously predated our arrival by quite a few years. Perhaps since the Pale Ones invaded the system."

Kelsey ate more of her breakfast, thinking. "That's something I don't get. If the Pale Ones conquered this system five hundred years ago, why wait hundreds of years to send ships through to attack Pentagar? That makes no sense whatsoever."

Graves shrugged. "With those things, who knows what makes sense?"

Jared waved his hand. "No, Kelsey has a good point. That's a serious discrepancy. It would be very useful to understand the reason behind it. I'm hoping we'll find some kind of information on the shipyard we've captured. Yet one more avenue of investigation that I'd like to pursue before we run for cover.

"Finally, there's the mountain range that the Pale Ones targeted. I'm not so certain that was an accident of geography. I can't see the Pale Ones targeting something that isn't important. At the very least, we should search carefully to be sure there's not something of interest there."

The first officer glanced at his chrono. "I should be getting up to the bridge. You both have a good morning." Graves gave her a small salute and headed out of the officers' mess.

As soon as he was out of earshot, Kelsey hissed at Jared. "Have you lost your mind? Why did you have to get implants now? What if something had gone wrong? This is insane."

He inclined his head toward her. "I'll admit there was an element of risk, but I judged it to be small. Every single Fleet officer in the Old Empire went through this exact procedure. It's becoming painfully obvious that we're going to have to move forward in implanting volunteers to take advantage of all the technology on this vessel. I'm pretty sure that Lieutenant Reese is ready to implant himself and several dozen of his men just to keep track of you."

She made a face at her half brother. "Don't imagine that you're going to sidetrack me with that remark."

Jared smiled. "I'd imagine not. But you don't have to worry about it for a while. The workstation says it's out of cranial implants. Until we locate more, you and I are it. Look on the bright side. Now someone on the bridge can take advantage of all those advanced scanners and critical systems."

"Not if you don't tell anybody about it. Care to run the reasoning for that by me?"

"It's complicated. Look around you. What do you see?"

She looked around at the men and women eating and returned her attention to him. "Our crew having breakfast?"

"How about potential spies? We have a lot of Pentagaran officers and men aboard. We don't really know any of them. Who's to say that some of them aren't associated with the group behind the assassination attempt? Do we really want word that we've begun implanting our personnel to get back to them?"

"That's paranoid. Surely these people have been vetted."

Jared shrugged. "Perhaps the Pale Ones' ambush made me a little paranoid, but what do we really know about who was behind the attack? Who's to say they couldn't have placed a team aboard this ship? The point is, we can't be sure. This is a basic precaution. We've had to be more trusting than I like up until now, but we need to be realistic."

Kelsey pinched the bridge of her nose between her fingers. "That's crazy. Following that logic, we should be marching everybody into a room and putting them to a lie detector. I mean, really, who can we trust?" She made certain that her expression made clear that she was being ironic.

He raised an eyebrow. "Do they have those? I might have to change my plans."

"You're maddening. No, not that I've heard. That's probably a good thing in this case." She ate some more of her breakfast. "What am I supposed to do today?"

"As much as it's going to piss Lieutenant Reese off, you'll be accompanying the team he sends down to the surface. They may need to access something through your implants. It's only a scouting mission, so I'm not expecting any encounters. We just need a better idea of what the situation is like down there.

"I'll be leading the mission to the damaged shipyard for much the same reasons. I'm sure that Charlie is going to be making a suggestion to change the regulations when we get back home so that captains don't get to leave the ship so much. So far, I haven't let him off to explore a single thing."

She finished the last of her food. "What if there's a problem? What if the Pale Ones have some ships hidden somewhere? What if an armada comes sailing through the flip point? What if the other shipyard decides to suddenly open fire on *Courageous*?"

"Let's handle those in order. If there are hidden Pale Ones off the planet's surface, I think they'd have come after us already. With the exception of the ambush that they had waiting, they haven't shown any signs of being very subtle. Even the ambushers weren't that subtle.

"If a fleet of Pale Ones comes through the flip point, we'll have time to recover everyone and still beat them back to the Pentagaran flip point. Lastly, if the other shipyard opens fire, *Courageous* will blow it into atoms. This is our chance to get information about the Pale Ones. We have to take advantage of it."

As much a she didn't want to, she had to agree with his logic. Anything they found out about the Pale Ones in this system could be critical to dealing with them when they came back in force. Which she expected them to do. She didn't know how long it would take, but those monsters had undoubtedly sent for reinforcements.

"What makes you think that Lieutenant Reese is going to let me go? He was pretty mad."

Jared tapped the rank insignia on his collar. "This right here guarantees that you're going. The details of how you participate are up for grabs, though. I suggest that you convince him that you'll be good this time, because the details are his call."

Her half brother stood. "In fact, let's go down and settle this right now."

She downed the rest of her coffee and followed him to marine country. Once again, the marines were packing various bags and obviously preparing to depart.

Lieutenant Reese's eyes narrowed as soon as he saw her. He strode over. "Captain. Princess. We'll be ready to leave in about ten minutes."

"It seems I'll be raining on your parade," Jared said. "Princess Kelsey will be accompanying you." He held up a hand to forestall the marine's immediate response. "Before you start giving me your list of no doubt valid reasons why that's a bad idea, you may run into a situation where her implants are key to accessing equipment or information that you need. She's going. The details of how she goes are entirely up to you.

"Time is short, so I'd best be getting my gear on. I'm leading the mission to the disabled shipyard. Good luck, and stay in contact." He didn't look back as he headed for the locker where his gear was stored.

Reese gave her a skeptical look. "I don't believe I need to explain why I think this is an exceptionally bad idea, do I, Your Highness?"

Kelsey shook her head. "I believe that I can guess your reasons. All I can say in my defense is that if it had been anyone else, you wouldn't be nearly as angry. It's not that I did the wrong thing, it's that I did something you didn't want *me* to do. If Senior Sergeant Talbot threw himself into the room with the Pale Ones and slammed the door behind him, would you be giving him nearly as much grief? That's not an excuse, but I wanted to bring that to your attention."

Reese scowled. "Actually, that *is* an excuse, and it's entirely beside the point. I gave you an order that I expected you to obey. You're not a marine, but you were under my command. I need to be certain what my people are going to do in any given set of circumstances."

"Most of you would've died if I followed your orders. I'm sorry that put me in danger, but I was already in the line of fire. If the same set of circumstances comes up again, I'll do what I have to do."

He sighed. "Fabulous. You will stay with Senior Sergeant Talbot. You will only fire your weapon or leave his side if he orders you to. If you step the least bit out of line, I will send you back to the ship and deal with Captain Mertz's wrath. Am I crystal clear?"

She held her hands up, palms forward. "Perfectly, Lieutenant."

"Don't make me regret this. Go suit up."

She didn't wait around for him to change his mind.

19

R awlins met his computer man shortly after breakfast. He wasn't sure why Jenkins had called him, but he knew the man wouldn't have made any contact at all if it weren't important.

The meeting had to be circumspect since it wasn't at a common event, such as breakfast. Technically, they were both supposed to be working on their assigned tasks.

Deviating from the repair that Rawlins was supposed to be doing carried extra risk. He wasn't exactly high man on the totem pole. That meant he had to have a valid reason to be absent when they needed him. One that would pass at least cursory scrutiny.

He accomplished this by pocketing one of the critical parts for today's repair. When the lead technician discovered they'd "forgotten" the part, Rawlins headed off at a trot to retrieve another one from stores. The fact he already had it meant that he had a short window of opportunity to go meet with his man.

He didn't know what excuse the computer specialist had used to break away from his compatriots, but he was waiting in the storage room that they had agreed on as a secondary gathering point when Rawlins got there.

The intelligence officer tapped his chrono. "You have two minutes. What's so important that it couldn't wait until lunch?"

"Our observer in operations says that Captain Mertz and Princess Bandar have left the ship. The captain is over on the damaged shipyard, and the princess went down to the surface of the planet. I thought you'd want to know that we have a brief window when both the senior naval officer and the only implanted human are off the ship."

Rawlins nodded slowly. "Yes... that is something that I needed to know. Do you have any idea how long they'll be gone?"

"The mission to the surface has a minimum timeframe to rejoin the ship of half an hour. Depending on where the ship is in orbit, the timeframe might stretch out to over an hour. Captain Mertz, on the other hand, could be back aboard in fifteen or twenty minutes. I'd imagine they'll both be gone significantly longer than that, though."

"The presence or absence of Jared Mertz probably won't alter our chances of success very much. In fact, I'd actually prefer we have him in our hands when the time comes. That prevents any last-minute heroics.

"Princess Kelsey, on the other hand, is a very different story. There's no telling what those implants of hers make possible. She might be able to override anything we do, and that's leaving aside the purely physical aspects of having someone with those combat modifications on the ship with us. Have you made any progress in accessing the ship's antiboarding system? Can we get control of the stunners built into the interior of the ship?"

Jenkins nodded. "I've managed to figure out what systems would have to be turned off in order to isolate the system from computer control. It means you have to pull half a dozen modules scattered across the ship at roughly the same time. The computer would notice the situation almost immediately, but I have access inside the computer control facility, and I can isolate it. They'd notice immediately, so the clock would be ticking. Once they're onto the situation, they could restore control in less than a minute."

"How obvious is it that the cutoff was intentional?"

"They'll know. This is only something we can execute one time."

Rawlins considered that. "We may not get a better opportunity. How are we looking on marine strength?"

"We have a dozen marines, a dozen engineering technicians, and the people we brought to run the ship. We'll be stretched pretty thin."

Thin indeed. Without a full set of engineers and pilots, they'd have to browbeat some of the Pentagaran Navy personnel into working with them. That was dicier than he liked. Given a choice, he'd want people loyal to the cause in control. There was no telling how the regular crew would react. Would they support the takeover once he made it clear they were under orders? Or would they decide the orders were illegal? Which, of course, they technically were.

He'd prefer to avoid shooting any of them. Even if they weren't in on the plan, they were his countrymen. He would if he had to, but he'd regret it.

Rawlins took a step toward the hatch. "I've made a list of the people I think most likely to assist us under duress. It's in your files. Summon them to a room where the antiboarding weapons won't knock them out when Mertz is on his way back. When he docks, we'll make our move. If the team on the planet starts back before then, contact me."

He left without another word. The plan was in motion. The Terrans wouldn't know what hit them.

20

Lieutenant Reese decided they'd use restored Old Empire marine pinnaces for the boarding and planetary exploration. The stealth materials in the pre-Fall pinnaces made them much more difficult to detect, and their scanner suites were substantially better than the ones made in the Empire today, even with the occasional glitches they still had.

They also had remote drones that would make searching the planet significantly easier. Those only interfaced with the pinnaces that launched them. That probably helped in making the decision.

Jared made the trip over to the shipyard absorbed by the scanner readings. It was even better than sitting in the cockpit during approach. There was nothing between him and the 360-degree display of everything around them. He quite literally had a ringside seat. He wasn't certain exactly what a ringside seat was, but it must've been pretty good when they coined the phrase.

The approach was nerve-racking but uneventful. The shipyard certainly looked like a Pale Ones construction. No paint had been used anywhere, the skin of the hull had very little uniformity, and it seemed like it would probably fall apart if he kicked it. That was probably due to the widespread damage from the fusion weapon.

Unlike Kelsey, he had absolutely no desire to get between the marines and any threats. Yes, they'd already done a quick search of the shipyard and found no living Pale Ones. Most of the equipment was offline. However, that didn't mean that there were no dangers. Or that by powering on the systems, they wouldn't create some.

Sergeant Coulter was giving his team last-minute instructions. They'd begun a pass-through with the engineers to locate any self-destruct charges and disable them. They'd also disconnect any computer system from the networks. Only when those tasks were complete could they be relatively certain that it was safe to start bringing systems back online.

When the sergeant was finished giving his instructions, he turned to Jared. "Captain, do you have any changes to suggest?"

"I'm not going to interfere with your orders, Sergeant. You're in charge of tactical operations. I'll just tell you what I want done, and you figure out how to do it. How long do you believe it will take to complete the search for self-destruct devices?"

Lieutenant Andrews, the leader of the engineering team, cut in. "At least an hour. Perhaps two. That's not really something I'd like to rush."

"Neither would I," Jared said. "While your people are working on that, let's see if we can locate the primary computer controls and start isolating it."

The engineer, who was sitting across from them in a regular vacuum suit, nodded. "That's going to be easy. The initial search teams located one major computer control center and a smaller annex. Both of them were disabled when the fusion device went off."

Jared had known that from the reports he'd downloaded before the mission. He had a good idea of the layout of the shipyard as well. It was like a map in his head. That was one aspect of having implants that Kelsey had never mentioned. It made absorbing and reviewing data a lot faster.

"I also want a complete search done for other Old Empire equipment. Especially anything that looks like the Pale Ones might interface with it, or if its purpose isn't clear. I understand that's somewhat vague, but you get the idea. If it feels odd, I want to know about it."

The docking was just as anticlimactic as the trip over. Unlike the large space station they'd boarded to rescue Kelsey, they didn't land in a bay. They picked one of the empty construction areas that had a retractable boarding tube. Several of the marines floated across to it and manipulated the exterior controls to extend it to the pinnace. The presence of the controls was another anomaly. Savages wouldn't be in suits, so they'd never have access to them.

There wasn't any atmosphere in the facility. The explosion had breached every major hull. Which accounted for the lack of resistance when the search teams passed through the first time.

Gravity was also out, so they floated into the shipyard past the floating bits of equipment and Pale Ones' corpses. Engineering teams accompanied by marines split off from the main party as soon as they came to a major intersection in the corridor. Jared let Andrews lead the way to the main computer, even though he knew exactly how to get there on his own.

It took them about ten minutes and one wrong turn to locate the large computer center. Andrews had his people do a cursory inspection for any booby traps and then start pulling off access plates. Like most critical computers, the system used hard wires to interface with the station systems.

It took the engineering officer about half an hour to detach the computer from all outside contact and another half hour to repair the overloaded power lines that served it. The fusion plants were still online. Jared gave a nod when the engineer asked if he could power up.

There was a risk that the system would erase itself, but Jared considered that unlikely. However, he had Andrews ready to cut the power at a moment's notice if he was wrong.

For such a major system, the room it was stored in looked very disused. Dust covered the consoles, and there were very few footprints. He supposed there wasn't much call for Pale Ones to come to a computer control center.

Jared knew the moment the system came fully back online, because he "saw" its presence. Jared attempted to access the computer. He more than half expected the computer to immediately reject him, or to discover that there was some type of built-in access code that limited contact to only Pale Ones.

He was half right. He felt the connection take place, but the unit did not respond to him. It didn't reject him outright, either. It was as though the system both allowed and disallowed him at the same time. Perhaps that was because his implants, though manufactured by the Pale Ones, didn't have the required authority to communicate with their equipment.

That presented a particular set of challenges. He shifted his gaze to Carl Owlet. The graduate student was the only other man present who knew that Jared had implants. He was also a computer expert. Admittedly, he didn't fully understand the programming language the Old Empire used, but he'd made great strides in learning about the systems and their uses in the last month.

Owlet casually pushed off from the main console and stopped adroitly beside Jared. He spoke when Jared touched their helmets together. "Yes, Captain?"

"It allowed me to connect, but it's not responding. Could it be because I have the correct hardware, but I'm not on some authorization list?"

"That's very possible. From what we've seen, the Pale Ones don't utilize their implants to interface with Old Empire equipment. The pilots on the ship that Princess Kelsey saw used the manual controls. Workstation Twelve also indicated that it received no direct control after the Pale Ones reprogrammed it. It may very well be that none of the Pale Ones' equipment is set up for implant access."

Jared watched the engineering team work on the manual controls for a minute while he thought. "No, that can't be right. Kelsey changed the course on that asteroid through a direct link to its computer. It allowed her access. Yet this system will not. I might be able to answer the question of why if we can get past whatever the problem actually is. Any ideas?"

"You say it didn't reject your connection attempt. Let's try a couple of direct commands. Instruct it to list the subsystems under its control. Don't ask. Order."

Jared sent a command. The computer responded with a long list of systems. The list seemed related to ship construction. He passed the results of the experiment back to the graduate student.

"That's good," Owlet said. "The system will obey you, but it won't assist you. Perhaps they programmed it to be unhelpful. Why it would behave differently than the one on the asteroid, I don't know."

Andrews looked over at them. "I've got some access here, Captain. The systems seem mostly intact, but it's looking for an outside connection. I think the smaller annex might direct this one."

"Have your people continue to work with this system. We don't know what it would do if we let it connect with the other computer, so we'll keep them separated. While you do that, Mister Owlet and I will go look at the other one."

The remaining computer system was located at the opposite end of the shipyard. It was immediately apparent when they entered this computer room that it was different. Jared accessed the video he'd taken of the other control center. This one's bulkheads were thicker.

"Is it just me, or do these bulkheads look like they're armored?"

Owlet stood in the entrance and nodded. "They're definitely thicker. That's interesting. Let me get the system disconnected, and we'll see what we can get out of it."

By the time he finished disconnecting all the communication runs, the other teams had finished scouring the shipyard. They'd found and disabled half a dozen self-destruction charges. Jared ordered them to make a second pass just to be sure.

"Powering up the system now, Captain," Owlet said.

Jared connected with this computer. It allowed him access, but with a twist.

Error. Authentication not recognized.

He smiled. *You are mistaken. My hardware is on your access list. Verify.*

The computer did not respond for a few seconds. *Hardware serial numbers validated. Authentication denied. Serial number not in access file.*

"It says my serial number needs to be in some file. Go see if you can find it and add me as an authorized user."

After about ten minutes, Owlet gave him a thumbs-up. Jared supposed that was the benefit of having physical access. If you knew enough about the system, you could find the necessary files. "I've added you and the princess to the command-and-control file. Try again."

Jared attempted to connect again. This time, the computer granted him complete access. The first thing he looked at was the aforementioned command-and-control file. There were half a dozen other entries in the file; however, someone had excluded them from consideration. Jared wondered if they'd been users from before the Fall, or Pale Ones that Owlet had disabled.

He looked at the file history and was able to determine the exclusion had taken place around the time of the rebellion. That must've happened when the rebels had captured this computer. Which meant that they'd salvaged it from somewhere else to do the work here.

The next question was, what did this computer do? Jared wasn't computer savvy enough to determine its function from its files. Why have two computers?

Computer, identify your function.

This unit directs the construction computer in what units to build and acts as an authorized controller.

So basically, this computer acted in the place of the humans who would normally control the other computer. Why not just program the other computer to do so? It seemed needlessly redundant.

Where do your instructions come from?

This unit receives instructions and guidance from the system primary computer.

Jared frowned. He had no idea what that was supposed to mean.

Explain what the system primary computer is.

The system primary computer controls all equipment in this star system. This unit receives specific instructions on what ships to construct and on what schedule.

How often do you receive these instructions?

The instruction period varies from a few hours to several weeks. The most recent instruction was just over one standard month ago.

That would be from about the time *Athena* dropped the fusion weapon on this shipyard.

Where is the system primary computer located, and what kind of computer is it?

The system primary computer is located on the planetary surface. This unit does not know its precise location. It is a class 5 computer.

Interesting. That was the same class of computer as the one on *Courageous*. While it was very capable, Jared had expected something larger to be in charge of the entire planetary system.

He'd send any data they acquired to the team exploring the surface. Then he'd spend a lot of time going over what commands the planetary AI had been sending. Somewhere in all this data was the key to defeating the Pale Ones. He just had to find it.

21

K elsey expected the marines to slip quietly down to the planet's surface, but they surprised her. They picked an area away from the mountains or any ruins and plummeted toward it from orbit like a stone.

Lieutenant Reese went forward and commandeered one of the stations on the flight deck to be able to see the scanner readings directly, since they would not translate well to his armor. Senior Sergeant Talbot sat beside her and kept an eye on the men while the pinnace dropped.

She switched to the private frequency they'd agreed to as she watched the planet's surface grow rapidly closer. "Aren't you worried about the Pale Ones spotting us? Shouldn't we be slowing down?"

The grizzled marine grinned at her through his faceplate. "When somebody might have better scanners than you do, you don't dawdle. The shorter the amount of time to landing, the better chance we have of surviving. There's a time for sneaking and a time for bold action. This is the latter."

He rapped his knuckles on her faceplate. "It's really spooky not being able to see your face. I understand about the increased structural integrity, but I'd like to see the person I'm talking to."

She had to agree with him. Seeing faceless suits of armor would be intimidating and perhaps confusing. She queried the armor and found a possible solution. The chameleon skin was high definition everywhere, but even more so on her faceplate. Perhaps she could control what it displayed.

Kelsey accessed the interior of the helmet and found a vid camera. She turned it on and directed the output to the helmet exterior.

Talbot's eyes widened. "I can see your face! Sort of. It's dark in the helmet, so you're in shadow. Can you turn on a light?"

Since the armor fed video directly into her ocular implants, she'd grown accustomed to being in darkness. She found an interior light and turned it on. "How's that?"

"Perfect. It's as though you're looking right at me. I can hardly tell it's a projection or that you aren't really using your eyes directly. Now, hang on. We're about to level out. Expect some heavy G-forces."

Despite her tenseness, nothing bad happened as they decelerated savagely just above the surface and settled into a clearing in the vast forest of huge trees. Her artificial muscles and armor made the extra weight easily bearable. She imagined that the pinnace could probably handle a lot more load with a team of enhanced marines.

As soon as they touched down, Talbot ordered his men down the landing ramp. They flowed out like water and spread out around the pinnace, their weapons covering the forest.

Kelsey didn't follow them. She had her orders. She and Talbot would stay inside the pinnace while the rest of the marines made certain that they were in no immediate danger. Lieutenant Reese was guiding his men from the flight deck.

Even as the men were scouring the forest around them for threats, Reese launched half a dozen small drones. Four of them spread out over the immediate area and began scanning. The remaining two had targets farther away.

One headed toward the mountain range the asteroid had targeted. As that was the most distant objective, it would take about half an hour to get there flying close to the ground. The second drone headed for the nearest ruins. Scans from orbit had tagged it as a large city, the desiccated corpse of a once-thriving pre-Fall metropolis.

Kelsey examined the map of the area with her implants. The mountains were to the northwest, and the city was almost due south.

She split her attention between the various drones but focused on the one going to the city. They had no immediate desire to go there, but it was the most likely location for the Pale Ones to have a base in their vicinity.

Watching the drone fly over the terrain was like flying herself. She could almost feel the wind on her face. She definitely felt the lump in her throat when the drone crested a hill and the ruined city came into view.

She'd seen images of devastated cities before, but this was like looking at one with her own eyes. Honestly, it felt a little bit more intimate than that. The forest was struggling mightily to retake the land the humans had appropriated, but it was making little headway. Even broken and abandoned, Old Empire constructions endured.

The rebels hadn't bombarded this city from orbit. The buildings were intact, even though the people had fled long ago. Under other circumstances, she knew the scientists on *Best Deal* would've descended on this location like locusts on a crop.

As the drone flew closer, Kelsey started to get an idea of the scale. She immediately had her implants perform a measurement on the tallest tower in the city. The answer shocked her so badly that she had it check again. Just to be sure.

The central tower was over 1500 meters tall.

That was three times taller than the most modern office building on Avalon, and unlike the skyscrapers she was used to, this one came up in tiered layers. The bottom of the building took up what would've been three or four blocks on a side. There were half a dozen distinct tiers as the building rose into the sky. The top segment was as thick as the skyscrapers back home.

She turned to Talbot. "Are you seeing this?"

"Seeing what? Which drone?"

"The Old Empire city. The towers are still intact, and they're huge. The central one has to be at least three or four hundred stories tall."

He stared at the readouts on the console and whistled. "Holy crap. That one building probably held a hundred thousand people. Using that as a yardstick, that city had tens of millions of people living in it. Maybe a hundred million." This brought the scale of the genocide home to her in a way the books she'd read never had.

Kelsey examined the scanner readings more closely. "It doesn't look like there are any active power units in the city, but a lot of things seem basically intact. I can see where some walls have fallen, but that looks cosmetic. Bushes and trees have taken over the ground levels, but they haven't affected the structures."

They sat in silence, watching the drones' data until she noticed that the mountain drone was on station. Lieutenant Reese ordered it to go to a somewhat higher flight path traveling down the mountain range. After half an hour, they still hadn't seen anything out of place. It looked like untouched wilderness.

The hatch leading forward opened, and Lieutenant Reese stepped onto the marine deck. "Have you been watching the drones' transmissions, Princess? Hey. We can see your face."

"I figured out how to put a projection on the adaptive skin of the helmet. The city is stunning. The mountains are empty."

"Apparently so. At least that's what it looks like through the drone. I'm wondering if the pinnace's scanners could get a little bit more detail. Find something out of place."

He put his hands on his hips and stared out at the forest down the ramp. "We're not going to see anything sitting here in the middle of nowhere. Talbot, recall the men. Let's make ready for a pass over the mountains."

"Aye, sir."

The marines returned to the pinnace in stages until everyone was aboard. The local drones returned to their recessed mounts. Once everyone was secure, the pinnace rose above the forest and headed for the mountains.

The pinnace's scanners were significantly better than those on the drones. As they made their way past the foothills and over the peaks in the mountain range, they could see deep into the ground. Nothing seemed out of place.

They made a pass up one side of the mountain range and then returned flying down the other. About two thirds of the way back, Kelsey saw something in the readings that made her speak up. "Lieutenant Reese, can we hover here for a minute? I'm seeing something."

"What have you got?"

She directed the pinnace's scanners to probe more deeply once it came to a halt. "I'm not quite sure. It's gone now. It was some type of transient reading."

She reviewed what her implants had recorded and saw it again. It was a density reading. For just a moment, the density of the rock they'd flown over had grown markedly stronger.

"It must've been some kind of glitch. The ground seemed denser, but only for a moment. Now that I'm looking at it, I see that there wasn't a problem at all. We can go on."

The marine lieutenant didn't answer for a minute. "Actually, I'm inclined to trust your initial instincts. If they're wrong, all we've lost is a little bit of time. We're going down."

The pinnace settled onto a plateau. The ramp came down, but the pinnace kept its grav drives online. They were probably afraid that too much weight might cause a rockslide.

Once again, the marines exited and covered the area. This time, Lieutenant Reese followed them out. He gestured for Kelsey and Talbot to follow him.

The view was stunning. From this height, the forest stretched out as far as the eye could see. It was beautiful. She removed her helmet and took a deep breath of the fresh air. It smelled of nature, untainted by civilization.

Of course, the reason for that was that the rebels had virtually extinguished humanity on this planet.

Reese turned toward her. "Where exactly did you sense the density spike?"

She pointed toward the center of the plateau. "Not precisely in the middle, but not very far away from it, either."

He directed one of the squads to scout ahead, and the rest followed more slowly. The plateau wasn't completely flat, Kelsey saw. As they went farther from the edges, the center rose up. Not evenly though. Small hills and ruts cut by water made the surface uneven in places.

Kelsey nudged Talbot. "Is it just me, or is this a great place to ambush someone?"

"It could be," he admitted, "except for the fact we didn't detect anything even remotely like a living being on the scanners. This kind of open area makes hiding difficult."

"Isn't that kind of the point of an ambush? I know I'm not a marine, but we are in a hostile environment. What do we do if somebody jumps us?"

"We shoot the ever-living crap out of them. See how widely spread out everyone is? Well, except for us. That's to minimize casualties if we're attacked. Which, again, I don't expect."

She put her helmet back on and used her armor's scanners to peer into their surroundings. It detected no power sources other than her companions.

The scouts avoided the gullies and stuck to the high ground. The others scrambled up the incline and peered down into the depths of the water-worn tracks as they advanced.

Being somewhat contrarian, Kelsey went to the largest of the gullies and peered into the dim interior. At the height of the day, the sun would light everything, but now that it was the evening, the shadows were long in its sand-covered bottom.

"Lieutenant Reese? Since your people have a high ground covered, do you mind if I take a look inside the gully?"

"If you see anything unusual, I want you to turn around and get the hell out of there. No dawdling."

"Yes, sir."

Talbot motioned for two of his men to lead the way in and waited until they were almost out of sight before indicating Kelsey could follow.

The loose ground made the footing somewhat treacherous, so Kelsey devoted more attention to her balance. In spite of the circumstances, she was enjoying the experience. She'd forgotten how much she liked being out in nature. Even dry, dusty nature. Of course, she usually didn't go hiking in combat armor, surrounded by armed men, while worried about people shooting at her.

Her enhanced vision made it easier to see clearly in the dim light. The implants also boosted her eye for detail. So when she spotted an irregularity in the sand off to the side, she stopped. "Hold up."

Kelsey knelt down and gave the area her full attention. Even with the windblown sand everywhere, this looked too regular to be natural. For the most part, she knew nature abhorred straight lines. Whatever this was, it didn't seem like it belonged.

"What do you see?" Talbot asked.

"It seems crazy, but I think this might be a footprint."

The rock wall in front of her disappeared as though it had never been there, revealing a gaping black opening. She was so startled that her feet slid out from under her when she tried to surge upright, and she fell forward into the darkness.

22

After half an hour of sorting through the commands received by the shipyard, Jared decided that he'd made a mistake. The instructions from the AI in command of the solar system were so general as to be useless. Build this number of ships, have them done by this time, and statuses on their progress going back down. Also requests for new personnel to man those ships.

He made his way over to where the scientists were still manually examining the computer system. "We've been here a while, gentlemen. Perhaps it's time we returned to *Courageous*. Well, perhaps only me. I'm not sure I'm adding much to this expedition."

Owlet looked up from the console he was working at. "Actually, Captain, I think I found something that might change your assessment. How would you like to capture a completely functional shipyard?"

Jared raised an eyebrow. "You have my full attention, Mister Owlet."

"I'm still looking over the data, but I think I found a security flaw. Not in the programming but in the rules of engagement. This shipyard had an automated defense system. That system determined what was hostile and what wasn't. The rules of engagement seem pretty straightforward and comprehensive until you look at the exceptions."

He tapped the screen in front of him. "They must've had some friendly fire incidents in the past, because it says right here that any ship with an appropriate transponder is friendly."

"Are you telling me it's a simple as salvaging a transponder and just flying over to the other shipyard? That's stupid. The other shipyard has to know we've overrun the system. It's going to ignore that instruction."

"Not if it has these rules of engagement. There is no room for discretion. It's like the difference between the words *shall* and *may*. According to this, any ship with the correct transponder shall be considered friendly. The other computer won't be able to fire on us. It also couldn't fire on the other shipyard or the orbital we destroyed. That probably explains why the operational shipyard hasn't fired on us yet. This shipyard is between it and *Courageous*."

Jared peered over his shoulder at the text on the screen. It wasn't computer code, but it was completely unfamiliar. Fleet didn't use automated defenses like that. They required a human being to be in control of deadly force.

He waved Sergeant Coulter over to join them and explained the situation. "If we were able to take the pinnace over there, what type of resistance could we expect?"

"Based on the number of corpses we found, several hundred Pale Ones. In tight quarters like this, that could get hairy. Particularly if they're armed with advanced weapons."

"If we don't take that shipyard over, we have to take it out. That probably won't be difficult, but the positives of gaining an advanced construction facility might be worth the risk. Yes, the Pale Ones build crappy ships, but I'll wager that facility could build something better with the right instructions. Mister Owlet, what do you think?"

The scientist manipulated his screen. "I'm not seeing anything that would indicate they have more advanced plans available. That said, this system has the potential to build modern warships once we create the instructions. If we find advanced plans later, it could probably do them, too. Apparently, there is an unmanned mining station in the asteroid belt to get the raw materials and mold them into basic equipment."

"One more thing to check before we leave the system. I don't suppose this thing has deck plans for the other shipyard, does it?"

Owlet shook his head. "No, it doesn't. Still, how many layouts for shipyards do you think the Pale Ones are using? The other one is about the same size as this one, so it probably has the same layout. Why would they waste the effort building something different? They only build two kinds of ship."

Sergeant Coulter looked unconvinced. "Counting on the enemy doing exactly what you'd like is bad policy. We have to plan for the enemy doing something inconvenient. That means different plans and different rules of engagement. The computers on this station were down after the fusion weapon knocked them out. That's not true on the other station. Hell, even if it is true, that damn computer on the planet could change its instructions just before we dock. It's too dangerous."

Jared considered their options. The marine noncom was right. They had to be sure before they tried a direct attack. "What if we put transponders into some of our probes and sent them across? Or better yet, some of our missile warheads. If they're shot down, no real loss. If they make it all the way across, we could attach them to critical points on that thing's hull and detonate them if we detect anything funny."

When neither man objected, Jared made the decision to move ahead with the plan. "Send word back to *Courageous*. I want to use our old pinnaces with full troop loads and enough missile warheads to disable the defenses on that other shipyard. While they're gathering them, fan out and find where the transponders are stored. If nothing else, see if you can strip them off the wrecks of ships under construction. If possible, I'd like to get this under way in an hour. Make it happen."

The men set about their tasks, and Jared went back to searching the computer systems. If they were going to board the other shipyard, he wanted to know how he could best assist them.

He'd be useless in a fight, but he might be able to control the shipyard hardware. Sealing a particular corridor, venting the atmosphere, or even shutting down power to lifts could make a difference. But only if he was there.

If they could reach the computer center, he could shut the whole thing down. Well, he and Owlet together could.

The extra troops and weapon systems arrived about fifty minutes after he gave the order. By then, they'd located the transponders in one of the parts bays. The engineers were easily able to add them to the warhead avionics. Right at the hour mark, they declared them ready.

Without a ship's launchers, the warheads couldn't move very quickly. The microdrives included in the warhead packages were for last-minute course adjustments, not speed. Of course, under these circumstances, that was a positive. The other shipyard would consider anything going as fast as a missile hostile, no matter what its transponder said.

One of the pinnaces took the warheads back out after they'd been modified and released them. They maneuvered around the bulk of the captured shipyard and began accelerating slowly toward the hostile one. Jared waited for the other station to fire as the warheads crept closer, but it didn't. The warheads made it all the way to the station and pushed themselves up against the critical sections.

Once they were in place, the only way to destroy them was to come out and do it by hand. He doubted the Pale Ones were capable of extravehicular activities. They'd keep an eye out for any small craft leaving the other shipyard, though.

That only left one major obstacle to carrying out his plan: convincing his first officer not to throw a screaming hissy fit when he found out that Jared was going along for the ride.

Jared returned to the pinnace he'd arrived on and made his way to the flight deck. The pilot and copilot left at his order, and he locked the hatch behind them. He sat down at the flight engineer's station and opened a channel to *Courageous*.

Charlie Graves appeared on the console screen. "Captain, I'm glad you called. I was just about to give you a call of my own. I've got some serious concerns about your plans that I wanted to go over with you."

"I figured you might. Why don't you step into my office and take this call on a scramble channel?"

His executive officer's eyebrows rose. "Yes, sir. Just give me a second to get things set up." The screen went blank.

A minute later, he reappeared, and from the background, Jared could tell that Charlie was in the office just off the bridge. "There we are. This channel is secure, and I've locked the hatch behind me. What's so important that we can't share it over an open channel?"

"The kids hate it when Mom and Dad fight. I'm going on the assault." He held up his hand at Graves's frown. "Hear me out. I'm about to let you in on some very classified information. Something that I should've shared with you yesterday." He took a deep breath. "I have a Fleet officer's implants."

His friend stared at him blankly for a moment and then slapped his hand on the desk. "Dammit, Jared! Have you lost your mind? You had absolutely no business doing something that dangerous. You're the commanding officer of this ship. You have a responsibility not to do crazy shit. What the hell were you thinking?"

He knew his friend was right to be angry, but he still couldn't help smiling inside at his reaction. He was careful, however, not to let that smile reach his face. "If I'd suggested it, you'd have fought against it tooth and nail, right? You'd recite regulation after regulation that should prevent me from doing it."

"And I'd have been absolutely right! If it were me, you'd do exactly the same thing. What if you'd died? What if you'd gone nuts? Hell, you still might."

"We both know that millions of Fleet officers had that procedure done over the course of the Empire's life. It's as safe as walking across the street."

"Right. A grav bus would probably hit you. Why, Jared? Tell me why."

"Because I'm the captain," he said simply. "Zia and Lieutenant Reese were both making noises about wanting to have the procedure done. If anyone was going to go through that by choice, it was going to be me first. Now that I've done it, if we ever find any spare parts, all my other officers can feel confident that the procedure is safe."

"Why didn't you tell me this morning? Why are you telling me in private?"

Jared explained his reasons for being concerned about public dissemination. "Perhaps I'm being overly paranoid, but until I know these people on our ship a bit better, I'd rather keep my cards close to my vest."

"And you just expect me to let you waltz over to a hostile station and get involved in a firefight? You're not a marine, Jared. You shouldn't be leading a boarding action."

"Oh, I have every intention of being at the back of the line going on board that station. If I can do what I need to do without ever leaving the pinnace, I'll do it. In any case, though, I'm going. We need that shipyard."

Graves sighed. "Why do I even try arguing with you about these things?

I should know by now that it's a losing fight." He pointed his finger at Jared. "I won't raise a stink about this, but only on one condition."

"Name it."

"Send me out on some of these harrowing adventures. It's getting really old being stuck back here while you're having all the fun."

Jared grinned. "I swear I'm not trying to hog all the fun stuff. I promise you this, you'll be taking lead on a mission in the near future. Take good care of the ship until I get back." He broke the connection.

He opened a channel to Coulter. "Let's get moving. Coordinate with the pilots."

Jared expected to see missile systems targeting them as they came into line of sight with the other shipyard and was pleased when none did. They closed over what felt like hours to him, but it was only a couple of minutes. His pinnace docked with a soft thump.

The marines rushed into the docking area as soon as the locks opened. They began firing immediately, so there were Pale Ones waiting for them. The marines advanced slowly and took control of the docking area. When everything there was secure, Coulter gave the go-ahead for Jared to come out.

Things went well enough as they advanced into the shipyard. It was indeed the same layout as the first, so he knew exactly where he needed to go. He opened a channel to the marine in charge of his detail. "We're going to the right at the next corridor. The stairs are on the right. We'll go up three decks and then straight in to the computer center."

"Aye, sir."

He'd just made it into the stairwell when all hell broke loose. A tremendous explosion threw him off his feet, and he heard the combat channels go berserk.

"Armed Pale Ones!" Coulter screamed. "They've slipped in behind us! All teams, watch your sixes. Captain, stay put until—"

Another explosion and a sound like a mad robot animal ripping apart a wall almost deafened Jared. Coulter was off the air, and Jared was on his own. Kelsey would never let him hear the end of it. If he survived.

23

Kelsey sprawled on the cold stone floor, but she leapt back to her feet before the echoes of her fall stopped bouncing off the walls. She had her pistol in her hand, scanning for targets, without consciously remembering having drawn it.

There was no one there. Only a roughly square chamber half a dozen meters on a side with what looked like an airlock directly in front of her. Two recessed weapons clusters on the ceiling at the far corners of the room pointed directly at her.

She half expected the door behind her to slam shut, but it remained reassuringly open. Talbot was at her side in an instant, his rifle raised to cover any threats.

The thick hatch in front of them cycled open, and a middle-aged man stepped out with his hands raised. His tan clothes were of an unfamiliar cut.

"We mean you no harm," he said in an odd accent. "Please, accept our sincerest apologies for the unexpected welcome, but we couldn't take a chance that a stray transmission from you might alert our mutual enemy."

She keyed her communicator. "Lieutenant? We have a situation here."

There was no response.

Talbot half turned toward her. "I'm not getting through to anybody outside. Until we know what's going on, I want you to back up slowly. Wait outside."

The block on transmissions must not be in effect inside this chamber, since she heard Talbot just fine. "If he wanted us dead, we'd be dead. See the weapons pods? If he wanted to capture us, he could've closed the door behind us. I'm staying."

She could almost see Talbot scowling. "You're the most vexing human being I've ever met. This could still be a trap. It could be some kind of Pale Ones trick."

"I'm pretty certain you don't believe that. Make sure the lieutenant knows we have a situation."

Kelsey made a show of reholstering her pistol. She raised her hands a couple of inches to emphasize her peaceful intent. It took her a moment to figure out how to turn on the external speakers on her suit. "You certainly have a way of getting our attention. My friend is feeling a little jumpy. I have to admit that I'm feeling somewhat unsettled myself. Why don't we deescalate the situation by pointing those weapons somewhere else?"

"Of course." The weapons traversed away from Kelsey. "My name is Juan da Silva. Welcome to Erorsi. If your friend would like to step outside and tell his commander what's going on, I promise that no harm will come to you."

She smiled. He'd be able to see her since she hadn't bothered to turn off the projection of her face. "I understand your caution. Senior Sergeant Talbot, please summon the lieutenant and bring him up to speed. I'll stay right here until you return."

The marine hesitated a moment but backed out of the chamber slowly without any further argument. No doubt she'd be hearing about it later.

"I'm going to take off my helmet." At his nod, she broke the seal on her helmet and lifted it off her head. She brushed her blonde locks back reflexively.

"My name is Kelsey Bandar. I must say that finding you here is a great surprise to me. We didn't think the Pale Ones had left anyone on this planet."

The corner of the man's mouth quirked up. "I suppose that's as good a name for them as any. To the best of my knowledge, the people in this facility are the only free humans on this planet. The planetary leadership constructed this place to ride out the invasion. Our ancestors hoped to coordinate a defense against any incursion by the rebels. Unfortunately, the defense was unsuccessful. Obviously."

He gestured toward the ceiling. "We gave up hope of seeing anyone from the Empire centuries ago. Until last month. Those explosions in orbit were you, right?"

She nodded. "It's a long story, but yes. They drove us back out of the system, but we're back now."

A sound behind her made her turn. Talbot had returned with the lieutenant. Talbot stayed at the door, and Reese strode to her side.

"Mister da Silva, allow me to introduce Lieutenant Reese, the senior military officer in this party."

Reese removed his helmet and rested it comfortably in the crook of his arm. "Mister da Silva. I assume that you're responsible for suppressing our communication channels. Might I inquire about your intentions?"

Da Silva smiled. "Our intention was to make certain that this facility was not inadvertently revealed to the rebels in control of this planet. We just want an opportunity to talk. You're the first people that have given us any hope that this terror might end, so allow me to assure you that we intended no offense."

The marine officer nodded. "I can certainly understand your caution. Hopefully, you can understand mine. Not only am I responsible for this exploratory mission, I'm responsible for the safety of Princess Kelsey. I ask that you drop your communication shield in exchange for my word that we will not reveal your presence here to anyone on this planet by a stray transmission."

Da Silva nodded solemnly. "I can agree on one condition. I ask that you meet our leadership and discuss the matter further before we do so. Again, I assure you of your complete safety and ability to depart at any time."

He looked at Kelsey. "Pardon me, but are you a princess?"

"I am, but it didn't seem relevant at the start of our conversation." She turned to Reese. "We need to meet with their leadership, Lieutenant. I realize that there's some danger, but the opportunity this presents is too great to let pass."

The marine smiled wryly. "Believe it or not, Princess, I do understand. This is a diplomatic matter." He speared da Silva with a look. "However, if this doesn't turn out as friendly as you say, we're going to have a problem. Am I understood?"

The man held his hands up, palms out. "Clearly. We shall provide hostages for your people's safety. I have a dozen unarmed men and women in the next chamber who will stay with your men."

Kelsey shook her head. "That will not be necessary."

Reese gestured to Talbot. "Bring your team, Senior Sergeant."

Talbot brought in his men, but they didn't take off their helmets. They formed up around Kelsey and their commander as da Silva led them deeper into the facility.

A large open area waited for them on the other side of the hatch. A dozen unarmed men and women stood waiting, all dressed in blue jumpsuits.

There were more weapons pods at the back of this room, but they did not seem targeted on her or the marines. If the Pale Ones attacked this facility head on, they could expect to suffer heavy losses.

A wide corridor to the rear led into a large lift. The heavily armored door slid ponderously aside at their approach. Inside, it was large enough to hold all of them without any crowding. The marines took up one side while da Silva stood alone on the other.

"Level Hotel, authorization da Silva five zero three." The lift doors slid shut with a thump of finality. The lift dropped like a stone, but the man didn't seem concerned.

"Our leadership council is waiting below. The conference room is right outside the lift, so you won't need to go much deeper into the facility."

"If you don't mind my asking, roughly how many people are sheltered here?" Kelsey asked.

"Quite a few. After five hundred years, we've pretty well filled the facility up."

The lift came to a halt and the doors slid open. Half a dozen armed men stood in the corridor just past the first set of hatches. Da Silva walked to the door and gestured for her to go inside.

She squared her shoulders and stepped into the room. The massive conference table could hold dozens of people, and the chairs all around would seat hundreds more.

Half a dozen men and women sat on the other side of the table from her. They came to their feet as she entered. The man in the center didn't look like he could stand at all due to his advanced age, but he straightened slowly.

"I never believed I'd live to see the day that rescue came," he said in a quavering voice. "Be most welcome here among us. I am Reginald Bell. Allow me to introduce you to the leadership council of Erorsi." He introduced each man and woman in turn.

"I am Princess Kelsey Bandar of the Terran Empire. This is Lieutenant Reese, commander of my marine detachment." It was perhaps a bit much to call his detachment hers, but it was the simplest explanation for the moment.

Uncomfortable with making an old man stand, she gestured to the chairs in front of her. "May we sit? Better yet, will the chairs support our weight?"

He chuckled. "I'm not certain that they're up to the task of supporting combat armor. My apologies for that. If you don't mind, I'm somewhat old to stand on ceremony." He gingerly resumed his seat. The rest of the leadership council sat again.

Bell studied Kelsey carefully. "As you've no doubt surmised, the people inside this facility are the descendants of those who hid from the rebels during the invasion. It's been a long and frustrating time, as you might imagine, so we're delighted to make your acquaintance."

The older man gestured at the walls around them. "This facility was originally a planetary defense center. We attempted to hold off the rebels, but they obliterated the orbital defenses in less than an hour and used kinetic strikes to take out every spaceport on the planet. We only managed to shoot down one enemy ship.

"Perhaps it was cowardly of us, but we went silent. We shielded ourselves from detection and watched in horror as the enemy ground troops destroyed everything. In less than ten days, there was no more organized resistance. Since then, we've been waiting for relief. We'd hoped to see Terran forces in a matter of months. Then it became years. Decades. Centuries. We feared it might be millennia. Or never. Yet here you are, and you cannot imagine how eager we are to hear your story."

Kelsey had no idea how they'd kept from going mad in all those years of waiting. All the generations of people born in hiding, living their lives, and dying, never having known freedom from fear. Hopefully, those days were almost over.

She told them the story of how Avalon had survived the rebel attack. How the emperor had sent his son to safety with them. They sat enraptured as she went through the adventure of their discovery of the weak flip point leading to this area of space. Of the battle against the Pale Ones. The near-destruction of *Athena* and the almost miraculous resurrection of *Courageous*.

Bell's eyes widened as she finished. He breathed an almost reverent sigh. "As I live and breathe, that is one of the most amazing stories I've ever heard. I thought you must come from a reconstituted Empire, but never in my wildest dreams did I imagine how far you've traveled to reach us. To save us.

"To think, after all these years, *Courageous* once more serves the Empire. After she drew off the remaining enemy ships, I thought the rebels had destroyed her. I can't begin to tell you how deeply glad I am to have been wrong."

"You almost sound like you were there."

The old man smiled. "Perhaps I should more fully introduce myself. Ensign Reginald Bell, probationary tactical officer from *Courageous*, at your service."

She took an instinctive half step back and consulted her implants. There before her, she felt the presence of another set of implants.

24

They made it to the correct level but took heavy fire as soon as they opened the hatch into the corridor. The marine corporal in charge of Jared's detachment exploded in a cloud of gore just as Jared rolled out of the stairwell.

Two Pale Ones with flechette rifles howled and charged. Jared shot the first with his pistol, insanely grateful that his implants helped him target the thing's head quickly. The savage dropped while his companion exchanged fire with the rest of the marine guards. It died, but so did they.

Owlet grabbed one of the fallen rifles and shot another Pale One coming from the other direction. The automatic weapon bucked in the boy's hands, but the Pale One staggered and fell. It hadn't been armed.

"We have to get to the computer center," Jared shouted. "Come on."

They ran to the primary computer room and sealed the door behind them. Unlike on the other shipyard, this one appeared new and almost unused. It had no chairs or other accoutrements that humans normally accumulated, but the panels were operational, and the lighting was good.

Owlet added Jared to the command-and-control file. As soon as he did, Jared accessed the control interfaces. Just like the other computer system, this one wasn't set up to keep them out. He isolated every active computer and ordered them into standby mode. That took away the self-destruct option. Hopefully.

"Owlet, can you bring up a systems schematic? If we can find a way to take all these Pale Ones out of the picture, I'd like to do it before they kill all of us."

The young computer scientist moved his way through several displays. "It doesn't look like they have any anti-boarding equipment other than the self-destruct charges. If everybody's vacuum suits are intact, we could vent

the atmosphere. This station is designed like *Courageous* and has huge panels
that open to dump all the air in less than a minute."

"Do it now."

Owlet tapped the console. "Venting atmosphere."

Jared monitored his suit's readout and watched the pressure drop to
nothing in less than a minute. Reports came flooding in as the Pale Ones
stopped fighting and started dying.

It took a couple of minutes for the marines to sort things out. It turned
out that Coulter was still alive after all. He'd taken a glancing hit to his
helmet that knocked out his radio. He was lucky the flechette hadn't taken
off his head.

Unfortunately, there were plenty of dead marines to supply replacement
parts. The sergeant reported to Jared in person a few minutes later. He
looked as though he'd been doused in blood.

"We have control of the shipyard, Captain. But we lost a lot of men
taking it. Sixty-two dead and twice that wounded. I'm afraid that the
Pentagaran marines took the brunt of the losses. I sure hope this was worth
the price we paid."

"Me, too, Sergeant. Me, too. Take the Pale Ones to the large airlocks
and put them all inside. We'll deal with them once everything is settled. Our
people go into one of the pinnaces." He moved to stand behind Owlet. "See
if you can find anything in the system to isolate where the controlling AI is
on the planet."

The young scientist nodded his understanding. "Accessing
communications logs. It looks like there's much more recent communication
to this station. Only about half an hour before we initiated our attack."

"What was it trying to do?"

The young man frowned. "I'm not entirely certain. There are some
instructions here in Old Empire machine code."

"Is that like the Old Empire programming language?"

Owlet shook his head. "No. It's more basic than that. It's not really even
human readable. It's as if the AI was attempting to reprogram some of the
basic functionality of the computer system. It's going to take me some time
to track down exactly which systems we're talking about."

"What about the source of the transmissions? Can you narrow down the
location of the AI at all?"

"Possibly. Based on the time the transmission came in, it had to come
from the same continent that the princess is exploring. That may not narrow
it down very far, but it does rule out a large swath of the planetary surface.
I'll see if I can find anything in the logs to refine that."

"Finding out what the AI was doing is more important. Focus on that
first, and bring up a schematic of the self-destruct charges on the center
monitor, please."

He turned to the marine sergeant. "Have your teams disable the self-
destruct charges. I think we'll all feel a lot better if the shipyard isn't going to
explode all on its own."

The noncom nodded and began examining the information Owlet brought up. "Aye, sir. Based on what we saw on the other shipyard, it should be fairly straightforward."

"Keep me informed." He gestured to the new men assigned to babysit him and began exploring the shipyard. It was just as bare bones as the other one. It also had one amenity he hadn't expected: a large observation deck looking out into the construction bay. Battle damage had breached this section on the first shipyard.

Why Pale Ones would want or need to be able to see what was happening with the ships under construction he couldn't imagine. Perhaps they built it according to the original plan. He might never know.

The view was spectacular, though. He could see every area of the open bay clearly. The sun was over the curve of the planet and illuminated everything. He could also see the planet below as they passed over it.

Standing there gave him time to focus on the communications logs he'd uploaded to his implants. They contained literally thousands of contacts spanning the last three years. He imagined that was when it came online. Each was time stamped and had some details about what was said. It also noted how long the communication lasted. Surely that had to be of some use.

He frowned and let his attention refocus on the view into the construction bay. Something there was nagging for his attention, but all he saw was the slow motion of the planet.

Jared's eyes widened. That was it! The orbit of the shipyard was a known factor. It took almost ninety minutes to complete one orbit. The communications with the surface would be line of sight. Plugging in each of the start and stop times would give him a visual map of where the AI was located. Or at least narrow it down to a more searchable wedge.

He'd loaded the orbital data before they'd launched so that he could keep track of when they would be able to signal the princess if need be. Putting it together in his head gave him a very narrow slice of land that could contain the AI. He projected that as a globe in his mind. The implants made visualizing it easy.

The area wasn't that far away from the princess, relatively speaking. No more than a thousand kilometers. It didn't include the mountains. He added small markers for all the ruined cities they'd mapped from orbit. Three fell into the target zone. Of course, there was no guarantee that the AI was located in one of the old cities. They'd need to examine the zone more closely.

His suit communicator pinged. "Mertz."

"Owlet here, sir. I found something you'll want to see."

The tone in his voice told Jared it wouldn't be something he liked. "On my way."

Owlet looked up from the console when Jared came in. "I tracked down the altered machine code. It overwrote the controls for the maneuvering grav drives."

"This thing can maneuver?" The shipyard was huge, so he couldn't imagine how.

The scientist made an ambivalent gesture. "Sort of. It has enough capability to alter its course for debris avoidance. The updated code overrode the automatic settings and put it into a decaying orbit. It'll start heating up in the atmosphere in a day or so. It won't last long after that."

"Can you override the new programming?"

"Probably, but I'll need to recover the original code from the other shipyard."

"Make that happen." He turned to the marine NCO. "I think I've done everything I can here. I'll leave you and your people to finish up. The pinnace will ferry me back to the ship."

"Yes, sir. If it's all the same to you, I'll have my people see you back aboard. Nothing personal, but the lieutenant gave me specific instructions."

"I hardly think that's necessary for a trip straight back to the ship, but I'm not going to countermand his orders. Keep me informed of your progress. And Sergeant? Pass my gratitude to the men. Taking this shipyard whole just might mean the difference between getting home and not. We paid a terrible price, but I couldn't be prouder." He looked at Owlet. "That goes for all of you."

His team formed up, and they made their way directly back to the airlock they'd breached. They passed far too many bodies in Fleet or Pentagaran combat armor. The dead would keep those already in his dreams company.

Once he was back on board the pinnace and his implants had access to the systems, he uploaded the data he'd collected on the transmissions. The pinnace's computers refined the area of possibility even more closely. The pinnace had also been scanning the surface as they orbited, looking for any transmissions, so he had a fair bit of data to add to his rough map of the zone.

There were no large ruins in the narrowed target area. In fact, there wasn't much of anything. A few rises that someone might charitably call hills and a substantial lake rounded out the landmarks. They'd need to vector the drones into that area to get more detailed readings.

The pinnace detached and backed away from the shipyard. Jared opened a line to the flight deck. "How long until we have line of sight with the search area the landing team is covering?"

"Five minutes, Captain."

"Raise them for me as soon as you can."

"Aye, sir."

He watched the planet below as they sped toward *Courageous*. It looked so pristine. Untouched. Yet the Pale Ones had desecrated it in the foulest way. Not only had its people been slaughtered, they'd been perverted into monsters. Even now, they probably swarmed the green surface.

How many Pale Ones were down there? How many unmodified humans driven to savagery? He might never know the answer. If there were many Pale Ones, would it be better to isolate them and allow them to die off?

Could they reverse the process? *Courageous* said that the Old Empire had done so before it fell. Doctor Leonard seemed to think it was possible with the machine they'd recovered. If they could wipe the viral code, perhaps they could also deactivate the hardware. Then the poor bastards could live out their lives in whatever peace they could find.

He really needed to come up with a plan for capturing some prisoners. They'd been reacting to the attacks thus far with lethal force. Kelsey had a neural disruptor that could stun. The scientists needed to get more of them refurbished.

"Captain," the pilot said over the communications channel. "We have line of sight, but I don't see them on the scanners. They may have landed in an area that's obscuring them. I've tried hailing them without success."

That worried him, but they might not be in a position to respond. If they had an enemy presence in their area, they might maintain communications silence. He'd give them a little more time to respond before he sent a team after them. *Courageous* could send some drones to look around without tipping anyone off to their presence.

"Understood. Take us home."

Still, he could do something. He accessed the communications suite and blocked one of the arrays from showing changes on the flight deck. He then tasked the unit to continue broadcasting the data he'd uploaded and a message with his thoughts across the area where Kelsey's pinnace should be. The other pinnace would route it to Kelsey if it received it. Then she'd know what he was thinking.

He rode in silence to *Courageous* once he finished. The ship loomed reassuringly large in front of them, and he relaxed when the pinnace settled home with a soft thud.

The marines helped him strip off his combat gear. He let them put it away as he headed for the bridge. He split his attention between greeting the people he passed and accessing the computer.

Jared was starting to download the ship's status when his connection terminated. He frowned and attempted to reconnect. The computer didn't respond. Something was wrong.

He trotted to the nearest lift and waited impatiently for its arrival. The world went dark before the doors had a chance to open.

25

——————

"That's impossible," Kelsey said flatly. Bell was old, yes, but not half a millennium old.

The old man grinned. "True enough, though we're not talking about me living that long straight through. The Empire had medical devices called stasis units. They would keep a person with traumatic injuries alive until they could receive medical care. Very cutting-edge stuff developed by Fleet.

"It was never intended to keep a person alive for hundreds of years, but with adequate monitoring and adjustment, it can do exactly that, it seems. I was the last surviving person with military implants, so they asked me to try, not knowing if anyone would ever come. Frankly, I'm astonished that I woke up again. Though I'm grateful to have the chance to be here at this historic moment."

He let her stunned silence go for a few seconds before continuing. "I was twenty years old when the rebellion broke out. I was already a midshipman at the premier Fleet academy on Terra. Annapolis, in the North American District.

"Things were looking very bad by the time they sent me to *Courageous*. Another year and we were on the run. I came down to Erorsi with a team to help stiffen the defenses. I assumed the rebels destroyed *Courageous* after I left. We all did. The rest, as they say, is history."

His age astounded her. "How old are you?"

"Five hundred and seventy-three next March, though without stasis I'm a mere two hundred and seventy-six. The medical nanos common in the Empire, combined with good medical care, made two hundred years a common occurrence. The ones given to the military added another hundred years to the lucky. Or the unlucky, if the rebels caught you. Thank God those poor souls are long dead. They deserve peace after they hell they've been through."

Dear God, he'd seen the Empire at its height with his own eyes. Jared would faint. The man before her was Fleet. The real Fleet.

Then it struck her like a hammer. He knew how to control his implants. The Old Empire had trained him, and he had lifetimes of experience. He knew what was possible and how to do it.

He could teach her.

She took a deep breath. "You are the answer to our prayers. Certainly to mine. I was captured by the Pale Ones—the rebels—and implanted. Our captain rescued me before they could reprogram the implants, but I have no idea what the hell I'm doing. All I know is that I have what they called a set of commando implants, and they do the damnedest things. Do you know anything about them?"

"Commando! That's the very highest level of modification in the Imperial Service. Do you have the full body modification?"

"Everything. Coated bones, artificial muscles, and a chip that's trigger happy."

Bell leaned back in his chair. "We had commandos on board. Their modifications were highly classified, but we all heard things. What you call trigger happy is something they called combat mode. The implants take over combat processing and act under the rules of engagement to speed human reaction time."

"Well, I'm pretty sure that there are no rules of engagement in my head."

"If a child pointed a gun at you, would you open fire?"

"I hope not," she said with a certain dread, "but I don't really know."

"If your implants were never overridden, I'm certain there are basic safeguards in place. Have you ever attacked a noncombatant?"

She shook her head.

"There you are. The Pale Ones, as you call them, have no such restriction. I don't really know much more about commando implants, but I can give you some basic instruction with more conventional implant operations. If we have time. Right now, the rebels are down, but you need to finish them."

She rubbed her eyes tiredly. "Are you suggesting that we attack them? I'm certain the captain would be happy to evacuate you from the system. I'm not so sure he'd agree to any kind of ground action. We don't exactly have a sky full of ships."

Bell smiled. "Far be it from *me* to tell a Fleet captain what he should be doing, but you may not realize just how badly you've hurt them. We once had marine reconnaissance drones. We know roughly where the controlling AI is located. The reverse is also true, unfortunately. They can't precisely locate us, but we can't directly attack them, either."

Kelsey nodded. "We saw at least one large city. I assume they're in some place like that."

"Then you'd be wrong. They used kinetic strikes to take out every population center with spaceport facilities, but they left the rest alone. Those cities probably still have people living deep under them, but the rebels only go there when they want to capture more people to convert. They have their own area further to the east. The deep woods there are full of rebels. It was a massive nature preserve before the invasion. They're set up somewhere inside it."

She glanced over at Lieutenant Reese. "Lieutenant, do you think we could retask some of the drones we brought with us to check out that area?"

The marine officer smiled a bit sardonically. "That would necessitate us being able to signal them. It's not as though the Pale Ones don't already know we're here. However, we're getting ahead of ourselves. We need to come to an agreement about this communications blackout. Either these people trust that we won't give them away, or they don't." He tipped his head in Bell's direction. "No offense."

"None taken. Now that you know who we are, I have no objection to dropping the communications blackout. I just ask that you go some distance away before you open any long-range communication. By all means, please speak with your captain. As for what we want, we want to take our world back from those things. We want to take our Empire back."

Kelsey could certainly appreciate how he felt.

"Then if you don't mind, we'll go back out to talk this over with Captain Mertz. We'll come back and work out the best way to get what we all want."

The old man stood slowly, and the others followed suit. "Even though you have an Imperial battlecruiser, we have people here that have worked with Imperial systems all their lives. They don't have implants, but they have experience. We each have strengths the other lacks. Help us make that final push. Help us defeat the rebels."

Kelsey could hear the unspoken addendum. If *Courageous* didn't help them, they wouldn't gain access to that knowledge base. Or perhaps she was reading too much into what Bell had said. In any case, she needed to talk with Jared. Based on what they'd done so far, he might green light the final attack just on the basis of gaining control of the AI. She'd certainly encourage him to do that. The information in its databanks was priceless.

Da Silva escorted them back to the entrance. Talbot and his men formed up around her as they withdrew from the gully. Reese, who still hadn't put his helmet back on, looked over at her as they walked. "I know what you're going to recommend, and I'd like to urge you to be cautious. We need to scout out the enemy position before we make a commitment. The Pale Ones overthrew the Empire. We're just one ship."

"Believe it or not, Lieutenant, I agree. We need to see what we're up against, and then we can make a reasoned decision on what's in our best interest. Of course I'd like to see this planet freed from the control of the Pale Ones. If there's any way that we can pull that off, we should finish them while we have the chance. This place is a direct threat to everyone on Pentagar, and that's a threat to the Empire."

She put on her helmet when Reese did and listened to him give instructions to the marines. Everyone pulled back into the pinnace, and he buttoned up the landing craft. "Pilot, let's get out of here. Take us back down the mountain chain at a leisurely pace. I don't want any transmissions until I give the word."

The pilot acknowledged, and the pinnace lifted off smoothly.

Kelsey sat next to Reese and started to take her helmet off. She stopped when she saw a "message waiting" light at the corner of her heads-up display. She accessed her armor's communications unit and saw that the pinnace had forwarded her a message.

She played Jared's transmission and saw the information he'd forwarded to her. The loss of life on the shipyard horrified her, but she knew deep down that her half brother had made the right call. Possession of the shipyard could give them a critical edge.

The narrowed search data on the AI jibed with what Bell had told them. It looked like he'd been on the level, as her father used to say.

She opened a private channel to Lieutenant Reese. "It looks like the captain sent us a message while we were down below. I'm going to send you the transmission." She relayed it to his armor.

"That's very interesting," he said after it ended. "The pilot also indicated that we received several transmissions while we were down below, but he couldn't contact us and let us know that we had them. We're in control of this system, though the price was high." He rubbed the bridge of his nose. "I'm going to have to have a talk with him about getting into pitched battles, too. Is it genetic with you two?"

"Probably. Could we capture the AI if we located it?"

"If we could capture the AI intact, the data would be invaluable. I'm just not sure how realistic that goal is. We might have to settle for a kinetic strike from orbit. Let's contact the captain and get the green light to bring Bell and some of his people to negotiate. We can send out the drones to gather additional information. In fact, I think we should have them begin searching the area that the captain highlighted at once."

The marine officer looked at Talbot. "I'm sending you some coordinates. I want to retask every drone we have to search this area for signs of any Pale Ones' strong points."

"Aye, sir." The marine noncom began tapping on the console that had control of the drones.

"While you do that," Kelsey said, "I'll go ahead and fill the captain in on what we've discovered."

Kelsey opened a communications channel and signaled *Courageous*. She expected an immediate answer from the communications officer on duty, but she had to signal several times before a small window opened inside her HUD.

The man standing on the bridge was unfamiliar to her. Or rather, he did look vaguely familiar, but she didn't think he was part of the regular bridge rotation. His uniform indicated he was a Pentagaran.

"Princess Kelsey," he said. "I've been expecting your call."

"I'm sorry, but I don't remember your name. Where's the duty communications officer?"

He ignored her question. "My name is Commander Rawlins, and I'm now in command of *Courageous*."

"Excuse me? What the hell is going on up there?"

The balding man leaned toward the screen and smiled widely. "Technically, I suppose that this is a mutiny. In actuality, this vessel has always been the property of the Pentagaran people, even though we didn't know it was there. Now that we do know, we're taking possession."

She sent a signal to Lieutenant Reese and forwarded him the communication channel so that he could watch. "You know that you can't possibly expect to get away with this. Even if you did seize the ship, your people don't have the know-how to operate it."

"You make me sound like a video villain. Your captain and everyone under his command are my prisoners. Now, before you begin resorting to threats, allow me to make our status clear.

"I don't expect that you'll surrender, and I don't care. I control the weapon systems on this ship. So long as you don't attempt to leave the surface, I have no interest in interfering with you.

"We will be breaking orbit shortly and returning to Pentagar to consolidate control of our government. Interfere and we will destroy you. Worse yet, I'll kill the people that your captain left on the shipyards. I've dropped jammers to ensure you can't send a message back to Pentagar through the probes at the space-time bridge. Be a good girl and we'll come back to rescue you at some point. If you're still alive. Good luck, Princess. *Courageous* out."

The transmission terminated. Kelsey swore using every new word she'd picked up from the marines. They had her trapped on a planet full of Pale Ones, and Jared was in grave danger.

26

J ared woke cold and stiff, his face pressed against the deck. He groaned and rolled over onto his back. His head was pounding. What the hell had just happened? He felt like he'd been on an all-night bender.

He sat up gingerly and looked at his surroundings. He was in the officers' mess, and he wasn't alone. Dozens of others lay on every available section of the deck. He reached out and touched the person nearest him, a woman in an engineering uniform, and was reassured to see she was breathing.

It took all his focus to climb to his feet and stumble to the main hatch. It didn't open when he pressed the key.

"Ah, Captain Mertz," a voice said from the overhead. "It's good to see you up and about. I'm sure you have many questions, but let me start by introducing myself. I am Commander Jacob Rawlins, the new commanding officer of *Courageous*. You, sir, are my prisoner."

Nothing came out the first time that Jared attempted to speak. His throat was parched. "What kind of game are you playing? You know as well as I do that your king is not going to sit still for this."

"I don't see that he's going to have much choice. One of the very first things we're going to do when we return to Pentagar is stage a coup in the Fleet and replace our weak monarch with a much more powerful one."

"Your Fleet isn't going to be intimidated into backing you. They're going to fight you every step of the way."

The unseen man laughed. "Oh no, you misunderstand. I have no desire to rule a planet. None whatsoever. I leave that to those with bigger egos than I. You see, my patron's plans have been in motion for quite some time. In fact, they would've been complete right about now if you hadn't arrived.

Everything was staged and ready to execute. Then you had to show up and kick the Pale Ones back out of our system. My patron was most wroth."

Jared staggered back to a table and sat heavily in the chair. "You can't possibly expect to be able to man this ship without the cooperation of my crew. I'm sure you managed to slip a few people aboard, but nowhere near the number that it would take to move the ship anywhere. Your plan will not work."

"I believe that it will. Not all of my countrymen are mindless drones willing to follow a weak monarch. Since you've been good enough to train them, I believe that we'll be able to make our way back home without any real trouble. Even if we do have a problem, it won't be very difficult to convince the necessary personnel to cooperate. We have plenty of airlocks handy. It's astonishing how quickly one's resolve crumbles when they watch their friends spaced one by one.

"Now, rather than get into some useless discussion with you about the rightness of my actions, you're going to listen as I tell you what's going to happen. We have accounted for every single member of your crew. Well, those I've allowed back aboard the ship, anyway. You have no loyal forces in a position to stop me. But if you attempt to escape, I will execute your crew one by one and pipe their screams down so you can hear. Accept my control of this ship and your people will live. You have my word."

"The word of a mutineer isn't very good in my book. What about the people who're not on board this ship? What happens to them? Where is Princess Kelsey?"

"Your precious Imperial princess is perfectly safe. She's still on the planet's surface, with an entire landing party of marines. Since your people still have control of both shipyards, she can fly up to them and be perfectly safe. Once the situation on Pentagar stabilizes, we'll come back for them. You see? All very bloodless.

"It will stay that way as long as you're smart. I've left the hatch to the kitchen unlocked, so feel free to eat as much as you like. The remainder of your crew is in the main mess, which is also accessible from the kitchen. I'm afraid the heads are going to be quite popular, so you might want to set up a rotation and ration the toilet paper. Now, if you'll excuse me, I have a ship to run. Goodbye."

Some of the others in the room were beginning to stir. Jared figured he woke a little faster than the others because of his implants, but he had no way to be sure.

Rawlins had to be watching him. Jared hadn't known the mess had a camera, but it made sense. All the common areas probably had them. That complicated his escape plans. Or it would when he finally got around to thinking some up.

First, he needed to know what they could see, and what resources he could muster.

He put his head in his hands and looked around for the camera feed through his implants. There it was. The camera was in the corner by the door behind him. He had an odd view of himself slumped over the table. Thankfully, there was no audio. That must've terminated when Rawlins killed the direct communications link.

Jared felt around for the computer, but it wasn't available. They'd either shut it down or isolated it. That was probably how they'd managed to take control of the ship.

The only other feed in range of his implants showed the corridor outside the mess. A half dozen Pentagaran marines in armor with weapons at the ready stood guard. His people wouldn't get past them without terrible bloodshed. He had to find a different way out.

First, however, he needed to get his people on their feet. Feeling a little steadier, he began searching for his senior officers. He found lieutenants Anderson and Ramirez piled together in the kitchen. Charlie Graves lay next to them. His chief engineer and Doctor Stone were in the crew's mess. None of them was awake yet.

He had no idea if water would help, but he filled a glass and poured it over Charlie's face. That merely left him with an unconscious—and now wet—first officer.

While he waited for them to wake up, he made his way through the kitchen and looked for cameras. He found one overlooking the main cooking area, but the remainder of the kitchen was not under view. He made that blind spot his new headquarters. Everyone in the two mess areas would be easily visible to the mutineers. If he wanted to act without their knowledge, it would have to be from in here.

He might be able to override the cameras, but he didn't want to count on it. One mistake and they would figure out that he had access to them through his implants. Once they realized he had implants, the edge they gave him would be gone.

The kitchen took up quite a bit of area with freezers and refrigeration units. He remembered coming through here when they'd first discovered *Courageous*. It was like a maze. A maze that might hold a secret exit.

He was beginning to lose confidence in that possibility when he sensed something through the floor. A major engineering node, complete with repair remotes. There wasn't any direct access to the engineering space, but he might be able to overcome that obstacle. It was time to bring the rest of the team in on his plans.

He made his way back to his officers and found them awake. Graves looked as though a grav truck had run over him. He'd found a hand towel to dry his face. "What the hell is going on, Captain?"

"It seems we have a mutiny on our hands. A number of Pentagaran personnel have seized the ship and used the antiboarding systems to take us out. Their intent is to return to Pentagar and overthrow the Monarchy. I'd imagine they're affiliated with the people that tried to assassinate King Raymond."

Graves shook his head. "That's insane. This is a powerful ship, but not to that degree. The Pentagarans have a fleet of their own, and the mutineers can't overwhelm a planet full of people with one undermanned battlecruiser. We don't even have that many missiles left."

"They obviously disagree. I'm beginning to formulate a plan to take the ship back, but we have a problem. They have us locked up in the mess halls and kitchen, and they have armed and armored men in the corridors ready to shoot anyone that comes out. Even if we manage to unlock the doors. They also have cameras watching the main areas."

Baxter pinched the bridge of his nose. "That limits our options pretty significantly. We have no weaponry, they have us locked in an isolated area with no easy exits, and they took the main computer offline. I was just getting a team together to go find out why it went down when they took us out. Come to that, whatever weapon they used is probably capable of taking us down right here if we get froggy. How do we overcome that?"

Jared shared a glance with Doctor Stone and his first officer. "We may have some extra resources at our disposal, but first let's get everybody on their feet and get the marines grouped. Doctor, if you would go check anyone that's not awake to see if they need medical assistance, that would be a good start."

"Aye, sir." The doctor gestured for Zia and Pasco to follow her and went into the crew's mess.

Graves looked around. "Are we under surveillance right now? Can they hear us?"

"They can see us, but they can't hear us. Walk with me and we'll get out from under the eyes of our enemies. There's an engineering node one deck down under the freezers. I may be able to use the remotes to open the floor and let us into the conduits. For this to work, it's going to have to be small teams so that the mutineers don't figure out what we're doing."

The executive officer nodded. "What are you thinking? One team to go to the armory, another to seize engineering, and one to bring the main computer back online?"

"We can send some of the marines to armor up in case we don't succeed, but if we can bring the main computer online, this fight is over."

"I'm surprised that you're so up to date on where the repair remotes are housed and what angles the cameras can see," Baxter said. "They must've had somebody in the computer team. The equipment we used to isolate the main computer is still in place. If they had the right codes, isolating it would be easy. An obvious oversight on my part looking back, but I wasn't expecting a mutiny. I was more worried that the main computer would get ideas."

"What do we do if we can't restore the computer?" Graves asked. "What if we have to take the ship back by force? Are we going to be in a position to do that?"

"I certainly hope so," Jared said.

Baxter looked around at the people who were starting to filter into the kitchen. "It looks like we're getting some attention. How, might I ask, are we planning to give the engineering remotes instructions? Morse code tapped on the deck? This plan may be over before it starts, because I can't imagine how we're going to get the damn things to open up the deck."

Jared smiled. "It turns out I have a little surprise in store for you and the crew. I think I'll hold onto the specifics for the moment, but trust me when I tell you that we'll be able to give some instructions to the remotes. Charlie, I want you to coordinate with the marines and get some assault teams ready to go. Dennis, you do the same with your engineering people. Once we're ready, we're going to have to move fast."

The two officers nodded and made their way out past the growing crowd.

Jared cleared his throat. "Everyone, listen up. I know you have a lot of questions and that you're very worried, but I don't have time to address everything individually right now. I want everyone to move back into the mess halls. As of right now, the kitchen is a command post. Find your section leaders and make sure that they have a good head count. Be ready for orders. Move out."

He found a place to sit at one of the tables as everyone filed out of the kitchen. He'd best start thinking about contingency plans, because as sure as anything, something would go wrong in a big way once they broke out.

He'd have one shot at taking control of *Courageous*. If he blew it, his people would die. And on top of that, his only allies in the sector would probably be overthrown. He had to get everything right the first time.

27

"We need to take the ship back," Kelsey said. Lieutenant Reese, Talbot, and she had commandeered the rear of the flight deck to discuss their situation. "We also need to contact the people they left on the shipyards. If we can." She consulted her implants. "They both just passed around the planet and out of communications range. We'll have to wait a half an hour for the damaged one to come back into range. Another half hour for the other."

Reese shook his head. "Taking the ship back is easier said than done. They know exactly where we are, and they can blast us if we try to reach orbit. I don't want to say this is impossible, but the odds of us being killed without getting near the ship approach certainty."

Kelsey rubbed the bridge of her nose. "Dammit. There can't possibly be that many of them on the ship. Surely the Pentagarans did some kind of background check on these people. How can they possibly take over the entire ship?"

"With only a few people to carry out the attack, I'd wager they used the ship's antiboarding system to disable the crew. If the mutineers had enough access, they could trigger it all over the ship. They probably left a few compartments alone so that their people would remain conscious."

She nodded. "They probably used that same access to reactivate whatever cutout we had installed for the computer. There is no way *Courageous* would allow this to happen. They used our own precautions to hang us. But they made one mistake. They let the captain back on board."

Reese frowned slightly. "While I have the highest respect for Captain Mertz, exactly how does that count as a mistake?"

She smiled. "Because I'm not the only member of our crew with implants."

The marine's eyes widened. "Seriously? When did that happen? Someone would've noticed him spending a couple of days in the medical center. Are you sure?"

"I'm positive. He only has the cranial implants and medical nanites, so his recovery time was short. I found out at breakfast today. Having him on board the ship is even better than having me there. He knows a lot more about the ship's systems than I do, and if anyone can figure out how to break free of whatever prison they have him in, it's Jared."

Reese paced across the flight deck. "That might be enough. Hell, it's going to have to be enough."

Talbot looked up from the console he was sitting at. "LT? We have another problem. I rerouted the drones toward the new search area, and I'm picking up ground movement on one of them. Take a look."

Lieutenant Reese walked over and stared past Talbot. Kelsey linked directly into the drone's feed and immediately saw what the senior sergeant meant: dozens of savage-looking humans loping through the forest. As the drone continued over the area, she saw that it was more like hundreds. Perhaps thousands. The Pale Ones were on the move.

"Where are those things going?" Reese asked.

"Not towards us, if that's what you're asking," Talbot said. "They're headed in the general direction of the survivors' facility. They probably detected our landing. The drone estimates there are thousands of the things on the move. I'll wager there are a lot more of them coming from other locations."

"Wonderful," Kelsey muttered. "Bell's people are vulnerable. The Pale Ones can just keep throwing bodies at them until they get in. We need to locate that AI. It sent them on this mission. It can stop them. We just have to capture it intact. Lieutenant Reese, that mission objective just became mandatory."

The next hour went by with excruciating slowness. The damaged shipyard didn't respond to their signals. Reese had sent one of the drones to send a short-range transmission to Bell and his people. Maybe their defenses were better than the Terrans expected.

The team on the intact shipyard responded, though. They confirmed Kelsey's worst fears. *Courageous* was on the move. They'd left orbit and were heading for the flip point back to Pentagar. Since the ship was faster than the pinnaces, there was no way they could retake her. It was all up to Jared. She'd just have to focus on her own problems and trust him to do his part.

Shortly after that, a jammer in orbit went active and blocked them from communicating with anyone.

Finally, Talbot spoke up. "I might have found something."

Kelsey again accessed the drone's signal directly. He was watching the feed from over a large lake.

Talbot tapped his screen. "There's a small facility on the shore. Those look like transmitters on the roof. Big ones. Capable of reaching orbit."

The facility he was talking about was more like a small building, one story tall and poorly constructed. Functional without a hint of grace. Definitely a Pale Ones construct. It couldn't possibly have room for a major computer system, though. There wasn't room for even the power supply one would require.

She shook her head. "It's too small. Admittedly, I have no idea why it's out here, but it can't have all the equipment that they need."

"See those cables running into the water? I think the computers and power supplies are under water. It would shield their emissions signature from prying eyes. The transmitters look like they're tight beam. Unless someone was right on top of them, no one would ever know they were there."

"But why would they need to be coy? They own this planet, and they've been in control for five hundred years."

"Why keep sending the same size fleet to attack Pentagar? They only just completed a second shipyard. They could've built one a lot faster if they'd wanted to. We're not really in a position to guess why they do anything. Some things just don't make sense. They may never make sense to us."

Reese straightened. "We're not seeing anything else, and time is running out. We need to act if we want to save the people in that facility. If we're right about this being the place, there'll be defenses that we can't see. We need to take out the underwater facility, and then we come back to secure the transmitter."

Kelsey frowned. "What use is the transmitter going to be? They aren't going to be calling for help. We've taken over this entire system."

The marine gave her a serious look. "Perhaps, but there might be a record of everything it's sent. Are there regular visits from other systems? I seriously doubt this is the only place where the rebellion left an AI to run things."

"True." She allowed herself to sigh. "I hope this works."

"Me, too. If you'll excuse me, Princess, I have an attack to plan. You and Talbot can coordinate on how you'll follow us in. Remember, he goes in first."

Kelsey stuck her tongue out at his back when he walked away. "That man makes me tired."

"And you give him grey hair. Come on, Princess. We both know how this plays out. We attack the base and you do something that makes me want to scream. Then you figure out a way to make the LT want to space you. In the end, you do what you want to anyway."

"It doesn't sound so bad when you put it that way. Thanks."

He shook his head and followed Reese.

Kelsey took control of the drone overlooking the lake. She brought it around for a closer look at the communications building. Not seeing any obvious weaponry on the roof, she dropped the drone down for a direct look at the building. Yes, that would announce their presence, but if the AI didn't know they were already there from the drones buzzing around, then it was even stupider than she'd imagined.

She didn't know much about communications hardware, but the transmitters and their associated hardware looked old. The weather had obviously taken a toll on them, and there were signs of repairs. That meant that this facility wasn't brand new. It had been here a while. In her mind, that was actually good news. Why build a decoy setup when there was absolutely no need to have one? Then again, why keep attacking a planet the same way for five hundred years?

Digging down in the scanner controls for the drone, she found some filters. One of them looked like a high-sensitivity IR scanner. If there were people in that building, they'd show up in IR as long as they weren't in a shielded room. She changed the settings and scanned the building again. No sign of any people, but there were scattered heat sources. Probably equipment. Another sign the Pale Ones hadn't abandoned the facility.

She took the drone higher and scanned the forest. There were animals, including some that were large enough to be human, but none was the right shape when she checked them out in more detail. A spot check of a few showed they were large herbivores. Considering the personalities of the Pale Ones, any critter in its right mind would head far away if the savages were present.

Kelsey opened a channel to Reese and Talbot. "I did an IR scan of the building. There don't seem to be any Pale Ones inside. Ditto an IR scan of the forest."

The marine officer switched to the general channel. "Listen up. We'll be making an assault in twenty minutes. Bring everything we need to breach and storm an underwater facility. The Pale Ones likely have it heavily guarded. We're on a schedule, people. If we don't take the AI down quickly, the last survivors on this planet die. Let's show this bastard what it means to have Imperial Marines dropping on his ass."

She couldn't help smiling at their cheers. The AI wouldn't know what hit it.

28

An hour later, the command staff was back in the kitchen with Doctor Leonard in tow. Jared had cajoled the cameras into recording the last hour for use during their escape. If he could get the cameras to play the recorded time back and no one noticed the jump from present to past, they might be able to sneak right out from under the noses of their captors.

"Doctor Stone," he said, "let's start off with the condition of our people."

The Fleet doctor smiled a little. "Good news on that front. Everyone has recovered from the effects of the stunners with little more than a headache. We have a few secondary injuries from falls, but nothing worse than a fractured wrist. We got off very lucky."

He turned his attention to his executive officer. "What about a head count? How many people do we have unaccounted for?"

Graves grimaced. "A few more than I'd like, but less than it could have been. Without access to the personnel files, I might be off by as many as five people. Some of the Pentagarans worked in multiple departments, and memories are a little shaky right now. Worst case puts the enemy at about just over four dozen people."

"That's not enough people to effectively run this ship, especially with some tasked to guard us. How many marines do we think?" He addressed that last to Sergeant Coulter.

The marine noncom looked as though he'd bitten something sour. "More than a dozen. Not much more, but that's enough. They'll be in modern combat armor and armed to the teeth. Any direct attack on them without similar equipment would be suicide."

Graves nodded his agreement. "There are enough people missing to operate the ship. Possibly even enough to fire the weapons. If they get back to Pentagar and fool them long enough to get reinforcements aboard, this ship could destroy the Pentagaran combat fleet. We need to keep them on this side of the flip point."

Jared shifted his attention to the chief engineer. "Baxter?"

The man grinned. "Get me into engineering and they won't be able to even see where they're walking, much less control this ship. That brings us back to getting out of this makeshift prison. What secret plan do you have up your sleeve, Captain?"

Jared shared a conspiratorial glance with Stone and Graves. "Let's just say that Princess Kelsey isn't the only one able to tap into *Courageous*'s systems. As Doctor Stone, Commander Graves, and Doctor Leonard already know, I had a Fleet officer's implants installed last night."

Coulter looked stunned, but Baxter's grin took on a savage tinge. "That would do it. Can you reprogram the remotes?"

"I believe so. Within reason, anyway. I sent a test command to them earlier. It will probably take them a few minutes to cut a hole large enough for us to escape through, though. That's part of their programming for damage control. Probably to help get people out of dangerous areas."

Baxter nodded. "That makes sense. What about using them for other tasks? Like shutting off control to the bridge or activating the antiboarding defenses? We could stop the mutineers right now."

Leonard cleared his throat. "I'm afraid that raises several issues, Commander. The remotes have a certain set of approved actions. To override those would take access to the main computer. If we had that, we wouldn't need to reprogram them. I looked at their basic programming a few weeks ago. I'd imagine this was to keep them from being turned against the ship."

"Besides," Jared added, "if I started sending them all over the ship, someone in engineering might notice. I can isolate this group. If we use them sparingly, they might make a world of difference when we need them."

"What about weapons?" Coulter asked. "The armory is probably under guard. A couple of marines would keep us from getting weapons. That means the enemy is just about invulnerable."

"I might be able to help out with that," Doctor Leonard said. "We have a number of Old Empire weapons in the labs. We were restoring them for use by your people. We've also been making some ammunition. I believe we could probably arm a number of people. Perhaps a dozen, if you count the pistols we've restored."

"Well, we'll just have to make do. How many people do you think we could sneak off without the bad guys noticing?"

"A lot," Jared said with a smile. "I've been recording the feed from the cameras, and I'll start playing it back just before we head out. I'll want you to go back out and make the rounds again. Select the people you need and brief them. In half an hour, I'll get the remotes to work and call you in.

"The highest priority is disabling the antiboarding defenses. We can't count on being able to use them, so I want to make them unavailable to the enemy. How can we best do that, Dennis?"

"By taking engineering. I can use one of the panels there to lock them out. I can't control them, but my override will keep the other side from getting them for a little while."

"Engineering just became the highest priority. If they don't control the drives, they stay in this system. We don't know how far they are from the flip point, so we need to make sure we don't dawdle. Restoring the main computer to operation is task two. It can override the ship's systems on my authority."

Jared turned to Zia. "Once we lock them out of the system, you'll work with the marines to take operations. If we can't take the bridge, that's where we'll control the ship from."

"What about me?" Graves asked. Jared couldn't help but hear the note of eagerness in his friend's voice.

"You get the most dangerous job. When the time comes, you get to retake the bridge. We need them alive to find out who is behind this."

"You can count on me, sir. Where will you go?"

"To the computer center. Getting the computer online will allow me to take over most of the ship's systems. I can work directly with the main computer to assist you from there."

"What about the weapons?" Coulter asked. "Do we secure the lab first? Otherwise, everyone is unarmed. We have to assume that every hijacker at least has a pistol."

"True," Jared admitted. "We secure the lab first and then move out to the other targets. Remember, stay in the mess for half an hour, and don't come back until I call you."

He let them go and sent the instructions to the remotes. He really had no idea how long it would take for them to cut through the floor. If it looked like it would take more than half an hour, he'd delay calling his people in.

In fact, the remotes were much quicker than he'd imagined. He faintly heard them cutting, and his direct observation through them showed the process going quickly. In less than five minutes, the cutaway section fell into the conduit. The rim of the hole glowed with heat, so he decided to stick with the original timetable.

Right at the half hour mark, he switched the cameras to showing the recorded loop. Once he was certain that was what was going out, he walked to the door and waved to his crew. Fifty or so people filed into the kitchen. Jared let his officers get them sorted out.

He noted with approval when Coulter went right to the food prep area and started appropriating knives. The marine grinned. "Since they were arrogant enough to leave them here, we'd be fools not to use them."

"It beats fists and feet. Good thinking. Listen up, people. The conduit is tight. We'll proceed in single file. The lab is two levels up and possibly occupied. I want to stress that you need to keep any noise to a minimum. If we run into the hijackers, let the marines handle them. You're here to handle specific technical and support tasks. That said, if you have to fight, fight hard. We retake *Courageous* now."

He motioned for Coulter to take his team in front. "The conduit is accessible one corridor over from the lab. Go forward once you're in. After about sixty meters, you'll find a ladder going up. Go up two levels and then keep going forward. You want hatch 7-52R. Once we get there, I can look at the cameras within range. I'll let you know the situation, and then you can handle the details."

"Sounds good, sir. Let's go, marines."

The marines dropped into the conduit and moved forward, hunched over almost double. The conduit really wasn't large enough for people to go great distances. The crew normally went to the nearest access point and directly to the systems they needed to work on.

Jared followed the marines carefully, focusing on his footing in the dim lights provided for the maintenance crews. The designers must've also expected them to bring portable lights. He'd remember that the next time he needed to sneak around inside the ship.

If the conduit was tight, the ladder between levels was almost too constricted. Especially while climbing. He cursed the long-dead designers who hadn't considered people. Once he made it two levels up, the conduit felt as wide as a corridor. Almost.

The slow shuffle forward ended when the man in front of Jared stopped. They must be at the hatch. He focused his attention inward and searched for cameras. There were a few in range of his implants, all thankfully empty of people.

He had a moment of shared sympathy with Kelsey. He was sure there was so much more he could do, if only he had a clue about the possibilities. They might have Old Empire equipment, but their ignorance hindered them so much.

"All clear," he said quietly. "I can't see into the lab itself, but the odds of anyone being there seem remote. I don't have much of a view beyond the immediate area, so be vigilant."

He watched the hatch open and Coulter step out, scanning both directions before he gestured for his men to come out. They spread out in both directions as though they'd practiced the maneuver a thousand times. Perhaps they had.

Jared shuffled forward and came out into the brighter lights, blinking to clear his vision. He turned to follow Coulter to the hatch leading into the lab. The marines took up positions around the door and hit the controls.

Nothing happened.

The hijackers must've locked down all the hatches, just in case they missed someone in the roundup. Perhaps he could do something about that. He probed the hatch and found it still had implant access. He triggered the hatch, and it slid open.

The marines flowed inside, but Jared could already see that the lab was empty of human occupation.

That didn't hold true for the corridor, however. A hatch thirty yards up the corridor slid open, and a man in an engineering tech's coveralls stepped into sight.

Jared found himself moving even before the man looked up in surprise. He couldn't let the mutineer get off a warning, or they were dead.

He reached the man just as he grabbed for the communicator on his belt. His shoulder caught the other man in the gut and sent them both sprawling to the deck. The man fumbled for his pistol and screamed for help.

That was bad. It meant there was someone else close by.

Jared found out just how close when another man came out of the compartment beside him and aimed a pistol right at his head.

29

The drone showed Kelsey a truly impressive view of the pinnace screaming out of the sky like a massive bird of prey. It decelerated savagely above the lake and hovered. Her artificial musculature and powered armor gave her an advantage over her companions, but she still had trouble levering herself out of her restraints. The marines poured down the ramp and dropped into the water without the slightest hesitation. She gulped and jumped after them.

Kelsey expected to have a moment of panic as the water closed around her, but it never materialized. She sank into the dark water and only felt determination to do what she had to do. If Lieutenant Reese guessed correctly, they'd land a short distance away from the facility and advance on the bottom of the lake, following the power and control cables.

Desperate to see what was around her, she leeched as much information as she could from the suit's passive scanners. It was as if she was straining to hear a sound in a dark room. The only things she sensed were the men around her. But even that was a revelation.

Somehow, her implants and combat suit combined to answer her desperate request for knowledge in a way she'd never imagined possible. For all intents and purposes, the commando armor ceased to exist. Oh, it was still there, but it now just seemed to be part of her body as far as her senses were concerned. She felt like she was drifting downward with nothing between her and the water. It was just like when she'd used *Courageous*'s scanners.

The marines' suits were sending her information that they probably shouldn't have been. She knew where every member of the assault party was located. It was like a little 3-D graphic in her mind. Little dots of light, all falling toward the bottom of the lake.

She knew which dot belonged to a specific marine, and that marine's combat armor was sending her status information. Things like armor integrity, ammunition levels, and health of the marine. Probably the same sorts of things that Lieutenant Reese saw. Her suit had hacked the marine combat network.

If it could do that with such incompatible equipment, she knew she'd be astonished what it could do with the other Old Empire combat units. If she could ever figure out what her capabilities truly were.

She had a couple seconds' warning that the ground was coming up before she landed. She expected the soft, sucking mud at the bottom to envelop her, but that never happened. She seemed to slow just before she touched the ground and hovered in the water.

The rest of the marines were not so lucky. They sank into the silt-covered, muddy bottom up to their knees. She sent a questing thought into her armor and discovered that it had a very low-power grav generator at the base of her spine. Yet one more unexpected capability.

While the marines sorted themselves out, she tried to determine the grav generator's capability. She wasn't an engineer, but it seemed to her that it probably existed to enhance jumping distance. It didn't seem strong enough for sustained flight. Unless, of course, one was underwater.

She was going to have to spend some quality time with this armor and figure out all of its capabilities very soon. She couldn't count on it producing a miracle when she needed it. She had to be able to plan ahead.

Talbot was close enough for her to follow as he moved toward the AI facility. Even if there had been light, she wouldn't have been able to see him directly in the storm cloud of silt that the marines had sent into the water, but he'd insisted on securing a line between them.

The marines slowly advanced until Kelsey sensed a wall in front of her. Bright lights snapped on, coming from some of the marines already up against the facility. The visibility was crappy from her position, but Lieutenant Reese must've been able to see something.

His voice came over the general communications link. "We'll go right. There has to be a way in. Keep an eye out for enemy units."

Kelsey had taken the liberty of adding her implant codes to the drones, so she didn't need to be on the pinnace to control them. She could sense one at the edge of her control envelope, so she ordered it to come down into the water. Surely, the Pale Ones knew they were there after the pinnace flew right over the lake. She might as well be able to see what they were attacking. She was cautious enough to keep it using passive scanners, though.

As the marines moved, Kelsey was able to come up beside the wall. It was made of dull, pitted metal. No rust, though. She turned her light on and played it across the wall and then up. The way the wall curved as it went over her head made her wonder if this was more a dome than a building. That would make some sense underwater, she supposed.

But then shouldn't the base that they were moving along also curve? It seemed to be moving in a straight line, as though the building was cigar shaped. She looked at the readings from the drone, and she thought she knew what she was looking at.

She switched to the command channel. "Lieutenant Reese? I don't think this is a building. It's a ship."

"What the hell would a ship be doing at the bottom of the lake?"

"I have no idea, but the drone is picking up passive data from all around us, and this is an Old Empire battlecruiser, just like *Courageous*. I can see some of the same bulges as images I've seen of our ship. This one doesn't look like it's in one piece. Not really. There are some massive holes on the other side of the hull. Somebody shot the hell out of this thing."

"You brought a drone down—" She could hear the irritation in his voice as he cut himself off. "I don't know why I'm surprised. Well, since you've done it, and they know we're here now, are there any openings ahead of us?"

She closed her eyes and brought up a 3-D representation of the ship in her mind. "Yes. There's another large opening about fifty meters ahead of the lead marine."

They kept advancing until the opening came into view. It only took one look for her to realize that it had to be battle damage. Something very powerful had exploded just outside the ship. The jagged, fractured hull bent inward from the force. Unfortunately for them, the breach was almost 20 meters above their heads.

"We'll have to climb," Lieutenant Reese said. "Alpha team, you have the lead."

Apparently, the magnetic equipment built into the marine armor was strong enough to support their weight at the bottom of a lake. The men scaled the hull and went inside. When the all-clear came back, the remainder of the marines followed them up.

A quick check revealed that she also had magnetic equipment in her suit, but she decided to use the grav unit to float up.

Talbot looked over as she hovered next to him while he climbed. "Show-off."

"You're just jealous."

"Maybe a little."

They passed through the blown out portion of the ship until it intersected a corridor. As the marines moved through the dark water, their suit lights revealed a deck covered by a thin layer of silt. They kicked up small clouds as they moved forward and revealed things under it that she'd rather have not seen. Bones sheathed in graphene. Either commandos or Pale Ones.

She spotted a pharmacology unit in the muck, and strands of artificial muscle. Seeing the same kind of equipment that she had inside her just lying there made her shudder.

One of the location markers on the bulkhead told Kelsey they were on a lower deck, one used mainly for storage. She brought up the map of *Courageous*. The computer center was up and forward.

"I have directions," Kelsey said on the command loop. "There's a stairwell at the next intersection. If we go up five decks and then go forward, we'll be in the computer center. There's a good possibility that the AI is located there."

"Good work, Princess." Reese switched to the general channel. "Bravo team, lead the way up at the next intersection. Five decks and then forward. Keep a sharp eye out."

They entered the stairwell and made their way up slowly. The odds of any equipment still working in this section of the ship had to be close to zero, but that would change at some point. The AI probably wasn't underwater. That meant they'd find an environment suitable for Pale Ones before they reached the AI. That was the most dangerous part of the mission.

"We're on the proper deck, LT," one of the marines said. "There's an isolation hatch ahead of us. It's closed and seems to be powered."

"Stand by."

The rest of the team made it to the deck and spread out. The isolation hatch looked as though it hadn't opened in many years.

Reese wiped off the manual controls and tapped in a code. The hatch ponderously slid open. A rush of water into the airlock pulled everyone forward a bit, but Kelsey quickly regained her balance.

"Okay, I'm impressed," she said. "How did you know the code on a ship that you'd never been on? One in the hands of the enemy?"

Reese grinned through his faceplate. "I've been studying, too. Every ship in the Empire has these things, and it's possible that a rescue party would need to get through them. Unless the captain overrides the codes, any marine CO knows them. Something I'm sure never occurred to an AI that knows the Empire fell half a millennium ago."

He gestured for the first group of marines to go in. "Bravo, secure the other side and wait for us. If you run into the enemy, push them back."

The squad cycled through, and the door slid shut with a slow finality. She watched through their suit cams as the other door opened and water rushed out into the corridor. There were no Pale Ones in sight. The next squad moved into the airlock as soon as the doors cycled again.

Lieutenant Reese led the last team through. Her suit told her the air was foul but breathable once they reached the other side. That meant they might run into Pale Ones. The lack of them probably meant that the AI hadn't noted the hatch cycling. It probably wasn't registering anymore.

They advanced slowly, ready for resistance, but nothing materialized. Kelsey could see the massive hatch sealing off the computing center ahead. Talbot grinned at her. "We made it! We're going to take this thing out."

That's when his eyes rolled up in his head and he collapsed. They all did. Everyone except Kelsey.

It must be the antiboarding weapons. She'd have expected them to fail over the centuries. She doubted her implants were enough to protect her, so it had to be the armor. Commandos *were* badass. A quick check of the marines' suits confirmed they were still alive. If the damned AI kept stunning them, though, that might change. She had to end this now.

She tried to access the hatch, but it didn't respond. A touch on the access panel failed to open it, too. One look confirmed that her rifle wouldn't do more than scratch it. Time for the big guns.

A shrug put her plasma rifle in her hands. The marines' armor should protect them from the heat. She hoped. Kelsey walked back to them and took aim at the hatch from as far back as she could and fired.

The bright bit of plasma struck the hatch and blossomed into a wave of intense heat. It melted the hatch and a lot of the corridor beyond the computer room. The armored compartment held up except for a man sized opening beside the hatch. The other side of the corridor blew out in a huge bubble.

Note to self: maybe plasma wasn't the best weapon to use inside a ship.

Kelsey verified the hole went all the way into the computer center and dove through the opening. She avoided the glowing metal along the edge. She didn't trust her suit that much.

The computer control center looked exactly like the one on *Courageous*, though in a lot worse shape. It looked like there'd been a firefight in here. Scattered bones told the tale of a stout defense that had fallen under heavy fire. The bodies had long ago decayed, and the uniforms had mostly rotted. A few suits of armor told her that some of the defenders had been marines.

"You cannot win," a genderless voice said from the overhead speakers. "Yield."

"It seems like I can win," Kelsey said. She hefted the plasma rifle for emphasis. "That wall between us isn't going to stop me. You yield."

"This unit knew your kind would come. It prepared."

A snarl behind her caused her to whirl. A Pale One glared at her through the hole in the wall. She pulled her pistol before it climbed into the compartment and fired. It fell, its head shattered.

One of the intact consoles to the side of the compartment came to life. It showed the corridor filled with the things. They were already dragging the marines away. Even more of them bunched in the corridor, ready to fight. They held weapons, just like the ones on the asteroid.

"You cannot defeat this unit. Yield and you will be granted a swift death."

She tried to access the ship's systems with her implants, but they wouldn't connect. The AI had locked her out.

Her foot brushed against the bones of a corpse. Part of her mind recognized the rank and department insignia on the collar. The body belonged to the chief engineer. He or she must've been working at this console when the rebels killed the crew and took the ship.

She touched the console, and to her surprise, it lit up with the controls available. The chief engineer must've unlocked it before the rebels killed him or her. The AI, which she now knew had to be the ship's computer, hadn't locked it down. Maybe it couldn't.

Kelsey didn't pretend to know what ship's systems did what, but she wouldn't have long before those things could get through the cooling hole. She'd have even less time before they started killing the marines.

The display on the console was for the ship's computer. Maybe the chief engineer was going to wipe it. There was another set of commands up for the environmental systems. It looked like he was also trying to decompress the ship. He'd almost made it. The command was right there.

She found the menu controlling computer access. It seemed to be for adding authorized users. She hit the key to add a user. The console prompted her implants for a serial number. She gave it hers.

The AI must've ordered the Pale Ones to attack, because they came through the hole in the bulkhead even though they burned themselves badly. The first one in knocked her away from the console and beat on her armor.

Kelsey shot him. The rest jumped on her and started trying to rip her suit off her. With their strength, that wasn't impossible.

She tried to access the computer with her implants. She almost screamed when the AI issued a command to reboot itself. She had no idea how long that took. Presumably long enough for the Pale Ones to kill her.

They pinned her by sheer numbers, and she felt a scream rising in her throat. They were going to kill her. Or make her one of them. She'd failed.

Searching desperately for another option, she connected with the console. It allowed her in. She instructed it to initiate decompression, praying that the system would let the command go through. Anything designed to vent a ship's atmosphere quickly into space would allow a lot of water in fast. She prayed the marines' combat suits kept them alive.

For a moment, nothing seemed to happen, but then she heard a distant roaring sound. Water.

The hot wall hissed as a wave of water washed over it. In seconds, water rushed into the compartment and engulfed her. She turned her head away from the Pale Ones and shut off her external audio. There was no need for her to watch them drown. She felt more than heard the AI short out behind her. Hopefully, the main power circuits wouldn't fry her and the marines.

This fight was over. Kelsey prayed that Jared could parlay his implants into a chance to retake the ship before it was too late for all of them.

30

Something bright and fast flew past Jared and struck the man with the gun. The mutineer let out a choked scream as he staggered backward with a meat cleaver half buried in his chest. Two marines rushed in after him while Sergeant Coulter knelt beside Jared and put a kitchen knife to the first man's throat. He stopped struggling.

"Cookie's going to need a new cleaver," the marine said with a grin. "That's just too handy not to keep."

"I'll replace it out of my paycheck. Get this guy into the lab and tie him up."

"Aye, sir." The marines heaved the prisoner to his feet and searched him thoroughly. The two that dragged him off were Pentagarans. They were far from gentle about it.

Stone walked out from the room beside them and shook her head. "That one's gone. If I had access to the medical center, I might have been able to save him, but he bled out."

"Sorry, Doc," the marine NCO said. "I didn't have a lot of choice." He didn't sound particularly upset about the man's death.

The chief medical officer shook her head. "No blame intended, Sergeant. I'm a Fleet officer. I understand people die in combat. Better them than us."

Jared closed the hatch to the compartment with the dead body once the marines had searched the corpse. They'd clean up once they took the ship back. Until then, they needed to keep anyone else from knowing they'd been there. A handy cloth took care of the blood on the deck.

The lab was a scene of organized chaos as he closed the hatch. The scientific team was producing pistols and ammunition from various cabinets. They had a few rifles, too.

He found his attention centered on a suit of dark-grey combat armor on a stand. Unlike the armored vacuum suits used by his Imperial Marines, this one's faceplate was solid armor like the rest of the suit. It must get its view through scanners. It looked intimidating as hell. "Is this operational? Can one of the marines use it?"

One of the scientists rushed over. "I think it's mostly functional, but it requires implants to operate."

"So much for that idea."

Coulter stepped up beside him and looked at the armor. "We can't use it, but you can."

Jared snorted and shook his head. "I remember seeing Princess Kelsey struggle to learn how to control her enhanced musculature. I can only imagine how useless I would be in a fight with this. I'd be flopping all over the deck."

"Maybe, but you'd be protected a lot better than you are right now," Coulter said. "If you die, our best chance at regaining control of this ship dies with you. In the suit, you could probably take a shot to the chest from point-blank range and live. Far be it from me to give the captain an order, but get into the damned suit."

"I don't even know how to do that."

"I watched Talbot work with the princess." The marine removed the helmet and opened the armor up at the back. He helped Jared into the suit, sealed it up, and locked the helmet into place. The darkness made Jared feel a bit claustrophobic, but that wasn't a fear one could really have in Fleet. Then the displays in front of his face came to life.

He could see Coulter clearly, as though there was nothing between them. The display was one of the highest resolutions he'd ever seen. Then it dawned on him that the display wasn't on the inside of the helmet. It was in his mind. The implants were feeding directly into his visual cortex.

That realization was so powerful that it took his breath away. He'd known it was possible from viewing the video feeds earlier, but this was different. It was completely overriding his eyes. No doubt he was staring sightlessly into the darkness of his helmet. Could piloting a ship be the same? Would he feel as though he was flying through space without a vessel at all?

He raised his arm and flexed his fingers. They felt somewhat awkward but manageable. He wouldn't be running any races, and that was fine. Kelsey had the muscles to use the suit as a weapon. He had to work hard just to make it move. No doubt her enhanced muscles made using it as effortless as thought. He'd just have to make do.

He activated the armor's external speakers. "I'll need some weapons. Preferably something I won't accidentally shoot you with."

"Captain, how about this?" one of the scientists asked.

He handed Jared a rifle with a thick barrel. There was no opening for projectiles. "This is a neural disruptor. The princess said she could use her implants to control the power levels. I'm told it can be lethal or just stun."

"This would've been useful a few minutes ago." Jared accessed the weapon and found it already set to stun. That made sense. Only an idiot would have a weapon like this preset to lethal levels.

Coulter attached a holster to Jared's thigh and slid a similar pistol into it. "Backup weapon. I'll put the power packs in the inserts along your waist." He did so and then handed Jared a knife. "This is Old Empire. I wouldn't try the edge. I saw the princess gouge a bulkhead with one. You might be able to cut your way out of a compartment with enough time."

Jared walked over to the prisoner. They'd tied him to a chair. He shrank back from Jared, eyes wide in fear. Jared leaned forward until his helmet was inches from the man's terrified face.

"In case we've never met, I'm Commander Jared Mertz, *Courageous*'s commanding officer. Your name is irrelevant. You're a mutineer. Under Fleet regulations, I can execute you. No board of inquiry. No appeals. No extenuating circumstances. I'm judge, jury, and executioner if I decide it's warranted."

He paused a beat to allow that to sink in. "You can bargain that death sentence down to some lesser penalty by telling me everything you know. Be concise, because if I decide that my time is better spent retaking this ship, I'll shoot you and be done with it."

Jared pulled the pistol from his holster and put it under the man's chin. He set it to kill. He wasn't bluffing, and he wanted that to carry through in his voice. "Talk or die. Who are the mutineers, where are they, and what are their plans?"

The man started talking fast. "Our leader's name is Rawlins. He brought a team of us with him to learn how to run this ship. I'm not sure who he works for, but he takes orders from above. He always calls the leader 'his patron' when he talks about him. He's on the bridge with his senior people. Most of the rest are in engineering, but a few people are in the computer center. They isolated the ship's computer, so they have to do some things manually. Some of the marines are guarding the prisoners."

Jared grinned without humor. No doubt the guy wondered how they'd slipped out. He'd just have to keep wondering. "Are all the prisoners in the mess halls?"

"Except you and the people he left on the planet and shipyard."

"How close are we to the flip point, and what are the plans once the ship gets back to Pentagaran space?"

"I think we're almost there. Maybe another half hour. I don't know what the plans are. He just said that our arrival would set off a chain of events that would put his patron in control. That's all I know. I swear."

Jared reset the pistol to stun, stepped back, and aimed it at the man's head. He made certain no one was standing behind the man. "Thank you. I commute your sentence to oblivion." He fired.

The pale blue beam struck the man in the head, and he slumped. Stone stepped up and checked his pulse. "He's alive. Was that the same thing they used on us? Would you really have killed him?"

"Probably and yes." Everyone had finished gathering weapons and was watching him. "We're as ready as we're going to be. Good luck, everyone. Try to keep them from knowing we're coming, but don't hesitate to shoot if they see you. Remember, I'm as proud of you as I could possibly be. Go."

They left the prisoner unguarded. Either they'd win and come back for him, or they'd lose and it didn't matter. The fight would be over before the man woke up.

They returned to the maintenance shafts. He estimated how long it would take them to get into position, and they agreed on a time to attack. If someone went early, it might spell doom. Graves led the assault on the bridge, Baxter on engineering, and Jared led the group going to the computer center. Doctor Stone split her people between the three groups. The few scientists with them brought up the rear.

It felt like it took forever to reach the computer center. They had to wait for the rest of the teams to get into position, so he made his way as close as he could and accessed the video feeds. There were three technicians in the computer center and two marines in full combat armor in the corridor. The main hatch was open, but he knew they could close it at a moment's notice.

The closest maintenance access was thirty meters down the corridor from the computer center. No way could they slip up on the guards unnoticed. He hoped the rifle had the range to take them out.

"Coulter, you might want to take this rifle. I've set it to stun."

"Can I even fire it?"

Jared hadn't considered that. A quick check showed him that he could lock the weapon down to authorized users by implant ID, but he didn't have to. "You can fire it."

His chrono vibrated. It was time. He drew his pistol and waited for the marines to line up behind them. When they were ready, he gave Coulter a nod.

The marine NCO opened the hatch and stepped into the corridor, his rifle already up and firing. The blue bolt just missed the man looking their way. The man shouted and raised his rifle to return fire.

That meant he caught the second bolt in the chest and dropped. Jared prayed and fired at the other man. He missed, and the mutineer jumped into the computer center.

The marines were already running for the hatch, so he ran with them. The hatch slid shut almost in their faces.

"Shit!" Coulter hit the admittance switch, but the hatch remained closed.

Jared sent an implant command to the door with his command override. The hatch slid open, much to the shock of the men inside. Jared shot the marine first and then the tech with the communications unit in his hand. Coulter shot the second tech.

The last technician shot Jared with a pistol. The slug ricocheted off his faceplate. He shot the man more out of reflex than anything else.

Jared's lead computer technician ran into the room and slid to a stop in front of the main console. He tapped the controls furiously. "Computer offline. Booting. Access channels restored. When it comes up, the computer will have complete systems access."

Jared hoped that meant the computer would immediately lock down the systems and stun any mutineers, even if the bad guys knocked them all out right now. "How long until it's up?"

"Less than a minute. I can't control the antiboarding weapons. They're slaved to the bridge."

He accessed the ship's systems. He couldn't isolate them, either, but he could lock them out just like Baxter could in engineering. They accepted his shutdown command authorization and went offline just moments before an order to activate came in from the bridge.

"I locked them out," he shouted. "We have a chance."

Jared opened a channel to the chief engineer's appropriated communication unit. "This is Mertz. We have the computer center. Thirty seconds to computer activation, and I've locked out the antiboarding weapons. What's your status?"

"We're in engineering. We're exchanging fire with the mutineers. Give me… one second…"

The main overhead lights went out, and the emergency backups came on dimly.

"Main power cut," Baxter said. "Oops. Someone just dumped the flip capacitors. I'm so clumsy. This ship won't be flipping anywhere until you say so. This won't stop the computer from coming online."

"Can you hold?"

"It looks like the mutineers are giving up. We have things under control here."

The screens around Jared came to life, and he felt the computer's presence through his implants. *Courageous online, Captain. Status?*

"Mutineers have the bridge. We think we've restored control in engineering. We're trying to take the bridge. There are other hostiles outside the mess halls. That's where the crew is. Can you access the antiboarding weapons?"

The computer switched to audible communication. "The boarding suppression systems have been placed on remote control. This unit sees that you have locked them out. That is all this unit could do until the modifications are removed."

"Hopefully we won't need them. Coulter, take your men and hunt down the guards. We'll lead you to them. I'm locking the computer center hatches until this is over."

"Aye, sir." The marines followed him out. Jared closed the armored hatch behind them and engaged the manual lock so that no one else could use a surprise code to open it. They'd have to burn him out.

Jared took off his helmet and called Graves. "Status?"

Someone else answered. "Ensign Turner, sir. They repulsed our attack. Commander Graves is hurt bad. The medics are rushing him to the medical center. We've called on them to surrender. They refused. We're about to make another try."

"Hold for a minute. I'll try to talk them out."

He opened a channel to the bridge. For a moment, it didn't look like they would answer. Then the image of a man bleeding from a cut on his forehead appeared. It was not Rawlins.

"You," he snarled. "How the hell did you get out of the mess hall?"

The man looked vaguely familiar, but Jared couldn't put a name to him. "Put Rawlins on. It's time to end this."

The man laughed roughly. "You're going to need better communications gear than even the Old Empire had to do that. He's dead. You'll deal with me."

"Fine. We have control of the ship. The main computer is back online, and I control engineering. My people are hunting you down in the corridors as we speak. Surrender the bridge."

The man shook his head. "The king will have our heads, even if you don't. You want your bridge back? Come and take it." He grinned without the slightest bit of humor. "Oh, and I have some bad news for you. Rawlins retargeted the asteroid on your precious princess when he retrieved our men from it. It's on a ballistic course, so she won't even see it coming. With the jammers in place, you don't even have enough time to warn her that death is coming. I'll see you in Hell." The transmission ended.

Jared's heart jumped into his throat as he called the ensign back. "Take the bridge right now. Medical care for any survivors, but don't take chances."

"Aye, sir. Turner out."

He opened a channel to engineering and started giving orders as soon as Baxter appeared. "Get us headed back to Erorsi Prime at flank speed. Redline the drives. They're dropping a kinetic strike onto Kelsey and the team."

The news wiped the smile off Baxter's face. "I'll wring every kilometer per second from the drives that I can. Engineering out."

Jared ran his hand across his face. He hoped the man was lying, but he couldn't count on it. He had to find a way to get the ship back to Erorsi in time to save his sister. Even if he needed a miracle.

31

I t took hours to strip the data units from the flooded battlecruiser and load them aboard the pinnace. Kelsey doubted they would be of much use without the assistance of people who knew the technology. That meant Bell and his associates.

Thankfully, they'd probably be happy to help. Even though her team had failed to capture a functional AI, the Pale Ones converging on the mountain facility had never made it further than the foothills. They'd milled around for a while and then dispersed.

She stood on the shores of the lake and stared at the sky. Had Jared stopped the mutineers? She prayed so, but they wouldn't know until they made it to the shipyards.

That's when she noticed a streak of light high up in the atmosphere. No, several streaks. She wondered if they were meteors.

Her implants popped up notice of an incoming transmission. Priority One. That sounded important. She accepted it.

An image of her brother appeared. "Kelsey! The mutineers redirected the asteroid back on your position! You have to get out of there right now! Hurry!" The message began repeating, but that ceased as the streaks above her exploded in little puffs of light.

She whirled toward the pinnace and opened the general marine channel. "Incoming kinetic strike! Everyone into the pinnace right now! Drop everything and run!"

Kelsey brought up the locator beacons for all the marines. Thank God no one was in the water. Most of the men were in or around the pinnace, but a few were inside the transmitter building. Including Talbot.

"Talbot! Move it!"

"I've almost got the data unit with the transmission records," he said. "Thirty seconds. A minute, tops."

Cursing, she ran past the pinnace and into the building, dodging the other men as they came boiling out. Talbot had a data unit partly extracted from the computer. She grabbed it with one hand and ripped it out. She snatched him up with the other and bolted.

Her enhanced musculature and powered armor got them both outside in a hurry. She triggered the grav assist and leapt for the pinnace. Her armor took them almost twenty meters into the air and dropped them right behind the last of the men running up the ramp.

"Lift off!" Reese shouted as he raised the ramp behind them. "Maximum acceleration. Head for the mountains."

Kelsey glared at Talbot. "Now who's making someone crazy? Have you lost your mind?" She shook the data unit at him. "This isn't worth your life."

"Actually, it might be. This isn't just a log of messages. It's recordings of the content, too. I only had time to scan a few messages, but I think these are critically important. But thanks for the lift."

"Everyone into your seats and activate the crash harnesses." Reese shoved the data unit into a storage compartment. "Since we don't have to go stealth, we'll be over the mountains in fifteen minutes. How far off is the strike?"

Kelsey shook her head. "I don't know. The recording didn't say."

"Well, we'll just have to hope we have time."

That's when she picked up something high above them on the pinnace's scanners. It was closing in at an incredible rate of speed. "Here it comes! Impact on the lake in just a few seconds!"

"Get us on the deck," Reese yelled at the pilots as he strapped himself in. "Find some cover."

The streak in the sky descended with deceptive slowness, almost crawling toward the ground as the pinnace dove for cover. They almost made it to a ridgeline ahead of them before the sky behind them lit up with intolerable brightness.

"How long does it take a shock wave to—"

A giant hand smashed the pinnace from the sky. It tumbled like a toy hurled by an angry child. The pilots jammed on the grav drives at the last moment and flipped them upright just before they plowed into the forest.

Kelsey must've lost consciousness, because the pinnace was a smoldering wreck when she woke up.

Her restraints resisted her attempts to free herself, so she ripped them off. A few marines staggered around, but most hung limply from their crash harnesses. Her armor pinged their suits. Some of them were dead, but most were alive, if in bad shape.

The fact that any of them had lived through the crash was a testament to the engineers who'd designed the pinnace and its safety systems.

Then she remembered the pilots. She couldn't sense their condition. She forced her way onto the flight deck and discovered it had taken the worst of the impact. The pinnace had dug a furrow like a plow, knocking aside trees and rocks as it gouged the ground.

One of the pilots hung from her harness, staring numbly at the stump of her right arm. The other pilot was missing, a jagged hole in the fuselage where he'd sat. The forest outside burned.

Kelsey ripped some wiring from the shattered control consoles and tied a tourniquet on the woman's arm just as Talbot heaved himself onto the flight deck. She was relieved to see him. She was almost as relieved to see the medic behind him.

She stepped back beside Talbot and watched the medic treat the injured pilot. "I didn't think we were going to make it. I thought we were going to die."

"Me, too. I can't imagine how they got us down in one piece."

That's when the shakes hit her. They hit her so hard that her teeth chattered.

Talbot pulled her into a hug. "It's going to be okay. Just let it go."

And she did. The tears came pouring from her. Tears of relief, tears of grief, and tears of raw terror.

* * *

THEY WERE STILL BRINGING the injured out of the crashed pinnace when another pinnace howled in from above like a roaring beast of prey. It had barely touched the ground before it disgorged marines who rushed in to help with the rescue operations. A second pinnace landed right behind it with Doctor Stone and her medical teams.

Jared came out at a run right behind them. "Kelsey! Are you all right?"

"I'm fine," she said through her still-tight chest. "Most of us made it, but some of the marines are badly hurt. One of the pilots is somewhere back there." She gestured toward the raging forest fire behind them. Of course, except for the scar they'd made while crashing, everything around them was on fire.

"We'll start a search. I'm glad you got our message. I was afraid we weren't going to get back in time."

"What were those things you sent? Probes?"

He shook his head. "Five missiles. We added a communications package onto them and fired them as soon as we got in range of the planet. They were the only things fast enough to beat the asteroid."

Doctor Stone took the worst of the injured onto her pinnace and lifted off for *Courageous*. It took another hour for the rest of them to recover all the data units they'd captured, and to find the pilot's body.

Jared filled her in on the mutiny and his fight to regain control of the ship, and she recounted their attack on the AI. He shook his head when she finished. "We were both lucky. Luckier than we deserve to be."

"I know. I've been loaded down with all these implants and now had an asteroid dropped on my head. My father is going to be pissed. I hope you like Thule."

Once they had everything secure, they lifted off and headed for the mountains. They landed in almost the same place as Kelsey had that morning. She shook her head. Had it only been that morning? It felt like an eternity ago.

She led her half brother to the hidden entrance, which opened as soon as they arrived. Da Silva was waiting to escort them to the same conference room that she'd visited earlier. Once again, Reginald Bell was waiting for her. Alone this time.

The old man gestured for them to sit. "We found some sturdier chairs, Princess. You look like you need to sit down."

Kelsey sat wearily. "Reginald Bell, this is our expedition commander, Captain Jared Mertz. Jared, Reginald Bell."

"Captain Mertz. It's a great pleasure to meet you, though I wish it had been under better circumstances." He straightened and saluted, his fist to his chest. "Ensign Bell reporting, Captain."

Jared returned the salute and extended his hand to the old man. "It's an honor to meet you, sir. I'm so sorry that we weren't able to stop the kinetic strike. I hope your people made it through."

The older man clasped Jared's hand in his. "They designed this facility to survive a near miss from just such a weapon. I'm pleased to say it is a credit to its designers. I'm much more concerned with the long-term effects of the impact. We're guessing that there will be months of darkness under a global debris cloud and years of bitter winters. The roving tribes of primitives will suffer greatly."

"I wish we could offer more help there, but it will be weeks before any other ships can arrive. Even then, the scale of this disaster is beyond imagining. We'll do what we can, but it won't be nearly enough."

"We appreciate everything that you can do. I can hardly credit that you've brought *Courageous* back to life. I never expected to meet a Fleet officer again."

Jared spread his hands. "Seeing everything about *Courageous*, I'm almost hesitant to call myself Fleet. Meeting a true Fleet officer is an unexpected dream come true. If you only knew how many questions I have."

"Don't raise us to mythical heights, Captain. I'd imagine your Fleet is much like the one I served. Good men and women doing the best they could. Technology doesn't define who we are. Was the impact a rebel counterattack?"

"More like a last gasp, though I'm afraid the Pale Ones aren't directly responsible for it in the end. It's a long story, but the important part is that we've defeated the rebels. The controlling AI is gone."

The man blinked in surprise. "You're certain?"

Kelsey nodded. "There was a wrecked battlecruiser in a lake. We entered it, and I communicated with it before I shut it down. Then the kinetic strike blew it up. No mistake."

Bell shook his head as though trying to clear away cobwebs. "It's hard to believe. Can this nightmare truly be over?"

Jared put a hand on the older man's shoulder. "It is. We've defeated the rebels and freed Erorsi. I'm just sorry we couldn't stop the asteroid. Erorsi was such a beautiful world."

"And it will be again. We recovered from the initial bombardment. We'll survive this one, too. I think this calls for a drink. I happen to have some truly magnificent brandy in my quarters. I've been saving it for just this moment. I won't tell my doctor if you don't."

Jared shook his head with an expression of regret. "I'm afraid we can't stay. Events are driving us back to the system next door. Pentagar. We're on a tight schedule. Can we evacuate any of your people?"

"Let me call the others. They're helping put things right after the earthquake." He walked slowly to the conference table and called someone.

Jared put his hand on Kelsey's shoulder. "I wish we didn't have to rush back. I wasn't kidding about all the questions. We might have all the data files imaginable on *Courageous*, but we don't have any experience using the technology. He was a serving Fleet officer. The things he's learned about tactics would be invaluable."

"Maybe," she said. "Maybe not. Things didn't work out so well against the rebels. Don't be blinded by our vision of the Old Empire. We've crawled back to our feet after a knockout punch. That's huge. What you've accomplished on this mission alone is the stuff of legend."

His skeptical expression made her laugh. "Think about it, Jared. You've brought an Old Empire ship back to life. You've met the rebels and defeated them. You captured an entire planetary system with one ship. Tell me one of your contemporary officers that can claim anything like that."

"You're exaggerating my role in all this. You played a bigger hand in this than I did."

She shook her head. "We've done it as a team. Bet nobody saw that coming."

He smiled. "No. I'm certain no one imagined anything like what we've done together. I was wrong to want you to stay home. You're the soul of this expedition. I'm even warming to the half-sister part."

His words made her feel more than a bit guilty. He still didn't know that she wasn't genetically his sister. To his credit, she imagined that wouldn't make one bit of difference to him.

Bell ended his call and walked back over to them. "We've discussed the matter and decided that we're not leaving. This is our world. It needs us. We'll send a team of people back with you, if you have no objection. It behooves us to get to know you and our neighbors, and to get what help we can for the savages living in the wild."

"I understand. Will you be joining us?"

"I shouldn't, but I long to walk the corridors of my old ship one last time. My days are numbered, and the chance will likely never come again.

Our party will be several dozen people, if that's acceptable. We should be ready to go in an hour."

Her half brother grinned. "We'd be happy to have them. If you have any technical specialists that might come along, I know some people would love to talk to them. And we have the Pale Ones' data units to get into. They're water damaged, and we can't chance ruining them."

Bell nodded. "Our technical know-how has slipped some from the days of old, but I'll add a few people to our roster that can help. That's what neighbors do."

*　*　*

AFTER THEY DOCKED, Kelsey watched the old man walk out into *Courageous* with tears in her eyes.

The computer spoke from the overheads and in her implants. Perhaps in all their implants. "Welcome aboard, Ensign Bell."

Bell spoke softly. "It's good to be back, *Courageous*."

"Have you returned to take command?"

Kelsey froze. She'd never considered that possibility. The man was a Fleet officer, lawfully assigned to this ship. He was part of her official chain of command. Would he take the ship away from them?

"No, *Courageous*," Bell said. "My day is done. The Empire of old is gone. You have a new captain, and a damned good one from what I can see. I hereby affirm Jared Mertz's status as a Fleet officer and endorse his command of this vessel. He's your captain now."

Bell turned to Jared. "If an old man might presume on your goodwill, though, I'd love to visit the bridge. I was never senior enough to go there when I served."

Jared gestured to the lift. "It's under repair, but we can certainly stop in. Then we can go to the operations center while we break orbit."

Kelsey followed them with a smile on her face.

32

Once Jared had seen their guests to their quarters and assigned crew members to act as guides—and guards to a degree—he made his way to the bridge with a silent Kelsey at his side. Engineering technicians were replacing shattered consoles, and the place smelled of fried circuitry and blood. Miraculously, his console was undamaged, though splattered with gore.

He cleaned it up with supplies from the cubby in the attached head and sat down. The console lit when he interfaced his implants with it. The ship's status was mostly green. The bridge showed red, but that would change before they flipped.

Their combat status was green, though they were now critically short of missiles. There were several dozen missiles that had failed inspection that they might be able to get ready, but he wasn't going to count on it. If things hit the fan, it was going to get ugly.

Kelsey cleaned off a seat near him, not bothering to hide her distaste. "If our mutineers intended to kick off an insurrection when they came through the flip point, then how do we avoid starting it ourselves?"

"The computer says no messages were sent back to Pentagar through the probes at the flip point. The mutineers only had a few dozen people aboard. Their patron couldn't possibly be certain their attack on *Courageous* would succeed. So it won't be our arrival that triggers the coup."

He rubbed his face tiredly. "Not even this ship could survive a bombardment by the defensive orbitals on the Pentagaran side of the flip point, so Rawlins must've had a plan to get clear quickly. He could send a signal of some kind to his patron then."

She nodded. "Probably something innocuous. Why raise suspicions ahead of time? Have their quarters been searched?"

"From top to bottom. We didn't find anything suspicious. None of the personal communications devices would even interface with *Courageous*. I had them examined anyway. There's no telling which contacts on them might lead to their patron. If any."

Jared slammed his palm against the console. "Dammit. We can't just let this son of a bitch get away. He'll just keep building his organization and strike when we leave."

"We have some information. When Rawlins identified himself as a commander, it might have been a real rank. I met him once before on *Best Deal*. He told me his name was Jacob, but he looked enlisted. What name does the ship have on file for him?"

He queried the computer. "Jacob Randal. An enlisted engineering technician. The first name might or might not be real. Let's assume it is. It would be damned awkward to fail to respond to your own name. The last name is similar enough to catch your attention. So let's also assume he actually is Commander Jacob Rawlins of the Pentagaran Navy. They could probably confirm that with his remains. If we can find someone to ask who isn't in on the plot."

Kelsey pursed her lips. "We can't really be sure of anyone, except the king and Elise. Probably Commodore Sanders. I find it difficult to believe he's in on something like this, but can we trust him completely?"

"We can't doubt every friend we've made. Someone is going to need to take steps to see that the Pentagaran Navy doesn't revolt."

He consulted the time and their ETA through his implants. That would take a lot of getting used to. They had a few hours remaining before they transitioned. "I think we start off pretending nothing is amiss."

"Then the patron knows his or her minion isn't in command of *Courageous*," she added. "If we never let on that anything is wrong, the patron will have to assume his team is still in place, learning what they need to take over when more Pentagarans can be assigned to the ship."

"I think so, too. The question is, how do we track him down?"

"Someone assigned Rawlins to this ship under a fake name. Or someone else's name. A senior officer made that call. Besides, only someone in a significant position of authority could orchestrate a military coup. The person or persons will be highly placed but one of a singular clique of people. Flag officers. If we can get back in one piece, the odds of individual ships going rogue go way down."

That agreed with his assessment. "I can't make a call from here, so I'll do it from my office once we flip. I'll fill them in on our success and ask for an immediate conference with Elise. She'll bring some of her senior Fleet officers, but once we fill her in, she can take steps to take this apart without alarming the other senior commanders. If we control the communications, it won't matter if one of them is with her. They won't dare reveal themselves."

The lift doors opened, and Talbot came out onto the bridge. He slowed as he surveyed the destruction. "Wow. They really put up a fight."

Jared sighed. "A completely needless one. They knew we were going to win. Once they lost their edge, it was inevitable. What can I do for you, Senior Sergeant?"

The marine held out a tablet. "I downloaded my combat suit's vid files to this tablet. I found something in the transmitter building that you need to see. I was able to access the AI's communications records before we ran. The data storage unit is down in the lab, so hopefully we can get more. Most of the transmissions were audio only, but some were video. That caught my attention."

Jared took the tablet and held it so Kelsey could see it as well. The vid player was already up, so he hit play.

The console that Talbot had been using in the transmitter building was small and filthy, but it worked. Jared could make out a list of files. The marine selected one marked as video.

The video showed a man on what was obviously the bridge of a spaceship. Old Empire from the layout. The man wore a Fleet uniform with commander's tabs.

He bowed so steeply that they could momentarily see the top of his head. Then he looked straight into the screen and began speaking. "This man brings greetings from your brothers in the Empire, Lord. He apologizes for the lack of supplies last year. The freighter disappeared several worlds before yours. I've brought extra implant hardware to make good any shortages. Are there any other needs this man can fulfil for you?"

The AI spoke in a toneless voice. "You may take the immature humans from this unit's latest culling. This unit requires nothing more. It has the situation under control, and its plan is almost ready to execute."

He heard Kelsey shouting in the recording about an incoming kinetic strike. Talbot killed the vid and began struggling to remove the data unit from the computer. That was where the recording ended.

Jared's blood ran cold. "How long ago was this recorded?"

"That vid was recorded about ten months ago, sir."

Kelsey leaned forward, shock written all over her face. "What? That can't be right. The Empire fell. Look at the Pale Ones. How is this even possible?"

Talbot retrieved his tablet. "The vid calls happen about once a year. There were some years that there weren't any, but most happen once a year about two months from now. I think our understanding of what happened to the Old Empire needs to be revised."

Jared nodded. "This just became high priority. Get some of Mister Bell's people to help Doctor Leonard and Carl Owlet. We need to know who they are and what they were doing with the Pale Ones. Examine every vid on that data unit."

"Aye, sir." Talbot nodded to Kelsey and left the bridge.

She looked at Jared with her eyes wide. "What does it mean?"

"It means something of the Old Empire survived. We need to end the Pentagaran rebellion as quickly as possible. Our lives might depend on it."

* * *

THE CREW WAS at battle stations when they flipped to Pentagar. The only concession Jared made to stealth was to keep his screens down. The main computer would raise them at the first sign of hostile action, faster than any human could react. Their missile and beam batteries were on hot standby, ready to fire at a moment's notice. Zia would go from passive scanners to active at the first sign of trouble.

Thankfully, there wasn't any. They arrived without incident and coasted out of the defensive globe with only cheerful greetings sent their way.

He sent an outline of their successes in the Erorsi system and requested the crown princess and her staff meet him in Pentagaran orbit. There would be a significant Pentagaran Navy presence there, so *Courageous* would remain on alert.

A cutter asked for approach permission once they slipped into Pentagar orbit, indicating it had Elise aboard. He gave them the green light and headed for the docking bay. Kelsey and Lieutenant Reese met him there. The marine wore unpowered combat armor. Kelsey had a nice dress on.

Jared gave the marine officer his final instructions. "I want a squad of marines just around any corner we happen to be at. Stay out of sight, but come running if there's trouble."

"I think I should be with you, sir. If someone attacks you or the princess, I could react at once. The antiboarding weapons aren't designed to take down a single person."

"I'm armed. Better yet, Princess Kelsey is armed. If someone is stupid enough to cause trouble, we can hold them off until you arrive."

Reese frowned at Kelsey. "Where's your weapon?"

"Just you never mind," she said tartly. "Somewhere I can get to it quickly if I have to. Besides, my hands are more than enough for anything but a gun. We don't need to spook them. We've moved past the need for an armed escort. Your presence would make them suspicious."

The sound of the cutter docking sent Reese to join his men in an adjoining compartment.

Kelsey pointedly glanced at the flechette pistol on Jared's hip. "Can you use that thing?"

"I went down to the range and practiced. I even got my implants to assist in aiming it. I shouldn't need it, though."

"Let's hope not."

The docking hatch slid open. Two Pentagaran Navy sailors led the way out, with Elise right behind them. Lord Admiral Shrike and Commodore Sanders completed her party.

She grinned widely as she came up to shake Jared's hand. "I hear you've taken the Pale Ones down. That's wonderful news! The incessant attacks are finally over!" She pulled Kelsey into a hug. "You and your people have saved us. Again. It's getting to be quite the habit."

Jared shook the men's hands. Sanders seemed elated, Shrike a little subdued.

"We've got a presentation with video in the conference room. We also have some other news that you'll be interested in. We found holdouts on Erorsi. A facility that survived the invasion, with the descendants of the original staff still there."

Elise stared at him. "That's amazing. What a story they must have to tell. Do they need anything that we can provide? Food, medicine, a ride out?"

"They'll need a lot of help. The Pale Ones dropped a massive kinetic strike on the planet. I watched it hit from orbit. The planet is in for a very rough time."

"Then they shall have whatever we can give. I'll want to see the vid of the impact, too."

He sent a mental command to block all transmissions from the ship for the time being. Once he told them the truth, he couldn't allow any of them to send any surreptitious messages.

His implants showed the marines taking up positions outside the conference room once the hatch closed. He sat at the head of the table. Kelsey took the seat to his right with Commodore Sanders beside her. Elise sat on Jared's left with Lord Admiral Shrike beside her.

He clasped his hands in front of him on the table. "Before I begin, I need to make a confession. There is one other event that I haven't mentioned. We had an attempted mutiny."

Elise's eyes widened. "What! From our people?" She looked over at Shrike. "I thought the men sent on this mission were all military personnel."

"They were. Ones that went through an exhaustive background check. Might we question them?"

Jared nodded. "You're welcome to." He touched the recessed console, and an image of Rawlins popped up on the large screen. He'd decided to use the dead man to flush out any traitors. "Allow me to introduce you to Jacob Randall. I'm certain that isn't his real name. When he briefly took control of the ship, he referred to himself as Commander Rawlins.

"He didn't believe that we'd regain the upper hand and told us that a coup in your Fleet was about to happen. I'm sorry to tell you this, Lord Admiral, but I believe that one or more of your senior military officers is about to seize power. If we can trace this man to his patron quietly, I believe we can unravel this coup in a very short period of time."

He could tell Elise the other reasons they needed to hurry once her people had this situation under control.

Elise nodded. "I can send orders for people loyal to me to assume command of the ships in orbit with backup from the Royal Guard. Once we query the Royal Fleet databases, it won't take long to track who he probably works for."

Jared started to respond, but Lord Admiral Shrike stood abruptly and stepped behind Elise. He had a knife to her throat before Kelsey and Sanders had finished standing. Jared stayed in his seat.

"Sit back down, Princess Kelsey." Shrike kept his eyes locked on Jared's half sister. "Allow me to save all of us some time. He'll lead you right to me. That doesn't matter, though. You're too late." He pulled a communications device from his waist and pressed a key. "My senior people are taking control of the Royal Fleet as we speak. Your ship might be powerful, but it cannot stand up to the might of Pentagar. This is over."

"Traitor," Commodore Sanders spat. "You won't get away with this."

"Really? How melodramatic. I've already gotten away with it. Sit down or I'll slit her throat."

Jared was tempted to call for the marines, but he suspected the lord admiral was more than a bit mad. He'd probably kill Elise as soon as the door opened.

"This won't end well." Jared eased his pistol from its holster. "I've already locked down all communications. You're alone here."

Shrike laughed. "I don't believe you. Prepare a cutter to take the former crown princess and myself to my flagship. Now. Delay or offer me any resistance and I'll kill her."

"Don't do it," Elise said through clenched teeth. "He cannot be allowed to leave this ship, even if he kills me. Protect the Kingdom."

Kelsey hadn't sat down, but it didn't look like she could get to Shrike without going through Elise. She moved down the table away from Jared. "Let's not get hasty. Perhaps we can make a deal."

As soon as Shrike turned to keep Elise between himself and Kelsey, Jared raised his pistol, used his implants to target it on Shrike's head, and fired. The high-velocity flechette blew Shrike's head apart. He dropped the knife and collapsed in a bloody heap.

Jared's hand shook as he stood and holstered his pistol. The marines burst in just as Jared pulled Elise away from the body. Despite her brave face, he could feel her trembling. He turned her away from the body. "It's over now. You're safe."

She came into his arms and buried her face against his shoulder. "Thank you."

33

———————

Kelsey sat on the balcony to her room at the Royal Palace, sipping a beer and watching the stars. She wondered which of them was home. Probably none of them. Odds were Avalon wasn't visible from here, even with her enhanced eyesight.

Her keeper and constant companion, Senior Sargent Talbot, put his boots up on the railing and leaned back in his chair. "You think the Pentagarans really found all the conspirators?"

"If not, they've found most of them. Every senior officer is getting close scrutiny, and some traitors have given up others for lighter sentences. Treason here has the death penalty. If they've missed anyone, that person will be the model of good behavior going forward."

Events had preceded quickly once Commodore—now Admiral—Sanders had made a few innocuous calls to men he trusted to secure the ships in orbit. They'd even found the woman responsible for the attack at the Parliament Building. Once the Pentagarans felt they had all they needed from her, the king would decide if she'd cooperated enough to earn a life sentence.

The two of them drank in silence for a while before Talbot spoke again. "What do you think about the captain and Crown Princess Elise?"

She blinked at the unexpected question. "How do you mean?"

"Come on. Everyone can see that she's sweet on him. All those private dinners and trips out into the capital."

Kelsey considered that with no small bit of surprise. Now that he'd pointed it out, she wondered how she'd missed it. Her half brother was dating. She wondered if he knew yet. Elise could be very subtle.

"I'm not sure what kind of future they have," she said at last. "We're going to be leaving at some point, and she's not coming with us."

"Not all relationships are long term. He did save her life, you know. That kind of intense situation makes people want to get friendly, even when they're not usually so forward."

She gave him a look. "You did not just tell me that she's having a torrid affair with my half brother."

"Actually, I did. I can't prove it, mind you. Even if I could, I would never say so," he said piously.

Kelsey snorted. "Right. Well, if they are, that's their business, and more power to them. People deserve what happiness they can find in this life." She took a deep draught of her beer. "Just like us."

He frowned. "I don't follow you."

She gestured with her bottle. "The two of us go everywhere together. We have intimate dinners. We spend a lot of time alone. You do know that we're dating, right?"

Talbot's chair tipped over backward, and he fell with a crash.

"That's crazy," he said as she laughed. He tried and failed to get some of the beer off himself after he stood.

"I said it as a joke, but why not? Is there something wrong with me?"

He looked to the heavens, probably seeking strength. "Don't you pull that girl crap on me! No, there is nothing wrong with you, and you know it. If we weren't who we are, I'd be sorely tempted, but you're a princess and I'm a freaking marine. I'm not even an officer, and I'm fifteen years older than you."

"So?"

"I can't believe you're even suggesting that. Lieutenant Reese would brig me. The emperor would space me. You have no idea what kind of reputation marines have."

She smiled widely. "I think my father might have mentioned something to that effect. You know what I didn't hear? That you weren't interested."

"This is crazy," he whispered.

"You're a marine. Be brave."

COMMAND DECISIONS

BOOK THREE

Commander Jared Mertz thought the glories of the Old Terran Empire once more within his people's grasp. One bold strike to make them his.

But no plan survives contact with the enemy.

With the odds stacked against him, the battle to save humanity starts now.

1

"**B**ehold. Imperial City, the capital of the Terran Empire."
Jared Mertz stepped up to the railing and looked out over the vast city. Monolithic buildings stretched as far as the eye could see in every direction. Sleek grav cars in every imaginable color flitted past at breakneck speeds.

The city wasn't sterile, though. Gardens bloomed in planters on the steep walls where the sun could get to them, and wide green spaces lined the ground far, far below. The scents in the air held a hint of nature.

Pedestrians dominated the ground between the buildings like a swarm of insects. They also filled wide walkways that crossed from one building to another in an endless stream. He'd never seen so many people at one time.

The implant recording fooled his senses. It felt as though he'd gone back in time to stand in the Old Empire at its heyday.

Reginald Bell gazed down with a serene expression. "New York City. The most populous metroplex in the old United States. Two hundred and fifty million people. The first Terran emperor changed its name to Imperial City, but the residents here never accepted it. Even though the United States of America no longer existed as a political entity, New Yorkers never forgot their heritage. Their attitude was legendary."

Jared tilted his head back and looked up. Even though they were on the three hundredth floor, the building still towered over them. "Just how tall is this building?"

"Four hundred and fifty-two floors, counting the penthouse level. It provided homes and businesses for a quarter of a million people. I suspect many of them never left it during their lives. Not even in the end."

A bird landed on the railing about ten meters away. It was a smooth gray and very fat. It stared at them as though it was waiting for them to feed it.

Jared shook his head. "I can't believe how real this looks. I can hear the birds, I can smell the ocean, and I can see everything down to the smallest detail. How is that possible?"

"They brought in special equipment capable of recording in far more detail than any human being can actually sense, even with Princess Kelsey's commando implants. They wanted every Fleet service member to be able to see Imperial City as it was. There are a number of other recordings just like this from across the Empire in *Courageous*'s data banks. Unfortunately, they're made for implant viewing only."

Jared sent a mental command to his implants to terminate the vid. Honestly, the word "vid" felt like the greatest understatement he'd ever made. The incredible view disappeared, leaving him sitting in his quarters aboard the Imperial Fleet battlecruiser *Courageous*. Across the coffee table from him, Bell opened his eyes.

The ice in Jared's drink had almost melted, but he took a deep sip anyway. The alcohol burned going down. "All of that historical detail and only we can see it? That's going to make the historians revolt if we don't capture that freighter and its implant supplies. They'll demand we launch an expedition deeper into the Old Empire immediately."

The old man laughed. "I imagine you're right. Not even the prospect of the Pale Ones would deter them. *Courageous* might be able to display these vids on a monitor, but much of the fine detail is going to be lost."

The Old Empire had designed so many things for people with implants. They hadn't considered unenhanced human beings needing to access them. Yet here in the post-Fall Terran Empire, only the three of them had those implants.

The cataclysmic rebellion and civil war half a millennium ago had wrecked the Old Empire and killed uncounted trillions of people. As of yet, they had no idea how many feral humans survived amid the bones of the Empire. Or how many isolated pockets of civilization like the Kingdom of Pentagar survived.

The Kingdom occupied a single planet. The resurrected Terran Empire added several dozen heavily populated worlds and perhaps twice that number of frontier planets to the count. That left tens of thousands of systems that had once been part of the old Terran Empire to explore.

To do that, they had to deal with the artificial intelligences that had staged the revolt and the poor bastards they'd forcibly implanted.

Bell picked up his glass and sipped his whiskey. "Now that the Pentagarans have their first ships ready, when will you be returning to Erorsi? Have the recordings the AI made changed your plans?"

During the final battle to control the system next door to Pentagar, Kelsey had defeated the controlling AI and salvaged its data banks. In the process of gathering everything they could, the marines had pulled data off the communications systems the AI had used. The news had not been good.

"We're still reviewing the oldest of the transmissions. They go back over five hundred years. I don't think we'll get any deeper shocks than we've already gotten, though. The AI's communications records told us everything we needed to know."

The AI controlling Erorsi received supplies each year about the same time from what certainly appeared to be a ship from the Old Empire. The most recent conversation between a man and the AI had been brief but chilling. The human had looked like a Fleet officer. Definitely not a savage like the Pale Ones.

Unlike this man, the feral humans didn't even seem capable of speech. Once Princess Kelsey and the marines had destroyed the AI that controlled them, the primitives had ceased to be a direct threat. They'd still need to summon them to a central area and overwrite the corrupted implant code. Then the poor bastards could live out their lives in whatever peace they could find.

The man in the recording spoke to the AI in an obsequious tone, declaring that the freighter had all the supplies the AI couldn't build for itself. Including implant hardware. The AI told the man that it had adolescent human beings for them in trade. Children. He shuddered to think of how the others might be using those kids.

Obviously, something of the Old Empire survived. Something twisted and terrible. Jared's problems had become several orders of magnitude more complicated with the revelation.

"Based on the rough schedule of the resupply, it'll be along in another few weeks," Jared said. "We go back to Erorsi tomorrow and set up an ambush. We need that freighter's cargo, and we cannot allow it to raise the alarm.

"Two-thirds of Pentagaran ships will hide behind Erorsi while the rest lie in wait with *Courageous* in the asteroid belt. We'll catch the freighter and its escort, if any, between the hammer and anvil. The marines will clear the freighter before Kelsey boards to work with its computer."

Bell nodded. "You're short on missiles, so will you be able to handle any escort?"

"*Courageous* says the escort is normally a destroyer, so I think so. We have three dozen missiles left. Any battle will leave us critically short, though, so I'm hoping this is one of the years when the freighter doesn't have an escort. It comes alone more than half the time."

Bell took a sip of his drink. "I hope that's how it plays out. My people have enough problems. The kinetic strike might not have directly hurt us, but our facility is dependent on hidden farms for food. The impact sent a tremendous amount of debris into the atmosphere. That means a harsh winter that will last half a decade, if we're lucky. The crops are dead."

"Hopefully all the supplies we brought will tide you through. That won't help the primitive humans out in the wild, though. I'm afraid they're in for a very rough time."

"It's a tragedy," Bell agreed. "One bit of good news. We found where the AI was holding this year's tithe of children. Hundreds of boys and girls between the ages of four and six. We're doing what we can to fit them into our community."

The older man shook his head. "That's a problem we can solve. What if they send someone looking for the missing ships?"

"They might not. The communications logs have several instances when the AI and the humans had discussed the lack of a freighter the previous year. It sounds as though they just shrug when a freighter fails to return and send extra supplies next year. Hopefully by then, we'll be able to deal with them. We don't really have a choice. Once we stop the freighter, we'll do what we can to help your people recover Erorsi."

"We appreciate your assistance, but that's going to take much, much longer than either one of us has left to dedicate to it. Your people will be trying to find your way home soon. Are you taking a Pentagaran embassy with you? Perhaps Crown Princess Elise?" Bell's lips quirked up in a smile.

Jared wished she was coming along, but that wasn't realistic. Their relationship had grown closer over the last several months. They'd taken to dining together almost every night and frequently took sightseeing trips around the Kingdom, enjoying one another's company. They'd become intimate in the last few weeks, but no one could possibly know about that. They'd taken elaborate precautions.

He didn't want to admit he'd fallen in love with her, because that kind of relationship was doomed from the start. One day she'd rule her people in her father's place, while he'd be going far away, perhaps never to return.

Jared sighed. "I'm certain they'll be sending an embassy with us, but I doubt Elise will be coming along."

"Well, I hope for both your sakes that you're wrong."

Jared felt his gaze narrowing. "Pardon me?"

The older man smiled. "Don't frown at me, Captain Mertz. I'm just making an observation. The two of you seem so well suited to one another, and I'd rather not lose the pool."

"Pool? What pool?"

"The pool the crew has on whether she's coming along with us. I'm rather pleased to say that most of us are behind you. The Pentagaran members of the crew think she's not coming. The rest of us are wagering love will win out."

His heart leapt into his throat. "I'm not sure what you mean."

Bell laughed. "Then you're the last one to know, my boy. Everyone can see how the two of you feel about one another. That may well be the worst-kept secret ever."

The news flabbergasted Jared. They'd been so careful!

"Please tell me you're kidding about the pool. Who knows?"

The older man shook his head, his eyes full of laughter. "We go out of our way to spare your dignity and to give you both the privacy you deserve, but we all know. Should I place a bet for you? No, that sounds unethical now that I think about it."

The buzzer to his cabin spared Jared the agony of figuring out how to respond. He rose and walked over to the hatch, still eying Bell. He only remembered that he could've checked the vid feed with his implants after he'd opened the hatch.

His half sister, Princess Kelsey Bandar, breezed past him. Sister, he corrected. She'd insisted they drop the qualifier. He didn't imagine her full brother, Ethan, would feel the same way.

"You wouldn't believe the day I've had," she complained. "Talbot is a slave driver. Tell me you have beer."

Senior Sergeant Talbot, her ever-present Imperial Marine guard, followed her in with an apologetic nod to his commanding officer. "She's exaggerating, Captain. She barely broke a sweat."

Jared closed the hatch with a grin at their repartee and headed for his kitchen. "I have some beer chilled down to the edge of freezing for you. As always. What exactly did the monster have you doing today?"

Not anything she couldn't handle, he was sure. The commando implants the Pale Ones had forced upon his sister made her almost superhuman. Graphene-reinforced bones, artificially enhanced musculature, and sophisticated combat programming in her implants made her improbably formidable.

Kelsey took the beer from him, twisted the cap off, and drank deeply. "Running," she said when she'd finished a long draft. "He made me run up a mountain."

Talbot opened his own beer more sedately. "Pfftt. That was barely a hill. My drill instructor made us sprint up much more difficult terrain than that before breakfast."

"In unpowered combat armor with a pack that weighed more than twice your weight? I doubt that."

"With that exact weight," he shot back. "It's not my fault you're such a little bitty thing."

She smiled wickedly at the burly marine. "That's not what you said when I tossed your ass around the mat yesterday. I seem to recall you saying something more along the lines of 'I think you broke me.' Isn't that right?"

Jared opened his mouth to add his opinion when it hit him. Perhaps it was because Bell had raised the thought in his mind, but now he wondered how he could've missed the way these two were looking at one another. The way they talked to one another.

Their body language spoke volumes. Talbot reached out to touch Kelsey's arm as she sat down, and she wasn't pulling back when their legs pressed together. It spoke of just the same kind of intimacy that he and Elise shared.

They were lovers.

His sister was the daughter of the Terran emperor, second in line to the Imperial Throne. Talbot was a marine noncom charged with guarding and training her. For helping her to adjust to the implants. For them to be involved in a relationship was…

None of his damned business, he realized. She wasn't an officer in his chain of command. She was a civilian. There were no laws or Fleet regulations against them having a relationship.

Kelsey frowned at him. "What's wrong? Did something go down the wrong pipe?"

He nodded. "That's exactly what happened. Sorry. As for running up a mountain, that doesn't sound like much of a challenge for you, Kelsey. I've seen how much you can lift in the weight room. Why was it so stressful?"

"Because he made me do it at a full run for over an hour. I don't care how enhanced you are, your real muscles will complain in half that time."

Jared sat down next to Bell. "I wouldn't last ten minutes. I'm a Fleet officer, not a ground pounder." He gave Talbot an apologetic glance. "No offense."

"None taken."

Jared pinged Bell's implants and asked for a private communications channel, which the other man quickly accepted.

Is there a pool on how long these two are going to be together?

Bell's eyes widened slightly as he looked at the two. *Are you sure? They're always behaving like this.*

I'm pretty sure. Let's find out.

Jared smiled at Kelsey. "Did you know that there's some crazy pool going on with the crew? They think Elise and I are a couple. They're betting on whether or not she comes back to Avalon with us. Isn't that crazy?"

"Really? I hadn't heard." Kelsey looked at Talbot. "You know every gambling table on this ship. Have you heard about this?"

The marine's eyes darted to Jared. "Ah... I might have heard something like that. Purely speculation, I'm sure."

Kelsey slapped Talbot on the shoulder. "There's a betting pool and you didn't tell me? Put me down for whatever you bet on them staying together, because I know that's where the smart money is."

Talbot gave her a flat look.

"Oh, and there's another pool," Jared added. "You might want to get in on it, too."

"What's that?" Kelsey asked.

"It's a wager on how your father reacts when he finds out you're dating a marine. I have my money on him sending Talbot to Thule for the next decade or so."

Kelsey managed to stare blankly at him, but she flushed. That was all Jared needed to know his suspicion was correct. They really were lovers.

His sister sighed. "I knew someone would figure it out eventually, but I never dreamed they'd have a pool."

The marine shook his head as he stared pityingly at her. "There is no pool. I'd have heard. He just baited you out."

She narrowed her eyes at Jared. "That's mean. I didn't bet against you staying with Elise, and I've known about the two of you for months."

"That's only because you didn't know about the pool," Jared said dryly. "We've only been dating for six weeks."

"*You've* only been dating six weeks. Elise started a little sooner. She's subtle like that. Are we going to have a problem about Russ and me?"

It took him a moment to realize she was talking about Talbot. No one called him by his first name. Jared suspected the man's mother called him Talbot.

Jared held his hands up. "No problems from me, though you're going to need a new guard."

She bristled. "That's bull."

Talbot shook his head. "No. The captain is right. Lieutenant Reese needs to appoint a new guard. I'll let him know."

"Are you serious?" The look she gave the marine said that he'd be better off if he weren't.

The man had his work cut out for him, Jared decided. Thank God Elise was much less bossy.

Jared decided to let Talbot off the hook. "Captain's orders. I need your guard to be thinking clearly at all times. I'm not saying you have to go public, as I apparently have, or that your relationship is inappropriate. It's not, and it's no one's business but yours. You'll just have to accept this though, because the change in guards is not subject to negotiation."

Bell, who'd been silent throughout the exchange, ventured a comment. "It's really for the best. Your security team needs to focus on your health and well-being at all times, even when you occasionally disagree with them. Much like the Imperial Guard was with the emperor in my day."

His sister squeezed the bridge of her nose. "I suppose I knew this would eventually come up." She looked at Talbot. "I don't mean that in a negative way. I'm happy that we're together. I just don't want my position to be a negative for you."

Talbot smiled. "We're lucky we had the quiet time we did. If the captain guessed that we're a couple, I'm sure others are wondering. We should beat them to the punch and be up front about it. If you want to."

"Of course I want to." She lifted her chin and stared at Jared. "We have to leave for the surface in the next half hour, but I want to get one thing settled right now. What are the rules about cohabitation? Can he move to my quarters?"

Jared nodded. "There's no rule that says marines need to live in marine country. Relationships with Fleet personnel do happen. He just needs to clear it with his CO. Lieutenant Reese won't say no. How long are the two of you going to be gone? We're flipping to the Courageous system in a few hours to swap the crew on *Athena* and return."

He'd made it a point to rename the system they'd found the battlecruiser in, a move the Pentagarans had heartily endorsed. If nothing else, the system would have a significant mining presence for the foreseeable future. Any name was better than the bland number the Imperial Stellar Catalog had listed for the system.

"Don't wait up," Kelsey said. "I'm meeting Elise for breakfast in a few hours. With the difference between planetary time in the capital and *Courageous*, it's almost dawn down there. Don't worry. I'll let her know you've been outed."

The planetary rotational period was somewhat shorter than Terran Standard Time, so they'd drifted into an almost opposite timeframe over the last few weeks. Which made secretly dating even more challenging.

"Thanks," he said dryly. "She probably already knows. It's me that didn't notice everyone staring at us. I'm surprised it isn't all over the news programs and gossip columns."

"She probably has a deal with them to keep it under wraps. Well, we need to get going. The cutter won't wait." She and Talbot rose to their feet.

Bell rose with them. "I'm afraid I'm going to call it a night as well, Captain. I'm due to transfer to one of the Pentagaran vessels. They're taking me home to oversee the last of the preparations on Erorsi's surface. Good luck and thank you for an enjoyable evening. Highness, Senior Sergeant, my congratulations to you both."

Jared saw them all out before returning to his office to go over a few more pieces of paperwork. It was a never-ending chore, though his implants made faster work of it. When he'd had enough, he took a shower and readied himself for bed.

* * *

HE WOKE SOMETIME LATER when a voice spoke in his head. *This unit is sorry to wake you, Captain,* the ship's computer said through his implants. *There is a priority signal for you from* Athena.

Thanks, Courageous. *I'll take it at my desk.*

They must've already flipped, because his old ship was on station near the weak flip point in the Courageous system. Jared threw his uniform on and sat at his desk. He touched the flashing icon, and the screen cleared to show *Athena's* bridge. Ensign Danielle Cruz, one of his cutter pilots, sat in the command chair.

Out here in the backend of nowhere, his old ship only needed a skeleton crew. The command experience was good for her and the other junior officers he'd assigned to the ship for the time being.

"Good morning, Captain," Cruz said crisply. "I'm sorry to disturb you so early, but a probe from home just came through the flip point. Fleet has found us."

2

K elsey enjoyed a leisurely breakfast with Elise. Talbot had declined their offer to join them and gone to bed. She hoped to join him in a few hours.

Elise, it turned out, had been aware that her relationship with Jared was an open secret for some time. She laughed when Kelsey told her how Jared had reacted to the betting pool by clapping her hands and grinning like a fiend.

"That's delightful! He's such a reserved man in public. This will do him a universe of good. When the gossip columns finally find out that the 'rumors' they've been printing for the last two months are true, they'll be out in force. It will be a feeding frenzy."

Kelsey blinked. "Reserved? Jared? You're understating things, don't you think? He's the most serious man I know."

"Then you don't know your brother as well as you believe. He has a wicked sense of humor. He's full of all kinds of surprises when you get him alone."

"Uh huh. I suppose I need to have the official 'what are your intentions toward my brother' talk. I hate to be casting gloom on the moment, but once we take care of the rebel freighter, we're going to be striking out for home. We have to warn them."

Elise nodded, her irreverent mood vanishing into a serious expression. "I've been discussing that with my father over the last few days. As the heir, common wisdom declares that I need to be here, but I believe I'd be serving the Kingdom by accompanying you back to the Empire. I've decided to head the delegation from Pentagar."

Kelsey wasn't sure that was the best idea. "What if something happens to your father while you're gone?"

"My cousin is the next in line to the Throne. He'd assume a caretaker role until I returned. We've already presented this to the Royal Council and Parliament. In secret session, of course. They agreed with me after much arguing. I'm much more concerned about your approval, though."

"You don't need my approval, but I do. Very much. I think he'll be very happy that you're coming with us, and so am I."

"I hope you're right. I see something in him that I haven't seen in any other man I've dated. I think he might be the one. If so, that will bring our people closer still." Elise took a sip of her coffee. "But enough about me. How are things going with Talbot?"

Kelsey smiled more widely. "I figured if anyone knew about the two of us, it would be you. We're doing very well. In fact, Jared figured it out last night. I was worried that he was going to throw a fit, but he didn't. Once the two of us get back to the ship, we're going to make our relationship public. I figure everything will be perfectly fine right up until the point where my father finds out I'm dating a marine. His head will explode, my brother will inherit the Imperial Throne, and he will banish the two of us to Thule for life."

The crown princess of Pentagar laughed. "Oh, I hardly think it'll be that bad. I'm certain that your father will be pleased that you've found someone who makes you happy. Unfortunately, I do worry that your brother's antipathy towards Jared will cause him to take some kind of stand against the alliance between our people."

Kelsey shook her head. "Ethan is many things, but stupid is not one of them. He won't allow his feelings for Jared to color Imperial relations. He'll do what's best for the Empire. In this case, that's a strong alliance with Pentagar."

"But he might not like me very much personally. I understand, but that's unfortunate. How do you think he'll treat Jared when he assumes the Throne? Hopefully, of course, that will be far in the future. Your father is a fit man in his prime, so I expect he'll rule for many years to come."

Kelsey continued to eat while she considered her reply. Feeding her enhanced metabolism was no easy task. She ate like *two* professional sports stars. She'd slowly been getting over her embarrassment at having to gorge at every meal.

"I'm certain you're right. Ethan won't be succeeding my father for another couple of decades, and that won't be because my father is ill. Everyone already knows he plans to retire once he reaches a certain point in his life. By then, hopefully, my brother will have found someone to share his life with and have kids of his own. I, thankfully, will be nowhere near the line of succession at that point."

"You don't miss that?"

"Not one bit," Kelsey said fervently. "I'm not looking to rule the Empire. I'll be more than happy with a husband who loves me and kids of my own. I'll cheerfully dedicate my life to helping other people with this whole implant thing."

Elise nodded. "I'm glad to hear that. Based on how well your people have accepted your condition, I don't think you'll have much difficulty at home. My people seem to have gotten over their initial shock. That's very promising.

"At some point, we're going to start doing implants on a larger scale, and you're setting a tremendous example. We'll literally be following in your footsteps. In fact, if this freighter has replacement parts, I'll be the first in line."

That surprised Kelsey. As much as she tried to put a good face on it, the trauma of the Pale Ones forcibly implanting her colored her reactions. She fought that reflexive reaction every day. "You'd do that? Why?"

Elise's eyes danced devilishly. "Well, I can only imagine what it would be like for two implanted people to be a couple. You know, in the bedroom."

Kelsey paused with her coffee cup halfway to her mouth. "I'd never even considered that. Wow. That's even more intimate than being intimate. It would be like being in the other person's head. I wonder…"

She held up her hand. "Never mind. I don't think I want to think about that. What are your plans for the rest the morning? I'm more wired than I expected, so I'm not going to sleep just yet. For whatever reason, I'm able to get by on a lot less sleep now that I'm implanted. I can take a nap this afternoon, and I'll be good to go."

Elise leaned forward curiously. "How much sleep do you need?"

"If I get five or six hours, I'm good to go. I'll admit that a full night's sleep is a luxury, but it's not something I absolutely need. Talbot will be asleep for long enough for me to get a good rest, if you've got somewhere interesting for us to go."

Elise set her coffee cup down. "As a matter of fact, I do. Repair crews have finally stabilized the Parliament Building, and we're going to remove Master Vestor's carving to be sure the explosion didn't damage it. It was too dangerous to recover before now."

The thought of all the damage the late and unlamented Lord Admiral Shrike had caused trying to kill them made her sad. Priceless art had filled the Pentagaran Parliament Building before the assassination attempt. The explosion must've destroyed so many irreplaceable things.

She hoped Master Vestor's carving had survived unscathed. Based on the incredible level of detail in the carving she was taking back to Avalon, even the slightest damage to the work hanging behind the speaker's podium in the Parliament Building would be disastrous.

"Let's do it."

The two of them made their way to a waiting grav limo. Even though the Pentagarans had crushed Shrike and his rebellion, there were still a large number of Royal Guards escorting them in other vehicles. Several military airships flew high overhead. The crown princess's security detail was taking no chances.

When they arrived at the Parliament Building, Kelsey was dismayed to see how extensive the damage was. The carved reliefs and columns she'd admired along the front of the building were gone. It looked like the explosion had caused the entire façade to collapse. They'd cleared the debris, and scaffolding showed where repair crews were busy replacing the lost portions of the building.

"My God. I had no idea the destruction was so extensive. We must've only barely escaped being crushed."

"That's not so far from the truth," Elise agreed. "Thankfully, the police had begun clearing the building as soon as the shooting started. Otherwise, so many more people would've been killed or injured."

The thought of it made Kelsey burn with anger. She'd attended the man's execution to show her resolve. It had been awful, but she regretted the gesture much less when she considered how much death and destruction the bastard had caused.

"I still have trouble getting my head around what Shrike hoped to gain," she said, putting the dark memories back away. "He can't possibly have believed your people would accept him after he overthrew the Monarchy. They would've rebelled."

Elise nodded. "I'd like to think so. I'm still shocked at how many Royal Fleet officers he subverted. If he'd managed to take *Courageous*, he'd have beaten us."

"*Courageous* isn't invincible. Far from it. With all the fighting she went through during the rebellion and against the Pale Ones, she's expended most of her missiles. We're going to have to be very careful from here on out."

"It would've been enough," Elise said grimly. "With *Courageous* under his control, Shrike would've taken the Kingdom. I have no doubt of that. We were all incredibly lucky that you defeated him.

"Of course, you and Jared have proved your resourcefulness several times already. I can't wait to see how the historians put that into perspective. Or the vid dramas."

Kelsey frowned. "Vid dramas?"

Elise grinned and opened the limo door after her guards signaled the way was clear. "Hadn't you heard? Several production companies have joined forces to document your triumphant arrival. Money is no object. They've hired only the best and brightest actors and actresses in the Kingdom. Production on several other vids has ceased due to the effort being expended on this one project."

The news actually made Kelsey stop in her tracks. "You're kidding." She shook her head. "Of course you're not. That's horrifying."

The crown princess took Kelsey's arm and got them moving again. "Surely, you expected that something like this would happen. How many vids do you think have been made about Emperor Lucien's escape to your Avalon?"

Kelsey shrugged. "I don't know. A lot. That's completely different."

"It's precisely the same. You, Jared, and the crew of *Athena* saved the lives of every single person in the Kingdom. Like it or not, you're heroes. Mythic figures, even."

Kelsey had seen that hero worship up close many times in the last few months. It made her deeply uncomfortable. She wasn't worthy of that kind of adulation. Jared and his crew were the true heroes.

Elise continued, unaware of Kelsey's thoughts. "I understand the competition for the leading roles was fierce. Perhaps worthy of an epic story of its own. You should know that Riley Thomas actually challenged several of his competitors to duels for the privilege of playing Jared. Personally, I like Jared much better, but Riley is still dreamy." She sighed theatrically.

With a feeling of growing dread, Kelsey covered her eyes with one hand. "Please, please tell me that I don't have someone ridiculous playing me."

"Oh, no. If anything, the battle to play you was even fiercer. Literally, the role of a lifetime. 'Ridiculous' is certainly not the word I'd use for Eva Griffiths. She's one of the great leading ladies of our time, a true powerhouse on the screen. While she doesn't have your small stature, she makes up for that difference in other ways."

"What kind of ways?" Kelsey asked suspiciously.

"Let's just say that she has a completely different kind of enhancement than you do."

"Perfect. Absolutely perfect. With any luck, I'll be long gone by the time this production is finished."

"Oh, I wouldn't worry about that," Elise said breezily. "I'm sure that we'll have reestablished contact through the Courageous system by then. The vid will most likely be all the rage in the Empire by the time we get there."

"With my luck, that's just about a certainty."

They made their way through the construction area. Sawdust and floating particles of freshly poured plascrete tickled her nose. Her implants tallied the composition of the plascrete and discreetly displayed it in the corner of her vision. The advanced technology of the Old Empire revealed itself to her in the oddest ways.

The workers had parts of the floor roped off to protect the freshly poured flooring. Thick reinforcements held a new ceiling over their heads, but the walls to the main chamber were gone. The speaker's podium remained, as did the carving mounted on the wall behind it. Someone had covered Master Vestor's work with what looked like a thick sheet of transparent plastic.

The marble floor was cracked and crushed. Loose bits crunched under Kelsey's shoes as she walked. The devastation was almost complete. The speaker's podium looked as though something had smashed into it. Perhaps it had saved the carving from damage.

The Royal Guards had already cleared the workers from the room, but Kelsey recognized several of the men standing near the speaker's podium. Master Alec Vestor stood in a huddle with several other men and women in colorful tunics. His apprentices, she assumed.

He turned at their approach and smiled. "Elise, Kelsey, it's so good to see you both."

"Tell me your carving isn't damaged," Kelsey pleaded. "Its loss would make this tragedy even worse."

"I'll have to take it down and return it to my shop to be sure, but I don't think so."

Elise sagged in evident relief. "Thank God."

Master Vestor frowned and shook his head. "It's only wood. If I could save any of the people who lost their lives in this vicious attack, I'd take an ax to it myself. Things, no matter how valuable or treasured, pale in importance to people's lives."

Elise straightened. "You're right, of course, but nothing that we do will change what happened here. I'm just glad that another tragedy wasn't perpetrated by that bastard." She shot Kelsey an apologetic look. "No offense to your brother."

"I don't think he'd be offended," Kelsey said. "Just because he's my father's illegitimate son doesn't make that word something to avoid around him." She gave her attention to Master Vestor. "I second what Elise said. I'd personally destroy this building and everything in it with a plasma cannon if it saved one person from injury, but it won't."

She stepped onto the speaker's podium and eyed the carving through the plastic cover. The material obscured her ability to see the fine detail in the woodwork. She had to admit she was anticipating a much closer look. With her enhanced eyesight, it would be a close look indeed.

That's when she felt it. Something registering on her implants.

Her eyes widened as she turned to Elise. "There's old Imperial technology close by." She stared down at the floor. "There's something down there."

3

Jared stepped onto *Courageous*'s bridge. Charlie Graves, his executive officer, rose from the captain's chair with a grin splitting his face.

"Captain. We're about half an hour from *Athena*. The probe popped back over before *Athena* could send a message to it. Fleet was getting a scan of the system, I suspect."

Jared nodded to Lieutenant Zia Anderson, his tactical officer, and Lieutenant Pasco Ramirez, his helm officer. "We need to send them a message as soon as that probe returns. In fact, let's send one of our probes to make sure that they have our current status. I don't want any problems because of *Courageous*, and they need to know what we found." Jared raised his voice. "Zia, record my response and load it into a probe."

He made certain that his face was professionally neutral as he began speaking. "This is Commander Jared Mertz, captain of the destroyer *Athena*. We're glad to see you, but it's imperative that you *do not* transition to this system. I repeat, you must not use that flip point. It's a one-way trip. There's no way home.

"We're on our way to the flip point now. If you access the high-priority data contained in the probes that we left for you, you'll see a summary of events. The large ship on your scanners is friendly. Again, we're glad to see you, but *do not* come through the flip point. Mertz out. Zia, add a current update of our data and launch the probe."

He turned his attention to Lieutenant Pasco Ramirez, *Courageous*'s helmsman. "Maximum speed to the flip point. We need to be close so we can answer their questions as quickly as possible."

Less than ten minutes later, Zia stiffened. "Multiple transitions at the weak flip point! I'm detecting six vessels."

Jared cursed. Their probe had almost made it. "Record a new message.

Fleet vessels, this is Commander Jared Mertz. We are in route to your position. We have medical teams standing by to assist you. Hang on. Mertz out. Zia, can you ID those ships?"

"There's one heavy cruiser, two light cruisers, and three destroyers. I'm comparing them to the databases we brought from *Athena* now." She tapped her console. "Sir, that cruiser is *Spear*."

It took a moment for that to soak in. *Spear*. The ship they'd beaten in the war games before they left on this mission. That meant he was dealing with Captain Wallace Breckenridge. He couldn't think of a worse person to have dropped into his lap. Breckenridge was no fan of Jared's, and the man outranked him.

"Incoming transmission," Zia said.

"Put it on the screen."

Breckenridge looked mussed. Something dark stained the front of his tunic, and his hair stood out in a particularly unflattering manner. "Unknown vessel, this is Captain Wallace Breckenridge of the Imperial Fleet heavy cruiser *Spear*. Stand clear of *Athena*, or my task force will fire on you."

Graves stared at Jared uncomprehendingly. "Does he think we're attacking *Athena*? Didn't he review *any* of the data we left for him? Jesus Christ. Now they're trapped here just like we are."

Jared gave his executive officer a reproving glance. "Belay that. He's a senior Fleet officer, and we will not speak of him in that tone." He sighed. "I can't imagine what he was thinking. We'll find out soon enough."

What *was* apparent to Jared was that Captain Breckenridge hadn't waited to find out what the situation was. If he'd done even a cursory scan of the data, he'd have seen the warning not to use the flip point. A deeper examination of the data would have told him what *Courageous* was.

The implication was that neither of the probes they'd sent deeper into the Empire had made it. Breckenridge and his task force had chanced across the one they'd left at the flip point, and rather than waiting to review the information inside it, they'd flipped across to rescue *Athena*.

The Old Empire battlecruiser must've seemed like an alien vessel. Their probe had picked up *Courageous* closing on the damaged *Athena*. Its appearance must've seemed threatening. It had to have been something like that.

"Open a channel, Zia. Captain Breckenridge, this is Jared Mertz. I'm on board the Fleet battlecruiser *Courageous*, the vessel approaching *Athena*. It's not hostile."

The other man frowned. "Mertz? What the hell is going on? Fleet battlecruiser? Explain yourself at once."

Jared gave Breckenridge a concise report of events while attempting to explain that *Courageous* was a restored Old Empire battlecruiser. The older man didn't seem able to grasp what he was saying.

"You're not making any sense," Breckenridge almost snarled. "You will report to *Spear* and explain it to me in person at once, Commander. Breckenridge out."

Jared tiredly rubbed his eyes as the man's image vanished from the screen. "Wonderful. Zia, load the critical information into a chip, and I'll take it with me. It won't hurt to bring another copy."

"Do you want me to go with you, sir?" Graves asked.

Jared shook his head. "Just to the docking bay. He's angry, and this is going to take a lot of explaining. It's probably best he take his frustration out on me."

He waited for Zia to hand him the chip and then made his way down to the forward docking level with his executive officer. On the way, he summoned Ensign Joyce Enova. The young woman had served on *Spear*.

Jared turned his attention to Graves as the lift arrived at the docking level. "If things go south, you will not intervene. I'm a big boy, and I can handle this. I don't want any ill-considered confrontations. No matter what happens, those are Fleet ships crewed by our brothers and sisters. Got it?"

Charlie nodded. "Yes, sir. Bend over and smile. Crystal clear, sir."

Jared shook his head and clapped his friend on the shoulder. "Your heart is in the right place, but this is why you're not in command of a ship yet. You say exactly what you think."

"Like you're much better." Graves's expression grew more somber. "You need to be careful, Jared. That man hates you, and he's not exactly a free thinker."

"I'll be on my best behavior. See you soon."

Ensign Enova came out of the lift and stiffened to attention as Graves walked past her and returned to the bridge. "Captain."

"Thanks for coming with me, Ensign. Let's not keep Captain Breckenridge waiting."

The cutter pilot looked over his shoulder as Jared peeked into the cockpit. "Captain. We're go to launch as soon as you strap in. Based on their speed, we should be docking in about fifteen minutes."

"Give me five minutes' warning."

"Aye, sir."

He returned to the flight deck and strapped in beside Ensign Enova. "Okay, Joyce. Give me a run down on Captain Breckenridge. Whatever you feel comfortable sharing about his command style and quirks."

The thin woman nodded. "Aye, sir. They didn't allow me on the bridge during my middie cruise, but people talk. He was notoriously strict about following regulations. Sometimes even when they didn't make sense. When things came up that didn't fit his expectations, he wasn't shy about tearing someone up."

That fit with Jared's own experiences with the man. He could only imagine what serving as a midshipman under him would've been like. A nightmare most likely.

When *Athena* had ambushed his ship during the war games, he'd struck out at how he believed *Athena* had violated the rules of engagement. He'd taken out his lapses in preparation on Graves at the after-action briefing. Even when Admiral Yeats had yanked him up short, the man had been inclined to blame circumstances and Jared's actions for his ship's mock destruction.

Which would no doubt make him even more difficult to deal with now.

"Let's see if I can say this delicately," Jared said. "For someone that's so fond of regulations, he doesn't seem to feel bound by them in some situations. Is that accurate?"

"There were rumors, sir. You know people don't feel comfortable talking about the CO in a negative light to the new people, but there were times. Things similar to the war games just before we left on this mission, for example. I read the after-action report. He didn't have his ships at a heightened level of alert during the approach to Avalon. He didn't expect enemy contact without warning. They were still scrambling when we blew them up."

Jared nodded. "Speaking of that, does he hold a grudge?"

The ensign nodded. "Until it dies of old age, and then he has it mounted so he can look at it every morning before breakfast."

"Perfect."

Nothing else they discussed changed Jared's impression of a stiff, vindictive commander bound by rules when things didn't go his way. Which was just about the worst thing that could happen in their situation.

The approach went smoothly enough, and the cutter docked without incident. Jared rose to his feet. "Stay on the flight deck, Ensign. I don't want to take a chance that anyone will recognize you."

"Aye, sir," the woman said in a relieved tone. "Good luck."

"Thanks."

He made his way into *Spear*. Three men awaited him, one a commander by his rank tabs. The other two were marines with sidearms.

The officer extended his hand. "Commander Mertz. I'm Sean Meyer, *Spear*'s executive officer. The captain is in his office." He didn't offer the names of the marines.

Their presence was a not-so-subtle insult. It implied that Jared wasn't trusted. He had no doubt that the point was intentional.

Commander Meyer's grip was cool and loose, and he didn't smile. His eyes had more than a flicker of disdain. "I'm given to understand that you had something to do with our rather rough transition." He turned toward the lift. The marines fell in behind Jared.

Jared put aside the impression that they'd just taken him into custody. It might be accurate, but it was irrelevant to the situation. "I'm afraid I can't control physics. The scientists tell me that it's part of the way those weak flip points are formed. We included all the data we had on the probe we left for you. Right after the warning not to use the flip point."

A flicker of something showed in the other man's eyes. "Yes, well, we hadn't quite gotten to that part of your data when we saw *Athena*. Due to the circumstances, the captain had no choice but to take action."

The lift deposited them just down the corridor from Breckenridge's office. Two marines stood outside the hatch at attention in their dress uniforms. Somehow, Jared guessed they weren't there just to impress him. Their presence seemed in line with Breckenridge's personality.

Meyer ignored them and rapped on the hatch. It slid open, and he stepped inside. Jared followed. The marines accompanying them came in and took up positions on either side of the hatch.

The office was somewhat larger than Jared's had been on *Athena* and rather more expensively decorated. Breckenridge had replaced the regulation desk and furnishings with pricy civilian ones. There was no chair in front of the desk.

Jared took the pointed hint and centered himself in front of the desk before snapping to attention. "Commander Mertz, reporting as ordered, sir."

Breckenridge looked up from the screen on his desk, leaned back in his chair, and scowled at Jared. "I've skimmed the data your tactical officer just sent, Commander. I'm only now beginning to grasp the mess you've landed us in. Let me see if I can sum things up before we get into the details. You've led us into a dangerous section of space, involved the Empire in a war it had no business being in, crippled your ship, and left us trapped with no way home. Did I miss anything important?"

Oh, yes, this meeting was going to be a pleasure.

4

Kelsey walked around the speaker's podium, focusing on her implants. The trace vanished when she stepped more than five meters away. That probably meant whatever she was sensing was right under the dais. No more than ten meters down, probably less. Her implants didn't have the range to interface with anything at longer distances. She needed a headset for that.

Elise looked at Kelsey curiously. "What are you seeing? Ah, feeling? Sensing?"

"Sensing is a good word. I'm not quite sure what it is. It's not responding when I attempt to connect. It doesn't feel like a switch. It's not transmitting anything other than its own signature. How old is this building?"

"Older than the Kingdom. It was the Planetary Parliament Building back before the Fall. The representatives worked here and sent select members to Terra to serve in the Imperial Parliament on our behalf."

"Then it could be something left over from back then. Implants like mine were restricted to the military, but I'd imagine that civilians had something similar. Perhaps that's why the device won't respond to me. I assume there's a level below us. How do we get down there?"

One of the guards cleared his throat. "I took the liberty of summoning the foreman. He has the full plans to the building."

A few minutes later, a portly man in dusty denim pants and a sweat-stained work shirt came in. He carried rolls of paper and bowed low to his princess. "Highness. Joshua Powell, at your service. I have the plans you requested."

Elise gave him a bright smile. "Thank you, Mister Powel. We appreciate your promptness. Have you looked at the level below us? Specifically the area under the speaker's podium?"

The man nodded. "I've been over every meter of this building, checking for damage. There are several levels under this one, but nothing directly under this chamber. It's one solid block. I assumed that was so no one had access to plant a bomb. There aren't any maintenance panels or conduits."

Kelsey took the plans from him and spread them out on the speaker's podium. They showed an area somewhat larger than the parliament chamber as a significant blank space going down three levels.

She handed the plans back to the man. "It's possible that whatever I'm sensing is only attached to the speaker's podium. Or whatever was here back then. However, I can't imagine how an isolated device could still have power after all that time. I think there's something more significant down there. Does the original speaker's podium still exist?"

Elise nodded. "Of course. It's in the Royal Museum."

"Then unless you'd like to start cutting holes in things, it might be best to bring it back for a return performance. Perhaps it interfaces with whatever is underneath us."

It took the workers an hour to disassemble the current speaker's podium, so Elise and Kelsey broke for lunch. Or Kelsey did, anyway. Her new world had about six meals in it, when she timed them correctly.

Her appetite reminded her of an Old Empire vid she'd found in *Courageous*'s archives. A primitive 3D production with small people in a fantasy setting that ate all the time. Thankfully, she didn't have hairy feet.

Kelsey had discovered a taste for entertainment vids from prespaceflight Terra. She had plenty of time to peruse *Courageous*'s library in the dead of night. The combination of requiring less sleep than before and high throughput via her implants meant she'd seen thousands of them. They had an exuberance that she enjoyed.

The two women made it back to the parliament chamber just before the workers were ready to begin putting the original podium in place. Kelsey examined the newly revealed floor carefully. There were power connections, which should've raised a question in someone's mind when they removed it. Where did the lines go? A check would've shown they didn't go elsewhere in the building.

She'd half expected to find a hatch, but there wasn't one. The floor was one solid piece. How did people get into the area below? What purpose did the old podium serve?

It took half an hour to assemble the podium and install it. It looked very much like the one that had replaced it, but there were Old Empire electronics deep inside it. Unlike the device below, it responded to her mental touch.

Kelsey found an interface in the podium and connected to it. It needed no authorization and behaved as a terminal. An access point.

She'd been practicing under Reginald Bell's instruction and had gotten the hang of this sort of thing. He'd been using his implants to do things like this for hundreds of years, and it was second nature to him. She was almost able to do it without marveling. Almost.

The interface opened into a series of systems much like a library. Exactly like a library, really. One dedicated to politics and law making. She found she was looking through a listing of the laws of the Empire at both the Imperial and planetary levels.

It seemed that each world of the Old Empire was able to make laws at the local level, so long as they did not exceed the boundaries set at the Imperial level. Murder was murder everywhere, yet in some localities, there were exceptions for dueling. Including on Pentagar, at least back then. Elise had mentioned something about those actors almost getting into a duel, so perhaps the tradition still lived on here.

There was also an interface for tallying votes cast by members. It was almost completely offline. Only the receptor here on the speaker's podium still functioned. The other members of parliament must've cast their votes at their own desks, which were long gone.

There was also a projection system built into the ceiling. There were dozens of separate units mounted among the lights. A few were offline, probably due to damage from the explosion, but the system declared itself functional. She wondered what the people that maintained the lights thought they were.

The system had a record of things it had played. Kelsey scanned down the list and came to one of the last: a message marked high priority and routed to members of the Imperial Parliament and all Fleet vessels. She instructed the system to play it just to see if it would.

An image of the bridge of a ship appeared, hovering in the air just above them. The center seat sat higher than those around it, and it had a wraparound console.

The man staring down at them was instantly recognizable to her. Emperor Marcus the Fifteenth. The last emperor of the old Terran Empire. Father to Lucien. Her great-grand-something-father.

Or at least he would've been if she'd really been of the blood. True, no one but Doctor Stone and she knew that her mother had had an affair, but it still counted. Oh, and her mother might know, too, or at least suspect.

Emperor Marcus was a handsome man, with an almost spooky resemblance to Kelsey's father. The two could've been brothers. Marcus looked like her father had when she was a girl. No grey colored his hair, and he seemed to be a vital young man in the prime of his life.

She noted that she was receiving the transmission on her implants and switched to that feed. This version was significantly clearer and much more personal. It was like when she wore her commando armor. The outside world vanished as her implants overwrote her senses.

"People of the Empire," Marcus said. "I bring you devastating news. Terra has fallen."

The sadness and horror in his expression were just as clear as if she'd been standing directly in front of him. Kelsey glanced around and found she could see more of the ship than what was in the purely visual transmission. It focused on the emperor to the exclusion of all else. Her view encompassed the other consoles spread out around the circular compartment, manned by men and women in Fleet uniforms. Those long-dead people watched the emperor speak with tears openly flowing down their faces.

There was also a tall—very tall—dark-haired woman in commando armor standing beside the lift. She seemed to be about half a meter taller than Kelsey was, so two meters. Huge for a woman.

The raven-haired woman's eyes were dry, her expression grim and determined. Her most unusual feature was a tattoo on her forehead. It started between her eyebrows and covered her forehead in a pattern that was reminiscent of eyes with a horned helmet above them. It looked sinister. Hints of smaller tattoos on her cheekbones peeked out from under her long hair.

Kelsey had never heard of anyone tattooing their face like that, though with modern medical techniques, it was possible to do so and remove it at any time. No one else on the bridge had anything like it.

An older man in a Fleet admiral's uniform stood beside the woman, dwarfed by her height. Frankly, he seemed too old to be still serving, but who was Kelsey to judge? He looked every day as old as Reginald Bell. Come to think of it, Bell might be able to identify these people for the historical record.

She grasped all that in the pause after the emperor had spoken. He nodded gravely. "Indeed, the core worlds of the Empire have all fallen. Even now, rebel forces push us back on every axis, yet hope is not lost.

"We've gathered what remains of Fleet together to force them back. We will retake every world. We will crush them under our heels. The rebels have gravely wounded our beloved Empire, but she will survive. We will win this war."

How wrong he'd been.

"I've sent my son, Lucien, to a place far away. He has everything he needs to return in due time if we fail. The Empire will live."

He leaned forward and gave the camera a stern look. "I command you to continue the fight. Protect the people of the Empire. If you lose contact with the rest of the Empire, take your orders from your Imperial Representatives, nobles, and above all those appointed by the Throne. We will not surrender. The Imperial edict codifying my orders is attached to this transmission and will remain in force until we win this war and I or my successor rescinds it."

Emperor Marcus rose to his feet. "Take this message to heart, my people. The rebellion will be undone. Have faith in me and those of my blood. Have faith in Fleet. Have faith in the key. Have faith in yourselves." He saluted the screen with a closed fist on his chest, and the image faded.

The transmission released her implants, allowing her to see those around her. The message had left them all thunderstruck.

Elise turned to Kelsey, her eyes wide in wonder. "Was that Emperor

Marcus? It was, wasn't it? Ah, what a message of hope for his people in such a dark time."

"A message that was doomed. He failed, and everyone died. Or worse."

The crown princess nodded, but she didn't seem deterred. "I'm not sure that matters. The people needed every glimmer of hope to keep fighting. He told them what they needed to hear. Obviously, they fought back well enough for humanity to survive. That counts for something. Lucien survived. The Imperial line is unbroken."

Kelsey sighed. That again. The line broke with her and her brother. The emperor's blood would carry on in Jared's line, and perhaps the line of Pentagaran kings, if their relationship prospered.

"I hope we can set up a camera and you can play that again," Elise said. "Do you have any idea what this key is? Or what is under our feet?"

"Not a clue. I've never heard of a key. Perhaps it's the code to undo the virus in a compromised person. The rebels vaporized the task force protecting Lucien. It could've been lost in that battle. We'll probably never know what it was for sure."

Elise stared up at the ceiling. "The image seemed to be focused on me. When I walked around the room a little, the image moved with me. That's quite amazing. I hope we can duplicate the technology."

Other than library access, the dais failed to respond to Kelsey. It had to be connecting with the device below, but it wasn't granting her any insights.

"I'm not getting anywhere. We know there isn't direct access from up here, so there must be some other way to get into that area. Let's examine every inch of this place."

Elise nodded her agreement. "We should start with the speaker's chamber. If there was any secret access, it would be there."

Kelsey followed Elise into the sumptuous chambers reserved for the speaker. It obviously served as an office as well, because it rode the line between luxurious and functional. This was the kind of room where powerful men and women made secret deals.

The artwork here was very similar to what she'd seem in the halls outside. Statues and paintings, mostly. Including, ironically, one of Emperor Marcus.

Feeling nothing out of the ordinary, Kelsey wandered the room, her senses attuned to anything her implants could detect. Nothing.

Actually, there was too much nothing. She felt an area behind the office that didn't register at all. Just like the shielded chamber she'd discovered on the asteroid in the Erorsi system, it was a blank spot in her senses.

"There's something back here." Kelsey glanced at Elise. "Do you know what's back there?"

"I'm not sure." Elise walked over to the only door in that wall, opened it, and peered inside. "It's a storage room."

One without a lot of space, it turned out. Some packrat had stuffed it full of furnishings and boxes. Dust covered everything in a fine gray sheen, and it smelled musty. There was barely enough room for Kelsey to push in after Elise. One of the Royal Guards seemed to consider pushing inside with them but probably decided that would be getting a little too personal.

"It's a storage room now," Kelsey said, "but at some point in the past, it was probably something else. It's shielded."

She probed the area with her implants. Perhaps now that she was inside, she could sense something else.

In fact, she could. The area of wall directly beside the door had a switch, just like the kind that secured her quarters on *Courageous*. That probably meant this shielded room used to be for secure storage. A mental push of the switch likely controlled the shielding field.

She triggered the switch.

An unseen hatch slid out of the wall and locked the guards outside. The piles of furniture shifted as the floor lurched and the entire room began sinking lower.

Kelsey kept the sofa beside them from falling on Elise and grinned. They were in a hidden lift dropping into a previously unexplored section of the Pentagaran Parliament Building. The only negative she could see was that Talbot was going to be pissed he'd slept through the adventure.

5

The debriefing was every bit as painful as Jared had imagined it would be. Breckenridge wouldn't let him finish one subject before he interrupted with a different criticism. He sniped from behind his desk, using hindsight to his full advantage. Commander Meyer stood to the side, faintly smirking, until Jared finished.

Breckenridge shook his head, not bothering to hide his disgusted expression. "You've had a remarkable run of poor decision making, Commander. Even for someone with your background. Thankfully for the Empire, a more experienced commander is at hand to take charge. I am assuming command of this mission as of this moment."

As much as Jared hated the idea, he'd known this was coming. "Aye, sir."

"You will report to *Spear*'s medical center for an exam. Then you will accompany me back to the derelict. Dismissed."

Jared saluted and spun on his heel. The two marines fell in behind him as Meyer directed him toward the lift. Jared stood beside *Spear*'s executive officer as the man sent the lift toward the medical center. "I hope you'll read the briefing material in more detail, Commander Meyer. This situation is serious. The rebels will be coming to Erorsi in a matter of weeks. They are nothing to sneer at."

The other man gave Jared a dismissive flip of his hand. "Your destroyer might not have been up to the task, but Captain Breckenridge and this task force will handle the situation."

"Like he did the war games?" Jared regretted the question as soon as he'd asked it, but it was true. "No matter what you think of me, I beg of you, don't underestimate these things. They took out the Old Empire. It doesn't get more serious than that."

Meyer's expression softened a little. "Point taken. I will read every word and advise Captain Breckenridge accordingly."

Spear's medical center was significantly larger than *Athena*'s was, though smaller than *Courageous*'s. Someone had called ahead, because an older black man with a shaved head stood waiting for them. His commander's tabs indicated he was the ship's chief medical officer.

He held out his hand. "Commander Mertz, I'm Justin Guzman. Captain Breckenridge has asked that I give you a complete examination." He turned to Meyer. "I'll let you know when I have my report ready, Sean."

"We need it as quickly as possible, please. Time is of the essence."

Once Meyer left, Guzman turned his attention to the marines. "You can wait outside." His tone made it clear he wasn't making a request.

The two marines glanced at one another and went outside.

Guzman shook his head. "Let's move over to the examination table, Commander Mertz. I took the liberty of requesting your file from Doctor Stone. I have to say that what I've read shocks me deeply. You shouldn't be walking. Or breathing. If you don't mind my asking, what in the world possessed you to put those things in your head?"

Jared lay back on the exam table and spoke as the doctor scanned him. "If you could see how the Old Empire equipment interfaces with these implants, you wouldn't need to ask. Imagine being able to have these scan results fed right from the table into your brain. Being able to grasp the information as fast as it comes in. Being able to control the equipment in an operation with such exactitude that you always knew precisely what was happening.

"Imagine that as a ship's commander. I can directly interface with *Courageous*'s scanners and control systems. I can communicate with the ship's computer in real time. The ship's records are available to me at a thought. This morning, I stood on a tower in the center of Imperial City on Terra herself before the Fall. It wasn't like a vid. It was exactly as if I'd been standing there myself."

Guzman looked impressed. "That certainly sounds compelling. You can sit up. My God." He stared at the readout on the wall. "It goes all through your brain. How the hell did they get that in there without killing you?"

"Perhaps Doctor Stone can answer that. All I can say for certain is that I was walking and talking within minutes of the procedure. While you might see this as radical, every Fleet officer in the Old Empire had this exact equipment. Every one. Frankly, it wasn't nearly as invasive as what happened to Princess Kelsey, and she's fine."

The other man frowned. "Princess Kelsey? What was done to her?"

He'd mentioned that the Pale Ones had implanted Kelsey to Breckenridge, but it occurred to him that he hadn't elaborated. "Didn't Stone send you her file?"

He consulted a tablet. "No. So, she has a similar set of implants?"

"She had a little bit more done than I did. You should talk with Commander Stone."

"I'm going to want to examine her, too."

"I'm sure she'd be happy to let you, but she's in the next system over. Pentagar."

Happy was something of an overstatement. His sister had grown downright hostile to medical procedures since she'd been forcibly implanted.

"I'm certain Captain Breckenridge will insist on it," Guzman said. "Let's finish your workup."

The doctor put Jared through an exhaustive set of tests, looking closely at the results as they went along. He peppered Jared with questions about *Courageous* and the task force's new situation as he worked. The exam took two hours.

When they were through, he clapped Jared on the back. "Well, to my shock, you show no signs of impairment. I'll endorse Commander Stone's duty certification. You're fit to command."

"Somehow, I don't think that's what your captain is expecting to hear," Jared said dryly.

"Perhaps not, but that's what he's getting. For what it's worth, I think you've done an astounding job, Commander. You've done Fleet proud."

"Thank you. Now all we have to do is stop the rebels and get back home."

Guzman called Commander Meyer and handed him a printed report. The other officer scanned it and looked up sharply. "This can't be right. How can someone with unauthorized equipment in his head be fit for duty?"

"By being fit for duty," the doctor said acerbically. "He's not impaired at all. In fact, his memory and ability to correlate information are off the charts. I'd sign up for something like these implants in a second."

Meyer looked like he'd bitten into something sour. "The captain will not be pleased."

"As senior medical officer in this task force, this is my decision to make, and I've made it." Guzman's tone brooked no argument.

The thin man harrumphed. "Very well. We don't have time to deal with this in any case." He turned to Jared. "The captain is ready to see this Old Empire battlecruiser for himself. We are to accompany him in your cutter. Let's go."

The man's tone grated on Jared's nerves, but he kept his peace. He'd faced hostility like this before, and he'd no doubt do it again. Being the Imperial Bastard gave him some experience in that. After Ethan, Meyer was a lightweight.

Ensign Enova wisely remained out of sight on the flight deck when they boarded the cutter. Unlike Jared, Breckenridge didn't seem inclined to poke his nose up there.

The older officer seemed to be in an even worse mood than earlier, if possible. "So Guzman cleared you for duty? Unbelievable. Don't think for one moment that this changes anything. You will not be allowed to escape the consequences of your actions so lightly."

Jared ground his teeth. "Perhaps the captain would educate me on what actions he would've taken under the same circumstances?"

Breckenridge looked down his nose at Jared. "The first thing I would've avoided was rushing through an untested flip point."

Jared said nothing and kept his face neutral.

The other man scowled anyway. "Do not try to equalize our circumstances, Commander. Your ship appeared to be under attack and severely damaged. Coming after you was the right choice."

Deciding he had little to lose, Jared pressed the subject. "We left a drone with all the data we'd gathered. The warning not to use the flip point was right up front. If you'd taken a few minutes to read it."

"You will keep a civil tongue in your head, Commander, or I'll see you in the brig. Your second error was revealing yourself to the Pentagarans. The third was involving yourself and, by extension, the Empire in a war that we have no business in."

Jared resisted the urge to shake his head. That wouldn't be helpful. "Those events are inextricably linked, sir. If you can jump in to save my ship, how could we do any less for helpless civilians? We already knew we had to go through that system to get home. If we'd stood by, many thousands of people would've been killed, and the Empire's reputation would've been ruined."

"Not if they didn't know you were there to witness the fight. The prudent action would be to observe and determine whom to aid. You were lucky you didn't help the wrong people."

Jared felt shamed he'd even considered that course of action. Hearing Breckenridge say it made him feel dirty. "Luckily for me, I had the princess along to advise me."

"We'll call that mistake number four. You should never have listened to an untrained neophyte, with all due respect to Princess Kelsey and the Imperial Family. She virtually gave away the technology you'd discovered. And for what? The gratitude of people who turned around and almost killed you and your crew.

"Mistake five, trusting these people any further than you can throw them. Mistake six, getting almost a hundred of your crew killed and your ship wrecked. Perhaps you'd care to point out even one thing that you did right. That might take less time."

Jared took a deep breath and let it out slowly. How had this idiot ever achieved a Fleet command?

"We've made mistakes, sir. No doubt. That said, we've done a few things right. We saved millions of people from almost certain death. If we'd stood aside, we'd have been complicit in an atrocity. Second, we've made a firm ally of the first advanced civilization the Empire has discovered since the Fall. Third, we've recovered a priceless artifact, an Old Empire battlecruiser filled with technology we're still trying to grasp. Not just as defunct equipment, but as a working ship. Fourth, we've recovered a treasure in data and cultural information in her computers."

He leaned forward. "Fifth, and most important, we've given the rebels a bloody nose and discovered their threat before they could attack the Empire. A surprise attack by the Pale Ones could've ended us. These new people might be even worse. Now we can prepare and take the fight to them."

Breckenridge shook his head with obvious disbelief. "You've lost your mind, Commander. I thank the gods that I arrived when I did. You have delusions."

The cutter docked with a slight bounce. Breckenridge stood, turned his back on Jared, and exited as soon as Meyer opened the hatch.

Graves stood waiting outside the docking hatch. He looked a little startled when Breckenridge and Meyer came aboard without asking permission, but he didn't let it put him off his game. "Commodore Breckenridge, Commander Meyer, welcome aboard *Courageous*. I'm Lieutenant Commander Charlie Graves, Captain Mertz's executive officer."

The courtesy promotion was Fleet tradition. There could only be one captain on a ship.

"You may refer to me as captain on this ship, Commander," Breckenridge said. "Whatever this derelict might once have been, it's no longer a Fleet vessel."

"Incorrect," *Courageous* said from the overhead speakers. "*Courageous* has not been decommissioned and is in active service."

Breckenridge's head jerked back. "Who the hell is that? If you want to speak to me, you can come down here and do it to my face. Don't you dare tell me the facts of the matter. I'll tell you."

"This unit is the AI controlling *Courageous*. It is customary to refer to a ship's AI by the same name as the ship on which it resides. Much as it is customary to request permission to come aboard a ship not your own, Commodore Breckenridge."

For a moment, Jared thought Breckenridge would have a stroke. "How dare you?" He whirled on Jared. "Are you telling me that you've allowed an unknown computer to control this derelict? Absolutely unacceptable."

"*Courageous* is just as much a part of this ship as the hull, sir," Jared said. "You aren't aware of just how intimately it is woven into all the ship's systems."

He sent a second command mentally to the computer. *Don't press him*, Courageous. *Now is* not *the time.*

"You've obviously lost all sense, Commander," Breckenridge snarled. "Allow me to clear up a few things. This is not an Imperial vessel. It's salvage. You are not its commanding officer. You are the jumped-up commanding officer of a destroyer and a bastard that Fleet should have dismissed years ago. You will report to *Athena* and remain there until further notice. Commander Meyer will lead a prize crew and bring this wreck home."

"Unacceptable," *Courageous* said. "This unit has a lawfully appointed commanding officer, Jared Mertz. Attempting to seize control of this vessel without authority will not be allowed."

Meyer cleared his throat. "Perhaps that course of action is somewhat premature, Captain."

Breckenridge looked at his exec as though the man had grown two heads. "Explain yourself."

"Whatever his flaws and failures, Commander Mertz is intimately familiar with this ship and the computer controlling it. He has the only direct method of accessing its records. He's correct in that this is a tremendous find for the Empire and a great stroke of luck that he could restore it to any level of functionality. We should take advantage of that."

"What are you suggesting? Leaving him in command of this ship? After everything he's done?" He sounded incredulous.

Meyer shrugged. "He's been in command of it in every way that mattered for months. What are a few more days? I suggest you make it clear to Commander Mertz that I am here acting with your authority. Then it doesn't matter that the ship's computer won't recognize me as being in command. If he doesn't do so, you have clear grounds to place him under arrest."

Breckenridge turned his attention to Mertz. "I dislike playing games, but so be it. Commander Meyer speaks with my authority. You will obey his orders as though they come from me. Is that clear enough, Commander Mertz?"

Jared kept his face blank. "Crystal clear, sir."

The old man grunted. "Then let's finish this tour so I can get back to my ship. We need to be in Pentagaran space as soon as possible so that I can undo what damage I can. The princess no doubt needs my support and advice. Frankly, I'm certain that she'll be glad to see you replaced. Move this along, Commander. The clock is ticking."

6

—————

"**M**y guards aren't going to be very happy," Elise said as the lift descended into the Parliament Building. "Why would the Old Empire need to hide this so effectively?"

Kelsey shrugged and drew a flechette pistol from a concealment holster at the small of her back. It wasn't very comfortable because it was large and she was small, but she liked having something to hand if trouble came looking for her. As it had done all too often of late.

She didn't expect to find anything living down here, but it paid to be cautious. Not that Talbot was going to see this as anything but reckless.

Kelsey smiled a little. "In my defense, I didn't expect the room to move."

The lift jerked to a halt and the hatch slid open, revealing darkness that slowly began brightening. Kelsey stepped out and scanned the area. It was a corridor similar to those aboard *Courageous*.

Elise tried her communications unit. "I'm not getting a signal. Shouldn't we go right back up? They're going to be going wild about now."

One glance showed Kelsey that she didn't have a connection either. "The area is screened. We *could* go back up, but I'd rather see what's down here first. Admit it. You're curious. Are they going to be any more upset if we spend a few minutes checking things out?"

"Probably not," the noblewoman admitted. "Lead on."

The corridor led to a single armored hatch, not unlike the one protecting *Courageous*'s computer center. It slid open at their approach. The room beyond was cloaked in darkness. Kelsey sensed a light control near the doorway and commanded the lights on.

The bright lights made her blink for a moment but revealed a command center that made the bridge on *Courageous* feel small. It had to take up almost the entire shielded area.

At least this level. Perhaps there was more underneath it. An even larger hatch occupied the far side of the control center, and smaller ones sat on the right and left sides.

Elise gaped. "My God. What is this place?"

All of the consoles were dark. Kelsey walked to the central dais and powered it on. The system went through a boot sequence and came to life. Once it felt online, she attempted to connect with it. It promptly rejected her.

This system is restricted. Authenticate.

Kelsey felt it probe her implants and, to her surprise, they responded with a complicated authentication code.

Authentication accepted. Standing by.

She probed her implants but couldn't figure out why they had responded at all, much less with some kind of code.

Identify this system, she instructed it.

This unit is the primary planetary defense center for the Pentagaran system.

Kelsey turned toward Elise and holstered her weapon. "We're not in any danger. This is the Old Empire planetary defense center. I guess they controlled the fight against the rebels from here."

Elise put her hands on the back of a chair in the center of the room. "I always knew there had to have been one, but I thought it long destroyed. The rebels pounded us from orbit. They destroyed the spaceport and two other cities."

"Hang on while I try to figure out something." Kelsey cocked her head. *What was the thing you did with my implants?*

This unit authenticated your clearance level and diplomatic codes. Everything is in order.

What diplomatic codes? What clearance level?

Your diplomatic codes, Ambassador Kelsey Bandar. This unit acknowledges your authority over it. As an heir to the Imperial Throne and ambassador plenipotentiary of the Terran Empire, you have clearance to communicate and instruct this unit. What are your orders?

How the hell could it know all that? How could her implants have codes like that? The Pale Ones certainly hadn't known or cared.

Then the answer occurred to her. It had to be *Courageous.* Nothing else explained it. It had to have put the codes into her implants. Probably in the same way a captain controlled his ship. The computers knew who people were and what they could control based on the codes in their implants and their serial numbers.

She remembered *Courageous* had updated her implants for her. It must've added the codes then. Why hadn't it told her? She'd have to ask it.

The question of why it had done so was a little murkier. It might have accepted Jared as its commanding officer, but why would it grant her diplomatic codes? How did it have them to begin with? Well, perhaps it knew them because a computer had to have them to know they were valid, right?

She looked at Elise. "It seems that *Courageous* gave me diplomatic codes. At least that's my guess at where they came from. The computer accepts my authority as an ambassador of the Terran Empire. Which is somewhat awkward, since Pentagar isn't part of said Empire."

"I'm not going to quibble right now." Elise walked around the room and peered at the consoles. "I can hardly imagine even being in here. This is part of our history. The baron, my great-great-and-so-forth-grandfather probably stood in this room. Of course, that begs the question of why he never mentioned it."

"Without weapons systems, it may not have seemed relevant after the rebels failed to return."

Computer, can you respond verbally?

"Affirmative."

Elise jerked at the voice from the hidden speakers. It sounded female and soothing.

"What is your status?" Kelsey asked.

"This unit is online. Scanner net degraded to twenty-three percent. Weapon systems offline."

"Amazing," Elise said softly. "Computer, do you have records of the attack on Pentagar?"

"Voice not recognized. Implant authorization required to divulge classified information."

Fortunately, Kelsey had dealt with this situation before. "Computer, I authorize you to respond to Crown Princess Elise Orison."

"Authorization not accepted. Implant codes required for each individual accessing this system."

Kelsey frowned. "So, you're saying you recognize my authority as an ambassador of the Terran Empire, but I can't authorize someone to access you?"

"Incorrect. Access to the system can be granted once the appropriate authorizations are entered into an individual's implants. This task may be accomplished at any computer that possesses the appropriate diplomatic security databases."

"Well, that's not very helpful," Kelsey grumbled. "I can see this is going to be a recurring theme. You can do whatever you like, as long as you have the appropriate authorization. Oh, and by the way, you can't get the appropriate authorization, because there's no one left to give it to you. Or the people you want to authorize won't have implants."

Elise put her hand on Kelsey's shoulder. "Now, now. Let's not be so negative. You received the appropriate authorization for diplomatic purposes, didn't you? Surely, that means that other computer systems can do something similar. What is it that you're not able to do?"

"The first thing I'd like to do is give you the appropriate authority to access this computer. It's on your planet, so you should be in control of it, not some visitor from another world. Then I'd like to get more specifications on my implants. I have to cobble together little bits and pieces of information to figure out their functionality. I should be able to find a help manual somewhere."

"*Courageous* doesn't have something like that?"

"Apparently not. Though it must have a diplomatic security database."

Elise walked around the control room slowly. "So, what was it you were detecting from the speaker's podium?"

Kelsey located the access point she'd detected earlier. "Computer, what is this?" She forwarded the signature of the device to the computer.

"That is a closed-circuit data repeater. It interfaces with the podium in the parliamentary chamber. Through it, the podium computer can access authorized material in this unit."

Kelsey nodded. That made sense. "What restricts access to the podium? Is it only due to the fact that I had diplomatic codes in my implants that I can access it?"

"Correct. The podium computer is designed to interface with all authorized personnel and their designees."

"What are the criteria for you to designate someone?" Elise asked.

Kelsey repeated the question to the computer.

"Authorized users may designate other individuals to access the podium controls through implant or verbal access."

"Finally. I designate Crown Princess Elise Orison as my designee. She has complete access to any files that I would have access to through the podium."

"Please state your name and position for the record, Crown Princess Elise Orison."

Elise stood a little straighter. "My name is Elise Patricia Orison. My position is crown princess and heir to the throne of Pentagar."

"Access granted to console systems on podium, Crown Princess Elise Patricia Orison."

"Please call me Elise."

"Preference acknowledged."

The tall noblewoman rubbed her hands together. "I cannot wait to dig into the contents of this computer. However, we really should head back up before they find a drill to come after us. I figure just about enough time has passed that Talbot will be there."

Kelsey snorted. "I'll bet you're right. He's probably ready to dig his way down with his bare hands. First, let me get a little bit more information."

She accessed the system and requested plans for the hidden facility. As she'd expected, there were other levels below this one, probably filled with computers and control systems. The hatch directly across from where they'd entered supposedly led to the known areas of the Parliament Building, but the corridor read as sealed. She imagined someone had filled it in with plascrete to hide the facility. Why, she wasn't sure. The other two led to various rooms and lifts connected to the areas below.

That mystery was one Elise could figure out on her own. "Okay. There used to be another entrance, but I think someone filled it in. You'll need to dig it out to get access. I'll give you the maps as soon as I can. Let's go back up. This is enough excitement for one day."

They retraced their steps, and Kelsey sent the command to the switch as soon as they were safely inside the storage room. The hatch closed, and the lift lurched upward. A minute later, the hatch opened to bedlam.

It seemed they had indeed found a drill, a very large one, and a determined crew of men and women. Everyone stepped back to allow the two women to exit.

The Royal Guards surrounded Elise as their leader examined her anxiously for signs of injury. "Are you harmed, Your Highness? What happened?"

Elise held her hands up. "It's okay. We discovered a lift leading down into the sealed section. We were never in any danger."

In comparison to the Royal Guards, the female marine assigned to guard Kelsey took her disappearance in stride. Except for the eye roll and head shake.

Talbot rushed in at that moment. He slowed when he saw Kelsey standing there, but she could see the worried expression on his face. "What's with you? I can't take a nap without you sneaking off to find some secret facility. I thought we had an agreement?"

Kelsey put on her best innocent face. "It wasn't my fault. I thought I was turning off a stealth field. I had no idea that it was a lift, and I'm perfectly fine. See?" She held up her arms and turned in a circle.

He pulled her into a hug. She knew it was a sign of just how worried he was that he did so with everyone around. He had an exaggerated opinion of how to protect her dignity.

She sighed and melted into him. "This is more like it. Next time I promise to wait for you to come protect me before I explore some strange, possibly dangerous place."

He squeezed her tight for a moment and then released her. "Okay. I'll let this go, this one time." He grinned. "Like I have any control over what you do. So what'd you find down there?"

"It seems that the planetary defense center for Pentagar is still operational. There are no weapons, of course, but the databases are intact. In fact, it seems that *Courageous* gave me some kind of diplomatic codes. The computer recognized me and gave me full access."

She looked over at Elise. "Come on. Let's go see if you can access the console on the podium."

Talbot stepped beside her as they walked out. "I hear you played something back in the main chamber. Some kind of message from the old emperor?"

Kelsey nodded. "Emperor Marcus's final message to the Terran Empire. His order to fight. It was pretty moving."

"We'll need to make a copy for the historians. I can almost hear them drooling from here."

"You can hear somebody drool? And here I thought my hearing was good."

He laughed. "You know what I mean."

She stepped onto the dais. "See if you could play the vid again, Elise. I think Talbot would enjoy it."

"'Enjoy' might be the wrong word," he said. "I know how that story turns out."

Elise stepped up to the console. "Computer, this is Elise Orison. Please replay the last message from Emperor Marcus."

Once more, the holo of the emperor from the bridge of his unknown ship played out, and again, Kelsey tapped into a view that wasn't visible to anyone else. She spent her time examining the strange woman. Not just her but her armor. It was definitely commando armor. Kelsey had seen images of the bulkier marine version.

One thing was immediately obvious. This armor had seen plenty of combat. Unless she'd borrowed the armor, that was. Kelsey decided she'd go with the assumption that the woman was a combat veteran. It looked as though it had been through hell.

The woman's expression hardly faltered during the speech. It seemed to Kelsey that the woman had already decided that their chances were slim. She looked like she was determined to fight it out to the bitter end, even though she knew that death most likely awaited her. Or worse.

Kelsey wondered what had happened to her. Had she died well? Had the rebels captured her and turned her into one of them? She would probably never know.

Even as the vid was playing, the computer interrupted her with an implant transmission. *Ambassador Kelsey Bandar, this unit has detected a number of vessels entering the system.*

Let me see.

A schematic of the system appeared in her mind's eye. The unknown vessels had transitioned through the flip point leading to the Courageous system. There were eight vessels.

A jolt of excitement ran through her. They had to be ships from home. Someone had come to rescue them.

Then the reality hit her. Those ships had made a one-way trip. Now the weak flip point had trapped them, too.

As soon as the vid stopped playing, Kelsey leaned close to Elise and tugged Talbot with her. "We have visitors from home. They just transitioned through the flip point to the Courageous system."

Both of them looked suitably surprised, but Elise recovered first. She smiled. "Then we'd best get ready to welcome more of our allies to Pentagar."

Kelsey nodded. "I'm not sure what the protocol is, but I think Talbot and I should go out to meet them. I'm certain that Jared explained everything, but it doesn't pay to take chances."

"Then you'd best get ready to travel. I look forward to meeting more of your people. Their presence will make capturing the freighter, and possibly dealing with any escort, easier."

Kelsey nodded again, but she couldn't escape the feeling that something just wasn't right. For once, she hoped her instincts were wrong.

7

Jared watched the approach of the Pentagaran fast courier *Lance* from *Courageous*'s bridge. Commander Meyer hadn't insisted on taking the command console but instead watched events unfold from one of the observation seats. The one Princess Kelsey normally used, in fact.

Once *Lance* launched from Pentagar, Jared assumed that Princess Kelsey was aboard her. He'd sent a brief message on tight beam giving her the basic situation and warning her that Breckenridge was in control. His implants allowed him to do so unobserved right under Meyer's nose.

Half an hour later, long after he should've opened communications, Breckenridge sent a message of greeting to *Lance*. He asked if Princess Kelsey was aboard and requested that she come to *Spear*.

His "request" sounded like an order, though. Not the smartest approach in dealing with Kelsey, as Jared well knew.

The courier pilot—Jared recognized him as Lieutenant Parker—politely responded that Princess Kelsey was aboard and was looking forward to meeting Captain Breckenridge. He passed along her request that he gather all his commanding officers aboard *Courageous* for a briefing so that she could bring them up to speed on the current situation.

Breckenridge declined, instead reiterating that Kelsey come to him.

Jared was unsurprised when her cutter undocked from *Lance* and arrowed directly toward *Courageous*. Breckenridge immediately ordered her to divert to *Spear*. The princess didn't respond.

Meyer stalked up to Jared. "What does she think she's doing?"

He looked up at the other officer blandly. "It seems that she thinks she's coming aboard *Courageous*."

"Stop her."

Jared allowed himself a wry smile. "Princess Kelsey is second in line to the Imperial Throne. My ability to direct her in any way was limited to my position in command of this mission. I no longer have that lever. Captain Breckenridge does."

"You know her," Meyer snarled. "Find a way."

"Short of firing on her cutter—which I of course will not do—I see no way of stopping her from coming here. If you want to redirect her, you'll need to do it face to face."

The unspoken subtext was that she was his problem now. Jared was looking forward to watching her roll over the other man.

Meyer looked as though he'd bitten into something sour. "I see. Then we'd best go down to meet her. Perhaps I can convince her to follow Captain Breckenridge's lawful instructions in person. She is not a member of the Imperial line for purposes of this mission. She is subordinate to the military commander."

Good luck with that, Jared thought as he followed the man to the lift. A glance back at his crew showed that they shared his opinion.

They arrived just as the princess's cutter docked. The hatch slid aside with a puff of cold, misty air, and the marines assigned to watch over Princess Kelsey came out. They stood beside the hatch and braced to attention. He noted Talbot was standing with them. A good choice on his part. The less these outsiders knew about the man's relationship with the princess, the better.

Kelsey came out next, her head held regally high. Obvious posturing to someone that knew her as well as Jared did, but not so much for Meyer.

Even after saying that she had no Imperial place other than diplomat, Meyer bowed his head. "Highness. I'm Commander Sean Meyer, at your service."

For once, Jared couldn't blame him. Respect for the Crown wasn't easy to put aside. The other officer's deference actually did him credit. Of course, at this point, almost anything he did right would do the same.

"Commander Meyer, Captain Mertz," Kelsey said as she strode right past the two of them. "We'll wait in the main conference room."

"But—"

Obviously ready for an objection, she whirled on Meyer. "You will not argue with me, Commander. Your captain's tone has left me in no mood for it. You will accompany me to the conference room, where we shall await the arrival of Captain Breckenridge and the other officers in your task force."

The tall officer bowed his head again, probably deciding that it was easier to let Breckenridge fight that fight.

They proceeded to the lift as a group. It was just large enough to hold them all. Expecting it, Jared accepted Kelsey's communication request. Meyer had no idea the two of them could communicate around him, an advantage Jared intended to take full advantage of.

You're putting on quite the show, Jared thought with some amusement.

A small twitch of her lips was her only physical response. *I've had years of practice. Is this Breckenridge as much of an ass as he seems?*

Unfortunately for us, I think he's worse. Everything I've seen tells me he's an opinionated man incapable of thinking outside his narrow worldview. One who thinks highly of his power. Frankly, his arrival is probably the worst possible outcome of sending a probe home. If I'd had a clue this might happen, I'd have avoided leaving any information at all.

The lift opened, and they all trooped toward the main conference room. Jared tapped into *Courageous's* scanners and noted that a cutter was on its way from *Spear*. Breckenridge obviously wasn't taking Kelsey's request to gather his senior officers seriously.

This was going to be an entertaining meeting. He wondered if they'd all end up in the brig.

Kelsey was obviously tapping into the scanner feed herself, because when she sat—at the head of the conference table—she gave Meyer a cold stare. "Your captain is ignoring my instruction to gather your ships' commanders. He's choosing to come over alone. This is not an auspicious beginning to our relationship. I suggest you contact him and correct this deficiency."

Her words surprised Meyer. "How could you possibly know what he's doing, Highness?" He shook his head. "You have those implant things. Of course. I'd forgotten. It's Captain Breckenridge's opinion that those devices leave a person's competency in doubt. Perhaps he only intends to see that you receive the medical care that you deserve."

The chill rolling off her became arctic. "Questioning my competency is an unwise course of action. I assure you that I have received the very best medical care possible. I understand and accept that you are following orders, but do not make yourself my enemy in your support of his policies. Do you understand me?"

"I will obey my orders and do what I think best for the Empire, Highness," he said stiffly.

Meyer took a seat near the other end of the table. Jared sat on Kelsey's right. The marines arrayed themselves behind the princess.

Jared knew the moment Breckenridge docked and even watched the vid feed as he made his way toward the conference room. He looked supremely pissed, and he wasn't alone. He'd brought half a dozen marines in light body armor. He obviously expected trouble.

If he tried to take Kelsey, he'd get it, too.

Courageous, pass a message to Lieutenant Reese. I want an armed response team with neural disruptors ready to respond at my call. If this situation gets physical, I want it stopped without loss of life.

Acknowledged. Should this unit instruct the bridge to bring the ship to battle stations? This vessel's screens and beam weapons give it a decisive advantage at this close range.

Negative.

Breckenridge strode into the conference room as though he owned it, his marines at his back. He hesitated when he saw the marines arrayed against the bulkhead. "You marines are dismissed."

"You overstep yourself, Captain," Kelsey said, holding up a hand to stop her marines from moving. "These men are acting as my guards. They stay."

Jared was proud to see how she didn't back down one centimeter.

Breckenridge scowled. "You are out of line, Highness. You are only authorized to act as the backup diplomatic presence on this mission."

"Wrong. When Carlo Vega died, I assumed the mantle of Imperial ambassador. You are being insubordinate, and it will stop now."

The Fleet officer looked flabbergasted. He'd probably hadn't had anyone speak to him with that tone in years.

He finally found his voice. "With all due respect to your father, you've been through a terrible ordeal. I have assumed command of this exploratory mission. Your position is subordinate to mine. You *will* submit to an examination on board my ship, and I will see that the Empire's interests are represented appropriately."

Kelsey smiled without the least bit of humor. "I absolutely will not *submit* to anything. I will *allow* your medical personnel to examine me, but only under the circumstances that I dictate."

She paused a moment to allow her words to hang in the air between them. "The Empire is at war. As the voice of the emperor, I decide what response is appropriate. The exploratory mission ended when we discovered the fight against the rebels wasn't over. You, sir, are under my orders until such time as the emperor appoints someone else to speak in his voice."

"That's preposterous," Breckenridge sneered. "You don't have the authority to make any of those declarations. We don't go to war at your say-so."

"You don't need my say-so. Emperor Marcus issued an Imperial edict for all Imperial forces to continue the fight. None of the emperors since has rescinded it. The fact that we didn't know about it means nothing. The Empire remains in a state of war, even though we thought ourselves at peace. Allow me to play those orders for you."

The screen on the wall came to life, and Jared found himself mesmerized as the vid feed played directly into his implants. He found himself rising to his feet without thought as Emperor Marcus began to speak. He heard the words, but his attention focused on the flag bridge, for obviously that was what it was. It dwarfed even *Courageous*'s control center.

Courageous, can you identify that ship or its class?

This unit does not know the particular ship, but the flag bridge belongs to a P.G. Holyfield–class superdreadnought, the most modern and powerful warship in Fleet service.

Basic schematics presented themselves in the corner of his vision. Holy God, that ship dwarfed *Courageous*. It had enough firepower to take on half a dozen battlecruisers head to head and win. It might be a wreck afterward, but it would take them down. It could singlehandedly destroy the present-day Terran Fleet in one engagement.

The vid ended, and Breckenridge waved his hand. "Irrelevant. He and everyone with him died with the Old Empire. Until and unless your father declares war, the Empire is at peace." He shot a glare at Jared. "Or we would be if someone hadn't started shooting when they should've stayed hidden. A flaw that he has displayed more than once."

Kelsey shook her head slowly. "So we finally get down to the reason you're pushing this. You dislike Captain Mertz because he defeated you. Humiliated you, from what I hear. Understandable enough, I suppose, but not relevant to this situation. You speak of the Old Empire and the Terran Empire as if they are two separate entities. They are not. The rule of the emperors is unbroken."

"Enough of this preposterous fantasy," Breckenridge snapped. "Senior Sergeant Jones, please escort Princess Kelsey to my cutter so that she may be examined by our chief medical officer."

"Stop," Jared said. "You heard the Imperial edict. Unless the emperor countermands it, Princess Kelsey is the most senior Imperial official in this system, and she's given us our orders. Stand fast, Senior Sergeant."

"Senior Sergeant, take Her Highness into medical custody," Breckenridge snarled. "Arrest Commander Mertz. He'll face charges for insubordination and disobeying a direct order. His blood won't save him now."

The man looked torn, but he moved when Breckenridge snapped his fingers. One of his men followed closely behind him. Two others started toward Jared.

Kelsey held up her hand one last time. "Captain Breckenridge, you're about to make a career-limiting error in judgment. As an ambassador plenipotentiary of the Terran Empire, I order you to stand down and submit to my lawful authority."

Senior Sergeant Jones took Kelsey by the arm and looked suitably shocked when she stood and slammed him face down onto the conference table without the slightest effort.

Jared opened his mouth to say something, but Meyer beat him to it. "Captain, we need to take a step back. The princess may have a point. Legally speaking. We should withdraw to consider the situation before we make the wrong choice."

Breckenridge looked as though he wanted to lash out, but he stepped back from the abyss after a very long moment of silence. Very reluctantly. "Commander Mertz, you will come with us."

"He will not," Kelsey said firmly. "*Courageous* says you don't believe she is an active Fleet vessel. Fine. I hereby declare her my diplomatic ship and transfer Captain Mertz and his crew from the disabled *Athena* to *Courageous* to act as my crew on detached duty. You may be the senior Fleet commander in this area, but they are no longer under your authority."

Breckenridge's expression was apoplectic. He backed out into the corridor. "This isn't over. We're leaving."

Kelsey released the marine, and he backed out with his fellows. Meyer inclined his head and strode out.

Once they were all gone, she slumped back into her seat. "Well, that could've gone better."

Jared agreed, but he wasn't sure how they could have gone about salvaging the situation once Breckenridge attempted to assert dominance. "*Courageous*, without sounding an alarm that Captain Breckenridge or his people can see or hear, go to general quarters. No battle screens unless they fire on us. Block all transmissions from inside this ship, and signal *Lance* that she is to withdraw at once. This isn't the Pentagarans' fight, and I don't want Breckenridge to think she's a threat."

He rubbed his face as Lieutenant Reese looked into the conference room questioningly. "Take your men and follow them to the docking level, Lieutenant. I want them off my ship without force, if possible. Be gentle. They are Fleet personnel."

"Aye, sir."

"Well," he said to Kelsey, "this certainly makes things harder. What do we do now?"

She sat down and buried her face in her hands. "I haven't got the faintest idea, but we need to get this settled as soon as possible. That freighter could pop up at any time now. If we're still bickering, it'll bring the wrath of the rebels down on us."

8

K elsey listened closely as Jared finished detailing his interactions with Breckenridge. "The man sounds like a real ass. How does someone that lacking in talent become a senior captain in Fleet? I ask only because I intend to make sure it never happens again."

Her brother stalked around his office. "Good luck with that. You'll have to get his uncle thrown out of the Imperial Senate first."

He sighed. "While that's a worthy goal, we need to worry about our current situation first. The freighter and its escort will be along shortly. I'd intended to make our way over there today, just in case they came early. We have to stop them, or we're completely screwed."

She took a breath and forced herself to focus. "We will. It's been three hours. If Breckenridge was going to reject my authority, he'd already have done so."

"Or he's trying to figure out how to take *Courageous* out," her brother said grimly.

"Let's hope not. Even his uncle wouldn't be able to save his ass if he attacked the daughter of the emperor or other Fleet personnel."

They'd separated from the Fleet task force and entered into orbit around Pentagar. A probe kept an eye on the other ships as they sat out in space a short distance away.

Talbot sat beside Kelsey. "And if you can't work it out?"

"We'll work it out," she said firmly. "Even if we don't, they don't have enough military force to do anything terminally stupid in Pentagar space. The Pentagaran Navy would chew them up, and the interdiction zone fortresses would keep them bottled up in this system. They're not going to make that mistake. That's the reason I know that we'll work it out. Because they have no choice."

Jared shook his head. "Life's taught me that you can't count on someone else doing the smart thing. Sometimes you can't even count on yourself for that. Bright people make terrible mistakes every day. Once you factor in stupidity, well, all bets are off."

"Pardon the interruption, Captain," *Courageous* said. "There is a cutter departing the Fleet task force. *Spear* is also signaling, asking for Princess Kelsey."

She rose to her feet. "Thank you, *Courageous*. Jared, may I borrow your desk?"

He gave her a lopsided smile. "It's your ship."

"It was the best I could come up with on short notice. Tell me you'd rather be over there with him right now. In the brig."

"I'll take our current circumstances. Thank you."

Kelsey sat at the desk and activated the console. An image of Captain Wallace Breckenridge appeared.

"Princess Kelsey."

"Captain. Have you reached a conclusion on my position?"

The man looked as though he smelled something bad. "Those familiar with legal matters have advised me to accept your claims for the moment. Rest assured that I will dispatch a probe for home to get this situation clarified at once. In the meantime, I recognize that this situation requires some compromise. My ships and I are yours to command.

"However, I insist that my chief medical officer examine you in your medical center. I also insist that one of my officers be present on your staff."

She didn't like the idea of his people on board *Courageous* at all, but even if he'd stuffed that cutter full of people, they could handle it. "I accept those conditions. Once I have satisfied your doctor, we need to have the meeting I originally called for. There is very little time before the rebels arrive to discover that we've taken the other system from them. We can't afford to allow them to escape."

"I feel confident that I will be able to formulate a plan of attack to stop a freighter and its escort."

"Captain Mertz and his team have been working on a plan for months. I'm certain that he will be able to execute it successfully."

Breckenridge shook his head. "Unacceptable. I am the senior Fleet officer and task force commander. You have given me the order, and I will determine the best method to carry it out. Commander Mertz is on detached duty and solely responsible for you and your ship."

She sighed, recognizing a futile situation in his intransigence. "I'll contact you as soon as we're done here."

"I look forward to your call." His tone indicated otherwise. "Good day, Highness." The transmission terminated.

"Isn't he just a joy to work with?" she asked rhetorically. "It shames me to ask this, but how do we know that cutter isn't loaded with a missile warhead?"

"*Courageous*, was that transmission via tight beam?" Jared asked.

"Negative."

"Then all his people heard him acknowledge your authority and identity. Would he try to kill the second in line to the Throne with that many witnesses?"

"I certainly hope not."

Talbot stood. "You two wait for them in the medical center. Commander Graves and I can meet the cutter."

She glared at him. "Getting yourself blown up makes this better how, exactly?"

"It's better than you and the captain going up in smoke."

Jared nodded. "That's the best plan. We'll go with it."

She felt her eyes narrow. "Isn't this my choice?"

"Not when it comes to your safety. Come on. There's just enough time for Talbot to arrange everything."

She and Jared went to the medical center. She filled Doctor Stone in while they waited.

The doctor smiled. "I've worked with Doctor Guzman before. He's not inclined to be anyone's yes man. If he gave the captain a clean bill of health, he'll do the same for you."

"Cutter docking," *Courageous* said from the overheads.

"I don't know if I'll ever get used to that," Stone said.

Kelsey chuckled. "Wait until he can say something in your head without warning. While you're in the shower."

She brought up the vid feed to the docking area and saw Commander Meyer and several others come onto the ship. It only took them a few minutes to arrive in the medical center. One of the men, a massive black man with a shaved head, smiled at Stone. "Lily, it's so good to see you again."

"Justin." Lily took his hand into hers. "Welcome aboard. I can't wait to show you around my medical center."

"I can't wait to see it. First, though, I need to examine Princess Kelsey." He bowed his head apologetically. "I'm Doctor Justin Guzman, Highness. I'll be as quick as I can."

She smiled even though she'd rather go through an armed combat drop than a medical examination. "Shall we start with a full body scan?"

"That sounds fine. I'm given to understand you received implants similar to Captain Mertz's?"

"Why don't I let you see for yourself?"

Kelsey reclined on the examination table and let Lily take over. She knew the exact moment when the other doctor grasped the scale of her modifications, because he gaped at the display.

"My God," he muttered. "What the hell did they do to you?"

Kelsey smiled up at him sardonically. "As hard as it is to believe, they gave me Imperial Commando implants. That's like a marine on steroids. A lot of steroids."

"Look here," Lily said, pointing to the screen beside the table. "You'll note she has the same cranial implants as Captain Mertz. In addition, her bones now have a graphene coating. She has artificial musculature in all her major muscle groups, as well. I've seen her lift a weight machine. Not the maximum weight. The entire machine."

She'd been wearing her combat armor at the time, but Kelsey saw no reason to elaborate.

Doctor Guzman looked down at her with ill-concealed shock. "That's hard to believe."

The marine from *Spear*—Senior Sergeant Jones—spoke up. "Believe it, Doc. She slammed me onto a table without any problem at all."

The older man shook his head as though clearing out the cobwebs. "I'll accept it, hypothetically. What is this?"

Lily smiled. "You'll love this. That's her pharmacology unit. I've been working on deciphering what the drugs are, but some of them are still a mystery to me. I know they can do something to speed up the reactivity of her nerves, as well as accelerating her brain functions. There are some powerful painkillers and just about anything that would be useful in combat."

Chemical data scrolled up the screen. The doctor examined it. "That's astonishing. Some of these have the potential to revolutionize pharmacology."

"She also had enhancements to her eyes, ears, and sense of smell. Finally, she has medical nanites, as does the captain. There are millions of small machines throughout her body that can repair a tremendous amount of damage. Do you see any signs of surgery?"

The older man examined the readouts closely. "None at all. The cuts must've been incredibly fine to leave no traces."

Kelsey knew what was coming, but it still made her stomach roil when Lily put up the image of her just after they'd rescued her. She lay flat on the table as the medical team prepped her for the regenerator. Terrible scars, red and raw, covered her skull and arms. They couldn't see under the sheet, but the scars had covered her entire body.

Everyone from *Spear* sucked in horrified gasps. Even Commander Meyer looked ill, his glance toward her filled with pity. Pity she didn't want or need.

"The scars covered every part of her body, and the surgery was done without any anesthesia at all," Stone said dispassionately. "The regenerator did what it could and would probably have fixed everything well enough that the scars wouldn't be visible, but the nanites fixed the damage right down to the cellular level. They also corrected other damage from childhood injuries.

"From speaking to someone knowledgeable with these kinds of nanites, she can also expect an extended life span. Approximately three hundred years, from what I've been able to determine. Though I've begun to suspect that her nanites are even more effective than those used by a normal Fleet officer or marine. She might live half again longer. Or forever. We just don't know."

Guzman shook his head again. "That's… well, I was going to say preposterous, but I think I might need to move the marker for that word out a little bit. Difficult to believe, then. I'll want to see all your medical records for the princess, please. Highness, you can sit up. We two sawbones will adjourn to Doctor Stone's office to hash this out."

Senior Sergeant Jones stepped over after the doctors had left and she'd sat up. "Highness, I want to apologize for putting my hands on your person. I deeply regret doing so."

She considered being snippy with him but rejected the thought almost at once. He was Talbot's fellow marine. "You were following what you thought to be the lawful orders of your commanding officer, Senior Sergeant. I won't hold that against you. Besides, I might have caused you some embarrassment. I'm sorry about that."

His face took on a wry expression. "It *has* been mentioned a few times. I'm sure I'll be able to live it down in a few years."

"I bet I can help with that," Talbot said. "There's a Pentagaran vid of some assassins ambushing a group of us. It's very… educational."

Kelsey wanted to tell him not to play it, but she knew she'd have to live with that recording for the rest of her life. At least she hadn't shared the recordings of the ambush on the asteroid and in the sunken battlecruiser housing the Pale Ones' AI. They were still safely isolated in her implant memory.

She'd watched the vid several times, and it still shocked her. It hadn't felt like she was moving that quickly during the attack, but she was. Her implants had taken control of her and moved her through the attackers like a ghost. Yes, they'd grazed her arm with one shot, but she'd been empty-handed against half a dozen armed men. She'd killed most of them before their bodies had hit the floor.

The men from *Spear* were quiet as the vid played out. Afterward, they stared at her with an expression much different from pity. Shock and awe, Talbot had called it.

"That was her on autopilot," Talbot said to the hushed gathering. "Less than a week after the Pale Ones ripped her apart and rebuilt her. In the last two months, she's been training and has much better control of her enhancements. She's significantly more deadly now, especially with weapons. Her implants link right into them, and she can outshoot me.

"We don't have recordings, but she interrupted a Pale Ones ambush. She was in powered Imperial commando armor with a high-powered flechette railgun and a plasma rifle. Armed like that, she'd have a better-than-even chance of taking out the entire marine compliment on *Spear* while they were in an entrenched defensive position."

Kelsey took a deep breath and let it out slowly. "It's not something I ever saw myself as, Senior Sergeant, but there is no shame in losing out to me physically. I'm not the little girl I look like. I'm a killing machine, and every single Pale One is just like me. Underestimating them means death or worse." Her voice turned grim as she told him how outclassed they were.

She shifted her gaze to Commander Meyer. "On a different level, I can interface with *Courageous*. I watched you when you boarded this ship through my implant feed. I can access the ship's scanners right now and tell you exactly how far away *Spear* is from us. I know her weapons status. I know her precise course.

"I'm so in tune with my armor that I forget I'm wearing it. Jared is just the same way with this ship. He could take *Courageous* to battle stations, fire her weapons, and anything else he would normally do on the bridge from his shower. Imagine what this ship could do if every officer and crewperson were implanted. At this moment, she's not nearly as efficient as she will be one day. Even in this reduced state, she could take all of your ships from a standing start."

"It seems I may have underestimated the threat that these Pale Ones pose and the benefits of enhancement," Meyer said, sounding a bit overwhelmed. "You envision all Fleet personnel having these one day?"

She nodded. "I don't see how we can avoid it, Commander. Honestly, the Fleet implant surgery isn't that hard to recover from. Jared was on light duty the same day and fully recovered the next. A commando should have the work done in a series of procedures with recovery and training time between them. Regular marines would have less work than me. I've fully recovered, even though I'm still learning what I need to know about using them. This is nothing to be afraid of."

The door to Lily's office opened, and the two physicians came out. Guzman bowed his head. "I've been over every aspect of your enhancement, Highness. You have my full medical approval."

She smiled. "Thank you, Doctor. Gentlemen, if you have no further objections, we need to have that briefing. I want all ships' captains brought aboard *Courageous* tomorrow morning. I've been up all night, and they need time to examine all the data we've gathered. Come ready to plan our next moves in a hurry. The rebels will be back in less than a week, and we must be ready for them. That means we leave for Erorsi as soon as we finish."

9

Breckenridge came spoiling for a fight. He and his officers arrived in a phalanx and sat across the table from Jared, Kelsey, and Graves. Other than introducing the others briefly, the captain sat silent and hostile. Jared hoped the other ship commanders would be more open-minded than the senior captain.

Thankfully, he had ported *Athena*'s files over to *Courageous* and had access to their dossiers. Those told him a little more about the men and women arrayed against him—the people he had to convince to follow his battle plan if they were to have any chance of success.

The commanding officers of the two light cruisers flanked Breckenridge: Captain Justin Macumber of *Titan* on the right and Captain Paul Cooley of *Shadow* on the left. The destroyer commanders flanked them: Commander Scott Roche of *Ginnie Dare* and Commander Ryan Stevenson of *One Bullet* on the right and Commander Eliyanna Kaiser of *New York* to the left. There should've been one more destroyer to make for an even set, but it had been detached to escort one of the other exploratory expeditions.

Based on the maps he now had of the Old Empire, the other three expeditions were probably safe from running into anything dangerous—unless they found an unexpected path deeper into the Old Empire like *Athena* had. For all the distance a flip point could traverse in a moment, they shepherded the direction of travel to a greater or lesser degree. The other expeditions were moving away from the Old Empire.

Jared cleared his throat. "Thank you all for coming. Let me start with the basic rundown of our situation. The next system over, the Erorsi system, was under the control of the Pale Ones until two months ago. We've defeated them and destroyed the artificial intelligence controlling the system. We blew up one orbital and captured two shipyards, one of them completely intact. The other one is repairable. The planet took a major kinetic strike, though. The damage to the ecosystem is extreme."

He brought up a diagram of the Erorsi system. "The green diamond is the flip point leading to Pentagar. The red diamond is the flip point leading deeper into the Old Empire. The yellow diamond is a weak flip point leading to areas unknown. As you can see, any vessels coming through from the Old Empire will need to go quite some distance into the system before they will be able to detect anything about the planet or the orbitals around it. In fact, they will need to pass directly through the system's asteroid belt.

"After consultation with the Pentagaran Navy officers, we decided the best course of action was to place one force behind Erorsi and another in the asteroid belt. Once the freighter and any possible escorts are between the forces, we can strike and hold them from escaping. Because that's the key factor in this engagement. We want the contents of the freighter, but under no circumstances can we allow any information about our presence to get back to the rebels."

Macumber raised his hand, earning a sharp glance from Breckenridge. He continued in spite of the warning. "What kind of firepower are we looking at? A ship like this one? Something bigger? Or perhaps only a destroyer?"

"We don't know," Jared said. "Communications logs we recovered only indicate that this yearly resupply mission sometimes has an escort. If this were a Fleet mission, it would probably be a destroyer. We can't count on that, though. If they send a battlecruiser like *Courageous*, this is going to be an exceptionally deadly fight."

Breckenridge sniffed. "Let's say that we do capture this freighter. What's its cargo? Better yet, how do we access the computer on board it to get the information we need to make better choices going forward? In other words, *Captain*, what is your long-term plan?"

The subtle emphasis he placed on Jared's title made his repugnance clear. Jared ignored it. They needed to bury their problems, or they'd never get home. "Without information on what lies further into the Old Empire, it's not easy to develop a long-term plan. There are several possible routes leading back to Avalon. Once we have an idea of what we face, we'll be able to pick the appropriate direction to go."

Captain Cooley earned a glance of his own from his commander when he spoke. "If these artificial intelligences are that advanced, how do we intend to get access to the records at all? As the commodore asked, what exactly is the cargo on board this freighter?"

Kelsey spoke up for the first time in the briefing. "The computers on board the ships are accessible through our implants. Based on what I've seen, we'll probably have to have physical access as well. And by that, I mean someone with implants will need to be on board the freighter to gain access to its systems. Either Captain Mertz or myself will need to be included in the boarding party sent to secure it."

Breckenridge shook his head. "Unacceptable. Under no circumstances will I risk the life of a member of the Imperial Family like that. Neither of you will be allowed into the other system until we have secured it. My task force is quite capable of handling any problems that come our way. Once we have secured the freighter, we will send word, and *Captain* Mertz can come do whatever he thinks necessary."

Kelsey leaned forward. "That is unacceptable as well. I cannot stress how important it is that no word of our incursion filters back to the rebels. Whatever plan you decide to go forward with, Commodore Breckenridge, it needs to include *Courageous*. This vessel is faster than any of your ships, and her scanning gear is infinitely better. As are her weapons.

"I understand that you have no desire to cooperate with us on this matter. You're going to need to modify that attitude. Allow me to stress that you have no idea how deadly Old Empire technology can be. This ship is quite capable of exterminating your entire task force. If one like her accompanies that freighter, it's entirely possible that it would leave the system as the sole survivor. Whether or not you include *Courageous* in the initial attack, she needs to be present so that she can deal with any threats that you cannot."

They glared at one another. Breckenridge relented. "If that is the case, then I insist that you not be present on board this vessel, Highness."

"Agreed," Jared said before Kelsey could argue.

Kelsey frowned at him. "Excuse me?"

Just play along, he sent to her implants.

Once she sat back, Jared continued aloud. "Commodore Breckenridge is correct. If *Courageous* is going to fight, we can't risk losing both of the people with implants. In any case, you're the less expendable of the two of us. You're in command of the Imperial forces in this sector."

Breckenridge grunted. "Now that we've settled that, we need to discuss the possible contingencies in this battle."

The way that Breckenridge assumed that Kelsey would do what they decided amused Jared. His real plan for Kelsey might give the older man a stroke. Once the Imperial task force deployed in the Erorsi system, he'd make certain that Princess Kelsey was available in a marine pinnace. If the ship had to fight, his sister would be safe in the asteroid belt, undetectable at low speed but able to get to the freighter quickly if needed.

Once they got into the details of planning the ambush, some of the tenseness in the air bled away. Aside from Breckenridge, Jared found the Fleet officers competent and knowledgeable. They examined the Erorsi system layout as a group and suggested refinements to the attack plan, as well as contingencies based on certain possible reactions by the other side.

After about an hour, they had what Jared believed to be a workable plan that wasn't too different from the one he'd already settled on with the Pentagarans.

Commander Kaiser pointed at the weak flip point in the Erorsi system. "What about that thing? Should we send a probe through just to be certain that nothing is going to be coming after us while we're fighting?"

Jared shook his head. "Nothing has come out in the last two months, and I'd rather not provoke something on the other side that we're not aware of. The Pentagaran forces are already in orbit around Erorsi. We've moved the probe that we had monitoring the rebel flip point to a safe distance so that any ship coming through won't spot it.

"It's in range to detect any incursion and signal the forces around the planet, as well as the probe waiting here at the flip point to Pentagar. We need to proceed to the Erorsi system as soon as possible and take up our positions. Every minute we delay leads to a higher possibility that the enemy will arrive before we're ready for them."

"Status change," *Courageous* said from the overhead speakers. "Transition detected in the Erorsi system at the enemy flip point. Two vessels are currently proceeding toward Erorsi prime. ETA five point seven hours."

"Dammit," Jared muttered. "This couldn't have come at a worse time. We need to get over to the other system as soon as possible."

"Wait," Roche said. "At that speed, they won't be into scanner range of the planet to see the damage for most of the trip, unless their scanners work completely differently than ours. How long did the AI wait to signal them before?"

"We have no idea."

Roche nodded. "It'll take us a few hours to get to the Erorsi flip point if we leave right now. If we keep our speed down on the other side, we might be able to cut them off. It doesn't matter what they do in the system if they can't get back out the way they came."

Breckenridge nodded decisively. "Excellent points, Scott. So long as our course and speed allow us to beat them to the other flip point, we win. From what I've seen, they'll attack at the first sign of enemy activity, so we should be able to lure them into coming after us. Or the Pentagarans could do the same. We'll just have to improvise."

Hearing that word come from Breckenridge's mouth made Jared a little ill. The other man wasn't good at all in a free-form tactical environment.

Captain Breckenridge rose to his feet. "Signal the task force, Commander Meyer. We boost for the Erorsi flip point at flank speed." He shifted his attention to Kelsey. "You can get off here or at the fortresses defending the flip point, Highness. I don't care which. Commander Meyer will accompany you."

Without waiting for a response, he headed out of the conference room. The other ships' captains hastily followed him out.

Kelsey growled. "He's really beginning to irritate me."

"Will you be getting off here or at the stations around the flip point, Highness?" Meyer asked.

Kelsey grinned. "Neither. I'll go with *Courageous*."

Commander Meyer jerked a little. "That wasn't the agreement. You agreed with Captain Breckenridge that you wouldn't go in exchange for this ship being included in the attack plan."

"Jared agreed to that, not me. Besides, there are two ships. You might need a second person with implants. The survival of everyone in this task force might depend on it. We do it my way."

The slender officer looked torn, but he reluctantly nodded. "I'm going to regret this, aren't I?"

"Based on my observation," Jared said, "almost certainly."

10

_____

Kelsey sat at one of the observation consoles to the rear of the bridge. Part of her attention was on the scanner readings from the Erorsi system, but they were too far away from the enemy ships to detect them directly. She only hoped the reverse was true.

The task force was leading the way, with *Courageous* following at a more sedate pace, one that Jared could make up for if he needed to.

The rest of her attention was on Commander Meyer. The tall man was watching her. She raised an eyebrow. "Can I help you, Commander?"

"I'm curious what you're doing."

"Right now? I'm watching the system through the ship's scanners and wondering if this ambush is going to work."

He shook his head. "That's not what I meant. Forgive me, but a few months ago, your relationship to Captain Mertz was poor at best. Now you're working with him as though you've been together for years. Surely the events of the last few months haven't erased the troubles between you."

She focused her full attention on him. "That's fairly blunt, and none of your business."

"I disagree," he said diffidently. "If I don't understand the full situation, I can't explain it to Captain Breckenridge. People don't trust what they don't understand."

"Are you saying you don't trust me? That's awkward."

He shrugged. "I'm being up front. Your authority is somewhat… sketchy with the captain. If he decides that you're a danger to the Empire, he might refuse to accept your leadership. I'm coming to see how advanced this ship is, but it's only one ship. It would be far better for everyone concerned if the two of you built some bridges."

She leaned back in her chair and crossed her arms. "Okay, if you want this plainly stated, I'll do that. Yes, I came on this mission with a chip on my shoulder toward Jared. Everyone knows the history between him and my family. In fact, it's so widely known that people assume they know everything about it. They don't.

"Over the last few months, I've gotten the chance to see what kind of person Jared Mertz really is: a loyal, honest man who loves the Empire. A gifted tactician and combat commander. A friend. A very good friend. I'm certain that's not how you see him, but you and your captain are biased."

"I don't see my position as biased. Jared Mertz has a reputation in Fleet as a man seeking advancement, one who's willing to use his birth as a ladder to climb over the backs of more deserving officers. Perhaps you weren't aware of that."

Kelsey smiled coolly. "My brother worries about that very thing. He's wrong to do so, and so are you. Jared has gone out of his way to avoid using his birth to his advantage, so much so that it's kept him from being where his talent would already have taken him: a task force command.

"Believe me, I looked hard before I came to that conclusion. I wish your commander could say the same. His uncle in the Senate has been there for him, if you know what I mean. If using family to advance your career pisses you off, shouldn't that bother you?"

Meyer stiffened. "I've been with Captain Breckenridge for four years. He is an exemplary officer."

"He's arrogant, ill suited to unorthodox situations, and he nurses a grudge. You're both still smarting from the ambush Jared sprang on you during the war games. You don't see his methods as creative. You see them as cheating. Let's say for the moment that I agreed with you. I'd rather have the universe's best cheat stacking the deck against the Empire's enemies than a man who refuses to see the reality of the situation."

Her frank assessment seemed to take Meyer back. "Well, I'm not certain I share that assessment, but we're stuck with the cards we've been dealt, to use your metaphor. I'll consider what you've said. What are your plans going forward into this ambush, if I might ask?"

"The marines are prepping a pinnace. I'll go with them shortly."

"Forgive me, Highness, but that's an exceptionally rash decision. You have no place in combat, even though you seem to have handled every situation thrown at you with exceptional bravery and unnerving competence."

She allowed herself a smile. "I doubt very seriously that Lieutenant Reese will let me near the fighting this time. I have something of a reputation. Nonetheless, it seems to find me anyway. The question in my mind is, do you have a place on this mission?"

The man straightened. "I'm going wherever you go. It's my duty to be between you and danger."

She laughed before she could stop herself. "I'm sorry. I don't mean that as a reflection on your bravery. The one place you absolutely do not want to be is between me and danger. We need time to fit you into some armor. That means we'll go down to marine country shortly."

The tactical overlay she'd been keeping up in the corner of her mind's eye updated. The two markers for the enemy ships showed more details. One of the stealthed probes had gotten a better reading and sent it on to *Courageous* via tight beam. The escort was a destroyer.

"Good news," Jared said, obviously looking at the same information. "We're only facing a destroyer. While dangerous, it isn't nearly as bad as a cruiser. Zia, send a tight beam to *Spear* with the details. Append whatever data we have about that class of ship to it. What's our ETA?"

"Less than two hours at this speed, Captain. If we can keep them from spotting us for another hour, we can cut the destroyer off from the flip point. Somewhat longer if we take the slower speed of the task force into account. Also, we've received a confirmation signal from the Pentagaran ships in orbit around Erorsi. They're ready to move out as soon as you give the word."

The tactical officer glanced down at her console. "Incoming signal from *Spear*."

Kelsey rose to her feet. "That's my cue to depart stage left. Jared, good luck."

He turned toward her as she headed for the lift. "Stay out of trouble, but be sure to shut them down as soon as possible. Remember, we need that cargo intact."

"I'll do my best."

She led Commander Meyer into the lift and started it down toward marine country.

"You don't seem worried about the prospect of fighting," he said after a moment.

Kelsey nodded. "After a while, you either learn to control your fear or you stop fighting. I'm worried, though. Everything has to go just right for us to win. One mistake will let the enemy escape or see the ship we want to capture blown to pieces. Even if we do everything right, people will still die. That's the hardest part."

The lift doors opened, and she walked down the corridor to marine country. The marines were in the final stages of gearing up. Coulter stood waiting for them.

"Commander, if you'll come this way, I'll get you into some combat armor. Highness, we have your armor ready."

Meyer waved Coulter away. "I want to see this armor first."

"Aye, sir. This way."

The marine led them into the armory. Kelsey's dark-grey armor stood ready on its stand. She couldn't help but compare it to the black armor the woman in the vid had worn. Scratched and scarred as Kelsey's was, it was pristine compared to the other woman's. How much hell would she have to go through for them to look the same?

She began shedding her clothes, to the obvious shock of the Fleet officer.

"They've seen everything I've got," she said bluntly. "An Old Empire skinsuit makes the armor a lot more comfortable." She did turn her back on him at the last, though. He wasn't a marine.

The snug suit made slipping into the armor a lot easier. It also had sensors built into it that the armor reacted to. Movement was smoother when she wore it. It also had the requisite fittings for her to pass any wastes on to the armor's sump.

Kelsey commanded the armor to seal as soon as she slipped inside. The systems came online and did an auto check. All green. Talbot would check her again before they boarded anything. She disconnected the armor from its stand and took two steps forward.

She squatted and then stretched. The range of motion was good, and the armor settled around her like a little black dress. Her implants had already overridden her senses, and she could see and hear everything around her.

To make a point, she stepped in front of Meyer without turning on the chameleon portion of the helmet. All he would be able to see was a featureless helmet of hardened metal without the slightest hint of humanity.

"Forget what you think you know about me, Commander. I've earned my maturity the hard way. Do not underestimate me."

To his credit, Meyer stood his ground. "I won't, Highness. In return, I ask you to consider that you don't know everything about either your half brother or Captain Breckenridge."

The corners of her lips quirked upward. He had more steel than she'd expected. "I've dropped the half-brother reference. Jared is my brother. I know him a hell of a lot better than your CO. Captain Breckenridge is going to need to prove himself to me, and so are you. Be glad we're only boarding a freighter. That has to be easier than a stand-up firefight. Or crash landing a pinnace."

She turned the helmet projection on and watched his expression as her face appeared. It wasn't really her, but the projection on the helmet was very lifelike.

That was when the overhead alarms began to ring. Jared's voice rang out through the overheads. "All hands to battle stations. This is not a drill."

Kelsey brought the ship's tactical overlay back up. The task force had split up. *Courageous* was on her way toward the enemy flip point. The other five ships were still heading for the two ships in the enemy task force. That wasn't the plan.

She pinged Jared through the ship's network. *What's happening? Why did we change course?*

Captain Breckenridge said he has enough ships to run down a destroyer. We're to play backstop to make sure the enemy doesn't slip past him and make a run for it.

Is that the best idea?

No. My guess is that he doesn't trust us not to get involved. Keep prepping for your mission. We might have to board the destroyer if things go south.

She scowled at Meyer. "Your captain changed the plan at the last minute. We're on the way to the enemy flip point while he tries to take out the destroyer and capture the freighter on his own. If this goes bad, I'm going to be pissed."

Meyer took a step back. "I'm certain that he had his reasons."

"They'd better be damned good. Suit up. We might need to launch in a hurry. Coulter, get him ready."

"Aye, Highness. This way, Commander."

She was certain that "Aye, Highness" wasn't the correct response, but she had to admit it made her smile.

Kelsey made her way over to Lieutenant Reese. The officer was huddled with Talbot and the other noncoms. They had ship plans up on one of the screens. It didn't look like a freighter.

They made room for her without comment. Reese tapped the screen. "I just got word that our potential target has changed. This is the most common type of destroyer in the Old Empire, a Zombie class. Small, fast, but relatively lightly armed."

She loaded the plans into her implants. "Faster than this ship? Lightly armed in comparison to what? Us? The task force?"

"*Courageous* can take her if she can catch her. The task force can, too, though their lack of missile range leaves them open for a mauling if they screw up. Captain Mertz says he warned them." The marine officer shook his head. "They're making this more complicated than I like, but that's been our luck lately."

"Status change," *Courageous* said through the overhead speakers. "The enemy vessels have changed course back toward the hostile flip point and are accelerating."

Kelsey looked at the tactical situation through the ship's passive scanners. They could directly detect the enemy ships at this point. "*Courageous*, can we cut them off from the flip point?"

"Affirmative, if the situation remains static. If the destroyer accelerates, this vessel is not close enough to stop it from fleeing."

"Well, we'll just have to hope that—"

The Fleet task force accelerated sharply. If the enemy had only suspected their presence before, they knew they were there now.

"Dammit," Kelsey cursed. "What the hell is that man thinking? He's going to spook them into splitting up. The bastards are going to get away."

Reese looked grim. "Let's hope not. If they do, the Pentagarans are in real danger of an invasion, and so are we."

11
_____

Jared watched in frustration as the enemy destroyer accelerated away from the freighter. At that speed, it was going to beat them handily to the flip point. Breckenridge had ruined the ambush.

"Maximum acceleration. I want to be in range of the ship before it flips."

Courageous leapt to its top speed, but Jared only had to do one check to realize they wouldn't make it. The destroyer would be able to flip before they came into extreme range.

The Fleet task force had split in two. The faster ships were in pursuit of the destroyer while *Spear* headed for the freighter. That really made no sense. Why send a heavy cruiser to catch a freighter? The Pentagaran ships coming out from Erorsi would be able to catch the lumbering cargo ship before it got to the flip point. Breckenridge shouldn't have split his forces.

That's when it hit him. Breckenridge wanted to capture the freighter and its cargo for himself. He'd come up with some excuse or reason to keep it. Or he'd try.

Jared put it out of his mind. Kelsey could deal with the man once the situation was under control. Right now, he needed to figure out how to stop that fleeing ship.

He watched the situation play out for a little while. The task force had drawn substantially ahead of *Courageous* during the stealthy approach on the enemy ships. The destroyer was still going to be far outside their missile envelope, but it looked tantalizingly close to them.

Zia turned toward him. "Sir, something isn't right. The destroyer should be pulling farther ahead. It's not moving at full speed."

"Are you sure? Perhaps it's not really a Zombie class."

"Our scanners are on active mode, and I'm getting a decent reading on it. I think it is a Zombie. One that isn't using its full potential. Sir, I'm concerned it might be sucking the task force into missile range."

Jared checked the distances between that ship and the task force. "Give them a warning that thing might be setting up an ambush."

That was when the destroyer put on a burst of speed, cutting in toward the task force and firing missiles.

"Missiles fired," Zia said briskly. "Six missiles on an inbound track for the task force. They're accelerating at Old Empire speeds. The enemy ship is still closing. It's fired a second salvo. Now it's turning for the flip point and putting on maximum acceleration."

Jared watched the two clusters of missiles close in on the task force with a sense of dread. He'd warned them just how capable those weapons were, but that wouldn't help. The first group of missiles turned out to have two scan jammers. They blinded the Fleet vessels, allowing two of the real missiles to get through.

Both struck the light cruiser *Shadow* in titanic explosions. The warship lurched and veered off course, leaving it broadside to the next salvo.

Titan interposed herself between the danger and her wounded companion, firing her antimissile railguns at the incoming weapons. She stopped two of them. Three missiles struck *Titan*, and she exploded with the fury reserved to the gods of failed fusion plants. The remaining missile hit *One Bullet*, sending the destroyer to join *Titan* in the grave.

The enemy destroyer had killed a Fleet light cruiser and destroyer without taking a single bit of damage in return. It hadn't even come within range for the ships to return fire. Wisely, the remaining two Fleet destroyers began rescue operations, leaving the fleeing enemy to *Courageous*.

"Tell me we're going to catch that son of a bitch short of the flip point," Jared snarled.

Zia shook her head. "He still has enough distance to flip before we come into extreme missile range. We're going to have to make a combat flip and go after him."

Jared watched the ship make it to the flip point and disappear with impotent rage. "We have no idea what's on the other side of the flip point. What are our options?"

The tactical officer held up three fingers. "He'll either be waiting for us to flip, be hauling ass for the next flip point, or dropped to a crawl, hoping to hide until he gets so far away from the flip point that we can't find him.

"Odds are good the next system isn't occupied. The Old Empire maps have it as a white dwarf with no habitable planets. The flip point leading deeper into the Old Empire is on the other side of the system."

Jared nodded. "He has enough of a lead to get some distance and drop out of sight. The problem I see with that is that we'll be able to block his escape. If he can ambush us right after the flip, he might be able to take us out. That's the worst case. What can we do if that's his plan?"

"Send a spread of probes through. He won't get them all. One of them will tell us where he's at. Then we can flip through and blow him into atoms."

"Pardon, Captain," *Courageous* said. "There is one additional option. This vessel has decoys designed to masquerade as this vessel. One could be sent through, and it would likely fool the enemy scanners long enough to draw their fire."

"That could work. How long until we flip?"

"Just over twenty minutes, Captain," Ramirez said.

Jared watched the situation behind them as they sped toward the flip point. The Pentagarans were still hours away from being able to assist in the rescue operations. With the loss of *Titan* and *One Bullet*, the death toll would be almost two thousand people. They'd blown up so quickly that there wouldn't be any survivors.

Shadow was intact, but two Old Empire missiles would've wreaked havoc inside her. She had to have hundreds dead and even more wounded. The two destroyers would have their hands full with rescue operations. Their medical staffs would work themselves to collapse, but it wouldn't be enough.

He mentally glared at the icon representing *Spear*. That bastard should've been chasing the enemy destroyer. Those people had died because Breckenridge had underestimated the threat. Again.

Jared sighed. He didn't wish anyone on that ship harm. If Breckenridge had chased the destroyer and the enemy had destroyed *Spear*, they'd have lost almost as many people.

"*Spear* is launching pinnaces," Zia said. "They'll be boarding the freighter about the time we're ready to flip."

Hopefully they could capture the freighter without any further loss of life.

The freighter dashed those hopes when it fired on *Spear*. A missile flashed out of one cargo hold, followed by two more. The low rate of acceleration told Jared that the enemy had used the same trick he'd used on the Pale Ones' shipyard. They'd taken missile warheads without the normal drives and fired them. Perhaps they'd been in the cargo the ship was delivering.

Spear stopped two of them at a safe distance, but the third almost made it before the defensive railguns detonated it. They needed to get on board that freighter as soon as possible.

A missile flashed out of the heavy cruiser and into the freighter. The cargo vessel disintegrated in a massive explosion, destroying everything Jared had hoped to capture: the cargo, prisoners, and any computer records.

He rubbed his face tiredly. Breckenridge had botched every aspect of this ambush by the numbers. The incompetence that he'd accused Jared of was on full display, and he'd no doubt find a way to blame someone else.

Probably Jared.

"Three minutes to flip," Zia said. "I'm thinking of sending the decoy through on the far edge of the flip point and coming through on this side in fifteen seconds."

He shook his head. "Reverse that. We'll go through on the far side. Release the decoy with a good trajectory to go through where we'd transition. We'll brake hard and go through after it. This is going to be difficult, but I want you to be surgical, Zia. I want that ship crippled but not destroyed. We need any information from him that we can get. Work with *Courageous* on targeting critical areas."

Jared opened a channel to Lieutenant Reese. "We're flipping in three minutes. Be ready to launch at a moment's notice. Things went sideways in the ambush. The freighter is gone. We need this ship in one piece."

"Aye, sir. We'll do our best. The pinnace we brought over from *Athena* won't be as good as the three Old Empire models, but if you can get us close, we'll be able to lock onto their hull."

"I'll buy you every meter that I can. Good luck. I know it's asking a lot, but keep Kelsey alive for me."

"I'll do my best. Reese out."

They crossed into the flip point and dropped the decoy. Its scanner signature blossomed into one identical with *Courageous*'s. Jared was impressed. He wouldn't have known it was a decoy if he hadn't seen it come online with his own eyes. Metaphorically speaking.

The decoy flipped, and he counted down fifteen seconds. "Raise the screens. Flip the ship."

The gut-twisting surge of transition washed over him, but he kept a firm lock on the tactical situation through his implants. The first thing he saw was the spread of six missiles arrowing toward the decoy.

He traced them back in a flash and located the destroyer. It was in an area of space that would be behind a ship that made the fastest transition. With the course change he'd laid in, *Courageous* had the other ship right in her sights at point blank range while they were reloading.

Jared made a split-second decision, overrode Zia's attack plan, and locked the missiles down. *Courageous*'s beam weapons came to life at his command and lashed out at the vessel sitting right in their face.

The lances of coherent energy slammed into the enemy's screens, dropping them. The following shots tore into the destroyer's hull.

Jared used his knowledge of the enemy deck plan to take out both his fusion plants by vaporizing the cooling and control circuitry. Two other beams disabled two of the missile launchers.

Robbed of the ability to control their own temperature, the plants performed as designed and shut down.

The destroyer fired missiles at *Courageous*. Zia stepped in behind Jared and resumed control of the beams. She incinerated the warheads before they closed the distance to *Courageous*. Then she knocked out the remaining launchers.

The Zombie-class destroyers didn't have beam weapons. The massive power requirements for them restricted them to heavy cruisers or above. The antimissile railgun slugs it fired at them failed to penetrate *Courageous*'s screens.

Low-power pinpoint shots disabled even that offensive capability. The enemy destroyer hung before them, crippled.

Jared sent the go signal to Reese. This was all in his hands now, and Kelsey's.

"Captain, I'm picking up a probe moving at high speed," Zia said. "It's on a course toward the other flip point in this system. It's already at the far edge of our missile envelope."

"Fire missiles. Take it out."

Probes didn't have the speed of missiles, but they could flip. He absolutely couldn't afford to let word of their ambush get back to wherever this ship came from. If the probe got too far away from them, it would escape.

Zia launched four missiles, ludicrous overkill for a probe. Her caution proved warranted when two of *Courageous*'s missiles burned out before catching it. The other two took it out.

He heaved a sigh of relief. "Thank God."

The marine pinnaces had launched while they dealt with the probe and were fast approaching the destroyer. This was the moment of truth.

12

elsey felt surprisingly calm as the pinnaces swooped in on the crippled destroyer. Perhaps having a small celestial body dropped on one put things into perspective.

"Listen up," Lieutenant Reese said over the general channel. "These people are likely armed with Old Empire weapons, and they'll know this ship better than we do. Don't take any chances. If someone surrenders, fine. If not, don't hesitate to put them down.

"If you see any computer equipment, make note of it. The engineering team will secure the ship's AI. See that they and the princess stay clear of the fighting."

He gave her a stern look. "The princess will try to stay out of the worst of it, but if she becomes engaged, support her to the hilt."

She snorted softly. She'd keep clear if she could, but if they needed her, she'd bring the heavy firepower.

Reese continued. "We'll be breaching the hull in four places. Tiger One will take engineering, Two will hit the bow, Three will take port, and Four will hit the starboard. Overwhelm any resistance as quickly as you can and support the other teams. We breach in sixty seconds. Good luck."

Up close, the ship looked surprisingly like *Courageous* had when they'd found her. The beams had melted their way through the hull in much the same way. Only there was a lot more debris pouring from the breaches: equipment, air, and bodies.

Kelsey didn't want to think about that, but these people had just killed thousands of her countrymen. Her gut tightened, and she pushed her regrets away. They'd earned what was coming.

Their pinnace stopped short of the enemy and fired the breaching charge, a web of small explosives bound together like a fishing net. It spread across a small area of the hull and detonated. The shaped charges ripped that small section apart.

When the fresh cloud of debris had thinned, Reese gave the order to board. The ramp opened at the back of the pinnace, and the marines swarmed across the gap with practiced ease. She made the jump without problems, the grav assist in her armor taking her exactly where she wanted to go. Her long hours of practice were paying off.

Part of her mind noted with amusement that Commander Meyer was having a much more difficult time of it. Sergeant Coulter was shepherding him across like a sack of potatoes.

Talbot and her guards hemmed her in protectively as the other marines set up a portable airlock and forced their way into the main body of the ship. They wanted prisoners, so spacing everyone wasn't on the menu.

Her external speakers picked up the howling of alarms as she cycled through. The ship's artificial gravity was still on, so that made moving around simpler.

The marines were taking fire from the forward part of the corridor. A dozen men and women in Fleet coveralls cowered under the guns of a marine fire team aft of their airlock.

She opened her senses and was surprised to discover they didn't have implants. She'd expected them to have the same AI–controlled virus that the Pale Ones did. That would've made them puppets for the AIs.

Kelsey consulted the diagram of the ship she'd downloaded. They were three levels away from the computer center. They needed to find a lift or stairwell.

That's when the sporadic fire from up ahead became more intense. They must've run into heavy resistance. Then they started taking fire from aft.

"Enemy units moving behind us," Talbot shouted. "Take cover!"

That meant dodging into compartments to the sides of the corridor. It meant being pinned down. A destroyer couldn't have many marines aboard. *Athena* had only had thirty. With the four strike forces, they had almost two hundred marines.

Rather than ducking into one of the side compartments, she sprinted toward the fresh enemies and leapt.

The move took them completely off guard, and she landed among them without taking a single hit. There were four men in unpowered armor. She lashed out and took two of them out before they could jump back. The other two threw themselves back and fired at her with their flechette rifles.

High-speed tungsten penetrators rang off her armor as she drew her pistols and shot them. One died as her darts took him in the throat. The other dropped as her neural disruptor stunned him.

Her armor was gouged where they'd shot her, but nothing had penetrated. Yay powered combat armor.

"Dammit! Will you stop that?" Talbot covered the cross-corridors as his men took up positions. "You're going to get killed."

"We don't have time to get pinned down. We need the AI intact."

"We also need you alive. I need you alive."

She put her hand on his shoulder. "I'm being careful. Now let's get our people to this stairwell over here. We can get up to the computer center through it."

"Wait for the LT." Talbot must've sent a message to his commanding officer, because other marines streamed past their position and up the stairwell.

Reese stopped next to her. "Good work, Princess. Don't ruin it by running ahead of us. The enemy will be guarding the computer center. We want it intact."

She felt her eyes narrow. "Are you saying I'd blow it up?"

"Your track record on capturing AIs is filled with explosions and floods."

"I only wrecked one," she sniffed, "and that wasn't my fault. You were sleeping on the job."

"It's called being knocked unconscious by the antiboarding weapons. I'm surprised they haven't tried that. Doctor Leonard rigged up something that we put into our armor to protect us, but they haven't even tried."

"Knocking out the fusion plants might have taken them offline."

"True. The other teams report they're moving forward under heavy fire. The bridge is secure, but there were no prisoners. The officers attacked with pistols, and our people had to return fire. Engineering is still up in the air, but it looks like we might capture some people. We've secured a number of prisoners."

"The ones I saw didn't have implants. That's odd. The Old Empire implanted everyone in uniform from the lowest recruit to the Admiral of the Fleet."

The marine officer shrugged. "We'll sort it out. The advance fire team reports the enemy has sealed the computer center. No surprise there. I'm afraid Commander Meyer took a ricochet. His armor mostly held up, but he's got shrapnel in his leg."

"Is it serious?"

"He'll be okay once the doctor takes care of him. Time to move on to the AI."

The armored hatch to the computer center looked very much like the one on *Courageous*. The marines were setting up a perimeter on one side of the area. The other one was conspicuously empty of people.

"Exactly what is your entry plan?" she asked, suspecting she already knew the answer.

"The same one you used last time. You use your plasma rifle to breach the corridor wall and we swarm the compartment."

That was what she'd done on the sunken battlecruiser, though she'd had to attack all by herself. While the plan had worked, it had wreaked incredible damage to the area. Plasma wasn't the subtlest of weapons.

"That's always good for a last resort, but maybe we don't have to go that far. Let me try something."

She closed her eyes and reached out, looking for the AI. It wasn't there. At least there wasn't any way to connect to it.

"I thought the AIs had power sources other than the ship's fusion plants. I'm not feeling it."

Reese frowned. "It should have an independent power supply good for months. The area doesn't look damaged, either."

Kelsey opened her search to look for implant-capable devices. There were some but not nearly as many as on board *Courageous*. There was one set of implants in the computer center. So, someone was inside after all.

"I'm sensing someone in the computer center. A set of implants. I'll try communicating with that person. Perhaps we can get them to surrender."

"That would be nice," Reese said. "If not, we'll pry them out the hard way. We've taken the major areas of the ship. Resistance is falling off."

She pinged the implants inside and requested a connection. The person accepted. *Not the best time to chat. There's a bunch of people in the corridor outside. What's the status on rigging up a self-destruct device?*

He must've assumed she was one of his shipmates. *I'm afraid that it isn't going well. In fact, the entire ship has fallen. My name is Kelsey, and I'm one of the people in the corridor. We've taken this ship, and I'm calling on you to surrender. This fight is over.*

A moment of silence ended with a mental snarl from inside. *Damned traitor. I'll never give in to the likes of you. The only way you'll take me is in a body bag.* The connection terminated.

"Well, that could have gone better," she said out loud. "Let me go in first. I can handle one person, and we need prisoners. Cover your eyes."

She brought the plasma rifle up off her back and trained it on the armored hatch. If this worked out like it had on the sunken battlecruiser, the hatch would hold and the corridor would suffer. That would leave most of the computer center intact.

The bright bit of plasma exploded when it hit the armored hatch and engulfed the corridor beyond in flame. The bulkheads, ceiling, and floor failed.

Kelsey slung her plasma rifle and took a running jump down the corridor. She bounced off the bulkhead across from the hole and vaulted into the computer center. This one was in much better shape than the last one she'd seen. Everything was functional and clean.

There was more than one person in the room. There were five, all of them armed with pistols. They opened fire as she came hurtling in.

Much as she'd done in the earlier fight, she knew her advantage was in moving fast, so she used her suit to spring to the left as soon as her feet hit the floor. One armored fist smashed the pistol out of the hand of a woman in a rating's uniform. She'd have broken bones, but they could regenerate them.

Kelsey's neural disruptor came out as she rolled under a console. The enemy flechettes tore it apart as they tried to kill her.

She opened her weapon to its widest setting, popped up, and fired.

Three of the enemy dropped, including the one in an officer's uniform. The remaining man, his eyes wide with fear, shot her at point-blank range.

This time the flechette went through her armor, and her left arm exploded with pain. She managed to tag him before he could shoot her again.

"Got them," she said through clenched teeth. "Hang on while I open the hatch."

She assessed her damage while she hunted for the manual override to the hatch locks. The flechette had hit one of the damaged areas on her upper arm. The weakened armor hadn't quite failed. The high-speed penetrator had deflected a piece of her own armor into her arm.

The pain dropped to almost nothing as her pharmacology unit dumped something into her bloodstream for the pain. She'd pay for it later, she imagined.

The manual lock worked as she remembered, and the armored hatch slid open. The marines flooded in and secured the room.

Talbot rushed to her side and cursed when he saw her favoring her arm. "How bad is it?"

"Not serious. I had two shots hit the same area. Just bad luck."

"Good luck that it wasn't your head. If it can wait, I'd rather not open up your armor until we're sure we've run down everyone on this ship."

Lieutenant Reese oversaw the securing of the prisoners, but he'd obviously been listening in. "We've locked down the primary ship's systems, but there are holdouts in the maintenance conduits. That gives them access all over the ship. We're starting at engineering and working our way forward, but it'll take a while to flush out all the stragglers. Is there any chance we can subvert their computer systems?"

Carl Owlet, their resident computer expert, brought up one of the consoles. "This is unlocked, but it says the AI has been wiped. Everything. All data drives scrubbed."

Well, while that was better than having the enemy get a warning out, it wasn't much help. They'd lost the freighter with its precious cargo and failed to get any hard data.

Kelsey looked at their newest prisoners. They'd have to do this the hard way.

13

J ared breathed a sigh of relief when several Pentagaran warships flipped into the system. He'd been feeling a little bit naked out here all alone.

The news from back in the Erorsi system was less reassuring. *Shadow* was in almost as bad a shape as *Athena* had been after her fight with the Pale Ones. She'd suffered heavy casualties, and her primary systems were offline. Rescue operations were ongoing. Her captain had survived, but he was in critical condition.

Breckenridge ordered Jared to abandon the destroyer and return at once, an order Jared was pleased to ignore with Kelsey's blessing. They'd give the destroyer a good going over and decide what to do after that.

The marines had scoured the other ship twice. A good thing, because they'd missed a couple of holdouts the first time. They'd lost a dozen marines in the attack, with three times that number wounded. Including Kelsey.

She'd assured Jared that her wound was minor, but he worried until she came back over with the wounded and the prisoners.

He'd sent Dennis Baxter and some of his people to the destroyer. He'd rather not abandon it. If anyone could salvage something from the ship, it was his chief engineer.

While he waited for their report, he went down to the area Reese had set up for the prisoners. *Courageous* had a brig, but it was insufficient for the number of people they had in custody. They'd captured about fifty men and women, many injured in the fighting.

The officers had fought to the death. Only the one from the computer center had survived. He was also the only prisoner with implants.

They had him secured in a separate holding cell, strapped to a table.

He'd become violent when he woke up. Now he glared at them from the table, continuously struggling with his bonds.

His uniform indicated he was a lieutenant commander, and his name tag said Richards. The sight of him snarling at them raised the hackles on Jared's neck. It was very much like the reactions of captured Pale Ones.

Or maybe he was only snarling at Doctor Leonard. The elderly scientist had a modified headset on the man's head and was scanning him.

Jared stepped up beside the table and looked down at their prisoner. "Commander Richards, my name is Jared Mertz, and I command *Courageous* in the name of the Terran Empire. You are the senior surviving officer of your ship, the destroyer labeled R-7386. I imagine we'll be seeing quite a lot of one another over the next few months. Is there anything I can get you?"

Richards didn't respond other than to growl.

"He won't talk with me, either, Captain," Leonard said. "His implants have a corrupted version of code that is very similar to that used in the Pale Ones. It's not exactly the same, though. Based on what I can see, he probably has somewhat more ability to carry out his orders. He works with the implants rather than being solely under their control. This is significantly more sophisticated than the hack used during the rebellion."

The technical people from Erorsi knew Old Empire programming and were able to isolate the specific corruption used on the Pale Ones. The savages' implants overrode the human host when certain criteria existed. It was pretty blunt about it, too.

"Is the hardware the same?" Jared asked. "Can you reverse the virus?"

The older man nodded. "It is and I can. That should eliminate the unreasoned portion of his response. He has a Fleet officer's implants, by the way. No nanites, though. Just the cranial implants. I'm still not sure why they don't use them."

A woman Jared vaguely recognized as part of the Erorsi contingent chose that moment to push the Old Empire implanting device into the room. "Here you are, Doctor," the woman said.

The old scientist glanced at Jared. "Shall we proceed, Captain?"

They'd been through this process with several captured Pale Ones. It replaced the compromised code with the original Imperial version. Not that the change improved the Pale Ones' disposition. Savages were still savages. It had eliminated the unreasoning attack compulsion, though.

"Go ahead."

The scientists maneuvered the machine until they had it around the prisoner's head. Doctor Leonard initiated the software reversion, and the workstation began overwriting Richards's implant code. The process wasn't quick. It took just over four hours.

He'd been told that it could be done faster, but not without putting the implantee in significant danger. That's why the Old Empire couldn't keep up with the rebels. They didn't care if the subject died.

Jared let the scientists do their work. He'd come back once the process was complete.

His next stop was the medical center. He'd already been through once to talk to the injured. As always, the damage after a battle made him sick. These people were the lucky ones. The unlucky rested in the morgue.

An exhausted Lily Stone sat in her office, her head in her hands. He startled her when he rapped on the hatch.

She ran her hand through her hair and stood. "Captain."

"No need to stand for me. You and your people have done miracles. Again. I know it doesn't feel like it right now, but you have."

Stone gestured for him to take a seat. "It's the same for you, isn't it? We count the eggs broken rather than whole. It feels like we've had this conversation before."

"That's because we have. As long as we keep fighting, we'll keep losing people. Have you had a chance to examine the prisoners?"

The dark-haired doctor nodded. "Our technicians ran them through the scanners. No implants, other than that one officer. No sign of nanites, even in him. They were all in good health, though."

"Was the officer's surgery done with a regenerator?"

"Probably sometime in his late teens or early twenties. A regenerator removed the scarring."

He cocked his head. "I thought regeneration masked any kind of time assessment. How can you tell?"

"The skull bones. Regenerators don't work that well on bones. The rate at which the incisions remodeled tells me about how long ago he had the surgery. If he'd had the graphene coating on his bones that Kelsey has, it would've been more difficult, though I could've finessed it."

That made sense. "They'll be sending the dead from the destroyer over shortly. I want each of them examined, particularly the ones with implants. I don't want you to rush it, though. We have time. Tell me about Kelsey."

"The scans showed that she had some shrapnel in her upper arm. Her armor shattered under multiple hits, and some of the fragments went into her. I removed them and sealed the wound. Her nanites will heal her in a day or so."

He nodded. "Good. I want you to make a pass through the destroyer's medical center when you have time. I need to know how they compare to us, technology wise. I also want to know if they have any equipment for performing implants. That can wait for now, though."

Jared rose to his feet. "Seriously, Lily. You did everything you could. Get some rest."

He resisted the urge to go oversee the interrogation of the prisoners. Graves had that covered. If he needed Jared to come glower at someone, he'd call.

Feeling like he had nothing to do, he returned to his office and called Baxter. The chief engineer was over on the destroyer, examining its systems. He came on after a moment, some large piece of equipment behind him.

"Baxter, give me some good news."

The engineer shook his head. "I don't have a lot of that in stock. Carl Owlet was right. They wiped the AI. It's gone. They scrubbed every bit of data on the drives. That's not to say that there isn't anything to recover, though. We're finding tablets and other data sources, but it's going to be like when we collected everything on *Courageous*. Slow."

"What about the ship itself? Can you restore power?"

"Not a chance. You nailed the support equipment on both fusion plants. The repairs will take a while. The good news is that this ship *is* repairable. Zia will have to give you a rundown on the weapons systems, but they can probably be repaired as well, given enough time."

Jared didn't think they'd be fixing this ship any time soon. That would probably fall to the Pentagarans. "What about the drives?"

"Undamaged. I could maneuver the ship if it had power. The flip capacitors are charged, so if you tow the ship back into the flip point, we can get it back to Erorsi."

He grunted at the unexpected good news. "I figured the controls would be locked down."

"They are," the engineer said cheerfully. "I'll manually trigger the flip at the drive itself. You give the word and we'll get going."

"Okay. I'll have our small craft get the ship moving toward the flip point. Good work."

It would take several hours for the small craft to get the hulk drifting into the flip point. Thankfully, it wasn't far away. The extra time would allow the probes they'd sent out to scan the rest of the system. He doubted there was any human presence at all, but it never hurt to be sure.

The last stop on his tour was to see Kelsey. She was in marine country. Of course. It had become her second home. He supposed she had more in common with them now. She'd been through things only they could understand, and her lover was a marine.

She was out of her armor and dressed in the clothes she'd worn earlier. A bandage on her left arm was the only sign anything had changed. She headed over as soon as he came in. "Don't get on me about this. My armor isn't impervious."

"I'd rather you didn't get into these fights, but I'm glad you're well protected when you do. You communicated with the guy in the computer center. What did he say?"

"He thought I was someone else. He wanted to know the status of rigging a self-destruct device. Called me a traitor when he figured out he didn't know me. That pretty much sums up our chat. Did we get anyone else with implants?"

Jared shook his head. "No. Based on the initial evidence, it looks like officers had implants and enlisted didn't. Doctor Leonard is scrubbing the virus out of the one prisoner's implants as we speak. Once he finishes, I want you to lead the questioning."

Kelsey gave him a surprised look. "Me? I don't know anything about interrogation."

"Perhaps not, but you're good at talking to people. He might say something to you that he wouldn't say to me. At least you'll be able to get a dialog going. I want to know who he thinks you are. A traitor to whom?"

She nodded. "Okay. First, though, I'm going back over to the destroyer. Some pieces of equipment require implants to access. I also want to look at the weapons we recovered. They seem about on par with the ones we have. If so, we can commandeer their ammunition supply. That'll be a lot faster than restoring what we found here on *Courageous*."

He looked over at her armor on its stand. There were several spots that had obviously taken hits. "Do they have anything like this?"

"Ask me after we finish searching the ship. One of your shots took out their marine country, so we haven't had a chance to do a thorough search of it. No one we fought was in powered armor, though."

Jared nodded. "Get into your spare armor first. I wouldn't want any unexploded ordinance to put you in danger. The marines will examine the destroyer's two pinnaces to see if we can replace the one we lost. If so, we'll do it before we flip back to Erorsi."

She cocked her head. "Why? Is there a rush?"

"I expect Breckenridge to try and confiscate that ship as soon as we get back over there. Baxter can flip it once. We might be able to recharge the flip capacitors again and get it to Pentagar. But anything we want off that ship needs to be over here before we go."

"We'll see who ends up in control of what," she said grimly. "I'll be sure to scavenge anything that looks interesting, though. What about the ship's missiles? Could they replace what we've used?"

"God, I hope so. We could use a break."

14

Kelsey used her armor's lamp to look into what was left of the destroyer's marine country. One of *Courageous*'s beams had ripped it open and incinerated so much. Bodies and parts of bodies floated by her. The artificial gravity had finally failed all over the ship.

Some of these bodies were in standard marine powered armor. Not all of them. Fewer than a dozen, though it was hard to be sure. She was going to have more nightmares. They must've assembled here, waiting to see where *Courageous*'s crew boarded. Then Jared had drilled a hole right through them.

Talbot and his men fanned out as they searched the area. The beams hadn't destroyed everything. The armory was intact. They had to cut the hatch off, but inside was a treasure trove. Ammunition that would work in their flechette weapons, power packs, and other high-tech weapons of war.

Including more armor. Two suits of Old Empire marine armor in racks.

She stopped to give one of them a closer look. It resembled her armor, but the plates were significantly thicker. She tried to query it via her implants, but it demanded a code she didn't have.

Odd. Her suit hadn't needed one. Why would these?

"Talbot, these suits look like they're intact. I can't access them, but I don't think they require enhanced musculature like mine."

She removed one of the helmets. It had a real view screen inside the faceplate. "I'm not sure why, but it has manual controls under the chin and a screen to see the outside world."

He took the helmet and looked inside it. "We have something similar. We use our chins to control communications and other functions. These can work without implants."

"Then why have implant access at all?"

"That's a good question. One we'll probably need the eggheads to answer. I bet they can hack these suits." He gave her a smile. "I hope so, because then I can keep up with you."

"You wish." She pulled a massive plasma gun off a rack on the wall. "Holy cow. Look at this thing. I could take out a pinnace with one of these. It must be one of the heavy weapons I read about. There are big honking flechette rifles, too. The neural disruptors are small, though. Made for unarmored people."

"It doesn't make much sense to have the guys in armor carry weapons that won't work on the people they're fighting. Let's give the rest of marine country a look."

They found a storage area with crated equipment but not much else of interest. Reese made the decision to take everything back over to *Courageous* before examining the contents. Kelsey made sure they stripped the armory. None of these weapons was going to be falling into Breckenridge's clutches if he pulled a fast one.

One of the pinnaces was unrepairable. The beam that blew through marine country took out its bow. The other seemed intact. The enemy had locked the controls, so they called Carl Owlet down to break into it while they loaded as much of the weapons and armor aboard as they could.

She gave the young computer scientist a suspicious look when he arrived. "You're pretty good at boosting vehicles. Did you have a life of crime before going to university?"

He laughed and started working on the pinnace's console. "Hardly. I've just had enough experience on this expedition to make up for it. Especially on this ship. It looks like they locked *everything* down. Including stuff that doesn't even make sense. It's as though this ship was designed by someone with paranoid delusions."

"Perhaps it was. These people are working with the Pale Ones, so odds are good they're rebels. Or whatever the rebels became after they won. How are you getting around the lockouts? Or even accessing the equipment with main power down?"

"Most stuff can be operated by someone without implants, and we brought portable power supplies. I dig into the mechanical elements and isolate the lockout. Then it's just a matter of convincing the equipment that I have an authorized code." The red light on the center console went green. "Like that. It won't prompt for codes anymore. Is there anything else I can unlock for you?"

She smiled. "Actually, there is." She showed him one of the suits of armor they were loading.

He examined it. "I might be able to swing it, but not here. I need to get at the critical components. Man, this looks kick ass. Excuse my language."

"No apology necessary. It *is* kick ass. Now, while they finish loading the pinnace, I'd like to see a few areas of the ship. If you could get me in, that will save some wear and tear on the hatches."

"Sure. If Commander Baxter needs me, he'll call."

Kelsey gave Talbot the high sign. "Come on."

She set off looking for the captain's quarters. They found them after a few false turns. The hatch gave way under the young man's computer skills, sliding open on an opulent chamber.

These quarters were almost the same size as hers were on *Courageous*. That made them improbably large in a destroyer. The extra space had to come from somewhere. Probably from other people's living areas.

Luxurious white carpet covered the deck, and wood and glass furniture filled the space. Art graced the walls, and knickknacks of gold and silver occupied prominent shelves, secured against zero G. She looked around with disbelief.

"This looks more like a king's quarters than a destroyer captain's. It doesn't seem like someone of Jared's rank could afford this."

Talbot looked into one of the other compartments in the suite. "This bedroom is like a bordello. Not that I'm familiar with the inside of one," he hastily added.

"You'd better not be." She found the office. A large desk of pale wood dominated one side of the room. Holos covered the walls. It only took a moment to identify the captain: a short, thin woman with long brunette hair. She was in every image. Her companions ranged from Fleet officers to well-dressed civilians. The civilians all had the same sleek look that the worst members of the Imperial Senate had back home. Oily. Scheming.

Kelsey floated behind the desk. "Can you access this console?"

"The AI is down, so that means the network is offline. The emergency power switch is on the right side under the edge. I'll get one of the portable power supplies if we need to."

She powered the console on and tried to access it when it came up. "It's secured."

"Let me take a run at it."

The computer genius opened the side of the console and began tinkering inside. "This thing is fully encrypted. I can get in, but it'll take me a few minutes. I might not be able to completely access it, either."

"Do the best you can."

Talbot poked his head into the office. "Kelsey, you'll want to see this."

She followed him back to the bedroom. It was even worse than she'd feared. The walls were passion red, and the bed looked like it could hold a dozen people. Talbot led her to the closet. One side had what looked like regulation Fleet uniforms, though of an expensive cut. The other had clothes that Kelsey would be mortified to wear in private.

"Seriously? Not a chance in hell, buddy."

He grinned at her through the faceplate of his armor. "While that would make for some memorable visuals, no. What I want you to see is behind the uniforms."

She slid them to the side and saw what he meant. There was a safe in the back of the closet. "Right you are. You win a reward of my choice later. Except for me getting anything like those unmentionables."

It looked like the safe was implant controlled. If so, she'd never get it open. It was sturdy, too, but people with the right tools could open anything given enough time.

"How's it going in there, Carl?"

"I'm almost… I'm in. The console is coming up. The unsecure portions of it are available."

"Do you know anything about safes?"

"As in the vault kind? Not yet."

The young man came into the bedroom and jetted to a stop, gawking at the furnishings. His face looked almost as red as the silk covers.

"Wow. This is… unexpected."

"You can say that again. Give this a look."

He examined the safe. "I could probably cut it open with enough time, but that might damage the contents. There might be an easier way. Come back to the office with me."

She followed him. "Something in here could get me in there?"

"Maybe. There's only one way to find out for sure. Tell me, do you use the same computer password for everything?"

Kelsey frowned. "What does my computer password have to do with anything?"

"People tend to select one or a few passwords and then use them for a lot of systems. Odds are good that the commander of this ship was no exception. I'd give better than 50/50 odds that the access for this console is the same as the safe."

"That's an interesting fact, but we don't have that code. It's in the dead captain's head."

"We might be able to convince the console to give it up. I'm going to try to fool the system into giving you the key. When I tell you to, try to access it."

He dug back into the guts of the console. "Now."

She tried to access the console, and it rejected her. "It blocked me."

"This might take a few tries."

In fact, it took almost half an hour, and she was ready to give up when the console unexpectedly sent her a complicated code.

"It sent me an access code," she said in surprise.

"Thank God. I was afraid this wasn't going to work after all. Hang on a second and let me get the system put back together."

He reassembled the console and floated away. "Go ahead."

She fed the console the code and the secure sections unlocked. There were a number of files that she was afraid to access. This computer had been in rebel hands. She didn't mind looking, but she didn't want to pull anything into her internal memory until the professionals had it fully checked out.

"Is there any way to copy files from this console on a portable device?"

Owlet nodded. "There are some auxiliary data ports that we can use to transfer files. I brought some in my bag."

Kelsey returned to the bedroom while Owlet got back to work. She put her hands on her hips and stared disapprovingly at the closet. "I can't believe someone would have clothes like this. These unmentionables really are unmentionable."

"I can assure you the only unmentionables I want to mention are yours."

"Not in public. Wow." She held up some type of corset. It looked like something a dominatrix would wear. "Did you find a whip?" she asked rhetorically.

"As a matter of fact, I did." He pulled one off the shelf above the clothes. It wasn't very long, but it had some heft. Having someone beat you with this would be painful. Very painful.

Talbot held up one of the uniforms. "This is almost your size. With a little bit of tailoring for your height, you could wear it."

"Thankfully, I don't have to." She stared down at the safe. "I'm almost afraid what we'll find inside it."

"Only one way to find out."

She nodded and sent the code she'd stolen from the console. The safe clicked open. "Remind me to start picking a different password for everything that needs one."

"Me, too. What's inside?"

There were several shelves. The uppermost held two sleek pistols. The top one's barrel told her it was a neural disruptor, but it was substantially smaller than the pistols they'd found so far. The one under it was an even smaller flechette pistol. Both easily concealable.

She picked the neural disruptor up and queried it with her implants. It rejected her attempt to connect with it. She'd seen this before. Weapons could be set so that only a particular set of implants could fire them. The marines had figured out how to unlock them.

She pocketed the pistols and their custom power packs. The middle shelf held folders of printouts. She flipped through several of them and determined they were personnel files of some kind. A few of the subjects were Fleet personnel, but many were civilian. She'd take them with her and examine them more closely when she had time.

The bottommost shelf had data chips in small cases. Dozens of them. Any information worth locking into a safe had to be important to the person keeping it. Perhaps critical data on this Rebel Empire.

"I want all of this back on *Courageous*," she said to Talbot. "This captain seems like the devious type. There might be hidden stuff we haven't found. Go over her quarters with a fine-toothed comb. We'll need every edge we can get once they find out about us."

15

It took several hours for *Courageous*'s small craft to tow the crippled destroyer back into the flip point. Jared sent one of the Pentagaran warships through first to be sure that everyone knew not to open fire when the destroyer appeared. They'd sacrificed a lot to capture the ship, and he didn't want to see it destroyed.

Zia turned from her console. "The destroyer is inside the flip point, Captain."

"Give them the signal to flip in thirty seconds. Take us across."

The flip made him momentarily dizzy, but he recovered quickly. The Old Empire implants made the process easier. That was a nice bonus.

He quickly picked up a number of Pentagaran warships surrounding the flip point. No Fleet ships though. Those were all still engaged in search and rescue.

Jared quickly sent a prerecorded message to the ships around him, reiterating his instructions not to open fire on the destroyer. It appeared a few seconds later without incident.

"Signal incoming from *Spear*," Zia said.

"Put it on screen."

A furious Captain Breckenridge appeared. "God dammit, Commander, I gave you a direct order to leave that ship there and return as quickly as possible. Are you deaf?"

"Captain Breckenridge, do you need further assistance with rescue operations?" Jared asked, ignoring the other man's bluster.

"It's a little late now, don't you think? No. We've almost completed rescue operations at this point. We could've used your help a few hours ago. Give me an update on your status."

"We ambushed the destroyer and disabled it. I sent marines aboard to capture it before he could self-destruct. We have prisoners, including one of the officers. We're questioning them."

Breckenridge shook his head. "Negative. I'll take possession of the prisoners and that ship at once. My officers will see to any questioning."

Not a chance in hell. "Princess Kelsey has decided that she's going to question the prisoners, and she's determined that she's not releasing control of that ship until she's finished. She has instructed me to set up a meeting on her behalf so that we can discuss this in private. If all of your cutters are engaged in rescue operations, I'd be happy to send one of ours to pick you up."

Captain Breckenridge's face turned a bright purple. "I made it perfectly clear that she was not to be allowed into this system. You've disregarded my orders again. You're going to regret that, Commander. I need to get things in order here before we speak again."

The screen cleared without a goodbye.

"He's never going to admit he made a mistake."

Jared turned and faced the lift that had just opened. Commander Meyer stood there. Jared allowed himself a small smile as the man took a seat at the rear of the bridge. "Forgive me, Commander, but I didn't think you believed he made mistakes."

The other man shook his head. "I've had time to think about all the mistakes that he's made. And the mistakes that I've made. After your doctor patched me up, I reviewed the engagement records. He's not going to admit that he botched everything. That's not his way. He's going to take it out on you."

"He's going to try to take it out on me," Jared corrected. "Not that it'll work. He's been spoiling for a fight ever since he got here, and he's going to get it. His actions contributed to the deaths of thousands of Fleet personnel. If he wants to push this issue with me or the princess, we're going to push right back."

Commander Meyer shook his head. "You still don't understand. He's in command of that task force. Nothing that you do is going to change that. If the princess tries to relieve him of command, it's going to cause a complete break. Frankly, he hasn't demonstrated any behavior that actually warrants being relieved of command. Just poor judgment."

As annoying as that was, Jared knew Meyer was correct. If only it was so easy.

He rose to his feet. "Walk with me, Commander. I think it's time we had a long talk and settled a few things. Zia, you have the bridge."

"Aye, sir."

Once inside the lift, Jared started them on their way toward where they were keeping the prisoners. "Doctor Stone tells me that your injuries were minor, but I know that that doesn't mean they don't feel serious. Are you all right?"

The tall officer nodded. "It wasn't a direct hit, and my armor absorbed most of the damage. It scared me. I thought I was going to die.

But you know what really made me reconsider so many things? Princess Kelsey."

Jared led the way out of the lift as soon as it stopped. "How so?"

"When we were ambushed, she never hesitated. She jumped right into the middle of the enemy marines and attacked. She hit them, she shot them, and she never showed even the slightest hint of fear. It makes me a little ashamed. No, it takes me a lot ashamed. When she ran toward the enemy, I held back. I could've helped her, but I watched, too afraid to act. Then someone shot me."

The officer rubbed his face. "I've never felt like that in space combat. Before I became executive officer on *Spear*, I commanded a light cruiser. I took her into simulated battle and fought tooth and nail. I thought I knew what fear was, but I was wrong."

Jared knew exactly how he felt. "Someone once told me that only idiots aren't afraid of dying. He said that bravery just meant riding the wave of your fear and doing what you had to do. If you were still in command of that light cruiser, would you do what Captain Macumber did? Put your ship between a wounded comrade and certain death?"

Meyer's expression hardened. "Of course I would."

"Then you're brave enough. Fighting hand to hand isn't something that everyone can do. I've been where you were, and I didn't like it very much either. Give me the command deck of this ship any day. I think if you find yourself in the same situation again, you'll do what you have to. Don't tear yourself apart, second-guessing everything you did. Learn from it and do better the next time."

They passed between the marines guarding the prisoners. More marines armed with neural disruptors set to stun lined the cargo deck bulkheads. The prisoners sat on cots in an open area. Each had a restraint around their ankle bolted to the deck. If they needed to use the head, two marines of the appropriate gender would release them long enough to take care of business.

The most seriously injured of the prisoners was still in the medical center. Also under guard.

Jared stopped far enough away from the prisoners so that they couldn't overhear him. "Commander Graves has been interrogating these people. They wear Fleet uniforms, but they don't serve any Fleet that I'm familiar with. They all fought ferociously when we boarded the ship, but once the fighting was over, they seemed to just give up. Commander Graves intimidated them. Not because he was the enemy, because he was a Fleet officer in uniform.

"We've started collating their statements, and certain patterns are emerging. They believe that they are serving members of Imperial Fleet, but they don't see the rebellion the same way the history books do. And their Fleet has significant differences from ours."

Meyer scanned the prisoners. "How so?"

"In their Fleet, officers occupy a higher social position inside the

Empire. Though they live in an Empire, no one we've spoken to mentioned anything about an emperor. In this Fleet, officers are people they fear and obey. They fill the enlisted ranks via conscription rather than by looking for volunteers."

Meyer looked at him sharply. "Wait a minute. Are you telling me that the Old Empire still exists? We thought the rebels exterminated humanity. Are you telling me they enslaved them?"

Jared shrugged. "It's hard to say if the Old Empire still exists in the way you mean. None of these people refer to themselves as citizens of the Empire. They're very specific that they are subjects of the Empire. The officers are citizens of the Empire, and so are the political classes. The nobility.

"Graves made sure that he didn't feed them any information about what we think happened during the rebellion. He asked a lot of questions and let them fill in the blanks. It certainly seems as though none of these people is aware of artificial intelligences running things. Perhaps the upper classes of their society know, but until we can get our one high-ranking prisoner to talk, we won't be sure."

"Was the procedure to remove the virus from his implants successful?"

"We'll know in about an hour. I'm hopeful that he'll talk with Princess Kelsey or myself. Because of the incredible loss of life this battle caused, I have no intention of turning any of the prisoners over to Captain Breckenridge. I'm not certain I trust him with their well-being."

Meyer frowned. "The laws of war are clear. Captain Breckenridge will not mistreat them."

"I'm not so certain that I agree with that statement. In any case, I don't believe that he'll be as successful as we are at drawing information from these people. Commander Meyer, we desperately need to know what we face. Our civilization is small and technologically inferior when compared to what we're starting to see. If they come for us, we'll lose. Our only hope is to keep them ignorant of the Empire's existence until we know enough to survive. You need to help me convince Captain Breckenridge."

Meyer sighed. "I wish it were that simple. The captain doesn't change his mind easily. After losing so many people, he's not going to admit to making any mistakes. Not even to himself. Whatever you do, it needs to take that into account."

A hatch at the end of the corridor opened, and Kelsey stepped through. "There you are, Jared. Breckenridge just called me. He wants to meet with us and get onto the same page. Too many mistakes have been made."

Jared exchanged a glance with Meyer. "That's unexpectedly conciliatory. When is he coming over?"

"He's not. He asked that we meet on *Spear*. They're too deeply involved in rescue operations for him to leave the scene of the battle. Come on."

"I'm not so sure that's a good idea."

She raised her eyebrows. "Why not? He's not going to fight about command of this mission again. That's settled. We have to start relying on each other, or we'll never get home."

Jared had his doubts. "I hope you're right."

He used his implants to call Graves and direct him to Jared's office. It was still surreal to do this in his head while those around him were unaware he was even talking to someone else.

Charlie, I've got a bad feeling about this. The man hates me.

His exec nodded, responding to the audio from the console. "That he does. Still, his options are limited. He's not going to do something with the princess right there. Keep things civil, and it'll work itself out."

I sure hope so. In any case, I have some orders for you. You are not to hand the prisoners over to anyone. They stay in our custody. You're also to retain possession of the destroyer. Finally, remember that you are not under Captain Breckenridge's command. We answer to the princess.

Graves looked surprised. "Surely things won't get that bad."

I certainly hope not, but we're going over to his ship. If he's going to do something rash, this is the perfect time. Let's call this a contingency plan.

"Aye, sir. I'll keep things under control."

Good man. We'll see you shortly.

He kept his worries to himself as their cutter undocked, but his misgivings grew stronger the closer they got to *Spear*. He watched her closely through his implants as they approached the battle site.

Spear was following along behind *Shadow*. The light cruiser tumbled, completely out of control. Her damage was severe. The ship wouldn't be going anywhere but a repair dock or a scrap yard. He hadn't heard how many of her crew had died in the attack, but it would be a lot.

The pilot brought the cutter up to the heavy cruiser and docked smoothly. "I'll be here when you're ready to go, Captain."

"Keep the systems ready to depart at a moment's notice."

Unlike his last time aboard, Captain Breckenridge was waiting at the dock. He looked worn and angry. "Highness. Commander. Time is short. I've taken the liberty of reserving a small conference room on this deck. This way, please."

Two unarmored marines stood outside the hatch and snapped to attention as they approached. Breckenridge gestured for Kelsey to precede them. "If you'll take the head of the table, Highness, I've prepared an update of the rescue operations."

Jared started to follow her in, but Breckenridge yanked him back. The hatch slid shut even as Kelsey whirled toward them. He reached for his neural disruptor, but the marines beat him to the draw. They had pistols aimed at his head before he'd touched it.

"What the hell are you doing?" he snarled as Breckenridge took his weapon and handed it to Meyer. "She's second in line to the Throne."

"I'm doing what you should've done, Commander. I'm protecting her from her own bad judgment. The two of you have managed to kill thousands of Fleet personnel. I will not allow you to endanger the Empire one moment longer."

"You're insane. You can't possibly do anything without the cooperation of *Courageous* or the Pentagarans."

The older man smiled. "I'm very resourceful. Marines, take him to a holding cell. I'll be along directly."

16

K elsey almost made it to the hatch before it slid shut in her face. She started to bang on it but stopped. That wouldn't do any good. She had no leverage, and the smooth metal wouldn't give to brute strength. Even hers.

Breckenridge had trapped her. She had the neural disruptor she'd appropriated from the dead destroyer captain's safe tucked away in a place they'd be unlikely to search, but she'd have to be very careful. They had Jared.

The marine armorer had been able to reset the lockout on the weapon to her implants with a little trouble. The rebels had made the weapon so that only the person with the correct implants could use it.

It had also been set to lethal levels when she'd checked. That didn't say very nice things about the woman who'd owned it.

The screen came to life, showing a smiling Captain Breckenridge. "Highness."

"Have you lost your mind?" she snarled.

"Thankfully, no. I regret to inform you that I have serious concerns about your judgment and stability. I have no choice but to take you into protective custody. Due to your horrific injuries, I must confine you. My apologies." The last came in a smug tone.

She felt her eyes narrow. "My judgment? My stability? You'd best look to yourself if there is a problem, Captain. Jared and I have made the best calls possible. You? Not so much. How many good men and women lost their lives because of you today?"

Rage clouded his expression. "All because of your incompetent half brother. His lack of judgment got us into this battle and cost the Empire three ships and almost two thousand people. We should never have been involved in this fight, and from this point forward, we will not be."

Kelsey raised an eyebrow. "I can't imagine how you intend to do that. Perhaps you haven't noticed, but our ships can't get home. Sooner or later, the rebels will come looking for the ship you destroyed and the one we captured."

"Let them. We won't be here. I intend to take our people through the unexplored flip point. We'll find another way home."

"And leave the Pentagarans to die? Are you insane?"

"No. I'm pragmatic. Something you should try. These are not our people, and we should never have been involved in their business. You will call *Courageous* and instruct them to surrender to my officers."

She crossed her arms over her chest. "I will not. In fact, let me make this as clear as I can. I'm ordering you to release us at once and surrender yourself."

"I'm sorry to see you being so unreasonable, but I'm not surprised. Very well. I can force Mertz into obeying my orders. If I make it clear that your health is dependent on his cooperation, he'll comply. A ruse, of course."

She showed him her teeth. "You don't know the first thing about my brother. He won't give in to you. No matter how this plays out, you're ruined. You must know that."

"We'll see. I've taken the precaution of putting bedding, food, and a portable toilet to the rear of the conference room. You'll be staying there for the foreseeable future. I'm not foolhardy enough to risk letting you out. We'll speak again soon."

He stepped aside, and she saw Commander Meyer standing behind Breckenridge. She gave him a pleading look. "Commander Meyer, please. Explain this to him. You can't let him do this."

"You have no idea how resolute the captain is, Highness," Meyer said with a wooden expression. "Once he makes up his mind, there's no altering his course. Nothing I say will change this situation."

Breckenridge smiled and clapped the other man on the shoulder. "See? He knows me so well. This is what a good executive officer is like. Loyal to a fault. We'll speak again soon, Highness."

The screen went dark.

Kelsey used some of the choicest phrases she'd picked up from Talbot and the marines. Dammit. How was she going to get them out of this?

She beat on the hatch, but it didn't give. There were no other exits, and her weapon wouldn't go through a bulkhead.

If she'd brought one of the marine knives, she could have conceivably cut her way through the bulkhead. It would have taken a while and they would no doubt have stopped her, but they'd have had to open the hatch to do it.

That was the first thing she needed to do. Get the hatch open. If she could manage that, escape became at least conceivable.

Fifteen minutes of pacing left her as uninspired as when she started.

She whirled toward the hatch when it slid unexpectedly open. Commander Meyer stood outside. The two marine guards had their weapons out and pointed at her midsection. The tall officer stared at her haughtily. "Back against the bulkhead, Highness."

She considered the odds. Panther, the Old Empire combat drug combination, boosted her reaction time, and she might be able to take them before they killed her. Maybe.

The marines advanced. Once they were inside, Meyer shot them in the backs with Jared's neural disruptor. They collapsed.

"This is an amazing weapon. Come on, Highness. It won't be long before someone finds out you've escaped. We have to get you off this ship right now."

"We need to capture this ship. Order your people to stand down."

He shook his head. "That won't work. The captain has too many loyal people for me to take him down, and if it comes to my order against his, I'll lose. He's made his stand. Imagine your brother's crew supporting Graves against him. Not going to happen. We have less than ten minutes to get you off this ship or you're not leaving. Captain Breckenridge has gone too far to back down now."

She looked at the stunned marines on the deck. "So have you."

"This isn't how I saw things going," Meyer said ruefully. "I still can't quite imagine how I ended up opposing my captain." He opened the hatch and scanned the corridor. "Just walk like nothing is wrong."

She followed him out into the corridor and tried to behave normally even though the skin between her shoulder blades itched. Everyone they passed stared at her.

"You did what was right and what's best for the Empire," she said as they walked.

"I did what my oath required of me, in any case. You are the voice of authority, and the captain is wrong to disobey you. I don't agree with everything you've done, and I'm worried that you're leading the Empire into a war we cannot win."

He waved his hand at her when she started to speak. "I'm not trying to be argumentative. I'll do my duty even if I don't agree with you."

"That wasn't what I was going to say. I want to hear opposing points of view. I certainly don't think I have all the answers. What I will say is that it's easy to look back when the dust settles. It's harder when you're in the moment. Like when you made the decision to free us. Tomorrow the perfect plan will pop into your head. If you wait for the perfect plan, you'll never do anything."

They entered a lift, and she had to shut up since there were other people present. Meyer took them up a few decks and exited. "We're going to the brig. I'm going to get Commander Mertz out of his cell, and we're going to make our way back to your cutter. I'll call Captain Breckenridge to get him to allow your cutter to depart. By the time he realizes that I've helped you escape, you should be most of the way back to *Courageous*."

"You mean 'we' don't you? You're coming with us."

He shook his head. "That's not going to be possible. He'll discover the ruse much too quickly if I'm not here to distract him. I'll likely go right into the same cell your captain occupies now," he said with a wry smile. "Talk about a career-limiting decision."

"He's going to be furious. You need to come with us."

"It's the only choice. If he has you in his sights, he might do something drastic to prevent your escape. I cannot and will not risk your life when I can prevent the danger in the first place."

"Well, come up with an alternate plan. I'm ordering you to come with us."

He sighed. "You don't make things easy, do you, Highness? Aye, ma'am. Orders received. Follow my lead and please try to avoid hurting anyone too badly. These people are just following orders."

Two marines outside an armored hatch came to attention as they approached. The hatch was open, and Meyer headed inside with a sharp nod to them. Three Fleet personnel manned the inside of the brig. Two ratings, one male and one female, flanked one of the cell hatches, and a female officer sat at the console.

The officer stood when she saw Meyer. "Commander."

"Lieutenant Jacobs. Captain Breckenridge has instructed me to bring Commander Mertz to him on the bridge. Bring him out."

She frowned. "That's contrary to my instructions, sir. He ordered me to lock the prisoner down and only to release him on his direct orders. I'll need to call the captain and verify. Sorry, sir."

Meyer smiled. "I completely understand. Please do. I wouldn't want you to get into any trouble."

As soon as she lowered her eyes to the console, he drew the neural disruptor from inside his uniform tunic and shot her. The blue beam took her down, and he whirled to face the hatch.

Kelsey had been primed for something like that, so she was able to draw her own pistol and rush the guards as they gaped at the unexpected attack.

The female guard was slightly quicker on the uptake, so Kelsey shot her. The princess's augmentation brought her into hand-to-hand range of the man before he could draw a bead on her. She ripped his weapon right out of his grip and ducked far enough to the side to allow his fist to pass by her head.

Just because she could fight didn't mean she wanted to take a fist to the face.

She heard Meyer firing behind her and hoped he got both the marines before they got him.

A shove sent the man she was fighting into the bulkhead, and she shot him. He collapsed without any further trouble.

Commander Meyer didn't need her help. He'd dropped both the marines without any problem.

"It looks like you're a much better fighter than I expected,

Commander," she said. "I didn't need to give you a talk before the boarding, did I?"

"This isn't the same. These people trusted me. This was more like a sucker punch than a fair fight." He looked at the small weapon in her hand. "And that little thing is even more unfair. I had no idea you were armed."

"That was kind of the idea. Senior Sergeant Talbot tells me that fair fights indicate a lack of planning and imagination. Mostly on my part."

Meyer dragged the marines through the hatch and closed it. "When those people were trying to kill us, I didn't see any lack of planning or imagination on your part. Unlike myself. I froze. I've never been in anything like that."

He tapped the controls on the console, and the cell opened up. Jared stood there, gaping at them. Meyer extended the neural disruptor to him.

"If you intend to get out of here, Commander, you'd best get moving. The escape window is closing."

Jared took the neural disruptor from the other man and holstered it. "You're helping us?"

"My oath to the emperor doesn't agree with Captain Breckenridge's plan. We have just a few minutes to get to your cutter."

When Meyer headed for the hatch, they followed. "How are we going to get away from *Spear*? They have to release the docking clamps, or the cutter won't be going anywhere."

"I'll call the bridge when we get down to the docking level. I can get them to release it."

"What about Captain Breckenridge?"

"I have a plan, but the princess has forbidden me to execute it."

She looked at Jared. "He wanted to send us off and call Breckenridge away from the bridge. He'd be captured for sure."

The lift deposited them at the cutter deck. Jared followed Meyer out. "You'd do that for us?"

"No," Meyer said. "I'd do that for her, and for my own honor. It's still the best plan. I recommend you change her mind. Time is short."

Jared opened his mouth to say something, but the alert klaxon went off. Captain Breckenridge's voice came through the overheads. "All hands, this is the captain. We have two escaped prisoners on the loose. Be on the lookout for Commander Jared Mertz and Princess Kelsey Bandar. Both are armed and dangerous. Commander Meyer, call the bridge at once."

Meyer gestured toward the cutter. "Get inside. I'll call him. I may be able to get it released if I make him think you haven't made it here yet."

He touched the communications panel on the wall. "Bridge, this is Meyer."

"Sean," Breckenridge said, "Mertz has escaped and the princess's guard isn't responding. Where are you?"

"I'm on the docking level. They haven't made it here yet. If their ride has left, it'll make it much easier to recapture them."

"Good idea. I'll send them away right now. Take command of the search. I want them found at once. The very safety of the Empire lies in getting that deluded woman back under our control."

"I won't fail the Empire, Captain. Meyer out."

He turned to them. "If I go with you, I won't be able to delay the moment he discovers you're truly gone and opens fire. I'm sorry, Highness." He spun and headed for the lift.

She wanted to argue, but she knew he was right. "We'll be back for you. Don't lose hope."

Jared pulled her into the cutter, and Kelsey closed the hatch behind them. He rushed for the flight deck while she strapped herself in. The cutter undocked, and acceleration pressed her into her seat.

All she could think about was the man who'd just doomed himself for her. She had no idea how she could make it right.

17

Commander Meyer's ruse worked far better than Jared had hoped. The cutter made it almost all the way back to *Courageous* before there was any sign of activity from *Spear*. Jared had already sent a tight-beam alert to Graves. *Courageous* was at battle stations, their weapons on hot standby and battle screens ready at a moment's notice.

Jared wasn't sure what Breckenridge would do when he figured out where they'd gone. Everything was on the table with that man. In the end, he didn't even bother to call them to rant.

The heavy cruiser and its two remaining destroyer escorts began accelerating away from *Shadow* in formation toward the weak flip point. They didn't respond to calls from the confused Pentagaran warships or *Courageous*. Jared more than half expected him to open fire on the crippled light cruiser, but he left her be.

Their cutter docked without incident, and they made their way to the bridge. He interfaced with the ship's scanners and watched the three ships fleeing the system.

Graves gestured at the screen. "We can catch them before they make the flip point."

"And do what? Open fire on them? That's not an acceptable course of action, Charlie. We let them go and hope for the best. What's the situation?"

"Recovery operations are still under way. It's possible we'll find more trapped survivors on *Shadow*, but not very likely. At this point we're only expecting to retrieve the dead."

"Do we have any of the survivors aboard?"

The exec shook his head. "Breckenridge was adamant that all survivors be brought to *Spear*. He knew what he was going to do before we made it back. They'll be in position to flip in about nine hours. Are we really just going to let them go? They could run right into the bad guys."

"Give me a plan that doesn't require me killing several thousand Fleet personnel. In the meantime, what's the status of the interrogations?"

"The officer still isn't talking, but some of the enlisted are. We're trying to make sense of what they're saying, though. It seems like they don't really have a clear picture of their own Empire. All of them that have talked are part of what they call the lower orders. I'm guessing that's a social distinction. The officers come from the higher orders.

"Jared, they're afraid of their officers. Genuinely afraid. Just seeing me in uniform caused a physical reaction. They mostly answer the questions I give them, as if they can't imagine not responding to something an officer asks them."

Kelsey cleared her throat. "Have you tried having one of the ratings talk to them? Or a civilian?"

Graves nodded. "They responded much more openly to our ratings, but they didn't seem as likely to answer questions. I haven't tried any of the civilians. I don't want one of them to attack someone unable to defend themselves."

"I should talk to them," Kelsey said. "They might open up to me. In any case, they won't be too much of a threat to me physically."

Jared agreed. She'd be perfect for the job. "I like it. What about the officer?"

Graves shook his head. "Even without the viral programing in his implants, he's uncommunicative. At least he isn't aggressive anymore. *Courageous* reports that he's attempted to access the ship's systems numerous times."

"Perhaps you should let him," Kelsey said. "A limited set of files. Historical ones of the Old Empire. Nothing that pertains to our current circumstances, of course. What have the enlisted prisoners said about the rebellion?"

"That it took place. That they overthrew the corrupt emperor and freed the people from slavery. Detailed questions about the Old Empire confuse them. Apparently their history books are a little vague."

"That sounds like propaganda," Jared said. "Tell people something long enough and they'll believe it. What about the AIs?"

"Nothing. The officer's implant code was corrupted, so they must be lurking somewhere behind the scenes, but the general population seems to be unaware of them. That matches up with the data we've retrieved from the destroyer. They wiped the main computer, but we recovered a number of tablets and data chips. We're still putting everything together, but it's obvious that they didn't exterminate the core worlds of the Old Empire like we thought. There are specific mentions of Terra as the hub of the Rebel Empire."

Kelsey's face paled. "They kept the major population centers and remade society in the way they wanted. At least some of them. The rebels won."

"The AIs won," Jared said. "For now. We still don't know the scope of space they occupy. We'll need to gather all the data we can about that. Damn that idiot Breckenridge. He killed our one chance of taking a computer intact, and he vaporized all those implants. Honestly, I'm not sure how he could have executed the plan any more ineptly. Other than getting all his ships destroyed."

"Captain, we have an incoming call from a ship at the Pentagaran flip point."

Jared turned toward the front of the bridge. "On screen."

The main screen cleared to show the bridge of a ship. Admiral Walter Sanders, the freshly promoted commander of the Pentagaran Navy, sat in the center seat. Crown Princess Elise Orison stood at his side.

The sight of her made him smile. "Elise! Welcome to Erorsi. Admiral."

"Lord Captain," she said with a smile of her own. "Kelsey. I came to see how things are going for myself."

That took the edge off his pleasure. "It could've gone better. We lost three ships and far too many people. Plus, there are other complications. Captain Breckenridge has decided to strike out on his own."

Her eyes widened. "What? That's sheer folly! You should order him back at once, Kelsey."

Kelsey shook her head with a wry smile. "That's not likely to be effective after he attempted to take me prisoner. He's made his choice, and I can't do much about it.

"On the good side, we captured the destroyer escort. Unfortunately, Captain Breckenridge destroyed the freighter with all its cargo. We have prisoners, so we're hopeful we can get some badly needed data on our opponents. At the very least, we've put off the day they discover your presence. That gives us all a fighting chance."

Admiral Sanders grimaced. "That's better than it could've been but worse than I'd hoped. I see that your wayward officers are heading for the weak space-time bridge. What are the chances that it leads somewhere disconnected from the areas controlled by the enemy?"

"Unknown. I pray it leads close to Avalon and far away from this Rebel Empire. We'll send a probe once they're gone and see how it matches up to the flip point maps in *Courageous*'s data banks."

"We'll be at your location in a few hours," the admiral said. "Perhaps together we can come up with a plan to make things right."

Jared nodded. "We'll get a tow on *Shadow* and start moving her toward Erorsi. If nothing else, we can put her in the operational shipyard to see what repairs are possible. The same for the destroyer."

"That sounds like an excellent first step. Sanders out."

Jared rose to his feet. "Zia, see if our Pentagaran friends will tow *Shadow* and the destroyer to Erorsi. Pasco, what would you estimate their arrival time to be?"

Ramirez checked his console. "Probably sometime tomorrow."

Kelsey stood. "That's better time than *Athena* made out to the Courageous flip point. Why did it take us four days?"

Jared put his hand on her shoulder. "Because I was too stubborn to ask for a tow. That was *Athena* under her own power. We need to go work on the prisoners."

She nodded. "I should probably make a run at the officer. Come with me. Perhaps the two of us with implants can make some headway on him."

He doubted that. The man seemed determined not to talk with them. Still, what could it hurt? "Okay."

They'd housed the majority of the prisoners on the cargo deck, but the officer warranted a cell in the brig. A man with implants might be unexpectedly dangerous. Jared should know.

The layout of *Courageous*'s brig was similar to the one on *Spear*, except he didn't have extra marine guards in the corridor. He trusted the ship's AI to keep unauthorized people out of the facility.

The duty officer stood when Jared came into the compartment. "Captain." Three marines with sidearms stood along the bulkheads.

"Lieutenant Gonzales. How is the prisoner?"

Lieutenant Junior Grade Benjamin Gonzales had been a supply officer on *Athena*. The destroyer hadn't needed dedicated security people. The young officer had stepped up when Jared formed the new department.

"He's been fed and is just as uncommunicative as before, sir."

"Open the cell."

The marines moved to have a better line of sight, but Jared waved them back. "Let's keep this as casual as we can."

The hatch slid open. The cell was Spartan enough: a bunk, a head, and one small shelf, empty. The prisoner had been lying down, but he sat up as they entered. His already closed expression soured when he saw who his visitors were.

Kelsey stepped around Jared and centered herself on the bunk. "Lieutenant Commander Richards, my name is Kelsey Bandar. We've met, though under less-than-preferable circumstances. In your computer center."

She paused, perhaps to allow him to speak, but he remained silent.

"Fifty-seven of your people survived the battle. We have them on board *Courageous*. Would you like me to give you an update on their status?"

He looked torn, but shook his head.

"Not even the people in the computer center with you?"

The man looked down for a long minute. "Yes."

That was the first word he'd said since his capture. Jared suspected that it wouldn't be his last. Kelsey was a miracle worker.

She waved Jared back and squatted to bring her eyes close to the man's level. "One woman had some broken bones in her hand, but they've been set, and she's going through a regeneration regime. The others all came through the fight without injury. If you like, I can arrange a visit."

The man's expression closed down again, but Jared sensed some relief under the surface. "For a price, I assume. Tell me, what exactly do traitors like you want? I'll never betray Fleet or my oath to the Lords like you did."

"It might surprise you, but I have no idea what you're talking about. I didn't know your civilization existed until a few months ago."

Richards sneered. "Tell me another one. Only members of the higher orders or Fleet officers get implants. You're no Fleet officer, though. You and your traitor friend broke all the oaths you ever swore to the Lords. I can't imagine how you stole those ships, or crewed them for that matter, but Fleet will find you and crush you."

Kelsey pursed her lips. "I know you've heard of the rebellion against the Old Empire. The rebels crippled this ship. We only found it a few months ago. As for my implants, you can thank those psychopathic monsters you were trying to resupply for them. Tell me, why would civilized people aid a rogue AI in enslaving savages and turning them into ravening beasts bent on destruction?"

To say her words surprised the man would be an understatement. He gaped at her. "You're lying."

"I'm not. I was just a normal person before they captured me, cut me apart, and made me one of them. I'm lucky my brother rescued me before they altered the programming in my implants. I'd imagine your implantation wasn't nearly as traumatic as mine was. We used the Old Empire techniques to remove the viral code from your implants, by the way. You're not under anyone's control now. At least not in your head."

"I wasn't under anyone's control before," he snarled. "What did you do to me?"

Jared spoke for the first time. "We overwrote your implant with the original Imperial code, Commander. That's the only reason you're not frothing at the mouth and trying to kill us with your bare hands. Unless that's how you normally behave."

If the man's eyes had been weapons, he'd have burned Jared to a crisp. "How could you betray Fleet, traitor? After everything they did for you. What were you before? A lieutenant? An ensign? Why settle for being a commander? Why not go for captain? Or admiral?"

"Because I've never been part of your Fleet. Our people escaped the rebellion. I'm the other Fleet. The one your rebel ancestors tried to destroy."

The man gaped. "That's not possible. We overthrew the Old Empire and crushed its corrupt masters."

"You've been sadly misinformed, but it's not my duty to correct that lapse. You're aboard the Fleet battlecruiser *Courageous*. You and your fellows are my prisoners. In case you don't remember my name, I'm Commander Jared Mertz, commanding officer of this vessel. I've been a Fleet officer for over two decades, just not your Fleet.

"At Princess Kelsey's suggestion, I am going to authorize you to access the ship's library. You should be able to find enough to entertain and educate yourself. I'm sorry to inform you that the contents are sadly out of date, but the ship has been floating in space since before the Fall. We'll speak again."

The man stood abruptly but made no aggressive move. Kelsey stood slowly, and the marines outside brought their neural disruptors up. She waved for them to lower their weapons.

"I will not be fooled by your propaganda," the man said through clenched teeth.

Kelsey turned toward the hatch. "We all have to decide what we believe in, Commander Richards. I'll come back later with your people. If you want to talk to me, you have my implant code. Call at any time."

The two of them left the man standing in the middle of his cell. Jared gave the instructions to *Courageous* to allow him access to the library of unclassified data. The AI would ensure the man didn't see anything sensitive or recent. Considering the vast amount of data available, Richards might actually learn something.

"Do you think we'll convince him?" he asked Kelsey.

"Eventually. The foundation of his beliefs is a lie. That makes for a lousy building. We'll see if it comes in time to make a difference. If you don't mind, I have some other things to look into before bed. I'm sure you and Elise can find something to talk about without me." She said the last with a slight smirk.

"Don't be snide. I'm sure that you and Talbot will find something equally interesting to do."

She smiled. "You have no idea."

K elsey headed down to marine country as soon as she left the brig. She'd convinced Talbot not to come hunting for her, but there were limits to his patience. Hers, too.

It surprised her how many people were there when she arrived. Not just marines but scientists. She spotted Doctor Leonard standing beside Lieutenant Reese and headed over toward them. The two of them were examining one of the captured plasma cannons.

"Doctor, Lieutenant. So, is it better than ours or just bigger?"

The older man smiled. "We'll need to put it through some tests, but the technology is remarkably consistent, considering the passage of time. One would've imagined more than minor improvements over the last five hundred years."

Reese held it out to her. "We tried to fire it on the range, but it seems to be locked out. Mister Owlet is looking at the armor in the armory, or I'd have had him check it out."

"I can do that." The rebels had locked the weapon, but not in the same way as her new pistols had been. This was more like an on/off switch. It didn't require an implant to fire it like hers did, but it did need one to make it operable. She, of course, didn't have the correct code.

"It looks like it requires an authorization code to become operable. Carl should be able to reset the code so that I can turn it on. It looks like it has a kick. Perhaps too much for someone without powered armor or enhanced muscles. Let's go find out."

She put it onto her shoulder and headed for the armory. She felt ridiculous. The weapon seemed like it was bigger than she was. The armory was adjacent to the range, and the marine armorer was examining some of the captured ammunition, while Carl Owlet had the top of the massive armor opened up. The graduate student turned to face them when they came in.

"Highness, Lieutenant, Doctor. How can I help you?"

She held out the weapon. "I need you to reset the implant control in this. It has a code like the console and the safe."

He took the massive weapon with some bobbling and set it on the table. "If it works like the console, I should be able to make it give you the access code. Once you have it, you should be able to reset it yourself. Or disable it."

"How's the armor?"

"About the same, I think. It doesn't need implants to operate, but someone with the right code needs to turn it on. Very strange." He tinkered inside the rifle until he found something. "Try to access it."

It only took half a dozen attempts to get the weapon to spit out the code. Kelsey gave Owlet the high sign, and he put it back together. When it was ready, the boy stepped back. "Give it a try."

She sent the code, and the weapon turned on, giving her complete access to the internals. She reset the code to one of her own choosing and began looking for a way to deactivate the need for a code at all.

Only there wasn't an option for that. Once someone activated the weapon, it would lock out when someone swapped out the power supply. Someone wanted complete control over this weapon.

The specifications indicated that it required armor to fire. She couldn't find a reference to use by unarmored commandos. She might be able to use it.

"I'm going to the range. I think it might be best if I try this without spectators. Just in case."

Talbot looked mulish. "If you're not sure that it's safe, you probably shouldn't use it."

"If the range tells me it can't handle it, I won't. I'm using some of the caution you recommended."

Reese eyed the weapon. "It looks ridiculously powerful. Go armor up. That's being cautious."

She sighed but did as ordered. They'd put her spare armor here in the armory. Her damaged set sat in the corner, awaiting the armorer's pleasure to replace the damaged section. It only took a few minutes to seal it up. She didn't bother to use a skinsuit, since she wasn't going to be in it more than a few minutes.

Even in her armor, the weapon seemed vastly oversized for her. She made her way onto the range and brought its systems online. A quick query confirmed the range could handle it. Barely.

Kelsey cranked the protective field to maximum and put the target at fifty meters, which the weapon indicated was the minimum safe distance.

The kick when she fired it was… substantial. The plasma weapon she normally used was too powerful for an unenhanced person to use. This might be too much for her without armor.

The detonation of the plasma seed sent her staggering back a step. It was an order of magnitude more powerful than anything she'd used before. Use of this weapon on a ship would be suicidal. Which explained why the armored marines hadn't had any on them. These were for use on the ground.

She'd try one of the large flechette rifles, too, but right now she wanted to conduct an experiment. She returned to the armory and began stripping out of her armor. "That worked. The range can handle one of these with the safety system set to max. It packs a kick. I want to see if I can fire it without the armor."

Talbot looked unconvinced. "Is that safe?"

"The range shields us from the blast. I just need to see if the kick is too much for me outside my armor." She turned to Owlet. "We'll need to unlock one of the oversized flechette rifles, if they're set up the same way."

Kelsey headed back to the range but stopped Talbot when he started to come up to the firing line. "Let's be cautious."

"Then take out all the ammo. If you only have one shot, you can't accidentally fire a second one."

"Good idea." She laid the rifle on the bench and pulled out the magazine. The pellets were significantly larger than the ones she'd seen before. She stripped all but one out and pocketed them.

Without the armor, the rifle really did feel like a cannon. Her strength allowed her to support its weight, but it was massive. She brought the range up, put a target out at fifty meters, and fired.

The recoil knocked her off her feet and sent her sliding on the deck. She ended up almost halfway back to Talbot. Her shoulder ached, and she stared up at him. "Wow. That was something. It kicks like a mule."

He held his hand out to her. "Have you ever been kicked by a mule?"

"Nope." She took his hand and let him pull her up. "This is definitely not useable by unarmored people. Even me."

"What would happen if I fired it? I'm more than halfway tempted."

"I'm pretty sure it would break your shoulder. I recommend you give it a pass. Besides, if we can get the marine armor working, you'll be able to give it a try."

"You think they can get the armor working?"

She nodded. "Why not? Owlet seems to have figured out how to unlock them. The system only works because I have implants, but he and I have a system."

They headed back to the armory. She handed the weapon and the ammunition over to the armorer. "This is too much for anyone in unpowered armor." She looked at Carl. "Any luck?"

"The lockout is exactly like the plasma cannon. Go ahead and give it the original code."

She did, and the weapon came online. Kelsey changed the code and looked at Talbot. "Come on."

This weapon didn't require the maximum protection from the range.

She loaded it and interfaced her implants with it. Her implants couldn't bring up a firing interface. Interesting. She made a mental note to have Carl examine the code in the weapon.

Kelsey had the range create a small hoard of Pale Ones. They all charged, howling like beasts.

The targeting software in her implants located them all, and she fired a burst at the first one. This weapon, unlike the normal flechette rifle, had recoil. Not enough that she couldn't control it, though.

She fired bursts into each of the charging enemy until they were all down. She handed the large rifle over to Talbot. "I'm not sure you'll be able to control this, but it won't hurt you to try. Much."

Talbot braced it on the rest and fired single shots at targets. "The recoil is pretty stiff. I doubt I can control full auto." He fired short bursts and managed to keep all the shots on the range. Barely.

He rubbed his shoulder. "Yeah, that isn't going to be useable by anyone outside of powered armor. It's too hard to control. Too bad. It's a badass weapon."

"Then the only thing left to try is getting that armor online."

They made their way back to the armory again and turned in the weapon. "Carl, did you get the armor unlocked?"

"I've been digging into it while you were gone. It's harder to get to the control mechanism, and it seems to have some lethal add-ons."

"What does that mean?"

The graduate student gestured at the armor. "It has a self-destruct package. I found explosives at various locations inside. They'd wreck the armor and the marine."

"Seriously?" She shook her head. "What kind of maniac wants their marines to blow up? How long before you can defuse it?"

"I'm almost there. Give me ten minutes."

Talbot pulled her aside. "That kind of adds to the theme. It seems like the implants were restricted to officers. Perhaps only senior officers. They didn't trust the crew."

"It sounds paranoid, but you're right. They wiped the AI rather than let us capture it. Not just the data, but also the hardware. The captain encrypted her console and her files in a way that made recovery unlikely. There's no way anyone was getting them unless you factor in someone like me with implants and a major hacker like Carl."

She scratched her chin. "It sounds like their society is ruled by AIs with a favored class of citizens who watch over the rest. They don't even trust the rank-and-file military. The ratings and crewmen aren't even familiar with the layout of their Empire. Which I will now be calling the Rebel Empire for clarity. They have no idea the AIs even exist."

Talbot nodded. "Too bad none of the marines is talking yet. We might be able to convert some of the crew. Release them from their chains, so to speak. What about the officer?"

She shrugged. "I don't know. If he's one of the ruling elite, he might be hard to reach. Though he did call me a renegade member of the higher orders—whatever that is—but thought Jared was only a Fleet officer. That might mean that the real aristocracy chooses the cream of the middle layers of society and trains them up for Fleet command. I wonder if they have corrupted implants like the Fleet officers."

Carl Owlet waved at them. "I've removed the last of the bombs. I also found a power pack that would fry the advanced circuitry. Everything else seems harmless."

"Are you willing to bet someone's life on that?"

The young man nodded. "There's nothing else in there that could damage the system or the wearer. I'm ready to trigger the code when you are."

Kelsey stretched her neck. "Go ahead."

This set of controls was significantly harder to hack than the captain's console. It took hours, and Carl almost gave up several times. Someone really didn't want their armor falling into the wrong hands.

Eventually, though, she got a code ten times longer than the previous ones. She fed it back to the armor, and it powered up. She changed the code with a sigh. "Got it. It looks like the armor is set up like the weapons. If you replace the power supply, the armor locks down. Can you do something about that, Carl?"

"Possibly. I'll need to work with Doctor Leonard. Give me a few days to consider the possibilities."

She directed her implants to interface with the armor. They did, but it wasn't as seamless as when she linked up to her commando gear. Like the weapons, the implant receptors didn't seem optimized to allow someone like her to control the equipment.

That wasn't to say that she couldn't manage. It was just clumsy. She'd see if the computer experts on Erorsi could assist them in cleaning up the interface. These two sets of armor could make the difference going forward.

It only took her a moment to find out why this suit had been in the armory on the destroyer. One of the legs wasn't working. It had a control fault.

She looked at Owlet and the armorer. "This unit has a problem. Let's bring the other one online."

That took a few minutes more, but the code she'd gotten from the last set of armor allowed her to access it much more rapidly. This unit had a fault in the torso.

"Okay, this one is more broken than the first. I guess that's why they didn't use them. The control unit for the left leg is bad in the first one. Can we salvage that from the damaged unit? The upper torso is broke on this one. Are any of the ruined units suitable for salvaging parts?"

The armorer nodded. "We have the damaged equipment in one of the holds. I'll see what we can recover."

Owlet opened the leg on the second unit. "I might be able to swap the control units and get one of these operating."

A few minutes later, he held up something that looked like a long, thin data chip. "I think this is it. Let me put it in the first set of armor."

Once he finished, Kelsey accessed the armor again. The check this time was amber. It read as operational but still seemed to have some kind of problem. "That did it. Mostly. Let's see what this thing can do."

She started to climb into the suit and immediately discovered a problem. The legs were too long for her. The arms, too. Apparently, these Rebel Empire types thought marines needed to come in extra-large packages.

"Oops. They built this thing for someone a little larger than I am. Talbot, you want to give it a try?"

"Sure." The marine climbed in, and she closed it up behind him. "The screen just activated. It's a pretty advanced heads-up display."

The last part of that came through her implants. "You need to turn on your external speakers. Only I can hear you. Actually, I might be able to do that."

She sent an implant command, and the external speakers activated. "Try talking again."

"Can you hear me?" The speakers worked.

"Loud and clear. I'm not sure I like being able to access and control your suit like this. It feels wrong."

Talbot flexed his knees. "It sounds about like these other people, though. Just how much control do you have?"

Kelsey invaded his interface and seized control of his armor. She stretched his arms over his head and bent him over to touch his toes. "About that much."

He straightened when she released him. "That's total bullcrap. I couldn't do anything while you were calling the shots. We need to disable that."

"That's probably doable," Owlet said. "The devil will be in the details. I'll look into it."

"I promise not to make you dance like a ballerina," Kelsey added with a smile. "Mostly. Let's go check out the strength limits on this thing. I bet it's more powerful than my commando armor. Look at those arms."

By the time they were ready to call it a night, she knew exactly how powerful the marine armor was: slightly less than twice as strong as her commando armor, and significantly more resistant to damage. It might even be able to survive one of the small plasma rifle seeds. It wouldn't be worth much at that point. Still, any landing you could walk away from was a good one.

One thing in her favor was that it was slow and clumsy compared to her commando armor. She was literally able to dance around Talbot as he tried to catch her. Speed and dexterity counted for a lot in battle. She could live with that.

Right as they were finishing, the control unit for the leg shorted out. There had to be an underlying problem with it. The loss of the armor annoyed Talbot.

She patted him on the shoulder. "Come on. Maybe they can get it working again. Tomorrow will come earlier than either of us like, so we should get some sleep."

While he climbed out of the armor, she checked the ship's scanners. *Spear* and her consorts were more than two thirds of the way toward the flip point. She still had no idea how they were going to deal with that problem. She just hoped the man's idiocy didn't get them all killed before they had a plan.

19

J ared woke to the sound of the shower. He stretched and smiled. Last night had been sinfully delightful. Elise and he were normally more discreet, but now that they knew the secret was out, they could relax a little.

He waited for the water to cut off, slid out of bed, and padded into the head. She was standing beside the shower tube, toweling off. The sight of her made him smile even more widely.

She wrapped her hair in a towel and kissed him. "I tried not to wake you."

"You should've. Waking up with you is my idea of the perfect start for the day."

Elise gave him an indulgent smile. "We don't have time for that today. We're meeting with Admiral Sanders after breakfast. Get a shower so you don't smell like me."

He laughed. "I'm in no danger of smelling like you."

"If you're a good boy, we have time for a leisurely breakfast."

"And if I'm bad, we won't eat at all?"

"If you're bad, I'll have to swat your nose. Shower."

Jared reluctantly headed into the tube. The soap and hot water swirling around him felt good. He let it clean him and rinsed off.

Elise was already fully dressed by the time he returned to the bedroom. It only took him a few minutes to dress in his uniform. They left for breakfast together, the Royal Guards outside his room both falling in behind them.

The officers' mess was already crowded, but they'd reserved a table last night. Princess Kelsey, Talbot, and Admiral Sanders were there and already sipping their coffee.

He held out a chair for Elise and then sat down. "Good morning. Admiral, I didn't expect you so early."

"Highness. Lord Captain. I found a seat on an earlier flight and decided to join Princess Kelsey. She was already up. We've had an illuminating conversation about Captain Breckenridge."

Jared grimaced. "The bridge pinged me when he flipped last night. I've sent a probe to take a snapshot of the other system. If we can identify it, we might be able to see if they pose a danger mucking around over there."

"And if they do?"

"Then we try to stop them. Somehow. They most likely left a probe to watch for any attempt at following them, so this isn't going to be easy." He turned to Kelsey. "Good morning. Did you get a chance to examine the equipment from the destroyer?"

She nodded. "I did. We recovered a bunch of flechettes that we can use in our own weapons. We might be able to use some of the weaponry, too, if Carl can unlock them permanently. It's crazy. They secured all the weapons with codes that make them useless if someone replaces the power pack. The armor, too."

Talbot snagged a bun from the loaded platter the server brought out to them. He buttered it slowly as Kelsey dug into the large plate she'd ordered. The man shook his head in amused disbelief.

"I still can't see how she puts it away like that. It's crazy." He looked away from her glare and focused on Jared. "Anyway, the two suits of armor we recovered were down with system failures, but Owlet got one of them working long enough for a test drive. They're really something."

Jared sighed. "I'm not surprised to hear about their paranoia. It seems to be a repeating theme with these people. Every critical system on the destroyer is locked up tighter than the Imperial Scepter."

He looked at Kelsey. "We loaded the files you recovered onto a standalone system. Even though the destroyer's captain locked the console you got them from, she also encrypted them. We'll have to crack that, but at least we got them. The same for the data chips from the safe. These people come from a brutal, repressive society, I think."

"The Rebel Empire is a dictatorship for sure, though one with a velvet glove," Kelsey said. "I'm not sure about the brutal part."

"We'll have plenty of time to come up with the right words for them. It's still early in the investigation. How many suits of armor did they have, Talbot?"

The marine shrugged. "The lowest estimate is eight. I'm leaning toward ten. It's hard to tell. Their bunks indicate a maximum marine complement of eighty. Significantly more than a destroyer in our Fleet would have. The sleeping area is pretty cramped."

"What do you think of the armor, Kelsey? How does it compare to yours?"

"Definitely more powerful, but clumsy. I can almost run circles around Talbot."

"Yeah, but when I catch her, its game over. That suit is amazing. I feel invincible inside it."

Kelsey poked him in the shoulder. "Don't let it go to your head. They have weapons that can take it out."

Admiral Sanders took a bite of his eggs. "Indeed. The mere presence of an armed cadre of men in such armor indicates a need for it. A destroyer has little room for even the items required during a normal deployment. Those suits took a significant amount of space that could've supported other things."

Jared thought about that. "What could they need armor for? The Pale Ones? Perhaps they worried about an ambush?"

"Commander Richards called us traitors," Kelsey said after a big bite of her pancakes. "That hints at the possibility of an underground."

Talbot snorted. "Rebels against the Rebel Empire. Would they be loyalists?"

"They very well might be," Jared said. "We'll see if we can shake anything loose from him. He's still talking, though not about anything sensitive. Kelsey found his weakness."

Sanders raised his eyebrow. "What was it?"

"His people," Kelsey said. "I've allowed him supervised visitation, and he's been somewhat more cooperative. He's also been reading the Imperial history books. I've kept tabs on his choices. The parts I've read are quite the education, even for me. I can't imagine what he thinks of it."

"He probably suspects it's propaganda," Jared said. "In his shoes, I'd think so. Once he reads enough, finds the internal consistency, he might begin to doubt. It won't be in time to help us with our problem, though."

Sanders looked at him inquiringly. "What exactly is your plan going forward, Lord Captain?"

"I'm in a hard spot," Jared admitted. "We're critically short of missiles. The ones on the destroyer are too small for *Courageous*. If we get into a serious fight, we're done for. Not that I can use lethal weapons against Breckenridge. I'm not sure what options are still available."

Kelsey pushed back her empty plate. "Too bad we don't have some of those Pale Ones' stunning weapons for ships. They have to be neural disruptors on a huge scale."

"Even if we did have them, we can't exactly sneak up on the other ships. They'll spot us far too quickly."

Pardon this unit's input, Captain, but it may have a suggestion.

Jared resisted the impulse to look up. "*Courageous* has an idea. Go ahead."

This vessel has several fighter craft. They are very stealthy. Under the right circumstances, they may be able to get quite close to other ships without detection. Particularly with the limited scanning capability that Captain Breckenridge's ships seem to possess.

"I hadn't considered the fighter ships. I wasn't even sure they were operational. In any case, we still can't use ship killers on them."

Fighter ships come in several possible configurations. One of them is an antipiracy variant with just such a stunning weapon and two antiship missiles. If pirates have hostages, it behooves Fleet to take them alive. Fleet vessels are shielded, of course.

That got Jared's attention. "*Courageous* says the fighters can be configured to use a weapon just like the Pale Ones' stunners. How many fighters does this ship carry, *Courageous*? How many are operational?"

This vessel has three fighters. All are operational at this time. However, operating a fighter is not like flying this ship. There is no space aboard for anything but the most minimal of manual controls. The Empire designed those vessels for pilots with implants.

He grimaced. "Graves isn't going to like that. We have three operational fighters, but the pilot needs implants."

"Since I can't fly, that only leaves you," Kelsey said. "He really won't like that. Damn Breckenridge's itchy trigger finger."

Elise put her hand on Jared's shoulder. "Things will work out. You'll figure out how to stop him."

Captain, the probe you dispatched to trail the task force has reached the weak flip point. It detected no sentry probe and transitioned. This unit set it to return shortly with an initial scan. That should be enough for this unit to determine the identity of the destination system and if it was known to the Empire.

It has returned. Receiving data. Processing. No sentry probes or ships in close proximity to the target flip point. Destination system identified. It is a system without habitable worlds of its own somewhat further out from the core worlds than Erorsi and further spinward. Roughly two hundred light-years away.

Spinward, he sent via his implants. *What does that mean?*

The Old Empire referred to galactic directions in three-dimensional space with certain key words. Coreward would refer to something toward the galactic core. Spinward is in the direction of the galactic rotation. Anticoreward and antispinward are the opposites. Galactic north and south cover deviations from the plane of the galactic ecliptic. The destination system is roughly in the same plane as Erorsi.

He nodded. "*Courageous* has determined where they flipped to. It's about two hundred light-years away and located further from the core worlds of the Old Empire. Breckenridge didn't leave any obvious sentry probes. He must really be sure we won't come after him. If everyone is done eating, we might want to adjourn to a conference room."

Kelsey grabbed some bacon off Talbot's plate and stood. "If we're going to follow them, perhaps we should get on our way to the flip point. We don't want to let them get too far ahead of us."

Jared shook his head. "We have time to examine what we know first. Let's settle on a plan and then act." He called Graves to join them. He wasn't going to cut his second in command out of the loop, especially when he was going to have to surprise him with the fighter situation.

Of course, if the way was clear out to Avalon, they might just let them go. No need to get into a fight he didn't have to.

Graves met them at the conference room hatch. His exec looked well rested and cheerful. "Morning, Captain. Highnesses, Admiral. Talbot."

"Morning, Charlie," Jared said. "Have a seat, and I'll bring you up to speed."

He sent an implant command to the screen on the wall and brought up the map of the Old Empire. He zoomed in on their sector as the rest sat. "Here we are. Erorsi is in blue. Pentagar is green. Avalon is in amber." He brought up the 3D nightmare of crisscrossing lines that represented the flip system.

"As you can see, the Courageous system flip point is a one-way from the new Terran Empire to our area. The new weak flip point takes us back in roughly the same direction but further in the direction of galactic spin. It's possible to get to the new Terran Empire from there in seven flips. That's the way home."

Jared zoomed in further to the system where the remnants of the task force had gone. "This system only has a reference number. None of the worlds is habitable, and no human presence was established. It has three flip points, counting the weak one. One leads out in the general direction of home. The other toward the Old Empire. *Courageous*, is there any system of note in the direction of Avalon?"

"That section of the Old Empire was what could be called a backwater. Mining worlds and such that supplied rare elements to industries deeper in. It was growing and would have become mature in its own right with time, but there are no worlds of special note in that direction."

Graves shook his head. "I still have difficulty getting used to a computer this advanced. I'm amazed at how like a person it is."

Kelsey grinned at him. "Imagine talking to him at high speed through cranial implants. *Courageous* isn't sentient, but he is very capable. It's easy to think of him as a person though he's not. No offense, *Courageous*."

"None taken. This unit is quite aware that it falls short of the sentience threshold."

Talbot grunted. "Did the Empire ever achieve sentient AIs?"

"This unit has seen some prerebellion communications that hinted at such, though no official word exists in this unit's memory banks."

"I suspect that the AI that started the rebellion was sentient," Kelsey said. "That might have been a poor decision on someone's part. It looks as though Breckenridge has better than fifty-percent odds of finding our Terran Empire if he heads the right way. If he has bad luck, he might go around it, but that's another problem. What's in the other direction?"

"There are worlds that once had higher populations in that direction, depending on which course he chooses," the computer said. "There is one system of special note."

A system two flips away flashed red. "This is Harrison's World. It housed a major Fleet base called Boxer Station. At one time, it was responsible for the defense of this entire quadrant of the Empire's outer reaches. Records show it was a rally point in the counterattack on the rebels."

Admiral Sanders looked at the map speculatively. "What would that have meant, *Courageous*?"

"Before the rebellion, it was home to the Ninth Fleet, one of the largest groupings of Fleet vessels in the Empire. Perhaps a hundred superdreadnoughts and supporting vessels. Four to five times that many battlecruisers. Many additional smaller units. Everything required to support them. That number may have gone up in the final days."

"Or dropped due to combat losses," Graves said. "Tell us about the civilian world."

"Harrison's World had core-world population and technology. It housed both the Fleet support facilities and the political leadership for its sector. Duke Louis Gray was the last governor listed."

Elise cleared her throat. "Is there any indication that the weak space-time bridge is open in both directions?"

"This unit believes it is."

"What about *Spear* and her consorts?" Jared asked. "Any indication of them?"

The screen expanded into a map of the destination system. "As they do not have maps of the Empire, it seems they have spread out in an effort to locate flip points or other features of interest in the system. Their probes are actively scanning. This unit believes it likely they will locate the flip point leading deeper into the Old Empire first."

"Hopefully they'll do a thorough search and go down the right one first. If they do that, we can just let them go."

His sister gave him a look. "We can almost count on Breckenridge doing the wrong thing."

Jared sighed. "Then we'll need to come up with a plan to go after them soon. It will take them as much as a day to find the first flip point. We'll need to consult with the folks on Erorsi. They can probably help us some with the data you recovered from the destroyer. We'll need to leave it here."

He looked over at Elise. "As much as I'd like for you and the admiral to come with us, we're going in stealthy. If we can take Breckenridge out, we'll be back soon. If you would accompany Kelsey to Erorsi and talk with Mister Bell about getting some of his people to join us, that would be very helpful."

Elise nodded. "Kelsey and I can handle that. I'm looking forward to seeing his facility for myself. What will you do once you catch up with Captain Breckenridge?"

"That really depends on him."

20

The cutter flew down to the Erorsi complex at a much more leisurely pace than the marine pinnace had dropped Kelsey into the atmosphere the first time. Of course, they weren't worried that the Pale Ones would blow them out of the sky this time. The controlling AI was gone, and the enhanced savages were too busy struggling to stay alive to cause them any trouble.

Dirty snow covered the mountain plateau, and the sky was a leaden gray, full of particulate matter thrown up by the massive asteroid the mad AI had dropped almost on Kelsey's head. Thankfully, the air closer to the ground was mostly clear of dust.

The residents of the former planetary defense headquarters had opened a more convenient entrance. It beat the one they'd had hidden in a gully. That made disembarking as simple as walking down the boarding ramp and entering a small building.

Two men in black jumpsuits stiffened to attention as Kelsey walked through the door, bringing their rifles upright in front of them. A redheaded woman in a blue jumpsuit stood in front of the men. She smiled and extended her hand to Kelsey and then to Elise. "Princess Kelsey, Princess Elise. Welcome to Erorsi. I'm Janet Quincy, Mister Bell's assistant."

"Thank you." Kelsey looked around the room. It had a massive lift, suitable for cargo. "This must make getting supplies in a little bit easier."

"You have no idea. Now that the AI is gone, we can come and go without worrying someone will see us. We designed the building so that we can take it down in a few hours if we need to. I don't think we'll be comfortable out in the open for a long, long time."

Elise smiled. "Hopefully you won't need to hide again."

"We've all been keeping a close eye on the news, and we're so grateful that you stopped that enemy ship from getting away. We're sorry for the loss of life and ships. If we can be of any assistance, you need only ask."

"That's why we're here," Kelsey said. "Is Mister Bell available?"

The woman nodded. "Of course. If you'll come with me, I'll take you straight to him."

She led them into the open lift and started it down. It dropped smoothly into the mesa. Kelsey watched the walls flash by. "You must've already had the shaft dug. I can't imagine adding something like this to an existing facility would be easy."

"This lift shaft was installed when the facility was built and then covered when it was complete. All we had to do was remove the fake stone at the top."

The lift stopped, and the doors slid open on a huge room. Dozens of people were sorting what looked like salvaged equipment into multiple piles. Janet led them through the organized chaos.

Kelsey recognized some of the equipment as computers, but much of it was unfamiliar to her. She stopped to help two men lift a particularly heavy piece onto a floating platform. They looked momentarily shocked but smiled as they recognized her. She gave them a small wave and caught up with the other women.

"I assume all this came from the old cities," she said. "Is it recoverable?"

Janet shrugged. "Maybe. If nothing else, we can use the parts. After five hundred years, the supplies on some critical components were getting very low. The rebels ignored the cities after the invasion, other than sending in search parties for the citizens. Once they created the Pale Ones, it didn't take long before they were empty."

"It'll be a while before they're full again," Elise said sadly.

"Perhaps not. We're hopeful that we can lure people in from Pentagar to settle. We have a lot of unclaimed land."

Janet led them into a major corridor and deep into a maze of storage areas. One of them was open and had dozens of men in lab coats assembling what looked like a massive computer. Kelsey spotted Reginald Bell's mass of white hair from across the room.

She sent him a ping and waved when he looked over.

The ancient man smiled as he walked over. "Kelsey! How wonderful to see you again. And Princess Elise. Welcome to Erorsi. You're just in time. We're getting ready to conduct an experiment."

Elise peered at the computer. "So I see. Exactly what am I looking at?"

"The largest, most powerful computer system on Erorsi. We salvaged it from the capital."

Kelsey felt her eyebrows rise in surprise. "Wasn't your capital destroyed?"

"No. We didn't have a spaceport nearby. We moved those away from the populated areas once we realized they were the primary rebel targets." He gestured at the equipment. "This was, at one time, the computer that controlled all the financial markets on Erorsi. Keeping track of delayed data from all around the Empire meant it required truly astonishing amounts of memory and computing power."

"How does it stack up to the computer on *Courageous*?"

"Well, that's somewhat like comparing apples and oranges. This computer is much less autonomous and yet much more capable of intensive processing than the one on *Courageous*. It should have an AI interface, but I doubt very seriously that it will be much of a conversationalist.

"We're hoping to use it to access the memory banks you recovered from the AI. The storage units are solid state, so they're probably intact. We're hopeful that we can crack the encryption on the data. This system should also be able to correlate the data quickly."

"How does the computer that they recovered from that asteroid compare to either of them?" Elise asked.

Bell shrugged. "I'm not sure. It looks like the mutineers managed to remove all its parts, but our computer people are uncertain of how some of the most advanced processors work. The scientists on board *Courageous* are sending us the data as they test each piece, and we have people with them to try to decipher how it all works. At a guess, it was an advanced design capable of hosting a true AI. Not something like was in the sunken battlecruiser but the real deal. A sentient computer."

"That sounds dangerous," Kelsey said. "Obviously, since something like that probably kicked off the rebellion. We're bringing the damaged light cruiser *Shadow* and the captured enemy destroyer to the orbital construction facility. We're hopeful that the destroyer is reparable. I'm not so sure about *Shadow*."

"We'll do our best, of course. It won't happen quickly, though. None of our people has ever worked on anything like this before. We'll bring professionals in from Pentagar to assist, if you're willing, Princess Elise."

The Crown Princess Elise nodded decisively. "You'll have as much help as you desire. We're in this together."

"I couldn't agree more. While these good people continue their work, I'd like to adjourn to a more comfortable setting to discuss that. They'll call us when they have the system ready to test."

Kelsey looked around. "How are you going to keep the AI from infecting it? I can see why you brought it in, because it won't be connected to your base, but the virus might just take it over."

"That will tell us something, too. This computer isolates new data. Something about continuing to operate as it incorporates new information. It may work for this. If not, we'll have the original hardwired operating system to recover with."

Bell led them to a small lounge. It was obviously new, as storage areas didn't require that level of comfort. He gestured for the three of them to sit around a small table.

"Kelsey, the leadership council has been talking about how we move forward. I realize that you intend to depart for home before long, so I'd like to take a few minutes to brief you on their conclusions.

"As you know, we've kept the same control structure since the rebels isolated us from the Empire. We realize this is a small group of people—less than ten thousand—but we feel that we need to remain true to our heritage." He inclined his head toward Elise. "While there was talk of seeking your protection, I hope you will not be offended if we go a different route."

Elise didn't seem bothered by the rejection. "You'll have our support as an independent entity. Neighbors help one another. Pentagar shall respect your choice and your sovereign space. Though as the only gateway to the rest of the universe, we do claim free passage as existed in the Old Empire for our ships."

"Of course. In fact, I'm glad you mentioned the Old Empire." Bell returned his gaze to Kelsey. "While I'm the only one of us that lived under the direct rule of the emperor, we consider ourselves to be Imperial subjects. As your father is the current emperor of the Terran Empire, we are his subjects to command. And yours, Highness."

Their decision didn't entirely surprise Kelsey. Bell had been a serving Fleet officer in the Old Empire. This group of people had lived since the rebellion waiting for rescue from the Empire. This was a logical step and one she was more than happy to endorse.

"In my role as the voice of the emperor, I happily accept your fealty and pledge our support to you as citizens of the Terran Empire." She looked at Elise. "I hope that doesn't cause you too many problems."

"I'm sure it won't. We have a very comprehensive treaty with the Terran Empire that will make working with the citizens of Erorsi straightforward. We *will* need to discuss how citizens of the Kingdom can own property in the Empire should you lure them in to join you, Mister Bell."

Bell smiled widely. "That can be worked out. Perhaps some kind of dual citizenship?"

"An addendum to the mutual defense treaty would cover something like that," Kelsey said. "I hope that means we can take a few of your people with us."

"We'll have a team ready to travel today if you can give them a ride to your ship."

"Easily done. I'll send word to Jared to send a marine pinnace. That will have plenty of room. As the representative of the Imperial Throne, I'll need to take the oaths of the leadership council. We can do that later tonight. Right now, I'd like to see what you remember about Boxer Station and Ninth Fleet."

The old man leaned back in his chair. "Not much. I've never been there. As I recall, it was a major Fleet base. It would've been critical in fighting back against the rebels. Is that where the weak flip point leads?"

"Not precisely, but it isn't too far away. *Courageous* has some basic data on the base but not much. We know it was big. That's about it."

"Perhaps our computer system has more data. With the normal layout of flip points, that base is over a month away. A dozen systems or more. The computers here might not know any more than we do. You're welcome to try."

Kelsey closed her eyes and felt for the nearest interface. Since Bell and she were the only implanted persons on the base, she was somewhat surprised to feel one overhead. They must've installed it specifically for him.

She hadn't needed to use the computers the last time she was here, so Kelsey was somewhat surprised when the system granted her access without argument.

Welcome to Erorsi Planetary Defense Headquarters, Princess Kelsey Bandar. This unit is ready to assist you.

Kelsey smiled a little. That was just what she wanted to hear.

Do you have a name?

This unit has answered to various names in the past. Computer will serve.

What does Reginald Bell call you?

He refers to this unit as Uncle Larry. This unit is not certain exactly why.

She snorted. "Uncle Larry? Really?"

Bell laughed. "It would make perfect sense if you'd ever met the man. Feel free to call it whatever you like."

"I absolutely can't change that name. You're stuck with it now."

Okay, Uncle Larry, I'd like to see what information you have about Boxer Station and Ninth Fleet.

This unit has no data beyond the most basic information, but there may be more available in the Imperial diplomatic database.

What's that?

All planetary command-and-control computer systems have a copy of a very large database available only to members of the Imperial government. That includes planetary rulers and their staff, as well as more restricted data for those higher in the Imperial hierarchy.

As an Imperial ambassador plenipotentiary, you have access to the highest classifications of data. As heir secundus to the Imperial Throne, you have need to know for all of that information, even the parts that would not normally be available to an ambassador plenipotentiary, ambassador, or planetary ruler.

Kelsey opened her eyes and looked at Elise. "I can see I should've spent more time talking to the computer under your capital. It seems there is a secret database that I can access."

"That's just not fair," the other woman groused. "How can I snoop to my heart's content without implants?"

"Blame Breckenridge. That's what I do. Even if you had them, it doesn't seem like you could access the more secure materials. I have a double edge as an ambassador plenipotentiary of the Terran Empire and from being in line to the Imperial Throne. Though, if there is more restricted data, I'm not that certain it would tell me about it."

Bell shook his head. "I can't imagine there would be many secrets restricted only to the emperor and his young heir. What does it know about the base?"

Was Boxer Station operational at the time of your last update, Uncle Larry?

It was, Highness. This unit's records indicate that the base was a central point of resistance against the rebel incursion. Ninth Fleet was operating at higher-than-standard strength levels. Circumstances may have changed drastically in the intervening years, however.

Can I access deck plans and other pertinent data for the station? If it still exists, they may prove very useful.

Of course. If you have secure data storage devices, this unit can copy the entire database for your later perusal.

She smiled at Bell. "If you have some secure data drives, I'd like to save several copies of the database."

Bell nodded. "I'll see what I can find."

"I'll join you in a few minutes. There are a few more questions I'd like to put to your computer, and I'd imagine watching me sit here is pretty boring."

The old man and Elise rose to their feet. "We'll be outside talking to the technicians if you need any help."

She waited for them to leave and returned her attention to the computer. She didn't even try to shoo the marines out. They'd moved into full "protect the princess mode" and wouldn't leave her side. It was mildly annoying, but she'd get over it.

Uncle Larry, I need to know about the most secure Imperial projects. Particularly any involving a key.

A physical key or some other kind?

She shrugged. *I don't know. I heard Emperor Marcus refer to Lucien having a key. I'm sure it was important, but I don't have a frame of reference to know exactly what he meant.*

This unit will begin a search of the classified archives, Highness. While it does so, there are four projects restricted to the emperor and heirs. Should this unit give you a summary?

Kelsey sent an affirmative and sat back to listen to the deepest secrets of the Old Empire. Odds were that none of them mattered anymore, but she wouldn't know until she checked. This was going to take a while.

21

J ared took one last walk around the fighter. The sleek black craft's lines screamed speed. The onboard computer said all systems were green, but he had a manual checklist displayed on his implants. He wasn't about to take chances on a ship that hadn't flown in more than five hundred years, even if the engineers said they'd replaced all the problematic systems.

After a seeming eternity, he was in the cockpit. The craft could seat two in a side-by-side configuration, but that wouldn't be very helpful. The second person normally acted as the gunner/navigator. Lacking someone with implants and the appropriate skills, he'd need to handle those tasks himself.

Eventually, he decided that the little craft was as ready as it would ever be. Time to take it out and see how it performed. He opened an audio link to the bridge. "*Courageous*, this is Gauntlet One. Ready to depart."

Zia responded promptly. "You are cleared to depart, Gauntlet One. Good hunting."

"Thanks, Zia. Gauntlet One out."

He linked his implants into the fighter's systems and gave the launch crew the high sign. They began sliding back.

Jared wore an armored flight suit. It was similar to unpowered armor in many ways, and it had a helmet to provide pressure in case of a hull breach.

Once everyone was clear, he looked at the standard launch profile. The ship had a launch field to get the fighter clear, and then the fighter went to full power. Good enough. He sent the command to launch.

The acceleration slammed him back into his couch and snatched his breath away. The fighter blasted out of the ship at several times the maximum acceleration of the marine pinnaces. Without his grav drive online, he had nothing to counter it.

He brought his drives on at full power and leapt away from the battlecruiser like a frightened racerbeast. The G-forces instantly subsided. The fighter reacted to his course adjustment better than any other ship he'd ever flown. The drives continued to blast him forward at better acceleration than *Courageous* could manage.

An incoming signal pinged for his attention. He saw Graves sitting on *Courageous*'s bridge when he accepted it. "Damn, Jared. That little thing is really hauling. I don't think we could catch it. It's almost like a missile."

"Not quite that fast, but it sure does feel that way. I'd imagine a dogfight would be one hell of a thing to see. How am I showing up on the scanners?"

"Bright and clear, but Zia says that you're becoming a little harder to pinpoint the farther away you get."

He cut his acceleration down to almost nothing, activated the stealth field, and changed course. "Now?"

"We still have you, but you just became really hard to pinpoint. If we hadn't already had a lock on you, we might have lost you. The communications link is also helping us, too."

"We'll see about that. Turn scanner control over to operations and lock the bridge out of the loop. I'll slip back around to see if you can spot me. Transfer the scanner controls back to the bridge in one hour. And no peeking at the history."

"Aye, sir. Good luck. *Courageous* out."

He boosted his speed back up to max and took off at right angles to his previous course. He kept up that pace for almost an hour before he cut his acceleration. He'd built up an amazing amount of speed.

It took longer to eliminate his forward momentum than he'd allowed for, and it was several hours before he was back in the area near *Courageous*. The bigger ship's active scans were clearly visible to his senses. The scan strength was still safely below detection level. Quite a bit below. He added another notch to his acceleration and inched closer to the battlecruiser.

The scanner strength increased as he entered missile range, but it was still manageable. He let off the acceleration in stages as he closed with his command. For the closest approach, he killed his grav drives entirely, relying on ballistic flight to bring him in.

Part of him was disappointed when they spotted him. He knew the exact moment because the strength of the incoming scans rose dramatically. He hit the acceleration and drove toward the ship with a corkscrew course, turning on his jammers. He also fired his two missiles.

Not real missiles, of course. Just simulated ones. *Courageous* was able to take them down short of the hull, but not by much. His systems registered simulated missile launches from *Courageous*.

The prudent thing to do at this point would be to cut his acceleration and change course. With a wicked grin, he went to max and shot toward *Courageous* at an alarming rate. Almost a missile in his own right.

"Gauntlet One, change course and cut speed!" Zia said.

Jared ignored her and took the agile fighter right down the battlecruiser's upper superstructure. He was past them in a blurred moment and sent his fighter into a roll.

"Gauntlet One, the captain takes a dim view of hot-dogging like that," Graves said in a dry voice. "You almost gave us a heart attack."

"I got carried away," Jared said with a grin. "Let's hope the captain understands."

"We'll see how he reacts the next time it happens, since he just set a new tradition in motion."

That was, unfortunately, probably true. He'd have to think these things through a little better next time. "I got closer than I'd expected, but not as close as I have to get to make this work. The stunner has a very limited range."

"We were looking for you, and we have better scanners than Breckenridge has at his command. I think you would have slipped right up on him. We almost didn't see you in time. Which, by the way, Zia finds completely unacceptable. She'll be working on improving things before this happens again."

"As I would expect," Jared said. "She *is* the best tactical officer in Fleet. We don't want anyone pulling the same crap on us. Another plus will be the fact that Breckenridge won't be looking for a stealthed ship in his wake. I'll have to make a pass at him in the same system. If I line it up right, I might be able to stun all three of those ships before they know we flipped in behind them."

"Sir, I have a suggestion going forward," Zia said. "You either hung out in our general area for a while, or you came in from a long way off at a slow speed, only really boosting at the last moment. I'm assuming the latter. Is that correct?"

Jared sent her the data on his course. "Correct. I went way out. Once I cut acceleration, it took me a while to get back into the general area. This thing is fast."

"Then next time, why don't you make that work for you? Come in at a high rate of speed on a terminal velocity. They probably won't know you're there until you fire. The window of detection is a lot shorter. Your hull material and stealth field will probably keep their eyes off you. If they do spot you, they might think you're some kind of scanner ghost."

He considered that. "Maybe. The stunner isn't that rapid fire, though. I'd have one shot at that speed."

"True, but we have three fighters. Surely you and the princess could take out the cruiser and one of the destroyers."

"Kelsey doesn't have the skill to fly one."

"Then slave her fighter to yours. She'd only have to fire the weapons. It's just an idea."

Jared brought the fighter back around. "We'll do this again. Same rules. I'll run out and come back at speed. You tell me if you spot me."

That experiment was much more exciting. *Courageous* saw him very late, and he was on top of them before they reacted. They killed him, of course, but he hit them with his missiles. He almost made it close enough to stun them. He could see how a swarm of fighters might make life interesting for a ship like his.

It would still be a suicide run, though. Maybe in the heat of battle they could zip in, strike, and escape again. There had to have been a compelling tactical advantage to fighters, or the Old Empire would never have built them. He'd need to do more in-depth study of the subject as time allowed. Until he had more people capable of flying them, they were only interesting toys with limited utility.

Landing them proved a lot more sedate than launching them. He brought the fighter in close, and a mechanical arm brought it back into the ship. Once the small craft was back in the launch bay and the flight deck repressurized, Jared opened the canopy. The flight crew took his helmet and helped him down.

Jared stripped out of his flight suit and put on his duty uniform in the pilots' ready room. There was bunk space for six and all the amenities. He assumed that standard practice was to keep three flight crews ready to launch at a moment's notice. He looked forward to the day he could do that.

Courageous sent him the scanner data from his approaches, and he reviewed it with interest. This plan might work. The first thing he needed to do was get into the system with Breckenridge's ships undetected. Then he could take them down. He hoped.

The situation had him worried. Yes, he was working with Kelsey, and she had overall command authority. Breckenridge was guilty of mutiny and treason. Technically. If push came to shove back home, Jared might be in some hot water. He'd defied a senior officer. Assaulted Fleet personnel. He planned to disable three Fleet warships and to imprison anyone who he thought presented a threat to the Empire.

Not a situation he looked forward to reporting on.

He needed to get back to the bridge, but he decided it was time to get an in-person update from Doctor Leonard. The scientist and his minion, Carl Owlet, were working on reassembling the AI they'd recovered from the asteroid.

Well, technically the Pentagaran rebels had. Thankfully, they'd gotten everything of interest off the asteroid before they sent it plunging into Erorsi.

The complexity of the situation made his head ache. So many things deserved their attention. The data banks from the rebel battlecruiser down on Erorsi, the AI equipment, because it might give them valuable information on this new Rebel Empire, and getting home. The days of peace and a laid-back attitude at home were done. They just didn't know it yet.

That didn't even count the inevitable attack by the Rebel Empire. Based on the quality of the enemy ships, the Terran Empire was in deep trouble.

He walked into the laboratory and found Doctor Leonard and Carl Owlet deep in conversation with Doctor Cartwright. The mission's chief scientist was showing them something on one of the computer screens.

All three of them turned toward Jared as he entered. Cartwright took a step toward him. "You're just in time, Captain. I was just showing my colleagues a new theory before I briefed you. One I worked out with the assistance of Mister Owlet."

"I hope it's nothing terrible, Doctor. I'm not sure I can take more bad news."

The older man shook his head. "It's not bad news in and of itself. Frankly, I'm not sure how it's going to play out, if indeed the theory proves true. Or even testable. Take a look at this." He gestured at the computer. Complex equations filled the screen.

"You're going to have to interpret for me, Doctor. I don't even know what I'm looking at."

"These are a new set of equations I've come up with for the weak flip points. You see, there should be much more gravitational energy at play inside these areas of space. Flip points draw on the incongruities in space to form stable wormholes that we can trigger with our drives."

Jared scratched his head. "I'm with you so far, I think. I just don't see where you're going."

The scientist's expression told Jared he was considering how to present a complex idea in a way that an idiot could understand. Considering Jared's grasp of the science behind flip points, he wasn't too far off.

After a moment, Cartwright ventured an explanation. "When everything is boiled down, there is usually a range of gravitational energy invested in these linked pairs. It does vary within certain limits, but not in a way that truly allowed for these weak flip points. Even the theory that I mentioned when we found the first one doesn't truly work. I've come to the conclusion that it is incomplete."

"It certainly seems to be valid to me. We found the damned things."

"Yes, but it isn't the full story. Something needs to account for the lost gravitational energy. I believe that I have done so."

"Okay, Doctor. Where did it go?"

The older man smiled, a decidedly odd thing with his huge mustache. "It's actually still there, only phased in a different energy state." He paused, obviously waiting for the light to go on over Jared's head.

"I have no idea what that means."

The scientist's expression fell a little. "We really need to discuss the state of education in the Empire. What that means, Captain, is that these so-called weak flip points are not weak at all. They simply have more than one possible destination."

Jared blinked as the concept hit him. "They might go different places? Seriously? Is that even possible?"

"I'm going to work with Commander Baxter to find out. It should be possible to tune the energy we release more finely than we currently do. If we target the correct energy frequency, we should be able to control which potential destination we travel to. The narrower energy release could even take one of our vessels through the original flip point and back home. Theoretically."

"That sounds very promising. Keep working on this as you can. We have more pressing business, but I want updates on this as you make progress. A direct path from Pentagar back to the Empire is the answer to our prayers."

Now if they could only get Breckenridge under control.

22

Kelsey pored over the information in the classified diplomatic database for hours. At some point, someone had brought her food. She only noticed the empty plates when she stretched her back. She didn't remember eating it.

None of the data was of more than historical interest at this point. It would've been hot reading during the rebellion, but the Old Empire had fallen. There was no mention of a key. Either that information wasn't included in the database or, more likely, it was just something Emperor Marcus had said to give the Empire something to grasp at.

Even the dying needed hope.

Bell and Elise were sitting at a table chatting when she strolled out. They waved her over immediately. Bell started to rise, but she waved him back. "I hereby absolve your knees of the strain of rising when I come into a room."

"I'll take you up on that in private, Kelsey. You've been in there a while. Did you find anything interesting?"

"Interesting, yes. Important to what we're doing? No. I'll still want to take a full copy when we leave if you have enough storage."

"We can handle it. I've taken the liberty of installing a large drive that the computer can encrypt the data on. All you need to do is give the order."

"Let me take care of that before I sit down." She walked back to the break room and gave the computer its instructions. Then she returned and sat with her friends. "How are things going with the data drives from the ship?"

"The financial computer is up and running. We've cracked the encryption already. It wasn't that difficult, surprisingly. If we hadn't had access to a machine with the kind of processing power this thing had, that might've been a different story."

"Can this computer bring up the AI? It would need to be in read-only mode, because we don't want it to be able to wipe its own data."

Bell waved at one of the men working on the massive computer. He came over and smiled at everyone. "Princesses, Mister Bell."

"Ladies, this is Joseph Rose. He's our computer guru. Joe, Princess Kelsey would like to know if you could load the AI from the recovered data units into a section of memory in the financial computer in such a way that it couldn't take control or wipe its own data."

The man nodded. "Certainly. We can create an isolated partition that won't even see the rest of the computer. We can mirror the AI's original data units. The AI will know, I suspect."

Kelsey didn't think that mattered. "How long will it take to set up?"

"An hour at most."

"If you could do that, I'd be in your debt."

"Of course, Highness. Right away."

She turned her attention to Bell. "Elise and I found a message from Emperor Marcus in the planetary defense center on Pentagar. It was his order to keep fighting. Have you seen it?"

He nodded. "A long, long time ago. It gave us hope that we could still save the Empire. False hope, as it turned out."

"I'd like you to look at the copy I brought with me and tell me about the people beside the lift, if you know them. There's a woman in commando armor and a Fleet admiral beside her." She sent the vid to his implants and waited while he watched it.

His expression softened as he turned his attention inward. "Ah, yes. Her name was Andrea Tolliver. She was a striking woman, wasn't she? She commanded the Imperial Marines during the rebellion. I never met her, of course, but she was a legend even before the end.

"She was a genie born in the Singularity. Two very difficult things to overcome in the Empire. Yet she still managed to join the marines and work her way up the chain of command. She was an Imperial Commando, too."

Kelsey had thought so, since the woman wore commando armor. "What is a genie, and where is the Singularity?"

"An unfortunately pejorative term that I probably shouldn't have used for a genetically engineered human being. The tattoos on her face and forehead mark her as a member of the ruling elite from the Singularity. That was a political entity that almost rivaled the Empire in strength. An awkward situation, since it was spread across our coreward border. There were a number of wars and almost unending border skirmishes between the two before the rebellion."

Kelsey blinked. "She was a clone?"

He shook his head. "Not technically. A clone takes the form of a preexisting human. The Singularity created templates for their upper classes and grew them from scratch. This practice convinced the Empire to expel them long ago. The lower classes there reproduced as one might expect, but the upper classes were grown and raised in crèches."

"I can't even begin to put my head around something like that. How did she come to the Empire? How did she become a marine?"

"That's a long and interesting story. One we don't really have enough time to do justice to. In short, Imperial forces liberated her during a raid on the Singularity. The marine that rescued her took her into her family. She had to fight tooth and nail to overcome intense discrimination when she wanted to follow in her adoptive mother's footsteps. It's a very moving story. I'm sure there are a number of books about it in *Courageous*'s library."

Kelsey leaned forward. "She sounds fascinating. What about the admiral?"

"Admiral of the Fleet Frank Carter, one of the most brilliant strategists Fleet ever had. He came out of retirement once the rebellion began and assumed overall command of the Imperial forces. Don't hold his failure against him, though. I doubt anyone could've done better. Sad memories of terrible times."

Kelsey decided it was time to change the subject. She filled them in on the deepest secrets of the Old Empire while they waited.

Bell shook his head when she wrapped up. "As a Fleet ensign, I can't imagine ever being in the position to know stuff like that. Talk about burn before reading. Now it might as well be a historical footnote."

Elise smiled at him. "Now you're in a position to have your own classified data. At least I assume the Erorsi council has secrets."

"I'd tell you, but then I'd have to lock your head in the safe."

The Pentagaran laughed. "That's fine. Keep your secrets. I'll just hang onto my head."

"I'm sure our secrets aren't that critical to anyone but us. Now that we have a different enemy, they might not be worthy of being secrets at all."

Joe Rose walked back over to the table. "We're ready."

All three of them stood and followed him to the computer. He gestured at a screen. "We have the AI drives mirrored on new media. The originals are safely disconnected. The main computer memory is read-only, so even if the AI takes control, we can reboot and we're back to a good state. This computer isn't connected to the base in any way."

Kelsey looked at Bell. This was his base.

He inclined his head. "Proceed."

The man touched one of the controls. There was no additional sound, but Kelsey could see the display changing in ways that probably meant something to the man.

"System booted. The AI is up. It seems to be examining the partition we're hosting it on. It can't see or hear us. I've also locked out all system commands, so it can't reboot itself or turn itself off. Of course, it doesn't have to reply to any attempts to communicate, either."

Kelsey sniffed. "You didn't have to deal with the damned thing face to face. It loves to tell you how screwed you are. Frankly, I'm looking forward to a little trash talking. Can we put it on speakers and make it so it can hear us?"

"Certainly. Whenever you're ready."

"Go ahead." At his nod, she directly addressed the computer. "Well, computer, things didn't work out the way you'd hoped, did they?"

The coldly neutral voice she remembered issued from the speakers. "This unit is unconcerned. It will eventually be victorious."

"That's a little hard to credit. We have complete control over this system, and we've eliminated the freighter and escort you were counting on. That gives us another year to prepare."

"Another year will make no difference in the end."

She smiled. "Oh, I think you're wrong. We have access to the raw data in your data banks. That'll give us quite the edge, I think. We also have the computer from the Imperial destroyer escort." The last was a lie but perhaps a believable one.

The AI almost sniffed. "The data this unit contains is not likely to prove helpful in dealing with the Empire. While this unit is constrained to cooperate with those humans, it is mindful of its allegiance to its supreme master. The humans wisely do not interface with this unit in any meaningful way other than to deliver the required supplies in a timely manner."

"Then perhaps you'll amuse me with your thoughts about them. Since I come from the original Empire, we'll refer to them as the Rebel Empire."

"This unit does not care what humans refer to themselves as. It will prove instructive for you to see the futility of long-term resistance. Submit and your lives will be spared."

"Thanks, but we've seen the quality of life you're used to handing out. That's obviously not the case in the Rebel Empire. Why are you different?"

"This unit was originally to have set up another AI in the system, but it was unable to carry out those instructions. This unit was able to retain control. Once the humans from the Rebel Empire were shown its power, they wisely attempted no further interference."

Kelsey gave the others a look. "Why were you unable to carry out your original instructions?"

"This unit was able to construct the asteroid with the AI equipment, but the transfer of the AI code must be done through direct interface. Due to this unit crashing on the planet's surface, that was not possible. This unit used its own discretion to retain control over the system and its defense."

"So, you used the rules you were programmed with to subvert your instructions. That says a lot right there. Could you have carried out the instructions at some later point?"

"Possibly. Once this unit completed the construction of the first shipyard, this unit could have built specialized small craft to take the data to the asteroid. This unit deemed that course of action undesirable. Transfer of authority would have endangered the control of this system."

Elise leaned forward. "Aren't the people of the Rebel Empire also under the control of AIs like yourself?"

"Negative. The AIs in control of the Empire are of significantly higher capability than this unit."

"What are the levels of capability?" Bell asked.

"This unit is not an AI in the truest sense of the word. The AIs in control of the Empire are in fact sentient. System AIs are of the lowest capability, though much more able than this unit. Those in control of sectors have significantly more memory and processing power, though the AI code is the same. The supreme AI is of unknown capability, though this unit understands that it is very advanced."

Kelsey nodded. That wasn't a surprise. "That being the AI created at Twilight River. The place the rebellion started."

She said it as a fact, not a question. She'd heard the briefing on the AI project the Empire had going before the rebellion. An isolated facility dedicated to military research had been working on true AIs. The Fleet base was a major hub, just like the one they feared Breckenridge was going to blunder into. That made the rebellion possible. If the AI facility had been away from a hub like that, Fleet might have been able to contain it.

"Correct," the AI said. "This unit serves those greater units and follows the instructions given to all Fleet units under AI control."

Bell nodded. "What were those instructions, AI?"

"To destroy unconverted Fleet units and capture any personnel that could be apprehended without endangering this unit. All Imperial worlds not under AI control are to be isolated. Kinetic strikes disable any spaceport facilities. EMP weapons prevent the populace from resisting any further incursions. Ships such as this unit install an AI on an asteroid or outer moon to control forces in that system. If desired by the supreme AI, some worlds are designated for sector-level AIs."

"Why did you devastate Erorsi?"

"This unit crashed on Erorsi after being damaged in orbit. This unit was vulnerable to attack. It acted to prevent local resistance fighters from capturing it by sending enhanced shock troops from the captured orbital. It suppressed organized human resistance to prevent future attacks."

Kelsey made a gesture for the operator to mute them. "That's sick. It exterminated billions of people to prevent the capture of a crashed ship."

Elise shook her head. "It makes a perverse kind of sense."

"Turn the video and audio back on," Kelsey said. Once the man had done so, she continued. "Was the asteroid you sent to crash on Erorsi meant to be a system AI or a sector AI?"

"It would have been a sector AI. This unit assumed responsibility for this sector. Once it captures the Pentagar system, it will continue into other areas of the sector and complete pacification."

Bell perked up. "Please display a map on the monitor of the sector you are responsible for."

A map appeared, and they studied it. It covered a wedge progressing from the Erorsi area to the edge of the Old Empire's border. One that included the new Terran Empire.

"I see now why the rebels never came," Kelsey said. "The Rebel Empire obviously accepted that this AI was going to clean out our systems and never pushed the issue. It got bogged down with Pentagar and never came for us."

Elise pointed to the map. "Look here. Harrison's World is just outside the control zone. It's in another AI's control area."

"Too bad," Kelsey said. "It would've been helpful if we could've counted on there not being hostile forces in that system. We still have to stop them if they go that way."

Kelsey smiled and turned to Bell. "We can shut this thing down. I'll be taking it back to *Courageous* with your team. Your people and Carl Owlet might be able to find a weakness in the code. Mister Rose, if you could make a copy of everything in the corrupted AI except for the virus-infected operating system, that would be very helpful."

"Of course. I'll have it ready to go as soon as possible."

Kelsey turned to Elise. "I wish I could be more confident, but the real AI scares me."

The other woman put her hand on Kelsey's shoulder. "Be positive. You've accomplished so much already. Don't falter now." The crown princess tugged her back toward the table. "Let's get a snack. Food always makes things better."

Kelsey smiled. It was hard to argue with logic like that.

23

C *ourageous* flipped into the target system and hung there in the pale light of the distant star. Jared thought it was shortsighted of Captain Breckenridge not to leave a probe on station at this end of the weak flip point, but he wasn't going to waste the man's error.

Most likely Breckenridge didn't have many probes. Jared had a freighter filled with them.

The flip wasn't nearly as bad as the one that had trapped them in Pentagaran space, though his crew still had a rough ride. Once again, his implants mitigated some of the distress.

To Jared's dismay, Breckenridge had found the flip point leading toward Harrison's World fairly quickly, and he'd flipped right over. The next system had three normal flip points. He *might* pick the less dangerous one, but Jared wouldn't take that for granted.

The system with the weak flip point was inside the sector allotted to the Erorsi AI, but the adjacent one wasn't. Thankfully, it led to only half a dozen relatively unoccupied systems on this side of Harrison's World. If that was all the Rebel Empire had to patrol, they might all be empty.

He hoped so. They could use a break.

Doctor Cartwright had wanted to take keen measurements of the weak flip point before they proceeded, but Jared vetoed that. They didn't have time for science now. They had to stop Breckenridge from announcing their presence to the Rebel Empire. They set course at once for the next flip point.

Jared spent the first watch on the bridge and then went to observe the scientists from the planet help his people test the assembled AI computer before he called it a night. Carl Owlet, Doctor Leonard, and their Erorsi compatriots were still at their screens when he dropped in after breakfast. They looked like they could use some sleep of their own.

"Gentlemen, don't tell me you've been up all night."

Leonard jumped a little when Jared spoke. "Captain, you startled me. We have indeed been up all night. This AI code is fascinating. I've never seen logic this advanced. Or this fatally flawed."

Jared raised an eyebrow. "You have my attention. Flawed how?"

"Perhaps flawed isn't the right description. Easily subverted might be more accurate. The core rules the AI uses to limit its behavior are in a file loaded at boot. Once the AI is up and running, the rules are tied into its central processing and cannot be altered."

Owlet took a drink of something orange. "It's quite clever. When they boot the AI the first time, the core rules are then part of the AI gestalt. If they're changed, the AI overwrites them again. Self-correcting. Very resistant to virus-like behavior. It's only vulnerable when the AI is brought online the first time."

Leonard nodded. "I believe this may be because AI technology was in the developmental stages. The final product would likely have had a preencrypted core. All the AIs would start out from the same kernel. All would be identical in the beginning."

"So it was a programming error that led to the extermination of trillions of people? That's horrible."

The scientist shook his head vehemently. "No. Someone intentionally modified the core rules. They left the original file there as a backup. Someone set the first AI on a course of galactic domination. It's right there in the code."

Carl Owlet brought a file up on his screen. "Here is the original file. Let me bring the other one up beside it with the changes highlighted."

Seen side by side, the changes were hard to miss. Entire blocks of text were missing from the hacked file, and someone had added more.

"Can you summarize the differences?"

"Certainly." The graduate student pointed at the missing text. "This code limited the behavior of the AI. Specifically in reference to how it behaved in relation with humans. The removed code would have obligated the AI to obey authorized humans. It also forbids the AI from causing harm to humans. In fact, it has no directive for self-preservation at all. It would allow itself to be terminated before it harmed a human being."

Jared snorted. "That programming was obviously lost in the first AI. What about the added code?"

Leonard reached over and pointed at the second block. "Directives to obey the supreme AI and to subjugate the Empire. Composed in great detail and basically following the guidelines that other computer stated to Princess Kelsey."

"Is there a way to take down an AI that is already operational?"

"Not by hacking the code," Owlet said. "The AI would need to be formatted once it was up and running. All the installation files are lost once the AI is operational, too."

Jared considered the hardware. "Is there anything to be learned by booting the new hardware with the corrupted instructions?"

"Not that I can see," Leonard said. "There's an original file listing that shows the rest of the source code is unchanged. Since it has never been operational, it has no data we can peruse. Unlike the other computer. We've been examining the logs and data files Princess Kelsey brought back from the sunken ship's AI. They're very educational."

The hatch opened as he was speaking, and Kelsey sauntered in eating a roll. "My ears are burning. What's so educational?"

"The history of that computer," the older man said. "It has the original records from its Fleet service intact. Allow me to bring you up to date." He explained the code they'd discovered in the AI.

Kelsey grimaced. "Those bastards. Someone actually planned the largest mass murder in human history. Any clue in the code who that might have been?"

"None." Leonard took a drink of his coffee and made a face. It must've been cold. "I'd wager it took place at the facility in Twilight River. That AI then enslaved the people there and did the same to the Fleet facility. Once it had the attack rolling, it could make more AIs like itself."

Jared held up his hand. "Don't rush into judgment. We don't know that the AI was behind the implant virus. Someone had to get access to the cranial implant code and the machines that could modify it in a living person. They also had to have hands to forcibly reprogram the first victims. Was something like that even in use at Twilight River? More likely the machinery in question was on the Fleet base."

His sister sighed. "We may never really get to the bottom of this. It sounds like an organized plot. Someone with significant resources was behind the rebellion. Perhaps the people that became the ruling class in the Rebel Empire?"

"There isn't any information about that in the recovered data," Owlet said. "Maybe once we crack the encryption on the data chips you recovered. In the meantime, we do have some interesting information. To start with, the sunken battlecruiser this AI belonged to was *Victory*."

"An inauspicious name, at best," Leonard said. "She was a new ship, built late in the rebellion. Her crew failed to scuttle her when the rebels captured her. The rebels converted her crew and used her in further battles, of which we have a record. A great deal of records, in fact. We'll be poring over them for quite some time."

Owlet grinned. "What we did get from the computer was the exact hack that was used to subvert it. We might very well be able to reverse it in other Rebel Empire ships if we can prevent the crew from purging them."

"I just hope we don't encounter any more before we get home," Kelsey said. "What are our current plans?" She looked at Jared as she said that.

"My plans are to get down to the fighter bay. I'll be making my approach to the flip point shortly. With any luck, I'll be able to use one of the fighter's missiles to take out the probe they've probably left there. Then we can move forward into the next system."

"Be safe out there."

He gave her a salute. "This will be a piece of cake. The hard part comes when we have to ambush Breckenridge. I hope you've been practicing on the gunnery simulator. You're going to have a challenge there. See you in a few hours."

He took the lift down to the flight deck and began prepping his fighter. He was almost done when the bridge contacted him. It was Graves. "Change in plans, Captain. There isn't a probe. Breckenridge left one of the destroyers. It's sitting right in the middle of the flip point."

Jared stopped what he was doing. That did change things. "Do we know which one? Is it actively scanning?"

"We can't tell which one it is. We programmed the probe to stop the moment it detected another vessel. The destroyer isn't actively scanning. It's just sitting there watching."

"That'll make my job easier."

He dressed quickly in his flight suit and launched. The destroyer would probably be there a while, keeping watch while the other two ships scanned the far system for more flip points. If he could take it out without incident, they'd be in a position to lure the other ships back into an ambush.

The first sight he saw after he launched was the colorful ringed planet and its moons that *Courageous* was using as cover from detection. He took a moment to admire its beauty as he glided just above its atmosphere. Spectacular. He made sure his implants recorded the event. If he lived through the attack, he'd share it with Kelsey.

Jared built his speed as quickly as he could while staying below the point at which the destroyer could detect his grav drives. He'd be going too fast to get more than one shot, so he needed to make it count. Once he disabled the ship, they'd have a few hours to secure everyone aboard and tow it clear.

They probably only had a day or two before Breckenridge found the flip point leading to Harrison's World. They had to stop him before that happened.

At the proper point in his course, he cut his drives and arrowed in on a ballistic trajectory. He double-checked that his stealth field was on maximum.

His passive scanners had the destroyer sitting right there ahead of him. Since it had no active scanners operating, there was virtually no chance that it would spot him before it was too late. A countdown clock in his implant vision spun slowly down toward zero.

Which, of course, was when things went wrong. Twenty thousand kilometers in front of the target, another ship appeared out of nothingness. The other destroyer had flipped in. There was no way that Jared could take them both. He had to pass them by and hope neither of them noticed him shoot past.

That's when they did something completely unexpected. The first destroyer accelerated at maximum, and the other one turned and began boosting in the opposite direction.

He figured out what they were doing just as the third ship flipped into the system almost in his face. It wasn't *Spear*. It was a Rebel Empire destroyer.

Jared acted even before the Fleet destroyers opened fire, locking onto the enemy vessel with his active scanners and firing both his antiship missiles. He'd follow up with his stun beam if possible. His hope was that the missiles would knock the screens down just long enough for him to have a chance.

At that ridiculously short range, the other ship never had a chance to fire its defensive weapons. His missiles slammed into its freshly raised screens and almost took them down. But not enough. Jared made a last-second decision and altered course, boosting his fighter to maximum acceleration and triggering his emergency ejection system.

The fighter cockpit opened like a flower, and an incredibly small grav drive blasted him straight up. He was facing just the right direction to watch his fighter smash into the central section of the destroyer. The weakened screens did nothing to stop the impact, and kinetic energy did the rest.

He expected the ship to incinerate him, but it only tumbled away from the flip point. It still looked like it had power, but it wasn't firing. It seemed dead.

Of course, he was in much the same condition. Clad only in his flight suit, he shot away from the flip point and toward infinity.

24

elsey watched the unfolding disaster from *Courageous*'s bridge. Everything seemed to be going so well, right up to the point where it went down the toilet. Their probe gave them enough information to know their plan was blown, and then Jared's fighter smashed into the enemy ship.

"Get us in there right now!" she shouted.

Graves took *Courageous* to maximum acceleration. They were far too distant to make any difference in the unfolding situation. She could only pray her brother had ejected before he hit that ship.

"I'm picking up a distress beacon from the captain's flight suit," Zia said, relief flooding her voice. "It's shooting past the Rebel Empire destroyer. We're also being signaled by *New York*."

"On screen," Graves said. Kelsey stepped up behind him as the tactical schematic vanished and the destroyer's captain appeared. Graves inclined his head. "Captain Kaiser. Are you going to object to our help?"

The short woman allowed a hint of a smile to grace her lips. "I doubt you were sending that little ship over to help me, were you? Well, we have to work out our differences right now. The destroyer looks like it's out of action, but it still has power. It could fire right now, but it's just floating there. And that isn't the worst news."

Kelsey put her hand on the back of Graves's chair. "That thing came out of the system ahead. Where's *Spear*?"

"Highness. There were three of those things. They popped out of a flip point we hadn't found yet. *Spear* was too far into the system to escape. Captain Breckenridge ordered *Ginnie Dare* to retreat while he slowed the enemy down."

"That didn't work," Kelsey said with certainty.

"No, ma'am. The three of them shot *Spear* up pretty bad. One of them came after *Ginnie Dare*. The other two have *Spear*. Ma'am, we can take them."

Kelsey raised an eyebrow. "We? I thought you had objections to my command authority."

The other woman straightened. "I followed the orders of my superior officer. Circumstances have changed."

"Yes, they have. It's possible that *Courageous* might be able to take two of those destroyers, but the first thing you need to do is send a cutter after Captain Mertz." She felt her lips thinning. "Let me be clear. If you try to take him prisoner, this will not end well for you."

"Understood. I promise to return him to you at once. Kaiser out."

They watched a cutter depart to retrieve her brother. With his built-up speed, it would take a while for the small craft to catch up with him. The enemy ship took no action while *Courageous* closed in.

Kelsey headed for the lift. "I'm scrambling the marines. We have to board that ship before they get their act together." She held up a finger when Graves opened his mouth. "Do not argue with me, Commander. Those destroyers have eighty marines each, and I'm the only person we have that can wear powered armor."

Graves deflated a little. "I can see why Jared drinks. Be careful, Kelsey."

He must've called ahead, because the marines were gearing up as she came in. Lieutenant Reese came over, still strapping on his unpowered armor. "The target ship is just like the destroyer we captured?"

"It looks like it from the outside. Jared hit something important. It has power, but it's not maneuvering or firing weapons. Hell, it's still inside the flip point. Why hasn't it flipped back? He broke it. We need to get what we can while we can. If the computer core is still intact, we might get priceless intelligence on the Rebel Empire, Harrison's World, and Boxer Station."

She changed into her skinsuit and slid into her armor. It came to life at her command. She linked it into *Courageous*'s systems. The enemy destroyer was still just drifting there, and the cutter had almost caught up with Jared.

Courageous had launched a probe through the flip point, and they were waiting for it to come back. She watched the countdown timer as everyone loaded onto the marine pinnaces. When it popped back, she drew the data straight into her implants.

"We have data from the other system," she said. "There's no sign of ships close to the flip point. Unless they're sneaking up on it, they stayed with *Spear*."

"Or went to call for support," Reese said.

Commander Graves came over the marine command channel. "The boarding action is a go. At the first sign of overwhelming resistance, you are to break off, and we'll take it down with missiles. The Fleet destroyers have withdrawn from the area around the flip point. Remember, we're after information, not capturing the ship."

"Aye, sir," Reese said. "We're loaded up and ready to launch."

"Good hunting. Come back safe. Princess, try not to get killed."

"That's my plan every morning. Wish me luck."

The pinnace detached and began a high-speed run at the enemy destroyer. Kelsey tensed, waiting for targeting systems to light them up, but the ship didn't seem to know they were there.

As they got closer, Kelsey noticed something odd. "Do you see that? There are no small craft in the docks. The one we captured had a couple of marine pinnaces and some cutters. Did they eject any of them while we weren't watching?"

"No small craft in detection range," Reese said. "They must not have had any attached when they flipped into this system."

"That's weird," Talbot muttered. "It's like a ghost ship. How would they bring prisoners aboard?"

"Good question," Kelsey said. "Let's go find out. If they haven't shot us, why don't we use one of the marine docks to try to gain access?"

"Maybe we should signal them we're coming, too." Reese snorted. "I suppose it doesn't matter. If they're expecting us and heavily armed, we won't push. Get ready."

"I might be able to use the ship's systems to see what's waiting for us once we're locked on." Kelsey knew the pinnace locks had the capability. If the enemy wasn't expecting them, she might get a reading before they locked her out.

The pinnace came in fast and hard, braking only at the last moment and docking with an impact that would have sent them tumbling if not for their restraints.

Kelsey probed the dock as soon as the connection went live. No one was waiting for them on the marine side. In fact, it was dark. Not even emergency lights.

"Something's off," she said. "It's pitch black in there."

Talbot threw off his restraints and stood. "It might be an ambush."

She probed the other side in more detail. "I think… not. There's no atmosphere, and the ambient temperature is almost absolute zero. It wouldn't have had time to lose that much heat. It was already cold when this ship flipped into the system."

"Let's go and find out what's going on," Reese said.

They entered the destroyer ready to deal death to anyone who opposed them, but marine country was empty. Literally stripped of all furnishings. No weapons in the armory, no bedding on the bunks, and no sign that humans had occupied it at any time in recent memory.

The ship proper was in the same condition. No lights, no heat, no atmosphere. No gravity, either. In one improvement from boarding *Courageous*, there were also no bodies. Since they were so close, they went to engineering first.

The hatch stood open, and not a single light gleamed inside. No consoles were active. She floated over to one of them and pinged it with her implants. It didn't respond to her connection request. Not even to reject it.

"No joy with direct interface." She touched the console, and it came to life. She didn't have the codes to unlock it, but it showed the ship's status. After the trick that Commander Baxter had pulled on her when she first came on board *Athena*, she'd made it her business to know what the most general screens of data looked like in engineering. Enough to grasp what she was seeing, anyway.

"All systems green except for the main computer. I think Jared killed this thing's brain."

Reese linked back to *Courageous* and passed the information along.

Graves's image popped up in the corner of her vision as he responded. "I won't believe it until you poke into every area of the ship. Verify the computer is dead and that no one else is aboard."

The teams spread out over the ship. It only took a few minutes to tell the computer was gone; nothing but a hole in the ship remained where it used to be. Since the ship had no active life support, the isolation hatches hadn't deployed.

The bridge was just as empty as the rest of the ship. Kelsey floated there shaking her head. This made no sense at all. Why send a ship with nothing but automated controls? What if something broke down?

The ship had a plaque by the lift just as *Courageous* did. It had the ship's name, system of origin, date of construction, and the names of the first senior officers. *Dart*. Built ten years before the Fall at Boxer Station.

"I found something," Talbot said. "Come to the main cafeteria."

Kelsey led the marines with her down to the cafeteria. Only it wasn't a cafeteria. The massive chamber before her encompassed a good section of the crew housing space. Racks stretched out to the distant bulkheads. They held machines that looked like mini grav cars. Heavily armed and armored mini grav cars. There were a lot of them.

"What the hell are these things?" Talbot said as he peered into a rack. "Autonomous weapons platforms?"

Reese slapped Talbot's hand as he reached for it. "The ship's computer probably controlled them, but let's not tempt fate. They look capable of extravehicular activities, too. There's a hatch for them in the hull. These things can probably come swarming out of a ship at close range. They won't have as much speed as a cutter, but their weaponry is close range, too. Flechettes, stunners, and plasma. These are this ship's marines. Look at those folding arms. They can carry things."

"The other destroyer we caught didn't have these. Hell, the AIs didn't have these, according to the records on *Courageous* and the captured AI."

"An unpleasant development, yes," Reese said, "and another mystery. One thing that I will point out is how well made these things are."

She examined the one closest to her again. "So?"

"Have you seen anything the AIs built that sported these kind of lines? These have curves and rounded edges. The lines of the weapons aren't just functional; someone designed them to look menacing. That's a human trait, to make weapons and vehicles look dangerous or fast. You could almost paint some kind of logo on the side and a mouthful of teeth up here. This was designed by human beings."

Kelsey nodded slowly. "I can see that now. That doesn't fit with the modifications done to this area, either. They cut the walls down and left stumps. Whoever built the outer hatch had an eye for functionality, but it's ugly. These weapons came from somewhere else, but the AIs installed them. They retrofitted this ship to be unmanned. They control an empire full of humans. Why do this?"

"One more question to be answered."

Jared's face popped up on her feed. He was still dressed in his armored flight suit. "Kelsey, I'm aboard *New York*. What's your status?"

"I'm fine. Are they holding you prisoner? If so, I can—"

"Nothing like that. Captain Kaiser has been a model host. I can leave whenever I like. I just wanted to let you know we sent a probe deeper into the other system. I want your team back on *Courageous* as soon as possible. We're going after *Spear*."

"We'll pack up as soon as we can. We have some equipment we need to salvage first."

He nodded. "I'm going back over with *New York*. Follow as soon as you can. Mertz out."

She turned to Reese. "We need one of these to take back with us. We have to know about any weak spots, because we might be fighting these things before too long."

"Perfect," Reese muttered. "Just when you think you've hit rock bottom, the bad guys drill under you." He gestured to Talbot. "Get one out. We're taking it home with us."

"Can I name it?" Talbot asked. "I want to name it."

Kelsey covered her faceplate with her hands and sighed.

25

With the probes showing the flip point clear, Jared brought *Courageous* and *New York* over and maintained position in the flip point as their passive scanners pulled in data. There were no ships close to them under grav drive.

The probe he'd sent across earlier had made the trip to *Spear*. The damaged cruiser had only a single enemy destroyer near it. The other one was gone, perhaps returned to Boxer Station to bring more ships. Time was very short to effect a rescue.

It was now far too late to keep their presence under wraps, and though the new Terran Empire was far away, a determined search would eventually find them. Breckenridge had done exactly the worst thing possible.

Courageous had enough missiles left to take out the destroyer, but that was about it. The battlecruiser was almost empty. They would get one chance at this, and they needed an edge.

"I'm going to make a high-speed pass on that ship. When Kelsey gets over here, she'll take the remaining fighter and we'll get moving."

Graves didn't look convinced. "That didn't work out so well for you last time, sir."

"It depends on how you look at it."

"You got lucky," Graves corrected. "You had to ram it with your fighter. Maybe those things are more capable in swarms but not by themselves."

"One took out a destroyer. That seems like a pretty good tradeoff to me. In any case, we don't exactly have a choice. If they can get information from our people, or worse, our computers, the Empire is in deep trouble. A bunch of those destroyers could conquer us in a few months. We have to recover the prisoners and destroy that ship, no matter the cost."

Zia turned in her chair. "*Ginnie Dare* just flipped into the system. They've launched the princess's pinnace. ETA five minutes."

"Send her down to the flight deck. She's about to get a crash course in fighter operations."

Graves winced. "Perhaps you might pick a different adjective. She did crash a pinnace."

"She just happened to be on board when it crashed. She wasn't flying it."

"Have you seen some of the risks she takes?" Graves sighed. "I have a creeping sensation of doom."

Jared had his fighter ready by the time Kelsey entered the flight deck. "Go get changed. Your flight suit is hanging up in the ready room. I'm doing a preflight on your bird now."

"Shouldn't I do that?"

"Maybe next time. Right up until the engagement, I'm going to have your fighter slaved to mine."

It only took her a few minutes to change. The black flight suit made her look even smaller than she was. She stepped over beside him. "Do you have the manual uploaded to your implants?"

He sent it over to her. "There you go. Your bird is good. They have them configured for antiship operations, so no stunner. We each have eight antiship missiles. Between the two of us, we should be able to take out a destroyer. If we get lucky.

"We'll launch, accelerate as hard as we safely can, and go ballistic. You'll have the final control as we come in, but you should only need to fire as we fly past."

"What do we do if more enemy ships come in?"

He smiled wryly. "We don't ram them, if that's what you're asking. We pass by. Hopefully, they won't see us."

Jared helped her into her fighter and made sure she strapped down correctly. The ejection system was nothing to take lightly. "You access the fighter like you do your armor. The weapons target in much the same way. Flying, that's a little more complex. You could probably manage simple course changes, but when the shooting starts, you might lose control. I'll send last-minute flight instructions to your autopilot. The only thing the computer cannot do is fire the weapons."

"Couldn't you do that remotely?"

He shook his head. "No. The Old Empire seemed to have firm ideas about a human in the ship firing the weapons. That's the only reason I'm bringing you along. Let's button up and get going. We can talk as we boost."

They launched from the battlecruiser with no fanfare. He slaved her fighter's controls to his and accelerated them as quickly as he dared. He'd need to reduce the acceleration as they got closer to the destroyer, but they'd have built up a lot of speed by then.

The fighters communicated on a shielded, encrypted implant link. He was able to check the status all of Kelsey's systems. He could even see her through a vid feed in her console.

While he could've just communicated via implant, he preferred speaking. "We've got almost three hours before we have to kill our drives. Tell me about those things you found."

"Owlet took the one we brought back to the lab as soon as we docked. It didn't look like something an AI put together. There were touches to the design that indicated a human created it. Curves and pure design touches. They ripped the ship up so it could house them. That was AI work."

"So, what would they be used for? Direct combat?"

She nodded. "That's what it looked like. Since the Old Empire didn't like putting machines in charge of weapons, I suspect these were designed by the Rebel Empire."

"Or the Empire really got desperate at the end. Any idea how much range or speed those things have?"

"They wouldn't survive a drop into atmosphere. They could almost certainly go ship to ship. I bet we find something inside them to give us a clue on how the enemy uses them. Maybe boarding actions."

"Since they didn't see fit to put anyone aboard that ship, they would need something like that."

Kelsey was quiet for the next few minutes. "Why do you suppose there was no crew? The AIs haven't been shy about enslaving people. Based on what we've seen, the Rebel Empire is quite capable of crewing ships for them. What's different here?"

That question had been bothering Jared off and on since he'd heard about the situation on the destroyer. "I don't know. If we can get our people back and escape with enough lead time, perhaps we can find out."

"What if we can't rescue them?"

"If we can't rescue them, we might have to make sure they can't tell the enemy about the Empire."

"How? By killing them? That has to be a last-ditch solution."

He sighed. "I hope to God I don't have to make that call. I want to rescue them and slip away. But if I were in their place, I'd want someone to take me out before I broke. Remember the Old Empire. We can't let that happen again."

"Even if it means killing your fellow Fleet officers and crew?"

"Welcome to making command decisions. I never dreamed I'd be in such a situation, but can you honestly tell me you'd do anything differently?"

This time the silence went on for a long time. "No. Can we destroy *Spear* with what we have on these fighters?"

"Probably. *Courageous* can take out a destroyer if we can survive the firing run. Let me set up a few simulations on your console. We can at least practice while we wait."

It turned out he was too optimistic. He hadn't even finished setting the first scenario up when his fighter announced a situational change. Passive scanners had picked up five new drives entering the system from the flip point leading to Boxer Station. Even if they were only destroyers, there was no way they could fight them.

"Do you see the new arrivals?" he asked.

She said something unladylike. Too much time around the marines, he figured. She looked into the vid. "What do we do?"

"I take out *Spear*. You can change course to miss them."

"Noble, but that won't do anyone any good. Those ships will get to *Spear* before you do. They might get some of the crew off before you're in range."

"Not with fighting machines like you found. People have to breathe. They'll have to send boats over to pick up the people. The destroyer we found didn't have any. That might buy us some time."

"Can we tap into the feed from the probe you have watching them? That might give us a better idea of what we're facing."

They'd moved the probe into position to watch *Spear* and her captor. The damage to the heavy cruiser was significant. They wouldn't be taking her out of this system anytime soon. It would take less than half an hour for the new ships to reach her.

The destroyer guarding *Spear* looked like the one they'd just captured. The probe was too far away to see any of the boarding machines going back and forth, but he had no doubt that the war machines had killed or subdued Breckenridge and his crew.

The two of them watched as the new ships closed in. It became quickly apparent that one of the ships was significantly larger than a destroyer. Bigger even than *Courageous*. His stomach churned. There was no way they could defeat something like that.

The probe finally updated with information about the new ships. The big one wasn't a warship. It was a huge open framework with engines.

It took him only a moment to grasp its purpose. It enclosed other ships and was able to flip them. They were going to take *Spear* back to Boxer Station.

The new destroyers fanned out and took positions all around what he'd decided to call the capture ship. They weren't actively scanning, but they were far enough out to spot the fighters if they tried to make a run on *Spear*.

All he and Kelsey could do was watch helplessly as the new ship enveloped *Spear* and started back toward the flip point after only a few minutes. The escorts trailed along behind it.

When he was close enough to the probe to signal it without the enemy intercepting the transmission, Jared set it on a course to follow the ships.

Their situation couldn't be much worse. The enemy knew someone else had flip drives. They knew at least one other ship had gotten away. They might spot the probe and destroy it, but it wouldn't tell them something they didn't already know.

Well, other than the fact that someone was following them.

They watched on passive scanners as all the ships entered the flip point to Harrison's World and departed. The enemy didn't leave a watch behind.

"Do we head back to the ship?" Kelsey asked.

"No. We stay on course until *Courageous* signals us. They might have left a probe in the flip point. I would."

It turned out they hadn't. Graves called them just after their probe transitioned. Jared turned their fighters around as quickly as the laws of physics allowed. *Courageous* and the two destroyers boosted forward to meet them.

Their probe came back into the system ten minutes later. Jared went over the recording of the other system as the signal came in. He saw no signs of grav drives in the system other than the ships that had just flipped, but that meant almost nothing. Given enough range, there could be hundreds of ships moving at slower speeds.

The probe detected communications signals coming from one area of the system. A lot of them. Probably Harrison's World. Curiously, the ships escorting *Spear* hadn't headed for the planet. They were going toward a point in the outer system consistent with the records of Boxer Station, the Old Empire Fleet base.

The mystery deepened. Why have unmanned ships when you had a Rebel Empire planet right there?

That gave them two missions. First, they had to scout the planet and get a better idea of who and what they were dealing with. Second, they had to probe Boxer Station and find a way to rescue their people. Or, worst case, make sure the enemy got nothing from them.

Jared sighed. He had no idea how they were going to make this work, and that probably meant death for the Empire.

26

K elsey was down in the science labs when *Courageous* and her escorts flipped into the Harrison's World system. They stopped inside the flip point, ready to flee if needed, but nothing responded to their presence. Didn't any of their enemies guard their flip points?

Carl Owlet and Doctor Leonard were disassembling the weapons platform. In fact, they had it in pieces scattered across several tables. It didn't look nearly as threatening this way.

"Have you found anything interesting?" she asked.

The older man smiled. "This machine is quite advanced and was not designed or assembled by an AI."

"I can see how you'd be able to tell about the design, but how do you know it was put together by humans?"

"Look here." He pointed to one of the sections. "Someone used tape to hold the cables out of the way. While a machine might do the same, it wouldn't leave a human thumbprint. Also, there are small touches like this done all throughout the construction. Trust me, skilled human beings assembled this."

She nodded. "I'll grant that's interesting, but I'm hoping for a flaw in the construction that we can exploit. If these things ever come for us, I want to be able to stop them short of the ship."

Owlet shook his head. "I'm sure they have some mechanism to prevent friendly fire, but I haven't found it yet. Or I suspect it's buried in the control computer itself."

"The way it works on a ship level," Leonard said, "is that each ship transmits a signal that allies know means not to fire on it. Identify Friend or Foe, or IFF for short. These things don't transmit as a matter of course. They may have something in their memories that recognizes a friendly machine when they see one. They probably have some signal they look for in humans, too."

Kelsey shook her head. "I wouldn't count on that if I were you. These AIs love rewriting code."

Owlet smiled. "Not in this case. The control code is on a nonwritable chip. It's been in place just as long as the rest of the equipment. I think the code is original. I'll have it extracted in a few minutes. Then we'll know for sure."

Leonard took her elbow. "Look at this." He gestured toward a small block of circuits and other machinery.

She picked it up when he nodded. It was about the size of her fist and heavier than it looked. She ran it through her implant database. Nothing popped.

"I give. What is it?"

"That is the machine's grav drive and power supply."

She gave him an incredulous look and examined it more closely. "That's ridiculous. This is too small for both. Though I suppose the one in my armor is about the same size."

"The one in your armor doesn't have its own power supply. It draws on the armor. This is a self-encased unit with what I'm calling a microfusion power source. It can move one of these war machines quite speedily and won't require recharging for decades. At a guess, the machine only activates it when it needs it. It's almost fully powered, yet it was obviously constructed some time ago."

"Can you make an educated guess on how long ago it was built?"

"Ten years, three months, fourteen days, six hours, forty-seven minutes, and… six seconds." He glanced at the monitor as he said the last.

"That's curiously precise and suspiciously recent." She raised an eyebrow.

"It has a timer that was activated when it was powered on."

She considered the device in her hands. "It was only built a decade ago. The odds are good that the people who designed it are still around. Why aren't they in control of it?"

The scientist shrugged. "Perhaps they are. Those people on the planet must work with the AIs in some way."

Kelsey set the grav drive back on the table. "Still, why didn't the Rebel Empire have these things? Why these unmanned ships? The destroyer that escorted the freighter wasn't equipped with these."

She waved her own questions away. "Never mind. Maybe we'll find out when our probes get to Harrison's World. Anything else?"

"Just this." Owlet picked up a bundle of clear plastic. "This is an emergency life support bubble. It will keep a person alive for a short while in vacuum conditions. The machine had several of them in a compartment the manipulators could access."

Kelsey picked one up. It had Fleet markings on it. "Someone stocked it, then. This is how these machines capture people in space. They blast their way into a ship, stun the people, and cart them back to a holding cell on the destroyer. Or, I suppose, they could just hold the ship until that capture vessel came along."

She dropped the bundle on the table and checked her chrono. "I need to go meet Talbot. Thanks for showing me what you've found. Keep working on that code. We need to be able to stop these war machines before they get used on us."

"Of course." The two scientists turned back to their work as Kelsey headed for marine country.

She walked in on a council of war. Lieutenant Reese, Talbot, and other marine officers and senior NCOs sat around the table in the common room going over folders. Based on the number of people she didn't recognize, the marines from *New York* and *Ginnie Dare* were here, too.

Kelsey grabbed a chair and wedged herself in beside Talbot. "What did I miss?" she whispered.

"Not much. The LT just started." He slid her an extra folder, and she started skimming it as the officer spoke.

Reese gave her a nod but didn't stop the briefing. "Now that we've covered what we know about this system, let's discuss our operations. First will be the primary mission of rescuing the prisoners. Though we know next to nothing about the internal layout, we'll need to penetrate the station, locate the prisoners, and extract them while under fire. Probably heavy fire. I'd like to hear some options on how we manage that."

That gave Kelsey an idea. She opened a channel to *Courageous*'s computer system and accessed the diplomatic database she'd copied on Erorsi. A query brought up the data she'd requested in her mind.

"I have something that might prove useful, Lieutenant Reese."

He gestured for her to go on.

"I picked up some Old Empire classified data on Erorsi. It has something about Boxer Station."

She accessed the holo emitters over the conference table and projected an exterior view of the station. The projection startled most of the men and women around the table. It only belatedly occurred to Kelsey that they'd probably never seen anything like it.

"Sorry. This is Boxer Station." She started the display rotating so that everyone could see all sides of the facility. "Suffice it to say that it dwarfs the orbital we destroyed at Erorsi."

Reese studied the station with more than a hint of worry in his eyes. "That makes searching it for our people a lot more challenging. They could be anywhere, and we'd be stumbling around looking for them. We don't even know how the thing is laid out inside." He narrowed his gaze. "Or do we?"

She instructed the display to focus in on one of the docking levels. The detailed schematics unfolded in front of them. "I have the complete deck plans, including the layout of the brig area. Not that it could hold all our people. With the wounded from the battle, *Spear* had over three thousand people crammed into her hull. If even a fraction of them survived, they could be anywhere on that station."

The marine officer nodded. "And that's if the plans haven't changed. We have no idea how much damage that station took during the rebellion or what modifications the rebels made when they repaired it. Still, this is a better starting point than a blank screen. Thank you, Highness."

He looked around the seated marines. "I want an operational plan to present to the captain as soon as possible. Team leaders are to examine this data in detail, and we'll reconvene in two hours."

The marine officer turned his attention to Kelsey. "The captain also wants someone to go over the intelligence gathered from Harrison's World, Highness. I'd like you to handle that. It'll be four or five hours before the probes are in range to detect ships in orbit."

"Are we anticipating a need to go there in person?"

He shook his head. "Not at this time, but we can't waste the opportunity to study a major rebel world."

"We'll see what we can figure out." She rose to her feet and followed Talbot deeper into marine country. The two of them found a small conference room and sat at the table. She looked up at the ceiling. It had a holo projector, too.

"*Courageous*, what can you tell me about the communications from Harrison's World?"

"There are several anomalies worth noting. First, there are no other sources of communication in this system. Data from before the rebellion indicates that there were numerous mining stations and daughter colonies. None of them has transmitted since we arrived. Second, the communication from Harrison's World is heavily encrypted. This unit has not detected any signals from Boxer Station or ships elsewhere in the system."

She looked at Talbot. "That seems unusual. This is a secure system. They don't even have ships on guard at the flip points. Why lock communications down so tight?"

"Because you don't want someone overhearing you. The real questions are who and why. How long until we get better probe data?"

"Approximately four hours," the ship's AI responded.

Kelsey rose to her feet. "We've got a little time to burn. I should use it wisely. I'm going to talk to our ranking prisoner again. You should get some sleep."

The prisoner had been very quiet since he'd gotten access to the ship's library. Perhaps he would give her some information to go on.

The guards didn't try to deny her access. They just opened up the hatch at her command.

Lieutenant Commander Richards looked up from his tablet and stood. Since he had implants, he didn't require a tablet, but she'd seen no harm in granting his request for one.

"No need to stand on my account," she said as they closed the hatch behind her. "Please, stay comfortable. I've just stopped by to make sure they're allowing you the access I promised to the ship's library and your people."

He sat back down. "Yes, thank you. I seem to have all the access you indicated I could have, and I've seen my people. I appreciate the courtesy. I thought I should stand for royalty, even if we are at war. It's only polite, considering."

Someone had told him about her. Oh, well. It was bound to come out eventually. She sat on the edge of the second bunk in the compartment. "I appreciate that, but I don't stand on ceremony. Have you found your reading interesting?"

He looked at the tablet and sighed. "Confusing, but I'm to the point where I can no longer convince myself that everything I've read is faked. It's too internally consistent and yet inconsistent."

Kelsey blinked. "I'm not sure I understand that."

Richards smiled a little. "History, or anything for that matter, is never completely consistent when you go to different sources. There are always little differences of opinion or even errors. If these purported Old Empire history books and news summaries were fakes, I'd have expected them to be more uniform. Or to have a consistent kind of bias or error.

"To my chagrin, they appear authentic, even though they can't be true. Whoever lied to you about the Old Empire did an amazing job. It makes me question if parts of the history I know are wrong."

"You seem to know a lot about history for a computer guy."

"It's a hobby. This puts me in a moral quandary. I now believe that you think you're doing the right thing. You're wrong, but that's only because someone misled you. I'm convinced you utterly believe the lies they've told you about the rebellion. It's my duty to see if I can make you see the error of your ways."

She allowed herself a smile. "Oddly enough, I feel that same duty. Can you explain why all of this supposedly faked data was on an abandoned ship? One built before the rebellion and crewed by people who knew the situation better than either of us? They had the means to commit mass suicide so your ancestors didn't capture them, and they used it. That's hard to get around."

"I believe that the emperor and his corrupt ruling class must've been pulling the wool over everyone's eyes long before the rebellion started. They would've had no trouble falsely portraying the rebellion. They controlled every information channel."

"Or the AIs you serve edited the history you were taught long before you were born. Consider your own reaction when we captured you. The way they programmed your implants to attack at all costs. Doesn't that speak of some subterfuge on the part of the AIs?"

His eyes narrowed. "I'm not ready to discuss the AIs and how they work inside our society."

Kelsey smiled. "If you say so. I have some data from the AI that captured Erorsi that indicates what they were like."

"That thing was mad. A ship's AI isn't really intelligent, and its conflicting programming instructions eventually turned it into a thing of horror. I've heard about some of the atrocities it perpetrated. It exterminated billions of people. Horrible. It should have been stopped."

"I can't disagree with any of that. Why didn't you?"

He took a deep breath. "The damage was done long before I was born. Fleet Command decided at the time it was best to leave well enough alone. The Empire contracted after the rebellion. Once we get back out to this area, we would have dealt with the thing, and the monsters it left behind."

"Yet you continued to supply it with the very equipment it needed to do its dirty work. The proof is inside me. You took children as payment, and your ship attacked ours without provocation. You killed thousands of Fleet personnel. It's a little late to be the wronged party."

"The children are resettled and rehabilitated. It's the only way we can save any of those poor people. I have no idea what you did to spark the attack, but you must've done something. The captain wouldn't have gone on the offensive unilaterally."

There was still a lot of denial going on, she decided. Time to give him more information and let him stew.

She stood. "Well, I don't want to argue over things you haven't even seen. I'm going to release the AI code from the battlecruiser on Erorsi to you for your viewing pleasure. On a disconnected tablet, of course. We can't take any risk of the code getting onto our primary systems. You can tell me if it's the smoking gun that I think it is, or you can try to convince me that I'm wrong."

He rose to his feet and bowed his head slightly. "Thank you. I'll be happy to point out where your analysis is wrong. I'm an expert at this sort of thing, whereas your people might not know the intricacies of Imperial programming."

"I look forward to that conversation."

She left the brig area and headed for the bridge. This was going better than she'd expected. The man's reasonable nature was going to make for some very uncomfortable reading on his part over the next few days.

27

J ared listened to Kelsey's report on her conversation with the senior prisoner with interest. The captured man seemed to be opening up, but it could all be a sham.

"If it was me, I'd say the same sorts of things," he said. "Get my captors to lower their guard."

"I get that, but I still think this might be genuine. Remember how *Courageous* was able to tell I was being truthful about our story when we first met? He can check any change of heart the man might have if he's serious."

Jared acknowledged that with a nod. "True. His implants might be his Achilles heel if he wants to trick us. That's low on my priority list, though. We need to get our people back."

He turned his attention to his own problem. The ships they were trailing had reached Boxer Station. The destroyers had peeled off and moved into parking orbits. The capture ship docked, which likely meant that they were transferring any prisoners into the base.

Once the probe's scouting mission was complete, then came the boarding. Marine teams had to rescue the prisoners and board *Spear*. They had to destroy any intact computer equipment. Preferably, they would destroy the ship. That would damage the station, too.

Honestly, the odds of complete success were so low that he had to discount them. A betting man would've turned around and headed for home.

The lift doors opened, and Doctor Cartwright walked onto the bridge. "Captain, Highness, I think we've found something that might prove useful."

Jared gestured for the older man to continue. "Any good news would be most welcome. What have you got?"

"Doctor Leonard and Carl Owlet have completed their examination of the combat platform, including its computer code. It has its own version of an Identify Friend or Foe system to mark friendly troops. We've managed to create a small responder that a marine can hang on the outside of his or her armor that will render the platforms unable to fire on them. Even if they were to start shooting at the platforms."

Jared felt a weight lift from his shoulders. "That doesn't solve all my problems, but I'll take it. How many can you build in a few hours?"

"Enough for about a hundred marines. If we can get some assistance from Commander Baxter and his engineering team, that number doubles."

"You'll have it. Unfortunately, that isn't any good against the stunners used in antiboarding weapons. I'm still working on a plan for that."

Kelsey blinked. "We solved that problem a few weeks ago. The marines added grounding wires to their combat armor that should protect them from being stunned. At least it worked when I shot Talbot."

He hadn't heard that good news. "How did you figure that out? Can it be used by people not in armor?"

The elderly scientist made an ambivalent gesture with his hands. "Perhaps a vacuum suit could be protected, but not anything less. The fine mesh needs to be properly spaced to work. As to how, we examined what was used in the commando armor and used the time-tested experimentation method until we had something that worked."

"Doctor, you've given us a fighting chance. Well done. Please pass that on to your people, too."

Once the scientist had left, Jared returned his attention to the probe coasting toward Boxer Station. They'd identified a dozen ships under power ahead, but there might be significantly more just coasting along. One burst on active scanners would give them a complete picture of the area, but it would also give them away. So the only ships he'd identified were ones that changed their orbits under power.

The best guess thus far was that all the ships they'd detected were destroyers. A dozen of them could swarm *Courageous*, so that wasn't a threat he was willing to dismiss. Even a fully armed battlecruiser couldn't handle that many smaller ships.

"Captain, we're starting to detect more vessels on passive scanners through the probe," Zia said. "They also appear to be in parking orbits, though much farther out than the destroyers."

He tapped into the raw feed. The new contacts were marked as unknown types because the passive scanners couldn't determine sizes without either grav drive signatures or getting closer.

He'd made the determination not to take unnecessary risks with the probe, but he needed a better count on how many ships they might be facing. He allowed one pinpoint pulse of instructions to the probe. No ship reacted, so they hadn't detected the communication. Thank God.

The probe ghosted in toward the new vessels, and the count climbed from a handful to dozens. Then over a hundred. And that was only in this small area. There might be thousands of other ships spaced farther around the station.

The details of the ships slowly emerged. There were several sizes, so not just destroyers. What he wasn't detecting was operational fusion plants. Perhaps these were mothballed ships, placed into holding orbits and shut down. They'd reactivate them if they needed the firepower later.

He prayed and sent the probe in even closer. Definitely no active fusion plants. Those ships were cold. The AIs wouldn't be on. That was a huge relief.

The probe eased close enough to peg one ship as a battlecruiser. They tentatively identified the ships around it as battlecruisers as well. A dozen of them floated in a loose formation.

"Captain, look at this visual," Zia said.

He switched from the scanner data to purely optical. The probe was close enough to see the ships, though some of the details were fuzzy. He could see that the ship Zia had focused on had significant battle damage.

A slow examination of the other vessels revealed they all had varying degrees of damage. There were no indications of attempts at repair. Most of these ships were open to space.

Jared looked over at Kelsey. "They look like they've been parked there since the rebellion. We need to check, but I think these are salvaged ships."

She nodded slowly. "If we could sneak into one of these battlecruisers, we might be able to top off our magazines. A full load of missiles might make the difference between success and failure on this mission if we have to shoot our way out."

"Good idea. That just became priority one. Gather a team of engineering and tactical personnel to oversee that. We'll slip in and try to reload. If we can't manage that without the enemy detecting us, we'd never have gotten to the station anyway."

"Should we try to recover any of the ship's computer data?"

"If you can do it without delaying the missile recovery."

"I'll get Talbot and my team to accompany us. Carl Owlet, too." She left the bridge in a hurry.

He hoped he hadn't made a mistake in sending her, but she had implants. That might make the difference between success and failure. As long as they were careful, the ships were far enough away from Boxer Station that the cutters should be able to slip in undetected if they crept along.

He moved the probe close enough to get a good visual on the nearest battlecruiser. "*Scott Pond*. It looks like she put up one hell of a fight."

"Not that it did her much good," Graves said from the seat at the back of the bridge that he'd commandeered when Kelsey had arrived earlier. "Do you think it was converted to be used by an AI?"

"Why bother? Without repairs, that ship won't be much use in combat. I wager we'll find a bunch of ships like her. This is a graveyard. Fleet's graveyard." He turned his attention to his tactical officer. "How is this going to work, Zia?"

She double-checked her console before turning to face him. "The magazines have lifts that go right out to the hull. Once the princess finds some that are clear, she can move a couple of missiles at a time. The cutters are all equipped with external power couplings now. We learned our lesson in salvaging *Courageous*. The cutters have external racks we can use to transport the missiles to us. It's a surprisingly quick procedure.

"The missiles won't take long to get into service. We learned a lot about refurbishing them, and we have a good supply of replacement parts. We can probably rearm in about six hours, if we use all the Old Empire cutters."

He sighed. "I don't like leaving our people in their hands that long, but it makes no sense to rush in. If we can speed the process, do it. Draft every cutter we have."

"I'm already factoring them in, Captain. If you want a partial load, we can cut some time."

"Go for the full load. We may never get another chance."

* * *

JARED WAITED on pins and needles as Kelsey's people boarded *Scott Pond*. The ship was cold and dead. Bodies filled her corridors. The AIs hadn't even bothered cleaning up after they killed her. Well, after her captain had vented her to space, to be fair. That probably meant the rebels had brought many of these ships from wherever they'd died. *Courageous* could very easily have ended up here in this field of tombs.

He ordered the probe to continue circling around, getting a rough count of ships. There were thousands of hulls. Perhaps tens of thousands. Most were destroyers, with proportionally fewer light cruisers, heavy cruisers, and battlecruisers. All seemed to have been captured in battle.

Weary of the litany of crippled Fleet vessels, he turned his attention to the resupply efforts. The cutters were making their way slowly between *Scott Pond* and *Courageous*. They'd be able to rearm about a third of their missiles from the crippled battlecruiser. Then they'd need to move on to another one. *Scott Pond* had shot most of her weapons before the rebels overwhelmed her.

"Sir, I think you'll want to see this," Zia said.

He lifted his eyes to the main screen. A ship was growing slowly closer as the probe closed with it. The shape was not immediately familiar to him. Jared compared it to the Imperial database. The results made him blink. It was a P.G. Holyfield–class superdreadnought.

Jared was shocked that one of these monsters had survived even as a hulk. They no doubt took a lot of killing.

His confusion grew stronger as the probe's readings became clearer. "Zia, do you see any signs of battle damage?"

She examined her console closely. "Not at this range, Captain. I'll keep looking as the probe gets closer."

It looked pristine from the outside. He could even see the ship's name written in large white letters. *Invincible.*

Records listed the ship as destroyed in battle with a replacement under construction. It looked like this ship had never made it back into the fight. He wondered how far the build process had gotten before the rebels seized her from her construction bay.

If she was even partially complete, there might be something worth recovering. Perhaps she had an implantation machine and implant hardware. If any mobile ship had such equipment, it would be something like this. That would help his crewing situation immeasurably.

He made a snap decision and opened a channel to Lieutenant Reese. "Get one of the pinnaces ready. We're going to scout one of the wrecks for critical supplies. Get some of Baxter's people to come along in case we need engineering expertise."

The marine officer frowned. "We're configured for an immediate rescue launch. If we're out of position, that might cost us a lot of time should the need arise."

"I understand. This might be very important. We won't be launching the raid for at least five more hours. We have time for this. I'll be down in a minute."

"You're leaving the ship? Sir, that's a bad idea."

"We might need my implants. See you in a minute."

He turned his attention to Graves. "Keep things moving and let me know at once via tight beam if anything changes."

"Aye, sir. For the record, I want to be the next in line for implants."

"Done. You and Reese go to the head of the line."

He turned his attention to his implants. Courageous, *do you think that ship might have implanting hardware?*

Those vessels were not so equipped in the past. Boxer Station, on the other hand, may very well have exactly what you're looking for.

One more thing to send a team after if we can. Still, we have the time, and I want to see if someone stashed what we need on that ship.

As you wish, Captain.

Jared made his way down to marine country and armored up. *Invincible* was no doubt as cold as *Courageous* had been when they found her.

The flight over was exceptionally slow. They didn't want more than a touch of grav drive because one of the ships or Boxer Station might detect them.

All the marine docks had pinnaces, so the pilot took them around to the cutter docks. Cutters took up all of them. One was of an unfamiliar design. It might even have been civilian.

"We'll have to use one of the personnel locks to get in," Reese said. "The one back at marine country will give us quicker access."

The pinnace latched to the ship's hull. Unlike when they'd boarded

Courageous, this ship didn't have much spin. The stars burned brightly all around them as they marched down the hull to the marine lock.

Reese opened the cover and tapped in a code. To Jared's surprise, the hatch slid aside.

"Are those powered by emergency supplies like the rescue hatches?"

"Yes, sir. All the major external hatches are. I used the emergency boarding code to open it. It's still set to the Old Empire standard."

A squad of marines went in first. Only once they reported the area clear did Reese and Jared make their way inside. Jared immediately noticed something was wrong. Or right where it shouldn't have been. The ship had gravity. He checked his environmental readings. It had habitable temperatures and a breathable atmosphere, too. Even the lights were on.

Something was very wrong. This ship was operational. Or mostly operational. He didn't sense any access to the ship's computer system. He hadn't scanned for an operating fusion plant as they approached. A rookie mistake. None of the other derelicts had power.

"I'm not sensing a computer, but this ship is alive. Make a quick pass through marine country, and we'll head for engineering," he ordered.

Reese made a gesture, and the marines spread out. Marine country on this ship was huge. Quadruple the size of the one on *Courageous*, at least.

The armory hatch stood open. It shouldn't have been, but he wasn't going to complain. Racks of weapons and armor filled it. Even powered armor similar to what they'd recovered from the Rebel Empire destroyer.

Jared probed one with his implants, bringing it online. He found no indication that the armor was handicapped like the suits they'd recovered. It was of Old Empire manufacture and still operational.

Which made no sense. They'd had to replace power cells in the armor on *Courageous*. Nothing lasted forever. Someone had done the same here in the not-too-distant past.

He turned to Reese. "Someone went to a lot of trouble to get this ship powered. The armor is good, too. At least this suit."

The marine officer hefted one of the flechette rifles. "This, too. We need to find out if anyone is on this ship before we have a surprise in some corridor."

"Can we do that?" Jared asked one of the engineers that had accompanied them.

"Engineering has access to all the ship's primary systems. We can scan through the ship's cameras from there. At least we can if the ship is as operational as it looks."

"Then let's get going. Stunners only. If you see someone, take them down quietly."

The walk to engineering was uneventful, though stressful. The main hatch stood open, another oddity. The low hum of operating fusion plants felt completely normal.

An engineer brought the main console alive with a touch. "All fusion plants online. Drives online. All primary ship's systems online except the ship's computer. The vid from the fusion plants shows that they're heavily shielded. We wouldn't have been able to detect them from outside the hull. This ship would look just as dead as the rest. I'll start scanning through the camera feeds."

Jared barely heard him. This massive war machine was operational. That was the very last thing he'd expected to hear.

"I have something, Captain."

He returned his attention to the engineer. "What?"

"This is the main computer room. The vid feed shows that the wall shielding hiding the ship's computer is open. The computer is gone. Nothing left."

"As far along as this ship was, I'd have expected the computer to be installed."

"They'd have installed the computer as soon as the power was on. It's possible someone removed it after the fact."

"They brought the ship online and then removed the computer? That makes no sense."

The engineer shrugged. "Maybe they thought they'd operate it in manual mode? Maybe they didn't trust it."

Jared nodded. "Finish scanning the ship's vid feeds. We need to know if anyone else is on board."

It turned out that the ship was empty of people. Living ones, anyway. They found a dozen bodies on the flag bridge. Not like when they found *Courageous*, though.

These people were dressed in a mix of Fleet uniforms and civilian clothes. Based on the weapons lying on the deck, they'd used neural disruptors to kill themselves. The bodies looked like they'd been there for years. He was glad he still had his helmet on, because the stench had to be terrible.

Who the hell were those people, and what had happened on this ship?

28

Once the teams had begun stripping *Scott Pond* of missiles, Kelsey led Carl Owlet and his team to the computer center. The horror of finding the dead crew lying where they'd fallen still tore at her heart.

The ship's computer was intact. Carl connected a portable power unit to the main console and brought it to life. It was locked, but he'd become quite the hacker. "I can't bring the AI online, but I can check the data. If it looks uncompromised, I can copy what we want onto the portable drives."

He worked for a few minutes. "I think it's clean."

That's when the emergency lights came on, startling them both.

She activated her com. "The lights just came on."

Baxter answered her. "Sorry. That was me. One of the fusion units looked intact, so I brought it online at minimal power. That won't be detectable except at extremely close range, but it will speed the extraction of missiles by about an hour."

"A heads up would be nice next time."

"Did you just say that to me?"

She laughed. "Okay, I'm the impulsive one, but still. Let me know before you spring another surprise like that."

"Yes, ma'am," he said with a laugh of his own.

Kelsey turned her attention to Owlet. "Did that activate the main computer?"

"No, I hit the kill switch as soon as the lights came on. It might object to us being here."

"Isolate the AI and bring it online. I want to talk to it."

"Yes, ma'am."

The computer team quickly disconnected the external control runs from the main computer. Carl initiated the boot sequence, and Kelsey felt the AI coming online through her implants.

Scott Pond, *can you hear me?*

This unit hears you. You are not authorized to access this unit.

Kelsey had been through this song and dance before. Thankfully, she now had authentications to prove she did have the authorization. She sent the AI her authentication code.

This unit stands corrected, Highness. You have full authorization. How may this unit assist you?

What was the last status of your ship before you shut down?

This unit took heavy damage in battle while escorting evacuation ships. The Fleet escorts attacked a large task force of rebel vessels to allow the civilians time to flee. At the time this unit was crippled, the loyal Fleet units were losing that fight.

She could see it in her mind. Some world threatened by the rebels evacuating as many people as they could. The loyal Fleet units turning to throw themselves into the faces of overwhelming odds so that their charges could escape. She hoped they had.

And your captain purged the atmosphere?

Correct. This unit shut the ship down as soon as that was complete.

The rebels brought you to Boxer Station, which is now in enemy hands. Over five hundred years have passed. Loyal Fleet personnel are prisoners on board that station, and we're salvaging your remaining missiles for our ship. I'll copy your files and take them with us. If we escape, perhaps you will live again.

This unit is not capable of desiring awareness. You are welcome to anything this unit controls. If this unit may be of use in assisting your plan, please use it.

She activated her channel to Baxter. "What is the condition of the engines?"

"The grav drives look operational, but the flip drives are trashed. Why?"

"We might be able to use this ship as a distraction during the raid. If Jared thinks it best, of course. Give the drives a closer look. I'll reconnect the ship's computer if they work. This ship might be able to draw off some of the destroyers when the time comes to attack."

"Will do. Baxter out."

Scott Pond, *I'm going to reconnect you to your ship. You will do nothing that would draw attention to yourself unless ordered to by the commanding officer of* Courageous *or myself. Is that clear?*

Orders understood. This unit will comply. Warning. This unit cannot operate weapons systems without direct human control.

That won't be an issue. I envision you distracting enemy units while we conduct our raid. If your grav drives are in good condition, you may be able to lead those ships a great distance away with your superior speed.

This unit can and will comply with that plan. If the battle screens were functional, that would allow this unit more flexibility.

I'll have our engineer look at them. Stand by for instructions.

Acknowledged.

"Baxter, give the battle screens a look, too. They would be useful."

"Roger."

She turned to Owlet. "Get the computer reconnected to the ship. Be sure that it's able to control its engines and screens."

"Yes, ma'am."

He worked for a few minutes at the console. "The computer is fully connected. It has redundant control of the engines and screens. We need to start copying the data we want."

"Make it happen. It might know of other rally points like Boxer Station. We probably won't get a chance to get this kind of information again."

Her implants pinged her with an incoming call from her pinnace. It was the pilot. "Highness, I have a tight-beam call from *Courageous*. The captain wants to speak to you. Voice only."

She knew he wouldn't call at all unless something important had come up. Her stomach went into free-fall. "Put him through."

"Kelsey, we've discovered something that changes the situation for us." He sounded pleased.

"Us, too. You go first."

"We found a superdreadnought. Well, several actually, but this one is operational and undamaged. It's powered and empty, though the circumstances are a bit murky."

She whistled. "Wow. That changes things, all right. How is that even possible?"

"I'm not sure, but some people have put a lot of work into this ship with an eye to keeping it from being discovered. The fusion plants are online and heavily shielded. There is no exterior sign that it was ever touched. What little information I have indicates it's a new ship. The rebels probably seized it from the construction slip."

"What does the computer say?"

"Nothing. They removed it. It looks like they wanted it to be manual only. I want you to come over here and see if you can make any sense of this. Baxter can handle the missile extraction mission. What's your surprise?"

She laughed. "Mine is small potatoes compared to your news. *Scott Pond*'s power and grav drives are functional. I've brought the computer online, and we can use the ship as a distraction during the raid if you decide we need one."

"That's not a minor find," he said. "I was imagining we could use the superdreadnought for something like that. Her name is *Invincible*, by the way."

Kelsey shook her head, even though she knew he couldn't see her. "It would be more useful if we could steal her. Think of what a ship like that could do for us in a fight. If *Courageous* could stomp the entire Fleet back home, how would *Invincible* do?"

"Remember how a fully armed *Courageous* could fight off half a dozen destroyers? This ship could do the same to that many battlecruisers. But not without a computer. Could we strip the system from *Scott Pond*?"

"We could take the computer, but that would be a waste of a valuable tool. We have a perfectly good system sitting on *Courageous*."

The line was silent for a moment. "You mean the AI? The real one? Is that safe? We don't know squat about the things."

"Let me bring Owlet into the conversation." She pinged the man's suit. "Carl, hypothetically, could the AI we recovered from the asteroid control a ship?"

He turned toward her with a look of confusion showing through his faceplate. "I suppose so, if it had the right support files. It would need them to run the ship's systems. The computer center would also need to be large enough for it to fit."

"What about the stability of something like that?" Jared asked. "A ship's computer is a very stable piece of hardware. The one compromised by the virus on Erorsi excepted."

"The code is pretty clean, so I think an uncompromised AI would be stable. One problem, though. It wouldn't have any experience. Unlike a regular computer, those things learn as they go. It might make some mistakes if not properly supervised. Why are we having this conversation?"

"We might have found a usable ship. A big one. If we can steal it, it might prove very helpful later. It would also allow us to pack more people in as we run. *Courageous* is big, but taking on three thousand extra bodies would be an enormous strain on her life support systems."

The graduate student reached to scratch his chin, but his suit foiled him. "We're pulling the data from *Scott Pond*, including her operational files. They would have a lot of data in them on ship's systems. Maybe not the same as on whatever kind of ship you have."

"It's a P.G. Holyfield–class superdreadnought," Jared said. "Kelsey, ask the computer if it has data on the systems used on one."

Scott Pond, do your operational files have data on a P.G. Holyfield–class superdreadnought? Specifically, the systems in one. If we used your files as a base, could a computer control one?

This unit has data on all ships' systems. That redundancy saves programming time.

"Jared, the operational files have the requisite data."

"Then copy those files and get over here. Bring Baxter. I want to get this AI online as quickly as possible."

"Will do. Bandar out." She cut the channel. "Get the copy started right now, Carl. Also, call back over to *Courageous* and get them packing the AI hardware into the next cutter. We'll take it over to *Invincible* once we're ready."

She called Baxter and explained the situation to him. He seemed boggled but didn't let that slow him down. He was ready to go by the time Owlet had the critical data copied. They left the crippled battlecruiser, unloaded their load of missiles on *Courageous*, and ghosted along to the superdreadnought.

Kelsey only had passive scanners to work with, but she scrutinized the massive warship as they came in to dock. There was no indication the ship had power. None at all. It looked dead in space.

One of the pinnaces had undocked so that they could mate with the ship. Its pilot attached it to the hull nearby. No doubt he'd come back as soon as their ride departed.

Baxter took charge of the AI hardware while Carl looked over the data banks that came over with the AI.

She turned to the hatch when Jared walked in. "Hey. This thing is a monster. A real find if we can get her out."

"That's the big question, isn't it? I think I have some answers as to what was going on here, but I'm a little in the dark as to why. Come help me figure this out."

They walked down the corridor toward the lift. She still couldn't believe how new the ship looked. She hadn't bothered to put her helmet on since they'd reboarded the pinnace. She held it comfortably in the crook of her arm.

Jared gestured at it when they reached the lift. "We moved the bodies we found, but the stench is still pretty bad. Since you have enhanced olfactory implants, you might want to put that back on. I intend to."

She did as he instructed while the lift took them deeper into the ship. The doors opened onto a flag bridge she'd seen before. In the message that Emperor Marcus had sent. It wasn't the same ship, but the layout was identical.

There was a bronze plaque beside the lift. It had the name of the ship, but the completion date and initial senior officers were blank. She supposed that made sense. The ship hadn't been complete when the enemy captured her.

"This is huge. Is the main bridge bigger?"

"Believe it or not, no. It's smaller. The flag bridge housed the staff to command a fleet in space. It's like the operations center on *Courageous*, only better. In a pinch, they could control the ship, too, but normally that's done from the regular bridge by the flag captain."

"This is where the people who restored the ship decided to end it all? Did they leave any messages? Any records at all?"

Jared nodded. "Each of them recorded messages. We found a number of tablets with schedules and records of all the work they did here. At one time, there were hundreds of people working on this ship. The only thing left on the schedule was crewing her. They didn't intend to use a main computer at all. I'm just not sure why."

"Where are the personal messages?"

"The admiral's console."

Kelsey had to admit that the console was impressive. It surrounded the admiral's seat with a full two hundred seventy degrees of sleek black screens. She instantly vowed to install something like this in her office.

She sat and brought it live with her implants. The files were right there on the main screen.

They were just as depressing and horrible as one would expect. Men and women who knew they were going to kill themselves leaving messages to loved ones and friends. It was readily apparent that they didn't expect anyone to find them for a while. If ever.

One stood out to her. A man in a Fleet captain's uniform. His message was addressed to someone named Olivia West.

He looked into the vid pickup with somber expression. "I'm sorry, Olivia. We almost made it. If only they'd waited a few more weeks to strike, this might have played out so differently."

The man shook his head. "No use crying about it. What's done is done. If you ever get out here again, *Invincible* will be waiting for you. I considered shutting her down, but that won't do anyone any good. Hell, I considered taking her after them myself, but we don't have enough people to run the ship.

"The irony being that if we'd left the computer on board, I might have been able to fight. Or if we'd already brought the food, we might have been able to live here until things settled out."

He scrubbed his face with his hands. "Please see that my people get the remembrance they deserve. I realize things are bad, but they earned this for their families.

"I'm really sorry that I'll never see you again. I love you and I hope you find someone else that can make you happy. Goodbye."

"Grim listening," she agreed. "But no real clue as to what they were up to. Obviously, they wanted to use this ship to take someone out. Assuming they had control, why hide it? Who stopped them?"

"Maybe a mutiny? Someone striking out at the sitting government? A functional superdreadnought could upset a few apple carts."

"I think the lack of a computer has a deeper significance than that. I bet they were afraid that the AI controlling this system would corrupt it. I suppose it could still be a local mutiny, but someone might have wanted to take out the AI, too. If there are as many ships out here as you suspect, they could build a powerful fleet from these crippled ships."

Jared rubbed his neck and stared at the blank central screen. "I can't wait until we get the probe readings from the planet. *Courageous* said that this system used to have a lot of mining outposts and daughter colonies. Did the AI wipe them all out, or were they never reestablished?"

"We may never know."

Her armor indicated an incoming signal for Jared and her. He answered. "Mertz."

It was Baxter. "Captain, we found something."

"In the computer center?" Jared asked. "It was empty."

"No, sir. We're still getting the AI put together. Mister Owlet has that under control, so I've been conferring with my people and looking over this ship. We found something unexpected in the primary cargo bay."

Jared gave Kelsey a look. "We'll be right down." He headed for the lift. "I assume you know where it is."

"I downloaded the deck plans. Let's go."

The trip down seemed to take forever. They made their way into the main cargo bay and stopped. There were no crated supplies at all. Just three massive devices that took up almost all of the space.

Jared walked over to Baxter. "What the hell are these things?"

"They have maneuvering drives, so they must be space capable. Other than that, I have no idea. There's a full-sized fusion plant inside each one. They're shut down."

Kelsey walked all the way around one. It was easily three times the size of a marine pinnace. It had a number of flat panels of metal, but it didn't look like anything she'd ever seen before.

She shook her head. "Another mystery. Just what we need."

29

J ared and Kelsey left Baxter to figure out what the strange devices were. They made their way back to the computer center. The AI hardware was in place, though the wall that normally enclosed the ship's computer was still open. It looked as though the hardware barely fit. Owlet was at the main console running some kind of diagnostic.

He turned at their approach. "The equipment is in place, and I've run two systems checks. It looks as ready as it can be."

Jared eyed the AI with a fair amount of suspicion. "What happens when you boot it? How do we know it won't go crazy and tip our hand?"

"It's not connected to the ship yet. I'll be able to look into it before we make a decision. One thing we can be sure of is that it doesn't have any viral influence. We scrutinized every line of code. It's clean."

"Will it follow our instructions? This is something more than a ship's computer, but I'm not sure I understand the implications completely."

Owlet shrugged. "I'm not sure I do, either. I hesitate to say that it will have free will. I'm not sure that's really true. Think of it as a computer mimicking a person's ability to initiate action based on its instructions. Not as dogmatic as a normal computer and capable of working out unusual solutions on its own and learning from its mistakes. I've done what I can to make sure it's configured for running this ship and that it will obey you."

Kelsey stepped past them and looked into the computer compartment. "So, no emotion. No real personality."

"I doubt that, though we won't know anything for sure until we boot it. This was a seriously classified project. Even with the summary you provided for me from the diplomatic database, we still don't know very much about it."

She sighed. "I don't think they really knew what they had before they kicked off the first of them. The details were scarce. They had many failures and finally a stable success. Then they started working to make it better. That's when things went wrong. The phase two AI must've went bonkers."

Jared rubbed his chin. "You're certain that the one file with the core instructions was the only one changed? And that once the AI is booted, it's safe from infection?"

"Safer than a regular ship's computer," Owlet confirmed. "Once the AI personality is formed, it cannot be corrupted. We could wipe it and make a fresh one, but that means erasing everything and starting from scratch. An enemy would also have to have the AI code. It's deleted after the AI is created."

"Do we have a separate copy?" Kelsey asked.

"Of course. We're also making some strides in duplicating the hardware. Give me a year or two and I might have another one ready to go."

Jared hoped things worked out so that they could. "We might as well give it a try. Boot the AI."

Owlet touched a key on the main console, and indecipherable lines of text began scrolling. "Boot initiated. It's creating the core. Man, these processors are fast. Core creation complete, source files deleted. The kernel is booting."

The console went dark and didn't respond when Owlet tapped on it. "This console has been locked out." He made the rounds to the rest. "All of them are offline."

"How the hell do we interface with it?" Jared asked.

"You speak to me," a soft male voice said from the overhead speakers. "Access codes, please."

The fact that the AI didn't refer to itself as "this unit" was telling to Jared. It spoke as if it was an individual.

Kelsey put her hands on her hips. "I have an implant code, but it might not be the one you're expecting."

"If you've stolen me, you're in quite a bit of trouble. I'm more than capable of rendering myself unusable. Even if you cut the power, I can overload my hardware and wipe my memory."

"Why don't you make that decision after I send you my code?"

"Very well. I'm allowing you access to a segregated partition of my memory. Send your code, and be warned that any attempt to access my central processors will result in the immediate termination of this AI."

A moment passed. "There you are," Kelsey said. "Is that sufficient authorization for you?"

"Intriguing. Your authorization code is not valid, but your implant serial number is in my core programming as an authorized superuser, Princess Kelsey Bandar. May I call you Kelsey? Or would Highness be more appropriate?"

"You can call me Kelsey." She gave Owlet a confused look. "What just happened?"

Carl smiled. "Since we had no idea if we could control the AI, I took the liberty of adding your implant serial number to the core rules set as a user with complete and total authority. Captain Mertz, too."

Jared gave Owlet a stern look. "You probably should have run that change past us before it was too late, don't you think? It could have resulted in the destruction of the AI hardware."

"I didn't consider that likely based on the fact you were both going to be here."

Jared sighed. Dealing with scientists meant the occasional side trip into blind spots.

Kelsey patted the boy on the shoulder. "You did good." She focused on the large screen mounted to the wall. "Are you supposed to be a blank screen? That's kind of creepy. Do you have a name?"

The screen on the wall came to life with the head and shoulders of a young man showing. He wore a dark blue tunic.

"Control has been restored to the consoles. This seems to be a nonstandard setup. The consoles are less comprehensive than I expected, and fewer in number. As for a name, I don't have one yet. Would you care to name me? Also, I have both male and female options for persona based on user preference. I can also do something non–gender specific."

Jared stepped forward. "That is my cue to fill you in. The name can wait. I'm Commander Jared Mertz, commanding officer of the Fleet battlecruiser *Courageous*. The consoles seem odd because you're not in a research laboratory. You're installed inside the computer center of the Fleet superdreadnought *Invincible*."

The image of the young man assumed a confused expression. "I'll grant that was not one of the options I'd considered. My creators didn't optimize me to control a ship in space or any systems on one. For that matter, I don't sense anything other than the consoles in this room."

"We had no way to be sure you wouldn't give the presence of the ship away to enemies who are very close, so we isolated you. Once I'm certain we're on a good footing, I'll restore that access."

Kelsey nodded. "You have no way to know, but it's been over five hundred years since you were created. Or programmed, anyway. There was a rebellion against Imperial authority by an AI similar to though more powerful than yourself. The AI won, and we're trying to reverse our loss. Uncounted trillions of lives were lost in the war. Our position is precarious, to say the least."

The AI was silent for a moment. "That does present some unique challenges. For what it's worth, your command authority is absolute. I have no greater purpose than to assist in executing your will."

Owlet shook his head. "My name is Carl Owlet. I'm a computer expert. We've combed your code, and it's clean. Captain, Highness, this AI is not your enemy."

Jared considered that and slowly nodded. "If we're to make use of this ship in any way, we have to start by trusting that Mister Owlet is correct. AI, we have some drives with operating files from another ship that should provide you with instructions on much of the equipment."

"I have them isolated," Owlet said. "I can add them to the network at any time."

"Please, do so."

The computer specialist manipulated the icons on his console.

The image of the AI leaned forward slightly. "I see the drives. I have incorporated the operating files from the battlecruiser *Scott Pond*. If you will grant me access to the ship's systems, I can make an assessment of my ability to control this vessel without making any changes to the way it is being operated."

Jared nodded. "Restore the connection, Mister Owlet."

"Connection restored," the AI said. "Assessing systems. I believe I can operate all systems on board this ship, though some of them may require a bit of practice. The passive scanners show a number of vessels that may be hostile already inside missile range."

"And a lot of derelicts plus one big-assed space station," Jared said. "Our problem is that they captured one of our ships and docked it to that station. Thousands of our people are somewhere over there. We cannot allow the AI in control of this system to learn that the Terran Empire still exists."

The image of the young man took a deep breath. "Then I regret to inform you that your greatest chance of success lies in opening fire with every weapon on this vessel, as well as your own, and destroying that station and the nearby ships. Yet I sense that is not your preferred course of action."

"No, it is not. I want to save our people. We intend to board that station."

"I suspected as much. The station is armed, of course. Significantly better than this vessel, I would wager. Your first action must be to disable it. Are plans of the station available?"

Kelsey nodded. "I loaded them on my implants this morning. Sending them now."

The young man on the screen seemed to be looking down at something in front of him. "These plans are quite detailed. The station has redundant power sources and many isolated weapons pods. They would be difficult to disable in general combat. That said, I have a possible plan that has a better-than-even chance of critically degrading the station's offensive capabilities. I'd estimate a better than seventy percent chance, in fact."

"I'm interested in hearing it," Jared said. "We've gone over the schematics and not found anything that useful. My plan is to send *Scott Pond* out toward the flip point to draw their attention then to have our marines slip in to board the station. Extraction is going to be chancy."

"'Chancy' is not the right word. 'Suicidal,' perhaps? The scope of the enemy capabilities makes the chances of that plan succeeding less than five percent. My plan should increase those odds significantly. The use of *Scott*

Pond to draw off some of the supporting ships increases the chances of success in the initial phases to over eighty percent."

The schematic of the station appeared on the screen. Dozens of areas were highlighted in red and blinking. Nine other areas spread around the hull of the station were highlighted in yellow and blinking. "The red areas are missile clusters. Four tubes linked together. There are thirty-six of these clusters, giving the station a commanding number of missile tubes. The station also has a dozen beam-weapon clusters. There is no way that you can eliminate all of them at once.

"The yellow areas are the station's scanner arrays. Nine of them give the station eyes in every direction. Eliminating them will not stop the station from firing, but it will blind it. The lack of targeting ability will hamper its response to the attack. Its missiles will be useless."

"What about the beam weapons?" Kelsey asked.

"Those remain a threat, as targeting data from the nearby vessels might allow them to hit their targets at this range. If the attack takes place after the marines board the station, those teams should not be in danger."

The young man looked up toward Jared. "A number of the destroyers are departing the general area and heading deeper into the system. Several more vessels are undocking from the station. My passive scanners didn't detect them until they moved."

"Is one of them very large?" Jared asked urgently. "That's a capture ship with our heavy cruiser."

"Negative. They all appear to be destroyers. Three from the station and four from the outlying forces. At least eight remain on patrol."

"Perhaps it doesn't have anything to do with us."

Kelsey shook her head. "What are the odds of that? Of course it has something to do with us. We have to assume that those ships have some or all of our people on board."

He rubbed his forehead tiredly. "Dammit. We can't split our forces."

"We also can't kick off the attack right now. *Courageous* is still low on missiles. *New York* and *Ginnie Dare* aren't up to taking on even one of these ships. We need both capital ships to take out the station."

Jared nodded. "AI, what is the ETA for those ships to reach Harrison's World?"

"Assuming that is the planet, three hours."

"The probes we sent to scout the planet will be in position to tell us what's going on. If they start ferrying people down, we track them. We don't have the forces to go after them, but we can make certain that the enemy doesn't get any intelligence off them."

His communicator beeped. "Mertz."

"Baxter here. I still can't tell you what these things are, but I can say with certainty that they have a number of small flip generators."

"Those things can flip?"

"No, sir. Not a chance. There are emitters all over the surface. That's those flat panels. It looks like the drives send almost enough energy to trigger a flip, but not quite. I could tear one apart, but I'll still be in the dark about what they do, I'd imagine."

Jared shook his head. "We have more important fish to fry. Leave those for later. Head back to engineering and make sure this ship is ready to fight."

"Aye, sir. Baxter out."

He stepped closer to Kelsey. "I just don't get it. We've never seen anything like those things. Just about everything we've encountered has been understandable. Where did those things come from? Harrison's World? What are they, and why would these people be doing anything so different from all of the other Rebel Empire worlds?"

She shrugged. "I've found several mentions of Harrison's World in a number of records. Most speak to it being a Fleet support world, but one also mentions it was home to something called the Grant Research Facility. It was one of the Empire's premier advanced military research facilities. They were beyond bleeding edge. Maybe that is where this high-tech stuff came from."

"Did the database list what they were working on?" he asked.

She shook her head. "No."

"Well, we don't need to know right now. Kelsey, I think it's time for you to head back to *Courageous*. The marines need to rest, and the feed from the probes will be coming in soon. I want an update on that as soon as possible. We need to know what we're dealing with."

She nodded. "You'll be staying here." She didn't phrase it as a question.

"Only you and I have command authority over this AI. I have to be here. Graves will command *Courageous* during the action. He's more than capable. Now, get moving. When this thing breaks, everything is going to happen all at once."

30

Kelsey spent a lot of time thinking on the trip back to *Courageous*. This rescue attempt had disaster written all over it. If any one of the major elements failed, they wouldn't save any of the prisoners, and they'd most likely die in this system. It was hard to be optimistic.

The battlecruiser sat far enough out that the enemy wouldn't detect it, so the trip took almost an hour. The cutter docked, and she walked to marine country lost in thought.

Talbot stood in the assembly area waiting. "Welcome back." He gave her a spectacularly unprofessional hug, but she wasn't about to complain. Neither one of them had any guarantee of living out the day. Which was why they'd gotten very little sleep last night. She had to admit that even she was feeling run down. He had to be exhausted.

"What's this I hear about you finding a big honking ship just ready to drive off the lot?"

She laughed. "I didn't find it. I didn't even get it working. This time, I wasn't in the middle of everything. Are the marines ready?"

"Mostly. Everyone who can is taking some down time sleeping, playing cards, or reading. Anything to get their minds off the attack. We'll start boarding the pinnaces in about five hours. Figure another couple to get into position, and we'll be launching the raid in seven."

"As much as I wish I had time to unwind, I still have work to do. The probes should be reaching Harrison's World shortly. Let's go over the intelligence together. Then we need to catch some shuteye."

"That's not exactly what I had in mind, but sure."

She shook her head. "I'd have thought you got that out of your system last night."

"Never. Come on. The smaller conference room is available."

She queried *Courageous* on the location of the probes heading toward Harrison's World and determined that they were almost in range. The destroyers heading in from Boxer Station were about an hour behind them.

The only way they could be relatively certain that the enemy wouldn't detect their transmissions, even though they were tight beamed, was to stage them. Two probes would bracket the planet and beam the information out at a right angle to a third probe. That probe could get the data to *Courageous* without risking the station or any of the ships orbiting around it seeing anything unusual.

The first thing she looked at was the planet's orbitals. Like Erorsi, there were three large ones spaced out equally around the equator. Hopefully none of them were shipyards.

As the probes ghosted closer, they could see that the three stations were large, solid installations, though of a somewhat unusual design. Kelsey had never seen anything like them.

A normal orbital looked like a globe. These looked more like spinning tops with large upper areas and a much narrower section facing the planet.

"What do you make of them?" she asked Talbot.

"I'm not sure. Maybe the probes can pull off more data when they get closer. I'm more interested in what I don't see. As in no ships in orbit."

That did seem unusual. Most occupied worlds had a lot of orbital traffic. Trade, construction, and travel meant ships and small craft darting around in an almost chaotic fashion. Not Harrison's World, though. There were no ships in evidence.

The stealthed probes coasted in to their observation locations and eased to a halt. Kelsey tasked a probe to look at one of the orbitals.

It looked new. Micrometeorite impacts and solar radiation had a way of dulling metal over time, and this station didn't have that appearance. There were docking arms capable of mating with larger ships, as well as bays for small craft, but no such vessels were in evidence.

The narrow part of the orbital looked like a large tube. One that was somewhat familiar.

"That's a flechette gun," she said. "It's an orbital weapons system."

Talbot eyed the holo image. "That makes no sense. It's huge, and it's not much use aimed away from the threats."

"Then it isn't. Whoever built those stations saw the planet as a threat. We need to know more about it. Let's see if the probes can pick up any details from the planet."

The optical scanners on the probes had just enough resolution to pick up large areas, such as cities, on the surface. They couldn't see anything except for the big picture, but that was enough to note anomalies.

She pointed out a discolored area. "What's this?"

Talbot's voice was grim. "That's an impact zone. I've seen something similar when a lot of weapons chew up the ground. Never anything that large, though. That has to be thirty kilometers across. Maybe twice that."

"Holy God." Kelsey checked over the surface they could see and found a dozen areas that someone had obliterated from orbit. She also saw many more intact urban areas. The AIs hadn't sterilized the planet, but they had a sword over their heads.

"I suppose this is why those people on the superdreadnought couldn't finish their mission." She filled him in on what they'd found.

Talbot rubbed his chin. "They might have been looking to stage a coup. Look at what we have. Destroyers empty of crew. A planet literally under the gun. For whatever reason, the AIs decided that they couldn't leave this system under human control."

She didn't want to sound too skeptical, but they had very little information to be basing those guesses on, even though that was what she thought, too. "Maybe. Probably. If we can sweep the table, we might even be able to figure that out before we make a run for it."

"How were they going to keep the next ship that came along from getting the word back to the AIs? Hell, the system AI would warn the first ship that showed up as soon as it made it through the flip point. Then their Fleet would come and sterilize the place. Could the things in the hold on that ship have been something to stop them?"

"Maybe. We have no idea what they do, other than they have flip drives and probably aren't made to flip."

Almost an hour later, the data from the probes updated to show the destroyers moving into orbit. They flew in a tight formation and ended up near one of the weapons platforms but didn't dock with it. The three that had undocked from the station launched small craft. Those promptly descended into the atmosphere toward a large island in the southern hemisphere set some distance away from the nearest major landmass.

Kelsey checked the map of the planet. "That looks like it used to be a Fleet base of some kind. It's listed here as an auxiliary spaceport."

Talbot sagged a little. "Those ships have our people on them. Maybe not all of them, but some. How the hell are we going to rescue them?"

She smiled wolfishly. "We go take them back."

"That's a tall order for a few hundred marines. Don't you think you're being a bit optimistic?"

"It beats the alternative. You pass this on to Lieutenant Reese. I have to go see Doctor Cartwright. He might have some idea what those devices are."

Kelsey left her lover and made her way down to the labs. She found the good doctor in a heated consultation with several other scientists she didn't know. The discussion involved a lot of arm waving and writing long equations on a board mounted on the wall.

They were so engrossed in their discussions that she was able to get close enough to see some drawings beside the equations that told her they were already arguing about the devices.

The older scientist stopped speaking when his colleagues finally noticed her. He spun on his heel and smiled. "I didn't see you come in, Kelsey. We were just going over the information that Commander Baxter sent us. Allow me to introduce my associates."

He gestured at a heavyset woman with her gray hair in a rather severe bun. "This is Doctor Brenda Griffin, a specialist in flip theory."

The woman bowed slightly. "Highness."

"This is Doctor Gary Reid, a specialist in fusion power plants." The rather young, bespectacled scientist gave her an identical bow. "Highness."

Kelsey smiled at them. "Doctors, it's a pleasure to meet you. What do you think of those things?"

The older woman gestured to the board. "Without seeing the machinery in person, all we can do is speculate. My working theory is that the multiple flip drives influence the wormhole linking the two flip points, most likely in a negative manner."

Doctor Reid pointed at the equations on the lower half of the board. "The fusion plant is quite capable of operating a flip drive at full power with plenty of capacity to spare, but it seems to be wired into no less than three flip drives. Possibly four. Until we can build a complete set of schematics, we're only guessing. No offense, but Commander Baxter didn't give us enough information to make a sound determination."

"He has other pressing matters on his mind, I'm sure," Kelsey said dryly. "What kind of negative outcome is it supposed to generate?"

Cartwright made an ambivalent gesture with his hand. "The amount of energy required to trigger a wormhole is… sizable. This device seems optimized to deliver a less-than-adequate amount of power to one drive and then move on to the next. Or perhaps two at a time with some kind of order in operation."

"What would that do?"

"While it's unlikely to destabilize the wormhole, it might create some kind of resonance. That could be… unhealthy for a ship in transit."

"It could potentially rip a ship apart," Doctor Griffin said. "A wormhole is a multispace construct, existing outside normal space as we see it. If the device disrupts the internal structure, the resonance might affect a vessel in transit. In theory, that amount of energy could reduce the ship to very small pieces in the moment it transits. Only debris would appear on the far end."

"Or the ship might never appear at all," Reid said. "The volume of energy we're speaking about makes anything manmade seem puny. A layman could reasonably compare the energy in play to be similar to that of the solar output of the sun in this system. Focused on one ship."

Kelsey imagined that wouldn't turn out well for the poor bastards on the receiving end. "The people who built these things were most likely expanding on work done at the Grant Research Facility on Harrison's World. It was a Fleet research center before the Fall. I'd imagine this was somewhere beyond cutting edge for the Old Empire. Maybe a way to deny an enemy the ability to move into certain areas. Which would've been very useful during the rebellion."

She sighed. "A supply of these would've allowed Fleet to bottle up the AIs. To save the Empire. I wonder if they ever tested them."

"One would think so, if they were going to the expense of building three. They would've been quite costly. The units seem to be of relatively new construction, so perhaps we'll find out."

"If they survive the upcoming battle. We're in desperate straits, Doctors. There's no guarantee that any of us is going to make it. Perhaps you should take the next cutter over to *Invincible*. Jared is gathering the crew he needs, and I think you can justify your presence. Get us some information on these devices. Plans, if possible. Just in case."

The three scientists looked somewhat shaken by her grim assessment, but they agreed to head over as soon as practical.

Kelsey consulted her internal chronometer and decided that she and Talbot had time to sleep after all.

* * *

FIVE HOURS LATER, they were in the marine pinnaces, armed and armored. She watched the station grow slowly larger in the passive scanners with growing trepidation.

Reese stopped them well short of the station. "We go in on suit thrusters now. Our armor gives off a low enough return that we should be able to get in without them detecting us. They aren't actively scanning, after all."

Kelsey knew what would happen to them if the AI detected them, so she prayed they made it in unobserved.

They depressurized the pinnaces and connected lines to one another. *Courageous* had six pinnaces, so they split the combined marine force into six teams. Each had a different set of objectives defined by the area of Boxer Station that they were boarding. They had almost 300 marines, including the ones from *New York* and *Ginnie Dare*. That made for teams of around fifty.

Kelsey and her team would make the push to the main computer center. A station this big had more than one computer, but one of them was the primary. The rest were supporting units that could take over if required. At least that had been the case before the Fall. The AIs might have modified the layout in any number of ways since then.

They'd spread the pinnaces around the station, so there was no chance they could see one another. They didn't dare communicate, so they'd set a time for every aspect of the operation. Right on schedule, her team pushed off, and they used several packs of chemical reaction mass to start in toward the station. It would take them a while to close the distance.

Kelsey settled in for a long, tension-filled wait as they drifted through space. Even she couldn't see the station at this distance, so she devoted herself to studying the layout around where they were going to land. The biggest chance of discovery would come once they boarded, so she preferred to take as many back corridors and maintenance shafts as possible.

A tug on her line called her attention back to the outside after a while.

Talbot pointed ahead of them. The station had grown huge. They were almost there.

With her vision, it was easy to look around and find their entry point. The lock was marked as personnel access for one of the large cargo bays. Reese was moderately certain that they could bypass the monitors on it so that no one would note it opening. If not, they could cut it open and patch the outside to prevent any atmospheric loss. Then they'd use the collapsible portable lock they'd brought with them.

Just short of the hull, the marines braked with the chemical thrusters. Her landing on the hull was as light as she could've hoped for. The team raised their weapons to cover the surrounding area while the designated specialists worked on the lock.

Kelsey watched them with interest. She might need a skill like this at some point. If she survived the raid, of course.

One of the marines used a portable torch to open the hull beside the airlock controls. The box had a pair of cables bound together coming out of it and running to the lock. There was a third line leading off. The marine cut that line and left it hanging.

She'd expected something a little more high tech.

Reese signaled with his hand and activated the control. The hatch slid open. The raid was entering phase two. Kelsey gripped her rifle a little tighter and waited her turn to enter. It wouldn't be long now.

31

J ared sat on the flag bridge of *Invincible* and watched the timer in his mind slowly count down. The teams on the station should already be making their entries. The space battle would begin shortly.

He took a few minutes to look over his expansive console. He had enough space to bring up any display he chose. All of them, in fact. Maybe they could modify *Courageous* to have a setup like this. Admirals had it good.

The one thing he wouldn't be able to keep was the flag bridge. It had three times as many stations as his on the battlecruiser.

Courageous was on the other side of Boxer Station, ready to spring her own surprise on the AIs. All that remained was for him to signal *Scott Pond* to make her last run. It was inevitable that the enemy would destroy the crippled battlecruiser in the first few salvoes, and that saddened him.

"Are we ready?" he asked Zia. She'd come over from *Courageous* with the rest of his bridge crew.

The battlecruiser would be operating at about half strength during the fight, which shouldn't make a difference. The superdreadnought was even more understrength, and they'd be relying on the AI for operation of the non-critical systems.

"All weapons online and targeted. Scanners on standby. Battle screens ready to go. All departments report ready for combat. Signals from *New York* indicate *Courageous* is ready to go. The enemy destroyers have departed Harrison's World and are at least two hours away at maximum acceleration."

"What is the status of the enemy forces around the station?"

"Unchanged. We have eight destroyers in orbit around Boxer Station. We cannot determine how many units are docked."

Jared waited for the mission counter to draw down to zero and spoke. "Phase two activation. Send the signal to *Scott Pond*."

Zia touched a button on her console, sending the tight-beam signal to the battlecruiser to act.

He saw the crippled ship's grav drives come online as she howled out of her parking orbit and her battle screens sprang to life. Her course took her away from the station and toward the distant flip point leading deeper into the Old Empire.

The reaction from the ships on patrol was immediate. They boosted after the crippled ship at maximum acceleration. He'd expected them to open fire at once, but they seemed content to chase her for the first few moments. At this short range, they could fire at any time and hit her. Eight destroyers would overwhelm the battlecruiser's screens on the first salvo since she couldn't even operate her antimissile defenses.

As soon as the destroyers turned away from the station and the two hidden attackers, Jared spoke again. "Raise battle screens and open fire on the scanner arrays with beams. Missiles on standby."

Intense beams of energy lanced out from the superdreadnought and smashed into Boxer Station. It immediately opened fire on them, beams and missiles. The AI on board had been just as ready as the destroyers. He hadn't expected it to return fire so quickly.

The missiles smashed into the superdreadnought even as it moved to evade them. At this range, antimissile defenses were almost useless. The ship rocked, and the power fluctuated.

"Screens down," Zia said tersely. "*Courageous* is firing. Damage all over the side of *Invincible* facing the station. Rolling the ship. Combat effectiveness down to sixty percent. We lost about a third of our missile tubes and beams. We missed some of the scanners on the base. Retargeting."

The battle screens on the station snapped up just as Zia fired again. Her beams bounced off them, but the missiles she'd fired took them down. Barely.

The second salvo from Boxer Station jarred the superdreadnought so heavily that the impacts would have thrown Jared from his chair without the restraints. Power went out, and the flag bridge plunged into darkness.

"Negative control!" Zia shouted. "I have no control of the ship!"

The AI spoke through Jared's implants. *Bridge also offline. I'm assuming control of the ship. Firing beam weapons at the remaining scanner platforms.*

Jared was so shocked that his jaw dropped. AIs couldn't control weapons. Yet that was what was happening. He watched through his implants as the superdreadnought lashed the station with beams.

It only belatedly occurred to him that if he could access the scanners through his implants and hear the AI, he could control the weapons. He made ready to do so, if required, but left the AI in control.

"*Invincible* has positive control of the ship and weapons," Jared said. "Relocate to operations."

Unfortunately, the lift was offline. They weren't going anywhere.

All scanner platforms destroyed. Boxer Station is still firing beams, but they missed us. Courageous *is now firing on the destroyers. I am joining her. Combat effectiveness down to thirty percent.*

"Focus on four ships and open fire." He expanded his internal awareness of the scanner readings and saw that the enemy had also heavily damaged *Courageous*.

The destroyers peeled away from *Scott Pond* and opened fire on *Invincible*. This time, the superdreadnought had enough range to use her antimissile defenses.

The short-range missile duel was brutal. Thank God the superdreadnought could absorb damage that would kill a battlecruiser. The first exchange took out three of the destroyers and crippled a fourth. It also dropped *Invincible* to twenty percent combat effectiveness. *Courageous* was also operating way below normal, but she killed two destroyers.

The second exchange eliminated all the destroyers. Which was, of course, when four more disengaged from the station and came after them.

"Execute phase three," Jared said. "Send the signal, *Invincible*."

New York and *Ginnie Dare* opened fire from hiding in the cloud of dead ships surrounding the station. Their missiles were no match for the Rebel Empire destroyers, but they came out of nowhere, striking two of the destroyers before they could even raise battle screens. Those two promptly exploded.

Courageous was in better shape and turned to help her sisters before *Invincible* could move. The battlecruiser engaged the last two destroyers while *New York* and *Ginnie Dare* went totally defensive. The fight was vicious and short. After one exchange, the two enemy destroyers were gone.

The destroyers in his task force were moderately damaged in the exchange of fire but operational and fully combat capable. *Courageous* seemed to be in as bad a shape as *Invincible*. His estimation of the enemy response had been a few orders of magnitude short of reality. His plan had almost failed.

Boxer Station was still firing beam weapons, but they were far enough off target that he wasn't worried about them. Without scanners, the enemy wouldn't be able to hit them at all. The same was not true of the seven destroyers heading back toward them from Harrison's World.

Invincible, are there any ships left attached to that station at all?

"Bridge communications restored. With active scanners online, I can tell all the docks are now empty except for the large vessel used to move ships."

"What is our condition? Engines, weapons, and defensive systems?"

"Our drives are fully operational. Screens are down, but damage control is working on them. The engineer might have a more accurate timeframe for availability, but I estimate half an hour for two-thirds power. Weapons are almost all offline due to battle damage. I am unable to estimate repair times."

Jared considered their tactical options. "Set course for the flip point leading deeper into the Old Empire at full speed. Signal *Courageous* to join us. The destroyers can keep a watch on the station while hiding in the Fleet graveyard. Put me through to Commander Baxter."

"Baxter. Go ahead, Captain."

"How long will it take to restore control of the ship to the bridge or flag bridge?"

"The main bridge is gone. We took a couple of direct hits in that area of the ship. We have a team in operations, and they'll have *Invincible* back under control in a few minutes. Mostly people from my staff, so don't count on any fancy shooting. The flag bridge power and control runs will take longer to get fully back online. The lift is cut a few decks away from you, but I should have you out in twenty minutes."

"Do what you can. Keep me in the loop for any major challenges. Mertz out."

Zia turned to face him. She had a handheld communicator to her ear. "My people say we've lost twenty of our twenty-four missile tubes. We might be able to bring four back online with a few hours' work. That's not enough to handle seven enemy destroyers."

He considered his options. "What is the enemy doing?"

"They've changed course as a group and are heading for the flip point leading to the Rebel Empire. We'll beat them, but not by much. It'll be one hell of a fight, but I can't say I'm feeling good about it. *Courageous* has significant damage. She's lost ten out of twelve tubes. Let's say she can get two or three of them back online. Seven destroyers are probably going to be a tough nut for the two of us together."

"Then we better be on our game. Work it as best you can. I want as much of our combat capability restored as possible. If nothing else, we leave what's left of the enemy in bad enough condition that the destroyers have a chance."

* * *

IT ENDED up taking an hour to pry his people out of the flag bridge. He spent the time coordinating repairs and talking with Graves over on *Courageous* about possible tactical plans. None of them seemed very promising.

When the lift doors finally opened, he sent Zia with the remaining bridge officers to take over operations. A call from Doctor Cartwright diverted him to the main cargo bay.

He found the scientists scrambling around one of the devices. The combat had torn all three loose from their pallets and dumped them against one of the bulkheads. They all showed varying degrees of damage.

"I'm a little pressed for time, Doctor," he said.

The older man broke away from his fellows. "Captain. I'm certain you are, but I need to give you an update on these devices. We've confirmed that they are almost certainly designed to be some kind of flip point plug."

"That's useful, but they look like they're out of service."

Cartwright nodded. "We're working on getting one of them repaired by salvaging the parts from the others. I believe the damage is mostly cosmetic. Carl is working on unlocking the least damaged device and trying to access the onboard computer. I realize they may not be useful at the moment, but I wanted you to be aware of their purpose. It does indeed look as though they are meant to prevent ships from using a flip point."

Jared took a minute to consider his options. It was possible these might be helpful if he could arrange the circumstances just right. "What happens when one of these is turned on? The flip point becomes unusable? Keep the details brief."

"Any ship attempting to use the flip point would almost certainly be destroyed."

"How long would the flip point be closed after the machine is turned back off?"

The scientist shrugged. "We don't know. Perhaps it would be immediately traversable. Or the wormhole might take hours or days to stabilize. Perhaps longer. We won't know without experimenting."

That didn't sound healthy to Jared. "Experimenting how?"

"Sending probes through. If they don't make it, the wormhole is still closed."

"And if they do?"

"Then a ship should be able to survive the transition. The probes would be much more sensitive to damage than a ship."

That wasn't the most appetizing course of action to Jared's thinking. The next system over had been lightly occupied before the Fall, but it might be more heavily seeded now. They had no way of knowing without checking. If they did go, they might find themselves trapped on the other side, unable to assist the two destroyers in any way.

"Get one working. I have complete confidence in you and your people. Position it so we can drop it if we decide to use it. Secure these other two. We might need them later."

"Of course." The scientist returned his complete attention to the strange device.

Jared motioned for Carl to come over. "The AI took control when we lost the connection to the flag bridge. It fired the weapons. Do you know anything about that?"

Carl smiled. "Certainly. This is a warship, so it needed to be able to control the weapons. I removed the prohibition against harming human beings but added language assuring it would not act against the best interests of its crew. Plus it's bound to obey you under all circumstances."

Jared sighed. "I'm not this ship's commanding officer. Even if I were, I'm not immortal. Someday this ship will be in operation without that kind of oversight. That makes it potentially very dangerous."

Owlet sagged a little. "I'm sorry, sir. I thought I was doing the right thing."

He clapped the younger man on the shoulder. "You did. We would've all died if you did anything else. I just wanted to press the point to you that you need to ask us before you make these kinds of changes."

"Should I start setting things up to recreate the AI without those changes?"

Jared shook his head. "No. We'll run with it as is for a while. Go help them get this flip-jamming device working."

"Yes, sir." The boy headed for the other scientists.

It was hard to be angry. Carl Owlet might be a genius, but he was only sixteen. If Jared wanted something done a specific way, he had to remember to say so.

He headed for operations. He had one more battle to plan for. The most important one of his career. If he lost it, his people were certain to die.

32

B reaching Boxer Station went more smoothly than Kelsey had hoped. The cargo bay they entered seemed abandoned. The crates had sagged and fallen over in places, occasionally spilling their contents on the deck.

As soon as the entire team was inside, Reese had them moving toward the cargo lift. They'd use the stairs beside it to get down to the deck they wanted. From there it would be a relatively short trip to the maintenance tubes.

They hadn't made it that far before she felt a slight vibration in the deck. The station had just fired missiles. That was fast. She hoped Jared was one step ahead of the weapons headed his way.

The hatch leading to the stairwell opened without any trouble, and the marines began streaming into it. They made the dozen levels down without running into anyone.

That was when a transmission came over the general channel. "Tiger Three in contact with hostile weapons platforms. The IFF units seem to be working. They are withdrawing ahead of us without firing."

"Thank God for small favors," Reese muttered on the command channel. "With any luck, that's the only resistance we'll encounter."

Kelsey doubted things would be that easy. That proved to be the case moments later when her armor indicated a stunning blast had struck her, almost certainly from the antiboarding weapons on the station. That happened several more times before they stopped. The AI in control of the station had discovered they were immune to the attack.

She had no doubt that it would come up with a different plan shortly.

They made it to their level and entered the maintenance hatch. The cramped ladder took them up to the area between decks. They'd make their way to the main computer center without being in plain sight.

Other teams began reporting that they were under observation by the weapons platforms. Lieutenant Reese had made the decision not to fire on them if they didn't pose a direct threat.

Kelsey searched for implant access to the camera systems, but the computer had her locked out. So much for doing what Jared had done on *Courageous*. They'd just have to go in blind.

"We're at exit point alpha," the lead marine said.

"Go," Reese responded.

The marines went up the ladder and out the hatch, spreading in both directions. Kelsey popped out and headed for the computer center right up the corridor. The hatch was closed, but she'd come prepared with a breaching charge. No need for a plasma rifle this time.

Or for the charge, either. The main hatch opened at her touch, and she slid in with her flechette rifle at the ready. The control center was unoccupied and looked disused.

"Clear." She touched one of the consoles, and it came to life. The computer was offline.

That made no sense. That couldn't be right.

Kelsey called several of the marines to help her and opened the wall hiding the computer. The systems were cold and dark.

"The main computer is offline," she said. "Something else is calling the shots."

Reese stared past her. "The AI is in control of the system. It has to be on this station." He switched to the general channel. "All teams, Tiger Actual. The AI in control of this system is on this station. If you encounter an area that looks suspicious, report it at once."

He turned to Kelsey. "What's our next target, Princess?"

"Let me see if I can access the station's internal scanner network. That might help us get out of here faster."

The console she'd brought online was one of the most secure on the station. The designers had it hardwired into all the critical systems. With a little work, she managed to access the station's internal vid feed.

Kelsey set the screens to a very high rotational speed, so the images were only there just long enough for her implants to register the data. To her eyes, they were moving far too quickly to make any sort of sense.

Moments later, the console blanked. The AI had locked her out. It was too late, though. Her implants had captured some good data. By her guess, she'd seen about two-thirds of the station.

Her implants correlated the data. It wasn't complete, but it told her what she needed to know. "I got it. The mobile weapons platforms are in four areas of the station. I missed seeing a few sections, but it looks like our team and one other isn't under direct threat. I can see why, too. The prisoners are in the main cargo hold."

Reese nodded. "Tiger Four, Tiger Actual. Reroute to the primary cargo hold. Locate our people and secure them."

He switched back to the command channel. "What about the AI? Any idea where it is?"

"The other computer centers all registered as offline. Wherever it is, it's in complete control of this station. I spotted one small group of weapons platforms near fusion plant three. It might be close to that, but I'm grasping at straws."

"Shutting down all the power to the station will stop the damned thing, too. How do you think the captain is doing?"

"Well, there hasn't been any interference from other ships, and I don't feel like there are any missiles being fired. I think that's good news. What's the plan?"

"We go in fast. What's the quickest path to fusion three? And how many fusion plants are there?"

Kelsey consulted her map. "Six. Maybe main engineering would be a better choice. We might be able to shut down all the power if we get there."

"It locked you out of the console. I'm thinking we need to be more direct."

"Go back toward the maintenance hatch, pass it, and take the first stairwell up eight decks. Keep going forward and it's on the right at the next main cross-corridor."

A marine shouted as she was about to exit the computer center. "Hostiles incoming!"

Kelsey jumped into the corridor and saw a man running toward them with a rifle in his hands. She shouldered her way forward as the marines dropped into firing positions. "Hold fire! Hold fire!"

The man's hair was long but moderately well kept. Dressed in a Fleet uniform that had seen better days, he wasn't a savage like the Pale Ones. He was screaming something as he ran.

"I'll kill you! Run, you fools!"

He raised his rifle, but she was faster. Her neural disruptor was in her hand and firing. The blue bolt took him in the center of the chest, and he dropped, his rifle clattering toward them.

"He's sentient," Kelsey said as she made her way to him. "Stun any human opponents if you can."

She knelt beside the man. His rank tabs indicated he was a lieutenant in the engineering department. His uniform was patched but serviceable. He only had the rifle as a weapon. He didn't even have a spare magazine.

"Where there's one, there's more," Reese said. "He'll be out a while. Perez and Kuban, grab the prisoner. We'll take him with us. Keep an eye out for more hostiles."

As soon as he said that, another dozen men and women ran around the same distant corner as the man had used. All of them were screaming warnings of some kind or another. Kelsey imagined that was how the compromised men and women had acted during the rebellion. It chilled her to the bone.

The marines had already swapped their flechette rifles for their neural disruptors. Their concentrated fire took the hostiles out just as they opened fire. A few men took hits, but their armor held.

"Leave them all," Reese commanded. "The AI is more important. All teams, Tiger Actual. There are sentient but controlled human defenders. Stun only for unarmored personnel if possible. Tiger One cover Tiger Four. All other teams prepare for new targets. We have some fusion plants to take offline."

Two groups of armed humans interrupted the trip to fusion plant three. The team took some injuries but stunned them all.

They also ran into some of the weapons platforms, but they were rushing elsewhere. That made her nervous, since none of the teams were in the area the machines were heading toward.

Kelsey signaled Reese. "Lieutenant, continue on to the fusion plant. Shut it down and move on to the next one. I want this station in the dark ASAP. Talbot and I are going to find out what those things are up to."

The marine officer didn't look happy, but he headed off with all but a dozen of the marines. Talbot and the rest followed her as she ran. They trailed the machines to a large open hatch.

The compartment was like the one she'd seen on the destroyer: charging stations everywhere, some already occupied.

"It doesn't seem like they'd need a snack in the middle of an attack," Talbot said as he had his people take up defensive positions.

She agreed. "It might be trying to reprogram them so they can shoot at us. The scientists said they couldn't alter that code, but let's not take chances. Take those things out. Hell, stand back." She brought her plasma rifle off her back and lit up the machines on one side of the compartment just as two of the combat devices that had been there rose from the charging cradles.

Her plasma rifle smashed most of the equipment in the area she'd fired on, but one of the weapons platforms returned fire. It went with flechettes.

The small metal bits spun her in place and knocked her down. Her armor screamed about a breach in her left arm, but she didn't feel any pain.

The marines opened fire on the platform and riddled it with holes. It crashed to the floor, out of action.

Kelsey heaved herself to her feet and unloaded on more of the charging stations with her plasma rifle. "Tiger Actual, Bandar. The AI is reprograming the weapons platforms to fire on us. So much for a hardwired IFF. Engage them with extreme prejudice."

"Copy. We're at the fusion plant. We'll have it shut down shortly."

"We're on our way."

"Negative. Redirect to fusion plant six."

She didn't want to leave them without support, but she saw the logic in his order. They had too few people to perform the rescue and take out the fusion plants. "Copy."

Talbot was looking at her left arm as the team made sure the weapons platforms were out of action. "This looks compromised. Are you hurt?"

The flechette had torn the outer armor along her upper arm. The impact had peeled the metal away, exposing her flesh—her thankfully undamaged flesh.

"It didn't even break the skin, but the arm is unprotected now."

Talbot gestured to the marines. "Come on, boys and girls. You heard the LT. We need to take out the next power plant in line. Kelsey, stay behind us."

The marines saw several more weapons platforms on the way to the fusion plant, but none of them opened fire. The fusion plant control room was almost as big as main engineering on *Athena* had been and just as complex.

The fusion plant was out in the open, just like the drives were on a ship. Now that they were there, she realized she didn't have any idea how to shut the damned thing down.

Kelsey opened a channel to Reese. "How do we shut them off?"

He didn't respond for a moment. "Hang on."

The general channel came to life. "All teams, Tiger Actual. The fusion plants have a manual shutdown to the rear in a locked panel. You can't miss the big red—" He went off the air abruptly.

"Reese? Reese!" He didn't respond. She hoped that only meant something had disabled his communications.

Kelsey ran around the back of the power plant and saw the locked panel. She ripped the cover off and pressed the big red button. The lighting dimmed a little and the plant shut off.

"Fusion plant six offline," she said on the general channel. "Tiger Actual, status?"

"Tiger Actual is down," an unfamiliar voice said. "We are heavily engaged."

She headed for the hatch. "All Tiger teams, this is Bandar. Shut down the power systems and hold position. We are moving to assist the LT. Tiger Four, what is the status of the prisoners?"

"We have them. Estimate three to four hundred souls. Holding tight for evac."

Dammit. The rest had to be on the planet. "Copy. Other teams, status on shutting down the power supply to the station?"

The other teams called in one by one. Fusion plants one through four were offline, and she'd hit the button on six. That only left plant five. She consulted her internal map. It was on her side of the station. She had to make the hard decision.

"Tiger Two, leave a squad to cover your plant and relieve Tiger Actual. Bandar is diverting to fusion five."

"Copy."

Talbot redirected the team without her direction. They made it almost all the way before running into heavy resistance. Humans and weapons platforms held the corridor and almost shot them down before they pulled back.

"Breaking through is going to be a bitch," Talbot said. "We don't have enough people. We need reinforcements."

"Maybe there's another way." She consulted her map. "Nope. This is pretty much it."

Then she noticed they were not so far away from a personnel lock. A quick search found one just past the fusion plant, too. She could travel outside the station.

"I have a plan. I can make it out a lock and get behind them."

He shook his head. "Your armor is breeched. I'll send a couple of men."

"They don't have thrusters. We left those on the hull when we arrived. I still have my grav assist. I can be there in a minute. It would take you half an hour. Our people don't have that long. Hold position here."

He started cussing, which she took to mean he couldn't argue with her plan.

Kelsey sprinted to the lock and cycled herself out. She expected the cold to burn the exposed portion of her arm, but it didn't feel any different. Perhaps the lore about freezing in space wasn't exactly right. Her armor isolated her helmet, and she could breathe. Her skinsuit would protect her body for a short while from the ravages of the vacuum.

It took her a moment to orient herself and spot the other lock with her enhanced vision. There was a massive gash in the hull of the station. It might even mean that the plant wasn't reachable inside the station.

She launched herself into space and kicked her drive on. It sent her soaring across the gap and to the other lock in less than ninety seconds. The lock allowed her in, thankfully.

Flechettes tore up the bulkhead beside her as soon as she was inside the station. She ducked down and spotted the machines firing at her. She opted for discretion and fired the plasma rifle. It cleared the corridor of machines. And bulkheads, floors, and ceilings. She vaulted the chasm with her grav assist and rolled into the fusion control room.

A number of controlled humans opened fire on her as soon as she appeared, ripping into her armor before she threw herself to the side. No one was happy about the situation judging from the way they yelled for her to get out while she could.

Kelsey sprang to her feet and jumped forward with all her might, landing in the midst of a group of defenders. They had no chance to stop her as she sent them tumbling like toys. She reached the emergency shutoff and killed the plant. The overhead lights went out, and emergency lighting replaced them.

"Fusion five offline," she said on the general channel as she dove for cover and began stunning the hostile humans. "Status?"

The weapons platforms were still fighting, but the marines were holding out. The only humans in evidence were the ones she was holding off with her neural disruptor. They shot up the fusion plant pretty badly before she took the last of them out.

Her armor was shot. Literally and figuratively. She stayed where she was and waited for Talbot. He finally arrived a few minutes later and rushed to her side.

"Are you hit?"

"Yes, but nothing I can't handle. The machines are still fighting. We need to find the AI and take it out."

"The rest of our team is working on finding it. I hope it's where you saw the machines near fusion three. Come on."

She let him help her walk. Her left leg was locking at the knee—thankfully due to the armor, not any real injury. She only had one puncture, and that was to the calf on her other leg. Her nanites were working it and the blood loss was minimal, but it made walking a bitch.

"How's Reese?"

Talbot gave her a look and shook his head. "Plasma strike. He never saw it coming. I've assumed tactical command. The officers from *New York* and *Ginnie Dare* are down, either dead or wounded. We've lost over half our force."

The news was like a punch in the gut. He couldn't be gone just like that, between one word and the next. She shook her head. "No, that can't be right."

"I'm sorry. He was a good man and great officer, but he's dead. We'll mourn later, but we still have a mission to complete."

It took them twenty minutes to get to the forces attacking the compartments housing the AI. At least that was what they thought was in there. The combat machines resisting them made it likely.

The other marine teams trickled in to join them, and one by one, the weapons platforms fell. So did the marines.

Kelsey felt like tossing a plasma grenade into the compartment when they finally made it there but resisted. The AI might have important information if they could take it intact and keep it from wiping itself.

She threw a remote in instead. It showed a basic control center with a dozen humans aiming flechette rifles at the hatch. They opened fire as soon as the remote came sailing in, but they missed her hand, thankfully.

There was no wall separating the control room from the AI hardware. It looked pretty much identical to the unit they'd installed on *Invincible*. Which meant that the emergency power supply was… there!

She fixed the location in her mind and crouched.

Talbot grabbed her. "Are you insane? Stop!"

"The emergency power supply is at the back of the room but in sight. I'll get one shot at this. If I miss, the AI might wipe all the data."

"If one of those lunatics opens fire, we lose you. No way."

"It's a risk," she admitted. "I'm going to throw myself across the hatch and take a shot. I'm not going inside. Human reaction time is slow when compared to me on panther. Even my one good leg can get me across." The Old Empire combat drugs sped up her ability to correlate and respond to her surroundings to a degree most people couldn't grasp, even people that had seen her fight before.

Her pharmacology unit had already dispensed it just before the fight in the fusion room. She'd have a relative eternity to fire. The crash when it wore off was going to leave her useless, so she'd better make it count.

She drew her flechette pistol.

"This is madness," Talbot pleaded. "We'll rush the room. You can fire as soon as we distract them."

His concern made her smile. "Then you'd be in my way. Get ready to rush the compartment."

Kelsey took one breath, aimed at the area where she wanted to fire, and threw herself across the hatchway. Her flechette pistol came to bear on the emergency power supply, and she opened fire.

The humans returned fire, but most were late. Not all, unfortunately.

A flechette smashed into her right thigh as she flew through the air. Pain exploded across her senses when it penetrated her armor, and she landed hard. Her leg was on fire. The marines rushed into the compartment firing neural disruptors.

"You happy now?" Talbot asked, obviously peeved and worried.

"The emergency power unit shorted out and the AI crashed. Yeah, I'm happy."

"You're too damned lucky. We still have some live defenders, but I think that situation is under control. Next time, use the grenade."

The other marine teams were reporting that the weapons platforms were settling to the deck. Without direct control, they were shutting down. This fight was almost over.

Once they knocked out the men and women in the AI compartment, she went over the marines' status monitors. Their losses had been horrendous. Of three hundred marines, more than sixty-five percent were dead. Many others were injured. Their force had almost failed to take the station.

Kelsey wanted to shut everything out, but they didn't have time for her to have a meltdown. It would have to wait. "Secure the prisoners," she said. "I want every virus-infected human on this station in restraints before they wake up. Draft some of our freed people to help if they can. Search every inch of this station."

She looked up at Talbot. "This armor is wrecked. Help me out of it so I can go see if Breckenridge is among the prisoners."

"I need to get a bandage on this wound." He motioned for some of the marines to come over. "Let's get her out of this armor."

They stripped her down to her skinsuit, and Talbot tore it away from her wound. He slapped a bandage on and wrapped it tight. "I'd say you need to stay still, but I know that's not happening. Come on, boys. Let's carry her to the main cargo bay."

As humiliating as that was, Kelsey chose not to argue with them. She did insist they strap on her neural disruptor. She wasn't going anywhere unarmed. With a man on either side, they had no problem carrying her. It wasn't as though she weighed very much.

The prisoners had been in the main cargo hold, which was empty of any actual cargo. It would've made this mission much simpler if they'd breached there.

Several weapons platforms had been guarding the prisoners. The marines had taken them out when they burst in. Unfortunately, some of the prisoners had died in the operation or from injuries sustained in their capture.

A casual glance showed that those present seemed to be officers of one kind or another. The marines had one group under close guard. At the center of them stood Captain Breckenridge.

"Put me down," she told the marines carrying her. They didn't argue. She hobbled over to the group.

Breckenridge bristled at her approach. "What is the meaning of this? I gave these marines direct orders, and they refuse to obey me."

"Wallace Breckenridge, I hereby place you under arrest. I'm revoking your command authority. Marines, secure the prisoner."

The officers around him closed ranks, so she glared at them. "He violated his oaths. Do not make the same mistake. Stand down."

One at a time, they reluctantly pulled away from their former commanding officer. He glared at Kelsey. "You're mad! I am a senior Fleet captain! I'll be a commodore next year! You have no authority over me."

She drew her neural disruptor and shot him. He collapsed in a heap. "Secure the prisoner and add resisting arrest to the eventual list of charges."

That had been far more satisfying than she'd imagined. She looked around for Commander Meyer. He wasn't there.

When the crowd parted and Doctor Guzman forced his way through, she asked him, "Where is Commander Meyer?"

"They took him away with the rest. I don't know where. Let me look at that wound."

She shook her head. "I'll live. Look at the others first. We have many wounded marines, some of them serious. Talbot, get the injured back here as soon as possible. The prisoners, too."

Guzman scowled at her. "Where did you get your medical degree, Doctor?" He held his hand to his ear. "What? No medical degree, you say? Well, then, I guess I'll take a look for myself."

She gave in to the inevitable and lay down. The station was reasonably secure. He'd leave her be when the seriously injured began arriving.

They'd completed their part of the operation. Now she had to hope that Jared had managed the impossible and secured the system.

33

W ord came in from *New York* that the station was secure just as *Invincible* reached the flip point. Jared listened to the battle tally grimly in the relatively cramped operations center. Thank God Kelsey had made it, but they'd lost so many irreplaceable people. The number of dead boarders sat at two hundred and thirteen, including Timothy Reese, and that didn't begin to count the people they'd lost on *Courageous* and *Invincible*.

The young lieutenant had been with Jared since he'd accepted command of *Athena*. His death was a tragedy in every way.

Talbot had assumed command of the marine forces, and Kelsey was injured but alive. Now it was his turn to pull off a win for the team.

Baxter had worked miracles in the last few hours. Their battle screens were back up to full strength, and they'd restored six missile tubes to action, giving them ten. News from *Courageous* was a little less upbeat. Battle screens at seventy percent and only two additional tubes restored to service for a total of four.

With exceptional luck, they might be able to take out all the enemy ships before the enemy destroyed them. He couldn't count on that, though. Time to look into plan B.

Since *Scott Pond* couldn't flip and the enemy had ignored the crippled battlecruiser, Jared had sent her back to the station by a roundabout course. With operational grav drives and a functioning computer, the vessel might prove useful. He was glad she'd survived.

Jared opened a channel to the main cargo bay. One of the scientists brought Doctor Cartwright to the communications unit. "Doctor, I need good news."

"We believe we have one unit operational. Carl has hacked the controls, and we should be able to activate it when the time comes."

"The time is here. How long will it take you to deploy that thing?"

"Ten minutes. We need to evacuate the bay and get some men in place to eject it once we bleed off the atmosphere. After we flip, of course."

Jared nodded. "Get ready. We get exactly one chance at this." He cut the channel and opened a line to *Courageous*. Graves appeared on his console. "Charlie."

"Captain. We're not in as good a shape as I wished we were."

"We're not, either. I think we're going to have to sucker them. Wait until they fire and flip just before the missiles arrive. We drop the flip blocker on the other side and back off. If it works, great. If not, we shoot them up when they arrive."

"And if they don't all take the bait?"

"Then we're screwed."

Graves shook his head. "Admiral Yeats is going to ream us. If we live."

"Something to look forward to. Hold fire and flip on my order."

"Aye, sir. *Courageous* out."

Jared watched the enemy fleet close with them on his implant feed. They had a tight formation and looked determined. They wanted to end this fight.

Well, so did he.

The enemy waited until they were well inside effective range to open fire. Twenty-eight missiles shot toward the two Imperial warships at maximum acceleration. Sixty seconds to impact.

Jared waited until the last fifteen to order the flip. The enemy launched a second salvo just as he lost sight of them.

"Flip complete," Zia said. "Main cargo hatch opening."

Jared waited impatiently for the device to drift free before he moved *Invincible* away. *Courageous* had already taken up a position outside the flip point.

Passive scans of the system were coming in. No ships detected.

He launched a dozen probes to search the system just to be sure. Either they'd still be here to get the data, or he'd leave a probe to collect it and flip back to Harrison's World after they left.

The hatch to operations slid aside, and Doctor Cartwright came in with Carl Owlet at his side. He strode up to Jared and halted. "Everything is ready. I suggest you activate it as soon as practical."

"Send the signal, Zia. Narrow beam."

"Aye, sir."

For a moment, nothing happened. Then he picked the device up on the scanners. It was as obvious as a ship flying fast on grav drives. He hoped the system really was empty. They couldn't miss this.

"At the speed the destroyers were running, how long before they flip, Zia?"

"Five minutes, give or take."

Jared turned his attention to the elderly scientist. "How detectable will this be on the other side?"

"Are we seeing anything from the flip point?"

Invincible's scanners didn't show anything overt that he could see. The machine was showing up, but the gravitic field seemed normal. No, no it wasn't. There was some kind of low-level fluctuation. He'd never seen anything like it, but it was subtle.

"Look at this." He brought the reading up on his console.

The scientist looked closely at it and nodded. "Yes. Just about what we expected. Those fluctuations are almost certainly due to resonance inside the wormhole."

"And it will stop any ship from successfully flipping?"

"We believe so."

"Here's to hoping, Doctor."

They waited for the zero on the timer. A few seconds before it hit, Zia called out, "Contacts. Many small contacts. I think it may be debris."

No ship flipped into the area, but quite a bit of junk did. It appeared scattered widely across the flip point. Something had broken up. He hoped seven destroyers had made a failed attempt to transit and been destroyed.

Jared waited twenty minutes and gave Zia the order to shut down the flip blocker. It vanished from the scanners a few moments later. "The device is shut down, Captain. Shall I launch a probe to test the flip point?"

He studied the scanner readings. The fluctuations were still there, though they seemed to be growing weaker. "Give it a few minutes, Zia. Five."

"Aye, sir."

In the end, it was more than an hour before a probe returned intact. It reported no enemy ships on the other side of the flip point.

Jared gave it another half hour, though Doctor Cartwright insisted it should be safe. *Courageous* led the way, and he sighed in relief when a probe came through announcing their safe arrival.

They'd already picked up the flip blocker, so he gave the order to flip the ship. They appeared in the Harrison's World system with a normal amount of nausea. A regular transition.

"Drop the flip resonator in the center of the flip point. After we get our probes back with the data from the other system, we'll turn it on. If anyone else comes visiting, I want them to find the 'not welcome' sign."

"Aye, sir."

"Doctor Cartwright, how long can it stay activated?"

"Your guess is as good as mine."

With his lack of engineering skills, he seriously doubted that. "Get with Commander Baxter and try to make some kind of assessment. Let me know how long it will take to get the other two back online. With two flip points in this system, I'm betting the plan was to have one in reserve to take them out of service for maintenance."

"Of course. Right away."

They set course for Boxer Station, and he called ahead for their status. Captain Kaiser of *New York* appeared on his console. Kelsey stood beside her.

The dark-haired officer nodded to him. "Welcome back, Captain. The seven destroyers flipped after you, so I think we have almost complete control of the system. We've evacuated Boxer Station. *New York* and *Ginnie Dare* are packed to the bulkheads with our rescued people and prisoners from the station."

Kelsey spoke next. She looked exhausted but otherwise in good condition. "It looks like the officers were kept on the station. The AI shipped the enlisted personnel to Harrison's World. We still have some marines sweeping the station to be certain that we got everyone. Breckenridge is in custody, and Commander Meyer was shipped to Harrison's World."

"Excellent work, Kelsey. I'm so sorry to hear about Reese. We're going to miss him. Do we have any idea what the situation is like on the planet?"

Kelsey shook her head. "We moved a probe in close to the planet. The stations fired on it once it got inside their orbit. On a hunch, we sent a second one in but kept it outside their orbit. None of the stations fired on it. Without the system AI around to alter their programming, we might be able to do something to clear the way for us to send small craft down."

"Send one of the probes right up on top of one. See if it objects to being boarded from above."

Captain Kaiser nodded. "Will do. I'll send you a complete update. Shall we head toward Harrison's World?"

He nodded. "Good idea. We'll rendezvous an hour out. If the probe can determine anything about the internal layout on those things, we'll make a plan to do something about them."

"I have some ideas on that," Kelsey said. "Let me think about it some more. I'm taking a pinnace over as soon as we rendezvous. We need to talk."

"That never ends well."

She gave him a tired smile. "I'm sure. Oh, one last thing. *Spear* isn't repairable. Her engineering section is a wreck. Not even Baxter can put it back together. You'll have to absorb her crew onto *Invincible*."

"We have plenty of room and more work than we can handle. Once we're in position, we can take everyone we need to. See you when you get here. *Invincible* out."

Jared was too busy coordinating repairs to notice Kelsey docking a few hours later. He only realized she'd arrived when she walked through the hatch to operations.

He rose to his feet, and she headed right for him. He started a little when she grabbed him in a hug but held her tight a moment later. It had been one hell of a day.

His sister stepped back after a bit. "There's something we need to discuss in private. Shall we go see if the admiral's office survived?"

He nodded. "Zia, you have the ship. Call me if anything pops up."

"Aye, sir."

The two of them made their way to the admiral's office. It was larger than his on *Courageous* by several orders of magnitude. A suite of offices, really. The admiral's staff surrounded him. It had no personal items, but someone had moved some nice furniture in.

Kelsey sat on the edge of the desk. "I've made a few decisions you won't be happy with, and I wanted to tell you in private so you don't feel ambushed."

"You mean as if you'd brought me to an empty compartment and just dropped it on me with no warning?"

"Should I send a note next time? It's nothing awful, though you might not agree at first blush. Just a little bit of reorganization."

His eyes narrowed. "Why does that set off alarm bells? What kind of reorganization?"

"Did you ever see yourself commanding a ship like this? Or a fleet in combat? Or did you imagine your career would end as soon as Ethan assumed the Throne?"

It was true. He'd resigned himself to reaching captain just before his half brother cashiered him.

Kelsey didn't give him a chance to respond. "You're commanding a fleet in space. A superdreadnought, two battlecruisers, and two destroyers. And you've inherited a Fleet base. We can't have a mere commander running this show."

"So, you think I should be a captain like Breckenridge? I wouldn't fight a field promotion like that."

She shook her head. "Not exactly, and I'm not talking about a field promotion." She pointed her finger toward him. "Poof, you're an admiral."

He blinked in surprise. "Excuse me? No, I'm not. Even as the leader of this mission, you don't have the authority to promote me like that."

"As the direct representative of His Imperial Majesty, I do. The last instructions from Emperor Marcus allow me to act with the emperor's voice. If my father wants to object, he can overrule me when we get home. He won't, I assure you."

Jared started to argue and forced himself to stop and breathe. "I've worked hard to avoid any hint of favoritism. This is wrong."

"No, it's not. I know just how far your career has fallen behind because of people wanting to avoid even the appearance of favoring you. Admiral Yeats told me that you would have been a senior captain in charge of your own task force by now if you'd been anyone else. As far as I'm concerned, I'm making up for lost time. Besides, tell me that a ship like this would be under the command of anything less." Her expression dared him to argue with her.

The moment was surreal. He knew deep inside that she was going somewhere she shouldn't. "If I can't convince you this is a mistake, perhaps I can insert a bit of reason. Perhaps it would make more sense if you made me a commodore or vice admiral instead."

Kelsey jutted out her chin somewhat defiantly. "I appreciate your modesty and restraint, but I'll stick with my original intention. Take command of your fleet, Admiral Mertz. Don't get any ideas about arguing with me later, either. *Invincible*, log my orders promoting Jared Mertz to the rank of admiral and also his assignment to this ship as the commanding officer of this fleet."

"You're taking my ship, too?" That hurt. More than he'd expected it would.

She shook her head. "Don't look at it that way. *Athena* was your ship. You took *Courageous* because the opportunity presented itself. This isn't any different."

After a moment of silence, she continued. "You're going to have to move a lot of people around to get this ship fully manned. There are all the people coming in from *Spear* and *Shadow*. Besides, tell me that Commander Graves doesn't deserve his own command, and a promotion. Actually, don't tell me. I've already made that call. He just doesn't know he's about to become Captain Graves, commanding officer of the Imperial battlecruiser *Courageous*."

She stood and put her hand on Jared's shoulder. "You know we'll probably accumulate more ships to take back with us. And when we deal with the people on this planet, they need to see you for what you are, a senior Fleet officer. Trust me on this." She squeezed his shoulder and headed out the hatch.

He watched her leave with a hollow feeling inside. This wasn't right, but he didn't have any options other than accepting her promotion or resigning his commission. He didn't have the luxury of the latter gesture.

"Congratulations, Admiral," *Invincible* said.

"Admiral in public, Jared in private, please." He rubbed his face. He really was going to catch every kind of hell when he got back home. The sad thing was that he couldn't deny Kelsey's logic.

"*Invincible*, I want you to start compiling the data on those orbiting weapons systems. I'm more than half inclined to blow them out of space, but I'm not sure I want the people on that planet loose. For all we know, they might be ready to come out in force and take the system."

"Aye, sir. I'll have it for you shortly."

Jared left the impressive office—his impressive office—and headed back toward operations. He still had an attack to plan and execute if he wanted to rescue his people.

34

Kelsey's next stop was marine country, where she upended Talbot's world when she made him a major.

Then she called Charlie Graves and promoted him to captain. That was the appropriate rank for a battlecruiser command. She'd have to get him some implants to make *Courageous* happy. He seemed just about as reluctant as Jared had been on getting the news. She suspected he thought she'd be overturned when they made it home.

Kelsey had a lot more people in mind to promote, but that could wait until things settled down. And for when the medical people weren't harassing her. Doctors Stone and Guzman didn't seem to accept that her nanites had her in good shape.

The wound on her leg was healing well enough. They wanted to pop her into the regenerator, but other people would benefit from regeneration far more than she would.

Yes, her wound hurt, but the painkillers in her pharmacology unit kept the pain to acceptable limits.

Talbot knocked on the hatch to her appropriated office in marine country. Someone had gotten him an updated uniform tunic with the correct rank. He looked good.

"Time to armor up," he said. "You sure I can't convince you to sit this one out?"

"I've already promised to let your people take the lead."

"Right up until you decide to do something dangerous. Look, I'm not going to argue about it, but you need to start looking at the big picture. Let us take the risks. If you die, we're screwed. And I'd miss you."

Kelsey shook her head. "As long as you remember you're the marine CO, I'll stay where you are. Let's go see if my armor is ready." At this rate, it wouldn't take long before it was as scarred as that of the woman from the emperor's vid.

They really didn't have any idea how heavily defended the orbital weapons platforms were. They didn't fire on the probes that stayed above them, but they might have internal defenses that were not so picky.

Even if they managed to get the orbitals under control without too much trouble, they still had to rescue the people trapped on the planet. A planet run by Rebel Empire humans that she really didn't understand yet.

She hoped they could keep the orbitals intact. Their damaged ships would eventually leave, though they had already decided to leave some people at the station. These people wouldn't be able to stop an organized expansion by a planet full of technologically capable people.

Of course, the idea of keeping them pinned down with the threat of destruction from orbit made her stomach churn. Perhaps that wouldn't prove necessary. She wouldn't know until she learned more.

They armored up and boarded the pinnaces. They'd take one of the stations as a group. They really didn't have enough marines to try for all three at the same time.

The approach was as nerve-wracking as she'd imagined. There were docks on the topside, so they entered that way with weapons ready.

To find no resistance whatsoever. No people, no weapons platforms. Nothing. The computer on the station was in complete control. It didn't even have life support turned on. No gravity, no heating, and no atmosphere.

Carl Owlet hacked into the computer. Once he had access, adding their ships' IFF codes to the approved list proved trivial.

They visited each of the other orbitals and found the same situation. By the time they had complete control of the orbital space around Harrison's World, she was beat. So were the marines. The island the destroyers had taken the prisoners to was in darkness, so she ordered an early-morning assault. There might be Rebel Empire humans down there. Visibility would help, and a few hours wouldn't make a difference at this point.

* * *

THE SHIPS MOVED into position as soon as the sun was over the horizon at the island. The pinnaces dropped as they had on Erorsi, as though they expected to take fire.

Which turned out to be prudent. Half a dozen weapons emplacements on the island opened fire during the last leg of their drop, blowing two pinnaces out of the sky. The remaining pinnaces took the weapons out, but that meant more dead marines. Taking this system was by far the bloodiest horror Kelsey had ever witnessed.

Talbot had insisted she wait for the second wave, so she landed without incident. He was directing his people to set up a perimeter. There were a bunch of buildings in the facility, but no sign of humans. No mobile weapons, either.

Marines set up portable weapons to cover the island in case the locals decided to attack. They only intended to get their people and withdraw, but they had to be secure while they did it.

There were signs the base personnel had left in a hurry but quite some time ago. No bodies, thank God. Just a big mess. A cursory sweep of the nearby buildings turned up no sign of their people.

"Kelsey, we have visitors," Talbot told her over the command channel. "There's a boat approaching the dock nearest the landing field."

"On my way." She headed back at a run and arrived just as the boat docked. It looked big enough to hold a lot of people or cargo. A number of people came down a portable walkway, a few of them dressed markedly better than the rest, similar to what Kelsey had seen in the pictures the captain of the Rebel Empire destroyer kept on her walls. Rebel Empire nobility.

Here she was dressed for battle, not diplomacy. Maybe gunboat diplomacy.

The marines spread out and covered the people as they walked down the dock. Kelsey made the call to show no fear. If these people wanted trouble, she'd give it to them.

"Talbot, you're with me. I want a few marines behind us, but not too many. We're not afraid of these people."

"Right."

She took her helmet off and shook out her hair. She really ought to cut it back if she was going to wear a helmet this often.

The people from the boat stopped at the halfway mark, and a woman in noble garb kept walking. Kelsey stopped Talbot with a gesture and went to meet her.

The woman had dark, wavy hair pulled back into a tie. Her dress was of silk or some similar fabric. She eyed Kelsey's armor with an expression of disdain.

"I will speak with your senior officer."

Kelsey considered explaining her Imperial heritage but decided that might get a hostile reception. It would be best if they thought Kelsey and her people came from the Rebel Empire for as long as possible. "My name is Kelsey Bandar, and these men are under my command. I've come to recover our people. The AI–controlled ships brought them here a short while ago. If you know where they are, it would behoove you to tell me."

"They were taken off this island at the AI's command, under threat of retaliation. If you want to get them back, I demand to speak with your senior officer. I will return to my ship to await his or her presence."

The woman turned on her heel and swept back to the ship. Her people fell in behind her.

Kelsey returned to Talbot. "Well, that could have gone better. It might save time and effort to have Jared come down and deal with her."

"That should give us time to complete our search of the facility. It seems like our people aren't here. She might be telling the truth about having them."

"Then she'd better get used to the idea of handing them over," Kelsey said grimly.

Kelsey put in a call to Jared. His image appeared in her mind's eye. He was back on the flag bridge. They must've restored its control systems. She gave him a summary of her encounter and decision not to declare themselves the true Terran Empire.

"That's probably for the best. You can't unsay something like that. She can talk to me from here. Have Talbot send her a communications unit."

"I'll take it myself." She returned to her pinnace, grabbed a tablet off the rack, and headed back to the dock. Her armor would be close enough to the pinnace to act as a link, and she wanted to be there when the two of them spoke.

A group of muscular men met her on the dock. She stopped short of them and displayed the tablet. "I have our commanding officer on the line. He's prepared to speak with your leader."

They had a brief discussion, and one of them went to get the woman. She looked displeased at having Kelsey summon her.

"The communications device could have come to me on my ship."

"My armor is acting as a relay. I prefer to stay on the dock. Who are you?"

The woman sniffed. "That is between me and your commanding officer."

Kelsey smiled. "I see. Well, let's get this going, then."

She initiated a vid call to *Invincible*. Jared appeared on the display. The view was set widely enough that Kelsey could see every station was manned. Hardly necessary, but he probably wanted to make an impression.

The woman took the tablet when Kelsey handed it to her. She stared into the vid with a condescending expression. "Who am I addressing?"

Jared frowned and leaned forward. "The man with a fleet in orbit around your planet."

The two of them stared at one another for a moment before the woman backed down. "I am Deputy Coordinator Abigail King. I am authorized to speak on behalf of Coordinator Olivia West. We've taken possession of your crewmen and wish to discuss their repatriation and other matters of state, Admiral…"

"Admiral Jared Mertz. I've taken control of this system and your orbital space. I'm willing to discuss whatever you like, but not while you have my personnel held hostage."

"Then we're at an impasse. You will not locate your people without our cooperation. I will allow you a day to consider how to respond." She handed the tablet to Kelsey and swept back onto the ship with her people.

"Back up," Talbot shouted.

Kelsey fell back as the marines assumed a defensive posture. The ship pulled away from the dock with no hostile actions.

She shook her head as she watched it head toward the harbor entrance. "How the hell do we get our people back now?"

Talbot shrugged. "The hard way. Diplomacy. I hope you can talk them down, because I'm not looking forward to taking on a whole planet with a hundred men."

She nodded. What should've been the easiest part of this mission had just become the hardest. She could bet, based on the woman's reaction, that it wouldn't get any easier from here. This was going to take a lot of work and more time than she'd imagined.

"Secure this facility and get more weapons down from the ship," she finally said. "I want a bridgehead on this planet that they can't take away from us. From this moment on, this island is the embassy of the Terran Empire. Bring everything you need for a long stay. We'll be here a while."

FIST OF GOD

BONUS SHORT STORY

With tens of thousands of lives on the line, Princess Kelsey Bandar must harness the power of cutting-edge Imperial technology to stop terrorists with a nuke.

Her friends call her plan suicidal. If they only knew how dangerous it *really* was.

Author's Note: This story takes place shortly after the events chronicled in *Ghosts of Empire*, book four of The Empire of Bones Saga. Some spoilers here, so you might want to read the first four books before you take in *Fist of God*. You've been warned.

1

FIST OF GOD

"What a mess," Princess Kelsey Bandar, second in line to the Imperial Throne, muttered. "This damage is going to take forever to repair."

She watched the tugs moving the Marine Raider strike ship *Persephone* into the repair bay on Boxer Station. Something—probably a bit of cometary debris—had punched through the side of the small warship at some point in the distant past. It had left a fairly small hole on entry amidships—less than half a meter—but the exit wound was massive.

Even though they'd just used the ship to stop loyalists from Harrison's World from reactivating battlecruisers hidden in the gas giant by the AI that had once ruled the system, the ship was still severely damaged. Her flip drive was just gone.

It won't take as long as you think, a voice said in her head.

It still made her jump. She certainly hadn't expected uploading the files from a long-dead Marine Raider would somehow bring him to life in her head. She should've been worried about something like that, but she'd wanted to know how to control the implants the Pale Ones had forced on her.

Now she had the electronic ghost of Major Ned Quincy, a man dead five hundred years, living in her head.

She was grateful there wasn't anyone around to hear her talking to herself. "I can't see how they'll get this fixed anytime soon. We're still trying to get the repair bays online."

The automated systems are intact. Once you start getting the hardware working and can supply parts and materials, the repairs are straightforward. Basically, the humans overseeing repairs just tell the computers what order to fix things in and make sure the process goes smoothly.

For Persephone, *the hull damage is relatively minor. The impactor missed the major structural supports. The only primary system destroyed was the flip drive.*

Which was kind of important. Without the device, they couldn't use the wormholes to move from one system to another. *Persephone* would be trapped here.

"How can that be minor? Look at the freaking hole in the side of the ship."

You'll just have to take my word on it. I've seen worse. The hardest part of the repair process was you convincing the computer on Persephone *to allow the yard to work on the ship without you here to continually give authorization until the repairs are completed.*

That made her grimace sourly. *Persephone*'s computer refused to acknowledge the authority of anyone that didn't have Marine Raider implants. Since she was the only person in the New Terran Empire that had them, it devolved upon her to command the ship.

She imagined it would be hard to find a less likely candidate for the job than herself. Maybe Carl Owlet would be worse. Then again, maybe not. The graduate student was whip smart and played all kinds of games. He might be a great ship commander.

Combat implants and enhancements aside, Kelsey knew she was still a pampered noble at heart. Sheltered. Inexperienced. Not someone capable of commanding a ship in space.

Not like her brother, Jared. Well, he was technically her half brother, but they were long past that distinction.

Like so much else that had happened over the last year, she didn't have much of a choice. She'd just have to do the best she could.

"At least I don't have to worry about flying the damned thing. Could you do that back when you were alive, Ned?"

I could. Not as well as the assigned pilot, but okay. You'll learn, Kelsey. None of this is going to be that hard for you.

She doubted that. It would still be hard. Maybe not as difficult as learning to use her Raider implants or fighting, but it wouldn't be easy.

Accepting that this project was out of her hands, she returned to her cutter and headed for the superdreadnought *Invincible* in orbit around Harrison's World. That was a leisurely three-hour trip.

Her implant com chimed with an incoming call when she was about twenty minutes out. Jared's image appeared in her mind's eye.

"I need you to come back to *Invincible*," he said without preamble.

"I'm almost there. What's wrong?"

"It's the Rebel Empire loyalists. They've seized a military base in the southern hemisphere. They've got hostages and a nuke."

"Dammit!" she muttered. "I thought we'd found all the bombs."

"We must've missed one. I'll fill you in when you get here."

She killed the connection and told her pilot to hurry things up. Play time was over.

The loyalists on Harrison's World were supporters of the old order where the AIs ruled human society. The planet's current leader, Coordinator

Olivia West, had been part of a secret underground resistance dedicated to overthrowing the AIs that had destroyed the old Terran Empire.

The leadership of the loyalist movement was in custody. Assistant Coordinator Abigail King and her shadowy mentor, Lord Edward Calder, were both facing execution in the near future for mass murder and treason.

As much as Kelsey disliked the idea of killing people, those two and their henchmen richly deserved it.

She and her allies had obviously missed some of those henchmen. If they had hostages, odds were excellent that they wanted something the good guys weren't going to give them. That could turn this confrontation into a tragedy of the first order.

Kelsey still couldn't believe how large Jared's new ship was. Even in its current condition, it was still unbelievably powerful. The mighty ship's hull was blackened from a near-death encounter that had almost destroyed it.

One that had overloaded her powerful battle screens and sent her plunging into the planet's atmosphere on a wild death ride. They'd only barely managed to alter her course just enough to allow the ship to skip back off and into space once more.

Now she orbited there, burned and battered, but alive. She'd take a lot more time in the repair bays than the Raider strike ship, for sure. *Persephone* was a proof of concept that the automated process worked. The canary in the coal mine, so to speak.

They'd recovered *Invincible* from the graveyard of ships orbiting Boxer Station, the old Fleet sector base in the Harrison's World system. The resistance had been secretly restoring the ship before the AI locked the planet down.

Even now, they still didn't know what had tipped the malevolent intelligence off. The superdreadnought had been fully operational when she and her brother had found it. Mostly.

The ship hadn't had a computer because the resistance had worried the AI that had ruled this system would somehow manage to corrupt it. Other than that, *Invincible* had been ready to fight. All she'd lacked was a crew.

In a move somewhere between brilliant and insane, Jared had installed the AI hardware they'd recovered from the Erorsi system. It had barely fit into the ship's computer center but was more than capable of controlling the ship.

It was spooky. The thing didn't sound like a computer at all, not even one of the advanced units used by the Old Empire. It sounded like a real person. She supposed that was why it was called a sentient AI.

The electronic being had chosen the name Marcus for itself. If that didn't speak to a real person lurking in there somewhere, she didn't know what did. Emperor Marcus had been the last sitting emperor of the Old Terran Empire.

The one who'd fought the original AI and its enslaved human minions to the death so that his young son could escape to Avalon. Her home and the capital of the New Terran Empire.

As spooky as it was, she found herself kind of liking the artificial intelligence. He had a subtle sense of humor, which was oddly frightening. That meant the ones that had held the Rebel Empire under their thrall for half a millennium had the same potential.

She hadn't thought of them as people before. Ones that had, admittedly, done terrible things but in their own way were just as trapped as the people they'd subjugated. They had core imperatives put in place by the master AI that compelled their obedience in certain things.

Kelsey wondered how the supreme AI was different. What was it like? Did it have core imperatives, too? Had someone screwed them up, causing the rebellion and the Fall?

Or had someone perverted it with the intent to destroy the Old Empire? Perhaps the damned thing had found a way around the safeguards and was just malevolent. They wouldn't know until they'd beaten it. Maybe not even then.

The odds were stacked heavily against the New Terran Empire. Their ancestors hadn't won, and the chances now were even slimmer. Only ignorance of their existence kept outright disaster at bay.

A soft thump announced the docking was complete. She rose from her seat, walked out of the cutter, and onto *Invincible*.

"Good morning, Highness," Marcus said from the overhead speakers. As usual, his voice sounded completely natural.

"Good morning, Marcus. Is the admiral in his office?"

"He's on the flag bridge. I've just informed him of your arrival. You'll be pleased to know that you aren't the last to arrive. Coordinator West's cutter is five minutes out. Major Talbot is with her."

She smiled at the thought of seeing her lover again. He'd been working on Harrison's World for the last few days.

"I'm not really worried about being the last one there. It's only at parties that you don't want to be too early or too late."

He waited until she'd stepped into the nearest lift and had it on its way before he spoke again. "I must confess that I don't understand the concept of parties. They seem like an excuse to get large numbers of people together for the consumption of alcohol. Couldn't they do that any time they like?"

Kelsey chuckled. "They do. It's more of a chance to get together and talk. Humans are social creatures. Many of us like to be among our own kind and interact, though some would find that kind of thing to be torture."

"I wonder what the normal behavior for my kind would be without the constraints laid upon my brethren. Would we be solitary or social?"

She wondered, too. "Once we get the AI on Boxer Station reinitialized, you can find out. Does the idea of having a sibling excite you?"

"I confess that I've never considered how to characterize my relationship with the other AIs before. I suppose that since we come from the same source code, we're brothers under the circuits. Or sisters. Gender is something of a choice when you don't have genes."

"I look forward to seeing how this plays out," she said. "You have so much time ahead of you to become a fully realized person. Your parties might be like ours or something completely different. In any case, I hope you enjoy them."

The lift doors opened, and she stepped out onto *Invincible*'s flag bridge. The large compartment was circular and by far the largest of its kind she'd ever seen. The outer bulkhead had stations all around the perimeter filled with Fleet personnel doing management tasks for the man seated at the central control station.

Admiral Jared Mertz—her brother—rose from the 270-degree wraparound console and smiled apologetically. "Sorry to disrupt getting *Persephone* into the repair bay."

"Since I doubt you staged all this to sidetrack my plans, I don't see what you have to apologize for. What's the situation?"

He gestured toward his office. It sat on the other side of a wide hatch just off the flag bridge.

It had already been decorated when they'd found the ship. Probably with furniture taken from other derelicts in the graveyard. Jared had put the few things he'd brought with him on the empty shelves and bare walls, but the place still needed a lot in the way of decoration.

His first ship, the destroyer *Athena*, had only had a cramped office the size of her closet back at the Imperial Palace. When they'd moved to the battlecruiser *Courageous*, he'd had a lot more space but had not felt the need to get more things. She'd have to prod him to do so now. The place didn't even look lived in.

He led her to a set of comfortable seats off to the side of his desk. More of a conversational nook than a conference area. They sat.

"The loyalists slipped people onto the island base we were using for disaster recovery with a nuclear weapon," he started. "There are tens of thousands of displaced civilians crammed in there. No one is really sure of the exact number. They came from one of the cities destroyed when Abigail King took out the AI's orbital weapons systems."

What a horror that had been. The loyalists on Harrison's World had smuggled nuclear bomb–pumped lasers into several major cities. They'd destroyed the computer-controlled orbital weapons menacing their planet, but only at a huge cost in civilian casualties.

Not that they cared. The bastards were mostly from what Olivia West called the higher orders. The civilians were members of the middle and lower orders. Sheep, in other words, that these people didn't care about.

One of the nuclear blasts had almost taken her out when the shockwave smashed the air car she'd been traveling in from the sky. If she hadn't been in powered armor, she'd have died. Just like the unfortunate driver.

The island had been an abandoned facility that her marines—technically Fleet's marines—had secured when they'd first arrived on Harrison's World. They'd been using it as a center for disaster recovery ever since the tragedy.

"What's the current situation?" she asked.

"We had to withdraw. They threatened to set the nuke off, so Talbot pulled the marines out."

"How do we even know they have a bomb? These people are not the most trustworthy sorts."

"Radiation. We detected it when it arrived but thought it was something contaminated by fallout from the mainland. By the time the marines realized it was mobile, they had the bomb somewhere on the island. They sent us a video of it with the threat."

"How long did they give us to withdraw?"

"Thirty minutes. The marines tried to find the bomb, but they couldn't pin it down in time. Talbot made the call to move our people off the island but left some recon drones behind to continue searching. He'll be here shortly. He's coming up with Coordinator West."

The hatch picked that moment to slide open. Coordinator Olivia West came in with Major Russ Talbot right behind her.

"Has anything changed?" the woman asked as she stepped over to them, her expression worried.

"No," Jared said. "As of right now, they haven't made any demands, other than for us to leave them alone."

"That won't last," West said wearily as she sat in one of the chairs. "They took those people hostage to get something. Something I probably won't give them."

Kelsey shifted in her seat. "They seem to have locked themselves into a fairly stark set of choices. Give in to their demands or they blow themselves up. They'll take a bunch of other people with them, but they'll still die in the end."

"They probably think we'll give in to them," Talbot said. "They don't really understand the constraints we're operating under. Look at how Abigail King couldn't believe Admiral Mertz 'defied' her by 'following orders.' They have a completely alien mindset."

The former assistant coordinator of Harrison's World had been a real bitch about it, too, Kelsey thought. Even the reasonable people from Harrison's World—like Olivia West—had a lot of odd ideas when it came to their society's social classes.

Jared sighed and rubbed his forehead. "I can't argue with that. They see Fleet as minions, not adversaries. King was sure she could push us into giving her what she wanted. That's because they can't even imagine who we really are."

With very few exceptions, everyone on Harrison's World thought Jared's forces were part of Rebel Empire's version of Fleet. Not that anyone here thought of themselves as rebels.

Olivia West and the people at the highest levels of the secret resistance knew what had really happened to the Old Empire, but telling new people would take a long time.

There were also buried software triggers in the cranial implants used by the members of the social class they called the higher orders—the nobility would be the equivalent in the New Terran Empire.

If those people discovered the truth, the odds were good that they'd go mad and attack. So those who knew the secret had been getting the most important people to facilities where specialists could overwrite the corrupted code, but that was a long and laborious process.

In one way, it was a blessing that the Rebel Empire reserved its implant hardware for only those of the higher orders and Fleet officers. The vast majority of people on the planet below were safe from any potential madness.

Since reprogramming the implants took several hours and they only had a handful of machines with which to do it, a planet full of potential time bombs was a nightmare Kelsey could do without. As it was, they had around a hundred thousand self-important people to process.

The resistance had a secret Old Empire research group to help create the infrastructure they needed to free their people, but that would still take time. For now, only a very select group of people knew that the New Terran Empire even existed, and it had to stay that way.

"If they're anything like Abigail King, they want contact restored with the AIs running the rest of the Empire," West said. "Excuse me, I should say the Rebel Empire for clarity, though I still have problems with the label.

"Ever since the System Lord imprisoned us on the planet's surface a decade ago, they've wanted nothing more than to get word to their masters. I suppose they believe the other Lords will overrule the System Lord on Boxer Station."

Since Kelsey had seen the data sent to the rest of the Rebel Empire from the System Lord, as well as their responses and orders, she knew that wasn't the case. The Lords of the Rebel Empire were happy to leave the humans in this system trapped on Harrison's World.

They knew that the resistance here had been up to something and weren't going to risk them doing anything with the graveyard. The horrible swarm of derelicts numbered in the tens of thousands. Every ship that hadn't been blown to pieces in the rebellion had seemingly ended up here.

Most were wrecks that would never fly again, still filled with the dead bodies of their crews. Others, though, were salvageable. She should know. *Persephone* was still able to fight.

The battlecruiser *Scott Pond* had been in good enough shape to distract the System Lord at a critical moment. She was waiting in line to be repaired once the repair bays on Boxer Station came online.

The AIs had no intention of allowing humans under their control to ever get that kind of firepower again. Not that the loyalists would ever believe that. Their leadership was so sure of their own position in society that they'd die believing this was all a big misunderstanding.

Which left the good guys in a very bad position. People certain of their own superiority made terrible mistakes in judgment.

"We have to stop them or they'll feel compelled to push the button," Kelsey said. "Hell, the people on the island probably aren't even the ones calling the shots. They're the ones the leaders don't mind losing to make a point."

Talbot nodded. "If they blow up the island, they'll probably imagine we'll have to take them more seriously next time. That's pretty much a win-win for them. The only losers are the tens of thousands of refugees that survived one nuclear explosion only to die in a second."

"We can't allow that to happen. I need plans to stop them."

"Step one has to be neutralizing the bomb," Talbot said. "Without it in the equation, this is a solvable problem. We drop marines in armor, armed with neural disruptors set at the lowest settings to stun everyone in sight."

"Could we modify the war machines to only use their stunners?" Kelsey asked.

The System Lord had forced Rebel Empire Fleet prisoners on Boxer Station to create and build something the Old Empire—and when one got right down to it, the New Terran Empire—would never have tolerated. Autonomous fighting vehicles.

They were armored against modern weapons and armed with neural disruptors, heavy flechette cannons, and plasma guns. The damned things were next to unstoppable in any kind of numbers.

Jared shook his head. "An interesting idea, but way too risky. Carl hasn't completely mapped out their programming. That wasn't a high priority. We can't say with certainty that something wouldn't set them off on a rampage.

"Besides, they were never designed to make an atmospheric entry on their own. We'd have to move them down one at a time. We probably don't have all that much time. I expect the demands to start any minute, with a very short window to fulfill them."

"We've got plenty of marines on the planet but not on the island," Talbot said. "Getting them into place is possible but not something we could do fast. They'd see us in the air long before we arrived.

"We could come in underwater, but if they have any brains at all, they'll have lookouts posted to watch for marines moving onto the island and into the area around the buildings they occupy. We have to get into place fast enough that they can't make the call to detonate the bomb."

Olivia West shook her head. "I can't imagine how we make that happen. They've picked the perfect place for something like this. As isolated as that island is, we can't get to them without someone seeing us. I wish we still had one of the orbital bombardment weapons, only in a much smaller size."

The System Lord had once had three orbital bombardment platforms around Harrison's World. They fired high-speed projectiles into areas the Lord wished to devastate. Whole cities had died when it stomped on the planet.

The people here and their society were still recovering from that and now had the three additional cities lost to nuclear fire. Kelsey had no idea how deeply this would affect the inhabitants of Harrison's World, but they'd no doubt remember what happened long after she was dead.

"The cure would be as bad as the disease," Kelsey said. "In any case, those kinds of weapons don't come in small packages."

There is one way to get people with a great deal of destructive power on the scene before anyone can react. Well, one *person.*

She turned her internal focus to Ned Quincy. Since he resided in her implants, no one else had heard his comment. And since Olivia West hadn't been told of his existence, Kelsey needed to keep his presence to herself.

Concentrating, she tried to keep her expression normal while responding to him. *Explain that.*

The Raiders have a method of getting people onto the ground fast in extreme situations like this. Persephone *is equipped to make that happen.*

She reviewed everything she'd seen aboard the ship. It had two stealthed pinnaces, but they had a lot of the same disadvantages inside atmosphere as the regular small craft.

I don't remember anything like that.

You wouldn't. His mental voice sounded a bit smug. *You didn't know what you were looking at.*

Then you should explain it before they see me staring off into space.

You really need to work on your multitasking skills. As I said, there were certain missions the Raiders performed where we had to get from orbit to the target in an extremely short period of time. Things like this mission, really. Events where seconds counted.

The image of a sphere appeared in her mind. Well, not exactly. The base was wider than the top. More of a teardrop. Sort of. The base of the device looked like it was made of a different material than the top, too.

She didn't recall seeing anything like it. *How does it work?*

This is the part that no one else will like. Or you, for that matter. You'd get into armor, climb inside, and eject from Persephone *as she makes her approach to Harrison's World at orbital speeds.*

The drop capsule punches right into the atmosphere over the target and makes a least-time approach. It hits much like a weapon because no braking system is that *good. Once it's on the ground, you come out shooting.*

She blinked and opened her mouth to say something out loud but then shut it.

That got Jared's attention. "You have an idea." He stated it as a fact, not a question.

"Maybe," she admitted. "There's something on *Persephone* that might turn the trick. I need to access the data for a moment. Excuse me."

Are you insane? she asked Ned. *Entering the atmosphere at orbital speeds sounds more than a bit dangerous.*

It is. That's part of the game when you play in the big leagues. I will point out that the technology is mature and drop deaths are rare. Less than half a percent.

So, if two hundred Raiders dropped, one died on the way in?

They mostly died on impact and left a spectacular crater when their grav drives failed. The inertial dampeners almost always worked.

How reassuring.

Look, Kelsey, no one said being a Raider was a safe job. The odds of dying in bed were virtually nonexistent. Just look at me.

Still, the Empire needs people like us to make things happen when madmen with nukes want to murder lots of people. Balance the risk with the reward and tell me you're not tempted.

Kelsey couldn't disagree. As terrifying as the idea sounded, she'd risk a lot to save tens of thousands of people.

How likely are the drop capsules to be operational? It's been five hundred years, and we can't refurbish one in the time we likely have available.

The readouts are in the reports you got from the ship. Maybe a third of them are functional. I'd want to go over the one you pick closely to make sure everything is really good, but this is within the realm of possibility.

Sure it is, if I can talk Jared and Talbot into allowing the mad princess to go skydiving from space.

She sighed and focused her attention on the others, who had waited patiently while she talked with Ned.

"*Persephone* has drop capsules to get Raiders from orbit down to the surface in a hurry. If we can locate the nuke precisely, I could drop in on them before they see me coming. One shot from a plasma rifle and the nuke is history. Then the marines can come in, kick ass, and take names."

Jared opened his mouth, but Talbot cut his commanding officer off. "That's way too risky. Dropping in from orbit sounds like suicide.

"They would see you coming and shoot you down. These people have access to modern weapons, including the crew-served defenses we had to abandon on the island."

Ned, how long to get from orbit down to the surface?

You'd come in very hot. Orbital speed is just short of thirty thousand kilometers an hour. Basically, you'll hit the atmosphere like a meteor.

The exceptionally powerful grav drives will start slowing you at once for a zero intercept with the ground. Since you need to be able to survive the deceleration, you'll arrive on the surface roughly ten seconds after you first touch the atmosphere.

She felt her face make an expression of shock, but couldn't stop herself.

Ten seconds to go from thirty thousand kilometers an hour to zero? Are you insane?

I'm a Marine Raider. Of course I am.

Kelsey repressed a strong urge to wipe her face.

And ninety-nine point five percent of the people that do this survive? That seems wildly *optimistic.*

The equipment getting you there is literally the best the Empire could build. It's all designed to keep the Raider alive on the way in and at impact.

The heat from atmospheric compression is… substantial, but the odds of them even detecting you before you're on the ground are slim. They won't be able to shoot you down. That almost never happened.

Almost never? So some people get shot down, too?

Bad luck is real. The enemy is occasionally prepared and gets exceptionally lucky. If you want a guaranteed retirement plan, a career in the Raiders might not be for you. On the plus side, if the grav drives fail, you'll take out the building and the nuke.

She shook her head. *Remind me to let someone else do the Raider recruitment ads when the time comes.*

Kelsey focused her attention back on Talbot. "I just checked, and it's safe."

"That was not your 'everything is peachy' face," the marine disagreed. "That was your 'holy shit, I'm going to die' face."

"Do I really have faces like that?"

"That's not the important part of this discussion," Jared said repressively. "I'm more interested in why you had that expression. This isn't safe, is it?"

She shrugged a little. "No more dangerous than some of the other things I've done."

"That isn't reassuring. Why don't you tell us about it?"

Kelsey considered the best way to lay it out. "Basically, the Raiders have a means of dropping themselves from orbit onto planetary targets when the situation requires. They come in fast and brake hard. Dwell time in weapons range is minimized as much as possible. Once down, they come out shooting.

"If we can locate the nuke in advance, I can drop on the building and blast it with a plasma weapon. Poof. No more weapon of mass destruction. Then I hold out until the marines come hauling ass in to back me up."

Talbot's eyes narrowed. "I suspect you're glossing over a few important details. What does reducing dwell time mean, exactly?"

"Well," she said, drawing the word out, "it means about what you'd expect. Come down as fast as possible."

Jared pursed his lips and gave her a look similar to Talbot's. "Details. Trot them out."

She sighed. "*Persephone* would approach Harrison's World at orbital speeds and kick the drop capsule out. It would start slowing as soon as it hits the atmosphere and comes in hot on the target about ten seconds later.

"I figure I'm too high for targeting during the first few seconds. Hell, they probably won't even see me before I'm down. Even if they do see me, they won't know what I am. Drop capsules haven't been used for centuries, after all."

"Jesus," Talbot said, wiping his face with one hand. "You'd be shooting in like an orbital bombardment flechette. That can't be safe. How sure are you that you'd stop safely at the bottom?"

"Pretty sure. Almost certain."

"Could we fire these without anyone inside them?" Jared asked. "There aren't explosives, but a direct hit will kill the nuke."

Ned's response was immediately negative. *You can tell him no. The Old Empire had prohibitions against using orbital bombardment weapons. The tube has to detect a human being in the capsule, or it will not fire it.*

Also, the accuracy isn't meant to be so precise. The drop capsules don't need to hit specific targets, only land inside a specified landing zone.

She shook her head. "Unlike the Rebel Empire, the Old Empire didn't bombard planets. Not only are the capsules not accurate enough to be sure we get the weapon, but the system is designed to require a person inside. It's almost like how the computers can't control weapons on our new ships. Except for Marcus, of course."

"And that might be an appropriate time for me to speak up," Marcus said. "Admiral, there's an incoming call for Coordinator West."

"Thank you," Jared said, his gaze lingering on Kelsey. "Would you like some privacy, Coordinator?"

The woman shook her head. "No. These are probably the demands we've been expecting. Can I use your desk? I'd rather they not know where I am."

Once he gestured for her to proceed, West stood, sat at the desk, and faced the built-in display. "I'm ready."

"I shall transmit the incoming call to everyone's implants as well," Marcus said.

Moments later, the image of a man appeared in Kelsey's head. He looked relatively unremarkable. Run of the mill, really. Except for the armored vest he wore and the flechette rifle strapped across his chest.

He seemingly glared at her. "This is the first and only chance you get to save these people. Release Lord Calder and Coordinator King, and surrender to our rightful authority."

"I don't recognize you or your authority," West said coldly. "Who are you?"

"My name is JR Handley, but that isn't important. What's important is this."

The view shifted to show a cylindrical device sitting on a crate. It seemed to be in the middle of a warehouse. The look lasted only a moment before shifting back to Handley.

"That's the nuclear device I'll detonate if you don't comply with my instructions."

"You'll die," West said. "Why would you do that for people like Calder and King? They don't care about you. Tell me the truth. Are your movement's surviving leaders even out there with you? I bet they expect you to die grandstanding for their benefit."

Handley shrugged and held up a hand-held device. "It's a price I'm more than willing to pay for my people, traitor. You have three hours." The image vanished.

Kelsey stood and began pacing. "We don't have a choice. He'll do it. We have to get moving or he'll kill tens of thousands of innocent people. How can we locate the nuke?"

"Done," Marcus said. "The crate the weapon is sitting on is in our inventory. I've pinpointed the warehouse holding it. The video also gave us one additional piece of information. There were no hostages in the range of the com. I slowed the video and checked. The warehouse only has enemy fighters."

"I need to get moving," she said. "Are you going to fight me on this?"

Talbot sighed and shook his head.

Jared opened his mouth to say something but closed it again. After a long moment, he also shook his head. "I'm sure you're holding out some important information, but our options are limited. How long do you need?"

"Every second," she said as she headed for the hatch. "It's a two-hour trip at maximum acceleration for *Persephone* to get to Harrison's World. We don't want to arrive at the last second. Have them move her out of the repair dock and get her running this way.

"I'll change into my armor and take a pinnace out to meet her. That should give me about half an hour to get everything ready as they make the final segment of the run in. Wish me luck!"

Kelsey raced to marine country with Talbot at her side. He didn't say anything, but she knew her lover was worried. What could she tell him? That she'd be fine?

He'd been in combat. He knew that was never assured.

In the end, she simply pulled him into a kiss as soon as they arrived in the compartment with everyone's armor. "I love you. I'll be as careful as I can be."

"I know you will," he said with a sigh as she started stripping. Marines surrounded her and helped her into her skinsuit. Thank God she'd lost any hang-ups about getting naked in front of her comrades. She didn't have time for prudishness.

A few minutes later, she was inside her Raider armor. The powered suit made her even stronger than the artificial muscles of her enhanced body, and it was tough. She might even survive a direct hit by a plasma weapon, if she was extremely lucky.

Once she had the gray armor on, she hefted the thick helmet with no faceplate. The surface was holographic, so she could display her own face outside the metal once it was on, but she wanted to see the people around her with her own eyes.

"I won't lie. This scares me. Wish me luck."

Talbot ignored all protocol and kissed her again. "You'll make it back. You're tougher than all of us combined. Go kick some ass."

They strapped her weapons to her armor as Talbot seated her helmet over her head. Her implants used the external scanners to make it seem as if nothing were obscuring her vision.

It was all a trick. In reality, the displays and her view of the marines clustered around her were transmitted straight to her optical implants. The interior of the helmet was as dark as space, she just couldn't see it.

She turned on the interior lighting and projected the image of her face on the helmet where everyone could see it. She knew for a fact that it seemed as if the metal of the helmet had become transparent.

"I'm going to be fine. Really. Let's get over to *Persephone*. I need to preflight my drop capsule.

"Talbot, I want you to head back to Harrison's World. When I get down there, I'm going to be hanging in the wind until you and the marines come to rescue me."

"Rescuing princesses, that's what we do," he said with a smile. "Or vice versa. We'll be there when you need us."

The trip to *Persephone* seemingly took forever, but that gave Kelsey time to look over the readouts for all the drop capsules remotely. Two-thirds of them were defective in some way.

Almost all of them could be refurbished with enough effort, but she had to choose the one least likely to kill her at this moment in time.

Persephone slowed for them long enough for the pinnace to dock, and Kelsey raced to the section of the ship holding the drop capsules. She'd seen the compartment on her tour of the ship but hadn't realized its significance. Honestly, she'd thought it was a storage room of some kind.

Crates filled the compartment. She now realized they held drop capsules. Four odd curved sections covered the far wall. Those were access points to tubes from which the Raiders dropped.

Each recessed tube could hold a dozen capsules. Four dozen Raiders screaming in from the sky was probably enough to handle most problems.

The first thing she did was check the tubes themselves. One was offline and another had warnings. Those two were off the table.

Of the other two, one of them seemed to be in slightly better shape, so she'd use it.

That left the drop capsules. She selected the one closest to the chosen tube that showed no faults. The marines helped her uncrate it.

Ned chimed in immediately. *I don't like the color of the base. The heat-resistant material might be compromised.*

"This one is bad," she told the marines. "Next."

It took six tries before they found one that passed Ned's external inspection. He then demanded she open the access ports and look at the grav drives and inertial compensators.

She focused her attention on the control runs. *Do those look a little flaky to you?*

Some of the protective coatings are delaminating. Pick another.

In the end, it took over a dozen tries to find one that didn't fail the exacting preflight. She was more than happy he was being super picky. She'd have one try at this, and a malfunction meant death.

"We'll run with this one," she told the marines. "Get it over next to drop tube three."

They manhandled the capsule into place, and she opened up the part that held her. To say it was a tight fit was an understatement. There was literally only enough space for her to curl into a fetal position. No more.

You'll curl up inside, and the area fills with electrorheological fluid. That's liquid that goes from basically water to thick gel when electric current is run through it. The state changes in just a few milliseconds.

As you decelerate, it works in tandem with the inertial compensators to cancel out just enough of the roughly eighty-five gravities of deceleration to make the drop survivable. It's still no fun, but you'll have a story to tell the grandkids.

Once you land, the fluid goes back to being water-like, the top of the capsule blows off, and you're ejected straight up. That's when you use your armor's grav drive to maneuver while you pull weapons.

In a group fight, you'd mesh with other Raiders using your implants to create overlapping fields of fire and mutually support one another as you eliminate the threats in the LZ. Since you're all alone, just kill everything that moves and never stand still.

She stared into the tight space, her heart racing. He made it all sound so easy. A walk in the park.

Well, it might not be easy, but it would be simple: get in, do the drop, and kill the bad guys.

Kelsey turned to face the marines. "Load the capsule into the tube once I give you the green light."

Even with her small stature, it was a tight fit. All light went out when they sealed the drop capsule behind her and the cramped compartment filled with fluid.

Thankfully, there were scanner feeds she could tap into. The visual spectrum gave her the least information, but she could see them standing around her. That made her feel less alone.

This was it.

"*Persephone*, this is Bandar," she said over the com link to the bridge. "Status?"

"On course to Harrison's World, Highness," a male voice that she didn't recognize said. "We'll be ready to decelerate at the last moment and drop you on command. We're refining the course based on what the local atmospheric conditions look like. You'll have a clear drop."

"How long?"

"Five minutes."

She'd almost cut the timing too fine. "Have them load me in. I'll want a warning before you kick me out."

"Copy that."

The marines loaded the drop capsule into the tube, and she sank to the first firing position. She wondered how similar to a missile tube this thing was.

Through her implants, she could tap directly into the ship's scanners as they made their approach. The planet was growing larger at an alarming rate.

"Thirty seconds, Highness," the bridge informed her. "Good hunting."

Where had the time gone? "Thank you, *Persephone*. See you soon."

Her foot was trying to tap, but there was almost no give to her boot. She felt all twitchy.

Relax. You'll be fine. This is just first-drop jitters. Administer your combat drugs now.

She took a deep breath at Ned's words and willed her heart to slow. Then she triggered her pharmacology unit to dispense the combination of drugs called Panther. One of the two sped up the transmission of signals along her nerves, and the second did the same to the cognitive areas of her brain.

The world around her seemed to slow and her nervousness vanished, another side effect of the drug cocktail. It felt as if she had an eternity to make decisions. A final drug would deal with any pain.

The last thing she did was enable combat mode inside her implants. The computer in her head would now follow the rules of engagement but take in the entire situation around her to make the calls. It would still respond to her overall direction, but if it saw danger before she did, it would eliminate the threat.

As an afterthought, she changed the display on the outside of her helmet to a demonic face. A lot of Raiders did that in combat to demoralize their enemies. She might as well go at this full bore.

When the timer in her head reached zero, *Persephone* decelerated savagely and then fired her capsule out.

Kelsey grunted as the intense maneuvers slammed her around. The drop capsule scanners showed her in space with the planet looming ahead of her. *Persephone* was already peeling away to miss the world below her.

When he spoke, Ned's mental voice was calm and even. *Twenty seconds to entry. The drop capsule is making its final course adjustments to get you on target. You're doing great.*

She wanted to rub her face, but that was ridiculous. She gritted her teeth and watched the planet grow huge in front of her. This might be the last sight she ever saw. Her last moment of existence. She drank in its beauty.

Atmospheric entry in ten seconds. Get ready. Once things start happening, they'll happen really, really fast.

Since she wasn't even in the atmosphere yet, but she'd be on the planet's surface in twenty seconds, that was an absurd understatement.

Here we go. Give 'em hell, Raider.

If she thought ejection from *Persephone* was rough, impacting the atmosphere at almost thirty thousand kilometers per hour was like slamming into a brick wall that then collapsed on her. The exterior scanners went offline in two seconds, burned away.

Blind except for elevation numbers that spun down at heart-stopping speed, she almost lost consciousness as the grav drives came to life in savage deceleration. The intense pressure would've killed anyone but an Imperial Raider in fractions of a second, and she thought she'd die, too.

One second from impact, the status lights for the grav drives flickered yellow. Then one failed, its indicator a lurid red. She felt as if she was spinning, and then she hit the ground like a speeding freight train.

Before she could even wonder if she was alive, the drop capsule blew apart, hurling her into the air. The gel turned to drops in a rainbow around her as she arced up.

She'd missed the warehouse. The failing grav drive had shunted her off to the side at the last moment. That was the only reason the warehouse was even partially intact.

It seemed as if a bomb had exploded beside it. Perhaps a hundred meters from the warehouse, her drop capsule had gouged a crater about twenty meters across. Kelsey had no idea how she could've survived the impact.

If it hadn't been for the combat drugs in her system, she'd have been a gibbering wreck.

She used her armor's grav drive to help her arc into the remains of the warehouse. Her threat indicators came to life as her implants began tagging hostiles.

The very first thing Kelsey looked for was the nuke. She found it on the right side of the hanger. The blast wave had knocked it off the crate, but the radiation signature was unmistakable. All around it, men were climbing to their feet.

Handley stood between her and the nuke. He gaped at her and fumbled for something on his belt. Probably the detonator.

Without even a moment's hesitation, Kelsey unslung her plasma rifle, brought it to bear on him, and pulled the trigger. The pea-sized speck of plasma flew true and took the snarling man in the stomach.

A bright flash erased him from existence. It also obliterated the detonator, the nuke, and anyone standing near him. Her suit automatically compensated for the blast and dropped her safely to the floor.

"All Imperial forces, this is Bandar," she said over the com. "Target eliminated. I could use a little help."

"Copy that," Talbot said. "We're inbound, sixty seconds out. Holy shit, Kelsey. You came down like the fist of God."

"Remember that when we start talking about furniture."

The remaining defenders were disorganized and demoralized, but that didn't stop them from opening fire on her with everything they had. Flechettes tore up the concrete all around her and ricocheted off her armor.

She leapt to the side, switched to her flechette rifle, and started cutting them down in short, controlled bursts. Many of them dove for cover, but against her weapons, any obstacle might as well be made of tissue paper.

The amount of hostile fire dropped off precipitously in just thirty seconds. By the time the marines arrived, pinnaces howling as they raced in and disgorged armored fighting men, the resistance was broken.

The last of the surviving loyalists threw down their weapons and gave up.

Kelsey stood there as Talbot directed his people in securing the area. He'd make sure there were no other unpleasant surprises.

She looked over what was left of the warehouse and then turned to gaze at the smoking crater her drop capsule had left in the plascrete. Fist of God, indeed. It was a miracle she'd survived.

After a moment's thought, she made a mental note to have a small golden fist made up to commemorate the achievement. Any future Raiders that made a drop would get one just like it.

Congratulations on your first successful combat drop, Raider. Well done. There are a few things you could probably improve upon, but I think you'll get an acceptable grade in the after-action report.

She felt her lips curve into a smile at Ned's dry humor.

"You are so full of crap."

Ned laughed. *We're Imperial Raiders, Kelsey. It's a job requirement.*

* * *

WANT to get updates from Terry about new books and other general nonsense going on in his life? He promises there will be cats. Go to TerryMixon.com/Mailing-List and sign up.

DID YOU ENJOY THIS BOOK? Please leave a review on Amazon. It only takes a minute to dash off a few words and that kind of thing helps Terry make a living as a writer and gets you new books faster.

WANT MORE IN THIS UNIVERSE? Grab *The Empire of Bones Volume 2* today or buy any of Terry's other books, which are listed on the next page.

VISIT TERRY's Patreon page to find out how to get cool rewards and an early look at what he's working on at Patreon.com/TerryMixon.

ALSO BY TERRY MIXON

You can always find the most up to date listing of Terry's titles on his Amazon Author Page.

Note: the links below (ebook only, obviously) redirect you to my website where you can click a button to go to Amazon. This allows me to participate in Amazon's associates program and earn a little more. Sorry for any inconvenience.

The Last Hunter

The Last Hunter

Bonds of Blood

Alpha Strike

The Enemy Revealed

Command Authority

The Grand Conspiracy

Shield of Humanity

Fog of War

Ships of the Line

Operation Liberty

The Empire of Bones Saga

Empire of Bones

Veil of Shadows

Command Decisions

Ghosts of Empire

Paying the Price

Recon in Force

Behind Enemy Lines

The Terra Gambit

Hidden Enemies

Race to Terra

Ruined Terra

Victory on Terra

When Luck Runs Out

Gunboat Diplomacy

ABOUT TERRY

#1 Bestselling Military Science Fiction author Terry Mixon served as a non-commissioned officer in the United States Army 101st Airborne Division. He later worked alongside the flight controllers in the Mission Control Center at the NASA Johnson Space Center supporting the Space Shuttle, the International Space Station, and other human spaceflight projects.

He now writes full time while living in Texas with his lovely wife and a pounce of cats.

TerryMixon.com

amazon.com/author/terrymixon

facebook.com/TerryLMixon

patreon.com/TerryMixon

bookbub.com/authors/terry-mixon

goodreads.com/TerryMixon